The REST OF OUR LIVES

Hall Bartlett

Random House
New York

Library of Congress Cataloging-in-Publication Data

Bartlett, Hall.
The rest of our lives.

I. Title.
PS3552.A76537R4   1988   813'.54   87-42664
ISBN 0-394-56145-7

Manufactured in the United States of America
24689753
First Edition

Book design by Debbie Glasserman

For
Cathy and Laurie,
My Beloved Daughters,
My Dearest Friends
The Inspiration of My Life
with My Love Always

To David and Scott,
Who Have Become My Sons
and Blessed My Life

To Joshua Scott and Laurie Oliver,
Who Are the Promise of Our Tomorrows

To Jay Allen,
Who Encouraged Me to Write This Novel
and Who Believed in It

In Memory of
Mr. Sam Goldwyn
and His Legacy
of Passion and Taste

"To love someone is to see the face of God."

—Les Misérables
Victor Hugo

Acknowledgments

I Wish to Thank:

Kate Medina, my editor,
for her sensitivity, understanding, caring, and inspiration.

Bob Colgan,
for never failing to believe in, support, and guide
the writing of this novel.

Barbara and Bruce Wiseman,
for "being there."

Marily and Gary Demarest for their faith.

Margaret Leonard,
for all that she taught me.

Janet Dourif,
who, together with her associates, prepared the
manuscripts with feeling and commitment.

Contents

The
PEOPLE

Book I

1

New York

*H*e stood there alone on the edge of the stage, looking out over a sea of seventy thousand faces. A single spotlight encircled him. His face was drenched with sweat. "His people" knew what this song meant to Rayme Monterey and their screaming quieted. He spoke passionately.

"Before I go, I'd like to sing the best song ever written about America. Woody Guthrie wrote it as he crossed our country on the backs of empty railway cars."

He adjusted the harmonica on the bar that hung around his neck. His guitar was strapped around his leather jacket. He bent his head to the mouth organ and closed his eyes.

He wasn't Hollywood handsome, but you remembered his face. It was craggy and his eyes were intense. Sweat glistened on his forehead and streamed down across his temples. The ridges of his cheekbones tightened.

He began to play. His harmonica and his guitar came together in a single musical line of pure tones. His Norfolk River Band, behind him, was still.

"This land was made for you and me." Woody Guthrie's song became Rayme's hymn as he sang it.

> "This land is your land,
> this land is my land
> From California to the New York island

> *From the redwood forest to the Gulf stream waters*
> *This land was made for you and me."*

A slim, dark-haired girl watched him from the wings of the stage that had been erected in the center of the outfield of Yankee Stadium. She was not a beautiful girl by ordinary standards. Her features were irregular, her nose imperfect, her mouth slightly too large. But her eyes held you. Radiant set. Trusting. And vulnerable.

Rayme Monterey had fallen in love with her when she first came to hear him sing, with some of her girlfriends, at the Blue Grotto in Norfolk. She had become Rayme's lodestone, his good luck charm, his promise of a future.

Her feelings were like her eyes. They were vulnerable but they were true.

She was Rayme's best critic. She told him what she thought of a new performance, or a new song. She "lived" his music. And from her, he had learned to respect the truth.

Night after night on the road, she stood there in the wings of whatever stage it was and watched Rayme. Then, afterward, when they were alone, they talked about the concert step by step.

Marny understood what Rayme meant when he said, "I didn't have anything to believe in—nothing at all—till I first saw Elvis performing up there on the stage. It was a miracle for me. The first time in my life I could relate to something. It became part of me—I had a way to tell the pain and hope inside of me. Rock 'n' roll was it for me. It became my life. I wrote songs about myself. I wanted to find out what 'me' is. I wrote about places I saw, people I knew, feelings I had— and went as deep as I could with them."

The stadium was dark now except for the light shining down over Rayme Monterey. In the style he had made famous, Rayme sang with a rasping voice, straining every muscle in his neck and throat, singing with all the tension in his concentrated body. He demanded your heart.

Rayme sang the last line with his head thrown back, his eyes closed, almost in prayer. There was a moment of silence in the huge stadium.

And then Rayme lifted his head and spoke the line that would become famous. It was not a studied sign-off. It was simply the last communication of a concert between Rayme Monterey and "his people."

Rayme looked over the huge crowd and asked: "Do you love me?"

The answer came back almost in unison from seventy thousand voices. "We love you—we love you—we love you."

The drums were picking up the rhythm now. The searchlights swept the faces of the people.

Rayme's voice rose above the crowd. "I love you, too," he said—a dangerous line, so often cheapened by overuse in the show business world. But with Rayme it was different. He believed it, so you believed it. He did love "his people," and they knew it.

Breaking out now in Rayme's theme, "Living on the Edge," his Norfolk River Band powered their way through the sign-off of the Rayme Monterey concert.

Rayme went straight from the shadows of his last good-bye, to Marny, in the wings. He embraced her and she clung to his body. His clothes were soaked through with sweat. He was exhausted and exhilarated. He pulled back from the embrace for just a moment and looked at her. She nodded.

"I'll remember this one. Something special about it," Marny said. And Rayme's face began to ease its tension.

"You were right about Woody's song. I felt it out there."

Marny spoke again. "Could we do something alone tonight?" she asked. "Forget the limo and the party and just go back to our old neighborhood by ourselves?"

Rayme looked at her and put his hands on the sides of her face. "Let's go," he said.

He grabbed a towel from a huge moving box in which some of his sound equipment had come. He hurried with her toward a side door of the makeshift stage. He turned back and waved to Skeeter Thomas, his big black sax man and his closest friend in the band.

Skeeter smiled at him and raised his right hand in a salute. Rayme raised his in return, and so did Marny. It was always their hello and good-bye to Skeeter.

Marny took a telegram out of her tote bag. "This came for you during the concert."

Rayme opened it.

Mr. Rayme Monterey,
Monterey Rock Concert,
Yankee Stadium, New York

I have written a co-starring role, inspired by you, for a new motion picture. I have followed your career for many years and what you stand for is in this story. Only you can play it.

I know you have refused numerous film offers because they won't give you any control over what you do. I will. I need to meet with you to explain the unique aspects of this project in relation to your career.

You will not be exploited in any way and I'll guarantee that in a written contract.

Please call me or contact me at the address or telephone below. I will fit my time to yours.

Sincerely,
Steve Wayland,
Wayland Productions,
1048 South Mapleton Drive,
Los Angeles, CA 90077
(213) 555-3674

Rayme turned to Marny and handed her the telegram as they started out the back of the stage. "We'll talk about it later," Rayme said, as hundreds of fans broke through the police cordon near the bottom of the bandstand stairs and rushed toward them. "Everything is on, just the same. Tonight we go back home."

2

The Subway

It was 1:27 on the subway clock. The district attorney would establish that later. Rayme and Marny had started down the M system stairs. The D train to Church Street in Brooklyn was three minutes late. Rayme and Marny huddled against a cement pillar, breathing hard from their run.

From the top of the IND subway stairs, five young hoodlums moved slowly down the steps. Their eyes were fixed on the couple below.

Out of the darkness, the subway train hurtled like an exploding snake, screeching to a stop at the 57th Street station. A few people got off. All the cars seemed empty.

Rayme and Marny got on. Rayme stretched his legs out on the seat in front of him and Marny squeezed up against him.

Rayme took his guitar from the case and ran his fingers over the strings. Marny spoke above the pounding of the train.

"Play the new one."

Rayme strummed the guitar. "Not finished," he said.

Marny kissed him in his ear. "Finish it now."

Rayme laughed. "It's not a subway song, Marny."

Marny whispered to him, "It turns me on."

Rayme's first songs in high school in Virginia had been about his family, the street where he lived, the grocery store, the ice cream parlor, the look of the tenements from the top of the family apartment—songs of the heartbeat of the city.

Like the one he was singing now. "You Take My Breath Away," it was called—about the first love in a boy's life. It was a rock song with a ballad melody. And soon Rayme's feet were tapping and Marny's, too. She knew the song was about her. She was proud of it.

Rayme glanced at Marny as he sang certain lines. He had a way of singing tender lyrics with his raspy voice that made them sound like poetry.

He held the chords in his voice, right after "breath." Then he headed into the ballad part of the song with the word "away." Each time he held his pause longer. And he knew it would work with the rock crowd. It was the kind of sound you needed in a song to give it a chance to make the charts.

Rayme was hitting the rise of the song when Marny screamed. Her scream was cut off by a hand grabbing her mouth, jerking her neck back.

Another pair of hands ripped her coat and blouse off, baring her slender, turned-up breasts.

"Spread your legs, you little cunt," a voice commanded.

Rayme couldn't move. A knife blade stretched across his throat. Four hoodlums completely encircled him so that he couldn't see the fifth one tearing off Marny's skirt.

Marny screamed wildly as he ripped open her panty hose and pulled her legs apart.

"Ever been fucked by a *man*, pussy?"

"Now, this is a cock," a second assailant laughed as he spoke.

She bit the hand that covered her mouth. The attacker pulled his bleeding hand away, yelling in pain. Three of the other assailants held Marny as one of them drove his penis into her. Her body jerked in pain. She tried to scream. Her voice was cut off. The rapist forced her legs around his neck and thrust himself rapidly into her.

"Wet my cock, you bitch—blow it all over me," he yelled out.

The train lurched violently. Rayme took his chance.

He sliced at the hand with the knife at his throat with a vicious karate chop. He drove his knee into the groin of the man who fell on top of him and then, in one fast movement, he jerked a gun from his leather jacket and fired six rapid shots into the men raping Marny.

The man actually in her fell flat on top of her. The other three rapists fell back, each of them struck by a bullet from the revolver.

The man with the knife, who had fallen against Rayme, raised his right arm and drove it down towards Rayme's chest. Rayme fired directly into the man's heart. The man quivered in midair, blood spurting out against his tank top. He was dead before he hit the floor of the subway train.

Rayme put his arm around Marny. She was screaming wildly.

There was blood on her thighs and on her stomach. Two of the attackers were dead, the other three seriously wounded.

3

Hollywood

he offices of the president of Mager-Golden-Lasky, the most famous motion picture company in the world, were imposing, vibrating with power and glamorous with memories.

Steve Wayland, a tall, powerfully built man with a strongly cut face, intense blue eyes, and dark tousled hair, walked down the long corridor of the Dana Building to the outer offices of the president. He thought of the death walks he'd seen in motion pictures, when the convicted man walked to the execution chambers. He was sweating. His stomach was ripping apart. Was this the end of the line for Steve Wayland, motion picture maker?

This was the last chance for *The Rest of Our Lives*, turned down by seven major studios, five mini-majors, and seventy-one independent sources of film financing.

The answers had been varied. The story was not "high concept." It couldn't be told fully and convincingly in one line—the superb example was a drug story making the rounds of the studios: "Romeo and Juliet on drugs." Everyone could catch it in the flick of a phrase. Didn't mean it was good. But it was high concept, the latest executive "Bible" in town.

Steve had tried it. He had explained that *The Rest of Our Lives* was a story about a passionate search for people to find meaning in their lives. What was a bigger common denominator for people of all ages than "the search"? Wasn't everyone searching for something? Survival. Money. Sex. Love. Power. Fame. Peace. Weren't all the great audience pictures that had made big money about some form of search?

From *Gone with the Wind* to *Citizen Kane* to *Casablanca* to *It's a Wonderful Life*, the four pictures recently voted the best of all time by the members of a famous critical society. What about the hit pictures of today? *E.T. Star Wars. Out of Africa. Platoon. Hannah and Her Sisters.* They were stories of the search for what people would do with the rest of their lives.

He'd almost gotten *The Rest of Our Lives* on track at Universal, but they wanted the biggest stars—that is, the greatest possible security. Only stars didn't mean security, Steve had argued. The biggest stars, Eastwood and Redford, had lost money when the pictures they were in weren't right for their audiences. It was the project that was the star. He couldn't sell that one.

So Steve took another direction. They wanted money stars, he would deliver money stars. How about one of the biggest rock heroes, with that critical big young audience—Rayme Monterey? So what if he'd never done a film? His concerts were selling out all over the world. Millions of young people would come to see him, no matter what his first picture was. Steve got some interest there. But he had to admit that he didn't have Rayme Monterey signed. And everybody knew Rayme Monterey had taken a position about motion pictures. He wouldn't appear in a movie unless he had approval of every scene he was in after it was done. No studio head in his right mind would ever give that permission. Steve had heard that over and over again.

The only real interest he had to offer was the selection of Magdalena Alba as the female star of *The Rest of Our Lives*. There was no way to gauge what Magdalena meant anymore at the world box office. She wasn't a "name" with the massive young audience demographs the studios were using (the number one demograph in filmmaking now was the thirteen-year-old girl in the United States who went to see each film she liked four or five times). How did you rate a great international star like Magdalena Alba on a demograph of thirteen-year-old girls?

It had been twenty years since she had made her first appearance in a François Truffaut film called *The Haunted*. She had still been in her teens then. By now she was a question mark. She didn't belong to the group of middle-aged stars like Sophia Loren and Catherine Deneuve, who had lost much of their world box office draw. On the other hand, she wasn't part of the young group of stars either, like Debra Winger, Kathleen Turner, Kate Capshaw, Kelly McGillis, Cynthia Rhodes, and Linda Fiorentino.

She hadn't been in a film in almost two years. Yes, there'd still be a significant foreign market for a film starring Magdalena Alba, but what would it do in the United States? And now, with the videocassette market so important, you had to do well in the domestic release to get the big results in cassette sales. The many millions of dollars possible in the cassette market were dependent on a wide-reaching theatrical release.

Steve had had all the clichéd negatives thrown in his face. No one ever quite came out with their opinion of him, but he was not exactly the most popular filmmaker in town, and he knew it. He also knew that this was his last chance. If he didn't get *The Rest of Our Lives* launched, with Magdalena Alba in the cast, and the possibility of Rayme Monterey, on a budget of six million dollars, then he could forget all the years of work and dreams, losing and winning, getting up and trying again.

There weren't many people at MGL in the quarters of the executive offices that afternoon, but Steve felt as if he were making his way through a screaming crowd to the ring. One last shot at the title. If he lost, no more shots at all. He walked by the huge photographs on the walls of the corridor. They were some of the reasons he was here at all. Academy Award-winning films and actors of every studio. Humphrey Bogart and Ingrid Bergman in *Casablanca*. James Stewart in *It's a Wonderful Life*. Clark Gable and Vivien Leigh in *Gone with the Wind*. Elizabeth Taylor and Montgomery Clift in *A Place in the Sun*. Greta Garbo and Robert Taylor in *Camille*. Fred Astaire and Ginger Rogers in *The Barkleys of Broadway*. Judy Garland in *The Wizard of Oz*. *Ghandi*. *2001*. Magdalena Alba and Robert Redford in *Anna Karenina*. *A Star Is Born*. Then, the unforgettable classic picture of the MGL luncheon, with 175 world-known stars there under contract.

Steve Wayland watched Jack Gregson's secretary as she led him into the handsome conference room, its large oval table actually built for MGL's *Knights of the Round Table*. Like most executive secretaries, this one reflected the temperature of the coming meeting. She was cold, polite, and arrogant. She had four standard looks, one for each of the usual occasions.

Steve recognized the "number-four look," the lowest on the totem pole. He remembered when Betty, this same secretary, had greeted him differently. That was before Gregson had taken the job, and Betty had been different then. In the one year since Gregson had become head of production at the studio, Betty had aged ten. She had been a warm-looking, well-tailored woman, full of vitality. Her eyes had glistened with interest when Steve had first met her. Now, Betty's eyes were set, her mouth tight in the corners, her face like a clenched fist. What the hell had Gregson done to her, Steve wondered?

"Mr. Gregson will be in in a few minutes. Can I get you anything?" Betty asked.

Steve shook his head. "No, thank you."

She went out quietly. He was alone in the large room, again reflecting on the power and tradition of world-famous MGL.

He sat down on one side of the table, facing the door. He put the tips of his hands together and closed his eyes, the way Lieu had taught him. His eyes burned. There were pains in his head. His tongue was dry. His stomach felt like a raw ulcer.

Steve forced himself to meditate. He concentrated on his interior being, hoped that calm would come over him. He thought of the serenity with which Lieu faced the tragedies of her life.

He was in perfect concentration when the doors opened and Jack Gregson walked in with his entourage of vice presidents: Jerry Clune, his young computing expert, two other men, and one woman.

Steve rose and started to shake hands, but there was no hand shaking. Gregson sat down at the head of the table as his lieutenants grouped around him.

"You alone, Wayland?"

Steve nodded. "Spartan's wife is in the hospital. She had a car accident, so he couldn't be here. He said he'd call you later."

Gregson seemed to be relieved. "Well, I don't think there's anything we can't finish up without him."

Gregson was a man of medium height. Elegantly tailored, with sandy hair, rapidly thinning, piercing dark eyes, on the small side, a thin-lipped mouth squeezed downward.

He was a street fighter out of New York's East Side who had battled his way up in the entertainment world. He'd been in distribution most of his life, but his ambition had always been to run the studio. Now, head of MGL production, dealing with real power, Jack Gregson had "made it" on all levels. He paid a man a hundred and fifty thousand dollars a year simply to pick out his clothes, teach him the right wines, and bring him the women.

"Let's get it over with, Wayland," Gregson said. "I had a couple of meetings with my staff here. They've gone over the material and figures." He nodded to the men with him and the one woman, tall, well-dressed, with a face that seemed cut by an axe from marble block. She was Gregson's "story consultant."

"Have you read the treatment, Jack?" Steve asked him.

"I don't have time to read, you know that, Wayland. You've been around here quite a few years. And I'll tell you why you're here. Because you've got Spartan Lee, that's why. I don't know why the hell he bothers to be your manager. Name me one big picture you've ever made."

Steve replied, "What's your definition of 'big?' "

Gregson took out a cigarette. Jerry Clune produced a lighter with one swift movement. "I mean a picture that made big money—hope that doesn't offend you, Wayland. You always seem to be asking for money to do your pictures, but they never really hit." Gregson's tone was sarcastic.

Steve looked at him. "I've made sixteen pictures. Fifteen of them made money. That's better than a .300 batting average—and Billy Wilder says that .300's a hell of an average for any hitter in our business."

"You don't satisfy stockholders with mediocre earnings. You survive, Wayland, I grant you that, but you haven't got a single thing that I can sell to my board of directors or my stockholders in New York. We're in business to make money. Unfortunately for me, the man who was here at the studio before me liked you. I guess you lost to him at golf or poker. You did *something* we don't know about. Anyway, we have three more picture commitments with you.

"New York would rather make one picture and buy up the other two than have a lawsuit over three pictures—but tell Spartan he's got to take it my way. Personally, I'd rather let you sue and keep you out of court for five years. It really doesn't make any difference to me. I'd just as soon be facing you in a courtroom as here.

"You know why I dislike you, Wayland? You're a loser with pretensions. You represent something I despise. You look down on people who admit they make movies just to make money. You think that's a disgrace. Well, I'll tell you the truth—everybody's doing everything to make money—that's all there is, and if anyone pretends differently he's a fucking liar.

"From what Louise, over here, tells me—and she knows more about stories than you'll ever know—stories that work as movies, that is, Wayland—*The Rest of Our Lives* is a gamble, like all your others. It's got something to say, I understand, something *you* want to say, but how the hell do you know anyone else wants to hear it?"

"Wait a minute," Steve interrupted, "if you've got a full report from your story department—" He glanced at Louise. She was looking at him icily. "You know my story is about something we all think about.

What do we all have but the rest of our lives? Everyone's out there trying for something, something we'll want for as long as we're in this life. The past is finished. The present is right on top of us. But the one thing that's ahead for every man, woman, and child is the rest of our lives. And you know damn well, Jack, every one of us has a plan or a dream for what we want to do with whatever time we have left. You certainly do. You've fought and worked to have what you want for the rest of your life."

"And I got it," Gregson answered, "because I did work for it and I never pretended it was anything else than what it was. Money and power."

"*The Rest of Our Lives* is about money and power," Steve argued. "And survival. But it's about caring and loving as well. And communicating—none of us lives in a vacuum, Jack. You have to agree with that. Do *you?*"

Gregson's voice turned satirical. He glanced at his story editor. "You know what's showing up on the demographs—you can read, Wayland. Action, comedy, and violence. *Beverly Hills Cop, Back to the Future, Rambo, Top Gun, Aliens, Lethal Weapon, Fatal Attraction*—"

Steve interrupted. "Look back over the biggest grossers in film history and the biggest award-winning pictures, too. Most of them are about relationships and people who care about each other. People who accomplish something in the world."

Gregson cut him off. "I'm not interested in awards, Wayland. Guys like you, they've always got their eyes on the awards, with studio money. My stockholders are interested in bottom-line dollars. Profits and loss, that's what it's all about, Wayland, and that's what you don't understand and never will.

"You're a menace around here. I've heard about your lectures at USC and UCLA—a lot of young kids around town listen to somebody like you, because they're looking for a hero. Well, this studio is not in the position of financing heroes.

"Tell Spartan Lee we are writing off your other two commitments, so we don't owe you one thing more out of that stupid contract someone else made, and then we're going to put up the six million for *The Rest of Our Lives*. But not one cent more, and you've got to go on the completion bond yourself.

"I want your house, your property, your screenplays, everything you have as insurance. If you go over budget, you go one dollar over, Wayland, everything belongs to the studio.

"That's the deal I'll make, and the only one I'll make. I've looked at the budget for this picture and I'm sure you will go over, and that's going to be a day I'll enjoy, when we cash you out, and you'll end up, after fourteen years in Hollywood, with just what you're worth—nothing."

Jack Gregson stood up with his lieutenants and walked out of the conference room. He looked back for a moment from the door. "You said you'd deliver Magdalena Alba and Rayme Monterey. They're part of this deal, but I happen to know you've never met either of them, much less talked contract. And Monterey is being held for murder as well as homicide. It's on the newsstands right now. How are you going to get him out of jail to make a movie, Wayland?"

4

Paris

As he stood on the raised fitting platform of Yves St. Laurent's Paris salon at 5, rue St.-Honoré, surrounded by the homage befitting one of the most adored, most copied, most gossiped about, most praised, and most envied motion picture stars in the world.

Around her, small groups of uniformed fitting women and sketch artists swarmed in clusters like a Roland Petit ballet under the watchful eye of Yves St. Laurent himself. The room was filled with the stereo recording of Rodrigo's "Concerto for Guitar," a favorite of Magdalena's.

Magdalena Alba stood on the raised platform in perfect modeling position, her exquisite body clothed only in long pantyhose made of patterned black stocking lace, the new Parisian rage designed by St. Laurent.

True to her often-quoted statement about her fabulous wardrobes, Magdalena Alba wore no brassiere. She had beautifully round breasts, high and firm with delicately shaded rose nipples.

The great Mexican artist, Diego Rivera, had painted Magdalena Alba just before he had died. The painting was called *The Fawn*. It was Magdalena from the waist up, naked, half-turned toward the painter, her exquisite breasts in striking profile. Her breasts, with the rose nipples, had become famous as the painting was photographed and duplicated all over the world.

It was a name that followed Magdalena Alba—"The Fawn."

Her face was porcelain cut, fragile, delicate, with a sensuous mouth, a straight, short, aquiline nose, and large oval blue-green eyes. Her hair, soft blond, was pulled high on her head, framing her face. Her skin was as fresh as a child's, softening her beauty.

With St. Laurent scheduled to do her entire new wardrobe for her transoceanic "celebrity cruise" on the *Royal Princess*, the many worlds of Magdalena Alba centered on this night.

Magdalena, standing on the raised platform in St. Laurent's central showroom, seemed to rise, literally and figuratively, above it all, in the electricity-filled atmosphere. It was the crowning of a queen, a half-naked queen, enjoying to the full the imposition of her physical personality on her "audience."

Her sexuality was as pervasive as her Yves St. Laurent perfume, Tryst. Her maid had sprayed the perfume in all four corners of the room and on the designer fabrics that one of St. Laurent's chief assistants began to drape around Magdalena's body, as St. Laurent supervised.

"This is you!" the slender designer exclaimed, as he watched a long piece of turquoise chiffon being draped around Magdalena. A striking redheaded couturier-in-training simultaneously turned the pages of a sketchbook in full color, with the lettering on the bottom of each page, "*Royal Princess* Wardrobe for Magdalena Alba, Yves St. Laurent."

There was an attractive drawing of St. Laurent's turquoise chiffon creation emblazoned across the page, the name given to the creation— "Magdalena Turquoise."

The chiffon was draped quickly over Magdalena's bare shoulders and pinned into a scoop neckline, leaving the upper half of her breasts exposed. The material was pulled in tight at her waist, then allowed to flow out in a circular swirl split halfway up her left thigh.

Magdalena turned slowly as St. Laurent directed his clusters of fitters around the bottom of the platform. She watched the many mirrors built out from the recess in the room in which the raised platform stood. She watched her reflection from different points of view; every angle of the dress that St. Laurent was creating showed.

Magdalena spoke to a young woman sitting at a Louis XIV desk near the platform. On the desk were three phones, a white leather appointment book, and an antique gold lacquered box.

"Sylvia, my necklace, please."

The young woman turned to her right, took a key case from her purse, and unlocked the box. She pulled out the third tray. It was a shimmering turquoise and diamond necklace, made up of twenty perfectly matched turquoise stones one inch in diameter and encircled with diamonds.

She took out the necklace, locked the box again, and nodded at the uniformed security guard standing behind the desk. He was watching her carefully, and he understood the silent instructions to guard the box.

Sylvia crossed to the raised platform, deftly stepped through the clusters of fitters, and fastened the necklace at the back of Magdalena's neck.

She gave Magdalena a hand mirror. Magdalena pulled up one Grecian-draped sleeve of turquoise chiffon and put it against the necklace. It was a perfect match. She held up the mirror to inspect it closely and smiled at Yves St. Laurent, standing across from her, watching in anticipation.

"*Magnifique!*" she exclaimed.

Yves St. Laurent gave a slight bow. He spoke simply and he meant it. "*You* are *magnifique*, Magdalena. The jewelry—the clothes—they are only made up for you—you are the original."

Magdalena looked at him. Both people understood each other. Both were sincere. They were too accomplished to stroke each other. They were superstars in a world that demanded superstars.

On the stereo, coming through the professional Dolby system of St. Laurent's establishment, Mireille Mathieu was singing.

St. Laurent directed his assistants: "A little tighter there. Fix that tuck just to the left of the waist. That's right. There's a wrinkle over there, on the right breast. Smooth it out. Yes, that's it."

He circled her in great pride as she held her pose without moving. He said, "Yes, yes, the hipline. Magdalena, your hipline is a designer's dream. So high and so well-formed—*merveilleux*." He took one of her hands and kissed it. St. Laurent continued, "The photographers are waiting."

Magdalena said, "Let me check once when the fitters are through."

"They're finished," he told her. He called for the fitters to step aside. They stood in a half circle around Magdalena. St. Laurent stood back two steps, inspecting his creation.

Sylvia and the security guard stood by the desk. The staff waited in silence while St. Laurent dialed the platform overhead light into a perfect shading.

Magdalena stood there like a painting, immobile in her pose, her head held high, her large oval-shaped eyes fully green now with the turquoise of the dress. Her lips were half parted, and as she looked up, one could feel the magnetism of the great superstar, the sophisticated woman of thirty-two major motion pictures, the subject of legends, a woman of power, beauty, and intense sexuality. There she stood, the creation of every sophisticated tool of beauty known in the world, the greatest couturiers, hairdressers and, makeup experts of all Paris—and yet she had a shy, vulnerable, childlike expression.

She was a girl, and this was a party for her.

She turned a full circle slowly, a ballet turn, so that the group below her could see every aspect of the dress and all the reflections turning in the mirrors of the room.

The room broke into applause. They realized they were seeing the blending of the art of two superstars, and that this showing was about to be photographed by every news service in the world.

At the end of the applause, Magdalena put her left hand to her mouth and slowly waved out a kiss to St. Laurent. "Ready."

St. Laurent nodded to two security guards at the back of the large fitting room. They pulled open the doors and four members of St. Laurent's staff ushered in a crowd of over 200 photographers and reporters representing every major newspaper in the world.

The two security men who had been guarding the jewelry box took their places in front of the raised platform, one of them with the box under his arm. They were watching and ready for any kind of intrusion on Magdalena Alba's position. Yves St. Laurent spoke to the press from directly below Magdalena's platform.

St. Laurent, above the din in the room, pointed to the wardrobe sketchbook. "It's an entire new wardrobe, gentlemen. Miss Alba will wear it on this special celebrity voyage of the *Royal Princess.*

"Forty-seven costumes, designed and made only once. Once, ladies and gentlemen, for Miss Alba. It is a privilege to design her wardrobe. I think this collection is the best I've ever done."

Magdalena spoke softly, "I can tell you, it *is* the best."

She spoke to St. Laurent so that the reporters would pick it up. Movie cameras, television cameras, cassettes, and microphones— everything was going.

Magdalena's security people and St. Laurent's staff had it all covered. They were like a well-drilled military unit. Everybody knew what he was doing, what he was supposed to accomplish, and how to accomplish it. Twenty-five people handled over two hundred people like a military machine. It was intricate, precise, a Rockette drill.

"Magdalena, what's your next film?"

She answered, "I don't know yet. I'll be going back to my home in Hollywood when the cruise is over, and I'll be ready to go to work. I'm looking forward to making a new picture. But I'm going to be very careful. There are certain things I want to say in my films from now on."

Another voice came from across the crowd, "Message films? What do they say? If you want to send a message, send it by Western Union!"

Magdalena, turning for the photographers, replied, "That's another old cliché—there isn't a good filmmaker in the world who doesn't make some kind of statement every time he makes a film. Films are autobiographical for a director who is an artist. He gives his interpretation, his view of the world, or part of it, or of a group of people, or at least of one person. Story is all-important, gentlemen, and now that I have my own company, I'm going to look for stories that I really want to do."

Another voice: "How old are you? Really?"

Magdalena smiled. She never allowed herself to get irritated in front of the press; she had learned that lesson a long time ago. You can't fight with the press and win. You have no choice. The cheapest reporter on the cheapest paper, the most inadequate critic, the most biased writer, they all have the advantage over any superstar.

Francis Ford Coppola had taught her that. He had learned it the hard way, he told her. Any critic in the world has outlets to the public. What he or she thinks or feels or wants to say is going to be printed, or broadcast, or televised. No matter how famous the superstar, he or she doesn't have that power.

Magdalena answered her questioner. "You've asked me that question all over the world and you know my answers better than I remember them. I'm quite sure, though, that I've never given my age. As a matter of fact, I decided very early to forget my age.

"I don't like birthdays. When I was growing up, I don't remember my family ever celebrating them.

"I've heard somewhere that you're as old as you look." She gave them her best smile. "I feel wonderful and I'm very grateful to all of you for coming and sharing this moment with Yves and myself and all of these people who worked so hard for this very special wardrobe for Yves's new season and for mine."

She gestured toward the people in the room. "As for how old I look," she said, and walked down one of the ramps that went directly out from the raised platform into the crowd of photographers and reporters who were being served champagne and caviar.

"I can't really say, I'll have to leave that to you. And, please," she gave them another big smile, "try to be kind."

With that, she did a model's turn at the end of the runway in perfect rhythm to Linda Ronstadt's "What's New," in which she revealed, strikingly, the long slit in her dress, her beautiful legs, the silky black lace pantyhose, and her full figure.

The reporters and photographers burst into applause—their answer to how old she was.

The photographers' bulbs went off from all sides as everyone closed in to a tightly packed circle at Magdalena's feet.

Sylvia was waiting for her in the dressing room, where a small table had been set with flowers, champagne, caviar, and finger sandwiches. Sylvia handed her a telegram. "Just arrived, Magdalena," she said.

Magdalena took off the turquoise necklace carefully. "Read it, will you, darling?"

Sylvia opened it and read it with growing interest.

Mlle. Magdalena Alba,
c/o Yves St. Laurent,
5, rue St.-Honoré,
Paris, France

Dear Mlle. Alba,

I would like to come to Paris to talk with you about one of the starring roles in my forthcoming film, *The Rest of Our Lives.*

Only you are right for the part. And yet I want to assure you that this is different from any role you have ever attempted. This part does not depend on your beauty or your "glamour."

I want to put on the screen, finally, the full woman I see within you. I want your mind and your heart for this role. It will be a challenge for you to create and I know that you can.

I will arrange my time for my trip to Paris to suit your schedule. Please let me hear from you at the address and telephone number below.

Sincerely,

Steve Wayland
Wayland Productions,
1048 So. Mapleton Avenue,
Los Angeles, CA 90077
(213) 555-3674

It was almost nine o'clock when Magdalena reached her doctor's office. As they neared the steps of the handsome old office building on Avenue Foch, she dismissed Sylvia.

"Darling, go home. There's still a lot of packing to do and Bob Redford might be calling from Utah." She glanced at her watch. "Tell him I can call him back in a few hours. I want to talk to him about the script. I don't think it's quite right for me yet, but be sure he knows how much I'd like to work with him. Also, see if Clint's in town yet. Please make a note, I must talk to him before he leaves. And cable Steve Wayland—tell him I'll be glad to see him in Hollywood, that I have no time now in Paris before the sailing. Go along now, and have Joseph give you dinner. It's been a long day."

"What about you?" Sylvia asked.

"I'll get something when I come home."

Sylvia asked, "Don't you want me to wait?"

Magdalena shook her head. "I want to drive the car home. I love to drive in Paris at night. Did you ever see that little film Lelouch made, when he drove through Paris at night, with cameras all over his car? He went everywhere. The Champs-Elysées, the Left Bank, the airport drive, everything. At full speed. I'll get a print and run it for you. What a cameraman he is! See you later, darling." Magdalena kissed Sylvia on both cheeks and went into the building of Dr. Loussard.

A young, attractive doctor was studying a row of medical reports when a nurse brought in Magdalena Alba. Magdalena kissed him as he came up to greet her affectionately.

She was dressed in a tailored sky blue velvet suit with a powder blue silk blouse fitted very tightly across her breasts. She wore a large sapphire cross around her neck, a diamond and sapphire ring, and matching earrings. Around her shoulders she wore a striking full-length white mink cloak. The contrast of the sheer white against the deep blue of the suit was exquisite. Her almond-shaped eyes were a glowing blue.

Dr. Loussard looked at her admiringly. "You look more beautiful than ever. How's the collection?"

"The best ever," Magdalena replied. "These are clothes that you can actually wear, for every kind of occasion. They really are quite lovely."

The doctor looked at her intently. "How's the press?"

Magdalena smiled. "Crowded, rude, friendly, unfriendly, just like the rest of the world. We get along. I've learned."

The doctor sat down at the edge of his desk, opposite her.

"You know, Magdalena, you're one of my favorite people. I didn't say patients, I said people."

She looked up at him and spoke quietly. "Doctor, why that remark at this particular moment? I know you, and I know that there's thought-fulness behind everything you say, particularly at the yearly medical examination. You've found something?"

"I don't know," he said.

Magdalena glanced back. "Really?"

"Really. I never lie to you."

"Well, then, you can tell me the truth now. What's wrong with me? Cancer?"

The doctor shook his head. "The scans are negative; so are the cancer blood tests. We don't have to worry about that, Magdalena."

Magdalena spoke with a little edge in her voice. "What *do* we have to be afraid of? What I hear behind your voice, Doctor, is fear—fear for me."

The doctor flipped the switch to the secretary. "I don't want to be disturbed."

He snapped off the button. The tension in him was unmistakable.

He spoke quietly. "We don't know. The same old problem with my job so often. We have to guess and hope."

Magdalena looked at the doctor steadily.

"Tell me, Doctor—the truth—we always have, you and I."

The doctor replied quietly, "I am telling you the truth. It may be a very rare disease—called dermatomyositis. It's sometimes related to lupus.

"There are five clinics in the world that specialize in it. One is the University of California in Los Angeles.

"We don't know what causes it or very much about it, except that it begins attacking the muscles and the tissues and spreads through the body unless it's halted."

Magdalena held her steady gaze. "Where does it end?"

The doctor reached over his desk and picked up a printed medical report. "Many times it can be arrested. There's no cure for it yet. But some people have had it for many years, treated it, arrested it, and have gone on with their lives and their work. Laurence Olivier is one."

"Larry has it?"

The doctor nodded. "For years. And he's had other health problems, too. They've all been fully reported in the papers and in his auto-biography, but, as you know, he goes on working. I think he's had every honor that your profession gives by now, hasn't he?"

"He's such an artist—everyone in the business idolizes him. I've always wanted to work with him." Her voice was resigned. "How long before you know about me, for sure?" she asked.

The doctor stood up, relieved to have gotten over the first mountain. "A few months. I have here the last full medical report from UCLA on dermatomyositis. It describes the symptoms and the treatment. I want you to read it because I want you to monitor yourself. When are you going back to California?"

She answered slowly, "We sail next month. I've already agreed to the cruise. Now I wish I didn't have to go."

"Why? It's perfect for you to have something like that on your mind, taking all your attention, and it won't hurt you to get pampered a little right now. Remember, my tests are inconclusive. You may not have anything. You haven't felt tired recently, have you?"

She shook her head. "No."

The doctor smiled. "Well, that's one of the very first signs. Fatigue. Chances are the tests don't mean anything. But when you go to California, I want you to see Dr. Alfred Arms. He and a Dr. Cahill in Thailand are the leading experts on this disease. I'll call Dr. Arms before you get home."

Magdalena put on her gloves. He slipped her long white cloak over her shoulders. He wondered again how old she was. He had never asked her and he had no idea.

There was not a line in her face. Not a mark on her body. Her strong, special personal perfume, mixed with the intoxicating odor of the new Yves St. Laurent perfume, Tryst, came in waves.

He was her doctor, her personal doctor, but he still felt her mystery.

She looked at him directly. The smile was sad. Again, the word he always thought of when she came into his mind—haunted. What was the story behind this woman? He had heard many rumors, but he didn't know the truth.

Her voice was soft, with a lovely feminine inflection. "Thank you, Doctor. You are a special man. You do not pretend."

The doctor smiled. "I can say the same for you, Magdalena."

Suddenly she stopped, just as she was turning away from him. "I have to apologize."

"For what?" he asked.

"I lied to you," she answered.

He looked at her questioningly.

"I told you I'd been feeling well." Her voice broke a little. "But it's true that for weeks I've been feeling tired. I thought it was just a little passing thing. Now, perhaps we have the answer."

The doctor was taken aback for a moment. "Let me call Dr. Arms. Let me give him your fact sheets and your laboratory tests.

He'll tell us what to do. We could start the treatment here. But, Magdalena . . ."

She looked up at him.

He continued. "Magdalena, you must go to the best place in the world—where they know the most. I don't have the benefit of their research here. I just don't know enough. Maybe they'll want me to start you on the treatment here. But you have to go as soon as you can."

She glanced at him. "How important is time?"

He looked directly back at her. "Very important."

She questioned him. "This, what did you say it was?"

The doctor answered, "Dermatomyositis."

"It can kill you, Doctor?" she asked.

"Yes," he answered.

She steadied herself for a moment, and he reached out and took her by the shoulders.

She questioned him again. "What is the basic treatment?"

The doctor answered, "I think Dr. Arms would advise heavy corticosteroid injections, the strongest antiinflammatory drugs available. And rest is essential."

She said quickly, "What are the aftereffects of these injections?"

"It's not dangerous. It's a little painful and there is some swelling."

Immediately, she was on him. "Swelling? Where? The body or the face?"

The doctor shrugged. "Some of both. But the corticosteroids often arrest the disease."

Magdalena asked, "How long does the swelling last?"

The doctor answered, "Well, sometimes for a long time, sometimes for good. It isn't a short-term process."

"Are you saying that my face might swell up and stay that way?" Magdalena asked.

"You would really have to ask Dr. Arms that. I don't have the statistics."

She cut him off. "But you know. I can see it in your eyes. The answer is yes. My face would probably swell up out of shape, and I would have to live that way. Well, Doctor, I can tell you right now. I will not take these injections. I will not have my face destroyed."

"Your beauty is really more important to you than life itself?"

She flashed back at him. "I'm not in love with life. Life has always brought me pain. My one security has been my beauty. I'm not going to turn that over to anyone but myself. So don't worry about me,

Doctor, and don't call anyone else. This is a private matter between you and me. Is it not?"

The doctor nodded. "It is."

She spoke to him softly again. She had regained control of herself. "Thank you, Doctor. Just forget about tonight. I was never here. And I want to tear up my examination reports. They belong to me. I've paid for them."

She stepped over to the desk, picked up her file, and tore it in half, then in quarters. She threw it in the wastebasket.

"Like everything else, Doctor, it was all an illusion. You had a dream. A bad dream. But you won't have it again. Good-bye."

She turned and walked out of the doctor's office, forever.

Her white convertible Rolls-Royce, the top down and neatly covered and the white leather of the seats gleaming immaculately, was waiting on the street in front of the doctor's office. She tipped the building porter who had been watching the car for her. And then she stepped into the car and quickly pulled away from the curb.

The whole area of Avenue Foch was quiet and deserted. There was little traffic and she made her way expertly through it.

She came to a halt in the shadow of the Place de la Concorde.

As she pulled away from the stop sign and sped down the avenue opposite the Louvre, Magdalena Alba was sobbing. There was no one watching her. There was nobody demanding that she hide her face or her feelings.

She had fought so many fights, and won. There was no human being who frightened her. And very few who challenged her. But how could she fight this terrible thing that was in her body, clawing at her energy, tightening in on her breathing, and clenching her muscles, terrible sensations that had begun to come upon her?

Now, she knew what was happening to her. It all seemed very clear. For weeks she had been sick, perhaps for months, for years.

No one knew how this thing started, or how long it took to manifest itself. Was it from those days as a child in the gypsy caves of Seville? Was it from her early days as a young girl modeling in Marseilles and sleeping with a loaded gun?

How could she possibly have contracted such a disease? This was the last injustice. Her life had started off without justice. A bastard child. Not even her father's name. Deserted and ostracized by both the poor and rich families who were her heredity.

Magdalena continued to sob. She pushed down on the accelerator, heading toward the Arc de Triomphe.

Death was stalking her now. But more than death. The one thing that had salvaged her life and made it livable was under attack. Her beauty. Her face. Her body.

Everything that she showed to the world, everything that her career and her position in life depended on, were threatened now.

She might not die. But her beauty would be gone. Terror struck the heart of Magdalena Alba.

The car sped up. She was an expert driver, and only her skill prevented her from crashing into other cars. As she turned and twisted the wheel, a lifetime of locked-up sobs was spilling out.

She cut into the inner lane around the circle of the Arc de Triomphe. She was in a line of fast-moving French taxis.

Her chest fell against the wheel in a sob and the horn of her Rolls blasted out at the taxi in front of her. The driver turned around furiously.

Magdalena swung the wheel to her left and ran up over the curb of the first level of the Arc de Triomphe. The car raced along at an uneven level, the left front wheel traveling on the curb, until Magdalena swung it back down into the street.

The traffic spilled wildly in all directions. It was everyone for himself, with this speeding convertible Rolls-Royce out of control.

Magdalena shot out from the circle into the side streets. The parade of nighttime prostitutes in their extravagant costuming scattered in every direction, afraid that the Rolls-Royce was going to go over the edge of the curbing again.

Magdalena raced out into a long boulevard leading to the country.

The speedometer climbed as she sped down Avenue Charles de Gaulle. Other streets, other corners whirled by, a nightmare. Avenue Roule, Boulevard Victor Hugo, Boulevard Saussaye. A jagged blur of swerving cars, screeching tires, a spinning steering wheel.

Magdalena sped through an intersection, barely missing a massive, gasoline-bearing truck. As the long tail of the truck moved sideways, she swerved to her right, parallel to it. The swinging end of the truck skidded by her. Forty tons of instant liquid fire missed her by four feet.

She swung the car hard left, down another road, and behind her she heard the screaming whine of gendarmes. She glanced at her rearview mirror. Two police cars were two hundred yards behind her.

Magdalena raced through a small suburb of Paris, down the main street and out the other side of the town. Two cars barely got out of her way.

The Rolls-Royce was coming down a hill. The police cars were still two hundred yards away, but beginning to slip behind.

Magdalena could hardly see. The tears clouded her eyes. But there was something on the road. She strained to see. She could hear faintly in the open car the scream of a child.

Suddenly she saw a little girl, at the bottom of the hill. She stood directly in the path of the oncoming Rolls-Royce, which loomed like some huge animal in the night darkness. The child was transfixed in fear.

Magdalena thought she recognized the girl, even in the night. The face was her own, back in a gypsy camp on Sacre Monte, near Seville.

She swung the car to the right and lost control. The car veered off the shoulder of the road, straddling a ditch and still racing. The Rolls rolled over three times, bounced in the air, and exploded in the night sky.

5

Beverly Hills

The fashionable movie-society crowd turned, table by table, to watch the exquisite Oriental woman being escorted to her table by Jimmy Murphy.

Her dark hair was parted in the middle, swept back into a perfect chignon. She was dressed in a long, form-fitting mandarin dress of rose brocade. It came up high at the collar, with tight sleeves, and was split at the sides to a point midway up her thighs, revealing her beautiful legs.

She was tall for an Oriental woman, and delicately featured. The nose was short, straight, and slender. The cheekbones were high, the jawline firm, and the mouth full.

But it was the eyes of the woman that were fascinating. They had a stoic acceptance of life, but flashed with independence of spirit.

For the jaded crowd that populated Jimmy's chic restaurant in Beverly Hills, Lieu Santo was something different. Someone to whisper about.

Now in her early forties, Lieu had been the greatest woman motion picture star of the Asian world before the ravaging of Cambodia. Cambodian-born, internationally celebrated, powerful, with her own studio and production company, she was a Cambodian heroine. She and her husband, a high-ranking military figure in the army of Cambodia, had been closely aligned to the United States. Lieu Santo had escaped from the boat people tragedy on a refugee plane from Thailand.

She had tried to find work as an actress in Hollywood, but her money, her possessions, and her power had been left behind in Cambodia. She was a fascinating, glamorous, gossiped-about world figure, who in the space of a year became a top executive in the Cambodian refugee settlement organization in the United States. The job and the prestige were high. The pay was low.

And now, her life had become her two sons and a desperate determination to recapture her place in the international film community of Hollywood. Her drive and ambition were famous in the town. She had been, for the last three years, associate producer for Steve Wayland.

It was to Steve Wayland's table that Jimmy Murphy led Lieu. Steve was sitting with Spartan Lee, his distinguished and world famous Japanese-American partner, friend, lawyer, and manager.

Both men stood up as Lieu came to their table in one of the prime corners of Jimmy's restaurant.

Lieu glanced at Steve for a moment, and then sat down on the opposite side of the booth from the two men. There were no trivial greetings. They were waiting for what she had to say.

"I've just talked to the hospital," Lieu said softly. "They're taking her in for surgery now."

Steve leaned towards Lieu, his hand grasping hers. "She's alive."

Lieu nodded. "Still in a coma. That's all I know for sure. She was thrown from the car before it exploded."

"Had she taken anything?" Spartan Lee asked. "Was she drunk? I never heard of Magdalena Alba being addicted to drugs. I can't believe she'd try to kill herself."

Lieu answered him quietly. "The suicide talk is just a rumor. You know how they are with film people. It's got to be bigger than life. It can't be just an accident. Either it has to be suicide or murder or dope addiction." She paused for a moment. "One of the prices you pay."

"You knew her pretty well when you lived in Paris, didn't you?" Steve asked.

"Not intimately. We were both members of a small film group of actors and writers and directors—she was someone I always looked up to."

"That says something," Steve answered. "I don't know many people you've ever looked up to—maybe none."

Lieu smiled. "I'm not as arrogant as all that. In fact, your country has taught me humility."

Spartan Lee questioned, "Steve, you can't recast Magdalena, you know that. That's part of our deal. You have to have Magdalena Alba, and you have to sign Rayme Monterey, too. One of them's in jail, and one of them's God-knows-what in a Paris hospital—dying, crippled, maimed—" He turned to Lieu. "When will we have word?"

Lieu answered, "I have one of my Paris friends at the hospital—a writer for *Time*—he owes us some favors. I told him to call me as soon as he has any facts." She nodded at her lotus design purse and patted the beeper inside. "I'm on call."

"I'm going to leave tomorrow," Steve said.

"New York or Paris first?" Spartan asked.

"Depends on what I hear from our friend from *Time*. I may not be able to see Magdalena for a few days—you know I've never met her."

"Gregson's stepping up the pressure on you," Spartan said.

"That bastard," Lieu said, in her cool, refined voice, almost making "bastard" a word of distinction.

Spartan added, "He sent me a big stack of New York newspapers with Rayme's picture on the front page. He's enjoying the whole damn thing, and he's demanding the papers be signed—by you and by me."

"Why you?" Steve asked.

"I'm giving him my word that your signature is good. That's all. It doesn't matter."

Steve flushed bright red. "Spartan, you're not putting any more of your own on the line for me. Otherwise, we'll call it off right now. I know you, Spartan."

"The papers reflect only what you and I agreed to, Steve—nothing from me but my word. But the picture can't go over budget. It can't even *look* like it's going over budget. I want you to understand that, Steve, because I've been over every fine line three times now.

"This is independent production at its purest. Your own money on the line—your house, your work, your screenplays, your career, your future—it's all on your back, Steve. Take it and make it work."

Steve sipped his drink. "Everything," he said quietly. "There's no way I can hold back the house? You know what it means to the kids."

"And to you," Lieu said.

"I know," Spartan remarked. "It's the biggest personal gamble a man could make. But some of the men you admire who built this industry took that kind of gamble. I know you can handle it. Who gives a damn if they're all waiting for you to go into the sewer? You've known for a long time how this place operates.

"You just get the picture," Spartan continued, "within the budget—and no one can change one thing. You've got complete control—one of the few times in the history of this business the filmmaker has absolute control. That's what you've always wanted, Steve, and that's what we've got now. The same as Spielberg."

"This is your time," Lieu said. "You can make a statement up there on the screen, just the statement you want, with *The Rest of Our Lives*. If you never make another film, this is your legacy. If I had it to do over again, I would trade half the films I made, stories that didn't really matter, for one picture that had my feelings in it—my ideas— a legacy of my own. Don't compromise, Steve. Don't cater to anyone. Don't let anyone influence you."

"She's right," Spartan added, "but, for God's sake, don't go over budget."

6

Holmby Hills

Steve felt they were violating his home. The "team" from Rodeo Realty was spread out over his colonial house like a swarm of locusts. The results were being computerized by a Rodeo Realty clerk, who was sitting at the dining room table. House, furnishings, art objects, paintings; only his children's rooms were locked off, not to be touched.

He had built this house just three years before. He had put all of his savings into it.

Since he'd left Chicago to go to college, he'd never had anywhere he'd really belonged. These were his roots. His Missouri roots, put down in the foreign country of California. Put down for himself, his two daughters, Kathleen and Lorelei, and his friends. This is where Steve had written the screenplays of the last few years, and had dreamed his dreams.

He had sketched all the rooms himself, and then actually built the house with a good friend who was an architect. Every day for a year and a half, he had gone to the property at six o'clock in the morning to check the progress. The one thing he had built in all his life, his first real home, a place where he could lock out the jungle, where he could watch the stars at night and sit around the fire, reading with his children and playing music and being part of their world.

Now he was signing everything over. It was part of the deal to make *The Rest of Our Lives*.

He sat in the back of the house on the garden stairs. The huge sycamore trees cast their shadows over the yard and across the chimney tops.

Soon he would go for the children. It was his weekend with Kathleen and Lorelei and they lived for these weekends almost as much as he did.

What would he tell them? Important things in their lives they had always talked through together, the three of them, since they were very little. Steve had tried to explain exactly what he thought and felt, even when they were too young fully to understand it. Now he was in another crisis in his life, and theirs. Never any more did he separate his life from theirs. They had become part of everything he did.

He asked himself honestly if he really believed that it was right for him to sign away the potential ownership of the house to the studio and to Jack Gregson? He knew that he became obsessed with his creative convictions. That had happened more than once. But now he had two others to think of besides himself. Was he simply feeding his own ego? Was he simply so desperate to "make it" in his profession that he would gamble anything for it?

What it came down to was that if he had only one more film to make in his life, would it be *The Rest of Our Lives*? Did this story have the essence of everything he believed? Did it have now, with the changes he was making in it, the emotional power that he wanted to put on the screen? Did it reflect everything he had gone through and felt deeply in his life? Wasn't that the whole point? Wasn't that the reason for his drive?

He had learned finally that the most artistic was the simplest. This wasn't a popular concept in these times of artifice and negativity. It wasn't "in" or "chic" to be simple. Tricks and effects and glitz had replaced content most of the time. He had to see that *The Rest of Our Lives* was "today," that it reached out and cut across audience boundaries, but also that it had some lasting value.

He knew that he would be working on the movie right up to the moment of production and all the way through filming—refining, absorbing life itself as it came to him, taking the gifts from the stars he was hoping to assemble, welcoming ideas from all the people with whom he worked so closely in the creative part of his production. That's why he had chosen the name for his film. It wasn't a trick title. It wasn't a catch phrase. It wasn't a jingoistic line. Simplicity—that was his goal. And if he could reach that goal, a story that would dramatize, in straight and simple terms, the drive to accomplish one's dreams in the rest of the life one had left, then that was what he was doing himself right here, and what he was questioning now. He wanted to make a film that would withstand his own test.

The Rest of Our Lives had to be worth everything he was sacrificing, and if it was, then he was doing the right thing, not only for himself, but for his children.

He was convinced that he could meet Jack Gregson's toughest requirements. He did not believe that Rayme Monterey would be indicted by a jury for homicide. Manslaughter was questionable, too. Of course, Rayme could be freed and then indicted again on the basis of "new" evidence. Steve did have to consider that possibility, but he had to take the chance Rayme would have enough free time for the film.

The role Steve had written for Rayme in *The Rest of Our Lives* was Rayme Monterey. Rayme and his people would recognize it. With the creative controls he was offering them, he didn't feel Rayme could refuse.

Magdalena Alba. By now, Lieu should have spoken with her friend at that Paris hospital. By now, Steve should have heard something. Magdalena had to live. This part in *The Rest of Our Lives* would challenge her, he was certain of it. Although they had never met, he had seen all her films. He had watched the growth of her talent, her confidence. Her authority. In his film, she would be a modern woman with all the conflicts of life in the arena of today's world.

He remembered how she had looked when she had begun, almost twenty years before, in Truffaut's film. She had played a tormented young girl deserted by her teenaged lover, forsaken by family and friends. Pregnant. And alone. Magdalena had more than played a part. Steve recognized that. The girl was playing something out of her own life, out of her own experience. She was completely inside the part. She wasn't acting; she was being. For twenty years the image of that girl's face, so raw with pain, so vulnerable, had stayed with Steve.

So, without ever meeting her, he had written a part he felt could be the greatest achievement of her career. He would have to talk her out of perfection in her makeup, her clothes, her appearance. That had become her trademark. But how was she going to resist this part, when she could prove, once and for all, that she was a great actress? This was a role Bette Davis would have killed for in her prime. Steve was sure of it.

He hadn't even told the studio yet about Robert Montango. He didn't want to hear all the comments that Montango was over the hill. Certainly they couldn't deny that he was one of the biggest motion picture stars of all time. And the part that Steve had written was truly Robert Montango's; it was written to his emotional power.

Finally, there was the fourth starring role. No one knew about Mary Jane Stuckey, the girl he had seen once in a joint in Sacramento, whom he now felt sure he had tracked down.

It was a kind of strip joint he'd seen her in, but Mary Jane had made the place into something else. She was the best jazz dancer he had ever seen. As good in her way as Alessandra Ferri was on the stage of the American Ballet Company in *Romeo and Juliet* or dancing with Baryshnikov in *Giselle*. Mary Jane Stuckey was another original.

The girl from Sacramento had come into his mind again and again as he wrote the treatment for *The Rest of Our Lives*, and then the screenplay. But since she had been disguised as Raggedy Ann in the Sacramento floor show, Steve did not know exactly what she looked like.

So he hired detectives, who had finally found her. He would know in a few days. They said she now called herself La Tigressa.

The four central players. Magdalena, Robert Montango, Rayme Monterey, and, he hoped, La Tigressa. If she were the same girl, she was perfect for *The Rest of Our Lives*.

He gave himself the answer he had hoped to find. Yes, he was gambling. His home and everything he owned, and owned in trust for Kathleen and Lorelei. But he didn't really believe that *The Rest of Our Lives* could lose.

And the reason he could gamble some physical elements of his children's lives was clear to him now, even as his gaze roamed across the back yard and across the back windows of their rooms. This was a house, and had been their home, and maybe would remain their home. But it would remain their home because the three of them were in it. If they moved, and had to live somewhere else, they would take their home with them.

As he reconnected with his convictions, his fear quieted. Whenever he thought about his children's security, fear grabbed his stomach. But what had he talked to them about so many, many times, despite their tender years? He had talked about a mission in life, as he had come to believe, that we were all here in this existence at this time for some reason—to do something—to try—to follow a dream. And you went for that dream with everything you had. Because meaning in life was not derived from money or power, or how big a house you had, or if there was a Rolls-Royce in your driveway—meaning was in relationships—family, first of all, then in your friends, and, finally, in what you did with your life. He had made his children part of his convictions and they understood him because of the time they spent

together with him. It wasn't only the books they read together, the
television programs they saw, and the films, the plays, the ballet, the
art galleries, and the concerts—it was just as much in the spontaneous
times, times spent just having fun. Playing games, barbecuing a Sunday
night dinner together, just, as the kids called it, "hanging out." Being
together, no matter how they differed, how they argued. They always
had a place to come back to.

If *he* didn't have the courage to follow his dream, if he didn't give
his children the opportunity to understand him and to be a part of
this, then everything he'd been talking about and sharing with them
for years didn't stand the test.

He made up his mind he would tell them tonight, in a way they
would understand. And he knew, without any reservation or doubt,
that they would be with him. That was the home they had built
together, the home of the heart.

How many hundreds of times had he taken the Santa Monica Freeway to 26th Street and driven along the countrylike streets to Wellesley
Avenue. There his emotional life was centered, and his two daughters
waited for him, Kathleen, eleven, and Lorelei, nine. How many hundreds
of times had he driven up to their mother's house? The attorneys had
agreed on every other weekend for him to have the children. As time
went by, and his wife, Melanie, remarried, much of the basic feeling
between her and Steve had come back. The friendship they had once
had, without the tension of a close emotional relationship.

It was only that they couldn't make it as man and wife. Looking
back he realized they hadn't known what man and wife meant when
they got married. He was twenty-four; Melanie was eighteen. It was
a ritual of youth, sexual investigation, and romantic dreams. Life
hadn't tested them yet. The world of advertising had prepared them
for a perpetual honeymoon.

After a family wedding in Brentwood, they had settled down in a
small rented house in Pacific Palisades and Steve had begun his fight
to survive in the fierce competition of the entertainment world. Now,
somehow, in Steve's mind, all those years came together as one moment in which they had been married, had two children, and then
grown apart. They had demanded too much of each other. A line
from Anne Morrow's Lindbergh *Gift from the Sea* flashed through his
head. "No one loves anyone all the time. But that is what every one
of us wants."

His children were the most important people in the world to Steve.
When he was with them, he had a world that made sense. He had

something to fight for. He had his dream, tight in his arms. It had been that way since they were born, and it grew as they grew.

He had barely slowed his car over to the curb when the door of the house on Wellesley Street opened and his two children were racing across the lawn to their father. Steve swept them into his arms, one on each shoulder. They clung to him. It seemed a long time since their last weekend together.

His heart surged with the love between him and his daughters. It was different from anything he had ever felt before. He was part of them. They were part of him. They needed him, and he needed them. They gave him tenderness, strength, and love. He gave his heart back to them.

He carried them back to the front seat of the convertible, and then went back to the entrance of the house where the girls' mother was standing. Their overnight cases were resting in the doorway. Melanie's face was soft.

"Hello, Steve," she said. She was small and girlish. Her fragility and vulnerability had always moved him. She had long blond hair and a smile that was irresistible. The anger and bitterness from years past had gone out of her face. Steve felt at that moment much of the same attraction that had first drawn him to her.

These comings and goings of their children no longer unnerved them both, but there was still a wrenching about it. It never seemed right. Steve felt he should be going into that home to find his children and his wife waiting for him. He wondered why he and Melanie had ever divorced. All the old feelings burned inside.

The home he had had with Melanie and his children was another home that had passed him by. How had that happened? He asked himself this question for the thousandth time as he looked at the lovely green-eyed woman who had been his wife for seven years, the mother of his children.

Was it possible that they had gone together, fallen in love, made love for the first time, rented a house together, worried together, laughed together, cried together? Was it possible they had never understood each other's needs or how to communicate their innermost feelings to each other? Were they the same people who had lied to each other and cheated on each other before it was over?

Why hadn't he been more open to what she was feeling, all the insecurities of her childhood? Why hadn't he been able to see the pain in her and her deep need for approval and appreciation? Were those needs any different from his own? Were they both so scarred by their own pains that they couldn't open their hearts to the pains of others?

The unpleasant, angry, tortured things that eventually happened between them seemed impossible as he looked into her face. Was it really possible that their marriage had been over for three years now?

Steve said hello to her husband and in one moment was thankful for the man's gentleness to his children, and at the same time hated him for being there. What was he doing there, being called "Daddy Jim" by *his*, Steve's, children? Who the hell was he anyway? He could accept the fact that this stranger was sleeping with his wife, but he couldn't accept the fact that he was taking away part of Steve's place as the girls' father. This stranger was the one who could kiss them good night in their beds. *He* was there. Steve was not.

In the end Steve was grateful to Jim for his kindness to Kathleen and Lorelei. And he was good for Melanie. But it was never easy for any of them.

He said good night and gave Melanie a handshake—a handshake, for God's sake! He had embraced this woman thousands of times. What was he doing giving her a handshake? This was his wife—no, it wasn't—not anymore. This was a stranger. A Mrs. Somebody Else. Broken away and disconnected from him. Once she had been Mrs. Steve Wayland. No one would ever call her that again.

If only he had really listened to what Melanie had tried to say. If only he had had the unselfishness to put her first to find out what agonies of the past she held. He should have been able to do something about it—after all he was the older of the two and the more experienced. But he had been expecting so much from her. As long as he had worked, as hard as he could, for both of them, then he felt he was to be loved and admired for that. That's the way he had seen it between his father and mother. He had thought that's the way it was. If only he had known more and tried harder with Melanie, they might still be together with their children. He blamed himself.

But it was like Chicago. Thomas Wolfe had been so right—who could ever go home again?

He took the two bags to the car and put them in the back seat. Lorelei still called him by his nickname, "Daddyboat." Kathleen was beginning to grow up now and called her father a very proper "Dad." But when they put their arms around him it was the same. It would always be the same between them. Two whole days ahead he had with them. He hoped they would understand about the house.

They were coming off the 405 freeway on the Sunset exit and heading for home. He had been catching up on everything that had happened at school during the last few days. Suddenly, Kathleen turned to him. There was a different look in her eyes and a different tone in her voice. He had noticed when they pulled away from the house on Wellesley that both girls had leaned out the window to wave good-bye to their mother until she was out of sight. She had stayed there, standing in the doorway.

"Dad," Kathleen said, "I know we've talked about it before, but I don't really understand—why can't we all live together like other people do?"

Lorelei picked up what her sister had said. "We asked Mom about it again tonight, when we were packing our bags. She always says the same thing—when we're old enough we'll understand."

"We are old enough," Kathleen cut in, "and we don't understand. I've watched you two together, every time you pick us up and every time you bring us home back to mother's house. You like Mom, don't you?"

"Yes," Steve said. "And I miss her. She's a wonderful person."

"That's what she says about you," Lorelei stated. "If you like each other, why are you apart? Why aren't we all together?"

Steve's heart sank as they turned up Sunset and down toward his house. "Sometimes when you love someone, it just doesn't work out. People can love each other, but sometimes they can't seem to live together. That's what happened to your mother and me. We couldn't seem to work out a way of living together that made us happy. We each needed certain things out of the marriage, and we didn't get enough of them, either of us, to make us go on trying. We both thought we were right. Now, I think I was the one who was wrong.

"I know how hard it is on you both. To tell you the truth, it's hard on us, too—your mother knows that—I wish I had a chance to change what happened, but I don't." Steve turned to look at them. "I'm sorry," he said.

It was 10:00 at night. Anna Garrett, the black woman who worked for Steve and whom they called "AGW," adding their own last name to hers, was with them in the study watching a cassette of *The Wizard of Oz*. As the end credits went up, AGW clapped her hands lightly. It was the automatic sign for bedtime.

"I'll bring them up in a minute, AGW," Steve said. "I have something I want to tell them. As a matter of fact, you should hear it, too, because you are part of this family."

Steve held both girls in his lap. They were already in their pajamas and bathrobes. He kissed each girl on her eyelids, the way they always wanted him to do at night.

"Kath, Lor, I don't know any way to tell you a story about this . . ."

Kathleen interrupted. "Yes, you do. You can make a story out of anything."

Lor chimed in, "Please, Daddyboat."

"Well, I'll try. But I want to be sure you'll understand so you ask me any questions you like later. Okay?"

The two girls nodded and settled comfortably back on the sofa as he started the story.

"Well, you see, there was this friend of mine in Hollywood who tried to make stories."

Kathleen said, "You mean stories with a prince, a Sleeping Beauty, and a villain?"

Lorelei spoke up. "And a dragon? And some dwarfs?"

"That's right," Steve said. "Just like the stories we tell each other, that we make up all the time—the hero, the villain, Cinderella. Well, this man I'm telling you about, he had two boys."

Kathleen interrupted. "Are you sure they weren't girls, Dad? Just like Lorelei and me?"

Steve laughed. "Yes, I'm sure. These were two boys. Not two girls. Now listen, because I want you to get the point of the story, okay?"

Lorelei looked at Kathleen. "Let Daddyboat tell the story." She punched her father with her elbow. "Go ahead," she added. Anna laughed.

Steve went on. "Well, this man wanted to make a film he thought might be important for many people. A film about what people do with their lives, and how they do it. About people who care, and people who don't care. About people who love, and people who don't love. He wanted to try to put everything that he'd learned, including all his mistakes, into a motion picture that people would understand in any language. And the longer he worked, the more this dream became important to him, because he kept seeing his two boys grow up—"

Kathleen interrupted him. "You mean two girls, Dad?"

Steve smiled. "No—two boys. He wanted to make something that might mean something to people who saw it, something they could relate to their own lives and most of all his two little boys might be proud of what he tried to do. Because, you see, he loved these two little boys very much, and they were part of everything he did, and every dream he dreamed."

The two girls pressed closer to his shoulder.

"And," Steve continued, "this man couldn't raise the money for this picture to be made, and he went to all the usual places. Rich, powerful people with money in the motion picture business. And no one believed in this dream. And they didn't think his movie would make money.

"Finally, this man had to risk everything he owned—even his house, the house he'd built for his two boys. That was the only way to get the money. If enough people went to see the movie, his house would be saved. If not, it would be taken away from him. And so, you know what he did?"

Kathleen's face had changed from a smile to a worried frown. "He asked his two boys," Kathleen said, "because it was their house, too." Steve nodded. Lorelei sat up and looked at him straight in the face.

"What did the two boys say?"

"What do you think?" Steve asked.

Lorelei put her arms around his neck. "They said 'yes,' because it didn't matter where they lived as long as they were together and as long as they loved each other."

"And because if he didn't fight for his dream to the end, he just wouldn't be their dad, that's all," Kathleen added.

"No question about it?" Steve asked.

The girls shook their heads. Steve stood up, carrying both of them, one in each arm. He looked at Anna. She and the girls knew everything, anyway. They always seemed to be there before him. As Anna stood up and started upstairs, she said, quietly, "Never going to happen. Because that friend of yours, Mr. Wayland, is going to make a real good movie. And everybody's going to go see it."

Steve smiled as the girls' arms went around him. Kathleen whispered in his ears, "Everybody!"

Lorelei added, "I'll get my whole school."

Steve whispered back, "My friend is a very lucky man."

Anna stood at the doorway as Steve put the children to bed. They said their individual prayers now, for their friends, their teachers, their mother, for Anna, and then for their father. Tonight they added a name: "And God bless Dad's friend who's making the movie," Kathleen said, and Lorelei echoed her prayer.

Steve reached out and held his daughters' hands tightly. "I want you to remember something," he said, "always. No matter what happens, no matter what mistakes any of us make, no matter what the problem is, as you get older, there's one thing you can count on and I can, too. I'm there for you. I'll always be there for you. As you are for me. That's our rock. A lot of things can happen in life, good things and bad things. But nothing, nothing, can change the fact that I love you both with all my heart.

"Rain or shine, good grades or bad grades, success or failure, we have our rock. And your love for me is my rock. You've shown me that love all your lives. That rock is our home every day of our lives. Houses can come and go. But a home is forever."

7

New York City Jail

Rayme Monterey was being held in a jail cell in New York City, pending the grand jury investigation demanded by the district attorney. New York City law gave the person waiting for trial the choice of being heard before a judge or a jury. Also, it gave him the right to waive his right to a jury if the charge were so emotionally loaded that a jury would not listen to the "legal" ins and outs of why he should be acquitted.

Rayme Monterey had chosen to have the investigation in front of a jury. If the grand jury indicted him, then there would be a trial for murder or manslaughter. If the grand jury did not indict him, charges would have to be dropped, Rayme would go free, and the district attorney would have to show just cause to call together a second grand jury indictment.

Rayme had chosen against bail. He and his attorney, Edmund Bradford Wilson, felt that the best thing he could do for his case was to speak out his feelings, not in any way run from the charges.

Steve Wayland walked down the corridor in the jail with the master defense attorney, who had been hired by Rayme's managers. Wilson was concerned, and Steve picked that up.

"There's no possibility of an indictment, is there?" Steve asked.

"There's always a possibility," Wilson answered. "When you're dealing with a jury, and a judge, nothing is certain. There are too many questionables."

"What about public opinion?" Steve asked. "I haven't heard one newspaper or one commentator come out against Rayme."

"The 'deadly force' theory has a lot of supporters, within the law, but this district attorney is not going to be impartial. He's got a political powerhouse going for his career here—with one simple motto—'What if everyone took the law into his own hands?' "

"You can't defend a woman against rape?" Steve asked.

"If Rayme had just shot the assailant who was involved in the rape, I don't think there'd be any problem. But shooting all of them—and two of them dead . . . that's what gives the district attorney his opening, and he's as politically hungry as any public official I've ever seen," Wilson answered.

"This is the kind of case," he continued, "a defense attorney dreams about. Before we're through with indictments and appeals, and everything else, the Rayme Monterey case will go down in legal history—and I don't intend to lose."

Rayme was picking out chords on his guitar, and stood up as the guard unlocked the cell door. He said, "Hello," to Edmund Bradford Wilson, and then looked curiously at Steve.

Steve offered his hand. "Steve Wayland. I don't know whether you got a telegram from me from Los Angeles. I sent it the day of the concert in Yankee Stadium."

A glance of suspicion went through Rayme's eyes. "Yeah—Marny—my girl—she had it when I came off the stage. I remember."

Wilson spoke up. "I brought Steve along because I know him. He's straight, and I think he can be useful to us."

"How?" Rayme asked.

"Getting you back to work," Wilson answered. "He's got a plan and I like it. Your chances depend a great deal on how you react to all this. The whole country's in a sweat about it."

"Everybody still pretty supportive?" Rayme asked.

Wilson nodded. "But you've got to know, Rayme, that the district attorney and his friends won't let the fire go out. They'll keep on this case no matter what happens tomorrow—it's going to be a political football for a long time—and it'll drive you crazy if you don't go back to work."

Pain flashed across Monterey's eyes. "My life is tied to Marny's—and do you know she hasn't said a word? Hasn't even recognized anyone since it happened. Not even me. I'm not going to leave her," Rayme said.

Wilson spoke quietly. "Listen to what Steve has to say. That's all I suggest. You've got time to think about it—you can give him some time, can't you, Steve?"

Steve nodded. "Some," he answered. "There's big pressure to start the movie in three months. In fact, it has to start then. It has to start by April of next year."

"I'm not doing any movie."

"You don't know what this one is," Steve answered.

"Well?" Rayme questioned.

"I want you to do one special concert," Steve said, "to reintroduce you to the West Coast—the date's in March, two weeks before the Academy Awards. Then, right after the awards, we start rehearsal for the film. You'd have plenty of time to prepare for the concert—the Greek Theatre will put in all your equipment."

Rayme looked at him piercingly and waited.

"This film is different from all those you've turned down," Steve continued. "You will have approval by written contract of everything connected with your own performance. If you don't approve of the film as we finally get it—your performance—you can take any part of it out of the film."

Rayme looked at him incredulously. "You mean, we could shoot the whole film, and if I don't like what I do in it, I could take it all out—legally?"

"That's it," Steve replied.

"I've never really thought about doing a film, I mean, no one who approached me would give me any approvals, so I passed. Is there a script I can look at? I've got a lot of reading time in here."

Steve shook his head. "It's not ready yet, I still need a few more weeks, and I want to try to write your part to you. What this story's about, Rayme, is the same thing you're talking about more and more in your concerts. And in your public life, too. You're concerned with people, with causes you believe in, the world we live in—I know it's more than lip service with you, because I've checked you out. You care passionately, and that's important to me, about your work and about other people.

"*The Rest of Our Lives* is about the search that all of us make for what we want out of life. I want to put into your part who you really are.

"Think of the millions of people who never get to hear you in concert, who will see you in this movie all over the world. No matter why they come to the theater, whether they're curiosity-seekers or groupies, or whatever, once they're looking at that screen, they'll hear you.

"I know you're good box office and on the front pages right now, and I don't deny that will help us pull big audiences. I'll take it. You're damn right I'll take it—because I want to reach every possible person we can. You have a great audience who will listen to you, and not only to your music. If this film has any message, it's to push everyone to make the most of his family and his work, and everything else he cares passionately about. And remember, I can't exploit you, because you can take anything out of the film you want, even your whole part."

Rayme looked from Steve to his attorney. "He means what he says, Rayme," Wilson spoke out. "I have a written contract in my office confirming everything he just told you. I wouldn't have brought him here otherwise.

"I want you to have some plan, Rayme, for your work. Some plan you want to pursue before you go in front of the judge and the jury."

Wilson turned to Steve. "I'm asking Rayme to defend himself, in a way, because I couldn't do it as well. No one could." Then, to Rayme: "I want you to talk about all the tough days on the Jersey shore—why you had to carry a gun—always—I want you to talk about Marny. I want that judge and jury to know you and to know about your life, and I want you to tell them that you're going on in the future, that you have a cause. This movie of Steve's fits perfectly, and it's the truth."

Rayme looked at both men. "I want to talk about it with Marny, when she's able to talk. If she's well enough to come with me, I'll think about it. Without her, forget it."

"I understand," Steve said, and he put his hand out to Rayme. "I know you two have some things to talk about. Thank you, Ed, for bringing me along. I'll be in touch." The guard unlocked the door and Steve stepped outside.

Rayme gazed thoughtfully after him. "How long have you known him?"

"About six years," Wilson replied. "His manager, Spartan Lee, asked me to handle his affairs. I don't know him intimately, Rayme, but Spartan does, and Spartan doesn't handle fakes or phonies. And from what I've heard about Wayland, he's as independent as you are. You can't buy him or sell him."

"Will that contract in your office stand up?" Rayme asked.

"It will," Wilson replied. "I've never seen another one like it out of Hollywood."

"How the hell can he give me those approvals? I mean, I could destroy the whole film, there wouldn't be any film."

"That's right," Wilson said. "But he's doing what he wants and he's putting everything he has on the line—every dollar he owns—every contract—to get that kind of freedom. This is one you've really got to think about, Rayme—and I'd just like to say one thing more. It's your life, but whatever happens to Marny, it must go on—you can't stagnate right at the heart of your career—you have to move on when we get you out of here—and we will get you out of here."

8

Louis Pasteur Hospital, Paris

The doors of the Intensive Care Unit of the Hôpital Pasteur swung open and Magdalena was wheeled out. She had been in Intensive Care for almost ten days, and was finally being released to her own private room. A rush of photographers and reporters, who had been waiting in relays since the word of Magdalena's accident had gone around the world, surrounded her bed as three nurses guided her quickly down the hall and turned toward the elevators.

Magdalena was conscious, and she'd persuaded the nurses to fix her hair and give her some makeup and lipstick. Two spots of glow covered her pale cheeks. The left side of her head was bandaged where the cuts had been stitched by the greatest plastic surgeon in the world, flown in from Brazil. But her hair had been fixed to fall softly over the bandaged area, almost disguising it. Her secretary had brought her one of her nightgowns and negligees. The negligee had a high neck which almost completely covered the thin line of the scar in her throat where the surgeons had had to perform a tracheotomy.

The reporters had researched the "accident," and the police had been called in. No one could prove that it had been a suicide attempt, and Magdalena Alba was now a favorite "daughter of Paris." Her popularity with the press was reflected in their sympathetic handling of the situation. Only Sylvia knew of the visit to Dr. Loussard, and Dr. Loussard had not betrayed Magdalena's confidence. So the reconstructed "accident" had Magdalena driving her high-powered car at a reckless speed, and trying to outrun the police when they followed her. Obviously, she'd heard the sirens.

Fortunately, when the convertible skidded into a ditch and flipped over, Magdalena had been thrown clear before the car exploded. She had been in a coma when they found her. The emergency tracheotomy had been done as soon as she reached the hospital, when the coma was deepening. She had a severe concussion and three cracked ribs on her right side. Her famous legs were cut and bruised and she had multiple contusions and lacerations.

Slowly, in Intensive Care, Magdalena had regained consciousness, and it was her wish to stay in the ICU until the tubes in her throat could be removed and she could present to the outside world some remnants of her image.

She had braced herself for this night when she knew the press would be waiting for her. She had checked herself in the mirrors the nurses had given her until she was ready.

There was no way to keep the photographers back. Instead, Magdalena's instincts and defenses took over. The reporters fired questions at her as the photographers clicked their pictures, moving in very close between the nurses, surrounding her.

"The people here have been wonderful," Magdalena said. "They've taken such good care of me." She patted one of the nurses near her, who was guiding the bed along the aisle. Now she turned to the other side, answering some reporters just above her head. "No, really," she said, "I'm feeling fine, just a little weak. No, I don't really know what happened. The car just went out of control. I saw something on the highway—a little girl—and I swerved to miss her."

A reporter cut in quickly. "But no one around the accident saw a little girl, afterwards or before."

"Well, there was one," Magdalena said quietly. "I could see her plainly, even the way she was dressed. Thank God I didn't hit her."

Another reporter asked, "Are you still going to make the anniversary voyage of the *Royal Princess*?

Magdalena looked straight up at him. "I have to, don't I?" She flashed her famous smile. "I couldn't possibly waste the incredible wardrobe St. Laurent designed for me. Of course I'm going."

"When will you be leaving the hospital?" another one asked.

"Very soon," she answered.

Yet another reporter questioned, "There are stories about you making a film in a few months in America. *The Rest of Our Lives*, I think it's called."

"I've just received a wire about that from the director, Mr. Steve Wayland. It came to me the same day of the accident, so I really don't know much about it yet. You can be sure of one thing. If I decide to do any film, I'll call you all in to have a drink with me before I sail. You've always been so kind, and I'm very grateful."

The crowd of photographers and reporters wished her a warm good-bye as the nurses hurried the bed into an elevator.

An hour later, Magdalena Alba was finally alone in her room. The doctors had made their last check, the nurses had given her medicine for the night.

Magdalena lay in her bed. She had called on all her stamina to survive the ordeal of the press. Now she propped herself up in bed and swung the bedside table around in front of her. A large mirror had been placed on it by her request.

Her suicide attempt had been thwarted. She had not escaped. She was still alive in the real world and now she had to fight it out. She braced herself. She clicked on the night lamp of the bed. Slowly, she began to check her face, her head, her arms, and then her neck. She unbuttoned the high collar of the negligee, which covered the scar from the tracheotomy. There it was. The still red, slender scar against the whiteness of her throat.

Magdalena felt more alone than ever before in her life. She slipped out of the bed and walked unsteadily to the hospital windows at the side of her room. They were large, double windows, locked from the inside. She pressed down on the levers and opened them, looking out over the lights of Paris. The magic city. The Arc de Triomphe. The Paris Opera House. The Place de la Concorde. Notre Dame.

The memories of her life flashed before her. Into her mind came the figure of the little girl on the highway in front of her speeding car. She had seen her so distinctly before she swerved out of her way. The face of that little girl was coming back to her now. She was small, about seven years old, dressed in green velvet, in a style of thirty years before. A voice was calling out to the little girl. It was her voice. She realized the little girl was herself, and saw a handsome, distinguished, dark-haired man, opening a box with the green velvet dress in it. Yes, that was it—that little girl was herself. And her mouth formed the words, "Father—*mi padre*—oh, *mi padre*."

Magdalena Alba was the illegitimate daughter of a Spanish nobleman, descended from the Alba family of the famed *Duchess of Alba* painting. Rodrigo Alba was a Spanish consul who served in various capitals of the world, a career diplomat.

One of his duties, when he was home in Spain, was to appear at local civic festivities throughout the country, particularly those which attracted tourists from abroad. The "Feri" of Seville, in April, and the Festival of the Bulls at Pamplona, made famous by Ernest Hemingway, were two of the big tourist events at which he made an appearance, representing the aristocracy of Spain.

In the huge gypsy caves of Sacre Monte, near Granada, Rodrigo Alba watched the famous gypsy dancers, the *gitanas*. These were the oldest and wildest of Spain's gypsies, who clung to their traditional ways of life. In the spring of 1950, the Feri of Seville filled the nights with passionate celebration.

Many of Spain's greatest flamenco dancers had come out of these caves. The gypsy families were illiterate and untamed. The Spaniards left them alone unless they were invited guests. The *gitanas* lived in their traditional ways, changing their customs very little from generation to generation; they were apart from modern times.

They moved from place to place in the winter, but settled in their traditional caves for the spring and summer. They made enough money from their tourist shows and exhibitions to last them through the year.

They lived in little hovels and huts, either in the caves themselves or surrounding the mouths of the caves. They were dark-haired, wild-eyed, graceful of carriage, and electric of movement. They fought often, lived by their own justice. Murders in the gypsy caves were not investigated.

Rodrigo Alba, recently a widower, went with a sad heart to the gypsy exhibitions in the spring of 1950. His chauffeur drove him from Luz Granada Hotel in Pamplona, up Sacre Monte to the caves, already filled with spectators for the night.

Rodrigo hated to face the evening. He'd seen the dancers a hundred times or more. The cave would be filled with smoke, the odor of many bodies. The program would be long and he would have to stay until its end.

There would be an official presentation to him, as a representative of the government, at the beginning of the festival. It was one of the most tedious parts of the consular service and without his wife to share it with him, he was particularly disturbed to go.

Three hundred yards from the caves, he heard the flamenco guitars, the clicking of hundreds of castanets, fingers snapping like pistol shots, and heels stomping out the savage rhythms on the stone floors of the cave.

A young *gitana* was added to the program, and that night Rodrigo

Alba's life changed. The young girl was a solo dancer from a neighboring tribe of *gitanas* who had just moved into the caves.

Her black hair streamed down to her waist. Her face was strikingly beautiful, wild and sensual with flashing, savage eyes. Her whole demeanor, her whole dance, *was* the sexual act. She had small but beautiful breasts, which almost slipped out of her bodice at the extreme points of her flamenco dance.

She had been well trained by her gypsy family. The arch in her back, the straightness of her neck, the curve of the legs, and the rounded, exaggerated thrust of her hips, all were in perfect flamenco tradition.

Her skin was milk-white, unusual in a gypsy, and her large green eyes slanted upwards, a trace of her Indian heritage.

She twisted and turned and then began to dance straight to Rodrigo Alba, as the most important Spanish aristocrat there. She challenged him, enticed him, flaunted herself at him, drew herself away from him, and danced a whole story back and forth to him.

The crowd recognized it and entered into it. When the dancer would approach him and barely stop short of his face with one of her intriguing moves, they would pick up the bullfight cry of *"Olé!"*

Rodrigo, enjoying the byplay with the crowd, stood up and took a red silk handkerchief from inside his pocket. He was always ready with this when he went to a bullfight to represent the government. At the proper time, if the occasion happened that way, he would take the red handkerchief out and assume the position of a bullfighter.

The occasion happened that way, on this night. He let the handkerchief fall open and then placed it on his hip.

The gypsy girl made a rush at it, and he stepped aside. The crowd yelled, *"Olé, olé!"* again, and laughed.

The beautiful dancer made three runs at him and he made graceful passes on each of them. On the fourth, she veered away from the handkerchief and, with her two forefingers sticking out like tiny horns, she "wounded" him in the chest. This was the ancient gypsy game of "taking a heart," and the crowd screamed with appreciation.

Rodrigo bowed toward her and lifted her hands and her head toward him. For one moment, they stood face to face, he looking down at her, she looking up at him. The gypsies knew what was going to happen. Before the night was over, these two people, whoever they were, whatever their responsibilities or duties or marital ties, would make love.

And long after midnight, in the fields between the Sacre Monte caves and Granada, Rodrigo Alba made love to Yolanda Mendosa, the new queen of the *gitanas*, sixteen years old, already mother of two children, and the common-law wife of a thirty-five-year-old gypsy merchant, Enrique.

Exactly nine months later, after a scandal involving the Alba family, and after Yolanda Mendosa had left her husband to live secretly with Rodrigo Alba, a little girl was born to her in a small, out-of-the-way hospital near Alabaicam, the old gypsy quarters of Granada. The hospital ledger, in the space reserved for the mother's surname, stated— "bastarda."

"La Bastarda" is still known in the caves of Pamplona as the most beautiful and haunted child ever born to a *gitana* clan.

Even as a baby, Magdalena Alba, as she later named herself, was an exquisite child, with all the refinement of hundreds of years of Alba aristocracy. The high cheekbones, the perfect nose, slightly tilted at the end, the noble forehead, the slim line of the jaw, the swanlike neck, even her full healthy figure as a little girl reflected her aristocratic father.

From her mother, she inherited the huge, tilted-upwards gypsy eyes, only they were blue like her father's, or blue-green, as her mother used to say, changing with whatever she wore. She had the stamina of the gypsies, and the passion.

Before she was four years old, the surrounding villages were full of legends about her, her birth and her heritage. Other gypsy mothers were jealous. Even the half brothers and sisters of La Bastarda hated her because she was different.

Six months of every year, Magdalena spent with her father wherever he was in residence abroad. Paris, London, Vienna, Salzburg, Rome. For those months of every year, she lived in palatial surroundings, as befitting the ambassadorial life. She was cared for by governesses, and tutored, even as a baby. By the time she was five years old, she spoke four languages fluently.

Her father, a renowned womanizer, was proud of his beautiful little daughter and took her with him most of the time. However, the nights were long and Rodrigo Alba was usually out for the evening. Magdalena used to pretend to be asleep, and then, when her governess was gone, would get up and search for her father. She would go to his room, crawl into his large bed, and wait for his return. Sometimes, he didn't come back until the next day, and she would fall asleep in his bed.

In the mornings, she would sit beside him on the bed as he took the blue lapis cuff links out of his handmade silk shirt and went over his schedule for the next day.

He had no idea how to bring up a child. One's daughter was a possession, a showpiece. And she was a remarkable child with such a sweet smile, and such an intelligent manner, that she captivated people wherever she went. He hated it when it came time to deliver her back to her mother.

The arrangements had been made. The money had been paid. Her mother had gone back to her gypsy common-law husband. Alba would have his daughter half the year, and her mother would have her the other half.

He tried to buy all the time, but Yolanda had been deeply hurt by the rejection of Rodrigo's family and Rodrigo's weakness in not standing up for her. This was the only way she could get even. She knew that Magdalena was Rodrigo's most prized possession, although not prized enough to be legitimized with her father's name. His family's opposition won out, with their threats to cut off his title and inheritance.

Yolanda found herself jealous of her child. Magdalena had the nobility and refinement Yolanda lacked, the very qualities she needed to hold Rodrigo, or to at least have him come back to her and make love to her.

They had had a wild sexual encounter, sleeping together all over the country, in the face of rising social criticism from the aristocratic set. She had had a sexual fix on him for many months and she would not let him go. But finally, the strict orders of the Spanish government to proceed to his post in London had ended the liaison. She pleaded to go with him, but he would not be seen with her in any of his career assignments.

He was seen, though, and happily, with his little daughter. Everywhere he went, he introduced her as Magdalena Alba. But still he would not sign the papers legitimzing her birth and name.

The six months of the year that Magdalena spent in the gypsy caves were a living hell. When she came home, the other children waited until her father was safely out of distance before physically attacking her. They beat her, took her clothes, stripped her even of her undergarments. They threw her in the mud purposely to dirty her up and make her one of them. They made fun of her, taunted her, teased her. And Magdalena's mother sat by and watched.

Each time, within a week of her return, Magdalena became a silent, numb member of the gypsy camp. She stayed out of her family's way. She was ready to fight anyone who approached her. She carried a stick almost as big as she was, full of rough nails, to defend herself. At night, when no one could see her, she cried for her father and wrote him little letters, for which she paid her few pennies to have smuggled out of the camp.

She knew that her father was sending money to her mother to take care of her, but she never saw the money or anything bought with it. The money was taken for the rest of the family. She was told by her mother that if she told any of this to her father when she saw him, she would not be allowed to see him again.

At five years old, Magdalena was plotting a way to escape the gypsy life forever, and to live with her beloved father. She would take care of him. She would be all that he would ever need. She would be safe and she would be loved and eventually, he would give her his name.

Once, when one of the little gypsy boys in the camp was taunting her as "La Bastarda," she swung her rough board at his face and cut it open with five of the nails. Gypsies in the camp felt she had a witch's power and they often talked of her as the little bastard witch.

Magdalena never saw her father again. He died in an automobile accident in Madrid. He was racing his Ferrari and he and his companion, one of the most beautiful models in Europe, were killed when he failed to make an abrupt curve in the road on the highway to Barcelona. The Ferrari had smashed into a stone wall and exploded.

Magdalena was not told until a year after it happened. She kept waiting for her father to appear and take her away for their yearly six months together.

The little girl kept alive by watching everyone and everything around her. Learning. Remembering. Fantasizing. She dreamed herself out of reality so that she could stand the tomorrows.

She separated the world into two camps. One was the beautiful, tasteful, luxurious world she had known with her father. The other world was poor like the camp *gitanas*, hungry, vulgar, animalistic.

Even at her young age, she felt the glances of the boys and men of the caves on Sacre Monte. She watched her stepfather possess her mother in front of all the children by the campfire. If Magdalena protested, she was brutally struck and would fight back with her feet and hands and nails. All of her life was a fight.

She nurtured her private world and her memories protectively. She discussed them with no one. She shared them with no one. She acted, talked, and worked alone. She had no friends, no confidantes.

Magdalena became a woman at twelve years of age. It was usual for the *gitanas* to mature early. Most of them married at thirteen or fourteen, in gypsy fashion, which was simply a matter of selection of your mate and somehow earning a living.

When she felt the strange stirrings in her body, her flat youthful chest growing into breasts, and her boyish nipples spreading into a seductive circle, she was afraid. The boys and men in the camp were following her now, making crude remarks, reaching out to touch her when she was asleep, surrounding her when she would go out and bring in the hobbled horses from down in the field below Sacre Monte.

She made a decision three months before her thirteenth birthday. She had a tree house down in the valley which she had built herself, up in the high branches of an old Spanish oak tree. She had taken a few books there, drawing paper, and writing paper. It was her hideaway.

The boys followed her to the treehouse. A group of young *gitanos*, seven of them, between thirteen and seventeen years old. They waited at the bottom of the tree and dared her to come down. She had on a pale blue cotton dress, no shoes, and a blue ribbon in her hair.

She climbed down partway and told them to get away and leave her alone. They laughed and took a position directly under the limb she'd straddled, so they could see up between her legs. They demanded more. They called her *puta*, and made remarks about her *concha*, and what they would like to do to it—what they *were* going to do to it.

Magdalena answered in her own way. She had two heavy stones in her tree house which kept her possessions safe from the wind. She took one of the stones, went halfway down the tree again, and dropped it on one of the boys, striking him in the head and knocking him unconscious, cutting his head open.

The cocky, vulgar-mouthed group of *gitanos* raced off, swearing and cursing at the *puta* in the tree. They would be waiting for her, they screamed, when she got back to the cave.

Magdalena quickly packed up the treasures of her tree house. She tied them in a large bandana and made a loop to hang around her shoulders. She scrambled down the tree. She looked back for a moment at her beloved hideaway.

Then, she walked over to stand by the unconscious boy. She knelt down and listened to his heart. She took a piece of his own shirt, ripped it off, and bound up his wound.

He was still unconscious. She put her hands underneath his armpits and dragged him over so he would be propped up by the tree. When the bleeding stopped, she looked down at him, shook her head in disgust, and started for the road. Not the road for the cave, but the road to Madrid and freedom.

By twilight, she had reached the lake just beyond Granada. The Sacre Monte Lake. She went to the edge of the water and looked around. No one was there.

She slipped off her dress. It had been a hot spring day and she was tired. She swam out into the lake, then turned over onto her back to float peacefully until the sun went down. She didn't see the farmer who had gotten off his horse at the edge of the lake near where she had left her clothes.

He was halfway toward her when she was awakened from her drowsiness by the figure of the naked man pushing his way to her through the water. It was still shallow where she was, and when she stood up, the water came just to the bottom of her breasts.

Her eyes met the farmer's. There was no question in her mind what was going to happen. She started swimming as fast as she could toward the shore, moving in a curve to escape the man.

He laughed and spoke vulgarly to her. "Where are you going, *Concha*? You've seen a man before—plenty of them, I'll bet—"

She was touching the shore when he stepped out in all his nakedness, his penis extended and dark hair curling all over his body.

He had never seen a creature like her. She stood in the full bloom of her young womanhood, her breasts large and ripe with lovely, soft-tinted nipples. Her hair was long and blonde. The Venus mound between her legs was honey-colored, turned darker with the water of the lake. The water was running off of her in rivulets and made her even more exciting as the last rays of the sun reflected in the beads of water on her face and across her breasts and hips.

She made one move for her dress and panties and her bandana, filled with her treasures.

The farmer quickly stepped between her and her clothes. He stood facing her and then started toward her, his penis still extending rigidly in front of him, long and hard.

"Come on," he said.

As he reached out for her, Magdalena scrambled behind her, searching for anything. Her hands came in contact with the reins of the farmer's horse.

She turned and stepped on a pile of wheat on the ground, vaulting into the saddle. She pulled the horse's reins up fast.

She was a capable horsewoman. Her father had taught her as a little girl. She wheeled the horse around so that he was standing on his hind legs, pawing the air with his front legs at this strange rider who now commanded him.

The farmer, seven yards away, laughed loudly. "What the hell do you think you're doing? You take that horse and I'll kill you, so help me God."

He didn't finish the word "God," because his own horse was coming at him—Magdalena had the horse's bit behind the jaw, painfully pushing his tongue back, choking him. The horse reacted the only way he knew. He powered into flight.

It was like the aim of a rifle. She rode down the farmer with his own horse, lifting the horse's head and front hooves again and again as they pounded into the farmer, crashing him to the ground.

Magdalena was possessed. The farmer was crumpled, his skull crushed by three different blows of the iron hooves of the horse, before she pulled up. The horse backed off slowly, looking at the dead farmer in front of him, smashed in the head and in the body.

Magdalena went over and looked at him, too. She kicked him with her foot. There was no reaction. Slowly, still watching the farmer, she reached back to where her dress was and put it on. She was trembling.

She got on the horse again and sized up the surrounding territory. On the side of the lake was a farmhouse. Maybe that's where the horse was from. She headed the other way.

As the sun set on the road to Madrid, Magdalena began to cry. Under her breath, she whispered, "Father, how could you leave me with nothing? God help me now."

The wind was blowing the curtains of the open hospital windows in toward her. The night opened its arms to her, warm and beautiful, and empty of pain. Magdalena took a half step toward the windows when she heard the door behind her open. She turned quickly.

Steve Wayland smiled at her. "Miss Alba?" he asked. Magdalena pulled herself out of her memories.

"Yes?" she replied.

"I'm Steve Wayland," he answered. From behind his back Steve took a large bouquet of violets, wrapped in lace cellophane. Magdalena smiled as she saw them. At the same time, she fastened her negligee around her throat, instinctively covering the scar.

"I'm sorry if I startled you," he said. "I just wanted to leave the flowers. I'm at the Plaza Athenée. Would you have your secretary call me when you feel like talking?"

Magdalena took the bouquet. "I love violets," she said.

"I know," Steve answered. She looked at him questioningly. "Most of the biographical material about you somewhere mentions violets. You got my wire about the film?"

"Of course." Magdalena smiled at him. "While I was talking to the reporters tonight, as a matter of fact, they mentioned it to me. They said there'd been some rumors about your picture.

"Your cable reached me during the Yves St. Laurent showing of his collection for my trip on the anniversary voyage of the *Royal Princess.*" She swayed a moment on her feet and immediately stepped to one of the two armchairs in the room. She seated herself and motioned to the other chair.

"Stay a few minutes. I'm wide awake. I haven't done anything but sleep for over a week." She smiled at him. "And this is one time we won't be bothered by other people. I think it would be good for me to talk about a film—your film—for a moment. Hospitals depress me."

"I know you're considering the Redford picture," Steve began. "I don't blame you. Robert Redford and Sydney Pollack, that's a pretty unbeatable combination."

"That's true," Magdalena said. "I am considering it. As a matter of fact, I have to talk to Bob. He's called me several times since the accident. Sydney, too. You know how it always is with all of us. We have several projects—you hope to find the best part. I always hope for something original, something different—I've reached the point where I don't want to make a picture unless it's special to me. Now, with the accident, I feel even more determined about that. So, tell me about your film. Did you bring the script?"

Steve shook his head. "It's not finished. But it will be soon—I'm going over the final draft. I can tell you one thing, though, Magdalena, this part will be different."

He looked at her for a moment and took the plunge. "You will play your age," he continued, "you will play a real woman living in today's world, with all the new advantages women have and all the new problems. The woman of our film has your courage and the pain I've seen in your eyes since the Truffaut film.

"I want to make a film with absolutely no tricks—straight—the way we all heard stories when they were read to us when we were children. I don't want people in the audience looking at unobtainable perfection—I want them to see the kind of reality they face and the choices they have to make for the rest of their lives."

Magdalena looked at him, her face alive with interest. Steve stood up. "Now I've stayed much too long for your first night back here. I didn't mean to do that and I apologize."

Magdalena glanced at him. "I asked you about your film. For days I've lain in there, thinking about my face and my pains and the accident. I'm intrigued with your idea. I want so much to read it."

"When it is finished," Steve said, "you will be the first. I'm going to stay in Paris until we have a chance to talk again. I came here because you're the only woman I want for this role in my film. I want to mold the part to you. If you don't agree to do *The Rest of Our Lives*, there isn't going to be any film. The studio has given me that ultimatum."

Magdalena smiled. "You are different, Mr. Wayland. You're giving me the ace hand before the game begins."

9

Rome

The drums of Africa echoed through the steaming Italian night. The chimes of the towering clocks of Massima Square in Rome, near the Trevi Fountain, rang out, then faded from the stroke of one in the morning.

The courtyard of the square was crowded with cars and taxis. The action was centered on the nightclub Afrique, at the northeast corner of the square. The doors of Afrique were open and people were lined up all the way to the street, listening to the drums of Tucheki.

Life-sized posters of Tucheki stood on either side of the doorway of Afrique, pictures of a large, powerfully built black man, naked to the waist, dressed in white Persian pants. He wore a wide belt around his waist, with a carved blue lapis imprint of his own profile on the massive belt buckle. On each side of his strong arms, around his biceps, were circled gold snake pieces with raised snake heads, ready to strike.

Inside Afrique, the real Tucheki stood on a platform, surrounded by humanity, standing, sitting on the floor, wedged into corner tables, massed into the bar. He swiveled from one drum to the next, in the arc of nine jungle drums surrounding him. Behind him and to his right were a full set of snares and percussions. To his left were two large kettledrums.

Tucheki moved like a panther among his instruments. He screamed out a tribal chant. Suddenly, he began to run in full circles, hitting the right drums on the right beats, faster and faster. Just as suddenly, he stopped dead and called out one animalistic scream, "Tigressa!"

The curtains split open behind the small raised platform on which

Tucheki stood pounding his drums. The spotlight overhead hit a turning, writhing form.

She danced out of the darkness, as though Tucheki had merely called her in from a dance that had already begun to transport her.

She was not an "act" Tucheki was introducing; she was his partner, and she embodied his driving African drums in the most primitive and sexual of dances. "La Tigressa!" The people yelled out her name.

La Tigressa was a striking girl, with translucent, fair skin. She was just a quarter of an inch over five feet five inches, slimly built but still voluptuous, with pointed breasts that rounded out in front of her. Her legs were long and set high into her buttocks, giving her that special high-legged look that is a sexual fetish with many men. Her waist was small, her hips beautifully curved.

Her long, dark hair fell loosely around her shoulders. It was parted on one side and moved freely. La Tigressa paid no attention to hairstyles. She knew that almost all men loved long hair, regardless of what the hairdressers said. She took care of her own hair, washed it, and she had never had a permanent wave. Her hair shone with life.

Her face was a work of art. She had deep-set dark eyes with heavy black brows. From her eyes, as well as her dancing, the name La Tigressa had been born. And now she was known across three continents, with America still ahead.

Her cheekbones were high and clean, her cheeks sleekly smooth. Surprisingly, she wore very little makeup. Her eyes were rimmed with thick-set, dark lashes that seemed to supply their own eyeliner and mascara. Her mouth was full, not a perfect feature, but sexually magnetic. When she smiled, which was only occasionally, her sparkling white teeth emphasized the size of her mouth. She had a tiny brown mole on her upper lip. Men, and women, too, found this one of La Tigressa's most erotic attractions.

La Tigressa danced through the crowd. The people made way for her. They pushed each other back so La Tigressa would come their way and dance through them.

La Tigressa was a born dancer, reflecting no specific style or training. No one knew her real name or anything about her background. She had sprung upon the South African nightclub circuits like the animal whose name she took.

She and Tucheki had appeared in a Monte Carlo gala a year before and had transfixed a world audience, from Sinatra to Barbra Streisand to Prince Rainier to Anthony Quinn to Prince Andrew.

La Tigressa was dressed in a costume of black and yellow striped satin matched in cut and design to the color and symmetry of an African tigress. It had become a fashion rage in Rome. Dresses and gowns copied it, even beachwear. The tiger stripes clung to her body and tapered in the front, finishing just above her nipples. The stripes wound tightly around her full hips and then cut away around her upper thighs, then split open over her extraordinarily long legs. As La Tigressa moved and "attacked" the audience to Tucheki's drums, the animalistic effect was complete.

La Tigressa never played to her audience, or any one man or woman in particular. She danced in her own world, to her own commitment, and to Tucheki's drums.

The bond between Tucheki and La Tigressa was absolute. She understood every nuance of his music and he anticipated every intrinsic move of her improvised dance. Because no show was the same. That was part of the agreement between Tucheki and La Tigressa. He let his own emotions and moods set the pace of his drums. La Tigressa danced to his "symphony" of the moment.

In the center of Rome's most famous "Dolce Vita," the most artistic collaboration on the Italian scene was pulling an audience from all over Europe. Critics were coming from Germany, France, England, even from Scandinavia, to see Tucheki and La Tigressa, who were booked for six months into Afrique.

No one knew Tucheki's background either. He and La Tigressa had suddenly appeared in Monte Carlo with no word about them, no buildup, no biographies, no public relations handouts.

Steve Wayland watched her pass his table at the ringside of Afrique. La Tigressa made that small dance floor a personal experience between her and the people gathered around. She danced to everyone, and yet to no one. She was on fire.

When Steve had seen her before, her face had been covered with dark makeup and a wig. But Raggedy Ann was unmistakable now. The body, the movement, the consuming passion with which La Tigressa danced was the same as the girl he remembered in Sacramento. He had gotten her name from a waitress there—Mary Jane Stuckey was her real name. No one else he'd ever seen danced the way this girl did.

The drums were stepping up. Tucheki was going into the climax of the dance, playing his nine drums with a savage and intricate crosscut rhythm. It was primal music. And La Tigressa was dancing with primal abandon within the most disciplined rhythmic texture. The drums exploded and La Tigressa exploded with them.

La Tigressa's dressing room, behind the stage at Afrique, was her oasis. Steve stepped from the darkness at the backstage area, and the dimly lit hallway, into a remarkable room. The walls were whitewashed and glistening. Flowering plants, carefully tended, decorated each of the four corners. There was a small bookcase along one wall and across from it a chaise longue, an antique, covered with two brightly colored afghans. On the wall behind the makeup table there was a collage of the great dancers of the last fifty years: Makarova, Baryshnikov, Alessandra Ferri, Nureyev, Fred Astaire and Ginger Rogers, and many more. The frame of the collage was old and scratched, reflecting its many traveling homes. Below it was a framed photograph of a desolate Texas town in the middle of a barren plain. There was a family grouping in the foreground.

It was unlike any backstage dressing room Steve had ever seen. La Tigressa had created for herself a tiny home.

She was just beginning to take off her makeup when Steve opened the door. There was a sign on it, a large hand-painted one, which read, "Do Not Disturb." La Tigressa glanced at Steve in the dressing room mirror and turned around quickly, instantly defensive.

"Didn't you see the sign?"

Steve glanced at it. "I knocked, but there wasn't any answer."

"No one's allowed back here. It's the rule of the club."

Steve closed the door behind him. "I spoke to Antonio. He made an exception."

"Why?" Tigressa asked.

"Because I've come a long way to see you." He paused. "Mary Jane," he added.

La Tigressa looked at him questioningly, paling underneath the makeup. "How did you know my name?" she asked.

"I found you a year ago—in Sacramento. But then I lost you—you see, I never did know what you looked like because when I saw you you were Raggedy Ann—" He looked at her with a smile. "Raggedy Ann," he went on, "to La Tigressa—I wanted to see for myself after my people thought they'd found you. I flew in today from Los Angeles. When you came out on the floor, I knew I'd found you again."

"How did you know?"

"Because there's one thing you look for and always hope you'll find—

an original. I found one in Sacramento and I found her again here tonight. You're the best modern dancer I've ever seen, Mary Jane, and I've come to ask you to play a starring part in a new movie of mine—" He took a card from his pocket. "It's called *The Rest of Our Lives*." He handed her the card. She looked at him with total disbelief. "There are several numbers there. My office, my manager. My publicity people. Check me out. When you want to see me, please give me a call. I'm at the Hassler."

Steve turned towards the door and glanced back at La Tigressa. "I've waited a long time to see what you look like under that Raggedy Ann wig and all that makeup. I didn't have the faintest idea that you were so beautiful. Good night, Mary Jane."

He closed the door and left La Tigressa staring at his business card.

Steve had reserved a terrace balcony table in the penthouse dining room at the Hassler, and the magical sight of Rome at night was laid out before them. In front of La Tigressa's place setting was a single rose with a note from Steve which she had opened when they arrived. The message read, "You are worth the search." She had thanked him, and scrutinized him carefully as the meal progressed, waiting for him to make a move on her. It must be coming in a different form than she had known before.

"I don't think I could do it," La Tigressa said.

"I know you can," Steve said. "In time, however long it takes, you're going to believe me. Now, I'm not going to tell you much about the story because I'm in the last stages of developing it. But I *have* found three of my four principal characters. You are the fourth. I only knew one of you before I started on this story—Robert Montango."

La Tigressa's eyes flashed with respect. "I always thought he was a great actor," she said. "I thought he died."

Steve smiled. "A lot of others think so, too. He hasn't made a film in a long time. You will have quite an experience working with him."

La Tigressa looked up sharply. "I can't work with Robert Montango. I mean, he is a great actor. When I was a little girl—" Her voice trailed off. "He's won Academy Awards, hasn't he?"

"Two," Steve answered. "But I guarantee you, on the day we start shooting, he'll be as scared as you. That's what makes Robert great. He's going to surprise many people in our industry all over again. He has more lives than a cat."

La Tigressa looked at him intently. "How are you so sure I can do it?"

"I play my hunches. I go with my instincts. And when I'm passionate about something, I don't step back to check it out or try it another way. This is one of those times, Mary Jane. Writing this part, I've thought of no one but you. I knew I'd find you. You have to play it."

La Tigressa studied him. "You're serious." This wasn't a question; it was a statement.

"Completely," Steve answered. "And I have plans laid out."

"What do the plans involve?"

"We're going to keep quiet about your starring in *The Rest of Our Lives* until we build up the campaign. My publicity head, whom I think is one of the best in the world at launching a new motion picture personality, is arriving tomorrow. I want to see that he has all the international media covering the benefit Festival of the Gods on Saturday night. I know you've agreed to be one of the stars, and it might be a perfect place to launch an international campaign on La Tigressa. Jake and I will work it out. I want you to begin to show up in the best of the New York press. Some important writers are friends of ours. And photographers, too. We're going for quality, not quantity. From the very beginning, you'll be introduced as a new star."

"I didn't think they did that anymore," La Tigressa said.

Steve answered quickly, "They don't. But we're going back, with this picture, to the way they did it before I was around. I remember that when I was a boy, growing up in Kansas City, motion picture stars were built steadily and imaginatively by the studios, whose people knew how to do it. They created a mystery that was part of the movies. Stars that were bigger than life.

"We're going to do it the old-fashioned way for this picture. I'm going to cover every base—because, Mary Jane, *The Rest of Our Lives* has to be a commercial success. We need the public to be waiting for this picture, all over the world. I've planned it that way and I'm writing it that way, because this could be the last motion picture I'll ever make, and I want to try everything I've ever felt about making movies and selling them.

"This is my shot—for one time, I'm completely in control. And I'll tell you, Mary Jane, I've risked everything I have to get it that way."

"And you'd take a chance without even testing me? With one of the star roles?"

Steve shook his head. "I'm not leaving anything to chance. I know about you. That's why I'm here in Rome. I came here to finally see exactly what Raggedy Ann looked like, how she talked, how she smiled, what was in her eyes, the most important thing of all for films. And I knew before I saw you in your dressing room what I wrote you in the card." He nodded at the rose in front of her. "You are so very much worth the search. And the search that each of us makes is what the film is about."

La Tigressa leaned back in her chair. She had stopped eating completely. "I'm waiting—" she said flatly and paused, "—for the catch," she finished.

"You'll have a long wait," Steve answered.

"But this doesn't happen," she said. "Not in my life—I've never even thought about motion pictures—"

Steve spoke up sharply. "But you have the passion. Wherever you've come from, Mary Jane, and whatever you've been through, that passion to reach out and touch greatness, not to be just another dancer, but to be an original dancer, an original person—you exude that passion in the way you look, the way you talk, with the expression in your eyes. You're on fire—and that quality, I think, is moving out of the world faster than we know. I look for it everywhere. When I find a person on fire, I try to involve them in my work and my life . . . people who care passionately about their dream—that's part of what the film is going to be about, too."

"When can I read the script?" La Tigressa asked.

"When I finish it," Steve answered. "I don't want to say too much more about it to any of the four of you, because your personalities are influencing the way I write the parts.

"And one more thing, Mary Jane. I don't want you to have any lessons, go to any acting school, or talk about this to anyone—I don't want your natural personality changed or altered in any way. It's you that I want on the screen—and I'll be working intensively with you when we get to rehearsals."

"You know, I have a contract at Afrique for three more months," La Tigressa said.

"They've agreed to let you go at least a month early, whenever we need you for rehearsals. Meanwhile, you'll just be doing what you're doing now. I'm counting on you not to say one word to anyone."

He looked at her steadily across the table. She shook her head, confused, but starting to believe. He wouldn't let her eyes go. Whenever she looked away, he found her again. Could a man like this believe in Mary Jane Stuckey of Marfa, Texas?

Four thousand people were jammed into Trevi Fountain Square, surrounding a circular stage built around the ancient fountain. At the back rim of the stage, Tucheki, standing tall against the dark Roman sky, circled his drums with pure animal energy.

The crowd, young and adventurous, uttered a cry as La Tigressa appeared, lit by a single spotlight at the top of the stairs of an old Roman house on the square. She danced down the winding stairs to Tucheki's drums. The crowd began to dance behind La Tigressa in groups, in pairs, or alone.

Jake Powers stood with Steve at the back of the crowd near Steve's limousine. The electricity of La Tigressa shot through the brilliant press agent, jaded with too many stories and too many pressures. He was a pale, petulant man with big brown eyes and a sour expression. His mind was fast, geared for his own protection. This could be a big new account and there weren't any star builders anymore.

Steve was right. If you had been around films and you had any showmanship and intuition, you knew it sometimes when you saw a new personality. The old cliché was true, about "star quality." La Tigressa was electric. In all those thousands of people, the essence of one person was dominating the night.

There was something mystical and strangely erotic about the mixture of the ancient civilization of Rome, the old gods, the modern degradation of the Trevi Fountain, the cobblestone streets of the square, the heavy humidity of the night, the sweat glimmering on Tucheki's naked chest and back, and the perspiration twinkling on the upper lip of La Tigressa, and on her breasts and hips as she moved with complete abandon, in perfect rhythm to the drums.

The crowd listened to the incessant pounding and began rhythmically to clap their hands. People were swaying back and forth in a sexual motion; they began to pair off, embracing without restraint. The drums and the primitive sexuality of the night, together with La Tigressa and Tucheki, swept away everything else.

Jake Powers would publicize this night, all over the world, as the "Orgy at Trevi."

A couple broke away from the group, ran across the small stage, and plunged into the fountain, kissing passionately. The crowd laughed and applauded. They submerged in the waters of the fountain, oblivious to everyone else.

The man lifted the girl onto him in the water. She reached her mouth out to him and flicked her tongue back and forth across his lips as if she were painting his face. Suddenly, he stopped her and sucked her tongue full into his mouth, and then moved her down hard onto him.

They set the crowd on fire, as Tucheki and La Tigressa made wide, sweeping circles around the fountain.

Photographers and television cameramen recorded the entire scene from every angle.

Steve turned to Jake Powers. "Step one, Jake. Cover the world."

Jake nodded. "Hell of a beginning. How do I top this?"

Steve spoke sharply. "Just remember, everything goes through me. We don't want any explicit pictures. We want illusion, rumor, gossip. What really happened at the Trevi Fountain?"

He turned and walked to his limousine. "I want every major newspaper and magazine, the top syndicated columnists, all the opinion makers across the world, and I want you to leak some special material to Rupert Murdoch, and to *People*. Remember, Jake, I want it all done with class; she's going to have the buildup I've heard about from the forties. She's Hayworth and Lombard, and all of them, in one girl. And from tonight she has a new name, one she likes. Stephanie Columbo."

"How did you come up with that, Steve?"

"She did," Steve answered. "She always wanted to be named Stephanie, and her favorite rerun on TV is *Columbo*."

Dawn was slipping over the ancient city as a chauffeured car pulled up before the steps of 112 Botticelli Street, in one of the oldest living areas of Rome.

La Tigressa got out of the car. She was dressed in a white skirt and turquoise blouse, with a heavy African gold necklace around her neck. She said good night to the driver and to Tucheki, who was in the back seat of the car.

She went up the winding staircase to the top floor of the apartment. The inside of the building showed its ancient heritage, a prized possession in Rome. She took a key from her purse to let herself into one of the two suites on the top floor. She stepped into a hallway, then into a large living room, with a high-vaulted ceiling.

She turned on the stereo system. From secreted horns around the room, Charles Aznavour sang of Paris in the spring.

La Tigressa walked from the living room into a large bedroom furnished with antiques. A four-poster bed, several hundred years old, dominated the rest of the furniture. Good paintings covered the walls, not paintings by the masters, but semivaluable works that showed the taste of the selector.

She stepped out through double doors onto the outside terrace. The view was breathtaking. The terrace was on the level of the highest church towers of Rome.

It was early morning. The church bells were ringing. There, on a daybed on the terrace, a man slept, slender, boyish-looking, in his late thirties, with curly dark brown hair.

She looked at him for a moment. Robert Slater, world-famous leading man and womanizer. Magnetic, menacing (on screen), and charming.

La Tigressa smiled, a smile of wonder and of joy, as though she had come home after a long journey. She approached the bed and looked down at Bobby Slater.

Slowly, as the symphony of bells rang out over the terrace, La Tigressa eased out of her clothes. Naked, she approached the bed and pulled back the covers. Bobby was naked, too. She could not yet believe that this beautiful man who could have anyone he chose was in *her* bed.

She looked down on him tenderly and kissed him on the mouth. He was deep in sleep and did not stir. She bent over him on all fours and began kissing his chest softly and then his stomach and then moved down to his cock. She began to lick it softly at first until he started to mount in her mouth, then she took it in her left hand and began to increase the pressure and movement of her tongue and lips.

Bobby began to twist in his sleep as she worked faster. His cock had grown very big now and was almost filling her mouth. He opened his eyes suddenly and looked at her. He took her face in both his hands. "I love you, Steph—Oh, God, I love you."

Every line he spoke seemed to her to be from a movie. She was right.

"Can I go on top?" she asked.

He nodded, and she spread her legs over him.

La Tigressa spoke softly. "I'm so wet. I've been thinking of you all night."

He nodded at the pillow. "You've been with me here."

She eased down on him. "Am I too wet?"

"No, no, I like it that way."

She held up for a minute. "Wait a minute. It's not in right. I want to have it in just right, all the way." She spread her lips with her hand until he entered her perfectly. Then, she lowered herself down little by little, enjoying every slow moment of it. "Don't come too fast," she said. "I need you in me for a long time."

He barely got the word out, "Promise."

She took his hands and put them on her breasts. Her head was tilted back. The moans in her throat were passionate. "Oh, my God, I'm coming, I'm coming. You're so big, sweetheart. Oh, I love you, I love you, I love you."

Her voice rose, her movements becoming swifter as she rode him. He glanced down as his cock almost slipped out of her; it was glistening now, and her creamy juice covered him. She jammed herself down on him and screamed.

"Was it a big one?"

She shook her head. "Almost, oh, my God, you've got the greatest cock in the world."

He looked at her with that instant male jealousy of possessiveness, suddenly snapped out of his passionate lovemaking.

"How many are you comparing me to?"

He lifted her off of him and moved her up until she was straddling his face. He looked up at her and then started licking her softly. Instantly, she began to move back and forth against his mouth.

He took her clitoris in his mouth and began to suck on it, closing his teeth carefully over it to excite her but not hurt her. He sucked on it in that way until she had an orgasm right in his mouth. She lifted away from him. She was so sensitive now that, for a moment, she couldn't stand to be touched or licked or sucked.

She looked down at him. "Nobody ever did that to me before. What are you doing? I mean, it's fantastic. I can't stand it, but I love it. I can feel my clitoris. That little man in the boat is standing straight up."

"My favorite little man in the boat." He flicked it again with his tongue.

She muttered, "Oh, my God, I'm coming again."

He picked her up and, in one graceful move, swung her around underneath him. Her legs were bent back, she was completely exposed and he was high over her. Her small, graceful feet were on his shoulders. He sucked on her toes for a moment, then pushed her knees back against her chest.

Tenderly, but passionately, he eased himself into her, pushing his cock to the very end.

Her voice was a whisper. "God, you're in my chest—I can feel you all the way—don't ever take it out. Don't rush it. Hold it." She looked up at him. "Let's come together. I love that more than anything. With you looking at me."

He looked down at her. "And you looking at me." He brushed back her hair with his hand.

She glanced at their bodies meeting. "Look at us. You're perfect for me. Look at our hair together. It's even the same color."

He laughed. "But the equipment's different."

"Oh, yes," she sighed. Her breathing was starting to come fast now. She spoke quickly. "I can't wait any longer. I'm going to come. Oh, it's going to be the big one now. Please, come with me. Let me have all your juice, your wonderful juice. Put it way up in me. Please. Oh, God, please, now, now, now!"

He drove it one last time deep into her and his body shuddered with his orgasm. She came at the same time, and they held on to each other tightly. Her nails ran long dark scratches down his upper arms, breaking the skin. She twisted and moved underneath him and never let him go, sucking with her other lips, sucking all his juices into her.

He said thickly, "I can feel your lips tight on me. It's the best thing I've ever felt."

She spoke between hurried breaths. "This is special, isn't it? What we have? We're bonded now—forever."

Slowly he eased out of her, inch by inch, and he looked at their juices mixed together, running out of her. With his finger, he took two or three drops of juice directly from her. He sucked the finger and then put it in her mouth so she would suck it, too.

He said softly, "That's us. Very life itself. You're my woman, Steph."

She closed her eyes. All the years of suffering, and wanting to die, had been worth it.

Bobby Slater was giving a party for La Tigressa at the Tiberia Club. That's what the telegrams he'd sent around Rome's jet-movie-society set said, but it was really all planned for his own announcement. The great exposure he'd had with the skyrocketing fame of La Tigressa had put him back in the news. So now he was signing for the first epic film to be made in co-production with China.

It was comeback time for the man who continually placed in the top five in the newspaper and magazine polls as "The Sexiest Man in the World." Tom Selleck had come up fast, and Mel Gibson, too, and now Stallone was back again with the tremendous success of *Rambo* and *Rocky IV*. But Bobby Slater still maintained the position he'd held for so many years, since he'd stolen and discarded the movie star wife of an actor friend of his.

Bobby left each woman with a special memory. With his friend's wife, ten years ago, he had locked her in an adjoining room, day after day, while he made violent love to a call girl in the next room. The sounds of her lover making love to another woman broke the young movie star's spirit and provided her lover with complete sexual submission.

It was a technique Bobby Slater had perfected. He was a combination of techniques, from the time he woke up in the morning, until the time he went to sleep at night. He had a technique for everything.

Now, tonight, he was announcing his return to the screen. The name of the picture was *The Young Emperor.* He was getting two million dollars for his role, and the publicity would be going all over the world now that he was back in the eyes of show business news as the lover of La Tigressa.

It had all worked out very well, according to his plan. He had wanted to have the most talked-about woman in Rome, the most desired woman in Rome, at his side everywhere he went. He wanted people to see how much in love with him she was. And the announcement of his new film at the Tiberia Club would be the perfect culmination of all his plans.

Bobby had made his plans after he saw La Tigressa dance on her opening night at Afrique. It had taken time to sell her on the publicity being good for her career. Magazine stories. Columns. Newspaper photographs. Wire circuit breaks. It all started that way. But no one figured that La Tigressa would fall in love. After all, as the Afrique's publicist had told Bobby, "Something happened in the past. I don't know what. But this girl, as sexy as she looks, doesn't want anything to do with men. Or women, either."

Bobby had smiled, and said, "Well, I'm a hell of a friend, you know that. We can make it look good, that's all."

Bobby had made it look good. He and La Tigressa had become the most sought-after couple of Rome's jet set and motion picture set, as well.

His publicists covered the world with photographs of the "new lovers." They were marvelously photogenic together, and Bobby educated her.

The preparation for the camera. The clothes for the camera. The hairdos for the camera. The "candid" photos. The party photos. The premiere and royalty photos.

The first two months of their relationship, La Tigressa got the benefit of Bobby Slater's years of being photographed and handling the press. She was street smart, and she learned fast. She never drank, she never smoked, she never took dope. La Tigressa cared for her body and her dancer's stamina, like the gold they were.

Bobby had a fetish of almost always wearing horn-rimmed glasses. It fitted his pose as an intellectual politicist. He pretended to care nothing about being a movie star. He was turning down offers every day, according to him.

La Tigressa noted everything, and she often thought to herself, after months of going with Bobby Slater, that she really didn't know him at all. He screened off the interior of himself from everyone.

La Tigressa took what was given to her. And little by little, she allowed her natural feeling for a man to come back into her life.

She liked Bobby's touch. She liked his intelligence. She liked his interest in a wide variety of subjects. She enjoyed the celebrity life with him. She hardly ever thought back to the past, not consciously. Her world had changed. Every night, except Sunday, the applause and the acclaim of Afrique waited for her. It was a charmed period in her life.

Stolen weekends in Paris, Monte Carlo, and Florence. Four special days with Bobby in Venice. Overnight trips to Sardinia and Naples.

And when they became lovers, which Bobby had cleverly maneuvered as being her idea, it was better than anything she'd ever known with a man. She let herself go and she became unquenchable. She wanted to make love to Bobby every day and every night. The hours in between became lost.

La Tigressa was making up for a lifetime of emptiness. She'd come fully alive under the careful tutoring of Bobby Slater's knowledge, mind, and well-practiced body.

A crowd of reporters and photographers surrounded the entrance to the Tiberia Club as La Tigressa and Bobby got out of their limousine.

The couple stopped and took the time to sign autographs and receive the homage of the fans.

As they walked into the Tiberia Club, Bobby's press agent was already handing out the prepared brochures announcing his signing to star in *The Young Emperor*. There were congratulations shouted across the room as Bobby checked his coat.

He noticed the Tiberia's new hatcheck girl. She was dressed in the Roman slave costume that all of the waitresses wore at the Tiberia. It was called the minitoga. It had been designed by Rafaelo, the newest couturier rage in Milan.

It was made out of white satin, threaded with gold. It was cut low, just above the nipples. The skirt fit very tightly and was slit in a double panel up both legs. The girls wore nothing under their costumes, and every movement of their well-selected bodies was animally attractive.

The girls selected for the Tiberia were among the most beautiful models and starlets of Rome. They were paid big salaries, and they were not allowed to date the customers. There were many bets among the clientele as to which of them would be the first one set up by a wealthy benefactor.

The hatcheck girl was breathtaking. She was olive-skinned, with green eyes, long black hair down to her waist, and breasts that burst out of her minitoga. You could see the outline of the nipples just barely held in by the scoop neck. Her full cleavage was showing. Her legs were long and voluptuously curved, and her buttocks projected out provocatively.

Bobby spoke to her in a whisper as he left his coat. "You've got the greatest ass I've ever seen. I want to fuck it tonight." As he handed her his coat, his fingers touched her exposed cleavage.

"Do you think you could live up to your reputation, Mr. Slater?" the girl asked.

Bobby smiled at her. "Always have," he answered. "You're resigning your job. I've got another one for you. We're leaving in fifteen minutes." He looked at her directly and continued, "Will you be ready?"

She looked at him insolently. "Wait and see," she said.

Bobby smiled, reaching over and taking La Tigressa's hand as she came from the other part of the coatstand, where another girl had helped her off with her cloak. Together they made their way into the party.

Everyone crowded around Bobby, congratulating him on his new deal. *The Young Emperor*, and the idea of making a picture with China, were the talk of the party.

La Tigressa had heard none of his conversation with the hatcheck girl, and she clung to his arm proudly. She was dressed in a Calvin Klein crimson silk jersey, long-sleeved, and fitted as if it had been sewn on her. Her dark eyes shone. She was with her man, and she was glad her party had turned into his party, with the announcement of his new starring role. She was happy to stay in his shadow.

There were rumors around the room that finally Bobby Slater was going to get married, for the first time. There were bets taken on both sides. It was known that La Tigressa never went out with another man, but she would say nothing about her constant companion.

Steve Wayland approached La Tigressa with Jake Powers. Jake had kicked off the "Tigressa Campaign" well. The "Orgy at Trevi" had been a big story around the world; La Tigressa had gone international.

Face to face, her sexuality hit Steve once again. The girl gave you a visceral reaction. She didn't try to be sexy. She didn't try to be erotic. She didn't try to challenge a man. She simply was an incredibly sexy woman, with the added charm of not trying to capitalize on it. Every man in the room was riveted on her. Every man wanted her.

La Tigressa came up to Steve the moment she saw him. She embraced him and Jake. Bobby Slater stuck out his hand and gave his easiest, softest smile. He was charming, irresistible, genuine. "Hello, Steve," he said. "What a nice surprise. I really appreciate your coming."

"Thank you, Bobby," Steve said. "And congratulations on *The Young Emperor*. You look the part tonight."

"That was the idea." Bobby smiled again. "I really have to apologize to Tigressa here, though. It's supposed to be her party, and then the news began to leak out about my picture, and we had to go ahead and announce it—you and Jake know the press . . . so hard to please everyone, isn't it?"

Steve looked at him. "Yes, it is, Bobby."

"It's all the same anyway, Bobby," La Tigressa said. "It's *our* party."

She was direct, simple, lovable. She was giving everything to the man she loved at her side. She didn't care about the spotlight for herself.

"I don't want to mix business with the pleasure of this night in any way," Steve said. "But I'm going back to California tomorrow, and I came to say good-bye."

Bobby was being pulled away by reporters. He looked back at Stephanie. "It'll just take me a little while—they need a story. Enjoy yourself. Steve? Why don't you dance with her? It's an experience. Go ahead."

Steve guided La Tigressa to the dance floor. As she moved by Bobby, her breast touched his shoulder. Her voice drifted across his face—a whisper—"I'll miss you," she said. Bobby smiled as his woman went onto the dance floor.

The orchestra was playing a South American beguine arrangement of "Night and Day." It was exotic and wildly rhythmical. Steve was a good dancer, and he knew how to back up a woman who was a better one. He backed up La Tigressa as she fired up the dance floor.

Five minutes later, Bobby Slater threw his coat around the half-naked, minitogaed hatcheck girl, and put her in his limousine. He gave the address of a resort on the Appian Way, twenty miles outside of Rome. He wrote something out on a piece of paper and gave it to his driver. Slater spoke in a soft voice.

"Send this wire to Tigressa."

He pulled the glass and curtain across the opening between the front and back seats, screening off the back. Immediately, Slater turned to the hatcheck girl and unzipped her minitoga. She was naked except for her black lace garter belt and her black stockings.

She unzipped his pants and took out his cock. The hatcheck girl didn't wait to be led. She swung her right leg around his body so that she was sitting, facing him, straddled over him. Slater began to suck her nipples, as she let herself down slowly on his extended cock. He smiled happily.

He'd been getting bored with La Tigressa. She was too crazy about him. It wasn't interesting anymore. Now he'd have a hell of a weekend.

And the paparazzi and all the newspaper and magazine people were back around him now. His career had snapped back. He was a star again.

Slater spoke to the hatcheck girl with a sense of humor. "You know, my driver doesn't get any time off all week. Shall we give him a break? I know he'd like to watch."

She was running one hand through her hair and sucking the thumb of the other. She nodded her head wildly. "Oh, yeah, yeah," she said under her breath.

Slater pushed a button by his side. The window and curtain separating the front seat from the back slid clear automatically. Bobby Slater looked at his driver over the hatcheck girl's violently moving body.

The driver adjusted his mirror so that he was looking directly at the hatcheck girl's back as she fucked Mr. Robert Slater. The chauffeur smiled, taking it all in.

Bobby spoke to him across the girl's moving body. "Happy weekend, Alfredo," he said.

The driver nodded. "And a happy weekend to you, sir," he said.

La Tigressa was putting on a show on the dance floor. Not for the people, not for Steve, but for Bobby Slater. She thought she remembered just where he was standing when she took the dance floor, but as she circled by the tables, twisting and turning in the intricate treatment of the beguine arrangement of "Night and Day," she seemed to have lost him in the crowd.

She knew Bobby loved to watch her dance. She had her greatest hold on him when she danced, except when she was making love to him. How many hours on different nights had she danced for him, completely naked, in her penthouse tower overlooking Rome?

It had taken time for him to work through her sexual blackout period. It had been years since she had let any man put his hand on her.

Everyone had assumed she was living with Tucheki, and that was a great cover for her. She had confided in Tucheki, and he had protected her. She hadn't wanted a man around her.

But Bobby was different. She had fallen in love with him when she was a very young girl, going to the Marfa, Texas, theater every week, and seeing Bobby Slater in a succession of leading man roles. She had grown up with him. He was *the* movie star, as he was for so many young girls the world over.

He was cute, charming, romantic, and mysterious. He had never married, so every girl in the world still had a chance. He never was hurt; he was always the one who hurt people. He left woman after woman, following love affairs of short or long duration, every possible item in his life splattered over the world's scandal sheets.

Bobby Slater was Hollywood. Bobby Slater, the romantic. Bobby Slater, the cocksman. Bobby Slater, the real macho of them all.

Bobby treated each woman differently. It was an "art form," he used to say. "There isn't a woman in the world you can't make fall in love with you, if you give her enough attention. Find out what she needs—whatever it is—sex, intelligence, taste, friendship, a confidant. Money. A place in the sun. Perversion. Dope. Alcohol. A father. A child. Whatever it is, each one of them is searching for something. Then you supply the need. Slowly, steadily or quickly, if they want it that way, you supply the need. And then, once they're coming after it, you withdraw it just a little. You don't return a few phone calls. You're out late, but not with them. No explanation. You disappear for a long weekend. You don't send flowers for a while, or pick up anything for them in a shop window. You stop writing notes. Now, they decide they can't live without you.

"Then, it's their pursuit. The ball is in their court. You let yourself be caught whenever you want a great fuck. And when that gets boring, and it always does, you get out fast, with some kind of blinding insult. Something that makes their egos burn. Then, they fight to get you back. Sometimes you go back for a night or two. You watch them die a little.

"And," Bobby said, "believe me, I've seen it. Every man who treats a woman like this beats out the man who gives her everything—every time.

"They're bored by the man who's always there. They want challenge. They want a put-down some of the time. They want inconsistency. They want you to keep them guessing.

"Most of all, they want an exciting fuck. And if you're too good to them, you're not exciting anymore. I learned that when I was a kid, and I've made it my business never to forget it."

Most of all, Bobby Slater knew that he had to stay in the public eye if he was going to maintain his position as a number one in the business. And he meant to hold on to that position for as long as he could. He'd kill for it.

When the dance set closed and the band took ten, Steve and La Tigressa made their way back to where they had left Bobby Slater. He wasn't there. And Jake Powers had a strange look on his face. La Tigressa sensed something was wrong. She turned to Jake.

"Where's Bobby?" she asked.

"He left," Jake said.

"Left?" La Tigressa asked. "You mean, with the reporters? A story?"

Jake shook his head. "I don't know."

La Tigressa forced herself into an eerie laugh that sent chills up Steve's backbone.

"It must be a joke—some kind of bet—you know how Bobby is," La Tigressa said to Steve and Jake, and the others around her. "Yes, that's what it is."

"I'll go look for him," Steve said gently.

La Tigressa swallowed hard. "No, thank you, though—I'm sorry— if you'll forgive me. I really am tired. I did two shows tonight, you know, and Bobby will be calling me at home. He'll know that I'd go straight home and wait for him there. Not here, with other people. We have an agreement between us." Her voice was rising in false confidence.

"You're right—it's probably some kind of interview," Steve said. "Bobby's feeling very high tonight with the picture."

"Yes, he is so excited," La Tigressa said. "You know, he's turned down so many things, waiting for this."

"Yes, I know," Steve said. "And this is a very important film—one of the first with China. May I take you home?"

"No, please stay and enjoy the party. Bobby would want you to."

"Then you must take our car," Steve said. "Come on, I'll go with you and get the driver."

La Tigressa put out her hand and tightened her fingers on Steve's arm. Her hand was shaking. "Thank you," she said.

La Tigressa stayed up all night, waiting. She met the dawn of the new day on the balcony of her penthouse apartment. Lionel Ritchie's "Dancing on the Ceiling" was playing on the stereo.

There was a knock at the door, and La Tigressa ran from the terrace, through the living room, and out to the hallway, and breathlessly opened the front door. She thanked God all the way. She knew there had to be some mistake. Bobby Slater would be there.

"Bobby Slater" was a special delivery boy from the cable service. She took the telegram, tipped the boy lavishly, and closed the door, ripping open the cable.

> I'm going into training for the picture, baby. It's going to be a 24-hour-a-day job, the biggest film of my life. I know you'll understand, because you're a professional. I can't give you the time you need anymore. I hardly have time for myself. I'll be pulling for you, though. You can't miss. Thanks for everything.
>
> Bobby.

La Tigressa read the cable again. Then she screamed out, "You dirty son of a bitch. You dirty—" Her voice broke, and she started to cry. She wadded up the telegram and then pressed it out again. She stumbled for the telephone. She picked it up and started to dial, but at the fourth or fifth number, she stopped, then flung the white telephone against the golden-edged mirror over the fireplace. The mirror smashed into ruins on the floor.

With both hands, she swept clear her antique Louis XIII desk. Two pictures of Bobby went smashing to the floor, with her books, her calendar, her appointment pads, her pens. She pounded the top of the desk in frustration, fighting to gain control of herself.

She wandered aimlessly out to the terrace, where she could see the sleeping city of Rome coming to life, with the dawn of another day. It made her feel more alone. The morning bells were starting, mounting in intensity in one cacophony of sound.

La Tigressa, the toast of Roman nightlife, with all the anger, all the hatred of her first twenty-three years, broke out against this new humiliation. She would get even. She screamed it in the face of the chorus of bells. "Goddamn you!" she cried.

She shook her hands high above the street of her penthouse terrace, and her sobs turned into hysterical laughter, drowned out by the hundreds of bells welcoming the new Roman day.

10

Holmby Hills

teve Wayland's workroom above his garage was filled with photos, stills, clippings, research, location shots, and a huge countdown calendar, all in a massive collage.

And hundreds of pictures of Magdalena Alba.

Another wall space was filled with photographs of Rayme Monterey at Asbury Park, at the Stonecutter, at the Roxy in Los Angeles, at Yankee Stadium, in Greensborough, North Carolina, on stage, backstage, with "his people"—a thousand faces of Rayme Monterey.

And over on another wall were pictures of "Stephanie Columbo"— dancing pictures, pictures with Tucheki, with Bobby Slater, in Rome, in Monte Carlo, in Africa, and several pictures with a tall, distinguished older man, his evening clothes covered with French government decorations.

Steve was still researching the life and the story of La Tigressa. He looked at the clock. It was three-thirty in the morning. One day after La Tigressa had disappeared from Rome. He couldn't sleep. There was a pot of coffee on the hot plate near him, and he poured another cup.

His desk was covered with papers and piles of notes, and half the floor had boxes of notes, and separated piles of writings. The opposite wall was a collage of Hollywood filmmaking—not of glamour shots, but of locations—famous pictures—personalities he revered, and in the center, a photograph of Sam Goldwyn.

Here Steve lived, working on a film. There was a daybed on one side where he often spent the night. Because here he could surround himself with the people of his film—not only their physical likenesses, but their stories, their fact sheets, their interviews. Here his film family lived and breathed and vibrated, and he came home to them every chance he got.

He had four large looseleaf notebooks on his desk. There was adhesive tape across each one, and then letters in red crayon.

One was marked, "Magdalena," the second one, "Rayme." The third was marked, "Robert," and the fourth was marked, "La Tigressa— Mary Jane Stuckey."

He opened the book in front of him. There were hundreds of pages of notes from his research specialist, Barbara Carr.

For the second time, he began to read.

MARFA, TEXAS

La Tigressa had started her life twenty-three years before, in Marfa, Texas.

Her birth had been turbulent, her mother's pregnancy with her a constant nightmare. Mrs. Stuckey had almost died the week after Mary Jane was born. Life was already a struggle, and it had only just begun.

She was named Mary Jane after two aunts. Her last name was Stuckey. She was a strangely exotic-looking little baby for Marfa, Texas, with a mop of curly black hair and large, dark brown eyes that looked out at the world with terror.

Mary Jane was one of five children in a family that owned a diner-restaurant in Marfa. Three girls and two boys. Her father was a drunk, and a wife and child beater. He had been arrested twice for assault on his own family by the time Mary Jane was four years old. She stayed away from him as much as possible.

Mary Jane's mother kept the family alive. She kept the diner going. At thirty-nine years old, she was already worn out and lacked only the daring to kill herself.

Mary Jane was always the outsider. She didn't get along well with her brothers and sisters, or with the customers at the diner. She used to look out from behind the counter at the strange people, some of them sitting just a few feet away. They were mostly men of the road, truck drivers, motorcyclists, traveling salesmen. Their talk was salty, their manners crude. As Mary Jane began to develop into a young woman, they couldn't keep their hands off of her.

Mary Jane hated men. Her father terrified her, her brothers taunted her, and the boys at school made fun of her. Her dresses were made over, her stockings sewed up again and again.

And then there were her teeth. There was no money for dental work in the Stuckey family. And when, in adolescence, Mary Jane had a tooth broken off, the dentist took it out and installed a spike instead of a tooth. Because there was no money for anything else, and at least the spike was durable. It was on her left side.

From that day on, Mary Jane stopped smiling. Her whole life seemed symbolized by the ugly steel spike sitting there in the middle of her mouth, for everyone to see. It didn't matter to Mary Jane that she was developing into a pretty girl.

When Mary Jane was sixteen she had had her first sexual experience. It wasn't a boy from school or a man from town. It was her own father.

Ever since she had begun to mature into a voluptuous young woman, her father had been paying attention to her for the first time. He didn't scream anymore, or slap her, or tell her to shut up, or spank her brutally; instead he kept pulling her onto his lap and running his hands over her breasts. Sometimes, he would put her over his knee to pretend he was going to spank her, and pull down her panties and caress her bare bottom.

Mary Jane was humiliated. But, for the first time, she found that she could get some space to breathe. A little spending money. A new dress. Some curtains for the room she shared with one of her sisters. She found that she got these things if, when her father pulled her over, she sat on his lap and didn't say anything when he reached inside her sweater and felt her nipples. She longed to have her own room, and be out of this hell.

Her brother was an alcoholic and went on long drinking bouts with her father. Her older sister was sleeping with everybody in the school and she had heard the boys laughing about the "school pump." She would never let any of them touch her, even though she liked her new popularity since her breasts had swollen and her hips filled out.

One night, when she'd been out on a date and came home about one o'clock, her father was waiting for her in the living room. He'd been drinking heavily.

"I knew you'd turn out this way," he said, "going around with your tits sticking out, wiggling your ass for all those little chickenshit boys at school. What do you mean, coming in here, one o'clock in the morning?"

"I didn't do anything," Mary Jane said tersely. "And don't talk to me that way."

"I'll talk to you any goddamn way I want, you little fuck," her father said.

He got up, stumbling out of his armchair across from the TV set. He walked over to his daughter. She looked at him levelly.

"Don't touch me!"

He slapped her hard across the face.

"You're my daughter," he said. "I'll touch you any time I goddamn want to. And you'll know it's a man who touched you and not one of those little pimply-faced idiots at your fuckin' school."

With one hand, he ripped her blouse off.

Her breasts were bare. Ever since she'd begun to grow up, she'd gone without underclothes. It was something she was famous for in school. Now, her torn blouse was open all the way across the chest, and her great tilted breasts protruded out. Her father took her breasts in his hands and caressed them.

"Goddamn tits of yours. Never wear a brassiere anymore. Walkin' around this house showin' them off—before you're through, the whole town will fuck you. And you'll love it. Goddamn, it's something when a man raises a daughter and she turns out to be a cunt."

Mary Jane struck him in the face with both fists, sobbing hysterically as she swung her arms. He caught her wrists finally and pushed her back against the console television. The late news was on and part of the picture slivered through her legs and around her thighs as she was backed up against the set.

Her father reached down and pulled off her skirt. Her beautiful white thighs and her dark triangle were completely exposed. Only her high heels remained.

In one fast motion, he unzipped his pants and forced himself upon her. She screamed. But he didn't care. With a violent movement, he shoved her down on the floor in front of the television set and forced her legs apart.

She screamed, "You can't. Daddy, you can't."

It was the first time she'd called him "Daddy" in many years. She was terrified. What if she had his child? What if she'd have an idiot growing inside of her? The world blacked out. The last thing Mary Jane remembered was her father on top of her, forcing her legs back, and thrusting himself through her pain and through her blood, deep into her.

She wanted to die. And she welcomed the blackness coming in as most certainly the blessed death she had so often prayed for.

Mary Jane survived. She was taken to the hospital by her mother, who made up a covering story. She was severely torn vaginally and had to stay in the hospital for two weeks.

Nothing was ever said about the incident. The doctors did a complete curettage and the gossip started outside the hospital. Which of the high school boys had raped this girl? There were stories about a gang rape by the football team.

By the time Mary Jane came back to school, she was no longer the virgin she'd been reputed to be. Somebody had gotten to her and fucked the hell out of her. They knew all about it over at the hospital. Everybody had gotten it straight. She became, overnight, the most famous girl in school.

Charlie Heckert was the best-looking boy in Marfa High School. He had perfect features, a beautiful body, and wavy black hair. He was a great dancer and he was always voted the best-looking boy in the class, and the sexiest.

Girls chased him, and there were many stories about his prowess as a cocksman. The general feeling around Marfa High was that Charlie Heckert could fuck any girl that he wanted, and there were even tales of orgies, with eight or ten other juniors and seniors having naked parties and changing partners.

After Mary Jane had returned to school for a while, Charlie asked her out. It was the first time any of the popular boys had ever asked her for a date.

He came for her in his Ford coupe. He brought her a corsage. And he opened doors for her everywhere they went. For the first few dates, he never laid a hand on her.

Mary Jane began to come alive for the first time in her life. She started taking the night shifts at the diner after school, carefully putting away her meager earnings so that she could pay the dentist to put in a false tooth where her steel spike remained. She never lifted her upper lip, so no one at the school had seen the steel spike clearly.

But at the Marfa High School spring prom, when Mary Jane's classmates saw her dance for the first time, a circle of teenagers surrounded her, spellbound by her prowess on the dance floor, and Mary Jane laughed her full laugh at Charlie Heckert, who suddenly froze in his spot. He was looking directly at the steel spike in her mouth. Then he began to laugh. They all began to laugh. And he kept looking at her long after she'd closed her mouth and resumed her tight-lipped expression.

From then on, Mary Jane refused to go out with him until she had enough money for the dentist.

After the dentist had replaced the steel spike, and a new white tooth remained there exactly matching her other white teeth, only then did Mary Jane share her terrible cross with Charlie.

That night, Charlie had ordered a special dinner at the Marfa Inn, a few miles out of town. They had champagne, and she got drunk for the first time in her life. She laughed again and again. She laughed whether something was funny or not. She laughed at his serious expression. She laughed at the waiter. She laughed at the food. At everything.

Her smile was a bright white flash of perfect teeth. A terrible burden had been lifted from her. For the first time she could remember, she had some confidence. She was not afraid of somebody turning away from her in horror when they saw the steel spike.

Charlie asked the five-piece band to play their favorite songs: "I Will Survive," "Ring My Bell," "You Don't Bring Me Flowers," "Ooh, Baby, Baby." There was no question in either Charlie's mind or in Mary Jane's that they were going to spend the night together.

When they were on the dance floor, she felt completely carefree; she put her arms around him. And then she began to dance.

Nobody at school, none of her family had known about Mary Jane's dancing. From the time she had begun to grow up she had loved music. It was the one time she could lose herself and pour out her rebellious feelings and her longings.

There wasn't any dancing school in Marfa. She didn't have the money to go anyway. She didn't want to take any of the dance classes in school because she knew she'd be made fun of again. She had no clothes to wear. She had no social graces.

But again and again, through her young life, Mary Jane had turned on her favorite radio stations and made up her own dances.

She had danced in empty rooms. She had danced in locked bathrooms. She had danced in deserted back yards. She had danced in fields, on the edge of the city. She had danced in juke joints when no one was around.

She danced in the diner when she did the cleanup detail and had no help. She would play her favorite songs on the jukebox and dance for her own pleasure. She originated intricate steps, and her body turned and swayed to the different rhythms she loved.

That night at the Marfa Inn, Charlie discovered Mary Jane's dancing. When the band finally hit a good number, she pivoted and twirled around him like an exploding firecracker.

The other people got off the floor. This time, there was no steel spike to stop her. It was a one-woman show, and Charlie was proud because this was his woman. She wore a tight sweater and skirt, with nothing on underneath. You could see every line and every detail of her body. She was exquisite.

Mary Jane and Charlie had the best room in the house. It was called "The *Giant* Room," since some of the crew of *Giant* had stayed there a generation before when they were making the film in Marfa. There were pictures of Elizabeth Taylor, Rock Hudson, and Jimmy Dean all over the house, many of them inscribed to the man and woman who owned the Marfa Inn.

For the first time in her life, Mary Jane felt she was somebody. The champagne took away the memories of her father and she made love with all her heart to this handsome young man, who was the hero of her life.

Suddenly, for Mary Jane, life became worth living. And she did not notice at first when Charlie, in the middle of the night, began to do some strange things she'd never even heard about.

When he approached her from the back, after they had made love several times, and he went in the other place, she thought he'd made a mistake. The pain was excruciating and she cried out. But her discomfort simply excited him more and he took her hips in his hands and brutally drove himself into her.

After a few moments, it hurt less, but she felt violated. And then, when he followed her into the bathroom, never letting her alone, she decided he must be a little drunk and she would just have to get through the night.

Anyway, she loved him. He looked so tall and handsome, standing there naked in the early morning light in the bathroom.

She took his cock in her mouth and sucked her own juices from it. He was getting excited again and he held her by the hair of her head. He shoved her mouth up to the very head of his cock until she thought she was going to choke, and then jerked her head by the hair back and forth, back and forth, till suddenly she felt his organ bursting and exploding inside her mouth. He came again and again, sending the hot white fluid all over her mouth and down her throat. It was an incredible sensation.

She didn't know whether it was right or wrong, but somehow she knew that Charlie Heckert had to be good. This was just normal, she told herself, another part of sexual experience.

Charlie took her by the hand and lifted her up so that her mouth was near his. She swallowed the last bit of warm come. It had a strange, salty taste.

She felt truly close to him now. They had done all these things together. They were one person. It was like the happy endings in the movies. It was worth all her sordid life. This beautiful man really loved her.

Charlie spoke quietly as he stroked her hair. "I love you, baby."

She pressed her head against his chest. She wanted to close the blinds and shut out the new day forever.

A year later, the tenderness was gone from him. They were married now.

Charlie Heckert and Mary Jane. They were a good-looking couple. They looked like the most popular couple of the 4-H Club, except for two minor flaws.

There was a touch of degeneracy building steadily about Charlie's loose mouth and somewhat dangling lower lip. You didn't pick it up at first, but you knew something was a little off. Then, it began to grow on you.

And, in Mary Jane's eyes, there returned some of the expression that had been there since she was a child. Doctors called it "hysteric." It was a mirrored look, reflecting her deep inner conflicts and, like storm clouds, predicted emotional thunderstorms ahead.

Charlie had become a mechanic at the Marfa Garage and Mary Jane worked at the drugstore as a clerk. Together, for Marfa's standards, they made a reasonable living. They had an apartment, a new Ford, two-week vacations, and unlimited boredom ahead.

They were like the dusty stale wind in Marfa itself. Just settling down all the time, not going anywhere. Rotting.

It was in the middle of summer. It was 110 degrees outside. There was no air-conditioning in the apartment.

Charlie came in the door. Mary Jane had a fan going in every room. She was wearing a slip, cut very low in front so that her breasts were almost bare. Rivulets of sweat ran down her chest and across her forehead and down her cheeks. There were sweat stains on the inner thighs of her legs, although she was, as always, very clean.

She prided herself on her cleanliness. And after her father had raped her, it had become an obsession. She douched often in an effort to finally, once and for all, wash away the stain of her drunken father.

In this hot weather, she took several showers a day and drank a continuous string of iced coffees.

Charlie slumped down on a dining room chair. His face and hands were clean, but his overalls were stained with grease. A wind stirred the curtains in the living room windows. The wind was a hot breath. The stereo was playing Paul McCartney's "Yesterday."

"Goddamn," he said. "I never remember it this hot."

She looked at him and poured him iced coffee. "I never remember it anything but."

They looked at each other. He sipped his iced coffee. She sat down across from him, and pulled up her slip so that most of her white thighs were showing.

He muttered at her, "You doing that 'cause you're hot, or is that supposed to be for me?"

She played the game back. "That's for you to figure out."

He motioned to the whiskey on the sideboard. "Get me a scotch, will you, baby?" He watched her hips sway as she walked to the little sideboard and poured him a drink. "You've got the most beautiful ass in the world."

She stood beside him, barely two inches away from his mouth. "I thought you'd stopped noticing. Charlie, why don't you like to fuck me anymore? It's great when it's hot like this. I feel all juicy."

He pulled up her slip and pressed his mouth to her. He sucked quickly on a piece of ice in the iced coffee and then he ran his cool tongue across her clitoris.

She moaned softly and then, suddenly, unzipped his pants and sat down on him.

Her breasts were out of her slip now and he sucked on her nipples as she rode up and down him, tightening the mouth of her vagina around the base of his cock. She grabbed him roughly by the hair and kissed him with her tongue, forcing her tongue inside his mouth so that it was moving in exact rhythm with their bodies.

In the intense heat, they both climaxed fast and she pressed all the way down on him as she came. She looked down at their hair, intertwined as their bodies met. She loved that. The big mass of curly black hair they both shared. She had waited all day for this moment and now it was over.

Slowly, he lifted her off of him and zipped up his pants. "You're a hell of a woman, Mary Jane. That's the way I want to die. Fuckin' you. What a way to go!"

Mary Jane laughed. "Charlie, does everybody have it like this? I mean, does everyone get along so well sexually? When you finally get around to it, that is?"

Charlie poured himself a scotch. "I don't know, honey, but from what I hear about those people who make those big sexual research jobs, some of these books, I've seen them in the library, they got every kind of statistic in there, who does what to who, how many times a day, what time of day, they even have a chapter where some people do it with animals."

"With animals?"

Charlie said, "That's right. They've got some stories in one of those things I read about where a woman gets herself fucked by a horse."

Mary Jane said, "That's impossible."

Charlie answered, "Well, read it for yourself . . . people do a lot of strange things—'specially in a place like Marfa—in the heat like this—there ain't anything else you can do. You know, this guy down at the place, named Pete, you may have seen him around there, great big guy, great build, been pumping iron all his life, you know, one of *those* guys—well, he's married, a little longer than us, and he says there's a lot of things he does that are really fun, I mean, you know, fuckin' around, that sort of stuff."

Mary Jane said, "No, I don't know what you mean."

Charlie answered, "Well, Pete says that he and his wife, well, they go to some parties with some people they know, they're married, too—and they all get to drinking and having a good time and then they change partners for the night, you know, this guy with the wife of another guy, and his wife goes with the fellow of her girlfriend and . . ."

Mary Jane asked, "You mean switching?"

"Yeah," he answered, "that's right, switchin'."

"I read about that in a book—no, I guess it was a magazine. Somebody left it in the drugstore. It's been going on all over the country. I can't imagine people doing that if they like each other. What did Pete say?"

"Well, Pete says he's done it three or four times, he and his wife, they really get a kick out of it, you know, you probably never see the people again. He says that it even heats up their own sex life when he and his wife have been fuckin' somebody else."

Mary Jane blazed at him. "You tellin' me you'd like to do that? You'd like to take me somewhere and have somebody we don't even know make love to me? While you're in another room making love to somebody else? Are you tellin' me that, Charlie Heckert?"

Charlie replied, "I'm not telling you nothin'. I'm a man who's done a hard day's work, I'm hot and I'm tired, and I come home to my wife, I'm just sayin' what went on today, just sharin' with you.

"You're always talkin' about sharin', Mary Jane. Well, I'm sharin' with you, and this is probably the most interesting thing that happened to me today because it's boring down there, every other day is just like the other goddamn day, but Pete had something else to say today, and we all listened. And that's all the fuck it is. You want to make something out of it?"

Mary Jane looked at him. "Do you?"

Charlie said, "No, I just want to get a shower, sit down and watch the ballgame, with nobody yellin' at me, 'n' have a good dinner."

And then he grabbed her and drew her into him, putting his mouth on her nipples again. "Then, maybe if this heat lets up a bit, I'd like to have another piece of the greatest tail in Marfa, and it's mine." He pulled her down on him again.

Four months later Charlie took Mary Jane to their first "couples party." They decided just to try it, to look around and see what happened. They went with Pete and his wife.

Pete was tall and brutish, with massive shoulders and biceps. His wife was a long-legged, full-breasted woman with curving hips and a provocative face.

The party was at the Marfa Inn, where sixteen months before Charlie and Mary Jane had had that memorable night, the beginning of everything. Now there was a small orchestra, plenty to drink, and a big crowd.

In a private dining room, off the main room, eight couples were having dinner. They were all married and they were all from Marfa or surrounding small Texas towns.

By the time they were pretty drunk, they started asking each other to dance. There was enough room on the floor in the small dining area for four couples. The band in the next room was playing "With You I'm Born Again."

Pete asked Mary Jane to dance first. Then Charlie asked Pete's wife, Susie, to dance, and the other couples interchanged partners. The last couple on the floor got to work fast.

The woman whispered into her new partner's ear, "I want to feel your hands on me, underneath my dress. Go ahead. Go ahead, feel how wet I am . . . it's because I've been thinking of you. I knew you were going to ask me to dance. Are you hard?"

He whispered, "Feel me. I'm ready to come."

She took his cock out of his pants and put it against her. She said, "Pull up my dress." He did. She whispered to him, her tongue licking his ear, "Put your prick against my clitoris, just like that."

He said, "Someone's going to see us."

She said, "So? Everybody here knows they are going to end up with somebody, not their husbands or wives, either, they're going to be fucking somebody and it's going to be about five minutes and we'll all be out of here. It turns me on to fuck in front of other people. I've done it before. Try it. Just lift me up now and put me on you."

He lifted her up, his hands below her skirt, and she folded his prick inside of her and wrapped her legs around him. They were still moving to the music. He began to thrust in her wildly. Then the other couples began to notice, until they stopped dancing almost completely and just swayed to the music, watching these two strangers fucking.

Mary Jane watched, absolutely frozen.

Pete leaned down to her. "You scared?"

Mary Jane nodded her head. "I don't think I like this."

She reached out to her husband, who was dancing with Susie. "Charlie, I want to go home. Now. We shouldn't have come here."

Charlie was drunk. "Sure we should. Don't be a party killer—I'm just going to give Susie here a quick shot between her legs, right, Susie, baby? You go ahead, be nice to old Pete there, he's never had anyone like you. You show him, you show him, baby, you show him what a great fuck you are and then we'll go home and I'll fuck you."

Mary Jane said, "I told you before, Charlie, we shouldn't have come here. I feel sick."

Charlie laughed. "You'll get over it, baby. Go ahead, Pete. Give her that big old Polish prick of yours."

Pete pulled Mary Jane against his body. He drove his hard cock into her belly. "Do you feel that, honey? Your old man ain't got any equipment like that if he lives to be a hundred and forty. This is genuine old Eastern European Polack prick, and it's stored up waiting for you.

"I've been thinking about fucking you ever since I first saw you with Charlie there at the place—man, you are a fine-lookin' broad. I used to watch you walk away, swinging that cute little ass of yours, and my God, I'm going to tear it apart."

He grabbed Mary Jane by the wrists and pulled her out of the room and down the corridor into one of the seven bedrooms on the main floor of the Marfa Inn.

Mary Jane couldn't believe what was happening. She fought, kicked, even bit Pete on the shoulder, but all he did was laugh at her while he pulled her clothes off. When she resisted his pulling the zipper down her back, he simply tore the dress at the zipper point.

Suddenly, he was on her, this huge bull of a man with masses of black hair curling all over his shoulders, chest and arms. The ape man, she thought, here is the original ape man.

Pete was not a gentle lover. He believed that all women enjoyed force and force was his forte. He didn't care whether she was ready for him or not.

He had a huge organ and he prided himself on how fast he was ready. What he never acknowledged was that he couldn't stay hard long enough to give any woman a real orgasm. But then, all he was worried about was his own. He wanted to get it off fast.

Suddenly, he was on top of Charlie Heckert's beautiful little wife with the great tits and the slinky ass. The thatch of curly black hair between her legs made him hotter yet, and he could see the beads of moisture on her lips. She was pretending not to want it, but she was already liking it.

He pushed her legs back until the muscles in her thighs cramped. He held her wrists down on the pillow and he kept his hands out of biting range, as she snapped at him.

He muttered at her, "You cunts, you're all alike. Putting on your airs around the place—acting like you're better than any of us. Well, let's see if you're as good a fuck as Susie. Yeah. I'm coming, baby, drink it, take it all. Here it is."

He drove his way into her, shuddered, and convulsed. Mary Jane lay motionless under him. Something snapped within her. She saw in one brief instant a terrible road in front of her. She felt powerless. At the end of that road would be death, and she couldn't wait to get there.

It was three fifty-five in the morning by the ship's clock on Steve's desk, when the harsh ring of the telephone jolted him back to the present. He was studying the massive leather book marked "La Tigressa—Mary Jane Stuckey."

There was a page of a faded Marfa, Texas, newspaper photograph, at the time of Mary Jane's graduation from Marfa High School and then her marriage. Even in those newspaper photographs, the eyes haunted you, there was so much pain in them.

And the one professional photograph, printed on cheap studio paper, of Mary Jane smiling her broadest smile. She was showing off her now perfect teeth. Her mouth smiled, but the happiness in her eyes was tentative.

When the phone rang, Steve had become completely immersed in Mary Jane's life. He wanted to walk in her shoes. Maybe he could find the keys, and then he'd know where to look for her. My God, he thought, how could any father possibly rape his own daughter? He had read about incest in the papers, and he knew there were national studies on child abuse, but he had never run up against it in someone he knew. His heart reached out to Mary Jane, wherever she was.

Maybe the phone was bringing more news about Mary Jane. Maybe they had located her. Maybe she was dead.

He picked up the phone. Steve's mother's voice was controlled and loving, as he always remembered it.

"Steve," she said, "I'm so glad that I've reached you. I tried last night before I went to bed, but I don't think you were home yet."

"No, I came in around midnight. I was in Rome, about the picture."

"Are you all right?" his mother asked.

"Sure," Steve said. "Fine."

"You sound awfully tired," his mother said.

"Jet lag, that's all. How are you and Dad? Ready for Christmas?"

"Well—" He heard a change in his mother's voice. It broke a little, but quickly she regained control. "Your father is going to have a little operation, Steve. A stomach ulcer."

"During Christmas?" Suddenly, Steve was on the alert.

"Yes," his mother answered. "It really seems best to do it now. It's a good time for your father to be away from the office. Christmas season is a vacation period for him now."

"Since when?" Steve asked. "I don't remember Dad ever having a vacation season. It's always been trouble getting him away, any time. What is it, Mother? I hear something in your voice."

Mrs. Wayland sounded tentative. "Well, Steve, we haven't told you because we didn't want to bother you. We knew you were getting ready for Christmas with the girls. It's your year to have them."

"That's right," Steve answered. "But what about Dad?"

"He hasn't been feeling well for the last six months, Steve," his mother said, "and lately he hasn't been able to taste his food, so the doctor made some tests—"

Steve interrupted. "What doctor? McElroy?"

"Yes," his mother said. "Why?"

"He's no good, that's why. Mother, we've had this talk so many times. McElroy's a fake. He's a society doctor."

"Anyway," Steve's mother said, "we can't change it now. They're going to operate in two days."

"Christmas Day?" Steve asked, incredulously. "No one has an operation on Christmas Day."

"The doctor had two cases scheduled on Christmas afternoon so he's fitting your father in. He's leaving the next day for a vacation in Aspen. We had to make the decision quickly. We didn't want to do it on Christmas, but we want to get it over with and take a trip. Your father's promised to take me to England when this is over with. It's just routine, Steve. They say he'll be out of the hospital in a week."

"That could be true with a stomach ulcer. But about the taste—how long has that been going on?"

"Well, maybe nine months. It's been getting worse. He didn't tell me about it for a long time. And now, everything tastes bitter—and I noticed he was eating hardly anything. But you know your father never complains."

"Has he lost weight?" Steve asked.

"Quite a bit," his mother answered. She paused. "Steve—I just wanted you to know about the operation. I didn't think it was right that your father be operated on without your knowing."

"I should be there," Steve said.

"You can't do that," his mother answered. "We know you're just preparing a picture. And Christmas—well, Steve, you've never missed a Christmas with your children, have you?"

"No, Mother, I haven't."

"Well, there you are. If this were anything more serious, I would tell you, Steve, but you know from medical school yourself, an ulcer is common and it's not very dangerous."

"Unless there's a hemorrhage," Steve said. "Then it can kill you."

"But it hasn't hemorrhaged," his mother said. "And you know that's true, or they would have operated by now. I've been watching him, making a daily report for the last month to the doctor." Her voice suddenly sounded weak.

"Mother, are you all right?" Steve asked.

The weary voice on the other end of the line picked up strength. "Yes, I'm fine, son. But I'll be glad when this is over."

"Tell Dad I'll call him tomorrow," Steve said.

"I don't know—I just got him to sleep an hour or so ago. He had a rather bad night."

"In pain?" Steve asked.

"No," his mother said. "Not in pain. But very disturbed, very nervous."

Steve tried to sound reassuring. "Well, Mother, an ulcer's like that. You can't eat right, and when you do eat, it hurts. You feel sick, and it weakens you to be fighting a lot of pain all the time."

"Do you think we've made the right decision, son?" his mother asked.

"Well, I don't know, you're there and I'm not. When you've got an ulcer acting up like that, it's wise to have a look and cut it out if necessary. I wish we had another doctor on it, though. Do you think Dad would accept a change?"

"Not now," his mother answered. "He's used to Doctor McElroy."

"I'm going to be in touch with you both, every day. And, Mother," Steve added, "you tell Dad we're going to lick this thing. Is Junior around?"

"I haven't seen much of him lately," his mother said, "because he's taken over everything at your father's business. He's been a real help. And Clarence and Molly have been loyal, as always," she added. "They take care of everything at the house and help me with your father. They're going to take us over to the hospital today."

"Give them my love," Steve said. "They just don't change, do they . . . they're great people."

"Steve," his mother said, "I've got to get organized, pack your father up for the hospital. You know how he hates being sick. He's got to have all his special things, his bathrobe and pajamas and slippers and radio and notepads and phones. We've been through it before."

"And most of all," Steve said, "he has to have you. He's a lucky man, Mother. He knows what it is to be really loved."

"Someday, Steve," his mother added, "I hope you'll find the woman who truly loves you. You sound lonely, Steve. I worry about you. Is the picture coming well?"

"The picture doesn't count right now—it's you and Dad—I'll call you every night. And remember, Mother, I love you both—"

"And we love you, my son," his mother answered. "Good night, dear."

Steve hung up the phone slowly, then held onto it, as though he were holding on in some magical way to his mother and father, and to the connection back to them.

A surge of energy flowed through his body. As he punched out a number, pulling the extension cord with him, he began collecting up key things around the desk and around the room. Pictures of Kathleen and Lorelei. The collection of clippings and research on Rayme, Mary Jane, and Magdalena. A budget still in work, crew lists, something from almost every folder spread across his desk.

"Get me Doctor Rubin," he said on the phone. "Yes, put it through to emergency. This is a friend of his." He raised his voice. "Look, this is an emergency. My name is Steve Wayland, and Dr. Rubin will pick up my call."

A just-awakened voice came over the phone. "Hello, Steve, what is it? Are you sick?"

"No, it's not me," Steve said. "It's my father. In Chicago. I'm not up on the latest in medicine, as you well know, but I don't like what I hear. I just want to ask you one question, Philip. Does a stomach ulcer, when it's in condition serious enough for the doctor to decide to operate, does it strongly affect the taste in the mouth—does it ever cause a continuous bitter taste?"

Dr. Rubin sounded thoughtful. "A stomach ulcer can discourage you from eating and cut your hunger. It's so damn painful when it's open. But the taste shouldn't be that much affected. Particularly turning bitter. Has he had other checks?"

"I don't know," Steve answered. "He's got a lousy doctor, a doctor he inherited from a friend of his who was the family doctor. I never trusted him. Tell me, Philip, does it have a peculiar sound to you? It does to me."

Philip Rubin's voice grew serious. "Are you going back for the operation?"

"Why?" Steve asked.

"Because," Dr. Rubin said, "I think you should investigate it. Go back, Steve. I know it's Christmas, but—make sure yourself."

"That's why I called you," Steve said. "I think I should go back. Thanks, Philip. Go back to sleep."

Steve flashed the phone and dialed another number. Lieu's voice came on, apprehensive but contained. "Yes?" she said.

"Lieu," Steve said. "I don't have time to explain now—I want you to get me on the first possible flight . . . I don't care what kind of a seat it is, or what kind of a plane, to Chicago. My father's ill—I don't know how ill yet—a lot of things have got to be handled—first, call my children in a few hours and tell them I'll call them from Chicago. Tell their mother the children will be with her this year."

"I understand," Lieu said.

"I don't know how long I'll be there, but we've got to keep synched up. I'll be at Memorial Hospital. You know what I'll need and what you'll have to do to get it—we've got to use all the leverage we have. I need a control center with special lines to all of you from the hospital—and the day after Christmas, Lieu, on Stage Six, at the Goldwyn Studio, I want all our team there, all of them, on the speaker system."

"I understand."

"Any word on Tigressa?" Steve asked.

"No," Lieu answered. "We're combing Italy for her. Spartan's hired the best detectives in Europe. What are you going to do about Rayme? The trial's coming up soon."

"Lieu, I want you in New York with him. I'm going to try, no matter what happens, to fly there for the trial. We've got to give him all the support we can. There are plenty of his other people, but he's got to feel it from us, too. He's looking for a lie in us, and he's not going to find it."

"Do you want me to go back there for Christmas?" Lieu asked.

"No. You've got your family. After Christmas. Could you do that for me, Lieu?"

"I'll go back Christmas night. And Steve—do you want anything done about Mr. Gregson at the studio? He'll find out about your going away and he'll start complaining that you're not on the job."

"I want Spartan Lee over there," Steve said. "Gregson's afraid of Spartan, and he's not afraid of us. It's Spartan's job to keep the lid on. And when you get me set up at Memorial Hospital, give Spartan the phone numbers. And, Lieu, please see my children before you leave, and explain why I had to go."

He turned from the desk as he put the last folders into his briefcase. He was facing the piece of wall behind his desk, filled with photographs and his favorite mottoes, things he'd collected, some just typewritten, and some in special calligraphy. Winston Churchill's quote was the biggest, because there were so few words. "Never quit," it read.

11

Memorial Hospital, Chicago

*T*he cab pulled up through heavy banks of snow in front of Memorial Hospital, in Chicago. Steve paid the driver and pulled his thin California trenchcoat around his shoulders. He'd forgotten how cold Chicago was in the wintertime. His rugged face was lined with worry.

The huge hospital loomed up in front of him, flanked by twelve-foot-tall trees, gaily decorated with Christmas lights. A towering Santa Claus beamed steadily from a ledge over the massive doors of the hospital.

Steve picked up his suitcase and headed inside. As he walked through the downstairs lobby of the hospital, toward the front information desk, he sensed the odor that always made him sick, the institutional smell of strong, germ-ridding peroxide cleansers, the stale anesthetics, the cigarette smoke. He hated it.

Christmas surrounded him everywhere, Christmas trees, Santa Clauses, and the season's music on the stereo. The music made him sad. "Rudolph, the Red-Nosed Reindeer."

Steve asked for the room of his father, Lawrence Wayland.

"He's on the sixth floor—but it's after visiting hours." The nurse was quite definite about it. "I'm sorry, sir, but there's no visiting until this afternoon."

He headed for the elevator. The nurse followed him from behind the desk.

"I'm sorry, sir, you can't go up now."

One of the elevators had just come down and its doors were opening. Steve walked into it.

"I think they're going to check me in, too. Will you watch for notification to come through? My office in California is arranging it. Steven Wayland?"

"I haven't received any instructions about it," the nurse answered. She looked around. No one was in sight. "All right, your father's room is 606."

The fine-looking older man lay immobile in the bed. His hair was brushed back, silver and grey, with a tapered widow's peak. His eyes were shut. His cheeks were chiseled in, worn down by sickness. The big body Steve remembered protecting him as a child looked emaciated. His shoulder bones were mere points in his hospital nightgown.

On the dresser, across from the bed, were a few personal things and a photograph, from younger days, of a handsome middle-aged couple and two young boys. The younger and smaller one was definitely Steve Wayland. The older boy was as blond as Steve was dark.

Steve bent over his father. He brushed back his hair gently with his hand. Steve whispered, "Dad . . . Dad . . ."

Steve bent down and kissed his father on the forehead. There was respect in the way he did it, and love. The older man still slept.

Steve looked at his father's chart at the foot of the bed. There were the usual hieroglyphics there, and some notes about his medicine. *Morphine* shots, three a day.

My God, Steve thought, what's going on here?

Lawrence Wayland moved slightly and sat up with great effort in the bed. His eyes were deep blue, penetrating.

A surprised smile hovered over his face when he saw Steve. It had been years since the terrible breach.

Father and son looked at each other. Steve had his dad's eyes, a lighter shade of blue, but just as penetrating. The years of bitterness fell away with one look.

Steve stepped quickly to the bed and put his arms around his father. There were tears in the eyes of both men. Flesh to flesh. Blood to blood. The bond, put to the test now at the very threshold of life and death, was steel strong.

The older man spoke softly, "You came."

Steve nodded. "The minute I heard."

Lawrence Wayland leaned back against the pillows. "You shouldn't have left your work right now—ruin your Christmas. It's only an ulcer. A damn nuisance, nothing more. Your mother told you that, didn't she?"

"It's time *we* had a reunion, Dad."

Steve's father took his son's hand in both of his and held it as tightly as he could. There was desperation in his grip. There was so much to say.

"Your mother and brother will be so glad to see you."

Steve said, "No more illusions, Dad, that's what separated us before. Mother will be glad to see me. Junior may drop dead."

His father's eyes fell. "Lately, ever since I got sick, some strange things have been happening—and they give me so much dope—I can't remember anything. And the nightmares. But enough of that."

He pulled himself up and put both his hands on the sides of his son's face as he'd done when Steve was a little boy.

"When I get out of here, son, you and I are going to make up for everything my blindness has cost me. I'm going to take the time . . . suddenly, when I woke up just now and saw you here—well, I never guessed that you'd come. That's the truth, son. But here you are. I don't think I've ever understood you. But what I see in your face— for a young man, your eyes are full of pain . . . not the eyes of a playboy."

He coughed and sank back into the bed with the big effort he had just made. He muttered, "I never forgave you for not coming into the business—I had a dream—I never let you have your own. . . . But it's going to be different, I promise you, son, for the rest of our lives."

"Dad, take it easy. We don't need to talk. I'm here. You're here. We'll fight the world."

His father began to turn grey with pain. He whispered, "We may have to . . ."

Steve had been there for hours when his mother came in.

Roberta Wayland was a lovely-looking woman of sixty-seven. Her soft grey hair was piled high on her head, immaculately combed. She wore a pastel lavender wool dress.

She wore a small diamond wedding ring, which Lawrence Wayland had bought with his first paycheck after leaving the Navy after World War I. He had bought it at Tiffany's. And even when his great success had come, years later, and he was able to give his wife more beautiful jewelry, Roberta always wore the tiny diamond ring he had given her for their engagement.

On her slim shoulder was a handsome diamond pin in the shape of the famed Carmel cypress trees. Underneath, lettered in small, tasteful sapphire script was the word "Windswept."

This was the name of the vacation home that Lawrence had bought for her, their dream home in Carmel. It was one of the great pieces of property left in the famed Del Monte Properties, and they had wanted it for a long time. Finally, they'd bought it. And now, in their later years, they spent six months of the year there.

Roberta Wayland came from pioneer stock. She had not had an easy life as a young woman. She had graduated from the University of California at Berkeley, and had taught school for several years before she married her childhood sweetheart.

Together, they had gone to Chicago, from the California they loved so much, because of the job opportunities there with the giant sprawling grain companies that bought and sold and stored the crops of the Midwest.

Forty-seven years they had been together, and they had had their tragedies and crises. But they were solid. And, as Lawrence reached out his hand to his wife, she took it, without tears but with confidence and support.

You could feel their relationship filling the room. And, as always, it moved Steve. He had never felt a part of their relationship, but he respected it and admired it.

Then, his mother saw him and moved to him quickly with happy surprise. Steve embraced her.

"What a wonderful surprise!" she said. "You didn't tell me you were even thinking about coming—when I talked to you on the phone— but how can you be here? It's Christmas . . . your little girls . . . ?" Her voice trailed off questioningly.

Steve cut her off with a look, but Lawrence picked it up. "I thought so," his father said.

"Mother, I rearranged the schedule a little bit," Steve answered. "The girls and I are going to celebrate Christmas when I go home."

Lawrence objected, "But it's only an ulcer operation. I would have been fine. You could have called in and just kept track of things."

Steve looked at his father, then at his mother. "I belong here."

His mother moved to the phone on the bedside table. "Let's call your brother—he'll be so happy to know you're here."

12

Board of Trade Building, Chicago

A pale, red-haired man with quick, intelligent eyes stood along the wall in the back of the huge "pit" where wheat and grain and corn of the future harvests were being bought, sold, and traded all over the world.

It was a wild and noisy nightmare for anyone who was not part of it. Four large circular trading pits were spaced out along the floor of the giant vaulted room. In large numbers and configurations on the constantly shifting electronic blackboards, above the grain pits, the markets of the world were swiftly changing in correlation with the bidding and selling on the floor.

At the five circular centers, hundreds of men were gathered, talking in a language of their own, gesticulating madly with hand signs, and giving and taking, in quick arm thrusts, pieces of paper with small notations on them.

It was the usual morning bedlam of the Chicago Board of Trade Grain Market.

A casual visitor could never understand what was happening. Men trained for years to become active traders in the pit. The frenzy and the tension produced hundreds of yearly ulcers and a slew of heart attacks. It was constant pressure. Millions of dollars of product and commitments trading hands in the intricate, almost hysterical, atmosphere of the pit.

Lawrence Wayland, Jr., stood with his back against the wall of the trading floor, his body rigid with excitement. His small, piercing blue eyes shifted from circle to circle, and there was a continual flow of signals from him to his men, trading in every pit.

Junior surveying the scene was reminiscent of General Patton on his way to Berlin. These were his armies. This was his soil to conquer, his land to take. Confidence emanated from him as he gave orders in every direction. He was surrounded with three assistants and a secretary, who handled a group of portable phones.

In the roar of the trading floor, the secretary reached over and whispered in Junior's ear.

"What are you talking about?" he said. "You mean he's calling from California?"

"No." She shook her head. "He's here. At the hospital. In your father's room."

Lawrence Wayland, Jr., looked at his secretary as though she had pulled a gun on him. The color drained from his face.

In that one instant, his complete aura of confidence was shot away. General Patton was gone. A private, stripped of all rank, stood there, suddenly indecisive.

The din of the trading pit still surrounded him. He took the phone and slowly pushed the button, cutting into the main line. He put his hand over his right ear to try to hear the unexpected voice on the phone.

"Larry?" the voice on the phone asked. "I just wanted to say hello. I'm out at the hospital with Dad and Mother."

Junior's thin-lipped face tightened. He couldn't think straight, with all the noise around him. The only word he could get out was, "Why?"

"I just thought this was one of those Christmases where we should all be together," Steve's voice came over the phone.

Junior muttered an answer that didn't seem to follow in continuity. "Christmas," he said. "Oh—that's right—how long are you going to be here?"

"A few days, I guess—I want to see Dad back on his feet—are you coming out here later today?"

"Yes," Junior answered. "I guess so—"

"I'll see you then," Steve said, and hung up. His glance went from his father to his mother. He shook his head. "He's the same," he said. "I've ruined his day—a bad penny turned up for him—I told you, Mother, I didn't want to call him in the first place."

She smiled at him—a worn, self-deceiving smile. "I *know* he's just excited you're here."

Steve answered drily, "Excited, yes. Happy, no. He'll never change, Mother. Just forget it. We've all lived with him a long time."

Where had it begun, how many hundreds of times had Steve gone back in his head to try to understand? As long as he could remember, his brother had hated him. But it had to have started somewhere. His mind always went back just so far and stopped.

Stopping at the first scene he could remember, on the roaring train of memories. He saw himself in the corner of the living room on Michigan Avenue. The house his mother and father had had when he and Junior had been kids, six and nine.

Junior had been bigger than he was then, and almost every day there was a beating. Steve was on the run from the time school was over until he found a way to defend himself.

The *way* was the letter opener in the red Moroccan leather case on the coffee table in the living room. It was sharp, and threatening.

That first time, he remembered, he had gone for the letter opener after Junior had come in from school, hunted him down, and crashed his nine-year-old fist into Steve's jaw. Steve was blinded with tears but self-preservation drove him to the letter opener. He grabbed it, pulled it out of the red Moroccan leather sheath, and backed into a corner of the living room near the piano.

He stood there, quite terrified, brandishing the letter opener in his right hand as Junior came after him. The weapon stopped his brother dead in his tracks.

Steve was crying as he shouted out his defiance through his tears. "You're never going to hit me again." He could taste the blood running out of his mouth where his lips had been cut by his brother's blow.

Steve shouted again at his older brother, "One step further and I'll cut you open. I mean it." His voice choked on sobs.

Junior, color drained from his face, was almost out of control.

"You think you're so smart," he spoke in a threatening voice for a child. "You think you're a big shot in school already. I'm going to make Mother and Dad take you out of that school. You're never going to go to the same school I'm in.

"Every time I look, you're there, sucking around, making up to the teachers and the coaches—I'm sick of you."

Steve was still crying. "You've always been sick of me. You've been looking at me in that same way ever since I can remember. I hate you."

Junior's mouth was trembling. "Someday," he said, "I'll catch you without that letter opener. Then I'm going to beat you up every day of your life. I hate your guts. I always have and I always will."

Steve had had the same question then that he had now—why?

"Why?" Now, thirty years later, Steve had a few of the answers. But nothing had changed in the relationship.

He had tried to cross the bridge of Junior's hatred, particularly after he had gained insight into what really was wrong in that house on Michigan Avenue and in that house on Mansfield Drive and then on Byron, and every house in which they had lived as a family. His own terrible fear of leaving home had given him the key.

And then, that conversation he had had on the phone with his father and mother when he was shipping out from San Diego for Vietnam. My God, what a twisted idea they had of duty and honor and responsibility.

Steve had been twenty years old then, just graduated from Princeton, Phi Beta Kappa. It had been an unbelievable senior year, with all the honors, and all his friends, and then there had been Nancy.

Nancy Thayer was a model with the Nina Blanchard Agency in Los Angeles. She was, literally and figuratively, the "California Girl." She had been on the cover of *Sports Illustrated*, the special spring "swimsuit edition."

She was nineteen, a graduate of Briarcliff in New York, and from a fine old family in Buffalo. Steve had met her at a Princeton dance and they had become closer as the months went by in their respective senior years. Nancy was Steve's date over graduation weekend, and Steve had introduced her to his parents then.

She was as acceptable as any girl was ever going to be to Steve's mother and father. Her parents were the Thayers of the Thayers' Department Stores of upstate New York.

Nancy was a perfect all-American-looking type with one strange twist. Her eyes were slanted in a somewhat Oriental fashion. They were violet-colored like Elizabeth Taylor's and, combined with her long chestnut hair, her pale complexion, and her voluptuous body, gave her that extra-special look of a California model.

She was "The Jantzen Girl," "The Minute Maid Girl," "The Estée Lauder Perfume Girl," "The Marina Girl," and the most successful new young model on the Coast. Her Eastern society background, her education, and her refinement made her a special catch in California and film society circles.

That summer, after graduation, Steve and Nancy led a love idyll. Steve had to report to the Marine Base at El Toro in September, so Nancy took the summer off from her modeling assignments and she and Steve lived out their love story.

The beaches at La Jolla and Trancas, beyond Malibu. The Hollywood Bowl, the Greek Theatre, and the Sunset Boulevard jazz clubs. The ranch at San Ysidro. The Del Monte Country Club at Pebble Beach. The old Steinbeck haunts of Monterey and Monterey Bay.

They never talked about Vietnam. They were both scared and they both knew it. Steve already had his wings, so he was going in as a Marine flying officer and expected to see action in Vietnam before the end of the year.

They packed their love story into twenty-four hours a day, seven days a week. They were attacking life the way Arnold Palmer, a hero of theirs, played for championships, the way a whole generation of Americans was preparing to "go for it."

They didn't understand the war, they didn't understand international politics, they didn't understand the nuclear age. Nobody really did, they thought. But they could understand beauty, the excitement of making love with someone you really cared about, the physical pleasure of being young, healthy, and attractive, and alive.

They drove too fast, laughed too hard, drank too much, remembered too much, and forgot too much. They placed their happiness and their lives in each other's hands. Steve and Nancy didn't ask each other any questions. They didn't want any clouds coming across their sky. Everything about them happened naturally.

He remembered the first night they had made love. They hadn't planned it, but it was something they had both known was coming.

Steve had driven Nancy to a special cottage he had rented high in the hills overlooking the Big Sur ocean, at the Highlands Inn. They had checked in, gotten the keys, and gone on to the cottage, which was on the westernmost edge of the Highlands Inn's property. The fire had been laid and Steve lit it as soon as he took their bags into the room.

Nancy looked around the rustic living room in her special way. Steve had noticed it when he first met her—Nancy possessed any place that she really loved. Steve watched her and the joy of simply loving this beautiful girl went through him.

Nancy felt his look and turned toward him. Neither of them said a word.

In the flickering light of the fire, Nancy began to undress. She never took her eyes off Steve.

There was a simplicity, a purity in the way she did it that transfixed him. It was an open and true commitment of the moment, a special one that belonged to them. Steve looked at her and was moved as he had never been moved before.

She stood there naked now, her arms outstretched in a simple act of love toward the man she loved. And Steve came to her and held her face with both his hands and then kissed her softly. Her arms went around his neck, her body pressed close to his, and then she lay down in front of the fire and opened herself completely to him.

Steve had never forgotten that night. He was sure that was the night that Nancy had gotten pregnant.

Nancy wanted to have the baby. And so did he. They decided to call their parents and be married before Steve reported to El Toro.

Nancy's call had gone well. Her parents liked him, felt they both were too young, asked them both to delay until Steve came back, but they didn't really fight the plan.

Steve would never forget the call to his parents. It came back to him now, as he sat in the hospital room, talking quietly to his mother and father. His father looked so changed, lying in the bed, in the hospital, dependent on the people around him. Steve remembered him as never being dependent on anyone. He had always been the aggressor, the man in command.

It was driven home to Steve right then that people change, conditions change, authorities change. What was the old cliché? The only sure thing about life was change. He didn't think about that too much when everything was running along in form.

Steve remembered that phone conversation . . . word for word. The dead silence after he told his mother and father that he and Nancy were getting married. That they were planning a small ceremony in Los Angeles before he reported to El Toro Marine Base, and wanted his parents to come.

His mother had finally been the one to speak. "But Steve, you're only twenty years old. You haven't decided on what you might do. What if you go on to medical school? Please wait. Please take time."

Steve had answered quietly, believing that they would come around, as Nancy's parents had. "We don't want to wait. We have to decide for ourselves, you know that, but both Nancy and I want you to be part of this, just like her family will be."

Steve heard his father's quiet, deliberate, but highly charged voice over the phone. "Steve, we have so many plans for you. With your record in college, there's no question you have your choice of professions.

"I have it all worked out for you. Start here. You'll be the youngest vice president in any major grain business in the United States. I want to set up a European division and I want you to head it. You'll be traveling in Europe four months a year. You'll go right to the top."

Steve's alarm system went off. "When did you get this plan, Dad—and where does that leave my uncle—and where does that leave Junior?"

His father's voice came back strong and sure. "There's room for everybody. But you're special, Steve. You've proven it. And I'm not going to let you go to any other organization. This is what I've been building for all these years. This is my dream."

"A dynasty?" Steve asked.

"You might call it that," his father answered. "You'll be making a fortune before you're thirty years old. And after you've spent a couple of years in the European capitals, then, after some life experience, marry Nancy or anyone else you want to—but not now, Steve. You're still a boy."

"The Marines count me as something else—and so does Uncle Sam, Dad," Steve answered. "I didn't invent military service, you know."

His father had come back on that, too. "Steve, I'm pretty close to the Washington scene. We have to be because most of the world needs our grain to keep eating. I can tell you, I have the inside information with the government that this war isn't going to go on more than a couple months longer. You'll barely get over there and they'll be shipping you back. Nancy'll be here waiting for you and both of you will come to Chicago, and we'll talk it over together, like a family should."

Steve replied quietly. "Mother, Dad—I don't want to get into an argument about this. I've been happier with Nancy than I've ever been in my life. I love her. She loves me. We want to get married before I go overseas. It's a natural feeling. Nobody knows what's going to happen. How long it will be. Who's coming home and who isn't. So, I just ask you, will you come to the wedding? It's going to be a month from next Saturday in Los Angeles at a little chapel. We've met the minister, we like him. He understands exactly what we're doing. Please come."

His father's voice was dead level now. "Are you saying, son, that no matter what your mother or I think or feel, you're going to go ahead and get married at this time, whether we're there or not?"

"Well, I hope you won't put it that way, Dad," Steve said quietly.

His father answered abruptly. "I *am* putting it in that way, Steve.

We're a family. We've come up from a very poor beginning. We've worked very hard."

"I know all that," Steve interjected, "and I respect you for it."

"Then respect us now," his father answered. "This isn't too much to ask when we've worked hard for you, too, to give you all the opportunities we never had. Is it too much to ask?"

Steve thought for a moment. Then he made up his mind. "Yes, it is too much to ask. We're going to get married when we planned, just the way we planned it. Will you come?"

"No, we will not," his father answered slowly. "We don't believe you're doing the right thing. If you, my son, whom I've loved so much, can do this to us, after everything we've been to each other, then I'm through with you. You're no longer my son."

"But Dad, I love you—" Steve's voice trailed off as the sound of his father hanging up reverberated in his ears. Slowly, Steve hung up, too.

He was stunned. His father, whom he idolized, through with him? Just like that? Because he was getting married?

Nancy's voice came softly. "Why didn't you tell them I'm pregnant? If they knew—"

Steve shook his head. "If they knew, then they would put the whole thing on you. Our decision would be even more of a mistake to them."

Nancy crossed the small bedroom of the apartment they were renting out on Trancas Beach Highway, past Malibu. She was in her terry cloth robe and her hair fell loosely around her face. Her orchid-colored eyes had tears in them. He kissed the tears away. She shook her head. "What are you going to do, Steve? I can't believe they'd react like this."

"It's hard for me to believe," Steve said. "But I'm not going to use our baby to change their minds. What counts is that you and I love each other and we have the right to decide what we want to do.

"We've tried to include them, and my father tries to take over— I've seen that all my life. He fought his way up from being an office boy for ten dollars a week, eating at a little Greek restuarant where the owner gave him free oyster crackers on the table so that after he had a ten-cent bowl of soup, he could put the free ketchup on the free oyster crackers and have them swell up in his stomach and take away the hunger—he was an educated, talented man, but there was no place for him when he grew up. He made a place. He won his authority. He's used to controlling lives. But he's not always right. You know, I've told you about my brother—"

Steve was walking up and down now. "I've been trying to find out what was wrong. How did my brother develop a hatred for everything in life—and how come I was always terrified to leave home—?"

He went up to Nancy again and held her close. "Everything I know about really loving somebody is coming from you—you've given me that because you're soft and tender and really caring—not just on a romantic night—but day in and day out. Nancy, no one was like that, growing up in my family—every day was a question mark. Were you loved? Weren't you? Were you approved—were you a failure? Growing up, for me, was as insecure as a leaf blowing in the wind. I thought that's the way it was with everyone—you've taught me the difference. And as much as I love my father, I know that what he's done is wrong."

He touched her stomach in which their seed was growing. "No child of ours is ever going to wonder at any time or any place whether he's loved or wanted or needed. Do you know I wrote hundreds of notes when I was a kid and slipped them under my parents' door, asking why they didn't love me or what I had done to get their anger or criticism. I grew up on a yo-yo. And . . . thanks to you, it's over. That was a yo-yo comment my father ended with, hanging up the phone like that. He's seen me jump when that's happened before. Well, I'm all through with that, Nancy. I feel like somebody, really somebody, for the first time in my life. Because you love me. Because you want me and because we're going to have a child together." He held her. "I love you, Nancy, and I'm beholden to you."

It was the last week before he had to report to El Toro. It was three days before their marriage. About four o'clock in the morning, Nancy had wakened with terrible pains in her stomach. She was hemorrhaging. Steve got her to a hospital an hour before the doctor arrived. It was seven o'clock in the morning when it was all over.

Would she be able to have other children, was Steve's first question to the doctor after being assured that Nancy would recover.

"Of course," the doctor said. "She's a very healthy girl. But this has been difficult on her emotionally." He looked up at Steve. "She wanted this baby very much."

"So did I," Steve answered. He was trying to control his emotions. "Can I see her?" he asked.

"In about an hour. She'll be a little fuzzy for the rest of the day. I had to give her several injections. The pain was intense." He paused. "I'm sorry."

Steve nodded.

Her skin was whiter than ever. Her violet eyes were closed. The perspiration of her great effort stood out on her face and across her upper lip. She wore no lipstick, her hair was tangled against the pillow. He took a damp towel from the bathroom and sponged her face. He had never felt so much love for any one person in his life. She was part of him. He didn't know how he was going to face leaving her.

He was leaving home all over again. Except that Nancy had become his home. She was where he loved. She was where he lived. She was where he laughed and cried. She was his world. And he had given over his heart to her, exactly as he had given over his heart to his mother and father when he was a child. He had not yet learned to give his love without giving over his whole being into the power of another person.

The violet eyes opened. Steve couldn't help it, he was crying. They both knew she had lost the baby. Their love was even deeper because of the sadness they now shared. Her arms went up weakly to his shoulders and pulled him down to her. She kissed him, kissed away his tears, and pulled his head to her shoulder as though he were a child.

Steve always had memories of Nancy when he began to think back.

What it might have been! She had so deeply moved him, and they had been wonderfully happy for those few months before he was sent to Vietnam.

Nancy had gone back to her family in Buffalo. For months she had written him every day and he had written every chance he had. But he had been away too long. At the end of a year their exchange of letters became fewer and fewer. No one could keep a relationship going, no matter what the poets said, for separations of such a time. A human being just wasn't meant for that. Long separations were disaster.

Steve planned to attend medical school. Nancy had been strongly rooted in her family life in the East, and she dreaded the long years of schooling ahead and the internships that would follow. Finally, she wrote to him that she knew something had happened to the magic they had had together.

Maybe if their child had lived? But she had decided to make her life where she had grown up, where she felt comfortable, where her family was close by. She hoped that he would wish her well. She spoke out in her own direct way, that the man she was marrying did not bring out the fire and the passion within her. It wasn't like her relationship with Steve. But he was a good man. He loved her. And she had no fear of the future, with him. With Steve, she felt life would always be on the edge.

Steve put his head back on the couch and stared at the ceiling. He was missing Nancy terribly now. He needed someone to help him. His family was breaking up, his father was dying, and he had to take charge, he had to take over.

If he and Nancy had only gotten married after she lost the baby— gone ahead with their plans—before he reported to El Toro. But they had decided to wait and get married in Buffalo, as her parents wanted, when he came back. He didn't come back for two years. And by then, the first real love of his life was gone. And now Melanie was gone, too.

Junior was nervous as he came into the hospital room. He looked at Steve, sitting on a bedside chair, holding their father's hand. Steve didn't move. No one did. Finally, Steve stood up and put out his hand.

"Hello, Larry," he said.

"You don't belong here." Junior was livid. "You're not a member of this family. Why didn't you stay in Hollywood and leave us alone?"

His mother was shocked. "Larry, what are you saying? Of course Steve's a member of this family. It was wonderful of him to leave his work and his children and come here. The least we can do is make him feel welcome."

Junior's face turned red. "What are *you* saying? You two have talked about it as much as I have. He doesn't care anything about our family, or our family business. He doesn't care anything about any of us. He just wants to live in the fast lane. Isn't that what you call it out there? Beautiful women, fancy cars. You're probably on dope by now. A cokehead."

Steve took a step toward him; Steve was about four inches taller and forty pounds heavier than his brother. The two men were almost head to head.

Roberta Wayland stepped between them. "What are you two thinking about?" she said. "Your father's going to be operated on tomorrow and his sons are fighting. Can't you stop, even for this?"

Steve muttered, "I didn't come here to fight. I came here to see you and Dad and try and help."

Lawrence Wayland muttered under his breath, "Cain and Abel . . . my God . . . always."

Junior picked up what his father said. He shook his head. "No, it's not Cain and Abel. It's the prodigal son. And goddamn it, if you and Mother flip out because the big shot from Hollywood decides to fly in and pay you a visit and see how sick you are—I don't buy it. You know why he's here. He thinks maybe you're not going to come through this operation and he wants to be here when they read the will."

Roberta's voice was barely audible. "Stop it!"

The nurse in charge came in and immediately the conversation cut off. She exchanged a flicker of a look with Junior as she gave his father a morphine shot.

Steve stepped up to his mother and kissed her on the cheek. "I want to talk to the doctor. I'll be back," and he walked out of the room.

In the scrub room next to the operating room, several doctors were washing up. Steve came into the room, called out in a low voice, "Doctor McElroy?"

A plump, middle-aged man, with glasses and a dissipated face, turned from one of the basins. He held his hands up so that the water would drain off. Dr. McElroy recognized the intruder. "Hello, Steve, I didn't know you were here. I thought you were in California."

"I was. I'm here now. My mother called me about this ulcer business. I smelled something. That's why I came."

McElroy's lip twitched. It was slight, but unmistakable. McElroy said, "What do you mean?"

Steve replied, "Mother told me how Dad was feeling. I've seen some of the medicine he's getting. How long has this been going on? It doesn't sound like an ulcer to me."

Dr. McElroy smiled sarcastically. "If my memory is right, Steve, you left medical school before you finished your internship. I don't believe you ever did start to practice. You went to Hollywood instead. I really don't think you're in a position to make a judgment about the patient, the treatment, or the illness."

He started to walk out of the room, but Steve barred the entrance with his arm.

"McElroy, I've just seen my father. He's full of morphine—he's getting three shots a day and three sleeping pills—he's lucky he can make any sense at all. I never heard of this kind of treatment for an ulcer. What about all the weight he's lost? And the bitter taste in his mouth?"

The doctor replied, "It's hard to get nourishment when you have an ulcer. If it's bad enough, you lose weight. That's textbook material, you know that."

"You've been the doctor he's trusted," Steve said. "Why? Because your partner was my dad's friend, and when he retired, he asked my dad to accept you. That's the kind of man my father is.

"You wouldn't understand that because I don't think you've ever been a good doctor or a good friend.

"But you better watch what you're doing. You've got my father's life in your hands. I think there's something much worse than an ulcer wrong with him and I think you do, too. And if anything happens to him, I'm holding you personally responsible. I'll have you up in front of the medical board of Illinois and your career as a doctor will be over. I know where the bodies are buried in this town. I grew up here, remember? I've got political leverage, and bank power, and that's what's important in this place. I'll use every bit of it to nail you, McElroy, if you hurt my father in any way."

13

Memorial Hospital,
Chicago

*S*teve stopped by the hospital desk on his way back to his father's room. Lieu had arranged a room just two floors below his father, in the same northwest corner of the hospital. He could make it up the stairs to his father's room in less than two minutes. Faster than the elevator. He thanked the nurse at the desk who gave him his keys, then asked if she had any messages for him. She handed him a telegram after she went through the stack of mail and letters she had been sorting on her desk. Steve opened the telegram as he started for the ground floor elevator. The message stopped him cold.

The wire had no greeting whatsoever, just his name, Steve Wayland, Memorial Hospital, Chicago:

> "ABSOLUTELY CANNOT DELAY THE START DATE OF YOUR MO-
> TION PICTURE, THE REST OF OUR LIVES, ONE DAY BEYOND
> CONTRACTUAL SCHEDULE. YOUR CONTRACT REQUIRES THAT
> YOU START ON APRIL 21 AND THAT YOU FINISH IN FORTY-TWO
> SHOOTING DAYS. ANY DEVIATION FROM CONTRACTUAL SCHEDULE
> CANCELS THE PICTURE AND WE'LL CALL IN ALL YOUR NOTES
> AND PROPERTY, INCLUDING YOUR HOME, WITHOUT CONSUL-
> TATION OR NEGOTIATION. JACK GREGSON."

Steve studied the wire for a moment. "You son of a bitch. Merry Christmas to you, too," he muttered. He wadded up the telegram and threw it into the sandy top of the cigarette disposal stand. "Someday," Steve whispered to himself. "Someday."

As he walked to the elevator, he passed a newspaper and magazine counter. Newspapers from Chicago, New York, and Los Angeles were spread out on the counter. There was a picture of Rayme on the cover of the *New York Times*, and articles about the coming grand jury hearing on the front pages of the other newspapers. He picked Rayme's name up in the headlines.

He bought all four papers, folded them so that the New York paper was on the outside, and glanced at the story about the enormous crowds of teenagers gathered around the New York City jail. Marny, the papers said, was still in the hospital.

"Jesus," he thought. "What a Christmas for everybody."

It was cold inside the hospital even though the full heat was on. But Steve broke into a sweat as he stepped into the elevator. There was no place to turn. He said a prayer as the elevator started to take him back to his father's bedside.

The "Walking Tall" killings across the country had become celebrated modern law cases, subject to front-page stories, editorials, and TV symposiums. The potential spread of vigilante acts was debated everywhere.

Was it legal to defend yourself and your family against armed, aggressive attacks? Was it legal, in the cause of self-defense, to kill a holdup man or would-be rapist? Courts all over the country were lining up to try these cases. And now, in New York, in the center of legal history and legal theory, a young rock singer, Rayme Monterey, had taken the law into his own hands, killing two men and wounding three others to stop the rape of his girlfriend.

Rayme had big stories in *Time* and *Newsweek*, and there were interviewers from every national magazine waiting to see him. The grand jury hearing was proceeding, and Rayme was being held in jail until that hearing before a judge and a jury.

In his twenty-ninth year, Rayme Monterey found himself one of the most famous idols of young people around the world. It was more than his songs now, more than his rasping voice, more than his rugged good looks, more than his "outsider" background. This rebel from a poor family, living in the dark ghettos of Newport, had become the new voice for an America that was reawakening to its old values, returning to its feeling of pride in itself, an America that Lee Iacocca read well with his nationwide campaigns for commitment, hard work, pride, and individuality. Rayme was more than a product of this new feeling of nationalism, worth, and commitment to excellence. He was part of it.

Rayme was dope-free and scandal-free. On all of his tours, he had talked to "his people" about the dangers of dope, and he lived the way he talked. His songs, more and more, had come to speak of poverty, social injustice, individual pride, and courage, and his most famous song, "On the Outside Lookin' In," exploded Rayme into the hearts of his contemporaries. They all identified, beginning with his own Norfolk River Band, each of them collected from the back streets of New York and the Eastern Seaboard. "Skeeter" Thomas, "Smokey" Candeleriza, "Mad Dog" Bralken, "Little John" Volkland, and the others.

A great mass of public felt that they would have done the same thing that Rayme had done. This dark, brooding, intense young man from Jersey had emerged as an American folk hero.

Rayme was bigger than Charles Bronson in his *Death Wish* movie vigilante role, bigger than the various actors who had played in *Walking Tall*, versions one to five. Like Clint Eastwood, this was the courageous avenger, a man who would fight for his family and his girlfriend, a man not afraid to take chances, a man who was up to meeting the problems of the modern world.

Even Walter Cronkite editorialized about the state of American justice.

William Buckley went back to the Earl Warren court to trace the gradual weakening of American law enforcement which had brought on such a need for self-defense.

The Rayme Monterey case became a national issue. Headlines and editorials. *60 Minutes*. *20/20*. A Dan Stratton special.

A month before the "subway killings," Mike Wallace had broken the news that Lee Iacocca had offered Rayme Monterey twelve million dollars to do a series of commercials for Chrysler. Iacocca had said publicly that Rayme Monterey was a perfect image for their company— integrity, commitment, a return to real American values.

Rayme had turned the money down. He admired Iacocca and what he had done for Chrysler, but he said that his integrity was not up for sale. If he made multimillion-dollar commercials, the young people who believed he couldn't be bought would feel betrayed again.

The president even commented publicly two weeks later about Rayme Monterey. But Rayme had cut that cord, too. He would not make any political connections.

Kathryn Manning interviewed the most famous ticket manager in the country, Ed Brooks of Up Front Tickets, and some of Rayme's fans.

Kathryn asked him, "If you had a week of concerts with Rayme Monterey, where would you put them on and how would they draw?"

"You couldn't ask me an easier question," Brooks replied. "If I had a week, I'd put on seven consecutive shows at the Los Angeles Coliseum. I'd guarantee a hundred thousand people there every night. As a matter of fact, I've already made him an offer."

Kathryn asked, "What did he say?"

Brooks replied, "I can't get to him right now, but I'm going to keep after him. Nobody else in the entertainment world, ever, could do that. Fill the Coliseum seven consecutive nights. Monterey could do it. And it's not just a momentary phenomenon. This Rayme Monterey thing has a life force all its own. If I could get him, it would be the entertainment event of our time."

Kathryn turned to a group of Monterey fans who were also guests of hers for this ABC Network telecast. She introduced a twenty-year-old junior honor student from the City College of New York, Jimmy Mack.

"What is it?" Kathryn asked. "Why is Rayme Monterey such a force in young America today?"

"He's different, that's why," Jimmy answered. "He's what Americans want to see in themselves—what we'd like to be."

A twenty-year-old UCLA student, Jane Cullen, spoke up to Kathryn. "He cares about the crowds, he cares about the people, he cares about us. He stands for something moral—and he tells you that the factory workers and executives are the same. That's what America is," she said.

Another young man spoke up, "No one else gives us five-hour performances, going all out, every minute. He connects with us. He doesn't sell out. We look up to him and he doesn't let us down."

"Look," a twenty-year-old girl interrupted, "the truth is, Rayme is the heartland."

It had really started to happen the year before for Rayme and his Norfolk River Band at the Roxy on the Sunset Strip in Los Angeles. Rayme had never been able to get booked at the Roxy, one of the key launching spots for new rock groups in the eighties.

The small Roxy was packed for his opening. A hundred rock groups played there every year, and they had a steady audience. Most of the people there for Rayme's show had only "found" him recently and really were not familiar with his music.

That night, when Rayme first played the Roxy, he went for the jugular. There were opinion makers out front. Clive Davis, the ex-head of Columbia Records, was there. Quincy Jones. Michael Jackson. The Beach Boys. The word was beginning to get around about Rayme Montgomery.

That was the night Rayme introduced his song, "On the Outside Lookin' In." It was an angry, passionate song about kids who had to keep running because they had no place to go.

Rayme was out front hitting his guitar with everything he had. His head was thrown back and a bandana that was to become his trademark was tied around his forehead to hold the sweat.

He always wore the same thing, boots, faded blue jeans, tank top and a worn leather jacket. There were no gimmicks.

Rayme Monterey would not be denied. He charged off the band-stand. His neck cords were bulging, his face crimson, the sweat rolling down his cheeks in spite of the bandana, his guitar swinging on his shoulders.

It was the first time the Roxy had seen any singer like this. He went down off the stage, jumped on tables, pushed chairs aside, sang into the eyes of the people. He attacked the audience. He demanded. He ran through the room, stopping at certain chords, screaming at them in his own rasping voice. The lyrics were simple, direct, repetitive and demanding. "On the Outside Lookin' In."

Rayme Monterey *had* been born on the outside. And he was singing to all of his contemporaries who felt the same way.

The Roxy went wild. He destroyed them. He wouldn't leave at the band break. He and his Norfolk River boys, with "Mad Dog" pounding his drums, never letting up the beat, simply outwore and outpowered the cynical L.A. crowd. He pulled them up on their feet. They were all clapping hands, rocking. He was swaying in front of them, pounding his feet with "Mad Dog's" beat, throwing off sweat like a racehorse driving for home.

His throat sounded like his vocal cords had split. But the beat went on. It was four o'clock in the morning before the Roxy closed down. And they were still yelling for more.

The crowd mobbed the small backstage dressing rooms, and Rayme had to stand up on a chair to ask them all to go home so he could go home. He thanked them and told them how much this night meant to him.

He and Marny had gone back to the motel where the Rayme Mon-terey group had rooms. It was all they could afford then, a place that image-conscious Hollywood called barely a "B."

Now, little more than a year later, at the time of the subway killings, Rayme Monterey was a rock superstar.

Lieu went every day to the jail to help him with the interviews, catalogue the mail, and shield him from the exploiters. Bit by bit, she built trust in Rayme toward her, Steve, and *The Rest of Our Lives*.

The Rayme Monterey case became a catalyst. A Gallup poll of the nation showed that the people were 94 percent in favor of Rayme. The people demanded his complete release from all charges. Corporations joined the petitions. But the New York District Attorney realized he had a tiger by the tail and wouldn't let go.

There were editorials praising Rayme for his refusal to be bailed out, to wait in comfort and privacy for the hearing. He could have written the check himself (bail had been set at two hundred fifty thousand dollars), but he wouldn't do it. He saw the interviewers in jail.

Now, every day around the New York City jail, were legions of teenagers and young adults.

Rayme had said once, two years before, in an offhand moment, that he didn't want to become the voice of the country's teenagers. "I want to be their heart," he had said. Critics had picked out this line and made sarcastic remarks about it. But now it was coming true.

He was careful of what he said, and he followed exactly the advice of Edmund Bradford Wilson, his defense attorney, and, in a secondary way, the quiet, polite opinions of Lieu.

In an interview with Mike Wallace for *60 Minutes*, filmed in his jail cell, Rayme answered Wallace with the simplicity and directness that had caught the attention of adult America, as he had already won the hearts of young America. Lieu was sitting beside him, in the cell, and, across from her, Edmund Bradford Wilson.

Mike Wallace asked him, "Do you think that rock and roll will last, Rayme? Do you think it's a serious purpose to devote your life to?"

Rayme answered him quietly, "All I can tell you, Mr. Wallace, is the first time I had a guitar I felt I belonged somehow—I practiced twelve hours a day—playing along with rock 'n' roll records. I was alive—it was like my song about the guy who's been walkin' down mean streets all his life, outside lookin' in, broke and alone, not carin' whether he sees one more day, and then suddenly he's alive and he's got a dream—he's on fire—you see, Mr. Wallace, rock 'n' roll is the only thing I ever was good at—I wasn't very good at sports, and I failed in school—there was no place for me—no reason to be alive until seein' Elvis on TV hooked me on rock and roll—and good rock 'n' roll takes everything you have to give—it has a meaning all its own— it's important—it makes demands—"

"But you admit," Mike Wallace probed, "that some of the excesses we see in the name of rock 'n' roll, some of the drug orgies, sexual ones, too, represent society—particularly young society—at its worst."

"There's good and bad in everything," Rayme answered. "But if you listen to enough rock 'n' roll—the excitement of it—the pain—the feelings—if you really listen to Dylan or Elvis at his best, or the Beatles when they were really writing, you'll understand this is music that will last.

"If you went across the country with us on our tours, you'd see the people I write about. Not just kids, but all kinds of people, looking for love and compassion. What I hope to say in my music is that people don't have to live without love—that we can help each other— give each other a hand."

"Have you been working since you've been here in jail?" Dan Stratton asked Rayme when he and the CBS crew came to take their turn.

"Yes, I have," Rayme said. "It's tougher now. I'm trying to get to the truth of all this. It happened so suddenly."

"I've read some outstanding music critics about your work, Rayme," Stratton went on. "One of them said, 'More than any rock singer I've seen, I feel that Monterey isn't aiming for the big money and the success—he's aiming for truth.' " He stopped and looked at Rayme.

"I hope he's right," Rayme said.

"Rayme," Tom Brookson asked him, in his television profile on the young singer, "when did it start for you? A lot of people think that you're just a sudden big figure in popular music. But I know you've been at it for over fifteen years. You must have begun in school."

Rayme nodded his head. "That's right. When I was a kid, barely hangin' on in high school and hating my life, I heard Elvis in a concert. I wanted to be like him. Most people don't know what a great singer Elvis really was. After that night, I had a reason to live. I didn't have as good a voice, but I had the drive."

"What about your songs on your last album, *Junction City?*" Brookson asked. "All of them seem preoccupied with social statements. And there's brutality—at least, the way I listened to it—as well as beauty."

Rayme looked at Brookson with new respect.

"That's what I was trying to say. Good music, I think, is like life— heaven and hell. Love and hatred. Ugliness and violence, as well as beauty. If your music isn't real, it won't last. Whether you're home or out there on the road, you've got to face yourself every day and ask, 'Am I really doing it? Or am I faking it?' "

Ted Koppel asked him about a John Lennon remark that he felt "psychologically naked when he went back to Liverpool and bumped into one of the old gang."

"No way anybody can run—from anybody, not even yourself," Rayme answered. "The crowds, the applause, the money, the people around you, nothing hides you from knowing who you are inside.

"I always go back home, every chance I get. It wasn't all so great, but my roots are there. All my songs, one way or another, go back to where it all began, my hometown, my mom and dad, kids I grew up with. I drive around my hometown, sometimes, all night, remembering faces, checking out the old hangouts—everyone's a story for me—in their eyes.

"You drive around where I grew up now and it sends a chill right through you. Like a giant took a big vacuum cleaner and sucked all the life out of it."

Peter Benning of ABC asked him what his best moments were. Rayme paused before he answered, "The best of all were with Marny. Then with Skeeter and Mad Dog and the rest of the guys. And then it's the people who show up out there in front—the kids there, waiting for you. On fire—not with drugs, but with our music—and you know you've lit the fire. That's what rock 'n' roll is about. That's what Elvis gave me. Give it all your passion. Really do something—be a person in your own right, going for it. Be your own hero."

"Have you got any more concert tours scheduled, Rayme, after this is over?" Koppel asked.

Rayme shook his head. "No, I don't even know where my head is now. I can tell you one thing, though, I'll never walk out on the stage again and sing songs about blue jeans and surfboards, like I did once.

"As I crisscross America on these tours, I see hunger—I see poverty— I see hatred—cruelty—unhappiness—but I also see celebration—the American way working—people putting out their hands to help—I see caring people.

"I want to try to bring people together. I want to try to have them understand each other.

"Growing up, I didn't want to belong to anything because once you admit that to yourself you have to take responsibility. That's the way I felt about this country. If you're American, that means you've got responsibility to the U.S.A. In this country we've got things to be ashamed of, but we've just as many things to be proud of—I believe in this country, with all its faults. It's free out there—and like Woody Guthrie said—'This land is your land, this land is my land.'

"If I ever start writing songs again, and singin' 'em, that's the kind of song I want to try for. If I can't really have something to say of value to the people that come to hear me, I'll quit. It'll be over."

14

Memorial Hospital, Chicago

Steve was exhausted. And he was terrified. He had tried to persuade his parents to postpone the operation, and as delicately as he could, he had suggested the incompetency of Dr. McElroy. But they were convinced he knew what he was doing, and they wanted to get it over with. They had the trip to their beloved English countryside to look forward to. They were as emotionally prepared as they could be. So the operation was on for tomorrow afternoon.

Everywhere Steve walked, as he followed the arrows to the back northwest corner of the fourth floor, Christmas Eve was in full evidence. Clusters of families surrounded every room. Small children, teenagers, mothers, fathers, uncles, grandparents—every room was overflowing.

The secrecy and isolation of the hospital were gone for this one night. The stereo played Bing Crosby's "White Christmas" and all the other Christmas favorites over and over again. And on every floor section, the nurses' quarters had brightly decorated Christmas trees, and Santa Clauses and reindeer strung up across the ceiling. Steve looked into each room as he passed, and in most of them he could see Christmas trees and decorations, and in some he could hear the family singing and the echoes of laughter.

Steve remembered a wonderful motion picture he had seen when he was a child. It was called *Death Takes a Holiday*, adapted from a famous stage play.

For twenty-four hours, no one in the whole world died, because Death, too, had to have a holiday. And in the story of this film, Death, impersonated by Fredric March, wanted to know the human experience, and found love in the form of a beautiful woman. The woman fell so much in love with him that she followed him to his destiny when Death's holiday was over.

Steve remembered Evelyn Venable, a delicate, aristocratically featured blond woman, looking into the dark and mysterious eyes of Death, vowing that she would follow him. It was the beginning of Steve's fight against death—to live so passionately, to live so well that death could never destroy his feelings.

Now, as he neared the corner room in the northwest section of the hospital, he felt death had to be cheated at this Christmastime. Death could not visit any of these gay and happy families on Christmas Eve. Death could not strike in the midst of such celebration and reunion. And this truce of sorts would have to carry over until Christmas itself, until his father was safe.

He put the key the nurse had brought to him in the door of 461. It was an emergency room. Normally it was used by interns, but they were on a reduced holiday schedule, and the hospital had let him have this room. He flicked on the light and smiled.

How had he ever been lucky enough to find Lieu—this extraordinary woman who worked her miracles every day. Three phones had already been put into the room.

One was a red phone, which meant instant communication with his children. One of the black phones was marked with adhesive tape, "Lieu." The other black phone was marked "Stage."

Steve was emotionally drained. He hadn't anticipated exactly how he would feel coming home after so long and seeing his mother and father—and his brother. He tried not to think about how sick his father might be. They would know tomorrow.

He went directly to the one suitcase he had brought with him, which was sitting on the bed. On top of Steve's clothes were his notebooks, his work materials, and pictures of his children, which he always took with him. He laid out the notebooks Barbara Carr had prepared containing the fact sheets on each of his four stars. He arranged everything for precision and speed. Then he loosened his tie, propped up the pillows on the bed, and stretched out. He deliberated for a moment before he took the red phone with the adhesive mark on it. It was connected immediately to Melanie's home in Santa Monica and the Christmas Eve celebration there.

Kathleen and Lorelei were waiting for his call.

"How's grandfather?" Kathleen asked.

"We'll know tomorrow morning, after the operation."

"When are you coming home?" Lorelei asked.

"Maybe it will just be a few days," Steve answered, "but I've got to stay here until we know for sure. You understand that. I've got to be with him and grandmother until he's safe. I'll try to call you every night. Now girls, I know this is our first Christmas apart, but we'll make up for it, after I come home. Ask AGW to keep the Christmas decorations up—the tree and everything."

"Daddy," Kathleen said, "before our dinner started tonight I went back into my room and I said a special prayer for grandfather. I asked God to watch over him tomorrow and to take care of him."

"I will, too," Lorelei said. "Every day."

Kathleen was holding it back. "Merry Christmas, Daddy. We miss you. We love you."

"Please come home as soon as you can," Lorelei said.

"I love you," Steve said.

Melanie put her arms around the girls and took the receiver. Steve's voice came over the phone.

"Thank you for helping. I know you're going to have a wonderful Christmas day."

"We will," Melanie said. "But we'll all be thinking about you. It's not the same for any of us, Steve. It just seems wrong that it's Christmas Eve and we're not going to your home like we always do."

"It's pretty incredible, actually, the way it's all worked out, isn't it?" Steve said. "I mean when you think of it, you all spend Christmas Eve with me, and I spend Christmas days at your place, for all these years, both you and Jim have done a great deal to make that possible. I don't forget it."

"We've all tried," Melanie said. "And I know it's hard on you not having the children all the time."

"Melanie?" Steve said.

"Yes, Steve?"

"Melanie," Steve continued, "I want to wish all of you a wonderful Christmas."

"I'll try to see that Kathleen and Lorelei get through this as easily as possible," Melanie answered. "Don't forget, Steve, nobody can take your place with them. Nobody."

"Good night, Melanie. Give the girls a hug and a kiss for me. And take care of AGW."

He hung up the phone and leaned back on the pillow. He shut off the light and turned off the sound system. He couldn't take the Christmas music anymore. The wind was blowing hard outside and it was snowing. For the first time in his life, Steve dreaded Christmas Day.

15

Memorial Hospital, Chicago

The long hallways of the hospital were silent now. Laughter, even footsteps were gone. There was no excited conversation, no bursts of childish glee. The illusions of Santa Claus and his pack of gleaming, beautiful reindeer had disappeared. The reality of death filled the small waiting room outside the operating area on Christmas afternoon.

The service clock on the wall above continued on, inexorably. The second hand, pacing relentlessly in its rigid continual circle around the surface of the clock, was like the raised hand of a boxing referee counting out each ten seconds of life.

Every person in the room continually looked up at the double doors connecting the hallway to the operating rooms. Each waited for a simple answer. Life or death. And every human heart there held its own secret of feelings about the life or death of the person connected with them.

Inside OR 17, two nurses worked side by side behind Dr. McElroy and an assistant surgeon. Sweat poured across the rims of McElroy's mask, down the sides of his face, across his ears where the mask was tied, down the back of his neck. His eyes, barely visible, were sunken in his head until there was only a flicker of white in the black holes of the sockets. The deep lines of exhaustion set around the corners of his eyes, across his forehead, and across his exposed chin and neck. His face was plowed by little armies of flesh, pulled tight and shriveled up by the long years of hiding, pretending, and faking.

The assisting doctor bent low over the surgical table. He looked at the white face of Lawrence Wayland, a man of courage and accomplishments, lying there unconscious with four tubes running in and out of him. His face was almost covered with the anesthetist's mask and the evidence of his life tapped out relentlessly on the big machines by his side, measuring his pulse, his blood, his cardiovascular reactions.

All the sentries of life were stationed around this human being who was worth, according to material estimates, exactly eighty-seven cents.

Lawrence Wayland lay in an anesthetized, image-filled hallucination as this group of human beings worked to remove the negative elements of death from his body and to preserve the healthy cells, blood, tissue, and muscle.

As Dr. McElroy cut even farther into Wayland's supine form, the faces in an arc around him knew that every breath resounding so solidly in the compact room could be the man's last. Each of them glanced up at the clock every few seconds.

The doctor assisting in the surgery looked down from the clock; McElroy nodded and stepped back to have his face swabbed again. His hands shook from fatigue. He pressed them down against the side of the operating slab to steady them. McElroy made one more deft movement with his surgical knife. He cut away the last piece of tissue, and another nurse removed it with clampers and put it into the refuse depository at the side of the table.

McElroy, in a hoarse voice, said to his assistant, "You do the cleanup."

The assisting surgeon answered, "Right."

McElroy stepped back and looked at Lawrence Wayland, a patient of his for more than thirty years. He felt nothing for him.

Wayland was a successful and honored man in Chicago. He was on the board of the United Illinois Bank, the Winnetka Country Club, the University Club. He even owned some stock in the Halas family football team, the Chicago Bears.

He was an integral member of Chicago's elite group of leaders, part of the small group that managed the inner financial business workings of "the heart of America."

Everywhere, Lawrence Wayland was known by a code almost alien in the amoral modern world: "His handshake is his bond." He never cheated, never lied. Never welched on a deal. He was a visionary in his business; he had been instrumental in the building of a large grain empire. Throughout a network of middle Western states, Wayland's grain elevators and his grain business had spread slowly but surely through the years. He was nationally known now, one of the most respected export dealers in grain in the country.

Now, everything he had worked so hard to build was a flicker of breath away from extinction, at least as he knew it. But as long as that little needle jumped with each breath, Lawrence Wayland was still tied to all the realities and all the mysteries of one human life.

In the waiting room, Junior sat drawn and white-faced with his wife, Marion.

"A matched set," Steve had called them from the time he had first seen them together. "A perfect set of bookends" was how an acquaintance described them.

Now, after fifteen years of marriage, they seemed more alike; both looked pale and bloodless.

When Marion Bunting had married Lawrence Wayland, Jr., it was a last choice for both. Junior, with his tight-lipped conservatism, his money-crazed philosophy, his frigidity, and his hatred of most people and ideas was not the man of Marion's early romantic dreams. But he, as well as Steve, had never been given a consistent sense of worth by their mother and father. Like many children, they were the extensions of their parents' egos. Failure of any kind was not tolerated. And love and recognition had to be won every day.

Junior had turned to hatred as a way of survival. And, step by step, he had built a life based completely on that premise.

He couldn't say exactly when the hate began to fill him up and flood him over. From the time he could remember, the world seemed antagonistic. He was one of those people who worked at being unlikable.

He had had one goal since his high school days: He would take over the family business. He would have power and money, and then the world would love him. He would build an empire on the foundation of his father's accomplishments. His only possible competition was his younger brother.

Then Steve went to medical school, and he was out of the way. Steve had declined his father's offer to join the family business, and Lawrence Wayland had been bitterly disappointed.

Junior had taken the hand of cards given to him and drawn from the deck until he had a full house. Day by day, year after year, he fed his parents stories about his younger brother—the story of a playboy, the story of someone who really didn't belong in the family, someone who didn't care about them. A good-looking, egotistical charmer, going after one woman after another, flashy, but with no substance. A real prodigal son.

Junior's only misjudgment was his conviction that his brother would never really come home again, and he would never answer any family crisis.

The most important goal in Junior's life was to destroy forever the younger brother who had haunted his life, won every award, slept with the prettiest girls, lived colorfully, and never buckled under the hard Puritan ethic of their father. His day would come.

Now, as the clock ticked away, Junior glanced at his wife. The time was now. Every second that the clock ticked, the life of the king in there was going. Junior was sure of it. He tried not to show the excitement that was beginning to build in him. The king is dead. Long live the king.

His plan was prepared. His father would probably have to have morphine every few hours. More than before. He'd be out of his mind most of the time.

Junior had all the hospital shifts on the sixth floor memorized. There was a half hour between 10:00 and 10:30, when the shifts changed. The family could get in the room then. No one paid any attention to the private rooms, particularly if there was a private night nurse. And Junior already had Miss Bracken, his father's night nurse, taken care of satisfactorily.

All that was left was to get Steve out of the way one night, his father full of morphine, and his paid-off lawyer there with the new documents, fully prepared and ready to go. He wondered how Steve would look when the new will was read. He had a moment's sympathy for his brother, but quickly dismissed it.

He looked at his mother. There she was, getting sucked in all over again by Steve's charm and his special ways. They'd always loved Steve more. He'd grown up with that. And now, even though Steve had left medical school and gone to Hollywood to make films, after a lifelong flirtation with the theater, after all the women, the headlines, the scandals, here he was, appearing at the end to look after what he thought would be his part of the fortune. Stupid son of a bitch, he never could figure things right.

None of them—his father, his mother, his uncle, his cousins—had ever discovered how cleverly he, year after year, had been stealing the family fortune. The trading on the stock exchange, using company money, strictly forbidden by the laws of the corporation, special trustee accounts for himself, his wife, and his children, so carefully hidden away from the company accountants, the special expense accounts across the country and in Europe. The network of loans with personal proceeds going to him and the interest and debt being allocated to the firm—he had structured it with brilliance and research. Every tax law, every single possible shelter, every deferment plan Junior had studied, understood, and used to his advantage.

That poor man on the table in the operating room didn't even understand modern business. His time was past. He had been moved out of the presidency of his own company by his son.

Junior had been merciless at the end. He had told his father to his face that he was through, that he no longer had it, that he belonged to the past. When the old man started to fight back, he found he had no power in his own company. It had all been taken, a little bit at a time, by this pale red-haired man, his son.

Inside intensive care, Lawrence Wayland's mind came alive. His eyes flickered and then opened. A nurse was standing over him, tabulating all the vital signs. There were tubes running in and out of the orifices of his body.

He felt the weight of an immense stone on his chest. He could barely breathe. His saliva gagged in his throat.

Gradually, he sensed he was still alive. He didn't know how long he'd been unconscious, but he knew from the terrible pain that wracked his body that something must have gone wrong. He tried to speak. He couldn't. Then someone came up beside the nurse. It was his wife. Her face eased from the terror of the last hours into a thankful visual prayer that the man she loved was still alive. Wayland reached out his hand feebly and she quickly took it. She was careful not to break, not to give away her real feelings.

His voice was thick, but distinguishable. "Bobbie—Bobbie, don't worry."

Roberta shook her head, still smiling. "Just think about getting well. Come home to us soon."

Wayland nodded, exhausted with his effort.

In the small waiting room, Steve was waiting for Dr. McElroy. Across the room, Junior and Marion watched him as though they were waiting for a trick.

Steve went up to McElroy. He glanced at the clock and challenged the doctor. "You're still going to tell me it was an ulcer?"

McElroy answered slowly. "No way we could have known. There

was an obstruction in the stomach. We had to work under a big handicap. His heart hasn't been that strong since the coronary a few years ago."

Steve answered back quickly. "Five hours on the operating table. His heart must be strong as an ox. First biopsy in?" Steve asked.

McElroy nodded. He didn't look up.

"Malignant?"

McElroy nodded again.

Steve continued, "Spread?"

McElroy glanced away. "To the liver."

"You goddamn idiot. You suspected this—or should have. You had to have an idea you'd made a wrong diagnosis. You didn't tell anyone in this family. You didn't follow up. You kept saying it was a simple ulcer case, covering yourself, because you weren't going to take a chance on a malpractice suit."

Steve grabbed McElroy's shirt and jerked him against his chest. "I swear to you, McElroy, you're never going to misdiagnose again. You're never again going to falsify reports to cover your mistakes. Months ago you had to know it might be cancer, didn't you?—but you wouldn't tell them about your mistake because you might hurt your practice and position."

Steve pulled a medical report from his pocket. "Here it is, in your own handwriting—I made the record custodian give it to me—signed by you when my father came to the hospital two days ago—probably terminal cancer—we could have caught it months ago if you'd just told us what you suspected instead of sticking with the ulcer story— you sentenced a man to die, and you know it. Well, you're not going to go on living your lousy life without paying. You're going to pay for this every day."

Junior appeared at his side. He spoke in an even voice. "How long has he got?"

Steve turned on Junior as McElroy left the room. "Tasting it already? How long have you been waiting for this, Junior?"

"Ever since we were kids," Junior replied. "Remember the day they put your portrait over the mantel—alone—I knew then you'd sucked them in—you were the one they bragged about—but now everything's different."

"You've done a beautiful job," Steve said. "He's dying twenty years ahead of his time, because none of you wanted to check on the kind of doctor who was taking care of him, on what was happening. You didn't do a goddamn thing. You never even bothered to find out . . .

his blood count, his pulse, his vital signs, a scan, the medicines—
none of it."

Steve was in a rage. "Can't you see Mother's sick, too? She's exhausted with worry and pressure. And where is the great son, the
foundation of the next generation—?"

Junior turned away, but Steve grabbed his shoulder and spun him
around.

"I hoped and prayed that as much as you hated me you might
possibly love him and Mother," Steve lashed out. "I prayed that you
would be true to something or someone in your miserable life. All
your life, Junior, all you really cared about is yourself and your fucking
money. And the power it brought you.

"Well, I hope it's worth it to you. The way you've lived, playing a
part, all these years, God knows what else you've done.

"Wasn't it enough to kill me off in their eyes? And your own?"
Steve hammered at him. "Do you realize how much I would have
loved to have a brother? Someone who was supportive of me, someone
who cared, someone I could care about?

"When we were little, once in a while, you were nice to me. It was
like a whole new world. I looked up to you. I idolized you. And you
put me away. Even as a kid.

"And now you say I'm not a member of this family. Well, I'll tell
you, Junior, I'm more a member of this family than you think and
I'm going to see to it that that man's life in there, that man who created
so many things for so many people, I'm going to make sure that his
life counts for something. I don't want people to look at you and think
that you're all that Lawrence Wayland left to this world."

Steve looked as though he was going to hit Junior, then he suddenly
turned on his heels and walked out of the room.

16

Stage Six,
Goldwyn Studios,
Warner Hollywood

No one was working that day at the Warner-Hollywood Studio (formerly the Samuel Goldwyn Studios), the day after Christmas, except the people on Stage Six. Stage Six had been Samuel Goldwyn's favorite stage. Steve had selected it for good luck.

There were eleven people gathered around a worktable with a mass of telephones on it. There were four empty chairs.

The phone call from Steve Wayland came through right on schedule and was put through the speaker on the table. A tall, attractive, brilliant woman, Steve's research specialist, Barbara Carr, was seated at the table with a stack of yellow pads and pencils.

This was Steve's basic staff. They had worked with him before, and they were gathered together now on this day after Christmas, awaiting his special word from the hospital in Chicago. Some of them were drinking coffee. Some of them were smoking. Some were pacing up and down. All of them were on edge.

Steve's voice came over the sound system. It echoed through this bare, cavernous stage, filled with the memories of so many Goldwyn classics.

"I think it's going to be a fight for my father's life here. I'll be in Chicago for a while. We've never worked this way before, but this is the way it has to be. *The Rest of Our Lives* must start by April twenty-first. The studio won't delay it. Roberto—"

Steve's production manager, Roberto Bakker, a slender, dynamic Dutchman born in Rio and one of the acknowledged production troubleshooters in the international film industry, paused, standing at the table. He turned around, facing the speaker, as though he were looking at Steve. There were other outlets arranged around the edges of the table so that anyone could speak to Steve without going to the main speaker phone.

Roberto Bakker talked quietly into one of the mikes. "I'm here, boss."

"Roberto, you're really going to have to flow with this one. Everything about it is so damned difficult."

Roberto smiled and lit another cigarette. "So, boss, what's new?"

"*This one,*" Steve answered. "Roberto, I want you to start with the budget we have, and bring it down. We can't go over by one dollar. If we do, they stop the picture."

A slender, dark-haired man with a handsome, rough face stepped to a mike.

"Steve, this is Gaylin. Lieu gave me the dates. I had a commitment, but I'm getting out of it. This one sounds crazier than ever. I've got to be in on it."

"Thank God for that," Steve said.

Gaylin went on. "But how are Roberto and I going to lay out any kind of a schedule when we don't have a script? Or, what script we have, Lieu says, is going to change."

"Gaylin, I'm rewriting to fit the people we have—it's coming well now. You'll have it soon. I can give you three key sets the first of the week."

An older man with an artistic, Slavic face and jet-black hair spoke into a mike. Boris Peters, Academy Award–winning art director, was one of the most brilliant men in Hollywood.

"Steve, this is Boris—no way we can get more time?"

Steve said, "We're stuck, Boris. We begin rehearsals April fourteenth and we start shooting April twenty-first. We can't be one day late. That's part of the contract."

Boris said, "Excuse me, but I have to ask this. Is the studio for this picture or against it? Are they creating an obstacle course here?"

Steve's voice came back. "I'll explain it to all of you when I see you. It's a unique situation. But yes, Boris, the studio *is* against the picture. They would be glad if we all dropped dead right now. We'd become a tax write-off, which is how they'd like to think about us."

"When do you think I'll get a finished script?" Boris asked.

Steve answered, "Soon—that's the way it has to be for now."

Boris talked seriously into the mike. "Steve, preproduction is so important. This seems impossible."

"I'm counting on you, Boris. You're the best there is, and I can't make the picture without you."

Boris smiled and lit his pipe. "You just made me an offer I can't refuse. Well, God help us."

A tall man, graying, with a moustache, talked into the mike—Frank Warner, the first sound editor ever to be honored by the Academy with a special award, for Steven Spielberg's memorable film *Close Encounters of the Third Kind*.

"Steve, Frank Warner here. I'm beginning to see why you want me in this picture for the complete production schedule."

Steve's disembodied voice spoke again over the speaker system. "Frank, you know what we did with the sound—what *you* did, I should say, for *Dishonored*. This is similar in that we don't know whether we're going to be able to get live sound, have to dub later, or tell part of the story with just sound effects.

"You remember how John Ford used to talk in those lectures of his—that you should be able to make motion pictures without any dialogue at all? Well, in *The Rest of Our Lives* we've got to develop a soundtrack that grows like the picture, from day to day, from scene to scene, in the creative process. For once I don't want the sound editor coming in after the picture's made. I want you there from the beginning. I want all of you there from the beginning. I want to use everything you have. Every idea. Every concept. David, are you there?"

The young English director of photography stepped up to one of the microphones. "Here, Steve."

"David," Steve went on over the phone line, "and Frank, Gaylin, Boris, Roberto, Bill Thomas, Catalina, all of you—there's a dangerous beginning to this film. We're going to go seven or eight minutes without one word of dialogue. No music. Just sound effects, Frank.

"David, I want you to run every picture that you haven't seen of Magdalena Alba's. What we get from her, and I promise you she's going to be better than she ever has been, has to carry us for the first seven or eight minutes, together with Frank's sound effects. We're not going to use any music, no beginning titles. I don't have to tell any of you that with all the noise and music of today's films, we're taking a risk. But I want this story to start that way. As real as possible— quietly. Our film has to grow on the audience. We have to take them inside our people.

"This could be my last film," Steve said. "If I fail, it probably will be. So this may be my last chance to work with all of you and to try some of the things we've talked about as we've made other pictures together.

"And I want all of you to know how much I need you on this one."
His voice reached out to some of the people he hadn't talked to yet
—to the elegantly dressed, sophisticated Bill Thomas, an Academy
Award–winning dress designer; to the script lady, Catalina Lawrence;
to Richard Portman, the maverick dubbing genius, uncontrollable for
some directors but a friend of Steve's and a veteran of five of Steve's
films.

Steve's voice sounded so present that the group was physically closing
together around the table.

"Barbara or Lieu in New York," the voice said, "will transmit anything I have, every day, to each of you. Please leave all your numbers
with Barbara there now, so I can keep up with her and so that she'll
know if you go out of town, or on holidays. I just don't know how to
plan this from day to day, until I know about my father."

There were various remarks from the group, wishing him well.

"I know you understand," Steve said. "But I want to tell you one
more thing. It's something I've always wanted to do, and by God,
we're going to do it in this picture.

"Every one of you is going to own a piece of this film. I own fifty
percent of it by my contract with the studio. My fifty percent is going
to be divided equally between myself, the cast, and all of you. We're
going to put ten percent aside to be divided between the members of
the crew, the people who are going to be working in your departments.

"It's an old cliché that no one makes a motion picture alone. But
we know it's true. I'm calling upon every one of you to give me
everything you've got, even if you don't understand what I'm doing.
I may not understand myself. But we're going to make a picture together. And it's going to belong to each of you, just as much as it
belongs to me. Barbara?"

Barbara Carr spoke up on one of the mikes. "Yes, Mr. Wayland.
I'm right here."

"You have the contracts?" the voice asked.

"They're all ready," Barbara said.

Steve spoke again. "Barbara will give each one of you the same
contract about your share of ownership and profits. Take it home.
Check it with your families. Check it with your lawyers. Each of you
will be committing to this project with this contract, and we will be
committing to you, not only in your respective professions, but as
profit participants of The Rest of Our Lives.

"What I would say face to face, if I could be there to say it, is that
we are a creative family. We are going to extend our family to the

cast, to our crew, and to everyone who works on *The Rest of Our Lives*. Each one of you has been picked—because you feel passionately about your work and about motion pictures. For the next year we will go through hell together, I'm sure of that. But I swear to you, when it's over, and we look at our film together, you will be proud. You will not have given a year of your creative life just to make another picture, to make a film that doesn't stand for anything. What we're going to do together can count.

"I'm grateful to you. I'll be in touch."

The line clicked off. The speaker system clicked off. The group huddled around the center speaker didn't move. The dream had taken hold of them.

17

Memorial Hospital, Chicago

hree days later, Lawrence Wayland was taken out of the Intensive Care Unit, back to his own room.

Private Nurse Bracken came on at 9:00 P.M. Lawrence Wayland was dozing sporadically, out of his head with morphine hallucinations.

Steve was at his mother's side at her home, where a new doctor was checking her over thoroughly after her many weeks of staying at her husband's side. Steve would go back to his father's room at midnight.

At ten-thirty, while the hospital was served by a skeleton crew, Junior and another man made their way to the sixth floor. The nurse on the main floor paid no particular attention. She recognized Junior and, in a case like this, late-hour visits were permitted.

The man with Junior was Robert Lydell, a thin, almost spindly man, forty-seven years old, with glasses and stooped posture. He'd been Junior's parents' lawyer for years, but as the control of the Wayland Company had been taken over by Junior, Lydell had gone with the new controlling head. He had been put on a heavy retainer by Junior, pledging, at the same time, his loyalty to Junior. Any allegiance to Lawrence Wayland, Sr., or his wife, had been erased from Robert Lydell's conscience by the simple fact of money paid out. Lydell was custodian of all the wills in the company structure, including Lawrence Wayland, Sr.'s and Roberta's. He had written the documents.

They were admitted to room 608 by Nurse Bracken. Junior immediately checked his sleeping father and then picked up the room phone and dialed.

Junior spoke into the phone: "Hello, Clarence?"

A voice answered, "Yes, Mr. Wayland."

"Is Dr. Roberts there for my mother's checkup? Good. And my brother . . . ?"

"He's with your mother," the voice on the phone answered.

"Then don't bother anybody. I'll call later," Junior said.

Inside his father's hospital room, Junior's hands were trembling and his voice was pinched with tension. He turned to the lawyer. "Give me the papers, Bob."

The lawyer and the nurse stood by his side. Junior looked at his father in the bed; his father moaned slightly. Junior turned to the nurse. "You sure he's asleep?" he asked.

Nurse Bracken spoke back softly, "Absolutely sure."

He turned to the lawyer. "You sign first, Bob."

"I checked the document this afternoon. It's simple. It's believable," the lawyer added softly, "and it covers the company assets your brother might claim. You'll have complete, unquestioned control, and nothing will go to him, or your mother."

The lawyer looked over at the sleeping figure of Lawrence Wayland, Sr.

Junior took in the glance.

Lydell signed all three documents. Junior handed them to the night nurse.

Nervously, she signed the three copies of the document, as witness.

Junior inspected the papers and the signatures quickly and nodded. "Wake him up."

The nurse moved Lawrence Wayland's shoulders slightly and he came out of his deep sleep with a start. His eyes rolled in his head. He couldn't focus them.

"Dad, sorry to bother you, but Bob and I have the papers that you wanted to sign, remember? You've been asking for them."

Wayland responded with some unintelligible words. He obviously was not in his right mind.

Junior turned to Bob. "Guide his hand so he can sign."

Lydell put his hand over Wayland, Sr.'s right hand and placed it in a writing position. Then he took a pen and put it between his fingers. Junior placed the first copy of the will in a position so that his father could sign in the right place.

"Right there, now concentrate, Dad, this will be over in a minute."

The lawyer guided Lawrence Wayland's hand in a shaky version of his signature.

Junior looked at the signature. "It's not his regular signature," he said.

Lydell looked at it closely and spoke in a low voice. "It's obviously his, though. You're all right."

Junior prepared the second will for his father's signature. His words were pointed. "*We're* all right."

"Well, of course, that's what I meant."

Junior glanced up at him. "I'm sure you did."

With Lydell guiding his hand, Lawrence Wayland signed the other two copies.

Junior leaned over his father. "Go back to sleep, Dad, it's all over and corrected, like you wanted it."

Lawrence Wayland nodded incongruously and slipped back into the tortured hallucinations of his morphine-induced sleep.

Junior clipped the wills together and handed them back to Lydell. "File these away in the safe," he said. "I want everything in perfect order."

"I understand."

Junior put his arm around Nurse Bracken. Her face was rigid. Junior confronted her. "Will he remember?"

She replied, "I doubt it. I gave him an even stronger shot tonight to be sure."

Junior spoke reassuringly, "You've done well, and you will be taken care of. Remember, all three of us are in this together. So, we'll all be quiet. Right?"

The lawyer mumbled, "For sure."

The nurse's voice was shaky. "I understand."

Junior picked up his briefcase, buttoned up his cashmere topcoat, and walked out of the room, Lydell following. Junior never looked back at his father.

Every day was a struggle to survive. Lawrence Wayland's lifeline wavered with each labored breath. His heart was stable, but his other vital signs were shaky and inconsistent. The days and nights were vigils. Dope-tormented nightmares for Lawrence Wayland, with small oases of clarity and reunion with his family. For Roberta, his wife, could take only one day at a time and try to put into that day or night the love that she had for her husband, so that in his wakeful conscious moments he would feel it and draw strength from it.

For Junior, each day that passed made him more secure that his plan would work, and, at the same time, worried that his father wouldn't die, would somehow miraculously recover, and that his twenty-year strategy to steal the entire family fortune would be destroyed.

18

Memorial Hospital, Chicago

At midnight, Steve was in his room at the hospital for a conference call with Spartan Lee in Rome, Barbara Carr in Paris, and Lieu in New York.

"Any leads on Tigressa?" Steve asked.

Spartan's voice sounded depressed. "None. We've covered all her favorite places, in Italy and in all the European capitals. But the good news is that the press doesn't know. They think she's on a vacation. We've sold the police on that one, too."

"I've got an idea," Steve said.

"Fire away," Spartan perked up.

"I've studied Barbara's research. I think Tigressa will go to the people who've always exploited her."

"Men," Lieu spoke up.

"Right on," Steve answered. "Bobby Slater destroyed this girl. Wherever she is I think she's hell-bent on finishing the job he and the other men started—on destroying herself. Get every name Tucheki can remember of the men who hung around Afrique, the ones who went to see Tigressa night after night. Check them all out. It's a shot."

"I'll go to see Tucheki now," Spartan said.

"Lieu," Steve asked, "have they let Rayme see Marny?"

"Not yet," Lieu answered. "But they've moved her to a special hospital."

"An asylum?" Steve asked.

"Yes," Lieu answered.

"Has she recognized anybody yet?" Steve questioned.

"No. She's never come out of it."

"Skeeter and the boys staying close?"

"Like glue."

"I'll get there as soon as I can," Steve added.

"He really appreciates your notes, Steve—keep them up," Lieu said.

"Barbara, I don't want you to leave Paris until Magdalena sails on the *Royal Princess*. And when she sails, here's what I'd like you to do."

Steve lay down on the bed. The most he could sleep at night was two or three hours. He was traveling on nerves now, and on his long years of training on film sets. The director had to be ready always, no matter how long the hours were or how exhausted the crew was. He was the captain of the ship. If he acted tired, if he lost his enthusiasm, if he fired down instead of up, the crew and the cast followed him instinctively.

Steve tried to sleep, even for a few minutes, but the thoughts of the challenge he had taken on with *The Rest of Our Lives*, what he was risking, what he had to keep preparing in the face of his father's critical condition, tore at him.

Couldn't his father's illness be another nightmare? God, how he wished that. If only his father could get well, if he could only pull his family together, then he could face anything. The problems of *The Rest of Our Lives* would then become exciting challenges. And he could get back that feeling of winning, of having the brains and the power to make the impossible possible.

Magdalena came into his mind, as she did so frequently since he'd seen her in Paris. He was filled with the image of her at nineteen in Truffaut's film. And with the way she'd looked in the hospital. When he had stepped into the room and found her at the open window, had she been planning to commit suicide? Had she been thinking about it? Had the car accident really been an accident?

There was that "alone" look in her eyes in the hospital room when she turned and saw him. But how quickly she had brought herself under control and slipped into her professional persona, even after her ten days in Intensive Care. And the tracheotomy. What that must mean to a woman as beautiful as Magdalena.

He pictured her arriving for the embarkation of the *Royal Princess*. He imagined her being escorted along the pier, followed by the photographers and the reporters—with the kind of control he had seen her exude on the screen. The pride, the bearing, the class. And the sexuality.

That had hit him even in the hospital room. The woman had an aura. You felt it. You couldn't get to the mystery. He had to come up with something new for the film—a new way to photograph her— he'd have to talk to David Thayer about that. Was she going to have the courage to do the part the way he was creating it?

The professional thoughts of Magdalena drifted away. Her presence seemed to fill that small hospital room. He longed for her to be there with him. He didn't understand it himself. But everywhere he looked in the room in the darkness, her face faded in and out like long film dissolves. Her eyes. Her voice. Her body. Her hands. The swell of her breasts. He hadn't felt this way, even for a moment, for years. Was it happening to him again? Was he creating an obsession, once more, to haunt his life?

For Steve, time was not divided into hours, or days, or weeks, but one continuously running time clock. Every second of that clock he willed his father to live. To hang on. Until somehow they could pull off a miracle.

He had information coming in from cancer specialists in New York, at Doctors Hospital, from Mayo's, from Scripp's Clinic on the coast. From every medical facility where experimentation in cancer cures was in advanced stages. Steve was in daily touch with them. He used every connection he had to open up channels to the best medical information. The walls of his room were filled with medical charts and diagrams. He felt as if he were back in medical school studying for exams.

By now, he knew most of the people at the hospital. The floor chief, the resident interns, the nurses, even the janitors. These people were used to living with life and death. They were used to seeing patients come and go, and simply disappear. They were not open to fear, because they had lived with it for so long.

And so, consumed with his fight for the life of his father, as Steve roamed the hospital day and night, he was sensitive to the lack of caring of most people, except for themselves. Instead, their concerns were baseball, girlfriends, gossip about money, and little areas of power and competition between doctors and nurses. All the network of human relationships of a modern hospital.

Steve seldom left the hospital. If his father was having a good night, he would go down to his room for a few hours of sleep. If his father was having a bad night, he would stay up all night in the room with him. If his father was comatose with morphine, he would rest until the night nurse called him.

Steve snapped off the light by his bed. In the distance, the last remnants of the transcontinental trains pounded across Illinois and echoed in his head. The loneliest sound in the world, he had always thought. And now it hit him again.

He'd grown up with those trains. The Santa Fe Chief, the Santa Fe Super Chief, and the Union Pacific vacation specials. He remembered those lonely train whistles through the darkness of the nights waking him from his sleep in his room in his parents' home in State Line.

They always spoke of the same things to him, those train whistles. Of separation, of leaving home. And now the head of his family was deathly sick, and no doctor's chart needed to tell Steve Wayland. He could see the life force that had been his father draining out of his body. The lines on his face were deepening. His eyes were unnaturally bright. His breathing was more and more labored. The clickety clack of the distant train reverberated in Steve's head. Then there was that other train of another day.

The Los Angeles train station. Steve's father settled his mother on the train, and then his father had stepped off the platform with his son and they had walked away.

Steve had asked his father, "When will I see you again, Dad?"

His father had looked at him intently. "Come back home, son."

Steve shook his head. "I can't."

His father said, "I've been waiting for you. I've thought about it all the time you were growing up. Wayland and Sons Grain Company. Our own empire growing right out of the wheat belt. Working together the rest of our lives—building something that would last. I fought for that. Don't tell me that's not just as important a cause to fight for as a movie."

Steve looked down at his feet. He was searching for a way to make his father understand. The big locomotive of the Super Chief was beginning to steam up. Passengers were hurrying onto the train.

His father kept after him. "If you don't come back now, I can't keep a spot open for you. How much money do you have in the bank right now?"

Steve shrugged his shoulders. "Well, maybe eight or ten thousand."

His father pressed him. "And your car's rented and your house has three mortgages on it. Your marriage is shot—Melanie told me that herself. And you have two children—damn it, son, think of your children."

"I do think of them, all the time."

Steve's father looked at him with pain in his eyes. "Steve, there never was a boy in Chicago, not one, who had a record like you. From the first time you went to school, number one. Even at Princeton, number one. Every friend I have was sure you would be somebody very important. The whole city was proud of you.

"Now you've been out of Princeton ten years, and you don't have a job. You don't have any money. You don't have your wife. You only have your children half the time.

"I'll tell you how that adds up to me, son. You're a failure.

"How did it happen after all your records, after all your prizes, now here you are thirty years old and you're a failure? Did you ever think how heartbreaking it is for your mother and me? To see you throw away your life? You have a chance to take over the presidency of our family company. You're throwing it away because you've got a crazy idea of how important motion pictures are. You have to admit it to yourself, most of it's just junk, not worth the time or money to even see, much less to make a career of."

Steve looked at his father. "That's what I want to do, Dad. Just like you wanted the grain business."

His father cut him off. "I didn't *want* the grain business. I had to have a job, so I took the only job I could get. It happened to be the grain business. That's where I got my chance and I took it.

"I did it so my family wouldn't have to fight as hard as I did, so my sons would have a chance to get the best education, the best possibilities . . . you were always special to me."

Steve muttered quietly, "When I did what you wanted me to do."

His father looked up. "What's that?"

Steve replied, "Nothing."

The conductors were calling, "All aboard!"

His father turned and they walked back to his compartment. "I don't think we deserve this, Steve. Your mother and I. We've always backed you up. Even when we didn't believe in what you were doing."

"What about Nancy?"

His father continued on as though Steve had said nothing. "You've got to take responsibility now. I've told my lawyer to save an equal part of the stock in the company for you. But only when you get Hollywood out of your system.

"And I'm not going to wait too long—our company has to grow and if not with you, it will grow with someone else."

His father stepped up the stairs of the Pullman car. He turned and looked back at Steve. "Don't expect me to pay the way for you, son. This is your last chance. Think it over."

He turned and went through the door into the inner part of the Pullman car.

"Dad!" Steve's voice was blown out in the shrill whistle of the train as it lurched into action. He stood there looking after the slim line of the Super Chief as it trembled into motion and surged away.

19

Memorial Hospital, Chicago

$\mathcal{S}$teve was shaken out of his recollections by the jarring noise of the alarm clock. In two hours he had to leave for New York. He had talked to the new doctor, Dr. Arthur Roberts, whom he had brought in on the case after he had thrown McElroy out. His father's vital signs were about the same.

Now he had to go to New York to be at the grand jury hearing. Lieu had told him that she felt it was very important for him to be there, for the sake of his relationship with Rayme Monterey. He would be back before midnight to take his place in the room on the sixth floor above. The night watch.

Before leaving, Steve stopped in his father's room. It was six-thirty in the morning and the hospital was already moving. His father was asleep. Steve bent down. The night nurse was going off.

"How is he, Miss Bracken?" he asked the woman. He also glanced at the charts.

"I think he's having less pain," Miss Bracken said.

Steve bent down and pushed his father's silver widow's peak into place. The childlike essence of the man seemed to be coming out as he got sicker. He talked about his youth more and more in his waking hours, when the morphine gave him short times to be himself.

Steve prayed that he could somehow keep his father alive until he was strong enough to be flown to New York, where Dr. Pack, the great cancer specialist, would operate on his liver. Dr. Pack was saving some people with liver cancer, an impossibility only a few years before.

There were no such liver experiments yet in Chicago, and no surgeon of Dr. Pack's genius.

In an envelope he left a note to his mother for the morning nurse to deliver. Then he bent over the side railing of the bed, and kissed his father's forehead. Even in his sleep, his father seemed to respond to his son's touch. He stirred, and a tender smile passed over his lips.

Steve had always been moved by this quality in his father. The man could be angry, dictatorial, dominating, but within his masculinity there was a core of gentleness. And now, as he progressed back toward childhood, that tenderness was more and more evident.

Steve turned and left the room. He was in no frame of mind to make the trip to New York, but it had to be done.

Lieu had been watching the Rayme Monterey phenomenon, and Edmund Bradford Wilson was still recommending that Rayme take Steve's offer, but nothing had really been decided with regard to *The Rest of Our Lives*. As far as the rest of the world was concerned, all hell was breaking loose with Rayme Monterey's personal story.

At the grand jury hearing, the judge had called for the defense. Edmund Bradford Wilson called Rayme Monterey to the stand. He looked out over the spectators, hundreds of teenagers, the reporters and photographers in the back. He nodded to Steve and Lieu seated behind his attorney.

Rayme told his story slowly. He looked at the judge face to face and then the courtroom, and the jury.

"I was asked to plead guilty by the district attorney's office," he said. "It would be all arranged. Temporarily insane . . . you all know how it comes down. I'd plead guilty. I'd get a sentence that'd turn into probation. I'd admit I broke the law. Then, I'd walk back out there free. But there was a catch, and here's what it is. I would have had to say something I didn't believe. I was supposed to stand up here in front of all of you out there—" Rayme was cut off by screams and shouts of support from "his people" in the audience. The judge rapped for order.

Rayme continued, "I was supposed to stand here in front of you and say I was guilty. That I didn't know what I was doing."

His eyes went around the courtroom. "I can't do it. If I came in here and lied, then everything I've tried to do would be a lie.

"I want to say something to you, Judge, and you, members of the jury. I respect this courtroom. I never put down the law—I'm not some jerk going around attacking the establishment to try to get an audience.

"But I tell you sure, if it happened today in that subway with—" Rayme paused, and with effort he spoke her name, "—with Marny, I'd do the same thing. I have the right to protect myself and people I love if we're attacked. I'd never just sit back and let someone—" and his voice choked up, "—let someone rape *anybody,* much less my girl.

"No law, anywhere, is going to make me believe that a guy can't protect himself and his family."

There was a roar from the teenage audience. The judge had to rap for quiet again. "One more outburst and I'll clear the courtroom," he said.

"I don't like violence, but ever since I was in high school, I've been carrying a gun," Rayme said. "I applied for a gun license, my dad made me, the same day I applied for a car license. My parents told me to do it, my friends told me to do it. And then, when I started to sing in clubs, my managers told me to do it.

"I grew up in some mean streets and I've sung in tough places and usually I don't get to go anywhere alone. That's hard because some-times you want to be alone. That night, Marny and I just wanted to go back to where she used to live in Brooklyn. Take a subway, go to see her folks, like everyone else gets to do.

"And I tell you, my girl, Marny Hiller, might not be in a mental institution, out of her mind if I'd only used that gun sooner. She's catatonic. And if I hadn't used it at all, she might be dead today.

"Most of the people in this country believe I'm right. I've received over fifty thousand letters since I was arrested for this grand jury hear-ing. Not one letter said I was wrong. If you decide otherwise," Rayme looked at the judge, "I think you will be ruling against the basic right of a man to protect his family from attack." He looked at the jury, from face to face. "What would you have done?"

Thirty minutes later, Edmund Bradford Wilson summed up his case, standing quietly, looking directly at the jury.

"We have no obligation, any of us, to submit to street violence. No one can walk up to me and threaten me or my family. If they do, heaven help them if I'm armed, because I know what the law allows. Rayme Monterey simply did what the law allows."

A changed man walked out of New York City jail, freed by the grand jury of charges of manslaughter and premeditated murder.

The district attorney made it clear to the reporters that his investigation of his case had only begun and that there were certain circumstances involving the three assailants who were still alive, who had only been injured in a minor way, that could very well result in a new grand jury investigation, which he, the district attorney, had the right to call for. Rayme Monterey might be free now. But the district attorney was determined to stay on this case. It was too important, not only for the city, but for the country. If Rayme Monterey walked free for good, the vigilante cause could spread throughout the United States.

The press, the photographers, and mobs of teenagers and young people shouted and screamed as Rayme came down the steps of the New York City jail with his attorneys, Skeeter Thomas, Lieu, and Steve Wayland.

20

Greenwich Village,
New York

Edmund Bradford Wilson had a refuge ready for Rayme. He'd arranged for bail when he first took the case, but Rayme didn't want to go out on bail until the grand jury investigation was over. He refused any suggestion of special handling.

Now, as his lawyer explained it to him in the company of Steve and Lieu, there would be appeals by the district attorney, an attempt to get a new grand jury investigation, with supposed new evidence that Rayme Monterey had shot the three survivors without provocation, and a general harassment from the D.A.'s office.

Rayme couldn't appear on the street without getting mobbed, and the press hounded his parents' home and the homes of the band members.

Wilson had secured a house in Greenwich Village that belonged to some friends of his. It was a good place to stay for a while. The house came with a cook and comfortable quarters.

They sat around the dinner table now. Wilson toasted his client. "A remarkable day in court. I knew my hunch was right. No one else can speak for you, Rayme. No one else should."

"You handled it just the way I wanted it, Mr. Wilson."

"Have you decided what you want to do next?" Steve asked. "I've got to go back tonight on the red-eye."

"I don't know, Steve," Rayme continued. "I'm not going to do anything, like I told you before, until we get Marny out of the hospital. If we get your dad out and Marny, then maybe we can have a talk in

California. I like that Greek Theatre idea as a test, but I'm not ready for it yet."

"What are you going to do about the interviews now?" Wilson asked.

"Lieu here can handle anything with the press. And I've got a specialist coming in to help you if you want it—a man named Jake Powers," Steve said.

"Yeah, I know," Rayme said. "Lieu told me about him and I asked Skeeter if he knew him. You know Skeeter Thomas, my sax man. He's heard of Powers, says he's an okay guy.

"But I want to think everything through myself, the interviews and everything else. I don't know. It all scares the hell out of me.

"Like 20/20, for instance. Kathryn Manning—she really asks those questions. I've seen her a few times. She goes after it."

"I've an idea," Steve said. "If you were to take someone like Kathryn Manning—they'd have a tremendous audience if they announced you were going to be on the show, that there was going to be word from you. And then, send her a tape, like your song about the farm workers—about people losing their jobs, about families having to move on, about the way you feel the country's going."

Rayme looked at Steve, surprised. "I wrote that song in jail. I've never sung it for anybody yet."

Lieu said, "I told him about it, and I sent him the lyrics, because I know Steve. Everyone's going to tell you, Rayme, that Steve's like the others, that he just wants to exploit you. But he's followed you for years. He's known every song you've ever recorded. He's been telling people about you for a long time, people who hadn't heard of you yet. There's a reason for that. You've tried to do with your songs exactly what Steve's trying to do in his films. You both have something to say about passionate, committed people."

Rayme looked at Steve and Lieu, then back to Wilson.

"I've talked to my band about you. I've asked them to find the lie in any of you. They can't. So, right now, I'm trusting you."

Steve spoke up. "Rayme, I have to know about the movie by the end of February. We're supposed to start in April, and there won't be much time to prepare."

"I'll try," Rayme said. "I want Marny's opinion when she starts to talk again. Right now, nothing's changed. But Lieu's given me all your phones, so we'll be in touch."

Steve turned to Rayme's attorney. "Did you give him the contract?"

Wilson nodded.

"I've seen it," Rayme said. "I showed it to the band, too. And none of the guys can believe it. If we don't like our parts, out we go."

He looked up at Wilson. "I've asked movie people I know here in New York. They say it's never been done."

The attorney nodded. "I think that's true. I don't think it ever has been done, the approvals Steve has given to you. And I can promise you one thing, Rayme. You'll never get them again. No one will."

21

Memorial Hospital, Chicago

*J*unior Wayland came by after work for a short time, and friends were allowed to visit on good days.

Steve spent those dark hours of the night with his father and he was there when his father would awaken.

Steve was afraid that something would happen when he wasn't there, and when his father's vital signs began to fail, Steve was in the room around the clock.

It was a few minutes after four in the morning on Wednesday night and Steve was alone with his father in the hospital. His father was breathing heavily. The sound in his throat alarmed Steve.

Suddenly, his father sat straight up in bed. It was the fastest movement Steve had seen him make in weeks. His bright blue eyes shone and his voice was strong as he spoke to Steve, looking him right in the eyes. There was a convulsion in his chest. His voice trembled slightly as he said, "Is this the finish?"

Those words chilled Steve. He would never forget them. In that single moment, with that single line, Steve, for the first time in his life, came face to face with the death of a loved one. They had been talking about the past, about memories, about hopes for the future when suddenly the cold figure of death had taken over the room. Steve could feel it. What had been a visiting room was now a death room.

He rang for the nurse and then put his arms around his father and let him gently down again onto his pillow. "That damn morphine really gives you ideas, Dad," Steve said.

He took a washcloth and sponged his father's head. Wayland's blue eyes were soft now. Steve reached up and took his father's wrist and looked at it, once so strong and powerful. It had shrunk and the veins were discolored from all the fluids pouring into him. It was a frail wrist now and the grip was pitifully weak. But it was still a grip.

A film of tears filled his father's eyes. "I love you, son," he said. "Maybe I loved you too much. I wanted so much for you, and I wanted to save you from getting hurt. Instead, I'm afraid I gave you more pain."

The words were halting but they were clear. Steve's guts squeezed. He sat down in the chair beside his father's bed, took his father's frail hands in both of his and kissed them.

If tonight his father was going to die, they were going to handle it with the courage and dignity that he had always seen in his father. He prayed to God he would have the strength.

He sat there for hours with his father, holding his hands, with his father's head tilted over the pillow so that he could see his son at his side. They didn't talk much, only a few words, but there was communion between them.

Around five in the morning his father fell asleep. It seemed to be a soft sleep. He spoke out as he slept in a child's words.

"Mother mine," he said softly. "Mother mine."

His body seemed to rock slightly in the bed, and then his lips formed the words again, "Mother mine. Mother mine." He was back in his childhood. His mother was there in her tenderness for him. His father, in his strength.

A fever seemed to come upon him. His eyes opened, he called out, "Why? Why? Why?" Then he spoke to his mother and father by their first names, Betty and Michael. And then he was talking to his older brother, Harry, long dead, and another brother, Daniel, and his only sister, Sarah.

And then, slowly, Lawrence Wayland pulled himself up in the bed. He looked at Steve. "My son," he said. "My son."

Something deep in his father's chest rattled, and another chill went down Steve's backbone. His father's head turned from left to right, and back again. He said, clearly, "This is the death watch, isn't it, son?"

Steve didn't know what to say, what to do. All he could say was, "We're together, Dad. I'm here. We'll always be together."

His father opened his eyes, brilliant blue they were. They always looked right through you. They seemed to know every thought and every feeling you had. Now they were looking through him again.

"Always, my beloved son."

And with those words, a noble and unique man died.

22

The *Royal Princess*

agdalena Alba stood for a moment at the top of the golden staircase which descended into the Royal Palace Dining Room of the greatest of the new ocean liners, the *Royal Princess*.

A murmur went through the crowded tables at the "late sitting" of the most honored guests of Captain Knudsen of the *Royal Princess*. It was a *Who's Who* of international celebrity on the anniversary of the first crossing to Los Angeles of this great ship. The eyes of everyone in the room turned toward the legendary star.

Magdalena stood silently, her eyes sweeping the faces of the beautifully dressed first-nighters. There was only one empty chair at the captain's table, the one to his right. Captain Knudsen rose from his place and crossed to the bottom of the stairs.

Like most of his guests, the captain had seen Magdalena often in films, and had read much about her during her twenty-year career. She was a legend, reportedly fabulously wealthy, powerful, mysterious, and extremely private.

Every woman in the room was immediately on guard. No matter what designer gowns they wore, no matter what great house had jeweled them, where their coiffures had been designed, or what physical culturist held them among their private clients, the women in that room felt envy. A dangerous presence had been let loose among them, like a wild cat in a jungle camp.

Magdalena no longer felt the familiar thrill of triumph that so often had throbbed through her body when she entered a room and knew that she was the most beautiful and most desirable woman there. Fate had changed her every conscious thought.

She could not get the disease, and the threat of the disease, from her mind. If all these women knew the truth, the envy and even hatred in the sea of faces around her might have changed. Not a woman here would want to trade places with her. And this would be her milieu for five days and five nights on the crossing of the *Royal Princess*.

She had decided to make her entrance on the very first night and give them what they expected. Then it would be over. Maybe she could be left alone, and she would have fulfilled all her obligations.

Magdalena Alba made a sharp contrast to many of the women in the room, who were overly thin and model-influenced.

Her choker of emeralds was set with octagonally pointed diamonds and covered the scar on her neck, which was fading away. Her ring, with the beautiful Kahali emerald from the Colombian jungles, glittered from the second finger of her left hand. Around her shoulders she wore a full-length, white ermine cape.

As she neared the captain's table, her arm placed through his, her eyes, for one second, betrayed her vulnerability. If you knew Magdalena Alba, you would have seen the momentary flash of fear and pain as she braced herself to greet the famous people.

It was this vulnerability which great directors, using their cameras intuitively, picked up and made the heart of her memorable performances.

It was this element that had catapulted her to stardom in *The Haunted*.

This was another "opening night," and one that would make special stories, special columns, all over the world. But no writer, and none of the photographers, would capture what Magdalena Alba was feeling on this night.

The fear was making her mouth dry. She was besieged by visions of the future. What future? When would the illness really take hold of her? She had gotten stronger in the few days that she had spent in Paris, talking to Steve Wayland, and was encouraged after her dismissal from the hospital. But as soon as Steve had gone, the depression had come back again.

She wished he were here now. Someone ought to be there, protecting her. No one ever had—even when her father was alive, he hadn't really protected her. He had shown her off, but he had put his own pleasures above her survival.

There was an interesting collection of people here, accomplished people like herself, and ordinarily Magdalena would have been fascinated to have dinner with them. But tonight it all seemed hopeless. There were no futures for her. She would never see any of these people again. It would only be more painful to get to know them.

Early in her life, Magdalena had learned the secret of one-on-one communication. She looked directly at each person as she spoke. Some of the women pulled back their claws as they heard her inquiring about their children. And Magdalena listened. She didn't interrupt. She did not speak about herself. This was not the image of Hollywood one expected. This was not the woman, seemingly, of many erotic adventures, which had been intimated in the media all over the world.

The silver-haired Captain Knudsen, a stocky, weathered Scandinavian, bent over and spoke quietly. "We're running *Anna Karenina* tonight at eleven o'clock. We're not going to be able to get everyone into the theater."

"Captain, I think you're going to be surprised. I doubt if fifty people come see a film tonight, with all the other things to do on board and the ship's nightclub open."

Captain Knudsen replied, "I'll make you a bet. If I'm right, I have the pleasure of taking you to dinner on shore. On our first night. You pick the restaurant."

Magdalena smiled. "Captain," she said, "I like that bet. Even if I lose, I win a prize."

The captain answered, "Agreed?"

"We'll see," Magdalena smiled.

The theater of the *Royal Princess*, which seated two hundred people, was jammed to overflowing. People were crowded into the aisles, sitting anywhere they could. There was eager anticipation and excited conversation in every corner of the room.

The lights went out. All eyes strained toward Magdalena Alba, sitting with the captain and his dinner group across two rows of seats at the back of the theater. The screen credits rolled and there was loud applause when Magdalena's credit came on, in letters eight feet high.

Suddenly, the viewers were in a train station in Czarist Russia. The train trembled to a stop, and people began to disembark. In her first appearance in the film, as Greta Garbo had done so long before, Magdalena stepped down from the train, completely covered with the steam of the locomotive. She was unrecognizable as the haze drifted around her face.

Suddenly, it began to fade away in little wisps, as she looked around for her relatives and friends. As the mists cleared, little by little, revealing the different parts of her face and her wide-set, beautiful eyes, the audience gasped with her beauty.

She was dressed in the period clothes of the time of Tolstoy's masterpiece, with her high-crowned Russian hat, her hair pulled back, and her smile of expectancy as she sought out her friends.

That soft smile betrayed her vulnerability. It was a breathtaking shot, derived from the Garbo movie, but the performance was unique. Magdalena never copied anything, and she'd agreed to do *Anna Karenina* only if she could do it in her own way with her own director.

The audience in the *Royal Princess* theater was into the adventure. Not only Tolstoy's famous love story, but an unforgettable performance with the star of the movie, Anna Karenina herself, sitting in their midst. Various members of the audience kept turning from the screen to look at the real woman.

Magdalena sat watching the film. Long ago she had learned to look at her motion pictures from a dispassionate point of view. She watched carefully her looks, her lighting, her movements.

The film was coming to its end, and Magdalena was overwhelmed by her feelings. Because, as in the film, she was nearing the end of her life.

Anna Karenina had given her body and soul to her greatest love, even sacrificed the custody of her own son, but Count Vronsky had, in the end, gotten bored with her. He had returned to his military friends and to the gay life he had had before. He found the love of his lover simply too great and too possessive.

In the railroad station, where the audience had first seen her, she made her decision as she looked at the powerful wheels of a rolling train. There was one last gigantic close-up, the camera slowly moving in until her eyes covered the whole screen—vulnerable, alone, haunted, and disillusioned. Then, over her eyes, in their moment of decision, came the screeching wheels of the train, and then a single, terrifying scream. The last utterance of Anna Karenina.

The lights slowly came up in the screening room. The women who earlier had hated this glamorous movie star on sight could not wait to give her their homage. Because Magdalena Alba *was* Anna Karenina.

The magic of true movie making had happened. The motion picture had taken a group of people of every kind of background and sublimated them into a passionate experience which they all could share.

* * *

It was 2:00 A.M. when Magdalena turned the key of her private suite on the upper deck of the *Royal Princess*. As she flicked on the light, her whole body sagging with the effort of the night and the meaning of it, she saw on every side visions of blue-purple.

The Magdalena Suite, named after her, was filled with bouquets of violets.

Her breath caught in her throat, and she stepped into the bedroom beyond. It, too, was filled with the flowers she loved.

On her makeup table was a package. She started to laugh and then to cry. Could it be? How could he have done that? He would have had to pay off the head steward to arrange the whole thing while she was at the dinner—it had to be Steve Wayland. Please God, she thought, let it be Steve Wayland.

She tore open the cover of the package. It was a white leather script book, and it was empty. She read the script lettering on the cover:

> For *Magdalena Alba. The Rest*
> *of Our Lives.* This will be
> the story that we make together.
>
> Steve Wayland

Magdalena Alba put the white leather script book against her and clutched it warmly. Oh God, she had needed so much something to hang onto tonight, and now she was in her room and able to be herself, and Steve had anticipated the whole thing.

She made a full circle on her toes, her face suddenly filled with life. Only a true romantic could have done this. How many times had she come back to a room on an ocean liner and found a beautiful jewel or four dozen roses, or perhaps a fur coat? Gifts from men for every kind of reason. But when did you walk into your cabin and find an ocean of violets?

Magdalena crossed to the porthole and looked out across the ocean, rippling in the moonlight. All she knew was that the *Royal Princess* was heading for America, and she felt just as alive as ever. And the evening had let her know she was still a beautiful and desirable woman.

There was life left at the end of this journey. The rest of *her* life. And who knew how long they had? Every day, every hour, was special. And there would be a man waiting who had given her a whole ocean of violets, and the promise of one more film—one more film that had to be her best.

23

Monte Carlo

onte Carlo was in the height of its season in the big casino. The beautiful people of the international set, the best-looking courtesans in Europe, the professional gamblers, the drug dealers, the would-be motion-picture impresarios. It was one of the few cosmopolitan playgrounds of Europe that had retained its glamour and excitement.

There was a crowd four deep around the large dice table. It was deadly quiet.

A huge amount, even by Monte Carlo's standards, was being bet by the woman in the white Halston evening dress, daringly cut in the back. Her hair was piled high on top of her head and fastened with a diamond-encrusted clip of a tigress. The white silk jersey evening gown clung in one sweeping, curvaceous swirl around her spectacular figure.

The back of the dress was completely cut away to the very top of the indentation in her hips. It fitted skintight around her hips and was gathered closely around her knees, then swirled out to the floor. A large solitaire diamond adorned the third finger of her right hand.

La Tigressa was on a roll, with five stacks of chips in front of her on the table.

Next to her stood a tall, immaculate-looking man in his fifties, dressed in evening clothes. He took a silver cigarette box from his coat and withdrew another cigarette. Instantly, one of the house men covering the famous casino was there with a light.

The tall man accepted the service with a polite nod. He smoked with a cultivated air, turning the handling of his cigarette into a ritual of sophistication. There was a cool, studied attitude about the man. He watched La Tigressa, and the crowd watching her, with heightened interest.

He beckoned to a waiter passing champagne. The waiter offered the glasses on his tray. The tall man shook his head. "My Taittinger," he said. The waiter nodded and left the side of the dice table quickly.

The dice rolled out from Tigressa's hand. She held both her arms out in suspense, calling to the dice, her eyes bright with unnatural fever, her red lips moist and parted. She whispered with husky sexuality.

"Come to mother," she intoned fervently. "Come to mother—come." The people gathered around the table were spellbound.

Here was more than a beautiful woman gambling for high stakes. This they saw every night, all through the year. There was something explosive about this woman, as though she were going to break open in some secret trauma.

The dice came up four, and the croupier returned them to La Tigressa. She picked them up and put them quietly to her lips, kissed them and flicked her tongue over their surface.

The tall man at her side watched keenly. The waiter brought in a new bottle of Taittinger champagne, opened it, and poured two glasses. The man gave one to La Tigressa and raised his own to hers. She took his silent toast, sipped her champagne, kissed the tall man openly on the lips, then kissed the dice, again flicking the little cubes with her champagne-wetted tongue. Her action was so sensual that it further excited the crowd.

She pulled her hand back quickly and threw the dice across the green-padded table. They rebounded off the padded edges and settled into position. A murmur went around the crowd, as four came up again.

La Tigressa turned to the waiter standing by. "Champagne for everybody."

The tall man at her side nodded to the waiter and approved it. Another stack of chips was shoved toward La Tigressa. She had a fortune now on the table. The tall man took both her hands, one holding the dice. He nodded at the table.

"You have a half a million there. Don't you think you should cash in now?"

Tigressa looked at him, her eyes burning too brightly. She shook her head. "I want double or nothing," she said.

He shook his head. "The house won't approve that limit."

Tigressa answered coolly. "They'll do whatever you tell them to do, Henri."

He leaned close to her. "Why do you want to do this?"

"I want the thrill of having more money than I've ever had in my life, and gambling it all on one throw of the dice," she laughed gaily. "Isn't that what everything is, Henri, in the end? A throw of the dice? Sooner or later, you crap out."

She turned and pushed all her chips to the line. The crowd gasped.

A tall, blond, middle-aged woman, beautifully gowned in an Oscar de La Renta black lace dress, stepped up to Henri. She had a handful of chips clutched in her jeweled fingers.

"Hello, Henri," she said.

The count bowed his head. "Good evening, Eleanor." He turned to La Tigressa. "Tigressa, this is my good friend from America, Eleanor Mitchell."

"I've been watching you play, my dear." She put her chips down alongside La Tigressa's. "I'm riding with you, if you don't mind. I think you're going to be lucky for me."

La Tigressa gave her her best smile. "Thank you."

La Tigressa raised her right hand once again and threw the dice out along the felt table. They caromed off the end of the table and spun out to the dreaded snake eyes.

Everyone—Henri, Eleanor Mitchell, and Tigressa herself—was frozen for a moment in a silent tableau. In one split second, a fortune had been thrown away.

Then, La Tigressa spoke to the croupier just as he made a move to pass the dice to the player on La Tigressa's left. "I want another chance. A hundred thousand dollars." She kept the dice clenched in her hand. "Agreed?"

Behind La Tigressa, several rows of people back, Barbara Carr turned to one of the floor captains. She handed him a fifty-dollar tip. "I need a private phone right away," she said. "I've got to call Rome."

The floor manager pocketed the fifty dollars. "Please follow me. It can be arranged."

Barbara took one last look at La Tigressa, and then followed the captain.

La Tigressa glanced around the table. The other players agreed to let this extraordinary gambler continue with the dice. Tigressa turned to Henri. "I want to try once more. That was all the money I had. I want a loan."

Henri sipped his champagne, never taking his eyes from hers. His voice was low. "What's my collateral?" Henri asked.

La Tigressa looked back at him. "What you always told me you wanted more than anything, when you came to Afrique."

She didn't need to spell it out. They looked at each other. They both understood what she was doing. Henri turned toward the croupier and toward the floor boss, who came walking up to check what was going on at the table.

"One hundred thousand dollars worth of chips for the lady," Henri said. He quickly took a notepad out of his pocket and signed his name to it. "For my account," he added, as he passed it to the floor manager.

The floor manager nodded. "Thank you, Count." He gestured to the croupier, who pushed a hundred thousand dollars' worth of chips towards La Tigressa's place. The crowd leaned in against the table as the sensuous and beautiful woman with the dark hair and burning black eyes prepared to throw the dice.

In five straight throws, La Tigressa made her point. And once again there was five hundred thousand dollars' worth of chips in front of her. La Tigressa turned to Henri.

"Do you want your hundred thousand back before I throw again?"

Henri shook his head. "I want our agreement riding on this throw," he said. "But win or lose, this is it."

She looked intently at him. "And if I lose, you collect your collateral."

He smiled and sipped his champagne. "Of course," Henri answered.

La Tigressa turned to the table. She started to move one of the five stacks of chips towards Henri. But then she made up her mind. She threw the dice once more for a million dollars or nothing.

There they were again, the most dreaded numbers on the dice table. Snake eyes.

In the space of seven and a half minutes, Tigressa had twice lost a half million dollars. There was a chain of electricity around the dice table. Everyone sensed that there was something even more here than the great amount of money involved.

The beautiful woman with the burning eyes looked up at Henri. She glanced toward the table, and the place where all her chips had been, as the croupier swept them in. Henri understood her request. He simply shook his head. She picked up her gold evening bag with the encrusted diamonds spelling out "La Tigressa."

"How about one for the road?" she said.

As La Tigressa turned away from the table, every man's eyes were on her. And so were Eleanor Mitchell's, who called after her, "Let's *do* have a drink later!"

She could feel the men's eyes watching the sway of her hips, naked under her dress. Their faces had all fused into one for her. Her husband, Charlie Heckert.

Charlie Heckert had moved from boredom to orgies to alcohol to cocaine, and he took Mary Jane with him, because he couldn't do what he wanted to do without her. And she couldn't escape him. He had told her he'd kill her if she tried to leave him. And more and more, he had gone out of control.

He could kill. Mary Jane believed that. She had seen the same streak in him that she had seen in her father.

Charlie had spent many weekends taking nude photographs of his wife in every possible provocative position. She was unfeeling now.

Mary Jane posed in every kind of degenerate way for him. She knew that he was showing these pictures around. In bars. Repair shops. Corner grocery stores. Service stations. He worked outside of Marfa, so that the whole plan wouldn't be ruined.

He did it casually. He'd be having a drink with some strangers in a bar, and the talk would quickly get around to women. Charlie would stay quiet and people would notice the wedding ring on his hand, and there was a kind of respect for him.

He was a handsome man, and socially glib. When the talk had gone on for a while, Charlie would nonchalantly say that he was really crazy about his wife, that she was beautiful and sexy, and they would ask to see a picture, and then he would pull out a shot of his wife. They were all degenerate photographs, calling forth the lowest possible sexual urge.

The pictures would get passed around and the men he was drinking with would get excited. They wanted his wife. Then he'd offhandedly pick out the guy who seemed to have money. He would wait for a chance to speak alone to that man, then ask him to the house for dinner . . . and maybe he'd like to meet his wife.

Picking up on that, the stranger would ask Charlie what he meant by "coming over to meet his wife." The answer was that for a certain amount of money, Charlie would fix it up for the man to fuck Mary Jane. He usually charged two hundred dollars.

Those were special nights. "The man who came to dinner."

It would be polite and homey at first, just the three of them. Mary Jane would dress in something revealing, and, of course, she never wore anything underneath her clothes. Her figure was as voluptuous as ever.

At certain times during the dinner or during the after-dinner drinks, she would sit across from the stranger and pull her dress up or spread her legs suggestively. Charlie would go out of the room for a moment and Mary Jane would just sit there, looking at the stranger from across the room. Then, she would put her hand down between her legs and start rubbing herself softly. Their "guest" would go crazy.

When Charlie came back he would wait for a sign and then excuse himself, saying he was tired and was going to bed, but there was no reason for their friend to leave; he should stay and have another drink.

And Mary Jane would motion quietly to the stranger to come to her in the living room. When he sat down beside her, she would take his hands and put them underneath her blouse. He would feel her wonderful ripe breasts and then she would reach over and rub the man's cock, grown hard underneath his pants.

On one particular evening, Charlie took the byplay another step forward. On that night he had gone to bed pretty early, and Mary Jane took the man who came to dinner to her bedroom. She had fixed it beautifully, with many feminine touches. There were also several strategic mirrors. She closed the door behind her and locked it.

The stranger said, "Are you sure this is safe? I mean, he's just in the other room."

She answered, "He sleeps like a dead man. Nothing could get him up." She laughed at her own joke. She went to the man and felt his prick again. "I've been waiting all night for you. Feel me."

She took his hand and put it under her dress. She was very wet. He immediately lifted her back on the bed.

She pushed him away. "I don't want to do it with our clothes on, I want to see you. And I want to be naked in front of you." She turned up the lights a little bit. "I want to watch you and me together," she said. "Fix the mirror, will you?"

The stranger moved the mirror to adjust it where he thought she would be when he went inside of her. She had removed her dress by now and he stripped off his pants and shirt. She pushed him back on the bed until he was lying down, then she knelt over him, raised his penis to her mouth and started giving it long, circular sucks.

His organ got hard in her mouth and she rubbed it up and down, rewetting it with her mouth. His prick stood up there in the middle of his body, gleaming tall and hard. Then, she sat on him with her back to his face, and told him to lie still. The mirror reflected her face, her breasts, and beyond that his cock going in and out of her.

His face was a foot away from her, watching her. Then, suddenly, she turned, straddled him, placed his cock inside of her and went down on him in a savage way, reaching back and massaging his balls. He came with his balls in her hand, while she squeezed them, and he came again and then rolled over on top of her. She spread her legs wide.

Charlie watched everything. He had fixed his little place in the closet and worked it out with his wife. There were two small holes in the closet where he could see it all. The bed and the mirrors were arranged perfectly.

Charlie Heckert wasn't able to fuck his wife anymore unless he first saw somebody else fucking her. As he saw the stranger enter his wife, he felt his organ swelling underneath his pajamas. He watched intently as the man spread his wife's legs and entered her again. He could see her, could see the man thrusting.

Mary Jane had completely retired from life. She had turned off. Mechanically, she stroked her lover, encouraged him, and held him. And inside the closet, Charlie was masturbating.

It was not long after that that Mary Jane had a nervous breakdown. She was only 19 years old, but the pain in her eyes was of someone who had been suffering for years. When she got out of the county hospital, she didn't call her parents, or Charlie Heckert, or anyone. She got a cab to the airport and flew directly to Los Angeles. Nothing could be worse than how she was living. Maybe she could die in peace.

Four blocks from the airport, she spent her last hundred dollars on a week's rent of a motel room at "the charmingly quaint Westward Ho." She blew her last ten dollars on something called a "top-flight minute steak" at the Hyatt Coffee Shop, and then walked down Century Boulevard looking for a waitress job. She found a combination bowling alley/café/bar-lounge called Nightflight. The big neon sign out front flashed intermittently "nude—girl—dancers." Mary Jane went in and asked to see the manager.

The manager's office was the essence of airport sleaze. Conversations were interrupted by the steady drone of jet airliners which flew directly over this part of Century Boulevard. It seemed to Mary Jane that everything in Los Angeles was noisy, moving, and big.

The manager spent all his free change on hair dye and pomade.

He was a poor man's Valentino, born fifty years too late. He looked like something out of an old George Raft movie. When he smiled, his mouth did a number. His eyes never changed at all. He had a wide space between his two upper front teeth and his tongue hissed through them.

He gave Mary Jane the chills as he looked her up and down.

"Where have you danced, kid?"

Mary Jane answered quietly, "Texas."

The man questioned, "Regular job?"

She shook her head. "No."

He waved his hand upwards as though she would know what he meant.

She looked at him questioningly.

He gestured with irritation. "Come on, take off your blouse. I want to see your tits. This is no dancing school, you know."

She looked at him, drew herself up, and unbuttoned her blouse. The blouse draped over her nipples. The man stood up and walked around her. With both hands, he pulled the blouse to the sides of her arms, exposing her full, rounded breasts. The nipples were large and crimson red.

She shook her head.

He didn't notice that her eyes were filled with hatred. He reached out and felt both breasts, squeezing them. Then, his hand moved between her legs. "Come on, you saw the sign out front, this is a nude dancing joint. Let's see your pussy."

She moved his hand away. She looked him in the eye and started to button up her blouse. "I'm a hell of a lot better dancer than any tramp you have in here. I'll dance topless, but not nude. I don't turn *any* tricks, I don't do *any* favors, with you or anyone else. I want to make an honest living."

The manager looked at her disgustedly. "All the girls dance nude in here, that's what we advertise and that's what we give 'em. You better learn to be nice to me."

Mary Jane fired back, "You better learn to respect me, you big son of a bitch. I'll make the kind of deal you'll understand. I'll dance tonight's show . . . topless. If you don't have more business tomorrow night than tonight because of me, don't pay me anything.

"If I'm right, I want two hundred fifty dollars a week to start with. I know you're paying the other girls more now, probably, but I don't want to hear any more of your fancy dialogue, and you keep your hands off me. I'm not for sale."

The manager went back behind his desk. "Then what the fuck are you here for?"

She answered him coolly. "To make a living, and the only thing I know how to do really well is dance."

He looked at her quietly. "Did you ever dance in front of a crowd—I mean, entertain a crowd? These aren't exactly ballet fans here, you know. They come for tits, ass, and pussy."

"I'm going to educate your sleazy crowd. You watch tonight. You either get a free show or I get a job. That's the best deal you've had in a year. What time do I go on?"

"Ten o'clock," he answered, "and you better not be late."

It was a tough drinking crowd. Travelers. Salesmen. Oil workers covering the area near the airport and out at the Long Beach oil fields. It was ten o'clock and most of them were already drunk. The disco music was so loud it hurt the eardrums.

The introduction was brief. From somewhere in the bowels of this filthy joint a tired, third-rate comic's voice made this announcement: "From Texas, give the lady a big hand, just arrived on the coast, hot from an all-star engagement in the Lone Star State, give her a hand, folks, Mary Jane Stuckey."

The recording started: "Eye of the Tiger." Nobody gave Mary Jane a hand.

A tired, faded velvet curtain parted. The spotlight moved around and finally picked her up as she stepped out in front of the audience.

Mary Jane wore a handmade Raggedy Ann doll outfit, consisting of a red-and-white jumpsuit with thin halter straps which kept her breasts from being completely uncovered. Her nipples rode high on her breasts and turned out beyond the straps. Her face was blackened, and her long black hair flowed free.

She was playing the part of a puppet, something she had often done when dancing by herself in Marfa. Her movements were all perfectly synchronized as though she were controlled by a master puppeteer. Her eyes stared straight ahead as though they were false eyes and her mouth stayed half open in a kind of defiant lip-curling look. As the rhythm went on, she began to dance wildly as though the imaginary puppeteer had been seized with hysteria.

It was something different for the bored customers. They couldn't see her face too well, but her figure was a ten strike. Mary Jane knew how to make up, and her dark eyes shone out from her delicately carved face.

The sexual effect of the Raggedy Ann dance with the erotic costume, and her hair tossing back and forth in a shining mantle, set the crowd crazy. The storybook character lent innocence to all the provocative moves of the dance, which turned on the audience all the more. Mary Jane went from one step to another, in a synchronized, individually choreographed modern jazz dance. It was not the tired old bump-and-grind of the pelvic circuit.

Her breasts moved provocatively and she deliberately let the halter straps slip down her arms. At each new exposure of her breasts moving wildly in her dance rhythms, the crowd yelled. They began to clap on the beat of her make-believe puppeteer's movements. On each beat of their hand claps, Mary Jane accented her dance from one seductive step to another, but always in the flow of the fast, rhythmical modern jazz dance. The crowd turned from its drinking and, for the first time, actually began to participate in a dance solo at the Nightflight.

Mary Jane felt a new kind of warmth. She forgot where she was dancing and for whom. All she knew was that for only the second time in her miserable, terrified existence, she felt as if she were validated. She had something. And she was getting a public response to her performance. It wasn't just her looks or her figure. The crowd was responding to something it didn't even understand—talent.

The manager looked out from behind the bar. He spoke in an aside to the bartender, who was clapping his hands. "Son of a bitch," he said, "the kid's got something more than tits and pussy."

Mary Jane became a star name in the subcircuit of sleazy nudie joints from Los Angeles to San Francisco to Reno to Las Vegas.

When she was twenty-one, she signed on with a troupe of girls to stage a legitimate nightclub act in South Africa. In Nairobi, they would open at the Sheraton. The show was going to be called Folies d'Afrique, and they had the same dance director as the Folies Bergère in Paris. This was a new creation of Folies Bergère, Inc., a copy of what they had already done in Las Vegas. And the featured dancer was Mary Jane.

It was in Nairobi, in rehearsals, that La Tigressa was born. Tucheki was part of an act of five Watusi drummers who had been brought in from the jungle and rehearsed for the show. Mary Jane had waited around one night after dance rehearsal was finished, before the show opened, to hear the drummers. That night, as Tucheki pounded out his rhythms of tribal Africa, Mary Jane took the floor spontaneously to dance.

She moved like an animal, with the same grace and sensuality as the big, silky cats. No one else from the show was around, except one person, the director of Folies d'Afrique. He happened to be leaving the theater office and investigated the sensual sounds and noises that were coming from the rehearsal stage.

He watched a young girl dancing in complete abandon, throwing her head back, imitating the sounds of the black drummers, initiating her own rhythms in her bare feet, and in her black wraparound skirt and midriff tie blouse. It was the sexiest dancing he'd ever seen.

Tucheki and La Tigressa were born. Three weeks after the show opened, it was La Tigressa and Tucheki.

Six months later, Mary Jane Stuckey, alias La Tigressa, was next to last on the bill at the Monte Carlo Gala.

24

Monte Carlo Raceway

They parked at the top of the hill overlooking the Monte Carlo Grand Prix course, down through the winding streets. In the moonlit night, the enchanted playground island of Monte Carlo looked as though it was projected through a diffused photographic screen—like an Impressionist painting—soft, ethereal, unreal.

The top was down in Henri's specially built convertible Jaguar. He turned up the fire of the opium pipe he had fixed in the back seat.

"You've never tried it?" he asked.

She shook her head. "Not opium," La Tigressa answered.

"It's the best of all," he said. "And you come down easier."

"I don't want to come down, ever," La Tigressa said quietly. "How do we do it?"

He picked up the pipe and inhaled slowly, with the ease of a man long accustomed to taking opium. He filled his lungs and all the passages of his face and his brain with the heavy, sweet smoke.

Then, he reached out for La Tigressa, pulled her into his arms, and put his mouth on hers. As La Tigressa opened her mouth, he breathed into her all the opium he had taken. He did it slowly, sensuously, in the way of sexual intercourse.

He was putting his kind of "magic" into her, pushing it into her, with his tongue and his lips. She inhaled fully, relaxing in his arms, and let the opium invade her mouth, her head, and her blood. Henri turned away and drew in another inhalation of opium. La Tigressa was waiting for him, her head tilted back, her breasts jutting upward, her whole body ready to receive him and the trip to ecstasy. She opened her lips and consumed the opium that he gave her.

Then, Henri started up the Jaguar. Before he began to drive, he sucked in again from the opium pipe and breathed it into La Tigressa's mouth.

"Are you taking me on the same way the race goes?" La Tigressa asked. "I always wanted to do that."

He nodded as he pulled the car away from the top of the hill. La Tigressa moved over, wrapped her arms around him, and slid her right leg over his so that she was straddling the leg that controlled the speed of the car. She kissed him hungrily.

"Fast," she said. "Very fast."

The wind was already rushing past them in the open car, as the car picked up speed. Tigressa pulled up her dress, tugging it past the tight gathering below her hips, and sliding it up over her hips so that her white stockings and garter belt were exposed. She caressed him, pulling open his shirt and moving against his body in the rhythm of the music.

Whitney Houston was singing over the car radio, "I'm saving all my love for you." La Tigressa whispered to Henri as she brushed her mouth past his, and licked the inside of his right ear.

"That's what I'm going to do," she whispered with the lyric, "I'm going to love you all the night through." She put his right hand down her naked back and pushed it under her dress, so that he could feel her bare hips. She was rubbing against his knee now and unzipping his pants.

The car was swerving. He fought to keep it under control. He was an expert driver, but half his vision was obscured now by La Tigressa.

He wanted to push her off, but then again he didn't. It was one of the most exciting things he had ever felt. The speed of the car, the open air, the race course of the Monte Carlo Grand Prix, the sweeping Monte Carlo beneath, and his "collateral"—this exotic, beautiful woman whom he had waited to possess for so many nights in Rome. He had known that she was sensual, but the way she was embracing him, caressing him, groping for him, rubbing against him, and kissing him he could not have imagined.

It was as though there was some wild core in this woman that had been split open. La Tigressa guided his hand to the zipper at the back of her dress at the very beginning of her hips. She took his hand in hers and unzipped the dress.

Then, in the moonlight, her hair blowing wildly about her face,

La Tigressa slipped off the shoulders of her dress and rubbed her naked breasts across his chest.

He pushed her away to see the road as the car careened around the curves, but La Tigressa was laughing now. Then she guided him in between her legs, thrusting herself on him, giving him just enough room to catch a glimpse of the route curving from side to side.

With him deep inside of her, she looked at him and laughed. "How do you like your collateral?"

25

Eastern Airlines Flight 714

The plane was coming in over Los Angeles, and it was always the same for Steve. The last hour flying in over the endless sea of lights below.

It was an unforgettable sight, but it scared the hell out of him. It always had.

How could one person's dreams or work or accomplishments be of any significance, really? Millions of human lives lay in intricate personal patterns and networks in that ocean of lights below.

It was late at night and thousands of people were watching television, probably Johnny Carson. Other thousands were going to bed. Thousands were saying good night to their children, or checking them while they slept. Thousands more were making love.

Just that staggering thought. Maybe a million people down there right this moment were making love. Down there right now, hundreds of robberies were going on. At least four murders, according to statistics, at least seventy-five drug raids. Flotsam and jetsam.

What difference did one life make? Why did everyone feel that his or her life was so damned important? Was there any universal force in the world? How could any God of anyone's imagination really keep track of all the world—could one universal force even keep track of Los Angeles?

Depression filled his heart. Two double scotches hadn't helped. He couldn't shake the feeling he'd first had when he was five years old and left home to sleep overnight at a friend's house. It was always "leaving home." No one could hang onto that feeling of being completely protected, even if he'd ever had it. And Steve never had had it. Now, his father was gone, that father who could never give him the love he'd sought until the very end. Thank God he'd gone back and had that time with him. It shook Steve to consider how he might feel if his father had died and they were still estranged as they'd been for so many years.

He thought about his mother. He would be the only one to take care of her, to be truly involved with her. She was getting older. She had a few friends. But she had lost the son she had never had—a man who had tried to steal everything his mother had in the world.

How would it feel to have a child grow up and do that, Steve wondered. What a terrible disease that was, the greed and hate that motivated his brother.

Steve longed for the family he had never had. If only his brother had given a damn about him. If only they could have come together like a family, at the death of their father. But they hadn't been able to. And now, his only brother had expressed himself very clearly. He had taken a position outside the family, and was out to destroy it.

Steve had stopped him. He had done what his father would have wanted him to do. He had protected his mother, and saved her security for all her life. But it was a sad story.

Everyone in Chicago knew about it now. Everyone "in" in Chicago really was contained in one major circle of people. And gossip spread like fire within that circle.

The Wayland family had always been a conservative, positive force in the community, which made gossip of bribery, forgery, family hatred, jealousy, medical malpractice, and legal malpractice particularly unpalatable. It was now a cause célèbre in Chicago and would be remembered for many years.

It had all come down to one brief face-to-face encounter with his brother. Steve had picked the place for the meeting—the boardroom of his father's grain company, the Board of Trade Building. It was a handsome office furnished with early American antiques. The oval table his father had chosen brought back memories. It was oval so that there was no "head position" at the table. That was his father's way. It was Lawrence Wayland's company, but he never flaunted his authority.

Steve was purposely late. Junior was pacing up and down in the boardroom when Steve walked in. They were alone.

Junior looked at his brother with fear and hatred. Steve walked around the table. He wanted to invoke his father's presence; he wanted Junior to feel it.

Steve spoke quietly to his brother. "We both know the facts, Junior. If you weren't frightened out of your head at being revealed to this whole community, you wouldn't even be here. So, we start from there."

Junior flared up. "We don't start from anywhere. We never did. Exactly what are you threatening?"

Steve smiled at him. "Bluffs are gone. You've faded, Junior. At exactly eight o'clock tomorrow morning, I'm having a press conference. If you don't believe me, just check the *Chicago Tribune*. The night editor will know about it. The press conference is going to be here—in my father's grain company."

Junior flared up. "I own this company now."

Steve looked at him levelly. "That's what your false will says. The will you persuaded Robert Lydell and Thelma Bracken to witness. I don't think you want the facts of your 'persuasion' to come out.

"I can prove, Junior, and I will prove, my father was given a heavy dose of morphine that night. There was no way, and I can prove it medically, that my father could have known what he was doing. Dr. Roberts will testify to that. And he opened the door to Dad's room on his rounds just as you were guiding his hand for the signature. None of you noticed him. Call him if you don't believe me. He didn't understand what you were doing but it's in his records of the rounds he made that night.

"I can't understand anyone as smart as you making a mistake like that. Who the hell is going to believe that my father, in his right mind, would turn his back on his wife of forty-seven years and not even leave her the house they've lived in together for more than three decades?"

Steve walked up to his brother until his face was just a foot away.

"Why? Why did you do this? Tearing up this whole family—almost killing your own mother—you would have killed her, you know—the shock of her own son stealing behind her back, getting a false will signed and then telling her what to do and how she is going to live on a dole-out from you."

Junior's mouth trembled at the corners. "The thing you care about is yourself," he lashed out. "You didn't get what you came back here for!" His voice rose in pitch. "Not a cent. Not one cent. That's what you get."

Steve replied, "That's all right for me. But when your own mother doesn't get a cent, and you turn your back on her, then somebody's got to do something about it. And there's no one to do it except me.

"Here's what's facing you, Junior. Tomorrow morning at eight o'clock, I'm going to file a lawsuit in behalf of our mother against you for fraud, for executing and planning a false will, for stealing from the family company, for a total of seven million, four hundred and fifty-eight thousand dollars."

Junior's face drained white.

Steve pulled out of his pocket a copy of a lawsuit in a blue-backed cover and threw it on the oval table in front of Junior.

"Here's an advance copy. An exact stipulation of how much you have taken from the employee's trust in Dad's company, from the cash reserve funds, from the company stock itself, from trading on the stock market, even to the compiling of trusts with company money, family money, Junior, for the benefit of your four children, and for all of them, you're the trustee, all the money circles back to you. I've had four men working on this since that will of yours was read.

"I would have bet that you couldn't have been stealing all these years. And I would have been wrong. There's probably more before we're through. And we're going to find every cent. But this much we have found.

"You're going to be sued by your own mother—by your own mother, Junior. She's strong enough to do it, and I will make sure she's secure for life. That's all I care about. Secure for life! She's got to have what Dad wanted her to have.

"But the point is, this is never going to go to trial, in fact, it's never going to be filed, Junior, because I have another document here you're going to sign."

Steve pulled another blue-backed legal document from his pocket and put it down side by side with the other on the table.

"—this document, without any official stigma attached to your name, and that's important in this town, you know, because I can ruin you here. You wouldn't be able to lift your head again. But I don't want that, for my mother's sake. I would love it, personally. But I care about your children and I love my mother. They're innocent victims of you and your sick connivings. So, I'm going to give you an out.

"You sign that paper, giving Mother back the property that she would have gotten under the will, enough of Dad's bequests to her so that she can live securely the rest of her life. Then we won't sue you.

"We'll let you get away with the rest of it. We'll let you live with yourself. There's no punishment greater than that. A man who tries to steal from his own mother. And the tragedy of it, Junior, is that you don't need the money.

"I don't know exactly what you're worth, but from what I gather, you'd never have to work another day in your life, even without your false will.

"It doesn't make sense. It's insanity."

He paused. Steve looked at his brother carefully.

"Maybe that's what it is. Insanity. I'd rather not believe that you have no conscience at all."

Junior spoke defiantly. "I'm not signing anything."

Steve shrugged his shoulders. "Fine. Eight o'clock tomorrow morning, your life in this community will be over. You won't be able to show your head. You'll never win. There are too many things going against you. You didn't do it with any moderation. You went for everything. It'll never wash. Your reputation is going to be ruined. Your children are going to suffer. You're going to lose everything."

He stepped up to his brother. "You've got exactly ten hours. I want that document signed and delivered to me, at our mother's house, by seven o'clock in the morning. If I receive it by then, no suit will be filed, and no press conference will be held.

"There's not a damn thing you can do about it, Junior. You knew that before you came here to meet with me.

"If you want to test that I have all the proof—the sworn testimonies, the photographic records, all the details—just go ahead and let me file the case. The newspapers will be printing these things front page every day for a long time. And this city will be living hell for you, Junior, and no one deserves it more."

At seven o'clock the next morning, the signed contract was delivered by Junior's chauffeur to his mother's home on Byron Drive. Once again, she controlled her stock in her husband's company. Once again, Steve's mother owned the house she was living in. Once again, she had livable income. Once again, she had her independence.

But the family of Lawrence Wayland, Sr. had been split apart by the money he had worked so hard to earn. The dream of a united family was gone. They would never be a family again. That thought dug into Steve as the plane began to descend from above the mountaintops to the valley leading to the sea which encompassed in all its breadth the city of Los Angeles and its suburbs.

He picked up his journal from the empty seat next to him. It was a large, worn, leather-bound volume, in which Steve wrote the notes of people and places and happenings he wanted to remember. He turned to the back where a top sheet read, *The Rest of Our Lives*, Screenplay by Steven Wayland. He noted on the top of the page:

It has to hit you raw the way all these weeks have been—the pain—the beginnings—the endings—life and death—and it has to be today, the rhythm of today. People have to find something to live for—

And then he printed the words below the notes he had just written:

Dedicated to Lawrence Mark Wayland

The plane was coming in for landing. The airstrip lights flashed by. Steve spoke to his father silently. "This one's going to be for us, Dad—you and me."

26

Los Angeles

*I*t was the longest time Steve had ever been away from his children, except for the picture he had made in Brazil.

As he drove to Egremont School in the Valley, directly from the airport, to see his "real family," Lieu gave him the latest information on his "movie family."

Rayme was living in Jordan Park, New York, where Marny was being treated in the Jordan Park Psychiatric Center. Only Skeeter Thomas was with him. Marny still didn't recognize Rayme, and now Rayme, too, had begun to retreat far within himself. No more writing, no more music. No more press.

Jack Gregson was applying the pressure. If Steve didn't have a signed contract with Rayme soon, Gregson said he could legally cancel the picture and foreclose on Steve. He had sent a specific message to Steve. "Fuck the excuses. I want some signed contracts in here, I want sets moving, I want preproduction in order."

Steve rubbed his face with fatigue. "What about Tigressa?" he asked.

"Barbara lost her after Monte Carlo. The man she was with, the count, swears he doesn't know what happened to her. She was living with him, and suddenly she was gone. Barbara believes him. So does Spartan. He flew in after Barbara called him from Monte Carlo. They both talked to the count twice."

"What about the dope rumors?" Steve asked.

"The count admitted that they did dope together—just routine—cocaine, he said. Barbara felt Tigressa was on harder stuff when she saw her at the crap table. Burning up, she said. Never saw eyes like that."

"And Magdalena?" Steve asked.

"She came in on the *Royal Princess*. I met her at the Wilmington Dock. She said she'd give you a definite answer on the picture when she leaves the Golden Door. She's accepted your invitation to go to the Academy Awards. She always does this Golden Door thing before a picture—she trains like an athlete. She looked very well . . . she seems to have fully recovered except for the scar on her neck—and that's fading away."

"Thank God she's well now and responsible. One out of three at the moment. And Montango?"

"He really doesn't want to make any more pictures. He has writers working on a play about Picasso. And he's got a successful career now painting and sculpting."

Lieu turned the station wagon into the curved drive of Egremont School. The drive was at the bottom of the hill. The school rested atop the sloping green expanse. Steve's heart quickened.

"I missed them so much," he said.

"I know," she answered.

They had been at the top of the hill, waiting, excused from class by Lieu's careful planning. They had caught sight of him, and they were coming down the hill. They were sprinting for him.

Steve stood watching them, his heart full. He had lived with death for so many weeks. He had experienced the hopelessness of the final closing of the book on this earth. But here was his father's blood, alive in his children, young, bright-voiced, and vital, their lifetimes ahead.

He remembered what Evelyn Troup, the great child psychologist, had said to him at the time of his divorce, "If you really want to be a good father, Steve, you'll do everything you can to help your girls fulfill themselves—not your dreams, but theirs."

He bent down as the two people who were his life ran into his arms. "The principal gave us the rest of the day off," Kathleen said. "She said if we came to school this morning, we could get off this afternoon. We wanted to go with Lieu to meet the plane."

"I know how strict she is," Steve said. "I'm glad just to get the afternoon. Now, look, sweethearts, we're going to pretend this afternoon there is no picture, there are no problems. Your grandfather is safe and at peace now."

"Oh, Daddy." Lorelei started to cry.

Kathleen said, "We'll never see him again."

"Oh, yes, you will," Steve said. "You know why?" He put his finger on Kathleen's heart. "He's there, inside of you. Everything he was as a man is still alive. All his best qualities are a part of whatever good there is in us, and whatever we do that is worth something. We've got to keep him alive, and make his life count for even more."

27

Hollywood

The presence of the man filled the room. Under the overhead light high in the ceiling of the room, all of which was windowed, he circled his work in progress like a possessive mother lion. The man was leonine himself. He stood well over six feet. He had a great mane of grey hair falling back from his forehead, a Hemingwayesque moustache, and a fierce, rebellious face.

A critic had once said, "Robert Montango has the passion of a bull and the tenderness of a flower."

Robert Montango was in the final week of readying his latest sculpture for the casting furnaces.

He was dressed in his sculpting clothes. The blue sailing pants and a white silk shirt cut in a "Three Musketeers" style, which was his own design. He wore a red kerchief around his neck, which he used to wipe the sweat that poured from him when he was in the process of creation.

"A Man for All Seasons" the newspapers called him now, as he prepared for his latest sculpture exhibition. He'd already had five shows of his paintings in different places in the world, and sold on the merit of his work, as well as on his name.

He was an Academy Award winner and had made 170 films; he was instantly recognized wherever he went.

He had recently finished two years of touring in *Ulysses, the Man*, and his performance had won him new acclaim all over the country.

It had been another beginning for Montango, a rediscovery of his acting talent, a new recognition of his power on the American stage.

When he walked forward at the end of *Ulysses, the Man* for his curtain call, with the rest of the cast already gathered onstage, he walked slowly, with eyes roaming the audience, as though here and there he recognized old friends.

By the time he reached the proscenium of the stage, the audience, wherever it was, in New York City or in Youngstown, Ohio, was on its feet.

They didn't have to be told about Robert Montango. He had touched their lives, almost all of them, in one way or another. And there was something about the man that even the theatrically untutored and inexperienced discovered for themselves immediately. His audiences knew they were in the presence of a legend.

Montango looked up as his manservant-butler-drinking companion-jogging companion-mistress hiding secret letter deliverer, El Blanco, entered the room.

El Blanco had started out to be a Mexican bullfighter, but he had been gorged severely in the hip, had retired from the ring, and had fallen into heavy drinking.

Montango had found him in an old bullfighter tavern, working as a waiter. He had reinstated El Blanco's ego, and hired him as a sparring partner for a boxing picture that he was about to make.

That was twenty-five years ago. The two men had drunk together, argued together, and dreamed together. El Blanco was Robert Montango's best friend. He had grown out of subservience and "entourage-ism" to a position close to equal friendship. Montango had made him financially independent.

Montango scowled at the interruption. "Well?" he growled, with a deep, booming voice that carried both power and threat. He was not a man you disturbed easily.

El Blanco spoke respectfully. "It's Mr. Wayland. He said it would only be a minute. He also said you knew he was coming."

Montango hit his head with the sculpting tool in his hand. "Jesus, Blanco, what the fuck do you think you're doing here? You didn't even give me a schedule today. Steve called me from Chicago. I told you to write it down that he'd be here today. You know Steve Wayland would never come here without an appointment. That's not his style. But you wouldn't understand about style, would you, Blanco?" He glared at the man.

El Blanco stood his ground. "What would you like me to do, maestro?" He had a soft smile on his face.

Montango took in the smile and growled again. "All right, bring him in, you know damn well what you're supposed to do. Steve Wayland is a member of my family, you dumb son of a bitch."

El Blanco bowed to his master. It was a tongue-in-cheek performance on both sides. These men enjoyed each other.

Montango stood looking at his creation on the dais workplace next to him. He made two tiny corrections with a scalpellike instrument, then turned to greet Steve. He embraced Steve, European-style, on both sides of his face, put his massive hands on Steve's shoulders, and looked at him steadily. The two men were almost the same height.

The man who had been yelling and cursing only a few moments before was now soft-voiced and warm. "I'm sorry, Steve. No matter how you feel about your mother and father, when the time comes, it's murder. They're tied to your gut."

Steve nodded. "Something good happened, though. We talked."

Montango lit up a pipe from his table of instruments. "He loves you, doesn't he?"

Steve looked at him. No explanation was necessary for Montango's use of the present tense. It said everything about Montango and everything about Steve's father.

Steve replied quietly, "Yes, now I know. He does. And it set me free. You and I have talked so many times, I wanted to come and see you, and thank you."

Montango again embraced Steve. "Mi amigo."

Steve looked away from Montango and then to the work in progress in front of him. It was a provocative piece of bronze, intricate in design.

Montango stood back to let his friend absorb his work.

The entire sculpture flowed back from the head of a classic goddess of eternal time. Her cheekbones were high, the bridge of her nose straight, her forehead broad and finely structured. The mouth was full and sensuous. The ears slender and symmetrical.

The streamlined hair and body of Montango's goddess streamed back into a labyrinthine body that flowed into a turbulent river and then came out again in intricate coils, so that there was a circular, no-beginning-no-end feeling to the entire sculpture. The earth mother flowed into the river and into the land and back out again as the river also flowed into the earth goddess.

They were the eternal woman, the river, and the land, one.

Steve circled it twice and came back to the head. He looked at it, then to the man who had created it, and then back to the piece. Steve was stunned. "God," he said.

Montango smiled. "Are you talking to the sculpture or to me?"

Steve looked at him with open admiration. "I don't know, Robert, it's hypnotic. I think it's the best you've ever done."

Montango patted him on the back with his big hand. "I knew you would like it, amigo—after all, we don't call you the last of the romantics for nothing. This is the most romantic piece I've ever tried." He stroked the woman's head of the statue.

Steve said, "What do you call it, by the way?"

Montango smiled. "*Woman.*"

Steve looked again at the face of the woman. "I can't help it, but I feel I know that face."

Montango sipped his drink. "Of course you know that face. You've got to know that face. That face is the face of every woman you've ever slept with. That's the face of your mother, the face of your first girlfriend, and your last girlfriend, your dream woman, the woman you never find.

"That's the face that's waiting for us somewhere, in some remote heaven or hell, to take us to her breast forever and calm our fears, satisfy our lust, and kiss away our rejections.

"That's woman, son—that's the earth mother—or I've blown it for sure."

Steve saluted him with his drink. "You haven't blown it, my friend. How wonderful to be talented in so many things, maestro. You have so much passion in everything you do. That's why I've written you into my film, Robert. Maybe not you exactly—but almost. You gave me the idea for the character and you've got to play it—it's a starring part—" Steve smiled as he added the billing.

Montango stopped moving for the first time since Steve had come into his studio. He looked at Steve. The bigger-than-life theatrical figure, Robert Montango, who strode instead of walked, who towered instead of stood, who orated instead of talked, had shrunk into vulnerable human size. His eyes showed the pain of rejection and the fear of hope. "Nobody's wanted me to do a film in the last five years, amigo. You know that. I'm passé. They've shoved me out to the elephant burying grounds."

Steve nodded at Montango's bronze figure, *Woman.*

"The hell you are—there's more talent and balls, and beauty, too, right there, Robert, in what you're doing at this moment in your life than in fifty of those kids starting out on television, with that push-button kind of acting. Robert—" Steve walked up to him. "—this may be my last film—you know all about that—I talked with you about it before I left—I didn't have the story worked out—but now—with my father dying—and everything that's happened there—the story's begun to grow.

"The whole time at home was a catalyst—the past, the present, the future, all thrown together and tearing me up—but the film is coming now. And out of it have come four leading roles . . . a family. One of them I'm writing in your likeness—the kind of man who built this country—a man of tremendous energy and accomplishment—a man who can be frightening—" He looked at Montango. "—just like you frighten so many people—and still a man who can be frightened himself. I've written you into it, Robert, and my father, too.

"You're still vulnerable. That makes you able to move people. You can't refuse me," he pushed. "I need you, amigo."

28

Jordan Park
Psychiatric Center,
Jordan Park

The crowds followed Rayme to a state house for the mentally ill, the one in the country, in Jordan Park, Jordan Park Psychiatric Center. They waited outside, several hundred of them, as the word spread throughout the town that Rayme was there. He never went anywhere anymore without two ex-FBI men. He did not follow in the tradition of the rock singers, like Prince, or Cyndi Lauper, who hired towering professional wrestlers. He preferred quiet, lose-themselves-in-the-crowd FBI efficiency.

He was taken to a special room where he could look through a door into a large "activity room" of a ward of women patients. His uncle had died in a place like this. He had never seen it, but his father had told him about it. He had heard about the treatment of "human garbage."

Now, Marny was here. The Jordan Park superintendent had the door unlocked for him. The superintendent wanted to send a guard in with him but Rayme waved him back.

Rayme walked through the room slowly. He searched for Marny.

But Marny was gone. Marny's body was there. But the eyes stared emptily from her face. Her spirit had fled.

He bent down on his knees in the corner of that "waiting room" and tried to touch her. But she withdrew against the corner of the wall, trying to escape this black-haired stranger who was coming after her. And when he reached out to touch her again, she knew she was going to be attacked again, and she was glad she had sent her heart and soul away. Because now no one, not even this dark stranger, could ever harm her again. She had fooled them all. She had gone away.

Rayme withdrew his hand from her face and crouched there on his heels, crying.

This frame of bones and loosely tangled hair and defiant mouth— it looked like Marny, but this was not Marny. He had lost her forever.

Her trauma had triggered the rheumatic heart disease of her childhood. Her heart gave out. Marny died two days after Rayme saw her in the New York State Mental Hospital at Jordan Park.

29

Seaside Cemetery, Norfolk, Virginia

Rayme held the memorial service in a church Marny had loved, on a hill overlooking Norfolk River.

Rayme would not allow the usual morbid funeral services or a coffin burial. Rayme had given instructions for her to be cremated and then taken her ashes along the edge of the ocean at Norfolk River where they had walked so often, and scattered them. It was his last good-bye.

As the wind picked up Marny's ashes and carried them out across the waves, a song came together in Rayme's heart.

"You will never leave me" were the words and the name of the song he wrote that day.

Now the church on the hill overlooking Norfolk River was filled. Rayme Monterey looked out over the audience. His father and mother were there, and Marny's parents, too. One of her brothers and two of her sisters had come. Rayme had flown them in.

He was sure all her family blamed him for her death, and maybe they were right. Marny had literally given her life to be with him.

Near the back of the church Rayme saw Steve Wayland, and Lieu was there, too. He nodded slightly as he recognized face after face. All the people who had grown up with him in Norfolk River. Beer joint owners, barkeepers, waitresses, the street people he had sung for in the early years. And people who didn't know him, who simply followed him and looked up to him as a local boy who had made it in the outside world.

Skeeter Thomas and the rest of the band sat behind Rayme, behind the altar space.

Rayme spoke quietly from the altar. "Marny and I talked about funerals once, after we saw a line of black cars turning off the road ahead of us, and heading up into a stone meadow.

" 'Whichever one of us goes first,' she said, 'let's never have anything like that. I want people to remember the good times. When we laughed together, and played our music—all of us. Promise me, Rayme,' she said, 'if anything happens to me, that's what you'll do. Never put me in the ground.' "

Rayme's voice broke, but he recovered himself, " 'Keep me free. Keep me alive in the music.'

"I've only written one song since all this. I wrote it last night, when I put Marny out into the ocean, free, like she said. The best thing we can do for her, and the best way to remember her, is with the music she loved and the music she sang. But first I want to play this new one for her. I think she'd like it."

Rayme started slowly with the plaintive lyrics, "Marny, you will never leave me."

It was Rayme Monterey at his best. Simple, heartfelt lines. He sang the first two verses by himself. Then underneath the guitar, Skeeter's saxophone came in, mellow and soft, and behind Skeeter the drums and the other members of the band.

They kept it quiet, following Rayme's lead. And then after the fourth stanza, they built. There was no false mourning here. They were going to play their best for Marny.

Marny's death was celebrated with the music she loved, as she had wished. And that was the service.

Steve and Lieu waited outside until everything was over and almost all the cars had gone. The boys in the band were still there with their wives and girlfriends. Rayme left them in front of the church and walked over to the top of the hill where Steve and Lieu were waiting. Rayme came up to Steve.

"I heard about your dad. Sorry. Lieu, we all missed you. Got used to having you around."

He looked back at Steve. "You need an answer, don't you? I remember. You start in about a month, don't you?"

"Not without you, we don't," Steve said. "I'd just like to say one thing, Rayme."

Rayme half smiled. "Are you sure?" he said.

Steve went on. "I felt Marny in there. I've known her only through you, Rayme, but I believe she is a special person."

Rayme looked at him sharply, reacting to his use of the word "is" and wondering if the con was on. He had never seen any in Steve yet, but he was still waiting for it.

"I don't want to presume," Steve went on, "but I'm going to say what I believe. And that's simple. It came to me when you were singing your new song about Marny. If you make the film, for her, you can reach more people than you ever have before." Steve looked at him.

Rayme studied his face. "You'll still give me approvals of what I do in the film?"

"I know you don't quite believe me yet. Try me, Rayme."

Lieu stepped forward and kissed Rayme on the cheek. Then she and Steve turned and started down the hill to their car.

30

The Golden Door,
Escondido

own the hills and woods surrounding the Golden Door, twenty-two women neared the end of their sunrise run. They were dressed in a variety of designer exercise clothes, a rainbow of colors in the morning sun.

The women were in excellent condition. They were caught up in the physical perfection fever that had swept the country. Each of them had a pattern of exercise, nutrition, and medical and physical care. Almost all of them had their own physical instructors in their respective homes across the country.

Actresses, race syndicate owners, television commentators, a Supreme Court justice, the president of a department store, the owner of two of the largest newspapers in the country. And a woman they all admired, Magdalena Alba.

They had come not necessarily to lose weight, but to tone themselves, emotionally, mentally, as well as physically; to absorb the serenity and spiritual involvement made possible by the Golden Door staff.

These were times to refire, to replan, to redream, away from the pace and chaos of modern life. As the runners headed for the swimming pool to cool down before breakfast, one of the staff came up to Magdalena.

"Excuse me, Magdalena, there's an urgent call for you."

Magdalena's eyes brightened. "Mr. Wayland?" she asked.

The attendant shook her head. "No, a Mr. Gregson."

Magdalena's face registered a trace of disappointment. "Do I have time to return the call before breakfast? I know how you are about our schedules. I don't want any demerits."

The attendant laughed. "Breakfast in fifteen minutes. You have until then."

Magdalena smiled and said, "All right, thank you."

She checked herself into the Golden Door at least once a year. If there was any place in the world where she could restore herself and fight any disease, she thought defiantly, *any* disease, it was here. It was like a home to her.

She took the phone in her room as she toweled off. Her face was flushed with the early run in the morning sun. Her blue-green eyes shone with health. She glanced at herself in the mirror. She *couldn't* be sick. There was no reason to see that doctor in Los Angeles. Not when she felt this good.

There were violets in her room now. They had been there when she arrived. Clearly, the man cared about her; she had felt that even when he left Paris. She looked forward to his calls; he was phoning her almost every night. Now, when she would see him again on the night of the Academy Awards, after she left the Golden Door, she would be at her absolute best. A new picture, perhaps a new love, surely, at least, time with a special man. It was good to be alive.

Jack Gregson answered the call back immediately.

"Hello, Jack," Magdalena said. "How nice of you to call."

"How are you feeling?" Jack asked.

"Never felt better," she said.

"You always did love that place," Jack replied.

"More than ever," Magdalena spoke up, sipping the orange juice that had been left at her bedside. "It's the only way to prepare for a picture—for me, anyway. It clears out all the cobwebs—takes away all the pressures."

"That's what I want to talk to you about," Gregson said. "I'd really like to come down this weekend. You can have visitors on Sunday, right?"

"Yes, I can," Magdalena answered, "but I really have made a rule for myself this time. I'm here for a month to get ready for my next film. I'm not seeing anyone, and I'm keeping to my usual daily schedule on Sunday."

"You're not seeing Steve Wayland?" Jack Gregson asked.

"No. I don't want to see anyone."

"I have something to ask you," Gregson said. "I've bought a great new book, I think you're going to love it. A terrific woman's story—

with a double part—twin sisters—only a great actress could pull it off. It's called *Victoria*. I want to talk to you about it."

"I'll be glad to discuss it when I get back, Jack. Sounds interesting."

"Can I send you the book?" Gregson asked.

"No, thank you, not here. I want my mind absolutely clear."

"Have you been given a script of *The Rest of Our Lives?*"

"No. I have a very beautiful script book to hold what he's writing now, Steve tells me. It's a story of today, and my part is different from anything I've ever played. It sounds very exciting to me."

Gregson's voice was edged with sarcasm. "*Sounds* is right. There's nothing finished. The few pages I've seen are changing all the time."

Magdalena was instantly on the alert. "*The Rest of Our Lives* is being made at your studio, isn't it, Jack? You don't sound like it."

"I'm only making this picture because we have a signed obligation with Wayland, and the deal was put together before I came to the studio. I wouldn't sign that man to make a motion picture if it was the last thing I did."

Magdalena spoke quietly. "He's a better director than anyone you've got, Jack. I ran all his films that I hadn't seen before I left Paris. Two of them were shown on the boat coming over here, at my request. His work with his actors is incredibly good. Simple, true. Don't you agree with me?"

"No," Gregson answered, "I don't. And frankly, I don't give a damn. His pictures don't gross."

"But they don't lose, either," Magdalena said. "Every picture he's made is good for our profession in general. Every one of them has been a relationship story about real people in the real world. We need films like that."

"Not me," Gregson answered. "Have you signed with him yet?"

"No," Magdalena said, "I haven't. I wrote him a note telling him that I would give him my decision when I see him at the Academy Awards."

"Well, that's good, that's very good. I want you to do *Victoria* instead. I'll give you twice as much money as Wayland can afford to pay you. The budget of his picture is six million dollars—the budget of *Victoria* will be sixteen million."

"That doesn't necessarily mean it will be a better film, Jack," Magdalena said.

"Will you do this, then, Magdalena? Will you promise to read *Victoria* before you give Wayland a definite answer?"

"Yes, I'll be glad to do that, Jack. But I'm warning you in all fairness, I've almost definitely decided to do Steve Wayland's film."

"Even before the script's finished? Magdalena, I've known you for seven or eight years. I've never seen an actress so demanding about a script. You don't know anything really about the part he's creating for you in *The Rest of Our Lives*. It's not you at all. It deliberately takes away your glamour, minimizes your looks, lessens every appeal you've got as one of the most desirable women in the world. It reduces you, Magdalena—all the things you've fought for when anyone's worked with you—the makeup tests, the hair tests, the clothes tests, everything perfect—in Wayland's picture, this all goes by the boards. It's not you at all."

"I'll make my own judgments about that when I have his script," Magdalena answered. "I believe in Steve Wayland, and I have a hunch that *The Rest of Our Lives* is going to be a new and rare experience for me. I don't want to repeat myself anymore."

"You won't with *Victoria*. Just read the book. It's one of the most demanding parts ever written for motion pictures. Two completely different complex characterizations."

"Jack, I'm sorry. I have to go now. We're on a regular army schedule down here, you know. No exceptions."

"Magdalena," Jack asked, "can I see you when you come here? I'd like to take you to dinner. I've always had a special feeling for you. You know that, don't you?"

"Yes," Magdalena smiled, "that *has* gotten through to me. That's one of your most memorable qualities, Jack. You never try to be subtle. Call me when I get back to town."

Jack Gregson hung up the phone and flipped a switch on his intercom. "Jerry," he said into it, "she hasn't signed with Wayland. Send *Victoria* down to her at the Golden Door. She didn't ask for it but she won't send it back. And if it's there staring her in the face, she'll probably read it. She can't resist reading anything that would be a starring role for her.

"If we get her into *Victoria*, she won't do *The Rest of Our Lives*. And that should be the end of Steve Wayland.

"But I want to cover every base. I've found out quite a few facts about the district attorney, Mahoney, who called for the grand jury investigation of Rayme Monterey in the first place. He's a political animal, like most of them. He can be maneuvered, not with money, but with political support. I want our boys in New York to do a complete research job on him. His whole life, his friends, his political campaigners, his entourage. I want to know every weak spot he has.

"If he doesn't get another grand jury indictment on Rayme Monterey, after all the publicity he's put out, he's going to lose some vital political points.

"We're going to back him up. We're going to hound him and push him. The day a second grand jury investigation is called for in the Rayme Monterey case, and he's arrested again, we can close the book on Steve Wayland for good."

Magdalena had finished her night massage and was ready for bed when a member of the staff delivered *Victoria* to her. It had come by special messenger. Accompanying it were three dozen roses. She gave the box of roses back to the attendant. "Use these for the dining room, will you, Helen?"

Helen took the long box. "But they're so beautiful! Don't you want them here?"

Magdalena glanced at the cluster of violets on her coffee table. She nodded at the violets. "No, I have what I want. Let everyone else enjoy the roses."

She closed the door and unwrapped the book. She laughed and shook her head, and put it down on the coffee table next to the script binder marked *The Rest of Our Lives*.

She was tired and yet relaxed from the day's exercise, swimming, and massage. She wondered where Steve was and what he was doing. She had written him about his father. She hardly knew the man and yet she felt somehow close to him. She wanted to learn what he was really like, who he was.

Her thoughts went back to when she had first arrived on the outskirts of Madrid, after running away from home. She was thirteen. She had no money. Her father had been the only one who had ever taken care of her. And then he had vanished. When he had been killed, he left no one and nothing for her.

She had been arrested for vagrancy after three days without food, sleeping in the park. Her dress was filthy, her hair matted, her face streaked with dirt. She was exhausted.

The police had taken her to the station. That was the first time she saw the judge.

The judge couldn't believe his good fortune. He could see the girl's figure under the soiled blue dress. The soft curve of her hips and her slender, shapely legs were clearly visible. He was an expert at devising his own justice. The law was simply a puppet, and he was the puppeteer.

He was in his late sixties, a tall, powerfully built man with shining black hair and noisy false teeth. He lived well in the country, in a house provided by the government. He and his quiet, forlorn wife lived with their two servants in a handsome Spanish house.

The judge sentenced Magdalena Alba to a year in the county jail, but commuted her sentence immediately to a year's probation under his own protection. She was assigned to work with the other two servants in his household and to a routine of exhausting chores. When the local police officials drove her to his home, he was waiting for her. He asked his housekeeper to have her report to him later, when she had been shown her quarters and had had a chance to clean up.

The judge kept a workshop in a small building in the back of his home where he also had a developing lab for his own photography. It was in this cottage back of the main house that he first talked to Magdalena alone.

The housekeeper had given the new girl one of her own dresses, which was several sizes too big. She wore no stockings, but her face and hair were now clean. The judge walked in a circle around her. It was impossible to disguise her figure, even with such a full dress.

The judge asked her, "Have you ever done any modeling?"

Magdalena shook her head.

The judge nodded toward his studio. "You know you're going to have to pay your way here. I've tried to do a generous thing and to save you from jail. But you have to work like all the rest of us. Come here for a moment."

He led her into the photographic studio. He darkened the lights and hit one of the small spotlights that shone down on the center of the room. He took her to the circle of light.

"Now, just stand there," he said, "and let me see if you can pose. I hope you can learn quickly. Slip off the dress."

She turned and looked at him sharply.

"All photographic modeling is basically nude," he said. "You know that. It's just like an artist painting a picture." He peered into his camera and adjusted it. "I'm going to make some tests," he said, "to give me an idea whether you might be any good, with some teaching and experience. You know, some people make a lot of money at this. Go on, get the dress off. What are you waiting for?"

He walked up to her and looked at her. She looked directly back at him. Then, with one swipe of his arm, he ripped the front of the dress and let it drop to the floor, completely exposing her. She didn't try to cover herself. A look of hatred came over her face.

Her voice was hard. "You're not going to give me a chance, are you?"

He answered, "I'm going to give you every chance, Magdalena, to get along in this life. We all have to do what we have to do. I make sacrifices here in order to uphold the law."

He walked up to her again and took her by the chin.

"Now, get something straight. When I ask you something—you don't question me, you do it. When I said take your dress off, I meant just that. Now, I'm going to take some pictures of you and I want you to assume some different poses for me."

She said, "I don't know what you mean."

He said, "I want you to pose for me. Different positions. Exactly as if you were making love."

Her voice was fearless. "I've never made love."

He saw she was telling the truth. His heart beat faster. You don't get many virgins at my age, he thought.

She asked him, "What do you do with them—sell the pictures for as much as you can get for them?"

He smiled. "You're going to make me a rich man!"

That same night when the judge and his wife were asleep, Magdalena stole away from the house. She avoided the police and went into the ghetto where poor cafés didn't ask questions of dishwashers who worked cheap enough. She would save every peseta she earned until she had enough for a tourist ticket to Paris. Paris would save her.

Paris was the magic city of her childhood. She had spent three winters there with her father at the consulate, and the memories were gay and romantic. She hadn't been born to be victimized. Paris became the hope she lived with . . . that hope was her survival.

When she finally boarded her plane for France, she had the equivalent of forty-seven dollars in pesetas, one suitcase, a promise to herself to return to the land where she had been born, someday, and reclaim her rightful birthright. "La Bastarda" would be back.

In Paris, Magdalena started as a waitress in the bar-coffee shop of the Plaza Athénee. She and her father had stayed there many times, when they were not in residence at the consulate. She remembered the bar-coffee shop having attractive young women as waitresses, catering to the wealthy of the world who stayed at the Plaza Athénée.

She had begun to speak French fluently again, with a perfect accent that she had learned as a child. She was to the Parisian manner born. In her tight and well-designed waitress costume, with her long, silk-stockinged legs exposed, Magdalena had one goal—to survive and to be independent. She never wanted to depend on anyone again—most particularly, a man. She was determined to take her place in the world and to live as her father had lived, luxuriously, elegantly, bowing down to no one. She drove herself relentlessly.

She worked five regular days and two overtime days a week at the Plaza Athénée bar-coffee shop. At night she studied to be an actress. She knew that her beauty was exceptional. She studied how to care for it. She studied how to walk, how to talk. How to develop her presence onstage or before a camera. She studied technique and style. She saved her money and saw every play and every film. She became fanatical, tireless, determined to make it, and quickly.

Magdalena went through three years of drudgery—working, lessons, exercises, casting calls, insults, propositions, rejections. She was determined to succeed without sleeping with a man. And she did.

She learned to go out with men, to lead them to a point, to appear to be gullible and then see what she could negotiate. She much preferred to be a friend to a man than to be his lover.

When she was nineteen she saw her chance. François Truffaut was making a film. There were a number of small parts, but each had an individuality. One role was for a young girl just about her own age who killed herself when her teenage lover deserted her after she became pregnant.

Magdalena went after that role.

When she went to see Truffaut, she was the thirty-fifth actress interviewed; she asked to read the scene cold. That was the end of the interviewing. She *was* the girl in Truffaut's story.

When the film premiered in Paris, none of her part had been cut. And with it was born a new actress "of tragic innocence," "of beauty and depth," "of emotional power," and "a woman of animal magnetism and unbelievable beauty." The reaction was the same all through Europe. It was a beginning.

Next came a costarring part in a Gaumont picture as the sister of Isabelle Adjani. Then a film in Munich for Wolfgang Peterson, the director of *Das Boot*, costarring Jurgen Prochnow. Together they were said to be the most interesting, sexually provocative team on the screen since Ingrid Bergman and Humphrey Bogart.

Magdalena was her own agent. She had a shrewd business sense. What she didn't know, she learned. She picked her own films. Magdalena had studied the great women movie stars of history. She had learned her lessons well. She made her public appearances rare and special. She was never seen unless she was exquisitely dressed, whether it was for the opera, a society ball, or buying toothpaste in a drugstore. She was always the "star." Her name became synonymous with glamour, elegance, style, and mystery.

No one knew where she had come from. No one knew how old she was. No one knew what her racial delineations were, since she spoke several languages well. Her friends were as rare as her appearances.

She had become a legend.

Helen came in with her bedtime tea and "vegetable cake." How did the chef make something that tasted so good and had only nine calories? She laughed with Helen about that.

"This wire came for you, Magdalena," Helen said as she handed her a telegram. "Good night."

"Good night, Helen, and thank you." She put the tray aside and opened the telegram.

> LEAVING NEW YORK FOR LAS VEGAS. I'LL CALL YOU FROM THERE. EAGERLY LOOKING FORWARD TO SEEING YOU. THE SCRIPT IS COMING FAST NOW. CAN'T WAIT TO DISCUSS IT WITH YOU. STEVE.

Magdalena held the wire for a moment, then pulled out the drawer of the bedside table. There was a small stack of cards and wires there, all from Steve. She turned out the lights.

She hadn't glanced at *Victoria*. She already knew, for better or worse, that she would make her next film with Steve Wayland.

31

Las Vegas

A movie screen–sized poster showed Las Vegas as one small island in the middle of the ocean. In large red letters, at the top of the island, it read, "Welcome to Hedonists." In the picture, the little island was peopled with faces— gamblers, hookers, tourists, high rollers, all wearing big smiles.

The "desperates" who also filled Las Vegas weren't pictured on the poster.

Steve glanced at the poster as he walked by, repelled and fascinated by the fact that it pulled your attention—in the noisy, slot-machine din of the airport, you couldn't get away from the sign.

The taxi driver gave Steve a curious look when he heard where he wanted to go—Paradise Ranch. It was almost midnight and the lights of the strip blazed a few blocks away. Barbara Carr had called in the name and address, after she checked out everyone at the crap table the night that La Tigressa had disappeared. Barbara had remembered the name of the exquisite older woman, Eleanor Mitchell.

"How long will it take us to get there?" Steve asked.

The cab driver answered with a bored grunt. "About forty minutes. It's going to cost you fifty bucks. Okay, buddy?"

"Okay," Steve said.

Paradise Ranch looked like a replica of the Ewing spread on *Dallas*. There was a large white Colonial-style house at the end of a tree-lined drive. Surrounding the main building were cottages serving the main house.

Everywhere there were trees imported and planted in the dry Las Vegas earth. There were uniformly dressed "ranch hands," all in white pants, white shirts, and blue neckerchiefs emblazoned with the words "Paradise Ranch."

A tall Japanese man in a tuxedo answered the front door. "Your name, sir?" he asked Steve politely.

"Wayland."

The Japanese man pulled a printed list from his pocket, and found Steve's name. "Oh, yes, Mr. Wayland," he said, as he stepped aside for Steve to walk into a two-story hallway with a graceful winding staircase.

"Mrs. Mitchell will be here to see you." He led Steve to a study filled with French antiques, expensive paintings, and thick carpet. "What can I get you to drink?" the Japanese man asked.

"Scotch, please."

The Japanese man went to a small bar at one corner of the study. "Chivas Regal?" he asked, as he took a bottle in his hand.

"That'll be fine," Steve answered. He looked around the study further. The bookcase held books that looked well read.

A tall, handsome woman in her fifties came into the room. She had a slim and elegant figure, her hair was swept up, and she wore a Bill Blass gown of soft pink. Steve turned and the two looked at each other for a moment. The woman put out her hand. "I'm Eleanor Mitchell."

Steve remembered what *Time* magazine had said. "The lady owner of the Paradise Ranch," Steve said softly.

Eleanor Mitchell smiled. She could have taken a place in any society group in the world. Steve noticed the necklace, the bracelet, and the one large diamond ring. He could tell they were real.

"I never believed what one story in *Time* magazine could do. From unknown to very known in one week," Eleanor Mitchell smiled.

"You surpass what the *Time* correspondent wrote," Steve said.

Eleanor smiled and dismissed the Japanese man with a quiet nod of her head. "You surpass your reviews, Mr. Wayland," she said. "May I call you Steve? Please call me Eleanor. Mrs. Mitchell makes me sound so—" She dragged the "o" out. "—so ooold!"

Steve said, "I don't think anything could make you seem old, Eleanor."

She sat down, and beckoned to the chair opposite her. Steve complied, nursing his scotch. "I feel like I may not be in the right place," he said.

Eleanor gestured to encompass the entire surroundings. "I learned this from the movies, Steve. There's a beautiful old line from before your time—I've forgotten who wrote it—it was an answer to a critic saying that 'Movies should be more like life.' The response was, 'Life should be more like the movies.' That was in the back of my mind when I built the Paradise Ranch."

Steve asked, "This *is* a working ranch, isn't it?"

Eleanor laughed lightly. "It certainly is. Hard work. We have to make money to survive. We make a great deal. Because—" She paused, and looked at Steve thoughtfully. "—we are ready to please every taste, no matter how extravagant, how bizarre, or decadent. I believe that everything has a price, Steve, and there is a price for everything here— a large price. But I don't believe you're here for any of the usual reasons."

"I need your help, Eleanor. I'm looking for a girl—a girl I want to put into a motion picture. It's very important to me. One of my staff believes she's here. She's probably in terrible shape. No one has seen her for five weeks."

"There are over four hundred girls here—and we have a constant turnover. I don't get to know them all or even see them all. Could you describe her? She could be here under an assumed name, of course."

Steve nodded. "I'm sure she is. She doesn't want to get found— maybe she doesn't want to live—"

"She sounds like she could be trouble for us. I don't like depressive suicidals here, and there are many of them in this work," Eleanor said.

"I'm not even sure that photographs would tell the story. Is there some way I could see the girls without them seeing me?" Steve asked.

"You're asking me to do something I never do. But as I said, every- thing has its price," Eleanor added.

"Are you a gambler?"

Eleanor nodded. "All my life."

"Twenty-five thousand dollars for you, if I find the girl; five thou- sand, if I don't," Steve said.

"All right. But, as you might expect, many of the girls are busy. Our peak time is just beginning, so it may take you twenty-four hours to see them all. And I won't charge extra for the entertainment. You can choose what you want to, Steve. One, two, three, a group, what- ever appeals to you. That comes with our bet—and you'll eat with me in my private dining room. I have my own chef I brought from Paris. He's very good and well prepared for almost every delicacy." Eleanor stood up and motioned to Steve to come with her. "Let's begin with the Monitoring Room."

The Monitoring Room looked like an electronic control center for a plant of some size. There were thirty television screens lined up in rows of ten each. There was a security man, dressed in the Paradise Ranch white, seated at the control panels.

Eleanor nodded at him. "Hello, Ben," she said. "For the next twenty-four hours, Steve here can make any request he wants. We're looking for someone."

Ben nodded. He was a serious-faced young man, two years out of Cal Tech Engineering School. This electronic room was his pride and joy. All thirty screens were lit up. There were dining rooms on the screens, dance floors, individual bedrooms, a living room where an orgy between ten different couples was taking place, a movie set for pornographic movies featuring stars of the porno world.

The total effect was unbelievable. One of the most advanced communications systems man had yet invented was here to serve the very strange sexual appetites of men and women. Steve had never seen such a centralized mass of erotica—live, most of it. In the individual rooms, all lavishly furnished, the coupling of pair after pair seemed ludicrous. Even with the subdued sound in this electronic room, the whispers, the sighs, the groans, the groveling of paid sexual intercourse seemed sad. Steve's eyes darted over the various sets, trying to study the girls' faces. Eleanor watched him, puzzled. Steve turned to look at her. He shook his head.

"Let's go to the Assembly Room," Eleanor suggested. "There should be at least two hundred of my girls there."

The Assembly Room was a large, rectangular room, half filled by a glass-encased kind of living room. The "living room" was two stories tall, and the glass encasement ran from the ceiling to the floor. Outside the glass, looking in, was a collection of men and women from all walks of life. The only thing they had in common was money.

Behind the glass were more than two hundred and fifty women, from eighteen to forty years old. They were sitting in groups, in a handsomely furnished room. A Bobby Short imitator played the piano at one edge of the glass-encased area: "It Was Just One of Those Things."

Immediately it became apparent that from the outside you could look in through the glass, but from the inside you could not look out. So, the two hundred and fifty women inside the glass cage of the Assembly Room were *living* there for a period of hours. There was food and drink, music of old standards and new rock numbers, a small dance floor where some of the girls danced with each other, and even several card tables where some of the girls played checkers and chess and backgammon.

There was every type of woman, from every race. White, black, brown, yellow, mixed breed. The only common denominator was that all the girls were immaculately groomed and dressed in evening gowns of different styles—and evening gowns were the only thing they wore. Many of the dresses were chiffon, transparent, gauzy, lace-patterned; all of them were elegant.

All of the girls were pretty, or striking, and had sexually provocative figures.

The "cage" took Steve's breath away. He glanced at the faces in the crowd, outside, looking in. Some of them were pressed up against the glass. The lighting was perfect, inside and out. It was soft, sexual, and illusory. Close to the glass, looking from the outside in, there was a gauzelike effect, like a silk screen in front of a camera, erasing lines, covering bitterness, softening hardness.

The girls knew, of course, that a sea of people was out there watching them, and that anyone who paid the price from that crowd, man or woman, could buy them, singly or in groups. Every girl wore a bracelet with a cutout of the Paradise Ranch main house, and inside that cutout, in large but delicately carved gold plate, was a number. This was the only identification mark on each woman.

Steve watched in fascination as a well-dressed man with a face ravaged with alcohol and dissipation went to one of the Paradise Ranch attendants at the back of the cage. The man whispered a number to the attendant, the attendant took a microphone, which obviously was connected to the inside of the cage, and called out the number thirty-one.

A striking redhaired girl in a pale green chiffon evening gown, cut low in the middle to reveal half of her full breasts, moved toward the door. Steve watched as the attendant unlocked the back door of the cage for her. She moved like a dancer, and her body undulated perfectly. Her red hair was swept up; her aristocratic face, refined bone structure, shone in the light. Her lips were half parted, her eyes flashing with excitement. Too much excitement. Steve recognized the special light of a drug addict.

He watched her meet the man who had picked her through the glass, put her arm in his, and go out the back of the full Assembly Room. It was like a shocking parody of a cotillion ball, restaged in Dante's *Inferno*.

The other girls in the "cage" stepped up their provocative activities.

Some made suggestive gestures to the glass they couldn't see through. Some who were seated pulled their dresses up, past their garter belts, almost to their waists. Some of the girls dancing alone began to do exhibitionist dancing, directly toward their unseen audience.

Eleanor spoke softly to Steve. "Not here?"

Steve shook his head.

"There's a whole new shift coming in in four minutes. That's why you see all the action. This is their last chance tonight."

Steve repeated her words under his breath. "Their last chance."

The shift change was on, and the attention of the onlookers heightened. There were over two hundred new women coming in, in groups or in pairs, as the other women left. It was like an after-dinner group at a big party, where the men go to one section for cigars and brandy, and the women to the other section for stories and gossip.

Steve watched the new girls intently. His attention wavered for a moment when a man shoved through the crowd outside the cage, pushing a wheelchair in front of him. In the wheelchair was an older man with no legs. He couldn't stand up. His friend lifted him right out of the wheelchair and held him so that he could get a clear view of the girls. He was making his selection. Steve was riveted by this exchange.

Then, as he turned back to the cage, he saw her.

La Tigressa came in by herself. Edna St. Vincent Millay's poem on the burning candle and "Oh, what a lovely light," passed through Steve's mind. Only weeks before, he had seen this girl in the glow of perfect health, disciplined art, and ambitious professionalism. They had not guessed then how "lost" she was. She was dressed in white satin, skin tight, floor length. Her hair was pulled back and tied with a white satin ribbon. She was burned dark by the Las Vegas sun, even her legs which flashed through the hip-length slit sides of her dress. She wore no makeup except her startling red lipstick, which was painted on like a slash across her dark face. Her black eyes seemed even bigger, dramatically dark against the background of the white dress.

At first, Steve thought she was ill; she appeared feverish. He had never seen her that way before. Her look was unusually bright, but didn't seem to fix on anything; rather, it seemed to burn inward, to some hidden world in which all earthly problems had faded away. Around her wrist hung her number, seven.

Eleanor watched Steve as his gaze followed La Tigressa, who instinctively went to the piano. The piano player had been replaced, too. Now there was a pianist, a guitarist, and a drummer. They began to pound out a Huey Buis song. They nodded at La Tigressa and she began to undulate slowly, picking up the tempo of the beat.

Her mind was back in yesterday. The body moved and jerked in the style of the Raggedy Ann act she had created many years ago. She pulled her dress up to move more easily. As she twirled around and hit the accent points of the tune in her own frenetic style, her dress swirled around her, and her breasts looked as though they would burst out of the narrow satin top.

She looked startlingly young, as if she were attending a debutante dance that had suddenly gone berserk.

Eleanor followed Steve's look. "The stripper?" she asked.

At almost that moment, La Tigressa unzipped the side of her dress and let her breasts move out, exposed. A murmur swept through the people outside the glass.

"She hasn't been here long. I saw her in Monte Carlo and invited her to come and see me. She never says anything to anyone about who she is or what she was before. Who is she?"

"How long has she been here?" Steve asked.

"Oh, six or seven weeks, I think," Eleanor answered. "She's in a group that brings the highest money, but she's always broke."

"Big habit?"

Eleanor nodded. "Never wants to come down . . . You want *her* for your picture?" she asked Steve incredulously.

"That's right." There was a line forming near the attendant who called out the numbers. He heard the first one ask for number seven.

Steve moved quickly toward the attendant. He turned to Eleanor. "You just won twenty-five thousand dollars."

Eleanor turned to the men lined up. The attendant said, "They all want number seven."

Eleanor smiled. "Later, gentlemen. Number seven's taken for the evening." She nodded to the attendant, who called out the number. La Tigressa just went on dancing. The attendant went into the cage and took her by the arm. She followed him like a child being led by a nurse. As the attendant brought her out of the cage, she looked at Eleanor and then at Steve. No flash of recognition came across her face when she saw him. She simply slipped her arm through Steve's and led him toward the back entrance.

Tigressa guided Steve to her cottage. Each of the thousand-dollar-a-night girls had her own place. It was small and tastefully decorated, and supplied with food and drink. Steve followed her to a large bathroom with a sunken Jaccuzzi tub. She didn't even look at him, but turned on the tub, placing towels by the side of it, and then she slipped off her dress.

She looked up at Steve. "Here?" She nodded at the tub. "Or do you want to fuck right away?" She had slipped her dress off so quickly that Steve couldn't stop her.

He bent down and shut off the tub. He looked at her.

"Mary Jane?" he said.

She looked at him with burning but strangely dead eyes. "My name's Lily—I'm number seven—that's what you called for, isn't it? Number seven?"

He nodded his head.

"Whatever you want to do, you tell me—if you want another girl to join us, I'll get her. Or another couple, whatever you want. You paid for all night. It's my job to satisfy you," she said.

"Put your dress back on," he told her.

She did what he said without any question, zipping it up the back.

"I want to talk to you, that's what I want," Steve said.

La Tigressa shrugged. "Whatever you say. I don't talk much, but I can listen." She led the way into the bedroom and opened a bar that fit into one wall. "Drink?" she asked. He shook his head. "You want a joint?" She took a box of cigarettes from the bar and offered them to him. He shook his head again. "Some coke? This is pretty good stuff—" She offered him a small bowl of fine white powder. He shook his head.

She smiled. "Oh, you're a free-baser, huh? Me, too." Now she took a small lighting apparatus from a drawer in the bar and started the free-basing process. She moved surely and accurately, placing the apparatus on the table beside the bed. "This is better than fucking, anytime. You want a heavy shot? That's what I do—it takes me through the night."

Steve's foot smashed into the bedside table, kicking it over, smashing the apparatus and putting out the flame of the cocaine mixture. He bent down beside the bed and took hold of La Tigressa's shoulders.

"Mary Jane! Mary Jane! This is Steve Wayland. I have a contract with you for a movie. I came to Rome to see you. Remember?"

Her voice came out of her fogged mind, vague, afraid. "I don't remember. I only know Lily—number seven—"

Steve went to the only closet in the bedroom and pulled it open. There were a few dresses hanging there, and one suitcase. He put the suitcase on the bed and piled the dresses into it, pulled the dresser open, and threw the lingerie and the stockings into it. La Tigressa watched him with no particular expression. Steve pulled the last dress, a white cotton daytime dress, out of the closet.

"Put this on," he told her.

"Never wear that in the cage."

Steve leaned down toward her again, and put his hand under her chin, tilting her face upward. "You're never going back in the cage, goddamn it. I picked you for my picture and you're going to play in it."

"I need some pills. I'm coming down like a roller coaster."

Steve pulled her up and zipped off her white satin evening gown. He pulled the cotton dress over her and zipped it up the back. Then he brushed her hair back from her forehead.

"You're going to do what I tell you, when I tell you. I don't believe that you don't recognize me. I don't believe you don't remember. The hiding out is over, Mary Jane. You're through at the Paradise Ranch, you're through in Las Vegas. I just bought you."

Tigressa began to shake. Her eyes dilated wildly. Her voice was hysterical. "Get me something quick—I'm falling!" She screamed, and ran for the bar.

Steve reached out, pulled her back, and snapped her around, facing him. He put his arms around her and held her hard. He pressed her head against the wall, until it was rigid.

Steve spoke to her in a low voice, as if to a sleepy child. "Mary Jane—hear me—please hear me—I know what happened. I know what Bobby Slater did to you. But you're going to get over it—you're going to forget all this—it's just been a bad dream—because you cared too much—you're going to get well and you're going to have help—"

La Tigressa was crying. She kept repeating over and over again through Steve's conversation, "Don't leave me, please don't leave me—please don't leave me. Charlie—" she called out to the past "—Charlie—hold me—please, please, don't, Daddy. Oh, my God, I'm falling, oh—oh—"

Steve held on to her tight. "You're going to come down, and I'll be there with you—you'll never be alone . . . and you'll get off the roller coaster for good."

La Tigressa sank into his arms, clinging on to him in her nightmare.

32

Los Angeles

t was a bare room, stripped of everything but two beds. Steve watched her coming out of a sleep that was even more harrowing than wakefulness. There were black rings of fatigue around her eyes now. Her body moved with great slowness, as though there were heavy weights pressing down on her. Her eyes opened and took time to focus.

Steve spoke softly, "Mary Jane?"

She turned to look at him. Her dry, crusted tongue moved slowly across her parched lips. "Got to have something—"

"There's nothing here. The doors are locked; the windows. There's nothing here but you and me."

She looked at him suspiciously as she ran her hands across her face and down across her body. Her eyes flashed suddenly with desperation. "Get me some coke," she said. "You've got the connections. I need it fast. I'll do anything you want."

"What I want you to do is to trust me. You've been coming down for over a week. You've never left this room. Neither have I."

She looked at him incredulously. "Well, where are we?"

"A place where they don't talk," Steve said. "The best treatment facility in the country—and they let me stay here with you like I told you I'd do."

"We've been here for a week?" she said. "I don't remember."

He spoke reassuringly. "I don't want you to remember, I want you to look ahead. You're one of the stars of my motion picture *The Rest of Our Lives*. Do you remember that?"

La Tigressa strained her eyes. "I've got to have something," she muttered. "I feel like I'm dying—I only wish I could."

He offered her some fruit juice, as he'd been instructed to do. The treatment staff had explained that an addict in withdrawal had great need for sugar, that the plummeting blood sugar levels were partly responsible for the tremendous feelings of rage and desperation. Only partly, though. Steve had been given a crash course in the disease of drug addiction, had been taught the right words to use, the right actions to take, but, most important, that a drug addict was the ultimate con artist, and that self-pity was the ultimate con.

"You're going to have those feelings. It's okay. We'll just sweat them out."

She grabbed the juice and threw it at him. "We? What the hell do you know about it?"

"We've all got our pain, Mary Jane. No one escapes."

She fired back at him, "Oh, yes, I can. You get me some of my escape powder and I'll show you how to take on all the troubles in this fucking world, and float above them. None of it really matters, anyway. Nothing's real."

Steve reached across and shook her. "Let me show you something," he said.

He pulled her up to the washbasin in the room and forced her head to face the mirror on the wall. She looked at the reflection of herself, tired, haggard, her burned-out face ravaged by opium and free-base.

"You're a beautiful woman and look at what you've done to yourself. Is that really you staring at yourself? Is that a face that's floating above it all, with no fear, with the feeling you can do anything in the world? The queen? Is that the face of a queen?"

His face moved behind hers in the mirror, and his fingers traced across the shadows of the eyes, the pouches under the eyes, the dry tissue, the pinched neck.

"I'll tell you what that is. The face of a human being who's killing herself—the face of an addict—"

She screamed, "There's nothing for me in this fucking world, so I get high! You're right. I'm a lousy, good-for-nothing junkie. That's what it's come to. I don't care. I just want to die."

Steve countered, "You don't have to live like this, Mary Jane. Ever again. You have a disease, drug addiction's a disease, and you're sick with it, just as if you had cancer, Mary Jane, except that there's a way for you to get better and stay better. It's going to take work, you'll have to get to know yourself and work on yourself, but it's not your fault, do you hear me? It's not your fault that you're sick, but it's your responsibility to get well. And first, we have to get the drugs out of your system."

La Tigressa pounded him with her fists. She screamed, "I don't want to work on myself, you son of a bitch. Don't you get it? I'm going to die if I don't get some drugs. Get me something, get me something, get me something! Now, now, now—"

He fought her clear across the room. In her hysteria she had a special strength.

She railed at him, and then she backed up against the wall and yelled with all her might, "Help! Help me! I'm being attacked! I'm being raped. I'm being raped! Rape!"

Steve looked at her. "Go on yelling till your voice wears out. No one will come. The people here know what's going on. It's all over. You're not going to get anything to blow you out again. You're not going to get anything here—but caring—and then you're going to walk out of here with me and go to work. We've got a long way to go, and we've got to do it fast. We've got to get your looks back, your health back, your skill back, everything." He walked across the room toward her.

She reached out to smash his face again, and he caught her wrists in both his hands.

"Mary Jane." He put his arm over her screaming mouth. "*You are cared about. You matter.* Not just to me, but to Tucheki, Barbara, Spartan, Lieu, all of us. You're not alone. You need to let us love you back to sanity, Mary Jane. Till you can love yourself.

"Now we need to get your strength up. We're going to get some food in here, and you'll have a bath. But don't try anything. They've seen all the tricks here, and they know you're a liar and a schemer. Drug addicts don't know what the truth is anymore. This is a special place, Mary Jane. Most of the staff here have been in your shoes. They were addicts, too, but they're clean."

She jerked away from him, putting her hands on her ears, trying to shut out his voice. Then, as Steve started to speak again, she spit at him full in the face. He pinned her to the wall.

"You can't get rid of me," he said. "You're stuck with me."

33

The Greek Theatre,
Los Angeles

"Ladies and gentlemen, Mr. Rayme Monterey," the voice came over the speakers.

Rayme was alone out there, the way he had started years ago, singing for dinner in the neighborhood pool saloon at Asbury Park. He was alone the way he had been before Marny. He and Steve had finally agreed. They needed this test, for him, for his fans, for the press, and for *The Rest of Our Lives*. No one could predict the way he would be received. And Rayme himself didn't know if he could perform as he had before. They would all find out tonight.

The last months had honed the man. Rayme hadn't known it then, but he had never truly fulfilled himself before. He had idolized Presley too much, and Dylan, and some of the others. He had never been quite an original. Now the tragedy of the subway, the grand jury hearing, and, most of all, Marny's death in the asylum had stripped him bare.

He stood there for a moment on the edge of the Greek Theatre in Los Angeles, at this special performance in the old amphitheater where he had had a great success years before. Rayme felt a new strength flow into him.

Life was one lonely, sad experience where you had to expect tragedy. Where dreams didn't come true, where reality blasted illusion. You simply had to rock back on your heels and go for it. Just for the pure momentary joy and the need to throw out there what you had inside of you. He had to go for it, whatever he felt. He had to share his feelings.

A great roar rose from the crowd, as though it had one voice. The huge reverberating cry: "We—love—you," again and again.

That really struck home, because Rayme, in happier days, with Marny at his side, would always stroll out onto the stage, face his audience, and demand what he wanted to hear.

"Do you love me?" he used to say. And the answer would come back from "his people," loud and clear.

Rayme stood there now, under a single spotlight with his guitar slung over his tank top. His mouth formed the words "Thank you," but the noise was still deafening. Rayme's eyes went up to the people in the trees surrounding the outdoor theater. He spoke into the microphone in his raspy voice.

"Tree people," he said, "I've missed you."

There was a burst of recognition from the tree people and the crowd. Then the applause began to ripple down and Rayme spoke once more into the microphone.

"I'm glad to be back in L.A.," he said.

He picked up his guitar, planted his feet, looked out at the audience, and began his newest song by himself, a cappella. It was about Marny. "You'll Never Leave Me." As Rayme began to paint the picture of the woman he loved, his Main Street Band crept in behind him. He sang of the girl he had found, the girl who had shared his dreams, the girl who could never leave him because he wouldn't let go of her. She was with him now in everything he did, in everything he wrote, in all his music.

The song picked up a beat in the second verse and began to throb. Rayme's voice throbbed, too, but not pushing as he once had done. As with all great singers, it was not the technical quality of the voice, good or bad, which stood out, but the personality of the voice. What mattered was the dramatic quality of it. The ability of the voice to carry an emotion, to go up your backbone, drive a fist into your stomach, shake your heart, stir your mind, excite you, bring you out of your seat, take you back into the deepest part of your heart. The band was rocking now and Rayme was into it.

But "You'll Never Leave Me" never became an all-out rock song. It was a hymn to a woman. It was a love song of modern times. It was a rock celebration.

Steve, Lieu, and Spartan Lee were in the second row. Rayme saw them and smiled. Steve turned to Lieu. Rayme Monterey was back at work; he was reaching the people as he never had before. Electricity was surging through the Greek Theatre.

"You'll Never Leave Me" came to an end. Rayme was rocking. His eyes were closed. His face was twisted in memory. And then, as he hit the last plaintive rocking note of "Marny, I won't let you go," his voice was a cry. His head was turned back, his eyes lifted upward. The spotlight closed over him. He stood there in the darkness, and there was silence in the Greek Theatre for a long moment. The audience had felt what Rayme felt. They would never let Marny go, either; and they would never let Rayme go. He and his song, the new Rayme and what he had to say, belonged to that audience, and they belonged to him.

"Rayme-mania," the critics would come to call it.

Rayme's new songs were serious, socially aware songs. He had gone back into his roots, his country, his generation. Rayme stood again in the spotlight, listening to the thundering ovation that had brought him back for four curtain calls. The audience wouldn't let him go. They were on their feet and pressed forward in an arc around the stage. They were crowded against one another, fighting to get close to him.

"Marny's here, Steve," Lieu said. "I can feel it."

"She must have been an exceptional girl," Steve said. "What I hoped for is happening. He's singing for her, and for everything they believed together. People are going to follow him more than ever—and for different reasons—there's a new dimension there. If we can only get him on film—just the way he is."

34

The Dana Building,
MGL—Hollywood

"You're going to have a hell of a lawsuit on your hands, Gregson, if you don't get off Steve Wayland's back. It's the goddamnedest harassment I've ever seen in the motion picture business. Every turn of the road, you're trying to persecute this man. You've already got a lien on everything he owns."

"And he's got six million dollars of our money!" Gregson screamed at Spartan Lee. "To do what he wants with."

"*If,*" Spartan rode in over Gregson, "*if* he delivers Rayme Monterey and Magdalena Alba, and if he starts shooting on April twenty-first, and if—if, if, if. He's trying to get this picture together, and all you do is nail him on every technicality you can find. *The Rest of Our Lives* buys off all your other Wayland commitments, Gregson. That was your deal, and we agreed to it. Now, why not leave the man alone and let him make the picture?"

"What picture?" Gregson asked. "I haven't seen a final shooting script of a picture that starts in four weeks. The construction department only has a few drawings from the art director. The prop department doesn't know what it's doing. We don't have locations fixed. We haven't even made wardrobe tests. And now I hear this dancing protégé of Wayland's who's been missing has shown up and is working with a psychologist, trying to get her marbles collected long enough to shoot the film. Then, today we get this fucking news that there's another grand jury hearing coming down on Rayme Monterey. What a collection!"

"Yeah, what a collection. You're right. For six million dollars in this market, where your average cost per picture at this studio, reported by your own publicity department, is sixteen and a half million dollars—that's the average. And we're giving you a picture at six million with the biggest rock star in the world, with Magdalena Alba, and with a new star I can promise you is going to be sensational. I honestly believe you'd rather lose the whole six million dollars, move in on Steve Wayland's lifetime possessions, and write off the rest of the loss. That's the truth, isn't it, Gregson?"

Gregson shouted back at Spartan. "For once you're right, Spartan. We don't need people like Steve Wayland around our business."

"No!" Spartan shouted back. "What you need is a bunch of guys sucking around you, bowing and scraping to you and turning out moronic pictures your computers tell you will be seen four or five times by thirteen- or fourteen-year-old girls. You're a goddamned disgrace, Gregson, as head of the studio, and I'm telling you now I'm bringing Ed Wilson in to sue you if you do anything more to stop *The Rest of Our Lives*. It's tough enough getting this movie made without you screwing around. If you don't believe it, try me. I talked to Wilson on the phone before I came here this morning. He's studied the contract."

"Go ahead, sue." Gregson rose from his desk. "That could stop the whole picture dead."

Spartan Lee stood toe to toe with Gregson. "If that happens," he said, "you will never have one of my clients, no matter what you offer, as long as you're head of the studio. You know, Gregson, you're making Steve Wayland a real cause célèbre. You might just lose, no matter what you think. And then it will cost you your career. You've seen everything flip around often enough in this business—and no matter what you think of him, you're dealing with a very talented man."

"Listen, Spartan, if you're so fucking sure of this client of yours and this picture, why don't you just auction it off to another studio? We'll sell the whole package for exactly what we've got in it—six million dollars. Why don't you let someone else sweat it out? Be my guest."

"I'll remember what you said. We'll get that in writing. The time may come. Back up your big mouth, Gregson."

Spartan turned around and walked out of the office.

"I can't speed up the legal processes any more than I have." It was the voice of Mahoney, the New York district attorney.

"And I can't speed up the backing for your political campaign until you deliver for me." Jack Gregson's voice was dead level on his personal New York line to his private office. "Rayme Monterey had a smash comeback concert out here the other night, and there's another one scheduled for the Los Angeles Coliseum—it's going to be used for the film. Everything he does intensifies the controversy, and you're on the losing end because your grand jury hearing failed to indict him."

"That was only the first round," the district attorney answered. "We're building up damaging testimony that the three boys Monterey wounded didn't threaten him or the girl. We're filling in their life stories—hangers-on—kids following hero leaders—street gangs—victims of society. We have to do it very carefully because when I request a second grand jury hearing, they're going to indict him for premeditated homicide and armed assault."

"How long before you can ask for a second grand jury hearing?" Gregson questioned.

"I can't move any faster than I'm doing now—if we don't get an indictment this time there won't be a third hearing. It could ruin me politically."

"I can ruin you politically, Mahoney. Don't you forget that. I need this hearing. I need Monterey served with a warrant, and arrested and held for the hearing. I don't want Rayme Monterey finishing this picture. I've told you before."

"Why do you want your own studio's picture stopped?"

"That's my business," Gregson shot back. "In the long run, in this particular picture, we're better off if it isn't finished. And if nothing else works to stop it—I've got to have this hearing of Rayme Monterey tied up. Two months at the most. And I don't want any advance publicity or rumors about it. Do you understand that, Mahoney? Nothing. Just let everything sleep. I want Monterey to feel perfectly secure until your men serve the warrants on him and arrest him. Do you understand that?"

"It's very clear," Mahoney answered. "But I want to tell you again, it has to be by the book. That's the way I run my office."

"Oh, yeah?" Gregson said. "If that's the way you run your office you wouldn't even be having this conversation—and I'm sure you know that I've had every conversation of ours recorded. If it ever gets known about what I'm doing for you with the city party chiefs, you couldn't be elected as dog catcher. Get the grand jury hearing set up, Mahoney, and get it in time, and you'll be sitting in the governor's office in a year."

* * *

David Thayer, Steve's young cameraman, was waiting for Steve in the projection room. "Okay?" David asked.

Steve answered, "Let's go."

David pushed a button that connected with the projection room upstairs. The film *The Accused* opened with a moving shot of Magdalena Alba, accused of murdering her lover, taking the stand in a courtroom. David watched incredulously as he saw a completely different Magdalena Alba on the screen. As she sat down in the witness chair the camera pushed forward into a close-up. The glamorous character of Magdalena Alba was gone. She was rough-edged. Cheap. Overly made up. Calculating.

Even the voice was changed. It was not the cultured, flawless voice of most of Magdalena's performances. Her voice was common, anxious to make an impression, and flattered by the attention of the reporters and the photographers in the courtroom. The accused radiated a coarse sexuality.

A moment came when she was asked by the prosecuting attorney how she made her living.

She answered with pride that she was an executive secretary. A wave of laughter swept the courtroom.

The face of the accused changed on the crest of the wave of that laughter. Her reaction to people laughing at her was a strike of the heart. Magdalena was emotionally naked in that courtroom. The laughter cut through her coldness and her brittle quality and washed out the defenses that covered her expression. There was deep pain there. The accused was exposed in her human vulnerability.

Steve pushed the intercom button. "Walter," he said, "can you roll back to the close-up where the people start to laugh?" The film ran backward. "Slow up," Steve said on the intercom, "you're almost there." The film slowed up. "There!" Steve exclaimed. "Stop it right there, will you, Walter?" The film stopped and the nine-foot-high close-up of Magdalena was frozen on the screen. Her eyes reflected a pain so deep you couldn't look away. They hypnotized you.

Steve walked up to the massive image, a tiny figure against the towering close-up. He looked at Magdalena's eyes on the screen, in such great proportion now, each eye eight feet tall and fourteen feet wide. Her eyes took over the whole screening room, reaching into every corner.

"David," Steve said.

David Thayer was at his side.

"David, I want you to make me big stills of the points in the film that we'll mark out. Walter," Steve raised his voice as he walked back to the intercom, "mark this frame in red, will you? I'll be giving you marks all through this film, like the others we've run on her. David's going to make stills of them in the morning."

"Will do," Walter said. "Do you want me to start rolling again?"

Steve settled down in his seat with David beside him. "Just a minute." He turned to David. "David, anything wrong with that shot, in your opinion?"

"Great shot," David said. "But it could be better."

"Got any ideas?" Steve asked.

"The eyes are so moving—they're marvelous eyes—but I don't think they're lit right. The cameraman wasn't using any pin lights."

Steve answered, "Her head's moving from side to side, up and down—how could you hold any pin lights?"

"Have to invent some way to do it," David said. "If we could get pin lights on both those eyes, so they're illuminated without her having to hold herself rigid, so anywhere she turns, wherever she went with her looks, her expressions—"

"You're right," Steve said. "That could make a difference—that could move us more, get to the audience more. Do you think you can do it, David?"

"We've got to do it," David said. "It *could* make a difference. Those eyes could be unforgettable if they were always lit."

It was three o'clock in the morning when Steve settled down in his workroom over the garage. The pages of his notes were spread out over the desk.

The notebook marked "Magdalena Alba" was open in front of him. He'd written hundreds of notes in the margins of the research pages. He put in another sheet near the back of the notebook, marked it "Magdalena's Close-ups." And underneath he wrote, "Must work out a way with David so that we keep the pin lights in her eyes."

He leaned back and tried to shake off his fatigue. He poured himself a fresh cup of coffee. Then he turned in his chair to look at one complete wall filled with the "looks" of Magdalena Alba, blowups and frames from all her pictures, like the ones he had selected earlier that night.

Every angle of her face, every expression of the eyes, every kind of makeup and hairstyle—they were all there in literally hundreds of pictures, a vast collage of images of Magdalena Alba. And here and there, pinned over them or in a tiny piece of clear space, were notes on the story of *The Rest of Our Lives*.

It was one of the many things he had learned from the Italian writer Cesare Zavattini. Surround yourself every possible moment with the characters of your story. Vibrations.

Steve had persuaded Zavattini to come to the United States to work on a screenplay. It had been one of Steve Wayland's early projects. He had fought to have Cesare Zavattini, the author of such classics as *Bicycle Thief* and *Miracle of Milan*, as well as the Sophia Loren Academy Award–winning film *Two Women*, do the screenplay of *The Forgotten Ones*.

Speaking only ten words of English, Zavattini had come to the Bel Air Hotel and secreted himself in a suite. He had torn out the pages of the Italian translation of the book they were adapting, *The Forgotten Ones*, and pinned them on the walls of his suite, together with all his own notes.

He refused to go out for three months, insisting on cooking pasta for Steve every night in the suite and having his other meals brought in. He would walk around the room with his vibrant Italian stride, his beret always tilted to one side of his head, gesticulating madly, his round face shining with his "juice."

"The family," he said, "you have to know the family—the people you write about. I'm locked up with my 'family' in this suite, all around me, and they'll never get away. Everywhere I look, every moment of the day and night, the people of our film and the events of their lives are here. I can feel them, I can touch them, I can smell them in these rooms. They fill me. I cannot leave them until we are finished."

And now, fifteen years later, Steve Wayland was surrounding himself with the people of *The Rest of Our Lives*. Magdalena from one wall. La Tigressa from another. Rayme Monterey from another. Robert Montango on the fourth.

His fatigue drained out of him, and the excitement came on him again. *The Rest of Our Lives* was beginning to happen. He had his four stars now. Sets were being built. And the story was coming together right out of the truth, as he felt it. It had to be a film that "crossed over" to audiences of every age group and every taste. After fourteen years and eight major films, he had it. He could feel it in the pit of his stomach.

35

Academy Award Night, Hollywood

*T*he sunken bathtub was made out of rose quartz marble. It was circular, set into a nine-foot round insert, completely surrounded by two marble steps to the floor. The entire bathroom was built in a series of circles. Each circle was set against wall-length mirrors alternating with wall-length windows looking out on trees and sky.

One side of the bathroom, completely flanked with mirrors, led to built-in closets divided into sections for morning, afternoon, evening, formal, and nighttime clothes. There were negligee ensembles with matching nightgowns and slippers, twenty fur coats in the cedar-lined fur closet, shelves for hundreds of pairs of shoes, closets for blouses and skirts, hundreds of evening dresses, and seventy-five suits for every occasion. Everything was in its place and ready to wear.

Chests of lingerie had been built into the walls, behind glass cabinets—places for a mosaic of silk stockings, handmade lace chemises, and embroidered slips.

Magdalena Alba's maid, Sara, had laid everything out for the night, each thing hung and assembled.

Magdalena stepped up to the level of the bathtub and let her black negligee fall away from her body as gracefully as a ballet dancer maneuvering a scarf in *Giselle*. She dipped her toe into the water, testing it, and then stepped into the pool.

She scrubbed herself slowly. She turned to a marble platform near the faucets which had been designed to hold bathing creams, cosmetics, and perfumes. She took a hand mirror from the base and began to apply her makeup, painting it on carefully and darkening the beauty mark on the left side of her upper lip. She inspected her hair from the front and the back, and changed a few of the highly piled curls here and there.

She rose out of the bathtub and observed her nakedness reflected in the mirrors with the air of a professional student. She turned sideways to inspect the flatness of her stomach, the curve of her hips. Yes, she was alive, and she was going to live every minute of it. She would make a new picture and put out of her head any dread of tomorrow. Who knew about tomorrow, anyway? It was only now that counted.

And tonight was a special night—Academy Award night—and she was going to see Steve Wayland again. It was another beginning.

She perfumed her body with spray, and then she softly sprayed inside herself. Her body tingled with the sharpness of the alcohol of the perfume. She sprayed down her legs, around her hips, and even her feet.

Magdalena then took out from one of the built-in wooden cabinets a pair of white lace stockings. She sat on the edge of the bench of her makeup table, stretched her right leg, and slipped the stocking onto her pointed toes and then up her calf and high onto her thigh. Then, the left leg. She selected a white lace garter belt. She fixed the belt around her narrow waist and pinned the garters to her white stockings.

The addition of this very small and simple piece of clothing had a startling effect. Seeing long stockings and a garter belt on a beautiful woman, otherwise naked, was a striking sexual experience for most men. Magdalena knew that, just as she had learned many things about men. How to maneuver them, use them, surprise them, challenge them. It was a game.

It had always been a game, and it always would be. You could never really deal directly with a man. Sex always turned into a game. And Magdalena was a master player.

She slipped on a white lace chemise. It was cut so that it did not cover her breasts, but hung straight down on the outside of them and went to the middle of her hips. It gave line to her clothes, but didn't minimize the shape of her body.

She stepped into the shoes Sara had taken out for her. They were high-heeled, open-toed, white lace, matching the lace of the dress that awaited her. Magdalena slipped the dress over her head and smoothed it down around her, fitting it to the curves of her body.

It was an antique white lace dress from Portugal. It had been designed by the Hollywood Academy Award–winning designer Bill Thomas, who made most of Magdalena's clothes in the United States, as Yves St. Laurent made her European designs.

This Thomas creation was one of his most memorable. It was Grecian in design, high-necked, long-sleeved, fitted very tight to the bodice and then flared out in a soft, white lace circle. It was elegant, queenly, understated.

Magdalena zipped up the back of her dress and turned in front of the mirrors. The dress moved gracefully with her, never falling out of line. That was one of Thomas's magical touches.

Her critical eye measured the back of the dress, checked her calf line. It had been designed to hit her leg at the perfect place. Magdalena smiled. Her perfectionist's eye approved what she saw.

She walked to the built-in safe in the wall, hidden by a white lacquered door. She dialed it open. Built into it were thirty small jewelry drawers, each with different collections of jewels. She chose emeralds bordered by flawless marquise-shaped diamonds. A bracelet of emeralds flanked by diamonds, and an emerald-and-diamond necklace which sparkled deep green against the whiteness of her dress.

Her eyes turned green with the emeralds. Her coloring, her hair, her complexion, the redness of her mouth against the whiteness of the dress and the sparkling jewels made a striking reflection in the mirrors as she turned and inspected herself.

Magdalena picked up her white lace gloves and her evening bag made of miniature pearls sewn together, with a single diamond "M" in script fastening the purse closed.

Steve was waiting for her in the den, having a drink at the bar. She stopped just for a moment, then walked toward him with her right hand outstretched.

"Steve."

"Hello, Magdalena. You look beautiful!" Steve exclaimed.

The personal magnetism of this woman, the animal sexuality, the mystery, the bigger-than-life sense, combining with the wave of perfume which engulfed him, had an actual effect on his heart. Adrenaline charged through him.

Steve reached behind the bar and picked up a bunch of violets.

"Always—my violets," Magdalena said. "You never forget."

"Could I fix you a drink?" Steve asked.

Magdalena sat down across from him at the bar. She brushed the violets against her mouth. It was a slight gesture, but sensual. "I don't usually drink, but tonight—I think this calls for champagne. It's there behind you."

Steve opened it, poured the bubbling liquid just as it was beginning to overflow the bottle.

"Bravo," she said. She raised her glass in a toast. "To your film."

Steve raised his glass. "To *our* film."

They both sipped their champagne. Magdalena shook her head. "The director's king. That's the way it has to be. As they say, 'It's a director's medium.' "

He smiled at her. "Then why do the stars get the big money?"

She suddenly turned serious. "Most stars don't last too long. They have to make the money while they can."

Steve looked at her. "I can't imagine you ever being less than you are now." For just a flash, he picked up the fear in back of her expression.

She covered quickly. "That's the nicest thing anyone has said to me for a long time. I was right about you. I liked you from the beginning in Paris, although one should never tell a man that."

"Who says?" Steve asked.

Magdalena smiled. "All right, Steve, I like you. You're not spoiled yet. Stay that way. At least until after the picture is over."

"Then you *are* going to do it?"

Magdalena gave a little laugh. "I didn't say that. We'll talk about it later. Ready?"

36

Academy Awards,
Los Angeles Music Center Pavilion

*T*he frail old man, walking with difficulty but with his head held high, entered downstage from the wings of the Music Hall Grand Pavilion in Los Angeles. Twenty-four television cameras, placed at different angles and positions in the great hall, were focused on him. More than a billion people around the world were watching via satellite. It was the greatest awards ceremony of any year, the annual awards of the Motion Picture Academy of Arts and Sciences.

The entire audience of Academy members, families, honored guests, foreign dignitaries, and the press of the world was on its feet. The applause was shattering.

The old man stopped for a moment, making his way across the stage to the podium. On television screens everywhere, the familiar face was in close-up. It was a gaunt face, with hollow cheeks devastated by his illness. But still a handsome face, with sensitive eyes, a noble brow, and the thin white hair carefully brushed into place. Here he was, the greatest actor of his time, beloved, perhaps, as no other English-speaking actor in history, a survivor of cancer and lupus, a man moving with great difficulty, but still on his own, a man still busy, going from motion picture to motion picture, receiving the acclaim and the love of his peers, his followers, and the press—Sir Laurence Olivier, now a Lord of the British Empire. His face turned, and his eyes sought out the great crowd before him, in the orchestra, in the mezzanine, in the balconies.

In a delicate gesture, he raised both his hands almost unnoticeably and bowed his head. When his head came up, there were tears in his eyes. They were not the tears of Lear, or of Othello, or of any of the great parts Sir Laurence had played on screen and on stage. They were the tears of the artist, of the man who had lived out the *Romeo and Juliet* of his life with Vivien Leigh, the tears of the elder statesman of the English theater.

Sir Laurence made his way more quickly now to the podium, where Magdalena Alba waited for him.

Magdalena had been chosen by the Academy when they found out she was coming to America. It had been five years since she had appeared on the Academy Awards telecast, and they had asked her to present the Special Honorary Award to Sir Laurence. Of course, they knew nothing of her illness. She was a great and glamorous star, and a desirable presenter.

Magdalena watched Sir Laurence approaching her to receive the Oscar she held for him. She, too, loved and respected Sir Laurence. He was her peer, above all others. Her arms went out to him as he approached and they embraced each other.

As they stepped forward together to the microphones at the podium on the northern side of the proscenium, Magdalena picked up the Oscar. She didn't look at the TelePrompTer, but she turned squarely toward Sir Laurence so that she could look him in the face.

"Sir Laurence Olivier, surely William Shakespeare was thinking of a man like you when he wrote his eternal words, 'This is a man.' I believe every single member of the Academy and certainly every actor and actress in our profession looks up to you with honor, respect, and, yes," she looked at him and continued, "and yes, Larry, with love. You belong to us, to the world, and to the ages. And this year, the Academy presents you with a special Academy Award for your lifelong contribution to the art of motion pictures."

There were tears in her eyes as she presented the Oscar to Sir Laurence Olivier, and another crescendo of applause swept across the huge auditorium. Sir Laurence bowed his head, then stepped to the microphones.

"Oh, dear friends, am I supposed to speak after that? Thank you for that beautiful citation and the trouble you have taken to make it, and for all the warm generosities in it. Mr. President and governors of the Academy, committee members, fellows, my very noble and approved good masters, my colleagues, my friends, my fellow students. In the great wealth, the great firmament of your nation's generosities, this particular choice may perhaps be found by future generations as a trifle eccentric, but the mere fact of it—the prodigal, pure, human kindness of it—must be seen as a beautiful star in that firmament which shines upon me at this moment, dazzling me a little but filling me with warmth of the extraordinary elation, the euphoria that happens to so many of us at the first breath of the majestic glow of a new tomorrow. From the top of this moment, in the solace, in the kindly emotion that is charging my soul and my heart at this moment, I thank you for this great gift which lends me such a very splendid part in this, your glorious occasion.

"Thank you."

Steve Wayland's eyes went back and forth from the stage to one of the television monitors which were mounted for the orchestra section of attending celebrities. The monitor was on Sir Laurence and then, for a moment, as he finished his speech, the cameraman double-cut to a close-up of Magdalena Alba in the shadows. She did not know that a camera would be on her then, and her expression was incredibly moving. The reverence and love that everyone felt for Sir Laurence was there, but there was something else, some unknown bond between herself and the man being honored. It was as though she were identifying with that special moment, sharing it, feeling it.

Steve was shaken by the close-up. He saw things in this woman, qualities that would change and deepen the woman she would portray in *The Rest of Our Lives*—if she agreed to do the picture. There was no other actress he wanted to consider for Magdalena's part. She had become the woman for his film.

37

El Cid,
Beverly Hills

l Cid was a small café on the south side of Beverly Hills, one block off Pico. It was one of a string of Latin restaurants that had sprung up in that location, many of them owned by Spanish families. El Cid was the one that was authentic.

The food was good, the atmosphere real, and the entertainment from the family members themselves was authentic flamenco.

When Magdalena and Steve came in, late, after the Academy Governors' Ball at the Beverly Hills Hilton International Ballroom, a ripple of applause circled the room. Magdalena Alba was theirs, and this was one of her haunts. They had not seen her for a long time.

They set up a special table on the edge of the dance floor. There was embracing and kissing and shouts of *brava* from the family of Castilians and the other Spanish people in the restaurant. They crowded around her table; Steve felt out of place. He watched Magdalena adapt herself from the formal Academy ceremonies to this Spanish family restaurant in a not-too-desirable area of Beverly Hills.

A distinguished older gentleman came forward and presented Magdalena with an ancient Spanish guitar. There was enthusiastic applause as the crowd insisted that Magdalena play.

She turned to Steve and, for one brief moment, focused her entire attention on him. "Be patient, please—these are my friends." She did it with such simplicity that Steve was warmed. She knew that he would stay there all night, as long as he was with her, but she was still paying him that special courtesy that so many people forgot when they were on a high.

Magdalena put the guitar on her lap against her white lace gown and hit an opening chord. She took command of the room. The people closed in around the table.

She played her favorite theme from Rodrigo's Concierto de Aranjuez. On the second chorus, Magdalena put back her head and slipped back into the gypsy world of her childhood. Her voice became a full-throated flamenco cry, bridging the centuries that gypsies have wandered the world. She no longer looked at the people surrounding her. She'd become someone else.

As she finished the haunting song, a dark, intense-looking young man dressed in dancer's clothes suddenly took over the center of the small dance area, smashing his feet into the floor with his heavy boots. His presence was directed only toward Magdalena.

It was the traditional salute of a flamenco dancer to the woman he had selected as his dancing partner. From the edge of the dance floor, the flamenco guitars followed the flashing boots into musical life.

Magdalena sat quietly in her chair. You could hear the crowd breathe with expectancy. Very softly, she started to clap her hands together in the flamenco tradition. The beats of her hands were sharp and soft at the same time, in exact rhythm with the boots of the man who was approaching her across the dance floor.

Now she clapped her hands faster. They made sharp cracking sounds. The crowd moved back, clearing the dance floor.

The dancer approached, never taking his eyes off Magdalena. She was looking back at him now, and the beat of her hands stayed with his increased tempo.

Suddenly, as the man neared the table, Magdalena stood up. She made two sharp, cracking beats with her high-heeled, lace-covered shoes. The crowd rippled with excitement.

Steve was photographing the scene in his mind. The lights, the shadows, the colors, the crowd, the faces, the guitar players, the flamenco dancer, and, finally, Magdalena, in all her primitive gypsy quality, covered with the sophistication of the finest designers and beauty experts. She was a gypsy queen who had conquered the world. She took one step forward toward the dancer and then swung into unison with him, pounding her lace-covered feet into the hardwood floor, her hands lifted over her head flamenco style, her body moving perfectly with the beat.

The crowd ringed the floor, as Magdalena and the flamenco dancer danced to the music. All the traditional flamenco movements were there, intensified by the personality of each of these dancers. Sexual electricity filled the crowd. Steve could feel it, and then he started getting angry. He was confused about what was happening. A blinding fury began to fill his heart, as he watched the ancient dance. It was a primitive courtship between the two people. The flamenco dancer up there was stalking Steve's date. Who the hell did he think he was? And what was this little pomaded Spanish fruitcake doing? And worse, Magdalena was buying it. At least, Steve thought she was. She seemed absolutely intent on her partner and all of her movements were sexual and provocative.

Then suddenly, as though she were reading his mind, she turned to Steve and began to dance directly to him, as the crowd opened a lane of bodies so that she could approach him. She danced her way back to her chair beside Steve, picked up the guitar in one rhythmic movement, and sang into his eyes. She sang with her lips half-parted, her skin glistening with the heat of her body.

She finished with a passionate striking of a chord, her head flung back in the best flamenco tradition. And then she looked at Steve and smiled. He looked at her for a moment, then stood up facing her and started applauding. So did all the people around him.

Steve knew it then. He'd never really been in love before.

38

Malibu

*S*teve's convertible cruised along the moonlit coastline of California, heading north past the Malibu colony and Pepperdine. Magdalena stretched back comfortably on the seat beside him, her head tilted upward, her eyes searching the night sky. "Tell me about *The Rest of Our Lives*. I understand you've staked your whole career on this picture."

"Where'd you hear that?" Steve asked.

Magdalena smiled at him. "After you left Paris, I asked around—the stories generally agree—only one studio would give you the money, any money—they settled your contract for one picture. You had to sign over all the residuals of your career, your story properties, and the mortgage on your house. Did you really do that?"

Steve nodded. "Had to. I'm not considered very commercial. I don't make those approved lists."

"Well, you've made a lot of other lists—some of the best critics, many of the universities; certain words keep appearing through the articles and the reviews about you. Words I like," Magdalena continued. " 'Individualist' . . . 'Independent' . . . 'Commitment' . . . 'A leader, not a follower.' "

Steve interrupted her, "And on the lists that really count, the money lists—'Lone wolf,' 'Rebellious,' 'Stubborn,' 'Never makes big money for us,' 'Obstinate,' 'A loser.' "

Magdalena turned to him. "I know something about losing—but that's not what I see in your work."

Steve asked, "You've seen some of my films?"

"All of them," Magdalena told him. "I'd seen some before, the rest

after I met you. When you put all your work together, it's of a piece—
it's one work, really, although it's on such a variety of subjects."

Steve asked her, "What's the piece?"

She stretched back in the seat of the convertible and faced the sky.
She pulled her coat up around her neck, enjoying the cool ocean wind
blowing into the open car. Her answer was thoughtful. "I've seen eight
films of yours, and every one of them has a different look, I think,
more than a look, a feeling—about passion for life and living with a
reason and going for it—that's the way I'd review your career, Steve.
And that's why I'm going to make *The Rest of Our Lives* with you.
My guess is this film is going to be the most meaningful you've ever
made, and entertaining and moving to a wide audience."

"Better be," Steve said.

Magdalena smiled. "You're truly open." She reached across and
touched his hand on the steering wheel. "I like people who are vulnerable. That's an important quality for me." She withdrew her hand.
"I don't know that I want to make any more films after this. But like
you, I want to make a statement. I'm tired of making love stories with
no reality, adventure pictures where I'm just on exhibition, or mystery
pictures where there's no real mystery. You're a relationship director
and I'm a relationship actress at heart. I want you to know out front,
I want to believe myself in this film.

"Remember the picture you made about the Puerto Rican family—
what the daughter said to her father when she left home to try another
way of survival?"

Steve picked up on her quickly. " 'I don't want to leave this world
without a trace I was ever here'?" he said.

Magdalena smiled. "I think we can help each other leave a trace,
and that's something we both need very badly. Agreed?"

He turned and smiled at her. "Agreed—Maggie."

She looked at him sharply. "Where did you get that? I'm not the
'Maggie' type."

"That's just it," Steve answered. "You're not and that makes 'Maggie'
right for you."

She laughed. "Some of your critics would like that line."

"It takes one to know one," Steve smiled at her. "Do you know
Artie Shaw's music?" he asked.

Magdalena glanced at him. "Of course—his records are very popular
all over Europe."

Steve went on, "When I was in school, one of my roommates was
a collector of the big band years, the forties. Artie Shaw was his

favorite—I heard those records of his for four straight years. And then a few years ago I saw him on television with David Susskind. It was a two-hour-long interview and Artie took the ball and ran with it. He talked about everything from music to painting to sports to women to physics—truly brilliant—and one thing he said came into my head a few moments ago when you were talking . . . he said that when a really good musician plays a note, it isn't just the note that's written on the lead sheet, but that note, played his own way, is unique—is different from the way any other musician in the world could play it—that is the thrill of musicianship—because the musician automatically puts into that single note all his life, all his experience, all his feelings and thoughts on life itself—love and hate and passion and humor—all those things combined in the musician's soul to create that individual note and make it unique. And that's why every piece of music ever written is played differently by every great musician.

"Maggie, for the first time in my life, I think I'm ready to play my note."

"I'm ready, too," Magdalena said.

39

Encino,
Los Angeles Valley

ary Jane Stuckey sat in a small living room in the new professional building near the corner of Ventura Boulevard and Woodley. It was a bright, cheerful two-room suite done in bright yellow, green, and white. Flowering plants hung on the walls and beside the doors. It was delicately feminine, and as you walked in, you felt you were entering a woman's home. A woman who was warm and friendly.

A small, pretty woman in a rose-colored dress and glasses pulled back on her dark hair sat down in a chair across from where Mary Jane was seated. The woman smiled at her, a welcoming "I like you no matter what" smile, a smile that had softened hundreds of people who had been fortunate enough to have the counsel and guidance of Pearl Sargeant.

"Can I get you anything?" Pearl asked. "A coke or a cigarette?"

Mary Jane shook her head. "No, thank you," she said.

Pearl leaned back and gazed at Mary Jane. The girl looked like a beautiful battlefield—the hair, the eyes, the fine white skin, the lovely figure, the full and voluptuous mouth—Pearl took in everything as she studied her. She also perceived the pain behind the eyes, the sad aura, the depressed state of this woman which aged her and conflicted so vividly with her natural beauty.

My God, what bone structure, Pearl thought. The therapist was also an amateur artist, and she photographed Mary Jane in her mind, so that she could reproduce this look on canvas.

"I don't mean to be staring at you," Pearl said. "But you really are beautiful. Steve told me."

"It's hard for me to believe you. I think I look like hell," Mary Jane said. "I suppose he told you something about me. The drugs and what I've been doing."

"I want you to be sure of one thing from the beginning, Mary Jane. I will never lie to you. I will never evade a question. Never. That's the number-one rule here. When I look at you and say you're beautiful, I'm thinking of your face and figure as they soon will be, when all the effects of the drugs have worn off, and when you're rested and working at your profession. Steve tells me you go before the cameras in about five weeks, so apparently we have to work fast."

"I can't do it," Mary Jane said.

"Why?" Pearl asked.

"I just don't have the energy anymore—I don't have the desire—this is the biggest chance in my life, and I don't care."

"You'd rather just lie down and sleep it away, wouldn't you—permanently?"

Mary Jane looked up, shocked. "How do you know that?"

"Mary Jane . . . can I call you that? I prefer it to Stephanie Columbo."

"I don't care—anything you want—doesn't matter," Mary Jane answered.

"I've met many intelligent, sensitive people in my life who at one time or another have considered suicide. That's the truth. The man most people consider the greatest single personality and talent of this century, Albert Schweitzer, collapsed for three years before he did his finest work. He was in three hospitals. He couldn't move out of bed for three years. He didn't want to live. But one day it all came back to him. The energy, the desire, the ambition, the brilliance.

"And I want you to know another truth. Depression—and we all suffer from it sometimes—lifts. It really does. You just have to hang in there. And that's what I'm here for. To help you hang in. I know enough about your life, because of what Steve has told me, to be absolutely certain you're going to make it. You're going to come back, and be stronger than ever."

"Why do you say that?" Mary Jane asked.

"Because," Pearl said, "you're a survivor. There are many people who have gone through something like you have, who have never survived. But you will. And what's happened to you will never happen again, I can promise you that."

"How can *you* do that?" Mary Jane asked, with sarcasm.

Pearl leaned forward. She was small in stature, but large in power.

"Because," she said, "we're going to work together here. And in my home, too. Every day when you're not in rehearsal. You're an addictive personality, Mary Jane. Your compulsion to do drugs, to escape, is an illness, like heart trouble or high blood pressure. We're going to discover within yourself exactly how and why you've given power over your life to other people—that's what happened between you and Mr. Slater, Mary Jane. You gave another person the power over your life.

"We must not do that. We can love with all our hearts. We can need. We can lean on someone else. But we still have to be able to stand alone. Otherwise, we give away our strength.

"I gave away the power over my life to other people when I was younger. That's how I got into therapy. I had to find a cure for myself or I would have been destroyed over and over again until there was nothing left. When I look at you now, Mary Jane," she reached forward and took the girl's hands, "I see myself."

Mary Jane didn't move or speak.

"You won't let yourself be destroyed. I promise, Mary Jane. That is the work we have to accomplish together."

She put her arms around Mary Jane, who was so much bigger than she was, and cradled her like a child.

40

The Roxy,
Sunset Boulevard,
Hollywood

It was almost closing time. The crowd had shuffled out; the Badlands had finished their last set.

In a back corner of the crowded room, Rayme Monterey sat by himself, in the Roxy on the Sunset Strip. He had on his dark glasses and an old-fashioned cap with a snap button on the brim. It was another step along the memory roads he was walking. This is where they had first begun to pay attention to him on the West Coast. Marny had been with him. The whole group had been with him.

Charlie Tuna, the leader of the Badlands, was talking to the band as they packed up, when something about the guy in the shadows, off in the back, caught his attention—the way the man brushed his mouth with his wrist.

Charlie Tuna walked over to the table and looked at the man. The man looked at him. Charlie stuck out his hand. "Rayme?" he asked.

Rayme nodded and put out his hand. "You play good," Rayme said.

Charlie sat down beside him. "You know, my guys will never go home when they know it's you back here—not unless you play with us. Everybody's gone—just for us, okay? Once?"

Rayme smiled. It was the first feeling of musical fellowship except for his own group he'd had in a long time. "I'd like to."

He was in his usual blue jeans, dark tank shirt, and leather jacket. They walked together up to the bandstand.

Charlie Tuna said quietly, "Boys—Rayme's going to play with us."

The members of the band looked up at the name "Rayme." There was only one Rayme to them—and it was the man they were looking at. But the rock brotherhood of style dictated quiet nods and glances. Rayme Monterey was one of them—whether they knew him or not. The lead guitarist offered Rayme his guitar. Rayme nodded his thanks, plucked at the strings for a moment, tightened one.

Charlie spoke up. "You hit it, Rayme—just so it's one of yours. We know 'em all."

Rayme felt back home again, and he swung into the opening chords of one of his first hit records, "Big Texas Man." His body seemed to catch fire from his own song and the beat of the Badlands behind him. He was moving sharply, his head rocking back and forth with the melody. "Big Texas Man" had been one of Marny's favorite songs, and she was with him up there on the barely lit stage of the Roxy with the deserted room out in front of them.

Charlie and the boys were good. They'd never expected to play with Rayme Monterey, and they were surpassing themselves. It was a rock jam, with different soloists winging out of each chorus, as Rayme turned to one after another. He led them in and out with his rock guitar. The place was jumping; nobody saw the couple come in through the back. They stood in the shadows and watched.

The girl's foot started to tap. It was Mary Jane, with Steve. Steve had been looking for Rayme, and the Roxy was one of his first stops. Badlands was the biggest rock group in town.

Steve looked from Rayme on the little bandstand at the Roxy, pounding out "Big Texas Man," to Mary Jane, at his side, tapping her foot against the beat in countertime. Over her pale, troubled face slowly came a look of joy, as though someone had pulled up a shade and let the light shine in on her. When the shade passed her eyes, they glowed with light.

Mary Jane turned to him suddenly, not missing a beat. "Did you plan it this way—our first meeting?"

Steve smiled. "Just happened—or maybe it was supposed to happen and I didn't know about it. Dance—get out there and dance—you're both doing what you were born to do."

There was a strange combination of elements in the darkened club. The band showed their surprise as they saw, behind Rayme's back, a beautiful dark-haired girl dressed in black leather slacks and a white sweater, setting the dance floor afire.

It was all improvisation. The beat was there, underlying Rayme's famous song about the big Texas man and the woman he'd finally met. Rayme turned around to follow the glances of the band and saw

Mary Jane spinning around the floor in a wild jazz ballet to his music. The song was coming to an end, but Rayme put in a filler. Charlie Tuna picked it up. Rayme threw back his head, his neck cords straining, the veins in his forehead bulging, pouring out all his energy in the Rayme Monterey trademark. The band behind him pushed the beat, Mary Jane picked it up, moving with abandon, free and loose. Now she looked at Rayme. He was looking at her. There was an electric connection.

He struck the last chord of his song, head thrown back with the final words of "Big Texas Man." Mary Jane did a fast twirl and gradually slowed down to end exactly with Rayme's last breath.

The singer and the dancer stood there, looking at each other. The band stayed quiet. It was a moment!

Then Rayme stepped down from the bandstand and walked up to Mary Jane. He didn't ask a question, but rather made a statement. "You're the girl in the picture."

She nodded. Her passion was gone. The electricity was gone. They were two damaged people in the process of building fences around themselves so they wouldn't be hurt again.

"How'd you find me?" Rayme asked coldly, fighting the sensual attraction of this girl. He didn't want to feel excited about a woman. He was too tied to Marny. The guilt of what he had felt watching the girl dance made him angry. At her.

Mary Jane turned and nodded toward Steve, who was still standing in the shadows. "Steve brought me here. We'd been to two other places, but couldn't find you."

Rayme turned toward Steve as Steve walked up to him. "You always turn up, don't you, Steve? There are times it's kind of nice. And then, there are other times—"

"Like tonight?"

Rayme nodded.

Mary Jane said, "I'm sorry we bothered you—we didn't mean to."

Steve spoke quietly to Rayme. "You're going to have to work together—you had to meet sometime, and this is the best way—each of you seeing what the other does best."

Mary Jane turned to Rayme. "I like what you say when you sing— I always have."

Rayme looked at her. "You dance like there's a fire in you. Never saw anything like it." With that, he turned around, waved to Charlie Tuna and his boys, and went out the front door of the Roxy.

Steve and Mary Jane looked at each other.

"I think you made a mistake with me—he doesn't like me and he doesn't want to work with me," Mary Jane said.

"Who says?"

"He's one of the rudest people I've ever met. I don't like him, either. He's a smartass. If I have to play many scenes with him, I don't think I can do it. I've got a terrific temper, I better warn you."

"Don't forget, you can be rude, too," Steve said. "And when you were dancing and he was singing, it was all there—I wish I had that on film."

41

UCLA Medical Center, Los Angeles

"I wish you'd come to see me sooner," Dr. Arms said. He was a fine-looking man in his late fifties, with a kind face.

"How long do I have?" she asked.

"Possibly your normal lifetime," the doctor answered, "if we begin the treatments immediately. Dermatomyositis is incurable as of now, but it can be arrested, and a breakthrough on a cure could come at any time."

"Arrested with cortisone?" she asked.

The doctor nodded. "What we call corticosteroid drugs are the most successful. We try to inhibit the body's immune system."

"Is there any way to avoid the swelling it causes?" she asked.

"No, but the medication affects different people in different ways. It's possible that you would only have swelling to a limited degree."

Magdalena turned and looked at the doctor directly. "In my face, isn't that right, Doctor?"

The doctor answered her matter-of-factly. "Usually the face is one of the places most affected. But, Miss Alba, a swollen face is a small price to pay for your life."

Magdalena sank into her chair in the spacious office in the research center of UCLA in Los Angeles.

The doctor continued, "I would like you to go to Pukhet Island in Thailand. It's a lovely and peaceful place and Dr. Cahill, a brilliant young research man, has the ideal conditions there to study and treat all forms of lupus and dermatomyositis. He has a special hospital that's more like a home. It really would be the best."

Magdalena cut him off. "That's impossible. I'm starting a new picture in a few weeks."

The doctor commented quietly, "You'll have to give it up or postpone it. You can't take on a strenuous schedule now. Rest is a very important factor in stopping this disease."

"But, Doctor," she said, "I have to make this picture now. For personal reasons. You see, Doctor, I was told in Paris that I had this disease and there was no cure for it and what I might have to go through even to arrest it. I suddenly thought, who can I turn to, who do I really trust, who really cares about the person rather than the image? I quickly came to an honest answer. No one."

The doctor glanced at her. "That's hard to believe. You're one of the most admired women in the world."

Magdalena shook her head. "No, Doctor, that's the image. But now, well, I've met someone, and there's just that small possibility that maybe he could love *me*, not the image. And suddenly . . ."

She smiled sadly, and then continued, ". . . suddenly I might have something, someone, to live for. That's rather a new feeling for me, and it's worth everything."

The doctor rose from his desk.

"Let's bring him in, let's tell him about this. If he loves you, he'll be the first one to want you to be treated. He'll help us."

Magdalena shook her head. "No. You promised me, Doctor, when I came in here, that this visit would be absolutely confidential and it has to be that way. If he knew, he might want to stand by me because he's looking at me now. But after my face began to swell—after my beauty was gone—after I was no longer an actress, a supposedly glamorous figure—after everything he knows me as is different and changed—no, Doctor, I am not that naive. I remember something in a biography of a great movie star, a quote from her, 'My lovers went to bed with the woman in the film, but woke up with only me.' Eternal love, as the stories go, does not exist outside the pages of stories. People can't live up to such an ideal. You know it and I know it. This man loves me, maybe . . . because I am who I am, and maybe because I look the way I do. So I will not take any treatments. To tell you the truth, Doctor . . ." She looked at him in all sincerity, ". . . as I told Dr. Loussard, if the price of stopping this disease is to lose my beauty, then I'd rather be dead."

"The way you look is really that important to you?"

She nodded, "Everything I have comes from the way I look. Everything I am. Without my beauty I have no life, I'm already dead."

The doctor shook his head. "Well, Miss Alba, I don't know that you can make it through a picture. How long is the shooting schedule?"

"Nine weeks," she said.

The doctor looked at her doubtfully. "You must come to see me every weekend. I will meet you here in the clinic or at my home on Saturdays or Sundays, whenever it's possible for you to come. I'm going to give you some vitamin shots and nutritional therapy to keep your energy up. It's possible I may have to give you a blood transfusion. And we'll do EMG's periodically. Electromyography. Muscle scans."

"Will the fatigue get worse?"

"Probably. Muscle weakness. And possibly skin rashes. And you may get progressively weaker. Watch out for anemia, soreness in the joints, and fever." Dr. Arms smiled at her. "I warn you, Miss Alba, I will keep fighting you until you let me give you the corticosteroids. Please think about it."

Magdalena offered her hand. "I won't change my mind," she said. "One thing I want to check again, Doctor. I was told this disease is not contagious. Is that absolutely true?"

He nodded. "Absolutely." He handed her his card. "My home number is there. Feel free to call me at any time. Your life is valuable. You bring pleasure to millions of people. Not many of us can say that. Think it over. There is a point, you know, when this disease begins to run wild. Once it is at that point, no amount of medicine or anything else will stop it. That's the risk you're running, taking on a new picture at this time. I want you to understand that. Nine weeks is a terrible gamble."

"I understand very well, Doctor. But I have to make this picture. If I leave it, the film will be shut down. That can't happen. Good-bye, Doctor."

42

Bel Air Hotel,
Bel Air

teve guided Magdalena up the curved stairway to the tower room. All by itself, surrounded by tall trees, gardens, and the mountains beyond, Villa 240 at the Bel Air Hotel was one of the most famous honeymoon suites in all of California. Steve had reserved it for the weekend.

He stood with Magdalena on the tower balcony, and they looked out over the lovely villas of what many believed to be the most romantic hotel in existence. A home, really, not a hotel. It was completely secluded; no one was in sight. A private world. Across from them and below, the famous white swans of Bel Air swam in the mystic glades among the gardens. It was a magical sight.

She turned to him, took his face in both her hands and kissed him softly. "I knew you would bring me to someplace like this—it means a great deal to me, Steve. Robert Montango told me you were the last of the romantics, and I'm beginning to believe him."

He took her into the large suite, radiant with candlelight. Bouquets of violets were scattered throughout the room.

Magdalena looked around, slowly looked back at Steve, then went to the violets on the coffee table, which held a letter from him.

She opened it and read, "Maggie, I've been looking for you all my life. And that is the truth. I love you, Steve."

"I love you, Steve," she said.

He put his arms around her tentatively. "I wanted it to be special."

She kissed him softly. "It was so important to me, to wait. I love you for understanding. I had to know you first. That's the way I am."

Steve kissed her more passionately, and she took his hands and kissed them and put her cheek against them.

Steve spoke quietly, "Will you marry me, Maggie?"

Magdalena looked up at him, her defenses gone, her sophisticated aura vanished. She was a girl again, a girl with a first love. "We'll talk about it after the picture," she answered. "Now—everything is so perfect—working together, our talks, the people we're with, the start of the picture. And tonight, our own real beginning. Please, let's leave it just as it is for the time being—"

She turned and picked up the overnight case Steve had carried into the room for her. She looked up at him, then kissed him and pressed up against him.

"I'll be back in a minute. Don't go anywhere."

She looked back around the room; she seemed to be photographing Steve and the room and the world outside, all in one glance.

"I want to remember everything, just the way you've made it."

She turned and crossed the narrow hallway into the large bathroom beyond. Steve went to the fireplace and lit the fire.

When Magdalena came back through the hallway, the sight of her took Steve's breath away. He was still dressed, although he had brought his overnight case in with Maggie's. He stood at one end of the room looking out at the trees in the garden and beyond to the pool in the moonlight.

She was wearing a pale blue negligee and nightgown of Thai silk trimmed in Irish lace. The nightgown was form-fitting to the waist, with a low, scooped neckline softly revealing Magdalena's perfect breasts. The negligee flowed in a train some four feet behind her, full at the waist, gathered together by a wide, sky-blue satin sash. Her high-heeled bedroom slippers were covered with the same sky-blue silk. Her hair fell softly down around her shoulders but was pulled back the way Steve liked it, revealing her strangely fawn-shaped ears, which intrigued all the great cameramen. Her porcelain skin was white in the candle-light, but her cheeks were softly flushed. The blue-green of her eyes was electric.

Her look was one of ultrafemininity, the receiver of love. As Magdalena told Steve later, "That's where men and women are so often different," she said. "For the men, sex seems to come first, the promise of love later. For women, at least for women like me," she said, "respect, consideration, to be cared for, to be held, to be treated with value and worth make a woman want to give herself to a man."

Montango had told him from the beginning, "This is a different kind of woman. You'll hear a lot of stories about her, but almost all of them are made up. This is a woman who places a high value on herself. None of the hit-and-run boys could even get started with her. Many of the famous lovers have called her frigid." As always, even her sexuality was a matter of controversy.

"Do you like me?" she said, standing there in front of him.

He laughed with the sheer incredulity of it. Here was one of the most desirable women in the world, legendary, famous, sought-after, and she was asking him if he liked her. He looked at her and then kissed her. She kissed him slowly at first, then passionately, putting her arms around his neck and stroking the back of his head.

She pulled her head back from his for a moment. "Well, are you going to make love to me with your clothes on?"

They both laughed.

For the first part of the night, Steve was a nervous lover. He was in awe of Magdalena, and it took her patience and understanding to enable Steve to make love to her. She told him it made no difference whether they actually made love that night at all. "They" were much more important to her than the physical act. She talked about other things and then suddenly he was at ease and his potency returned.

Steve had never known lovemaking in the way they created it together. This was no gymnastic test, or matching of physical abilities, or imaginative positions, or sexual fantasizing. There were no tricks about it. There was no acting. Steve had thought that sex, in many ways, had become overpromoted, packaged in every conceivable manner. He remembered the thrill of his first sexual experience, which was with a girl named Helene, and what sex had been like with Nancy and with Melanie—his first sexual experiences, in which there was mutual wonder and youthful dreams.

Now, the young people he knew treated sex like something you picked up at the neighborhood store. Everybody lived with everybody else, people changed partners after an evening's argument. Beautiful bodies burst at you from every billboard and every street corner. Sex no longer had subtlety. The wonder of it, the magic of two people lying together, the man inside the woman, the woman's arms around him, looking into each other's eyes in completeness and joy. Where had all that gone?

And now he'd found it again. A feeling more rare than he had ever experienced before. Because there was something about this woman that made everything important.

He thought of some lines from a play called *Four-Poster*. A father tells his son, in trying to explain sex to him, that there is a time he would come to know, when a man and woman who cared about each other lay together in a bed and the whole world came down to just them together, and the world had truth and meaning.

Suddenly, he was telling Magdalena what he was feeling. He was lying at this woman's side, his arms around her, her face just a breath away from his. And he was looking into her eyes, and he felt heart to heart, body and soul. And that's what he said.

"Maggie—right now—I feel we're one person. We're inside each other. I can feel you looking right through to me and when I look into your eyes, I feel that I'm looking right through to you. Right here, now, there is no game—there is no one on one—no lies—there's no ugliness—there's truth and God knows, beauty . . ." He reached out and brushed her forehead. "I'm more alive than I've ever been in my whole life."

"Make love to me again, Steve," Magdalena whispered. And then with a look in her eyes he didn't quite understand, she said, "I've never felt so alive in my life, either."

43

Bellagio Road,
Bel Air

The party was set up around Magdalena's pool. Steve watched her. It had been her idea. A party for his crew and their families.

There were forty people there, eating at tables of eight, encircling the pool. The music of *Flamenco Puro* was on the stereo and the party was Spanish style. Magdalena had cooked the paella and fabada herself, and she stood now at the outdoor cooking stove, an apron tied around her. She had learned to cook well, growing up in the gypsy encampment, and now she was loving to cook again, for Steve. He had most of his meals at her house, and when he was working late, she had something waiting for him there.

She had invited Kathleen and Lorelei to the party, and they were sitting at the table with Magdalena and Steve. Magdalena insisted that they sit on either side of their father; Steve watched how she made friends with them. He had known many beautiful women, and most of them did not want to be bothered with young children. None of them wanted young children to be in the way, between them and the man with whom they were involved.

Now, as he sat at the table, gaily decorated with Spanish colors, listening to the exciting and passionate strains of *Flamenco Puro*, he could not believe that the three people he loved most in the world were together with him.

Magdalena went from table to table, making sure her guests were cared for, serving those who wanted second helpings from the buffet. Many of the wives were surprised to see this famous actress serving them herself.

Magdalena was drawing out of every day, every bit of life and love and passion that she could. She screened out the future, and she waited until she was alone to think about her illness, and to be aware of the fear that lay within her.

At the end of the afternoon, at Steve's insistence, she sang several of the *Flamenco Puro* songs. Only Steve among the people there had ever seen her play the guitar and sing. Her strong singing voice completely surprised Steve's "family." Her voice was full throated, and her stance and manner took on the fire of the ancient songs.

As the guests left late in the afternoon, Steve prepared to drive his children home. He thanked Magdalena, and the girls embraced her; she had won them over.

"Thank you, Maggie," he said. "It was a beautiful afternoon for everybody." He kissed her, and then said softly, "I'll be back about eight, then let's go over to Trader's. You always like to go there Sunday nights. We can have a quiet dinner and an early night."

"I can't tonight, Steve," Magdalena said. "There are some friends of mine from Spain here," she said slowly. "I really have to be with them tonight—it's business, or I'd ask you to come with us."

Steve had never heard her be so vague, and he looked at her closely. "Well, all right," he said.

Magdalena smiled at him. "I'll call you when I get in. I want to talk to you before I go to sleep."

"All right, Maggie," Steve said. "I'll be at home. Come on, girls," he said. "How would you like to go by the Big Riders on the way home? They'll be open for another hour."

The girls clamored, "Yes, yes, wonderful, Daddy, let's go!"

The Big Riders was their nickname for the corner of Beverly and La Cienega, where there was an amusement park with all kinds of rides. Steve often took the girls there, and they had named it the Big Riders. They waved good-bye to Magdalena and went to the car.

When they arrived at Melanie's house, the children's mother wanted to talk to Steve about the girls' summer vacation and how they would divide their daughters' time. Steve stayed for a drink, and then he told them good-bye. They knew he would call them the next day. It was routine now.

Steve was sad when he left, but the children were resigned to the situation, and they knew they would see him soon. He drove away from the house in Santa Monica with the same terrible feeling in his stomach. He had gone in that day from the heights of pure happiness to the return of the loneliness he felt when he took his children back to someone else's home. They should be going home with him. That was the feeling he always had. It was as though a part of him were being cut off. And, for a moment, all the old doubts and sadnesses and guilts came pouring in on him. His children were part of him, and they should be together. Life was not the same when they weren't with him.

It would be another week or even ten days before he saw them now. Why? Why couldn't it have worked out? Why couldn't he and Melanie have really tried after the mistakes on both sides? Could he really not accept flaws in anyone close to him? Did he really demand perfection, as Melanie had said? His thoughts led him to drive by Magdalena's house on his way home. It was some kind of tie to the new life he had found with her—and now she was linked with his children, because they liked her, and he felt she liked them.

He turned off Sunset Boulevard to Bellagio Road after he came over from the Valley on the San Diego Freeway. Magdalena's house had become his second home.

A block away, in the early evening light, he braked his car and pulled over to the curb. He could see her clearly ahead.

Magdalena was coming out of her house with a man. He was older, distinguished-looking. Magdalena's arm was through his arm, and she was dressed for the evening. She was wearing her sable coat, the one she always wore when she was going to some special place for dinner.

Steve felt a terrible sinking sensation in his stomach. There was no one else with them, no evidence of any other "friends" in sight. As they got into the car, he sped down the street. He wanted to be sure that no one else was in the car. He prayed there would be. She had told him "friends."

It was a limousine. There was a chauffeur, the tall, distinguished man, and Magdalena Alba.

A fury seized Steve. There was no rationalization, no other thought, except that Magdalena, his Magdalena, had lied to him. He broke into a sweat. He had to stop himself from swinging around the other car, ahead in traffic, and pulling it over to the curb. What the hell was she doing with another man? All the triggers went off—triggers he had known all his life. He forced himself to turn up a side street and head for Holmby Hills. There was a terrible pain in his stomach, a pain he had known often in his life.

He went to his workroom over the garage. He looked at the small cluster of sayings on his wall. That one from Rinder, he thought. Why can't I make that work now?

"Yesterday's hurt is today's understanding and tomorrow's love." There it was, spelled out for him. That's why Rinder's quotation was there. It was something that had been given him by one of the women he had gone with. It had struck him because of his own insecurities and pains from childhood.

Why couldn't he take these words and make them work with his pain over Melanie? Why couldn't he make them work now, with Magdalena? So a woman had lied to him. A woman he trusted, believed in—he would have sworn—but what did that mean? She was a great actress. That's why he'd sought her out in the first place.

So she had seemed to commit—well, what did that mean? Everybody lied! Had he ever lied to a woman? Had he ever broken a commitment with a woman? Had he ever cheated on a woman? Yes, to all three. Well, why couldn't he accept the same thing from a woman he loved?

He'd never been able to figure that out. When a woman he loved, or even liked very much, lied to him or made love to somebody else, or backed out of a commitment, he was suddenly on a rocket. A rocket deep within himself. Exploding in pain. In his gut. Those moments became traumatic, obsessive, and there was a chain reaction all the way back—to where?

44

Holmby Hills,
Bel Air

It was early in the morning before Steve could finally drift off to sleep. The image of Magdalena with another man kept flashing through his mind. He'd seen her himself, coming out of her home, dressed for the evening.

Where was she? Who was she with? Was she making love to another man? He couldn't stop thinking about it. The thought of her in another man's embrace. The thought of her naked with another man. The thought of her opening herself for another man. The thought of another man kissing those beautiful rose-colored nipples. The thought of another man on top of her. He couldn't stand it.

He could hear her, the way she said so softly, "I want you." The way she moaned, the way she said, "Mi amor, mi amor," over and over again, and then—God, had she done that, too?

He twisted and turned in bed, and then the phone began to ring. One-thirty in the morning. One forty-five, one fifty-five, two-ten, it had to be her. Sure, she was going to call him and tell him good night and pretend that everything was fine and that she was really with her so-called "friends." Well, he was through. He wasn't going to answer the phone. She'd be in the picture and he was professional enough to keep himself in line and her, too. But he'd never hold her again. He'd never again kiss those full, red lips. He'd never again feel her tongue darting in and out of his mouth as she moved her voluptuous body against him. He'd never again hold her naked and feel the whole world full of meaning, coming down to just the two of them. Goddamn it, how could she do that?

He felt the pain in his groin now—the knot in his stomach. The bondage—that woman belonged to you and you belonged to her. And that bondage nobody could break—nothing—not even death.

What a joke. What a fool he'd been! Krakow, the psychologist, had been right. Searching for the perfect woman, always. There wasn't any perfect woman. There wasn't any true woman.

He'd thought Magdalena Alba was proof that there was meaning to the world. And now, through some goddamned man whom she had met somewhere—or was it a man out of her past—one of those European men she'd known—was it the man from her home? Who the hell knew? She was with another man—maybe many more—she was only with Steve because of the picture. All the meaningful times they'd shared; everything that had been said—it didn't mean a thing—how could she do that?

The phone rang again. He picked up her picture on his work desk and threw it at the telephone. It hit the receiver and the glass smashed. It ripped across the image—Magdalena Alba looking out at him, from the broken frame on the floor. He kicked it into the corner. He wished he were kicking her. He'd kick her into oblivion—until she couldn't hurt him any more—until the pain stopped.

He took another drink. There had been a long string of them now, but none of them knocked him out. He sat there in the shadows of his workroom above the garage. Where the hell was his life? Eight hours before he had been alive, vital, excited—he couldn't wait for the next moment of living.

Now his world had been kicked into a hat. He didn't feel anything anymore. He was numb. For God's sake, he was thirty-eight years old, and a woman could do this to him—turn him off, "dejuice" him creatively? Castrate his abilities? Goddamn her.

He hated her. He turned over in bed.

He never wanted her so much in all his life. Once more—he had to have her once more—just once more—then he would walk out, and kiss her off. The bitch. She was just a beautiful and expensive whore. The rumors had been right. Goddamn it, how could she do that—go out with another man?

He drifted off finally, around three in the morning. That was the last time he remembered checking the time on his watch on the bedside table. Images of Magdalena making love with another man, fulfilling his worst fears, filled his dreams. God, there'd never be another woman like her. He was stuck. He was hooked—he was bonded. Bonded. He was too mature to let that happen . . . been around too much . . . he'd had too many women.

Suddenly, Steve's eyes opened; he was on the alert. He listened. There was an unmistakable scraping noise against the outer wall of his workroom apartment over the garage.

He thought for a moment it was a nightmare, but it was real. His heart started beating faster. He'd never had a gun. He had planned to get one during the rise in violence in Los Angeles. Now he was caught.

The bedroom part of his workroom was right there, over the garage, two stories up, windows on every side. He'd designed it that way, for his writing.

What in the hell was going on—how would he defend himself? Somebody was coming up that wall and through the open window.

Steve always slept with the windows open. He loved fresh air. He'd never imagined a burglar might climb that wall. And how the hell was he going to defend himself against an armed intruder? He'd never learned any karate or any of the new forms of physical defense. He'd boxed some in college, but he hadn't had a real fight in years—even a country club fight. He'd knocked out an actor once who had berated him on the set—that was four years ago.

The scraping was getting louder and louder. And then he watched, fascinated, as in the dim shadows of the night, the intruder stepped from a ladder through the open window.

It was a woman in a full-length dark sable coat, her features very clear, even in the moonlight. It was Magdalena.

She stood looking at him sitting up in his bed. Then she called softly down to the bottom of the ladder which had brought her up to the second story and into Steve's workroom, "Pick me up in the morning, Sara. Nine o'clock."

There was a slight noise as the ladder was pulled away from the building. She stood there, looking her elegant and beautiful self, one of the most publicized women in the world, who took it as a simple matter that she had climbed up a ladder and entered Steve's room through a window at four o'clock in the morning.

"You didn't answer your phone," Magdalena said, as nonchalantly as if she were at an afternoon garden party.

"You bitch!" Steve said.

Magdalena asked him, "Aren't you going to ask me in?"

"You're already in," Steve answered.

"You should know me by now, Steve. I don't wait for answers. I want to know what's going on with my life. You don't answer the phone at three o'clock in the morning, I know something's wrong."

"Really?" Steve asked. "What could be wrong? Nothing more than you lied to me about tonight. Lied to me about 'friends' from Spain. Lied to me about how late you'd be out. Lied to me about why I couldn't be with you, with your Spanish friends. Goddamn it. Where were you?"

Magdalena stood her ground. "If I didn't know you, and what's wrong with you, this would be the end for us."

She walked over to him by the side of his bed. She had never looked more appealing. He had never desired her so much.

"I hate your guts," Steve said.

Magdalena smiled. "That's the other side of love. All the best writers have said that."

"What do writers know about love?" Steve said. "Philosophers . . . screw them. All I know is that when I saw you come out of your house with a man and get into that car, and I knew you'd lied to me about what you were doing, I got sick."

"You talk about love but you don't know what love is, Steve," she said. "You've got a real problem about possessing people. I'm not your possession. I won't love that way. What are you doing spying on me, anyway?"

"I just happened to drive home by way of your house. I didn't plan to," Steve snapped back.

"I love you, Steve," Magdalena said quietly. "With all my heart."

He started to answer, and she put her hand over his mouth.

"No, you're going to listen to me. And I want you to hear every word. I swear that since I met you I have never been with another man. I've never wanted to be with another man. I've never gone out with another man in the sense that you're talking about. But there are certain things in my life that I must keep private. I ask you to trust me. It's only about those things, when you question me, that I would ever lie to you, as I did tonight. Tonight was a personal matter for me. I had to do it. I wanted to do it. It had nothing to do with anything sexual. Or anything that should bother you.

"I didn't want to lie to you, but you forced me, with your questions about where I was going and what I was doing. Just because for one night we weren't together.

"I love you, but I can't feel that I'm being spied on, and watched. I want to make your picture with you. I want us to be together. I want us to try to create something together on film—like the child I would love to have with you. Look at me, Steve. Can you doubt what I'm saying?"

He looked at her and said nothing. He swallowed. She was convincing. He wanted so much to believe. Why couldn't he trust her? She had to feel what he felt.

She slipped off her coat and lay down beside him. "Make love to me. Mi amor, mi vida. You are mine, and I am yours. Give me room enough to breathe, Steve. That's all I ask. Trust me as I trust you."

45

Steve's Dressing Room, Samuel Goldwyn Studios, Warner Hollywood

Edmund Bradford Wilson's voice came over the telephone. "Steve, I've just got the word, straight from the D.A.'s office. There's going to be a new grand jury hearing on Rayme. No doubt about it. This district attorney knows he's got a headline grabber. He feels that sooner or later public sentiment will switch against Rayme. Or else the public will just lose interest in the case. And he's going to keep trying."

"This can't happen till the picture's over, can it?" Steve asked.

"The district attorney's trying to speed it up. I'd say it's fifty-fifty that Rayme will be served with a warrant before the picture's over. That could be great publicity for the D.A.'s office—no catering to special interests—handling celebrities the same way they would anyone else. You can write it yourself, Steve. It's an old ploy, but it gets headlines and political attention. And there's an election in the fall."

Steve asked, "If he gets served while he's on the picture, can we delay his appearance in New York until we finish shooting?"

"I'm not sure," Wilson answered. "It would be difficult. He's so damn big right now that it's hard to predict.

"I'm going to prepare everything I can ahead of time. Is there any chance of your delaying the picture, Steve? We could push them, try to get it over with, and hope Rayme's freed again—and then make the picture without a problem."

"No chance," Steve answered. "Gregson is just waiting for something like that. It would be a perfect excuse for him. I'm a week late now. We must start shooting in two weeks."

"So we're talking about ten weeks. We have to try and stall the D.A. and his staff."

"That's right," Steve answered. "If Rayme's served before that time, the picture's finished. I know you'll do your best, Ed. Please try every-thing. We just won't have a picture if anything happens to him."

"I understand. Talk to you later," Wilson said.

Steve hung up the phone in his dressing room in the studio. Lieu was fixing him a salad in the kitchenette. She had heard the conver-sation. As she walked into the small dining room with a salad and iced tea, Lieu spoke reassuringly. "It will never happen. You're going to finish your film."

46

Dorothy Chandler Pavilion, Los Angeles Music Center

"Georgia, sweet Georgia."

The refrain of the Ray Charles standard rang out through the Dorothy Chandler Pavilion at the Los Angeles Music Center.

Ray Charles was a thin, wiry man, and his supercharged body danced with his music. He kicked his legs off the pedals as the rhythm mounted, sometimes bringing them up clear over the level of the piano stool and to the edge of the piano itself. They were rubber legs, bouncing almost out of control in weird, strange, original dance steps, but always in rhythm with "Georgia." His head was back, his dark glasses shifting across his nose, his face trembling with emotion. As he finished, Rayme was on his feet. Everyone else followed.

It was an ovation. Magdalena watched Steve standing there, clapping his hands, raised high in the air. She smiled. That was one of the things she loved about Steve—he had the enthusiasm of a teenager. When he loved something, it was all out.

And Magdalena caught, in just a fraction of a second, Lieu's look at Steve. It was the first time she had ever seen Lieu's face without its passivity. There was a deep look about her. There it was, for one brief second, unmistakable. A look of absolute love. As a woman, Magdalena understood it all.

This fascinating Cambodian woman, with her poise and pride, and her stunning looks, was in love with Steve. And Steve didn't even know it. A feeling of identification came over Magdalena. This was a woman she respected and liked, who was in love with the same man she loved. And suddenly, Magdalena felt the urgency of her illness, the desperate desire to stay well, to live out the years with her man.

How much she wished she could tell him that the tall, distinguished man who had escorted her from her house the night that had caused so much trouble between them was her doctor, Dr. Alfred Arms. He had come to take Magdalena to his home for dinner, where his wife was waiting; the same night he had checked her, in his office in his home.

It was getting more difficult to disguise her problem from Steve. He wanted to know where she was all the time, what her appointments were, what meetings she had that he didn't know about. And she knew that doubt still lingered in his mind about that night he'd seen her with Dr. Arms. But how could she tell him who it really was?

She wondered what Lieu felt about her. She wanted the respect of this woman.

There were five days left before the beginning of rehearsal. *The Rest of Our Lives* was almost ready to start shooting.

47

Steve's Workshop, Holmby Hills

The detectives had done their work well. They'd come to Steve as the most expensive, highly respected international private detective firm in the world—the Courtwright Agency of London and New York.

It was after midnight in Steve's workroom when he spread out the reports and photographs over his desk.

This was the life of Magdalena Alba—everything about the past that had been missing.

The pictures covered more than twenty years. There she was, looking up at him as a young girl, already sensuous, already voluptuous. There she was in a Parisian soap advertisement, almost completely naked. In fashion ads, in early movie stills, as an extra in *Carmen*, barebreasted. Pictures of her with famous men in many countries, all rich and successful. Pictures of her being received by the Royal Family in England. At Ascot. At Deauville and La Scala. Hollywood stills.

Then there were typewritten reports tracing the origins of the woman who now obsessed him.

He couldn't get enough of Magdalena Alba. He wanted to make love to her twenty-four hours a day. He wanted to do everything with her. He wanted to undress her every time he saw her. He wanted those incredible breasts in his hands and in his mouth. He wanted to be alone with this woman. He didn't want anyone else around. He wanted to lose himself in her.

But the question that had hit him in the gut the night she lied to him came up again. She still refused to tell him the name of the man who had taken her out that Sunday evening. When Magdalena didn't call exactly the time she said she would, the alarm bells went off deep within him.

Sometimes she was out when he called. She wasn't in her beauty shop when he thought she was supposed to be there. He couldn't stand it.

Every possible black thought filled his mind. Was she seeing someone else? Was she reliving some old affair? Was she a woman who had to have more than one lover? Was she a woman who'd ever been true to any man?

He had sworn to her that he believed her. He thought he did when he was with her, but when they were apart the suspicions came back on him hard. He had no control of his jealousy. That old feeling he hated in himself had taken over.

One thing was certain: there had been other men in her life. Other men had slept with her, other men had touched her. Other men had kissed her. She had given herself to others. He didn't even think of the fact that he hadn't known her when those things had happened. He didn't think of his own affairs with other women, with the woman he'd been married to, with the women he'd almost been married to, and with the women he'd lived with for long periods of time. He thought of none of his own sexual experiences.

This woman had to belong to him. And how could she have done this to him? How could she have slept with anyone before him? How could she have allowed any man to touch her, how could she have allowed any man to enter her?

The terrible, sick feeling of "his woman" being made love to by other men struck him at all kinds of odd moments. He could be driving the car, and the emotion would be so violent he would have to stop the car and get out and walk around.

He was in a movie theater for a premiere. And he had to get up and leave the theater when he saw a handsome leading man, who had once gone out with Magdalena five years before, talking to her.

When he ran her pictures and saw her embracing other men, kissing them, letting them hold her body against theirs, he became enraged.

He'd felt this feeling before. He'd felt it with Nancy and with Melanie. But never like this. He'd fought to keep it from affecting his work. He had to know the truth, face it, control it. He'd decided to find out the truth once and for all, so that he could deal with it. The hell with rumors and imagination. He'd hired the best detective agency in the world to do an immediate printout on Magdalena's life. And now, alone in his workroom, he didn't want to read the reports or look at the pictures, but then again, he couldn't wait to.

The evidence was all there in front of him. The facts, figures, dates, confidential reports. No doubt about it, Magdalena Alba was a woman of mystery. Of intrigue, assignations. An expert in walking out on people. A collector of jewels, luxurious apartments, choice real estate. A woman of substantial financial holdings, all conservatively invested with financial masters in different cities in the world. Financial masters with whom she had been linked.

There was no way to escape it. Many men probably had possessed her. Expensive and powerful men. And God knows, Steve thought, what isn't contained in these pages.

Magdalena the prize! Magdalena the perfect woman. The ideal love he had sought all his life. The one flawless woman he had ever known. Beautiful, intelligent, sensitive, creative, and she belonged to him!

Doctor Krakow had warned him years before. He had been one of the last of Freud's original students, an old, old man from the Menninger Clinic who was practicing in Beverly Hills. A German intellectual, Jewish, one of the most brilliant men Steve had ever met. Steve had had the privilege of working with him for a year.

One day, the distinguished old German had tossed his head and looked at Steve with amazement. He said, "At last, I've seen a man who spends his life searching for the perfect love. Don't you realize, Steve, that this is the myth of myths—the search of writers and poets forever—the journey that has no end—there *is* no perfect love, unless some people far more spiritual than I find a perfect love with their vision of God. Here on earth, there is no perfect love. But men like you, and they are the stuff of legends, go on searching all their *lives* for perfection. Women fall in love with that, but they can't live with it. It's too demanding."

He had looked at Steve as if he were looking at his son. "Steve," he said, "give up this illusion. There is no perfect man—there is no perfect woman—there is no perfect love. Maybe you can touch that sometimes. But if you chase it, if you pursue it, it will always be an illusion, and it will ruin your life. You will profane the very idealism you seek. No one lives with pure beauty. Look past the glamorous facade of people you work with. Search for quality, honesty, caring, commitment, not for illusions and escape—you lead life as though it were an epic movie and you were the leading actor—make your actor as human and full of mistakes as *you* really are."

Was Magdalena another illusion? What did he really possess? A woman who had been possessed by many?

Men were probably part of a texture of every picture she had made. He'd heard about that many times. The relationships of stars. Those women carefully picked their mentors and seemed to fall in love with every director they had, always getting the benefit of that director's special considerations. And then when the picture was over, maybe there were one or two more films with the same combination and then there were new people. And new romances, new commitments. New breaking of those commitments. Was this the reality of their relationship?

Steve picked up the phone and called her at home. She wasn't there. She wasn't at the beauty shop. She wasn't at aerobics class. All afternoon, she was missing. He never imagined that on the same day that he had received the results of the expensive detective work about her, Magdalena was in Dr. Arms's medical quarters at UCLA. She was already beginning to feel the terrible drain on her vital energies that marked the inroads of her disease.

Steve turned the car off the road to the east, leading through the hills to San Ysidro. He had reserved the cottage for the night. They were going to talk about the "story" as it was evolving.

Both of them were quiet. They were used to these shared quiet moments now. They didn't have to talk. That was one of the things they valued most about their relationship. No one had to keep up a conversation.

Magdalena was determined not to show Steve the fear that was eating at her. Somehow she had pushed the disease out of her head during the last few weeks. She had felt well, filled with happiness. She had finally found a man who was strong enough for her, and not afraid to show a woman his love.

Steve was making his way through all her defenses. Little by little, day by day, she had found them dropping away, the defenses she had built up over the years.

Her day began when she saw him. The nights were over when they separated. And most of their waking hours were consumed with *The Rest of Our Lives*. The story was taking shape now, a modern relationship story with four powerful parts—based on true events—with moving, real circumstances and a passionate commitment to quality, people, work, and truth—taking a stand in one's life for what one believed—and in the context of modern realities.

She was thankful that her last film, and the last part of her life, were going to mean something.

Magdalena watched Steve taking the curves through the hills in Santa Barbara. The top was down, the way it had been that first night on the Malibu Road. She was remembering everything that had passed between them. She could never let him know. She had to salvage her strength.

What was so different about him tonight? He was quiet, but there was an electricity about him. His mouth was tight at the corners, and the lines from his nostrils to his mouth seemed deeper. His manner was a little rigid, even while he drove. He was usually so relaxed driving. But now, his fluidity and ease were gone.

"Where were you this afternoon?" Steve finally asked, casually. His light blue eyes had grown cold.

"On an errand," she said.

"Where?" he asked.

She laughed. "Just an errand, Steve. In Beverly Hills."

"For four hours?" he asked. "I looked for you. I called a few places— no one had seen you."

"How would you find me in Beverly Hills with all the people shopping, Steve? You've never looked for me before."

"I wanted to see you. I was worried about you. You weren't home," Steve said.

She watched him carefully. "What is it?"

"Nothing."

Magdalena reached out her hand, as she so often did, and touched his on the steering wheel. He moved away; Steve never did that.

She turned toward him. "Steve, what's the matter? Something is— I know you too well."

"You know a man in Rome named Pavardo?"

Magdalena looked at him quietly. "Yes, I know him."

Steve sped up, recklessly, on a curve. The car was definitely going too fast for this road. "Do you know him well?" he asked.

He was attacking her and the car on the road at the same time.

"Why do you ask me?"

"Does Villa Santana sound familiar to you—a villa with a famous reputation and a famous owner?"

"What is all this—what's happened to you? And slow down. We could have an accident."

"I didn't hear an answer."

"All right, Steve," she said quietly. "What has happened to you? Why all these questions? What are you getting at?"

"You know what I'm getting at," Steve said. "Pavardo. Italian producer. He set you up for three years. Did you live at his house, Villa Santana, as his mistress—for three years?"

She looked at him sharply. "That's none of your business."

He took another curve, the tires skidding. "Oh, yes, it is. What the hell were you doing, not going to bed with me, not sleeping with me for weeks, saying we had to be friends first, acting like the Virgin Mary?"

She slapped Steve across the face. His hands slipped on the wheel. The car skidded again. Her face was deadly white.

"Take me home!" she said. "Take me home!"

He yelled at her. "We've got a reservation for tonight, and we're going to keep it. At San Ysidro." He went on, "Pavardo has a great reputation—a whole string of women. And you were the mistress he loved the most. He spent more money on you and more time with you. And you got the picture contract you wanted."

"No one could ever buy me, do you understand? No one!"

The car was careening around the Santa Barbara curves, leading to San Ysidro, but she didn't care anymore. She was hitting him with both hands, screaming and crying. The car swung into an embankment just below the San Ysidro sign. It ran over two gulleys and smashed into the high road shoulder. Both of them were thrown against the dashboard.

Steve's manner suddenly changed. "Are you all right, Maggie?"

She was trembling, crying.

"I'm not Maggie. I'm not anything to you. For weeks, we've been together, and now, out of the blue, you come at me with these questions and accusations. I don't ever want to see you again."

She got out of her side of the car and started up the road toward San Ysidro Ranch and the clusters of individual cottages, landscaped into the mountain hillside. Steve followed her.

"Maggie, my God, I don't know what's happening to me."

Magdalena said, "I knew it. I knew it was too good to be true. You've been playing a game with me. I believed"—she was half crying and the words came tumbling out—"I believed you were different."

He pulled her into a recessed area on the twisting mountain road.

It was one of the small picnic areas the San Ysidro Ranch management had placed on different parts of the grounds, with secluded tables and benches for guests to use if they wished to eat outside. Steve took Magdalena by the arms.

"Leave me alone," she said. "I want to go home, but not with you."

"Maggie, I can't—it's true, I can't live without you. I can't stand the thought of somebody else in your life, ever. All those stories—"

"All what stories?" she asked through her tears.

"Stories about you from everywhere. God, I couldn't stand it, Maggie. Pavardo and others like him. Christ, Maggie, how could you do that?"

"What have you done, had somebody check out my life?" She looked at him incredulously, and then realized the truth. "You *have* had me checked out, haven't you? That's what happened. You put detectives on me and my life. At the same time I'm sleeping with you, you're checking me out, and you believe everything they say, whatever it is.

"You never grew up, did you? You're back in some dream world, looking for a holy virgin just made for you. Well, let me tell you something. I'm not ashamed of anything I've done in my life. I'm proud of who I am and what I have managed to become. And I thought you were, too. Whatever you've done to get information about me— all you had to do was ask me and save yourself all that money and trouble. If your idea of loving someone is to sit down and have them recite every love affair of their life, I would have done it for you. I would have tried to help you grow up. You're playing romantic games—you're trying to live out some childish dream of perfection.

"Who is perfect? Are you? When someone starts telling me something about you, and many have, I refuse to listen. I don't want an illusion. I want reality—I want to know it, count on it, and accept it with all its faults. And you've got faults, Steve, and this incredible jealousy is the worst. It will kill our love and friendship, too—I won't live with it—but I will try to help you get over it because that's how I love you. Whatever you are, I love you. And one more time, I said to myself, for the last time—I'm going to throw everything in the street. That's what the gypsies say. Throw everything out the window and into the street. And take one last chance that maybe in this crazy world, a man and a woman could really love each other. That's what I thought we had, Steve. And I've been more alive these last few weeks than I've ever been in my life.

"Some nights," she was crying openly, "some nights, I have been so happy with you that I've wanted the world to end right then, for us, anyway. So that there never would be any pain between us or any hurt or any disappointment. So we could live and die on that kind of high."

She glanced up at the sky. "We began in the stars, Steve. And you're dragging us down to the ground and worse. This is gutter talk—from you. Who did I sleep with, where did I get money? Did I sell myself? Am I really a whore? That's what you're asking, isn't it? Am I really a whore up for sale?"

"No, no, I didn't mean it," Steve said. "I didn't mean that."

"Yes, you did. And you want me to be a whore, don't you? Because then I won't be worth loving. Well, you're stuck, Steve. I'm not a whore. I'm a woman who loves you. And don't ask me why, for God's sake, because right now I'm thinking I'm the stupidest woman alive. But I can't cut you out of my heart. And I'll tell you something, Steve. You're the stupidest man in the whole world if you don't see what you have. You've told me about your hurts and rejections. How many of us have someone in this world who really loves us, whom we can go to when the outside world gets too much? That's what I am for you, Steve. I'm there with all my faults, with whatever I've done or been in the past—not to be judged by you and not to judge you—but to be just what we have become."

He put his arms around her. "Maggie, Maggie." His voice broke.

She drew back from him. "This is the last time, Steve. If you ever again question me about the past, if you ever again tear into me with your questions and innuendos, you'll never see me again. I'll walk out of your life. I'll walk out of your picture. I don't have time to waste."

She put her arms around him, at last. He clutched at her desperately. Then she looked at him and he dried her tears.

"Steve, there's one thing keeping you from being a great artist. I know that now, after working with you these weeks. I know what you can be. I know your gifts. But you spend so much time looking for perfection. There is none.

"What there are, are good things and good people, even if they are not perfect. You're your own worst enemy. Why do you think you have gone from woman to woman, leaving them when you find imperfections, when the tiresome and boring and unbeautiful things of just living day to day, just surviving, destroy your illusion. Someday you'll know that loving somebody includes everything. Their human faults, vulgarities. Things about the other person that are distasteful, unpleasant—things that you can hate and despise—but underneath all that is a bond, a connection that gives life meaning and joy. Steve, my life has been without joy almost always—until now. For God's sake, don't destroy us."

48

Office of the President, MGL

"What the hell do you think you're doing, Wayland?" Gregson said angrily, and threw the letter across his desk.

Steve glanced at it. It was one of the letters he had written to the members of his crew, to be delivered a few days before the actual beginning of the film. It was something Steve had done since his first picture, *Remembrance*. On that film, he'd had a crew of four. Now there were sixty-three.

Before each picture, he wrote a letter to each crew member. He hated all the "event" letters he got, which obviously were reprinted in a fancy way even with the person's signature duplicated almost convincingly. Someone wrote a master letter and a thousand people in the industry got the same letter. They could be done so that personal names could be inserted at the beginning. Who the hell did that fool? He preferred to get nothing if it wasn't really written to him.

So, Steve had written individual letters which he'd dictated on cassettes and Lieu had typed up. Most of the crew members had worked for him before. So it was easy to personalize out of the recollections he had of working with each one of them. The point Steve made was that he couldn't make the picture alone, that everyone had a contribution to make, and that he wanted each person to know why Steve wanted him or her to work on that project. Why he thought the film counted.

And with each letter went a script of the film that was about to begin. He asked for reactions and suggestions.

Sometimes in the past he had used suggestions that had come in from the crew. One of the best suggestions, in fact, had come from a maintenance painter.

The crews became bound together, with few exceptions, through the years. Often, a crew was treated differently from the so-called "artists"—casts, department heads, technical "stars." But Steve believed that everyone on a film had something to give, and he went for that. The personalization of the letters struck home.

Now, with *The Rest of Our Lives*, the letters had explained that the screenplay would come later in the week, because Steve was still rewriting. He asked for each man's and woman's loyalty to the project.

The letters spoke of the percentage of profits to be divided, pro rata, among the crew members. No one working on the picture was excluded from a percentage.

The letter Gregson had thrown across the desk was to a property master, someone Steve hadn't known before, who had been hired through the studio pool. Steve glanced at the letter, recognized the name of the prop man, and looked up at Gregson.

"What are you doing with this letter?" Steve asked. "It's addressed to one of the prop men we've hired. We've taken him off your maintenance payroll and put him on our film payroll. Since you don't have a job for him right now, it ought to make you happy."

Gregson shot up out of his chair. "Wayland, I've heard about these letters of yours before and the trouble they cause. You know damn well that every worker in the studio, when he sees some letter that some friend of his gets, wants to work on your crew. I know that's why you send them. And now you're talking about giving all these people points in your project. That's easy enough to toss off when the picture you're making doesn't have a chance to break even, much less make a profit. But it's seductive. And it's against the whole principle of the studio."

"That's why I like it," Steve fired back. "At least you get the point."

"You're goddamned right I get the point, Wayland. The point is, everywhere you go, you've got to try to change the system. You've got to do something different, whatever it is. Now, goddamn it, every workman on this lot is trying to get assigned to your picture. Every goddamned one of them. They bought all that 'creative family' bullshit— they can go home and talk about how they own one-eighth of a percent in a 'big picture.' And they lose their fear."

"Fear of what?" Wayland asked.

"The fear of losing their jobs—Wayland, you don't know one fucking thing about leadership. The way to get the most out of a man or a woman, too, is to have them afraid every single day that they may lose their jobs.

"From the time they wake up in the morning, I want every person who works for my studio to be afraid they might get canned that day. That means they're going to be on time, they're going to watch their coffee breaks, they're not going to be one minute late from their lunch period, they're not going to be bucking for fringe overtime—they're not going to be foreclosing on every single goddamn union rule. Because they know, if they work for me, that they could be gone tomorrow if they don't do what they're getting paid for. Fear, Wayland—that's what produces results."

"You're sick, Gregson," Steve said. "That's one thing that's wrong with some of this industry. Thank God there are studio heads who don't believe that's the way to treat people who work for you.

"Do you know, Gregson, that when Samuel Goldwyn made a picture in his studio, everybody on his lot went to the preview? Everyone was part of that picture. They were a team.

"And it was the same for so many of the people who built the studios. They tell me Irving Thalberg was like that. And Darryl Zanuck. And even Jack Warner. All these men cared about the companies they controlled and the films they made. If you ever studied the way this business was built, you'd know that.

"But you can't learn it through all the computers and the conglomerates and the stock deals and everything else that you work by, Gregson. That has nothing to do with people. And motion pictures are people. The good ones are about people and made by people.

"I'm telling you now, there's nothing in our contract that says I can't write letters to whomever I want, that I can't run my own picture, that I can't handle my crew the way I want to."

He stepped up to Gregson. "And don't call me in here anymore. That's not in my contract either. Stay away from me. Stay away from my picture. Live up to the contract, Gregson."

"You're the one who's not going to live up to it," Gregson fired back. "We're making the cost runs every day. And *that's* in our contract, Wayland. You're going to go over budget, just as sure as hell. And the minute you do, I'm going to pull the plug on you."

The two men looked at each other, then Steve walked out.

49

Stage Six,
Goldwyn Studios,
Warner Hollywood

The first day's rehearsal for *The Rest of Our Lives* was on Stage Six at the old Goldwyn Studios, now the Warner-Hollywood Studio.

Sam Goldwyn had used it for all his major pictures. Lieu had found Mr. Goldwyn's old conference table in a storehouse on the back lot and she'd had it refinished and collected the matching chairs from different storage places around the stages. In the center of the cavernous stage was the table. The finished scripts were in front of each place. The coffee mugs. The yellow notepads. One big stage light above the table cast a circle of illumination around it.

Steve's actors and his crew spread around the table. The atmosphere was like a briefing for a bombing run—between old friends. Steve had his hand on the script. "Every film that was shot on this stage in the Goldwyn days was a passionate attempt to make something of meaning. Many of those films have become classics, screening every day somewhere in the world.

"That's the kind of film we're trying to make with *The Rest of Our Lives*. Every one of you has a passionate commitment to your work, and so do the people in the story. We're going to have this week of invaluable rehearsal, Magdalena, Robert, Rayme, and Stephanie, so these parts can take on your colors, your feelings, your input."

He nodded to David Thayer, the cameraman. "David, I want every shot diagrammed by you and your crew. My notes have all been typed up and they're there for you—every scene illustrated with my storyboard drawings of the vision I have for the way to shoot that scene. Like the words of the script, those aren't frozen either. I don't want you to ignore my concepts, but I want you to improve them if you can. The film is going to be done as I visualize it, but if you want to change the way I visualize the shooting of any scene, I want to hear about it. I want to have your ideas back from you in storyboard form. There is no detail too small for us to get worked out before we shoot it.

"Boris?" He nodded at Boris Peters. "I've been over your sketches for the first four weeks' shoot. I've approved them all. I indicated a few small special things that I want in certain sequences.

"Frank?" He turned to Frank Warner, the sound effects man. "I want every extraneous sound track of every location we shoot. I've marked some scenes in the script that I will shoot without live sound coverage in order to save money. But I want the real sounds there when you and I dub them in.

"John?" He turned to John Hammell, the music editor. "I want you and Rayme to work closely. We won't do the score in this picture in specific time segments because I don't want to restrict Rayme in the way he works. I want all major and minor themes and songs to be recorded in full. Rayme and I have worked these out. I want you to keep an eye on each selection as we go along, so that we will have it in all forms that we need when you and I go to cut it up and dub it in for the musical track of our picture.

"Rayme, you can learn a lot from John. John, I want you to answer his questions as we go along. I want Rayme to learn film scoring. That's one of the best things we can give him in this picture."

Steve turned to Bill Thomas, his wardrobe designer. "I've approved the sketches for Magdalena's and Stephanie's clothes. Buy what you can and get those you have to make into work at Western Costume. We have to stay on budget, but the clothes must be right, too. You and I have bridged this gap before.

"Roberto and Gaylin?" He turned to Roberto Bakker and Gaylin Schultz. "We have to make the nine-week schedule. As my production manager and key grip, you will run this crew. As always, there will be problems and crises. You have complete authority from me to act. I will never cross the way you call it. What I expect in return is everything ready for me that I've requested when I get to the set. Every set, every prop, every transportation vehicle, every meal arrangement, every location—everything done to a T. Right?"

Roberto and Gaylin smiled and looked at each other and nodded. Steve was beginning to get in shape for the actual shooting. He was honing the people and himself. They'd all been through it. It worked.

Steve turned to Magdalena, Stephanie, Rayme, and Montango, sitting together in the middle of the oval table. "I want this film to stand on its own two legs and speak out through you. Everything in the story has happened this year or could have. In spite of all the demands the studio has put on this picture, the conviction has grown in me that we can make a film about people who are trying to make their lives count and have a voice in today's issues. *The Rest of Our Lives* needs all of you. The actors, the crew, the people around us. That's why I asked every one of you to come to what's usually an actors' rehearsal. This is our film, all of us, and it's going to say what we want it to say. It's going to do what we want it to do.

"We have six million dollars to make a nine-week shooting schedule, and we have to move. As long as we don't go over that six million, we can exist exactly like John Ford's cavalry that we all saw growing up as kids. Those John Wayne pictures where the soldiers squared off in a phalanx inside the wagons while the Indians kept circling. Well, the Indians are all around us, circling, but they can't break through unless we give them an opening."

He turned to Danny Chiaverini, the production accountant. "Danny, I want summaries every day. I need those computers telling me cost to date and cost to finish. The minute those figures demonstrate that we're going over the six million dollars, Gregson will be on my tail."

"That's right," Spartan said. "Don't give him any openings."

"Okay, Danny," Steve continued. "Watch it and keep us with at least a two-hundred-thousand-dollar margin for emergencies at all times."

Chiaverini spoke up. "You're going to have to make some cuts then, Steve. Construction and set dressing are already going to go over at least seventy thousand."

"We'll take it out of some other place in the budget," Steve said. "The sets have to be right. And Danny, every Sunday I want a meeting at my house with you, Lieu, and Spartan. You'd better be there, too, Roberto and Gaylin.

"And Jake," he turned to Jake Powers, "publicity is so damned important to this picture. We've got to plan it all the way through. We know we've got wide coverage with Rayme here, but we have to be careful that everything is handled with his approval and Ed Wilson's, too. It's a very delicate matter, we all know that.

"We've got to wind up with enough publicity around the world that there's a significant audience waiting, who quite simply are curious to see our stars. I'm depending on that, Jake—I'll cooperate with you in every way possible, but no one is to be exploited. Good taste is your style, Jake—I want this to be one of your best.

"And Spartan—" He turned to Spartan Lee. "I want Ed Wilson to give us a weekly report. We've got to stay ahead of Rayme's problems. If they move in on Rayme for a second grand jury hearing, tell Ed Wilson that I've got to have a fallback plan. Rayme's got to finish this picture with us."

Steve glanced around the famous old stage. "The sets we use will all be here. We start outside the studio, as you'll see by your schedules there, and then come back in for the last weeks. The closer we get to running out of time and money, the more confined we'll be, and that will be good. We'll be in here on the stage, controlling the schedules, the lighting, the cameras, the sound.

"Most of you," he paused and looked around the table, "I've worked with before. I wouldn't want to make any film without you. I'm going to need every support I can get. My neck is sticking 'way out there. You all know that story. And I know you're sticking yours out for me. Together we'll get the film we want. *The Rest of Our Lives* belongs to every one of you, just as it does to me."

50

Shoreham Apartments, Hollywood

It was the Friday night before *The Rest of Our Lives* was scheduled to start shooting. Stephanie had come back to her apartment after a full day of rehearsal at the studio. Steve had told her that morning that she would be working on the second day. He had told her that he believed in her, that he knew she could do it, and the sooner she broke the ice the better. She had been terrified, still was.

Lieu had helped her find the small condominium at the Shoreham, just above Sunset Boulevard. It was only ten minutes from the studio, twenty minutes from Pearl's, and fifteen minutes from Steve's—the three places where she spent her life now.

She had decorated the condo herself. There was a collection of old things, bought from some of the used furniture stores in Santa Monica.

Stephanie had a flair; nothing matched, but everything was coming together as a whole. There was an old rattan lounging chair which she had covered in crimson cotton. There were blue curtains she had made, appliquéd with white daisies. There was an old rolltop desk she was going to refinish herself. She had a tiny bedroom with a four-poster bed, a blue-and-white chest, and framed prints everywhere of the impressionist artists she loved. There were several brilliantly colored pillows in the corners of the rooms and some huge plaid pillows to lounge on by the fireside. Open on her desk was the shooting script of *The Rest of Our Lives*.

She had taken a shower and washed her hair, and was wrapped in the white terrycloth robe that the makeup department had given her. It had her name across the front pocket in blue script. She was proud of it. She had just finished drying her hair, listening to the stereo playing Kim Wilde's "You Keep Me Hangin' On." She began to dance around the room to the music as she brushed her hair.

She was scared, but she was excited. If Steve felt she could do it, if Pearl felt she could do it, maybe she could.

The telephone jarred Stephanie's world. Few people had her phone number, and so it had to be Steve or Pearl or Lieu or Barbara; she picked up the phone, knowing she was going to hear a "safe" voice, the voice of someone who was a friend.

"Hello," a man said. "Stephanie?"

For a moment she didn't recognize him. She had screened him out. But then it came on her fast, the way he said "Stephanie." Only one person in the world said it that way. It was seduction, in a word. Bobby Slater.

"This is Bobby," the voice said.

Stephanie paused for a moment. "Bobby—where are you calling from?"

"Downstairs," he said. "I wanted to surprise you. Could I come up? I have to see you."

A flood of emotions Stephanie had felt for Bobby Slater came in waves. Her heart surged. Her mouth went dry. Bobby Slater. The Bobby Slater who had left her. The Bobby Slater she had almost killed herself about. Bobby Slater. Her voice shook on the phone.

"It's number four-fifteen, Bobby."

"I'll be right up," he said.

Quickly, she ran to the bathroom and brushed her hair. She put on fresh lipstick. Oh, my God. Why hadn't she had him wait? Why was she seeing him at all? What was she doing? But she couldn't ignore the fact that her heart was pounding.

The doorbell rang. She straightened her robe, slipped on her high-heeled bedroom slippers, took a last look in the mirror. It's as good as I can do for now, she thought. She went to the front door and opened it.

Bobby was carrying a package. He was dressed in gray flannel slacks, a blue blazer, a powder-blue shirt, and a striped tie. His hair was cut in the new short style. He was deeply tanned. He looked like a god. She flashed back on the way she had thought about him.

Had she really been this man's woman for months and months? Had she slept with him hundreds of times? Made love with him all over Italy? Was this a dream?

"Come in, Bobby," she said quietly. God, she wished her heart would stop racing.

Bobby put down the package and put his hands on her arms, looking at her. "You look beautiful, Stephanie, just beautiful. I heard you were in top condition."

"I thought you were in China, getting ready for your film," she said.

"No," Bobby said, "the film's been delayed. Maybe for another year. Problems with the Chinese government. You know, getting thirty million dollars' worth of yen, with all the international transactions—" He threw up his hands. "It's so complicated. You know how films are."

"No, I don't, Bobby," she said.

"Well, you're in one," he said. "And I hear you've got one of the leads."

"It's a very special film. And we've got a wonderful director. You know, Steve Wayland."

"Yeah, I heard all about it," Bobby said. "Well, I'm really happy for you, Stephanie. You deserve the best."

"Can I get you something to drink?" Stephanie said. "And please, sit down. I don't know what I'm thinking about, just standing here. It's such a shock, Bobby, to see you again. I never thought I would."

Slater said, "I'll come with you while I get a drink. How about our old favorite, a Cock and Bull gin and tonic? I'll help you fix it."

She led him into the tiny kitchen. He got out the ice while she found the gin and tonic. Together, standing beside each other because of the small area of the kitchen, they fell into an old pattern of the way they used to make their drinks, with the music on the stereo. It was as if nothing had happened, as if they were suddenly back in Rome, getting ready for an evening out. As they finished mixing the gin and tonics, he said, "I brought you something from China. Open it."

He led the way out of the kitchen to the chair where he had left the package.

Stephanie thought of nothing for the moment, except that she was with Bobby Slater again, they were having their Cock and Bull gin and tonics, listening to music, and he had brought her a present. She opened it quickly. It was a white Mandarin dress beaded in ancient Chinese figures with rose, powder blue, and pale yellow beads. She held it up against her body. Then she walked quickly to the mirror in the bedroom, and looked at herself.

"It's so beautiful, Bobby. I've never seen anything like it."

Bobby stood in the doorway of the bedroom, sipping his drink. "It's copied from an old Chinese royal gown. The design has history about it. When I saw it, I knew it had to be yours."

She turned to him. "You're trying to tell me you were thinking specifically of *me*, in China? You really thought of *me*?"

"I've never forgotten you," Bobby said. "It's just that I—well, Stephanie, I needed a job. And there was no way I could take you to China with me. So I just thought it was the best way, to say good-bye the way I did."

She was trembling. "Oh, Bobby, I don't know . . ." she said.

"Put the dress on," he suggested. "I want to see you in it."

She looked embarrassed.

Bobby said, "I'll turn around." He did as he said, to give her some privacy. She slipped off the robe and into the dress.

"Ready?" Bobby asked.

"Ready," she answered. She was glowing. The dress fit her as though she had bought it herself.

"I've never seen you look so beautiful. God, I've missed you," Bobby said. He reached out and pulled her to him. He kissed her deeply, longingly, and held her body against him. "It's been so long. There hasn't been anyone else, Stephanie," he said. "I couldn't forget you."

Stephanie kissed him passionately. "I've never forgotten you, either, Bobby. I thought I had. I hated you. But, oh, God."

He picked her up and put her on the bed. He unbuttoned the Mandarin dress.

"Bobby, I don't know," she said. "I've got to get my brain together—"

"I'll do the thinking for both of us," Bobby said. "We're meant to be together. I'm back, Stephanie. I'm back to stay."

Quickly and smoothly, he slipped off her dress, unzipped his pants, and spread her legs under him. He pulled her under him roughly. He pushed into her; her feet still in the high-heeled mules, went up around his head, the way he liked it. They knew each other so well. It all came back in a blinding flash.

"Oh, Bobby, make love to me, make love to me."

"Here's your cock, baby," he said. "God, I remember your cunt, just the way it feels. All that hot juice of yours. Turn around." He spoke it like an order.

She turned around on her knees, her head on the pillow. He jammed his cock into her hard.

"I remember you, too, Bobby." Her breath was coming faster and faster. "Oh, my God, Bobby, please, together. I can't wait any longer, please, together, together."

He thrust his cock fully into her, and then held her hips with both his hands so that she was tight against him. He came at the same time, and she could feel him spurting inside of her.

Then, as suddenly as she exploded, she became as suddenly quiet. A million thoughts were going through her head.

Slater bent over and began slowly licking her breasts. He ran his hands up between her legs to her wetness, and put his fingers on her clitoris, beginning to massage it in the same rhythm as his tongue. Stephanie brushed his hand away from her, and pulled the sheet up around her. As violently as the passion had come over her, it had left. The Bobby Slater she had thought she knew had abandoned her, just like every man she had ever known. The truth was coming back to her now, and all the work she had done with Pearl—*The Rest of Our Lives*, Steve, Lieu—it was a different world.

Slater caressed her. "What's wrong, Steph?" he said. "You're different."

"Maybe I am," she said. She got up and put the towel robe back on.

Slater sat up in bed, casually. He put out his hand to hold hers, but she drew back from him.

"Come on, Steph," he said. "I want to feel you again. I want to make love to you again."

"There's a difference," Stephanie said. "You want to fuck me. You don't want to make love to me. I've come to understand that."

Slater glanced up at her, quizzically. "You got another guy, Steph?"

Stephanie shook her head. "I don't want another guy. But I don't want you, either, Bobby. You took me by surprise. You know, I really loved you. I don't think you understand the meaning of the word. But it's different now. Shaky, but different."

He gave her a sarcastic smile. "What happened? You decide to become a nun?"

Stephanie looked at him.

"I decided to become myself," she said. "I have talent, Bobby. I never realized that before. But the people I'm around now—they've been wonderful to me. I'm beginning to believe in myself."

Slater got up from the bed and zipped up his pants. "I wanted to talk to you a little bit about your picture, Stephanie. Got anything to eat here? Why don't we just have a quiet dinner and talk?"

Stephanie walked back into the living room and picked up a cigarette. Her hand was shaking. Bobby took the lighter from her and lit her cigarette. He put his hand on her shoulder. "What's the matter, Stephanie? Tell me about it. You know I always understood."

Stephanie jerked away from him. Her eyes were glaring. "You never understood anything. You conned me twenty-four hours a day. And I bought you, Bobby. You were a hero out of my little-girl days, a hero come to life. And I worshiped you. I'll never worship anyone again."

Now he changed his tactic. He lit a cigarette and sat down on the edge of the couch. "Stephanie, I want you to help me. For old time's sake."

"Help you?" Stephanie said, incredulous.

"That's right," he answered. "There's a lot of talk around town about *The Rest of Our Lives.* I heard about it the minute I got back from China. And today—"

"When did you get back, Bobby?"

"Oh, just a few days ago."

"And you just now came to see me. What was it you heard about the picture?" A look of recognition had come over Stephanie's face. "Now I'm beginning to understand. God, I thought I was finished with being so stupid. I should have known there was a special reason why you showed up here—"

Slater stood up again and approached her. "I came because I had to see you, Stephanie. I love you."

"Don't make me any sicker than I already am," Stephanie said. "What's the favor, Bobby? It's always something with you. I can smell it. I should have smelled you when you walked in the door. Better yet, I should have heard it in your voice on the telephone. Tell me whatever it is, Bobby, and then get the hell out of here."

"I want a part in *The Rest of Our Lives,* Stephanie," he said. "The word is getting out about what the picture is. And I hear one of the leads, opposite Magdalena Alba, hasn't been cast yet, and it could be built up for me. I've got the time to do it before we get things cleared away in China. I think I'd be perfect for it. Magdalena and I are about the same age—"

Stephanie cut him off. "You couldn't work in our film. It's a family. That's Steve's way. You're good sometimes as an actor, Bobby, but you're always out for yourself. You wouldn't fit."

"So Steve's the one who's getting it from you," Slater said. "I knew there'd be someone. You're too hot."

Stephanie slapped him. "Get out. Get out or I'll have you thrown out. I'll call the police."

Bobby laughed and reached into the pocket of his coat. "You're not going to call anybody. Nobody's going to get thrown out. Take a look at these. I have duplicates in my safe deposit box. One call and they go to the Associated Press and UPI.

"And then we'll auction them off to the magazines. *Playboy* and *Penthouse* would pay a fortune for one of them. Not to mention the rest."

He handed her an envelope. She looked at him, then at the envelope, then opened it. Inside were a group of three-by-five reductions of stills. They were photographs of Stephanie at work in Las Vegas— at the Paradise Ranch. She only had to look at a few.

Bobby interrupted her thoughts. "They're authentic. You don't have to go through them all. How long do you think you could keep your part in *The Rest of Our Lives* if these pictures got distributed in the right places?

"I've got a trade to make. The pictures, the copies, the negatives, for the part of the manager in *The Rest of Our Lives*."

He took hold of Stephanie roughly by the arms.

His voice was desperate. "I need that part, Stephanie. I need something right now. Something big, something important, something I can dramatize in the press. *The Rest of Our Lives* is the comeback picture for me."

She looked at him levelly. "You lost the picture in China, didn't you?"

His voice was angry. "*I* didn't lose it. They didn't know what the fuck they were doing. They rewrote the part. It wasn't good enough. It wasn't the lead I was promised. They double-crossed me. I quit."

She looked at him. "Sure, Bobby. Sure, you quit."

"I'll leave the photos with you so you can think about it," Slater said. "I'll need an answer in the morning. Nine o'clock. I know the picture starts in two days. And I know that no one else in this town has been cast. I've checked it out. I want to see Steve Wayland tomorrow. I don't care what his schedule is. You get him to do it." He gave her a disgusted look. "He'll do it for you. He wouldn't want to lose a good fuck."

Stephanie grabbed a brass candlestick from the mantel and flung it at him. He dodged and it slammed against the door and bounced back into the room. Bobby laughed at her. "You always did have a lousy aim, you cunt," he said, and went out the door.

* * *

"I shouldn't have seen him," Stephanie sobbed brokenly. "The whole movie can be ruined because of me. I'm coming apart."

"Promise me," Pearl's calm voice came over the phone. "Promise me you won't take one more call or answer the phone or the doorbell. Nothing until I get there. Do you hear me, Mary Jane?" The use of her real name seemed to steady her.

"I can't ever face any of them again—when this gets out—"

"It's not going to get out," Pearl replied. "Steve and Spartan can handle Bobby Slater. Now I'm on my way and you're going to be all right. I'll stay with you. You won't be alone."

"But I don't want to make the picture now, no matter what. I'm scared. I don't think I can do it. I really don't, Pearl—"

"It's your decision. No one's going to force you." Pearl's voice was quiet. She was sitting by the fireplace, as Stephanie paced up and down her living room. "From the time you started to work with me, Mary Jane, the very first decision you made was to take over your own life. Isn't that true?" Stephanie nodded. "Just as you did when you ran away from Marfa. You made decisions for yourself, and you succeeded, until you gave your life over to someone else once again. Bobby Slater is just an extension of Charlie Heckert, who is just an extension of your father. Do you see that connection?"

"I think so," Stephanie answered. "Pearl, I thought I was pulling myself together. I've been very shaky when I think about the picture actually starting. I'm just not sure of anything."

"This is a big decision for you," Pearl said. "Do you take this chance with the film—or do you turn away from it? Have you kept up your writing?"

"Yes, I have," Stephanie nodded. "I've written everything I can remember from the time I was born—just as you said—I'm into the high school part now. It's pretty terrible stuff, but somehow I feel better after I write it down—things I never told anyone."

"I want you to think about something seriously," Pearl said. "I worked with a prominent actress some years ago, who was almost dead from alcoholism. She was an addictive personality, too. But she went with me to AA—lots of people with drug dependencies are going to AA meetings these days—did you know that?" Stephanie shook her head. "You just substitute your drug of choice when you hear the word 'alcohol.' Will you go with me?" Pearl asked.

"I don't know," Stephanie answered. "I really don't know what it's about—it scares me—"

"You started on the road to controlling your addiction in just the way AA recommends—you've already affirmed their very first principle—that there's something greater in the world than one's self. That was the starting point for this great actress, and after a few weeks she started to write down her life story so that I would know everything she could remember, all the facts of her life. This kind of writing, incidentally, is the fourth principle of AA.

"Hers was a shattering story. And that's the way I think you'll find your answers for yourself. Because what you're going to do now about this film is related to all those pages you've written and what you haven't written yet, too. What's happened to you, how hard you've fought, how deep your needs are.

"For the rest of your life you can have freedom of choice. You'll be responsible for what happens to you outside and what happens to you inside. *Your decisions.*"

Stephanie had stopped pacing. She was looking down at Pearl by the fireplace. "It's mind-blowing," she said. "Thinking of what you do, helping people every day of your life. I think that must be the most wonderful job in the world. Steve talks about making your life count. I don't know anyone who makes their life count like you do."

"Nobody's work is fun all the time," Pearl said. "You have to get through the drudgery and the fear. Like you're doing now. Last week a young seventeen-year-old girl, after five years of never speaking—not a physical problem, just the desire deep within her not to communicate—for five long years she had not spoken to anyone in her home or outside her family. She had retired from the world—"

"I understand *that*," Stephanie said.

"She's come to me three or four times a week for all these years and I thought after last year, I'd give up. I felt I was taking her parents' money falsely—I just couldn't do a thing. Then, just last week in the middle of her time with me, when I was rattling on about something, trying to get through to her, suddenly she said right out of the sky, 'I hear you. I want to tell you something—I've been afraid. I thought I wasn't good enough or interesting enough or smart enough to talk. No one seemed to hear me anyway. No one listened. In my home or at school. So I did it my own way. I've lived in my own world. But now I want to come out, Pearl—I trust you. Help me.'

"That moment," Pearl said, "was one of pure joy. If I could help one person 'come out,' as this girl said, it was worth all the years. And Mary Jane, I believe that you're ready to come out. In your own way, you took refuge. You ran from the pain. You wanted to be lost. You know that. You've told that to me in what you've already written and said.

"I hope you'll go ahead and make the picture. I know that Steve wants you to do it. And I want to be working with you whenever you can. I'll be there for you and we'll go on working together, you and I—because it takes work and support."

She went over to Stephanie. "I want you to consider something. The middle-aged star I told you about finished her work with me, and by then she had more than enough pages for a book. One day she walked into my office and I told her it was our last time together. She didn't need me anymore. I took all of the pages of her story out of my file and gave them back to her. And then I asked her to submit her story for publication—not as a psychological treatise but as a human story. I felt that this woman could reach thousands.

"It took me time to convince her, but finally she published the book and it became a best seller.

"Think about it, Mary Jane. If you do the film and someday consider allowing your story to be published just the way you're writing it, you will have the power to get positive results out of all the pain you've been through."

"Do you honestly believe, Pearl, that I can make it through the picture? I'm so scared."

"You have the chance to reach many more people through your talents than I ever can," said Pearl.

"You've known a lot of movie people, Pearl—like the actress you've been talking about—do you think I could really be any good?"

"I've lived here for twenty-five years," Pearl replied. "I've heard and read about 'star quality.' I haven't seen much of that. But I think you have it."

Mary Jane put her arms around Pearl and hugged her. "God, I hope so."

51

Château Marmont Apartment Hotel, Hollywood

Bobby Slater walked into the lobby of the Château Marmont at thirty-five minutes past midnight. He'd had his favorite steak Diane at Chasen's with his stand-in and his hairdresser. They were with Bobby fifty-two weeks a year, on permanent salary. Part of their job was to be with Bobby at mealtimes, if he was otherwise alone.

Bobby went straight to the desk. "Any calls for me, Maisie?" he said to the blonde girl at the desk.

She looked like a former star, Ann Sothern, who had done a series of pictures playing a free and funny blonde named Maisie. The girl at the desk liked the way Bobby Slater always took time with her, like he did with every receptionist and every secretary. Bobby got inside information that way.

"No, Mr. Slater," Maisie answered. "No messages since you went out. I guess most people don't know you're in town again."

Bobby winked at her. "That's right, that's the way I want it. I am expecting one call, though, so give me a ring, will you? Whenever it comes in. I'll be up for a while. By the way, Maisie, what time do you get off?"

"Five o'clock in the morning. I've got this graveyard shift because it pays double."

"What do you do at five o'clock?" Bobby Slater asked.

Maisie smiled. "I go home. Unless I've got something better to do."

Bobby Slater smiled. "Why don't you come up to the room and

we'll talk awhile—I'll stay up and wait for you, and we'll have some breakfast."

Maisie smiled at him in surprise. "Really, Mr. Slater?"

"Call me Bobby," Bobby Slater said. "Sure—I've got some cassettes I have to run. I usually stay up until then, anyway. I'll certainly be *up* for you," he gave his full smile, "Maisie."

Maisie spoke almost to herself. "Breakfast with Bobby Slater? No one would ever believe it. I don't think I do."

"You will at five o'clock," Bobby smiled. "See you then, Maisie."

"Thank you, Bobby," she said, gratefully, as though the gods above had finally smiled on her.

Bobby went to the elevator and punched number five. Five-forty-two at the Château Marmont was his home when he came back from location. He had a place in Bel Air, an estate, but it was rented right now. When he got things straightened out on *The Rest of Our Lives*, he'd have to move back into his house, or rent another place. He needed acres to spread himself out. He needed a workout room, a projection room, a sauna, and places for a full staff. The Bobby Slater lifestyle.

He was glad to be back in town. He pulled out his key as he neared the room of his suite. It looked out over Hollywood, and they always kept it ready for him. He liked the Château Marmont because the New York crowd was there and many of the European film people, too. He picked up inside information at the Château Marmont about new scripts and inside deals.

He stepped inside the door of his suite and flicked on the light. Steve Wayland was seated on the couch in the middle of the living room, and Spartan Lee was in a chair near the couch. Bobby Slater hit his biggest smile.

"Gentlemen," he said, "what a surprise. I thought I'd hear from you, but not so soon."

Steve nodded at Spartan. "Is Ed ready?"

Spartan picked up the telephone on a coffee table. The ordinary phone at the Château Marmont had to go through the switchboard. Slater had always had a special outside line waiting for his visits. Spartan punched out a number.

"Ed?" he said.

"Yes, I've been waiting for you," Edmund Bradford Wilson answered.

"Sorry to keep you up so late," Spartan said, "but we didn't know what time Mr. Slater was coming in. He's just arrived. You want to speak to him?"

"Yes," Ed Wilson said.

Spartan held up the phone toward Slater. "Ed Wilson. He's got an answer for your request, Bobby, about *The Rest of Our Lives*."

Slater shook his head. "That's not legal ethics—an opposing lawyer is never supposed to speak to a principal."

Spartan smiled. "Well, you've learned something in all the legal cases you've been involved in. But you'd better learn a little bit about blackmail. This is one of the foremost criminal attorneys in the world."

Edmund Bradford Wilson's sophisticated voice came over the phone. "Thank you, Spartan," he said. "Can I quote you on that?"

"I know who Mr. Wilson is," Bobby said. He walked over and took the phone. "This is Bobby Slater," he said.

Wilson's voice was cordial. "Hello, Mr. Slater. I've been hired to protect Stephanie Columbo. We know about your visit, obviously, and we know about your pictures. Now we've got an ultimatum for you. You have every copy of those pictures, and the negatives, in Steve Wayland's hands, delivered to his office, sealed and marked 'Personal Only,' by five o'clock this afternoon, or I swear to you, Mr. Slater, you'll be arrested for blackmail no matter where you run to. Miss Columbo has chosen to share her problem with Mr. Wayland, Mr. Lee, and myself. And for your information—"

"You dirty son of a bitch!" Steve lashed out at Bobby. "Stephanie's offered to give up her part in the picture, rather than implicate us in any way."

"That's right," Wilson picked up on the telephone. "I heard Steve and that's right, Bobby. What she cares about is protecting the picture and the two people in the room with you now. So no matter what the cost to Stephanie Columbo personally, her career and her reputation, she's throwing it all on the table against you. You can't win, Mr. Slater. She's called in your hand.

"And I guarantee you, I'm going to have a warrant sworn out for your arrest at five o'clock tonight and the law enforcement officials all over this country ready to move, if those pictures and negatives are not delivered.

"Furthermore, if there is ever any further use of these pictures, if you hold back a set of these pictures or negatives and you decide to use them a year from now, the same thing will be true.

"We have a sworn statement, documented and witnessed, from

Stephanie Columbo, of exactly what happened. This will not be a civil complaint, Mr. Slater. This will be a criminal action. You won't have the connections to get you out of it. You'll go to prison when we get through with you, and it'll be a clear, straight case. Good night, Mr. Slater."

52

Shoreham Apartments, Hollywood

The jarring ring of the telephone cut through Stephanie's nightmares. She woke up in a sweat. Someone was answering the phone out in the kitchen, and Stephanie could smell the aroma of fresh coffee and bacon frying. Then she remembered. Pearl had stayed all night with her. She hadn't wanted to be alone.

Pearl knocked and came into the bedroom. She was smiling, and Stephanie began to believe that another day was possible, and then maybe another. It wasn't all over yet.

"Steve's on the phone for you."

"How does he sound?" Stephanie asked, fear in her eyes again.

"Excited about tomorrow and the start of the picture," Pearl said.

Stephanie looked at her as she got to her feet. "Did he say anything about—you know?"

Pearl shook her head. "Not a thing. I'm sure it's all taken care of. Come on, take the phone. Breakfast is almost ready." Her tone was casual and bright.

Stephanie slipped into her robe and picked up the phone. She started pacing again as she walked with the phone into the living room. It was a sunny California day, without smog, and the sky was crystal blue.

"Sorry to keep you waiting, Steve—I overslept."

"How long will it take you to get ready?" Steve's voice came over the phone.

Stephanie looked stricken again. "I didn't have rehearsal call for today—did I?"

"No—but the girls and I have been talking about it over here and we won't take no for an answer. The Sunday before every picture begins, we go to Disneyland. It's a promise between us we never break. We're going to take you with us. We'll be by for you in one hour."

Stephanie immediately headed for the kitchen with the phone. She looked at Pearl for support. Her hand went through her rumpled hair. "Steve, I can't," she said. "Pearl's here and . . ."

Pearl interrupted. "I'm leaving after breakfast. Whatever Steve has in mind will be good for you." She smiled at Stephanie and her voice dropped to a whisper. "Go on," she whispered, "you'll have fun."

"Steve, well—I just don't know. My hair's a mess."

Steve laughed on the phone. "Tie a scarf around it then. Listen, the girls are dying to meet you—they've seen your pictures in my workroom—you have to come. We'll see you in an hour." He hung up the phone.

Stephanie hung up too, and watched Pearl as she took the toast out of the oven. She looked down at her hands. They were trembling. "Pearl, I don't think I can do it—any of it—I'm not ready—"

"Come on and sit down here with me," Pearl ordered as she served the eggs and bacon. "It would be ideal if you were beginning the film six months from now. You'd have gone through all the steps by then—but that's not the way it worked out. We have to take the chances when they come—and this is your chance—now."

53

Goldwyn Studios, Stage Six, Warner Hollywood

The magic of the studio came alive at night. The long dark streets, the silent stages, the fronts, the New York tenements, the Southern plantation set. Everything changed once the glaring California sun went down.

Movies should be made at night, Steve thought. Motion pictures came alive in a darkened motion picture theater. He walked down the Western street hand in hand with Magdalena. The memories of John Wayne were there. How many times he'd come around that curve and galloped up to the saloon on that street.

Gary Cooper had made *High Noon* there.

William Holden had done some pick-up shots on *The Wild Bunch*.

Gregory Peck had stalked through these dirt roads in *The Gunfighter*.

Jimmy Stewart had fought the desperados here in *The Man from Laramie*.

Steve surveyed the street. "It's different here at night, isn't it?"

Magdalena nodded. "Magic," she said.

"I can hear the horses, the spurs, the music from the bars, the dance-hall girls, the villains."

Magdalena smiled at him. "That's the best part of you, Steve. It's still magic for you, isn't it?"

"Let's go see the trucks roll," he said.

In the darkness, twelve of the studio's massive location trucks were lined up. The name of the studio was on the side, and on the windshield of each truck there was a card that read *Production #861—The Rest of Our Lives—Steven Wayland Productions*.

A chill ran up Steve's backbone. These trucks were getting ready to move to location for the first day's shooting. He walked up to the gate.

Frankie Pavetti had been there since Samuel Goldwyn had bought the studio in 1936—over fifty years. Frankie had been twenty-one then. He'd seen the big parade come and go.

Frankie tipped his hat toward Magdalena. "Miss Alba, Mr. Wayland," he said. "I sure want to wish you good luck with *The Rest of Our Lives*. I like that title, by the way. Makes me wonder what the picture is all about."

"You're going to have four tickets to the premiere—if there is a premiere," Steve said.

Stage Six was dark, and Steve flashed on two worklights as he and Magdalena stepped onto the large floor. There was the full interior of an old house there—two floors, a wide stairway, a vaulted front hall, and eight other rooms. Steve stepped into the hallway and looked up at the high ceiling.

"I can't believe it," he said. "All my life, I dreamed of the exact sets I wanted, and the locations I picked."

Magdalena said, "I can't wait to start. It's very important that I do my best work in your picture. I want to approach every scene as though I were going to stop acting after *The Rest of Our Lives*."

"Never," he interrupted, "it would be an incredible waste."

She spoke softly to him. "I want you to promise that you will get the very best you can from me no matter what you have to do. No matter how angry I get."

He saw that she was serious. "I promise," he said. "This isn't just my movie, Maggie. It's yours."

"I love you, Steve. I can't believe I'm saying those words and feeling them. Where were you ten years ago, five years ago, last year?"

"Looking for you," he said.

He opened her dressing room with his key. Magdalena's name was already on the door. Her personal belongings had been moved in, including some books and a selection of her favorite records. And here and there were small bunches of violets.

Magdalena embraced Steve. "What can I say? You *are* the last romantic, Steve, and I found you. I thought they were all gone."

Steve took her by the hand and led her to the kitchen. A bottle of champagne in an ice bucket was sitting on the kitchen table. Steve popped the cork and poured two glasses. He touched Maggie's glass with his, then kissed her.

"You're going to have to be patient, Steve, during the picture. You don't want me looking old and haggard."

"Never. I want you looking flushed and excited, just like you are after we make love," he said.

She laughed. "Well, I hope you're not going to make love to me before every important scene I do."

"Why not? That's why you got the part." He pulled her close to him. "Now, close your eyes."

He took from his pocket a tiny box, opened it, and lifted out a small heart of clustered diamonds on a platinum chain. He fastened it around her neck.

"Open," he said.

She did. He turned her so she faced the mirrors. The diamonds sparkled in the light.

"I found it when I made a picture in Thailand. There's an old Thai proverb. 'The only real gift is the gift of the heart.' "

Magdalena kissed him. "I'll never take it off."

"I saved it. I'm glad I did." Steve raised his glass again. "There's another person we should toast. To Sam Goldwyn."

"You knew him?" Magdalena asked.

Steve nodded. "Just the last few years of his life. I was an apprentice and I was working here at his studio. The head of the sound department, Gordon Sawyer, liked my work and he suggested to Mr. Goldwyn that he should run a picture I was making.

"Mr. Goldwyn sent an invitation for me to have lunch with him after he saw my picture. In his offices at the studio he had a dining room, a kitchen, and a chef, and he still ate lunch there every day. He had different guests at different times and it was a prize everyone hopes for. To have an invitation for lunch from Mr. Goldwyn.

"The day I went there, the first day, I was plenty nervous. I was meeting one of the few giants of all time in motion pictures. A man who was not satisfied with anything but the finest of talent, a man of incredible achievement and courage who even distributed his own films."

Steve remembered Samuel Goldwyn looking at him with his piercing blue eyes in the elaborate dining suite at his studio.

"I ran your film, son," Goldwyn had said. "That's why I wanted to meet you. Your scenes are good. The dialogue—well, people didn't talk like that when I was making pictures, but I get around enough to know that everything has changed.

"Every morning I walk from my home to the studio; I have my car follow me a couple of blocks behind, in case I get tired. I go home the same way. I need the exercise, but I like to listen to the people in the streets, in the cars, playing with their kids, newspaper boys, all kinds of people. I always learn from that.

"They talk differently today. And you've caught their rhythm and their sound. Of course you should. You're today, I'm yesterday.

"But I tell you, son, some things don't change. Words change, but not feelings. Styles change but the human heart doesn't, not the mind, either. And that's always what was important to me. I wanted to move the heart. I wanted people to be a little changed for the better after seeing a Sam Goldwyn film.

"I wanted to bring them the best talent. Writers, directors, actors. And if something was wrong when I previewed the picture, I went back and fixed it, or scrapped it altogether. That's what I miss today. I see movies four times a week. I see everything that's any good here and from Europe, too. I've got only one measuring stick. Did I feel anything afterwards?"

He'd looked at Steve across the table. "You're not eating, son."

Steve had suddenly awakened to the fact that he hadn't touched his plate. He picked up his knife and fork. "I was listening, sir."

Mr. Goldwyn smiled. "That's a nice thing to do, to an old man. Listen to him—not many people do—even when you're paying their salaries. Damn it, strange thing to get old. You don't ever feel it's going to happen to you, too much to live for, too much to do.

"I never lost my passion, son, just my body did. I never got old, just my body."

"You'll never grow old, Mr. Goldwyn," Steve said. "Every day, I'm sure somewhere in the world a picture of yours is playing. In a theater, or on television, or on a university campus. Your work is alive. It's always going to be alive."

Mr. Goldwyn looked at him and then took another roll from the dish in front of him.

"Steve—that's your name, isn't it—Steve?"

"Yes, sir. Steve Wayland."

"That's right," Mr. Goldwyn said, "Steve Wayland. I remember everything Gordon Sawyer told me about you. He believes you're going to be one of our fine directors of the future. And I do, too. I want you to come here every week. My secretary will be in touch with you about the day. I want you to have lunch with me . . . I want you to tell me what movies I should see. I want you to be kind of a pipeline for me, Steve, to what's going on in motion pictures, particularly with your generation.

"Your generation will take over the industry, and that's as it should be. New blood. But I hope you'll really care about pictures.

"In the old days, a bunch of us got the bug. Like an infection. We didn't just want to make money, we wanted to make pictures. And we learned—but most of all, we *felt*.

"There hasn't been a day in over fifty years that I haven't been excited about motion pictures, usually one in particular, one I was dreaming of, one I was making up in my head.

"I wasn't always right, but I was right in what I cared about. I never let anyone change my mind."

He smiled. "That's not quite true. My wife changed it a few times, a few dozen times, as a matter of fact. We had quite a group in those days—Irving Thalberg, L. B. Mayer, Harry Cohn, the Warner brothers, Darryl Zanuck, Adolph Zukor, Cecil B. DeMille; David Selznick came along a little later, a great filmmaker.

"We all knew each other, we all fought like hell, we were all egomaniacs, and we had the greatest new toy in the world, and power. Power, Steve. It's intoxicating, but it goes like everything else. It changes.

"But I always remembered something I heard a professor say—it wasn't in school because I never got beyond the seventh grade—never had the money—but I read a lot and learned everything I could. I heard this professor say—his name was Erbin, he used to teach at Harvard, and he was giving this night course over at Columbia and I signed up for Philosophy. I just remember one thing that man said.

"He said, 'Remember, all of you, no matter what happens in life, what tragedies, what problems, return to your work, your work is always there. Not a woman, or a hobby, or any person, or any structure, but your real work—what you're here to do. Keep it and return to it.'

"It was his closing lecture. Looking back, I think about what this crazy bunch of us did, out here working day and night. Learning how to make films, building stars, signing people, putting together studios. It was a wild and frantic and wonderful time, and out of it came so many different people, but they all had a passion for their work—their passion was motion pictures.

"Now, even in my own studio here, even with all these independent companies that rent space from me, I don't see much passion, Steve. I don't see fire. You've got to be on fire to make a good picture, you've got to feel like you *must* make your picture.

"As my friend Bill Faulkner said, 'You write even if you have to *steal* to write.' That's the way he felt about writing, and that's why he was good. Well, we felt that way about pictures.

"And that's what our work is all about, son. That's a long way around to tell you why I asked you here to lunch today. Gordon Sawyer told me you had the passion and the fire. And I saw it on the screen in *Remembrance*. You *moved* me. You dealt from the heart.

"So, if you want to come around once a week and keep an old man company, and by the way, you're a hell of a listener, and that's important, then I'm going to try to leave you with some of the things I learned.

"And now," Mr. Goldwyn finished up his plate, "I've got to take my rest. If I don't, my wife will be phoning up here and checking on me and I'll start getting some new orders. They'll cut down my free time."

He stood up very erect, his proud jaw sticking out prominently, his bald head shining and his eyes flinty blue.

Steve put out his hand; he was in a daze. "Mr. Goldwyn, well, I don't know what . . . well . . . this has been just one of the most fantastic times of my whole life."

Mr. Goldwyn reached out his other hand and patted Steve on the shoulder in a gentle way. "Wish I was still making motion pictures, son—you'd be directing for me, and I'd be making your life miserable. You wouldn't get away with a thing." He laughed and patted Steve again and then disappeared behind the door to his living quarters at the studio.

Steve turned to Magdalena. He lifted his glass to hers. "To all the Sam Goldwyns who gave us this day and the chance to make *The Rest of Our Lives*. He paused. "Together."

Their glasses touched, and the first day of *The Rest of Our Lives* had begun.

The
FILM

Book II

1

Barbara Garibaldi

arbara Garibaldi checked herself in the mirror. Lines were beginning to show around her eyes and at the corners of her mouth. She made no attempt to disguise them with makeup. She left the lashes of her large, oval eyes untouched. She put on her soft red lipstick. Her hand trembled for a moment as she etched in the corners of her mouth.

She looked at the finished product. It was a lived-in face, handsome, defiant, aggressive. The face of a survivor.

She forced her hand into a fist to keep it from trembling as she put down the lipstick brush. Why was she so afraid? Wasn't this what she'd wanted? What she'd fought for?

She smoothed out her plain black dress, ran a comb through her hair once more, tried to put one unruly strand in place, and gave up.

She looked at her watch. She was late. She flicked out the bathroom lights, picked up her coat from the chair in the bedroom, and turned to glance around the room in the half light.

Things would never be the same again. Her eyes went to the wall above the bedroom fireplace. She had designed everything in that room. She had found the carved fireplace molding in Florence. The blue-and-white Delft tiles in Spain.

Above the fireplace were the photographs of her family. How she wished they were with her tonight! But she was alone.

She turned out the light, looked once around the room as though she were saying good-bye to all the memories there, went down the staircase, through the dining room, past the breakfast room and the kitchen. She stopped near the back door to punch in the computer alarm system. She made sure the outside lights were on in the front and back and then went through the portico to the garage.

She put her key in the lock to trigger the garage door. The station wagon was waiting for her. But was the dream enough now? She felt alone as she backed out of the garage, pushed a button to close the doors, and pulled out of the driveway.

Barbara drove through the neighborhood streets, onto the freeway to the central part of the city.

The faces of her mother and father flashed in front of her. Her life flowed on—every face she loved.

What was ahead to change her life was only a few minutes away. How was she ever going to face everybody?

She avoided the front of the building. She could see the mass of photographers and press people there, even in the distance, as she turned off the freeway ramp. She went around the back way.

The vast parking lot was deserted except for two security guards. One came over to investigate. He waved at her as she got out of the car and locked the door.

It was a clear, bright night and Barbara glanced up at the towering building with its Greek dome reaching for the sky. She was dwarfed by the majesty of the capitol building.

Sudden fear gripped her heart. Could she do it? She walked through the twelve-foot doors that flanked the center of the building at the top of the stairs. She nodded at the security guard watching the entrance. She smiled at him and crossed over the English glass floor tiles carrying the state seal, under the domed rotunda with its historical mosaics and paintings surrounding her.

She walked up the circular stairway, under the quartz crystal chandelier, her gaze passing from one historical painting to another. At the top of the stairs before she turned to her right to approach the reception hall, she took a deep breath. She straightened her dress, steadied herself, and walked directly to the doors.

The roar of the celebration was deafening. More than two thousand people were jammed into the reception room, which was strewn with banners, flags, confetti and noise makers, and people. A flood of hand-carried signs greeted her gaze. They all carried the words "What are we going to do with the rest of our lives?" Centered below that quotation were one-word questions. "Peace?" "Hunger?" "Health?" "Education?" "Relationships?" "Drugs?" "Commitment?" "Caring?" "Families?" "Integrity?" "Freedom?" "Individualism?"

The university band was playing at one end of the room on a raised stage. Behind the band was a huge banner covering the wall. There was a picture of Barbara, and then printed in large letters: WHAT ARE WE GOING TO DO WITH THE REST OF OUR LIVES? And then the name— Barbara Garibaldi . . . United States Senator from Michigan.

The reporters, photographers, and television newspeople pushed in on her from every side. She stood her ground.

Steve's voice sliced through the pandemonium of the reception hall. "Cut . . . cut it."

Steve looked directly at Magdalena, still completely one with the Barbara Garibaldi character she was creating, then at David Thayer who was strapped into the intricate harness on the Panaglide camera, one of the finest portable camera units in the world. The camera lens was still trained on Magdalena's face.

The reception hall was quiet now.

"Hold it steady, David. I want to take a look." Steve peered into the lens. "Don't move, Magdalena. I want to check your pin lights."

Magdalena was carrying her small tailored bag in front of her. The back of it was cut away to hold two tiny powerful pin lights set to shine up into her eyes.

"Do you see those pins in her eyes?" David asked him.

Steve pulled away from the camera.

"Perfect. Let's get set up for the interview scene. At the same time I want to run everything you've got on our TV monitor. What do you think, David? Did you get her all the way?"

"I never took my eye off the lens from the first shot in the mirror at the townhouse. We rehearsed all the moves, my boys behind me, guiding me until I could walk it backward. Through the house, down the stairs, into the car, all the way here, up the rotunda steps and right to this moment, we had the pin lights fixed for her eyes, every step of the way. We used the night shadows in places, and the passing highway lights, just like you and I laid it out—but what really did it," David looked at Magdalena, "was what she gave us.

"I thought you were crazy to try to open the picture this way. Eight minutes without a word spoken. In one, unbroken shot. Never breaking away from her. But she held it. And she put me through one emotional feeling after another."

"Her stream of consciousness," Steve said. "That's what we gambled on. If there are any technical problems we can do it again, but now we know we *can* do it."

Magdalena was listening to them but not moving from her position as the lighting team was already at work to set up the three cameras to shoot her, the full room, and individual close-ups of the reporters and photographers.

Steve embraced Magdalena.

"You've just given the film the beginning I wanted. I'm proud of you. There's going to be nothing but you on that screen, right up to this point, and you're going to involve this audience every bit of the way."

She whispered into his ear.

"I'm scared. You've taken away my protections, but it's exciting. I didn't even think about the way I looked."

"I want to show you something," Steve said.

Steve motioned to Magdalena's stand-in to step into her place so that the lighting could continue. He took Magdalena to the back side of the reception hall. Roberto Bakker had the television unit set up for him.

"Ready, boss."

"Roll," Steve said.

He and Magdalena stood side by side watching the TV screen. There was Magdalena in a close-up, looking in the mirror, checking her hair, and putting on her lipstick with her trembling hand.

The camera work was precise and the pin lights were in her eyes. You were immediately involved. You cared. Who was this woman? What was she going through? What was she afraid of? What had happened in her life?

Steve smiled and the tension eased out of his face.

"Maggie," he said excitedly, "there it is. Everything we've talked about—you're *inside* Barbara Garibaldi—you are this woman—we're on our way."

"I'm beginning to understand her," Magdalena said.

Steve took Magdalena into a corner of the room away from the others. "I changed my mind about the way I'm going to shoot the news conference."

Magdalena looked at him questioningly. "But the lines are going to be the same, aren't they? I've studied them and I think it's a good scene. I believe what Barbara says."

"It would pass," Steve said. "We can always go back and do it that way if my idea doesn't work, but I'm sure it will work.

"How many political news interviews have we all seen? It's always a scramble—reporters interrupt each other, the person getting interviewed interrupts the reporters, nothing is cut and dried. The interviews take sudden twists and personal antagonisms come out—and personal angles—particularly on election nights.

"That's what I want to hear, Maggie—forget the scene as I wrote it. It's not spontaneous enough—no matter how well you play it. You just said you know Barbara Garibaldi, right? I want this press conference like it would happen in real life. I don't want you knowing ahead of time what you're going to say—or what the questions are—or what the answers are. I want people to interrupt each other and stammer around and hesitate and fire back.

"We're shooting it with three cameras so we can gamble. I just want you to answer what comes, any way it comes—and I want you to remember your favorite critic, Sam Carrington, who always blasts your performances—one of the few you never charmed—one of the few who hits you every time out of the gate—I know how you feel about him and how much you'd like to tell him off—how much we'd all like to tell him off. Well, there's bound to be a Sam Carrington or two at every political news conference. If anyone goes after you now, just think of what he represents, Maggie—say the things you've wanted to say in the context of Barbara Garibaldi. I want you to feel free— keep it in mind who you are and what you've just been elected to and let it fly—*be* Barbara Garibaldi, with her fire and her guts."

Maggie looked at him thoughtfully. "You're never predictable, but this is the first time you've tried this."

"The first time *we've* tried it," Steve said. "But it's the only way to come close to the way it really would be. I want to see what you'll do with it."

"Challenging me?" Maggie asked.

"Always," Steve answered.

Maggie looked up at him. "Let's go."

The moment had come for Barbara Garibaldi. Henry Calvin had conceded. She had beaten the incumbent U.S. senator from the state of Michigan who had held this seat for twenty-four years. She had gotten 58 percent of the vote, the second-largest plurality in the history of the state. And here were the key people all together. The people who had nominated her and fought for her.

Jim Reardon pushed his way through the crowd around Barbara. "You won," he said. "Even bigger than we could have hoped. They listened to you."

"They listened to *us*," Barbara Garibaldi said. "To you and all these people here."

Jim Reardon, thirty-two years old, a veteran of four political campaigns, a brilliant young political manager, would probably go to Washington as her chief of staff.

He was a tall, slender man with a boyish face and intense brown eyes. He was good with the press but now the reporters and photographers were overwhelming. He could no longer contain them.

The networks had flown out their anchormen to cover this election. It was the first time that a woman had ever been elected to the U.S. Senate from Michigan. Reardon made a signal to the band to stop playing and the constituents pressed against the reporters, some of them separated from the new senator by fifty yards. Large television screens were placed high on each side of the reception hall to carry the interview. Groups of people crowded around those.

The press closed in around Barbara. Five questions were asked at once. The man with the loudest attack got to her first.

"Why do you think you're qualified to be a senator?" There was unmistakable sarcasm in his voice. The questioned rocked Barbara for a moment.

"I was born in this country and in this State," Barbara answered. "I'm obviously over twenty-one." She paused and there was humor in her voice now, sparring back to the sarcasm of the question.

"And I've never been convicted of a crime. I believe that qualifies me," Barbara added.

Another voice rode in right on top of her answer. It was Jack Jacoby, a Washington columnist. "What else are you offering the voters?" he asked.

"I ran for senator, Mr. Jacoby, because I think the government in this state and in this country can do more for all of its citizens, and I think people should have clear-cut, definitely stated choices. My whole campaign is based on choices. More than nine million people in this state have written my platform—they have told me what matters most to them for the rest of their lives."

Jacoby interrupted her. "What makes you think you can deliver?"

Barbara spoke back sharply. "Do we have to take political manipulation as a way of life?" Barbara asked. "People in this state have grown up with political corruption, they've come of age thinking it's natural: Pigeons fly, judges suck up money, rats bite, politicians lie. But if we take corruption and misery for granted, it'll hang like smoke over all of us for the rest of our lives; we won't be able to breathe. I've spoken with union men and women who never expect to see their pensions because some wiseguys poured the fund into their own yachts and limos. I've worked with dozens of high school graduates who can't read or write well enough to fill out a voter registration form. How can they get rid of the people responsible for giving them a noneducation? By taking responsibility for every vote they have and what's happening in our state.

"You want to know if I can deliver, Mr. Jacoby, well right now I'm taking step one: I'm taking responsibility. That elderly woman whose hand I held in the hospital, who spoke so softly I could barely hear her, whose financial back had been broken by one week in a hospital bed—I'm responsible for her. If you've got no home, if you live in a freezing crevice somewhere, you're on my list, I'm responsible. If you're scared to death of AIDS, if you have a son who has to fight if we go into a war, and if your whole family life is haunted by the threat of nuclear war, you want your government to listen and to try to work on those problems. I'm there now. I've listened. I'll keep on listening.

"All of you who voted for me, since you put me here, you're responsible, too. If you didn't vote for me, well, pitch in, we're still friends. Help me. Don't do it for me, do it for all the people we're responsible for. For the rest of our lives.

"We, you and I, Mr. Jacoby—all of us—we have the power whenever we bring the ises in front of the people, not just what you reporters write about it, with all your own prejudices and angles, but what the people are able to see and hear directly, then we find out what the people really think. We the people have the power. We've got to use it.

"That's why I ran for senator, Mr. Jacoby, because I think the government of this state and this country could do more for all its citizens. I'm going to Washington to speak for their platform, to argue for them and to fight for them, to take my best shot at making a difference. That's why I ran, and I believe that's why I was elected."

"You realize the prejudices against a woman in the political arena?" another reporter cut in.

"I'm not an innocent. I've done my homework; I've paid my dues. Whoever likes it or not, times are changing on many issues—including *women* in politics. I believe I can be a good senator."

Another network reporter rode over Barbara's answer. "Do you think you can do that better than Henry Calvin with twenty-four years of experience in the capital getting things done?"

"I think twenty-four years is enough—and the people of Michigan seem to agree with me."

Jacoby interrupted. "What do you have to say about Henry Calvin? Or are you taking the Fifth?"

Barbara turned to him sharply. She thought a moment before she answered. "No, Mr. Jacoby, I won't take the Fifth Amendment or anything. That has been a mark of all my press conferences in this campaign and I've promised to keep it. I won't dodge questions.

"Frankly, I don't believe in political machines. And I think that is what has gotten Mr. Calvin elected for term after term. Sooner or later history tells us that political machines run out of muscle. I think that's happened here.

"And now you answer me a question, Jack," Barbara continued. "Why is it when you show up at a press conference of mine I always feel like the lady in a knife-throwing act?" She slapped her breastbone and then her back as though his knives were going in. "Are *you* taking the Fifth, Jack?" she asked. She'd stopped Jacoby cold for a moment. The other reporters laughed.

NBC's anchorman spoke up quickly. "Where did your campaign slogan come from? Did you use the same advertising agency your father does? Did he hire them for you?"

"I can't afford my father's advertising agency," Barbara laughed.

Jacoby was after her again. "Was it your father's idea for you to run for senator? Do we have the old syndrome of political life here—a big money family deciding to buy its way into political power?"

Barbara cut him off. "If you are as good a reporter as I think you are, Jack, you'll go out and talk to the people of this state—not just here in the city, but out in the Michigan countryside—the little towns— people who never get covered by a network special, certainly not in a political campaign. Find out for yourself if there have been any votes bought, any jobs promised—any principles broken.

"My father has nothing to do with this campaign. In fact, he is very much against the idea."

She glanced humorously at Jacoby. "He has the same philosophy as you do, Jack—women should stay home, have children, take care of their man—and stay out of political life.

"The idea for my campaign came out of my own life. You all know I was divorced a few years ago," Barbara went on. "I have two children. Teenagers. Before I went back to school to get a degree, something I never wanted before, I took a look at my life and the children I was responsible for—and what I was going to do with all I had left—the rest of my life. And I decided to run for the Senate—I believe this question must be the central part of the life of every man, woman, and child in this state and everywhere else. That's how the campaign was born. It is not an advertising gimmick. It is something we have all said to ourselves. 'What am I going to do for the rest of my life?' "

Another reporter shoved forward. "We've all heard about the nine million postcard poll—who paid for the staff to handle this poll before you became your party's nominee for the Senate? It certainly didn't come out of your earnings as a teacher at Michigan State."

"You're right on that," Barbara shot back, "it certainly didn't. A teacher can hardly afford a decent life, let alone a political campaign. Thank you for bringing it up—it's one of the issues of my educational platform. As for where I got the money, it came from my inheritance from my mother."

"How many millions did you inherit?" another reporter asked sharply.

"It's a matter of record," Barbara replied. "It wasn't millions. It was two hundred fifty thousand dollars."

"Did you spend all of that on your campaign to get nominated?"

"Yes, I did," Barbara answered. "And I borrowed more on my house."

"Will you be reimbursed for the money you spent?"

"I don't expect to be," Barbara said. "It's no one's responsibility but my own."

The ABC anchorman interrupted. "We all know your father's automobile company is worth many millions of dollars. How much stock do you have?"

"None," Barbara replied.

"Will you inherit stock in the company?"

"Ask my father. I know nothing about his plans. We've never discussed it."

The CBS man overlapped her answer. "Where is your father? Where's your brother and sister and the rest of the family? We haven't seen any of them during your campaign. Where are they on your big night?"

"Working," Barbara said. "We're a working family."

"Yeah," Jack Jacoby said. "Your sister's a hell of a worker. When did she ever have a job?"

"When she was nine years old she was working ten hours a day at the London Ballet School," Barbara answered. "She was one of the best students they ever had until she injured a knee. She was just starting with the American Ballet Company and she was expected to become a prima ballerina in time—she was that good—and she worked that hard. Check the records."

"I have," Jacoby shot back. "But in the last four years she hasn't worked at anything except getting headlines. Jet-setting headlines—and rumors have it that she's heavy on drugs."

"I don't believe that," Barbara flashed back. "She lived with me for three years after our mother died. She's a superbly trained athlete."

"*Was*," Jacoby answered. "But not now."

"Have you ever seen her free-fall from an airplane? Have you ever seen her on the ski run at Vail? She's done those things even with the injured knee. There's nothing she won't try."

"That's what I've heard," Jacoby said. "Nothing or no one."

Barbara gave him a frozen look. "I said I will try to answer all your questions, but I won't discuss my family any further. None of them was elected senator. *I* was. Next question."

Another reporter stepped up. "Are you going to try to pursue in the Senate the educational reforms you've talked about?"

"I am," Barbara answered. Then she paused for a moment, thinking out her answer to the question. "I'm on the record for my belief in the war against illiteracy. I don't think we can solve the terrifying problems we have without higher educational standards—better teachers—better paid teachers, and working to eliminate the illiteracy in our country and everywhere else we can help and train students at every level in human communication.

"If a family can't communicate, a community can't relate. And if a community can't relate, we have what we have now—a world living under the threat of extermination.

"I'm going to the Senate with a committed program to fight for changes in the educational system—that's a number one for me."

Another network reporter spoke up. He glanced from Barbara Garibaldi to her young campaign manager, Jim Reardon, at her side.

"There are many rumors about you and Mr. Reardon. What do you have to say about them?"

"I am in love with Mr. Reardon," Barbara answered. "Next question?"

2

Lansing, Michigan

"You're going to have one hell of a fight, lady." Henry Calvin sat in the center of an arc of chairs in front of the large television screen in his study. The bank of phones on the desk in the south corner of the room were ringing continually. Calvin took in the cheers of Barbara's constituency all around her as she continued to answer the interviewers on the telecast from the state capitol.

"We underrated her, Henry," said a shaggy-haired older man at one end of the chairs. "I didn't think a woman could take this state. I really didn't." Henry Calvin got out of his chair as he flicked the remote control on the television and the huge TV screen went black. He walked over to the phones ringing on his desk. There were five of them. He snapped the buttons in quick succession, ending the intrusion of the telephone noise upon his thoughts. The calls were now going into an automatic recorder that could not be heard in the room.

"I would have bet against it," Calvin said. "In fact, I did bet against it—my whole career." He surveyed the four other men in front of him. "And yours, too, except—" He paused theatrically on his own word.

"There is no 'except,'" one of the men said.

"Yes, there is," Calvin answered. He picked up from his desk four large folders, each labeled with a name. He gave each of the men in front of him a folder. "We're still going back to Washington. I haven't worked for all my life to be beaten by a woman with some crazy idea that she really knows what the people of my state want. We just didn't realize what we were dealing with—now we do.

"Ever since the polls showed me that she had any chance at all, I've had an investigation going on about her and her family. I've been looking for ghosts. Not rumors, but facts. We all know every family has skeletons, but I can tell you I've come up with more than I guessed. I want each one of you to study this information and meet here again tomorrow morning at eight."

"How can we change the election?" another man asked.

"I've checked the state law and precedent with my lawyers. It's all in the folder. Just because a candidate's elected doesn't mean he has to serve. There's always privilege to resign. And if by resigning you save from becoming public knowledge the ghosts of the past of everyone in your family, including yourself, you've got a good reason to resign."

Another man spoke up. "That's blackmail."

"Not if it's handled with taste and diplomacy," Calvin answered. "If Barbara Garibaldi resigns, the governor names someone to replace her for two years. And who do you think that would be?"

Calvin was a big, imposing-looking man—everybody's idea of what a senator should look like; his body language and his voice reflected authority. "This kind of information is a political tool," he went on. "You all know that, and also you know it's a tool everybody uses. Once you enter the political arena, gentlemen, and I learned this a long time ago, you are fair game. Every single fact, mistake, and transgression in your life and in your family's life and in your friends' lives and in your appointees' lives is put under high voltage exposure. You all know how it is today what with the FBI, the CIA, computers, credit systems, phone lists—my God, which one of us has a really private life, and which one of us has never made any mistakes? Well, it so happens that this family, like so many other important families in our own recent history, is full of ghosts and transgressions. And none of this family has ever been under the kind of scrutiny that produces public information. Until now.

"Bill Donnelly, Eric Garibaldi's lawyer, will handle this just the way I want. He is the person closest to the old man.

"We're in a new age now, gentlemen. Everyone is fair game for the press, even presidential nominees and presidents themselves. Read the editorials. Listen to Rather, Brokaw, and Jennings. 'Character' has become a basic 'must' for political office. Americans want to believe their politicians are decent, moral, ethical people.

"I don't think the Garibaldi family can stand up—read the folder—the information we have, in many ways, could destroy this family, and Barbara Garibaldi. Certainly each of their positions would be changed"—he smiled at the thought that occurred to him—"for 'the rest of their lives.' The heat is on, gentlemen."

3

Stephanie Columbo

The New York intersection on East 14th Street was closed off by policemen and security guards. The Palladium glittered with a dazzling display of night lights.

Thousands of movie-in-the-making watchers and fans were held back by the ropes setting off the street, the crew, and the rented motor homes of the cast. A long black limousine with uniformed chauffeur stood waiting to drive down the street to the entrance of the Palladium.

Inside her dressing room, Stephanie was preparing for her first shot in the picture. The whole company had flown to New York the night before.

Bill Thomas and his seamstress closed in the tucks of Stephanie's black velvet gown. It was cut very low and the last-minute's work of the seamstress pulled the dress together at the end of the curve of Stephanie's hips. She knew she wouldn't be able to sit down in the dress, but there was a deep slit almost to the hips so that she could dance.

Bill stood back and looked at her. He motioned with his hand for her to turn in a circle.

"You make the dress, Stephanie. That's the way it should be. This is your first shot in our movie and nobody is going to forget you. I can guarantee that."

The seamstress looked up and down Stephanie's spectacular figure. Nobody *will* forget her, for sure, the seamstress thought, as her eyes moved down the seductive curves of Stephanie's hips. The dress was so simple in design and line that your eyes went directly to the woman.

"Give me a cigarette, will you, Bill?" Stephanie asked.

Bill took one out of his cigarette case, gave it to her, and lit it. Her hand was shaking.

"You're supposed to have the shakes. That's the reason you're shooting this scene first," Steve said, as he came up the steps of the motor home.

"Thank you, Bill," he said. "And Helen," he spoke to the seamstress.

Steve seemed younger than usual, and excited. His eyes shone as he looked at Stephanie. "You look exactly as I hoped you would."

"Really?" Stephanie asked, picking up his excitement.

Steve nodded at Bill and Helen, and they left the trailer. He closed his fist over her hand with the cigarette in it, and steadied her.

"This is opening night for you, Stephanie—and you look exactly like Christina Garibaldi should look. Every man who sees you will want you, and that is what Christina Garibaldi intends.

"I want you to walk out of this trailer and into that limousine and drive up to the Palladium and do the scene—remember, *you're* in control—for the first time in your life. The men come to you."

He turned her toward the mirror again. "Look at yourself, Stephanie. Remember when you stood like this, looking in the mirror at the sanatorium? *That* face is gone because of your guts. You've beaten it. You're standing there, an absolutely stunning, confident, strong woman.

"That's what you are now, Stephanie—even more than the character you are playing. Christina still has her need—a deep need. You have no more need. So I want all your vulnerability.

"This is your opening night, Stephanie—not for me, not even for the picture but for yourself. Ready?"

The crowd screamed as Steve took Stephanie to the waiting limousine. The three other members of her "party" were already in the car.

"You'll be there, won't you?" she asked Steve.

"Right by the camera. If you feel uncomfortable on any shot, come to me. We'll go off by ourselves and talk it over. Maybe you'll have an instinct that's better than my idea. If you do we'll go with it. I want you loose and free out there.

"And remember what we've worked on. In motion pictures, everything is the *eyes*. What you feel, what you think. Just lose yourself to Christina Garibaldi. Listen to those people applauding you already.

They don't even know who you are but they know how you look. That's for you, Stephanie. And I'm cheering with them."

He closed the door and headed for the camera and the long dolly track. David Thayer and Gaylin Schultz were waiting for him to begin Stephanie's first sequence in *The Rest of Our Lives*.

4

The Palladium,
New York

There was the usual crowd of celebrity groupies packed around the door of the Palladium as the long black limo pulled to the curb. First to appear was a short, thickset man who had captured world headlines for months as the most important middleman munitions dealer in current world conflicts. He courted the international elite and they courted him. He was swarmed over by the paparazzi, who did not get his picture, but closed in on the gorgeous woman who was the next to get out of the car.

She was strikingly beautiful, with her long hair falling loosely around her shoulders in her own famous style, photographed all over the world. She wore a full-length chinchilla coat, and the Sanderson gem collection of sapphires and diamonds, made so famous by Winston, sparkled from her necklace and bracelets. Her head was thrown back as she surveyed the mob pushing in on her. Her mouth was half open in the look of astonished pleasure that she had made famous.

Christina was like a child at a party. Except, for her, there was no more surprise. This was the way she was hunted and welcomed in every jet-set gathering across the world. She and her best friend, who was now coming out of the car. This, too, was a famous face—the South American beauty who had married the rock star sex symbol of the decade, and divorced him, and become a celebrity in her own right through her political activities in behalf of Latin America and, most particularly, her own country. Another notorious European munitions dealer was the last one to emerge from the limousine.

The two women were out front all the way. The crowd screamed their names and pushed in for autographs. Photographers fought to get in close with their flashbulbs.

The two famous multimillionaires from the Middle East, one, in fact, rumored to be a billionaire, followed the women in. Both men were much older than the women and they were obviously proud to be seen with them.

The security guards at the Palladium made a wedge in the crowd to get the party in. The club had set it up the way Christina Garibaldi and her friend liked it. They fed on the attention and center stage. They were superstars in a superstar world. If they understood anything in life, it was what it meant to be a superstar and to stay one.

The story had been whispered all through the evening inside the Palladium. Two of the most famous women of the world's jet set were expected with two men very prominent in world news. Their table was at the edge of the dance floor, the only empty one. The Palladium was jammed. Every person there watched the entrance of this special foursome.

The two women made their way to the ladies' room with a trail of studied glances following their path. This was glamour. This was money. This was power. This was envy, and hatred. The Palladium was electric.

The dressing room was supplied with perfumes, makeup, flowers. Two immaculately dressed Palladium women attendants were there to see to the guests.

Christina's friend went straight to one makeup mirror and began checking her makeup in the special lighting. Christina went into one of the stalls, and glanced around. She shut the door so that no one could see her; she huddled in a corner. Quickly, she unfastened her purse and took out a delicate blue lace handkerchief in a roll. At the center of the roll was a hypodermic needle. She picked up her skirt from the high slit in her dress, pulled it above her garter belt, slid back her panties to expose her left hip. Deftly, she inserted the needle into her flesh. She squeezed out the cocaine and quickly replaced the hypodermic in her silk handkerchief.

The attendant was outside waiting with a cigarette box and lighter. Christina took one and lit it.

The attendant's face was deferential, accustomed to servicing the wealthy and glamorous. She was memorable only for being average. Her manner was subdued. She was the perfect attendant for the Palladium.

She had started to work there three days before. Henry Calvin had word that Christina Garibaldi was coming home from the ski slopes of St. Moritz. One of the finest detective agencies in the world, Somerset's of England, had supplied the new Palladium attendant. They had placed her there armed with her unpretentious personality and the minute camera installed within her cigarette lighter. She was one of the most efficient undercover workers in the Somerset organization. She had been able to hold the lighter up over the closed door of Christina's stall and get her pictures in a few seconds.

Christina paraded through the crowd to the table at the edge of the dance floor. Her friend was right behind her.

She stopped by the table only long enough to give up her chinchilla coat to the maître d'. She touched the shoulder of her escort and passed her hand sensuously across his mouth. He took hold of her hand and held it to his lips for a moment and then stood up as she stepped onto the dance floor. She was almost a head taller than he was. The rock band immediately keyed into Tina Turner's "Break Every Rule."

There were a number of other couples on the floor but as Christina unleashed her dancing style, everyone else melted away. She was a show stopper. She knew it. They knew it. She took over.

Her eyes burned, her body slithered and jerked in rhythm with the music. She began to sing the song softly, barely mouthing the words, looking directly at her partner. He didn't try to match her dancing. He stood there, doing a kind of tentative rock step, while she danced up to him, teasingly. His head was just above the level of her breasts, which were almost completely exposed. Her legs, revealed almost to the hip by the slit in her dress, moved intricately with the rhythm. Every person in the Palladium was bewitched.

A reporter caught her eyes for a moment at the edge of the dance floor.

"How about your sister's winning the election?"

"Nothing to do with me," she answered as she twirled by.

Photographers crowded around the edge of the dance floor. She had told the manager that was what she expected if she came to the Palladium. She loved the excitement of it. It was the next best thing to being on stage.

The cocaine made her forget the pain in her knee, made her forget that her career was over and gone—made her forget the emptiness she felt. She was a show stopper and she stopped everything dead in the Palladium. High on drugs, she didn't think about the past or what she would do with the rest of her life. Only tonight. The crowd. The adulation. You could feel it, dense as the smoke in the Palladium. She was somebody! Certainly as important as her sister, any day!

5

Lansing

*T*he oversized billboards had become the talk of Lansing. They came at you every two miles of freeway 496, leading in and out of the capital city. Their simplicity was striking; Barbara had designed them herself. Jim had plotted the exposure in rhythm with the traffic. Eighty-five percent of the population of Lansing and its environs used those freeways every day. The symbol of Barbara Garibaldi's campaign became something to look forward to, breaking the freeway tedium, and the boring traffic jams. The key lines of the signs and the key illustrations changed every week. It was the same all over Michigan.

They were on the freeway now in Jim's convertible with the top down. They were both glad to be quiet after the long hours of crowds and commotion. They watched the enormous billboards come and go as they drove down the freeway, almost deserted in the late hours of the night. The large red letters against the great expanse of white keyed every billboard: WHAT ARE WE GOING TO DO WITH THE REST OF OUR LIVES? "The rest of our lives" was twice the size of the introductory line.

They had taken a big chance. The billboards were an innovation. There was no mention of Barbara Garibaldi, the campaign, or the election. There was simply one key photograph in the left corner of the billboard. It was a photograph directly relating to one of Barbara's issues. And each photograph told an instant, basic story.

One showed a man dying on a battlefield, his hands extended upward as though he were seeking an answer in his last seconds of life. Underneath that photograph in red letters that matched exactly the color and the design of the letters of THE REST OF OUR LIVES were the words WAR OR PEACE.

The next billboard had a photograph of three emaciated Cambodian children. The words under it were HUNGER OR COMPASSION. The next billboard down the freeway depicted an American family together at a holiday table. Underneath it were the words TOGETHER OR ALONE.

The next billboard carried a horrifying photograph of a decomposing drug addict, shooting a hypodermic directly into his arm. Underneath it were the words LIFE OR DEATH.

The issues of Barbara's campaign strung out, dominating the freeway, as Jim's car sped along. Barbara and Jim looked together at each billboard, including the last one they'd done on AIDS.

They knew that the campaign, followed up by the enormous card mailing and Barbara's going to every corner of the state, no matter how small the town, to talk to the people, had been keyed by Barbara's phrase "What are we going to do with the rest of our lives?"

"I remember the night I came to you," Barbara said, nodding at the last billboard going by. "We'd been talking the night before about us, you and me."

"And," Jim replied, "you said we couldn't look back at all the mistakes we'd made. That we had to look forward, all we had was the rest of our lives. It seemed so simple, but so right. I would have bet my whole marketing future on it."

Barbara smiled at him. "You did," she said. "My mother—I wish you'd known her, Jim; she would have loved you—she used to say whenever any of us had a big disappointment or a heartbreak, 'That's past. That's gone. What we do have is the rest of our lives.' I wonder what she'd think if she saw this campaign."

"She'd be proud of you," Jim said. "I've never seen anyone work harder or care more."

"Now I've got to deliver," Barbara said. "It's frightening when I think about it. I've got to crack Washington and all the resistance to a woman in politics. A woman in government."

"It's just beginning, Barb," Jim said as he turned off the freeway and followed a tree-lined country road heading north. "You could feel it all through the reception tonight. The first time the big boys have had a full shot at you—with no holds barred—we can get anything we want now—*Time, Newsweek, Fortune, People*—all of them. It's one of the best stories in years and you're up to it."

"But," Barbara said quietly, "am I up to being United States senator? Am I up to fighting for everything we believe? To not caring as much about being liked as helping change things? The cards have shown us that most of the people agree on what they want for the rest of their lives. Do we have a shot at getting some of this accomplished? I've talked so much about doing it, now I'm in the kitchen and I've got to take the heat."

Jim stopped the car on a hill overlooking the lights of the city. He turned to her, protectively. "I want to talk to you about the heat. When you won the election tonight, you went under a microscope that will stay there as long as you're in elected office. It's ten times as bad for you because you're rich, you're from a famous family, you're intelligent, and God knows you're beautiful." He reached out and touched her face. "I never saw you more beautiful than tonight, Barb."

She put her arms around him and kissed him. "Let's go home," she said.

"It's your home, not mine," Jim said. "It's your election, not mine. It's your money, not mine. After you answered the question about us tonight the way you did, the press is going to be all over our story. They'll start with the difference in our ages and then the other differences all down the line."

"And that's the very reason I answered that question point blank," Barbara said. "I'm proud that we love each other. I'm proud of you. I know who you are, Jim. I don't care what anyone else says. I've felt your love and support through all these grinding weeks and every trip and tour we've made. When it's been freezing and raining and the timetables were off and no one met us and no one gave a damn. The tougher it got, the tougher you got.

"Now I can walk into a crowded room like the one tonight and not see you. But I can feel you clear across it. It's grown between us so we're comfortable with each other. We can spend time together, like in the car tonight, in silence. Not having to force a word.

"Remember something, Jim. We were partners first. Friends and partners before we fell in love. Respect and loyalty are so important if we're going to last and build something. And I have those things with you. It's taken time and work and effort and caring on both our parts.

"It's what I've always wanted—a real partnership with a man on every level.

"We won together tonight. We won because we have the same ideas, the same commitment and because we've learned to love each other. I'll never give that up because of any gossip or any pressure— or any ambition. Forty years I've waited for this relationship. And now

it's been given to me. You've been given to me. I am so blessed, Jim."
She kissed him passionately. "Take me home now. Make love to me.
Hold me. I don't want this night to ever end. It's our night, Jim. I
want to share my life with you and I want to share your life, too. I'm
going for all of it. In forty years I haven't done that. I tried to be what
my mother and father wanted me to be, what my brother and sister
wanted me to be, what men wanted me to be—now I want *my* life.
I want to be what *I* want to be.

"And don't try to get out of coming to Washington. There's no way
I want to go on with this unless you're there."

Jim took her in his arms again. "That's quite a speech, Senator. I'll
think it over."

6

Detroit

*H*e had them on their feet: 2,524 union members who worked at the Garibaldi plant.

The figures were in. They were far behind the Japanese and German imports. Particularly in the low-price field, the Japanese had taken leadership in the world.

The gathering cries for national elections were "How do we get America back in the world market?" "Has America lost its drive, its competitive edge?" "Has America gone soft, lazy, self-satisfied?" The anchormen and the columnists were saying that the political party which could lead America back into its past work ethics would win the election.

Eric Garibaldi wasn't running for office. The Garibaldi Automobile Company was fighting for its life. They needed renewed loans and new loans in order for Garibaldi's plans to be executed. He was confident he could build a better and cheaper car than the Japanese, but it took money. And it meant new equipment, new casting, new dye machines.

Garibaldi shouted across the great hall. "They're all saying we can't do it anymore. That we've lost our guts and our balls. We're no better than third and fading." There was a roar from the workers, angry and defiant.

Garibaldi went on. "They say we're satisfied with what we've got. We don't want to work hard. We don't care who's ahead of us. All we want is our money, our insurance, our vacation pay. Screw the quality; to hell with the efficiency; so what, the Japanese and the Germans can do it better and cheaper.

"I'm asking you, and myself, too, are they right? Is this true? Are we finished with the top? Do we really not care if someone else does it better and cheaper?"

Almost in unison the shouts rang through the company auditorium. "No, no, no—never!"

Garibaldi's gaze swept the room. "I'm speaking for myself. Yes, it's my company, but I don't have a company without you. That's why every one of you has a participation in the profits of the Garibaldi Automobile Company. Some of you were with me at the very start when we built the first Garibaldi car—twenty-four hour days, going without salaries, day after day, and night after night, but we believed in ourselves. We knew we could do it and we did.

"I'm not going to throw it all away. I want you to be with me, but if you don't feel the way I do, you can check out now, and you won't lose any of your vacation pay or pension or medical or anything else.

"Everyone in this room has done a great job for me and for the Garibaldi Automobile Company—no regrets—but I can't stand to go on this way, being third or fourth or fifth and having other countries build the cars we should build.

"I want to know today, now, who's with me and who wants out. I don't care whether it's one person or ten or a hundred or a thousand. I want every man here who doesn't really care anymore, who's only in it for the money, to walk out of this room now—no regrets, no resentments.

"You can walk out or you can stay here and fight it out with me. It's up to you. And for those of you who go, I want to thank you for what you've given.

"Maybe I'm wrong. Maybe I'm just an old man with a dream that's worn out. Maybe this factory, where so many wonderful machines have been built and created, by you just as much as by me, maybe we should lock up and call it a day and a life. You tell me if we're finished."

There was dead silence. Garibaldi looked across the room, giving more than two thousand men a chance to make up their minds. A smile filled his face.

"Fine. Now let's get back to work. Let's send out the message that we're going to build the best cars. We'll take them all on. Right?"

The assembly hall exploded with shouts and cheers.

Susan was waiting for Eric Garibaldi as he came out of the assembly hall. She had been his executive assistant for fifteen years, his friend and lover for twelve. She was slender, elegant, and well educated. She had a degree in engineering. She had written a brilliant report not long after she came to work in the marketing department of Garibaldi's company. The report had found its way to him and he had sought her out. That was the beginning.

She now had the power and prestige of her position in the company, and there was an added bonus. Through the years, slowly and reluctantly, Susan had fallen in love with Eric Garibaldi. "Congratulations," she said.

"For what?"

"Your daughter's election to the Senate. I wish you'd been there. I watched it on television."

Garibaldi nodded. A smile cut the corner of his mouth. "Damn good, wasn't she?"

Susan nodded. "Like you," she said. "A second congratulations for your speech in there. I listened from the back. Vince Lombardi would have been proud." He gave her a quick look. She laughed. "What would you have done if they had walked out?"

Suddenly, Eric Garibaldi looked as vulnerable as a child. He shook his head. "I don't know. We'd have had to close down, I guess."

"I wouldn't have let you," Susan said.

"That sounds like someone else I knew once . . . Susan, I want to stop in here for a minute. Come with me, won't you?" He turned and entered a small building marked with a sign in front: BUILDING C.

They walked through the understated but handsomely decorated foyer. The walls held awards and citations from all over the automobile world as well as from the White House. They were framed alike in dark blue, the color of the carpeting.

Garibaldi entered the inner part of the building. There was one main room, oval in design. In the center enclosed by velvet ropes was the Centurion, the first car Garibaldi had built—a "million-dollar" car that he and a few men had built by hand—the beginning of the Garibaldi Automobile Company. The Centurion had a slender racelike design, an Italian inheritance. It was polished black enamel trimmed in red with red-leather interior. One of the best of the front steering designs with a compact and powerful motor.

The Centurion had been a smash hit all over the world and it had led directly to the financing and future of the Garibaldi Automobile Company.

On the wall behind the car was a large portrait of Garibaldi, not in his library or sipping a scotch or in any of the other poses typical of a business tycoon. It was a painting of the raceway. He was in his white racing suit at the moment he was coming out of the Centurion after its successful testing. One hand was letting go of the helmet, raised high over his head in his moment of triumph; the other fist in the air. A smile cut across his begrimed face. The Centurion was made.

On each of the other walls were photographs of the classic cars that had come down through the Garibaldi dynasty.

Eric circled the room, looking at the Centurion, remembering.

Susan watched him. "You know, I've come here so many times without you, and there's always something new for me. It's almost as if the car has its own life—it's like walking into a home and sensing the vibrations—the feeling that the things inside a house are, well, alive. I feel that about the Centurion."

Garibaldi put his arms on her shoulders. "You say it so much better than I can—everything I feel—I can't stand to think of—" His voice went to a whisper. "—God, I wish my son—" He shook his head. "It could all be his. A man needs to pass things on." He took her in his arms. "Susan, if anything happens to me, I want you to keep it running. I want you to keep the Garibaldi Automobile Company alive—you'll find a way—you know who my people are, you know who the leaders are—I've collected them, one by one. If I go down, don't let the company go down with me."

7

The Web

"'m sorry you have to see these pictures, Eric, but I had no choice."

Eric Garibaldi looked at the twelve photographs spread across his desk. Christina, her eyes bright, stunningly beautiful, her breasts half exposed, her mouth parted, an international sex symbol of the 1980s. He had seen these kinds of photographs of her for the last few years, in the newspapers and magazines covering her worldly travels and escapades.

But these were different. These were close-ups of a hypodermic, her dress pulled up, her left hip exposed. Close-ups of her unwrapping the hypo from her purse. Of her expert handling of the needle. Close-ups of her eyes reflecting the effects of the shot while she was still in the stall at the Palladium. It was all there. A world-famous woman shooting herself full of cocaine in a washroom stall at the jet-setters' favorite club.

"There are more pictures—from Europe—with known dealers in the rock crowd. From London, the Riviera, Turkey, and Rio. Somebody's been on her trail for a long time."

"Who?" Garibaldi asked hoarsely.

"Henry Calvin," Bill Donnelly, his lawyer, answered. "He's had a top private detective agency in England investigating your family since Barbara started to run for senator—just in case he lost."

"Barbara slaughtered that son of a bitch," Garibaldi said. "Okay, Bill, let's have it. What's his angle? As far as the Senate goes, he's lost the election, and that's that."

"Not quite," Donnelly said. "An elected office holder can always resign. Henry Calvin plans to stay in Washington—as senior senator from Michigan, named by the governor as the law provides. You know, Eric, Calvin's whole life is wrapped around that job. He *is* that job."

Garibaldi looked steadily at Donnelly, his face livid. "You talking about blackmail?"

"Not legally," Donnelly answered. "Not technically. They're being very careful about everything. Some of these pictures came to my house, as you can see, postmarked from Europe. Some of them from Philadelphia. No messages except phone calls from phone booths. There's nothing we can trace directly to Calvin. He's too smart to set himself up for any accusations.

"This English detective agency—one of the best in the world— they've made up quite a package. The ghosts of your three children, Eric." He paused. "And yourself."

Garibaldi glanced at him. "What the hell do you mean by that?"

"These people have enough on you to blow your whole company— at the very least, force you to resign. Everybody knows you're the most popular automobile maker with the unions, Eric. And the unions— well, everybody needs them. That's been one of the great secrets of the success of your company. Your record for integrity. You keep your word. That's the heart of your company."

"So," Garibaldi asked, "let them check anything they want to. There's nothing that isn't public knowledge about my company and that's the way it was built."

His lawyer's voice was quiet. "But that's not the way it started, Eric. Somehow they've found out about how you built the Centurion— where you got the million dollars when you were broke and out of a job and when the men around you had no money either."

Garibaldi was stunned. "There are only two people in the world who knew that. You and me."

"And then there were three," Bill said. "They got to that third person. One who knew that you sold to Venezuela two million dollars' worth of General Motors equipment that was unsold the previous year."

Garibaldi shot back, "That was part of my job. Assistant to foreign sales. We sold equipment that was out of date—marked down—a bargain."

"But this was a special sale," Bill said. "The details are all in the folder here. There are photostated documents, checks. I don't know how they got them, but they're there. They show, without any doubt, that you delivered to Venezuela one million dollars' worth of General Motors equipment—mostly tractors and trucks—and you got paid two million dollars. One million for the company and one million straight into the building of the Centurion.

"It's open and shut, Eric. Granted, no one's surprised these days to read about corporate fraud and inside information and deceit, but that doesn't fly with the Garibaldi Automobile Company or with the Garibaldi legend. Eric, you're one of the last of your kind who people believe in. You can't be bought or sold. You're a hero and a champion in a day when we don't have any—hardly any—certainly none in the business world."

Garibaldi spoke slowly. "I paid the money back to General Motors, in my own way, later."

"That's not the point," Donnelly said. "The simple fact that Calvin's people will lay out for the newspapers, magazines, telecasters and anchormen in language they understand is that Eric Garibaldi stole one million dollars and built an American empire with money that didn't belong to him. Your reputation goes in the sewer—the legend along with it. You've been called a lot of things in your career, but nobody's ever been able to call you a liar, Eric, or a thief. Or a fraud. These are the words they're tossing around in the report. Study it."

"But that was thirty years ago," Garibaldi said. "The Centurion's made millions and millions of dollars for GM. It's all on the record."

"All but what's in the folder," Bill said. "And they have material on Barbara and your son, too.

"They're going to smear the whole family, Eric, if Barbara doesn't resign. This has been carefully planned for six months, it's clear-cut, and I believe they mean business. Really, it's down to this—" he continued "—is the senatorship of Michigan for your daughter worth the exposure and disgrace of the whole family?"

"Do you think the public will buy this garbage?" Garibaldi pulled the folders out of the large envelope that Donnelly had brought.

"The public is very fast to believe the worst about people."

"Will Calvin meet with me?" Garibaldi asked.

"No," Donnelly said. "He'll stay remote from this. Supposedly, it's a committee we're dealing with, a group of people who don't believe a family like yours should be involved in the government of the United States. The 'character' issue in politics is with us in a big way now, and they know it."

"Will they meet with me?" Garibaldi asked "Any of them?"

"I'll send some feelers out," Bill answered. "But the Somerset Agency in London is the only concrete thing I have as far as who's actually involved."

"Use every contact you've got," Garibaldi clipped out. "I want to see someone who's connected to this sewer face to face. Maybe I'll just walk in on Calvin."

"He'll just deny everything. It's been well set up. And that kind of confrontation can go against you, Eric. You've had spotlights on you before, but nothing like the one that comes with important political office. From now on, you're public domain. There is no private life for any of the Garibaldi family since the moment the vote came in last night."

8

Father and Son

There were eleven black Africans in the a cappella group. Michael Garibaldi had brought them out of Zimbabwe. He had heard about them and he had gone there to find them.

They didn't know any English. They sang the African words a cappella intermingled with chants that weren't full words, but carried emotional meanings of their own.

They came in from the left wing of the stage, one by one, each in his own individual style, and moving to his own rhythms and his own experiences. They didn't play to the audience. They only half turned toward the audience. They played to each other.

The preview audience in the theater was still. They'd never seen anything quite like this one.

The choir circled loosely around Michael, looking at him, their faces alive with their music. Michael nodded to the back of the stage to a circle of kettle drums. Inside the circle two men, one white and one black, stood back to back, each facing a half arc of five drums.

Michael nodded his head and the fingers of the two men began to brush against the kettle drums, almost inaudibly. The singers picked up the quiet throb. Their voices began to accelerate the rhythm and they moved upstairs to the middle of the bandstand and encircled the kettle drums and the two men playing them.

The drums built gradually until the drummers were pounding out the rising currents of the rhythms with their fingers and fists, elbows, their whole bodies, crackling with the beat of the jungle drums.

The audience began to pick up the rhythms. People of all ages were tapping their feet, moving in their chairs. It was contagious. The rhythms were of the very oldest jungle heritage and the very latest rock heritage.

The singers danced with fire.

In the back of the theater, standing room only, Eric Garibaldi and Susan watched the closing number of his son's preview concert. Susan was moving to the beat.

Garibaldi looked from his son up there on the stage, his musicians and his singers, to Susan next to him. They were moving the same way, like most of the people in the theater. Many were chanting in the rhythm of the drums and the a cappella singers from Africa.

Garibaldi had never heard anything like this. It was wild and yet plaintive at the same time.

"What the hell's going on?" Garibaldi turned to Susan. He watched her moving in her own free style. She was completely caught up in the music.

"Michael's found it," she said excitedly. "This is his own—and it's going to make him a star. Look at the crowd. This is only a preview concert. Think of it, Eric—your son is going around the world with this new band of musicians from seventeen countries. No one's ever done anything like it."

Suddenly, the electric guitars came in at the peak of the drum crescendo. Michael was bringing in the brass now, muted, not overpowering, but strong and virile in the mix. He had three saxophonists doubling on clarinet.

Out of this strange cacophony of instrumentation came the sounds of the black choir with the power of the jungle drums continuing to pound through. The form of an old and familiar melody was beginning to take shape. At first it was only an audible outline, a suggestion that arrested one's ear for a moment and sent one's memory spinning. What was it? Where was it from? Where have I heard that? Something's coming together here—what is it?

The melody line didn't take shape with any of the instruments, not the reeds or the brass or the guitars. It began to form with the chant of the black men encircling Michael in the center of the stage. As they passed by him, each one gave him a touch, a kind of "five" in his own way.

Their voices were soft now, becoming part of the tapestry of music that Michael was making with his musicians. He had his guitar strapped on his shoulder. In the midst of the beat and the counterpoints, his guitar, alone, blending perfectly with the voices of his African choir, picked out pieces of the melody and brought them together out of the driving force of his rock band.

The people in the audience recognized, at last, the melody. "Amazing Grace." And the audience began to sway with it and clapped their hands with the beat. Then the black chorus picked up the handclapping and began to send it back to the audience, the noise level rising but not overpowering the melody. Michael brought the other guitars in, then the brass, then the reeds. This was an "Amazing Grace" that no one had ever heard before. It was Michael's own arrangement, the final song of his concert.

In the back of the theater Susan still swayed with the music, singing softly now the words that came back to her.

Michael, with "Amazing Grace" driving behind him, called down to the front of the stage beside him one by one, his new band. The electric guitarist from England. The saxophonist from France. The horn player from Italy. The guitarist from Spain. The lead horn soloist from Japan. The bass player from Germany. The white drummer from Russia. The black drummer living in exile from South Africa, formerly of Johannesburg.

This concept of Michael's, to build a United Nations rock band and tour the world, had been born after his supporting participation in "We Are the World." And now this was the big night. From *Rolling Stone* to the *New York Times*, this concert would be reviewed. Thumbs up or thumbs down.

The band was lined up across the stage, the a cappella choir holding everything together with their rhythmic chanting as the music stopped.

Now in unison, with only the sounds of the a cappella choir behind them, the band sang the last two stanzas of "Amazing Grace." There it was, finally, his dream, a United Nations band of Michael Garibaldi's in its only American appearance before setting off on a world tour.

The crowd was moving, cheering, still clapping in rhythm. Many gathered around the stage, crowding the aisles.

There was one final curtain call and onstage, for the last time, they were singing "Amazing Grace" right with the audience.

Susan was crying. Eric Garibaldi was choked up. "My God," he said, "I never understood what he was trying to do."

Susan looked at him with compassion. She shook her head. "No, you didn't, Eric, and do you realize this is the first time you've ever seen him in concert?"

The security guards massed around the stage door. Eric Garibaldi pushed one of them out of the way. "He's my son, I tell you. Let us through." He pulled Susan through the crowd.

There was another crowd around the dressing-room door. A girl in very faded blue jeans and a torn leather jacket was adding names to the list of people waiting to see Michael. Garibaldi pushed to the head of the line and started to go in the door. The girl stepped in front of him.

"I'm sorry, you can't go in there. Give me your name, please. And go to the end of the line."

Garibaldi looked at her steadily. "I'm his father."

"I'll tell him you're here," the girl answered, annoyed.

Garibaldi picked her up by the arms and simply moved her aside and set her down again. He opened the door and went in alone. Michael was speaking in African dialect to the leader of the choir. They both looked up at the intrusion. Michael froze. So did his father. They stood looking at each other, trying to bridge the years. All Michael could say was, "You came!"

Eric went to his son and put his arms around him. He hugged him tightly and kissed him on both cheeks. It was the first time in more than twenty years that Garibaldi had kissed his son.

"Why didn't you tell me you were coming, Dad? I'd have had seats and everything."

"I saw it—I saw you," Garibaldi said. "Most of the concert I didn't understand. It's too loud—and you can't hear the words—but at the end even *I* got the point. I'm proud of you, son. I never understood what you were doing."

He looked at the black man. "You were wonderful," he said. Michael translated for his father in a few words of African. The black man smiled. Garibaldi put out his hand and the black man took it.

Eric turned back to his son. "Do you think we could have a few minutes together? Something very important has come up." Michael spoke four words to the black man, who nodded and went out the door.

"Susan told me she gave you the message about the family meeting at our Bay House, but you said you couldn't, no matter how important it was."

"Dad, we're leaving for Europe in three days—I'm on an airtight schedule. I'm sorry."

Garibaldi said, "You have to come. The whole family's been threatened. Each one of us . . . you, too. We've got to decide what to do —fast."

"Threatened?" Michael asked. "Terrorists or something?"

His father shook his head. "No. Certain enemies of this family have been working a long time getting information about all of us. Digging up pasts that we never even shared with each other. It's all come up because of your sister's election. There are people who don't want to see her go to Washington. Unless Barbara resigns, they're ready to turn over documentation on all of us to the press."

"But they can't do anything to me, Dad. There isn't any—"

Garibaldi cut him off. "Yes, there is, son. I'm sorry you didn't tell me about it because maybe it could have been handled, but they're ready to go at us big."

From his pocket he pulled the picture of a mulatto boy standing on a beach looking quizzically at the camera. The boy looked twelve or thirteen years old. "Your son, Michael. They have the whole story. The abortion that didn't work. Your refusal to marry the girl. Her return to Haiti. And her complete disappearance from your life."

He looked at his son's face and knew it was true. Michael just stared at the picture and back at his father. "These things aren't very scandalous anymore."

"But," his father said, "when they see your show, I know what they'll do. They'll tear the image of your band apart. They'll kill its chances of being successful. They'll call you a racist and a fraud. You've got to come to the Bay House for the weekend, Michael. Each one of us has to decide what to do. We have to decide as a family."

9

Magdalena Prepares

She lifted the casserole out of the oven and put it on the breakfast room table where Steve was sipping his drink. She took the potatoes and vegetables out of the microwave. The mixed salad was already on the table.

Magdalena poured the wine. Several strands of her usually perfectly groomed hair had fallen down across her forehead. She was hot and she looked tired.

Steve laughed.

"I shouldn't be surprised after the party you threw for my crew, but it's still strange somehow to see you in the kitchen."

"It's much better than going out to a restaurant all the time."

Magdalena sat down and took the top off the casserole of Spanish rice.

"This is a recipe handed down through the gypsy side of my family. Rice is what we eat day after day, so we have to learn to make it in different ways. Now I didn't do this for you. I did it for my scenes tomorrow. I wanted to get back in the swing of things, feel how it is to take care of my own house, the cooking, and not depend on anyone else. The way Barbara Garibaldi takes care of her home and her kids."

Magdalena brushed back the strands of her hair.

"I've been going by school playgrounds, listening to the conversations when the mothers pick up their children. It's a world of its own. I've never had a family—never had any children—"

"You're doing everything you can to build a believable character," Steve replied. "You know, Maggie, there are interesting reactions with our own people about Barbara Garibaldi's political campaign—about *The Rest of Our Lives*. People are picking it up from the publicity. I hear rumors that both major parties are thinking about making some tests with our concept. And you know, if a political candidate from either party used that idea, used issues instead of their pictures and names all over the billboards or the posters, I think that candidate would really have something going for him."

"That's what you intended, wasn't it?" Magdalena asked.

"That's what I hoped for. If this picture doesn't touch people's lives, then we'll fail. That's why I rescheduled four more days in the real locations. Spartan's going to kill me, but we had to have the real places before we go back to the sets on the stage."

"Steve—I need you to watch me in those scenes tomorrow," Magdalena said.

"Worried?" he asked.

She nodded. "This is still such unfamiliar territory for me, no matter how much preparation we do. I've never been a woman like Barbara, and I've never played one like her. I've never been a mother. I've never really been married—I mean like Barbara was—for years and years and taken care of a family. I've always been outside all that. Now I've got to be inside it. Here and there—a glance, a touch, a look. Not the big dramatic scenes I'm used to."

Magdalena had felt the fatigue come on her again strongly the last week and at night she'd had fevers. She'd called Dr. Arms twice from Lansing and once from New York. He was monitoring the disease long distance. He was worried and she had heard that in his voice.

She had moments when she thought she should step out of the film now. But then the fatigue and fever would slip away and she would feel well again and excited. Tonight she was tired, and worried. Her scenes tomorrow would run the gamut of so much of Barbara Garibaldi's life in the film.

"Do you think I should go with the same makeup tomorrow?" she asked Steve.

He looked at her intently.

"I like the way you changed it tonight. You've given yourself two or three new lines and a suggestion of darkness under your eyes. You look harried and tired, but determined—that's exactly the look we need for tomorrow."

A flash of defensiveness went through Magdalena's eyes. Steve wasn't looking at her, but taking another helping of Spanish rice.

"This is good," Steve said.

Magdalena pulled herself together. She looked at Steve from across the breakfast room table and took stock of the two of them, sitting there, both in their work clothes, sharing a discussion of tomorrow's shooting.

"Yes, it is," Magdalena smiled. "It *is* good."

10

Going Home

"You're screwing up our kids! Don't you see that?" Barbara's ex-husband, Ted, lashed out at her. "Hell, you're talking about communication in all your campaign speeches, people relating, families relating—what about your own family—us—you and me—and Melly and Stewart? You've already split us apart, and now . . ."

"Let's don't get into that again, for God's sake," Barbara said as she jammed clothes into her suitcase.

"I want to get into it," Ted fired back as he stood by the window seat of the master bedroom. "You're my wife and . . ."

"I *was* your wife—past tense—past talk—past rehashing."

Ted's voice softened. "I want you back . . . the way things were."

Barbara turned on him. "Until I left you, all I had done my whole life was to be what someone else wanted me to be. The daughter my father expected me to be, the wife you expected me to be, the mother the children expected me to be, the woman I expected me to be. Then suddenly I was thirty-six years old and I had never really done anything on my own—I had never asked myself what *I* wanted to be—was I going to try to do something with my life or just let it flow by, a pleasant stream blending into many other pleasant streams?"

"You had your family," Ted said.

"And family is important to me," Barbara answered. "That's why I tried to hold it together long after I felt this way. And being a wife and mother can work for a woman like me, if your family understands that each one in the family should have a chance to fulfill himself.

To do something, to make a contribution, and try to be out there in the arena. Not live life as a spectator."

She looked at him and the anger left her voice. "Ted, I'm in the arena now, and I'm scared. I don't know whether I'll be any good at it. I know I have some good ideas, but it's hard in government to get your ideas across, good or not, and still harder for a woman. The people here, most of them anyway, believe in me. They think I can make some kind of a difference for them. I feel useful. I have a dream—" Her voice trailed off.

"I had one, too," Ted answered. "To go through life with you. I didn't need to be in the arena—we had enough money—and the company was there."

"But it wasn't yours, Ted. You didn't create a company, you inherited it. You didn't try to change it or improve it or diversify it. It was just *there*, and I just couldn't go on with that kind of life."

"Well, now you've got what you wanted," Ted said. "I don't pretend to understand it all—and the children—well, you're so much better with them than I am—"

Barbara walked back to her suitcases, finishing up. "I'm worried about Melly," she said. "I meet with the doctor every week and he feels she's finally pulling out of the anorexia."

"Every week?" Ted said. "How do you find the time to do that?"

"Our children come first. I'm sure they do for you, too. But remember that whatever I'm doing, wherever I am, the two children are first."

"Are you going to put them in school here when you go to Washington?" Ted asked.

"No, I don't believe in boarding schools for young children, you know that."

"I just thought, with your work and all—"

"Ted," Barbara said, "I was in three boarding schools after my mother died—remember? I hated them. I needed to be with my family. I'm not going to do that to my children. No. They'll come to Washington, too. They're going to go to public school in Washington and come home every night.

"I hope you'll come to Washington to see them during the school year. It's very important they have you to look up to, Ted."

"A father figure, you mean?" Ted said, somewhat sarcastically. "I imagine that your campaign manager will be around for that."

Barbara straightened up. "Look, Ted, since the divorce we've always been honest with each other. You have friends. I have friends. There's nothing wrong in that. I sincerely hope someday you'll marry again, someone who's right for you. I would be happy for you."

He looked at her. "I think you would," he said. "But I'm not happy about your campaign manager. I resent him and the whole goddamn idea of you traipsing around, a beautiful and glamorous political figure now, and sleeping with this kid. It doesn't become you, Barb."

She glanced at him. "I don't comment on the people you go around with. That's none of my business, unless it affects the children. I'd like the same courtesy from you."

"I don't care what you say. A woman in politics just can't be there for her children when they need her—no way . . . and then when there's a new man around . . . It's not good for the children. They're worried about you now. They don't see you enough. There's not enough one on one," Ted said.

"Are you really in love with him, Barb?" Ted asked.

"Yes, I am," she said.

"Do you two, how would you say it, 'communicate'? Do you relate with this Reardon guy?"

"It has nothing to do with his age. It has to do with his mind and his heart and his goals." Her voice softened. "We have the same goals, Ted. And I love that in him. He understands me."

"Like I never could?" Ted asked.

Barbara's voice went even softer. "That's right." She closed up the bags. Ted crossed over to pick them up.

"What's this command call to the Bay House all about?"

"I don't know yet, but I'm worried that something's wrong with my father. That he's sick and that he's going to tell us about it. It's been so long since the four of us were together—somehow we've all been too busy."

She checked her packing one last time.

"Now, you know the rules for the children. They'll try to con you and say that I'll never have to know about their comings and goings but, please, everything stays exactly the same. I want them free up to a point, but no matter how they complain, they're not allowed to stay out late. I don't want them being picked up by any new friends till we meet them and know if they're responsible. They can have anybody over they want, even to stay all night, as long as it fits in with your plans.

"I should be back in three or four days, at the most. I'll call you from the lake. I'd planned to take them to the country this weekend just to talk about the changes but, well, I know whatever it is, this reunion Dad's asked for must be vital."

"I'll do the best I can," Ted said. "What if they ask about your—?"

"Jim? I planned to talk to them about him this weekend, too. I'll do that as soon as I get back. You can tell them that. Well," Barbara looked around the room, "I hope I've remembered everything."

They started down the stairs together.

"Are you going to marry Jim Reardon, Mom?" Melly asked. Barbara and the two children were in Ted's station wagon. Ted was driving them to the airport. Barbara turned to the back seat. "I have no plans to marry him at the moment, no."

"We heard it on the news this morning. You were all over TV, Mom. Everywhere we switched channels, you were there or they were talking about you. *Good Morning America* said you were probably going to marry Jim Reardon. They showed some pictures of you two together. He's cute," Melly said.

"Yeah, he looks like he could be an older brother of mine," Melly's brother Stewart added.

Barbara laughed. "And like my son, I suppose."

"Well, not exactly," her son answered. "But he sure looks a lot younger than you do, Mom."

"You're beautiful, but he's cute," Melly said. "There's a difference. Now, Dad's good-looking, like a man."

"Thanks, Melly," Ted chimed in.

"How long will you be away, Mom?" Stewart asked.

"A few days. It's a family conference, something important. That's all I know."

"If it's family," Melly said, "why aren't we going?"

"This is one of those times," Barbara answered, "that your grandfather wanted to be alone with his three children."

"I'd like to go back to the Bay House," Stewart said. "It's been so long since we were there. I like that place. There're so many things to do."

"Well," Barbara said, "you're going to have a wonderful weekend with your father. I know it's going to be fun for the three of you."

"When you go to Washington, Mom," Melly spoke up, "we're going to stay here in school, aren't we?"

"No," Barbara said, "you're going with me. You're going to live in Washington. It's going to be a great experience for us, together."

"Are you kidding?" her son asked. "I can't leave school now. I'll make the basketball and tennis teams this year. And I've got my friends. Look, Mom, we could stay with Dad. Right, Dad? If we stay with him, you don't have to be bothered with us in Washington."

"Great idea, for once," Melly spoke up. "I've got the teachers I want next year."

Her brother piped in, "And the boyfriends."

"I do not," Melly said. "Besides, I want to be near the doctor." She felt sure she would score with her mother on that point.

"No, I'm sorry, but you're going with me. I couldn't get along without you. No way."

"You've got your boyfriend . . . you won't have time for us anyway," Melly answered. The heat was rising.

Barbara turned around. "I always have time for you."

"Look, Mom," Melly was suddenly incensed, "I'm not going to Washington. I'm not going to change schools. I've got some things going for me now here, finally—most of all, my friends. I'm not going to Washington."

"Melly, I don't want to hear any more from you like that. When I get back we'll talk and you can give me all your reasons. I'll always listen to you—and when you're old enough you can make all your own decisions. You will have the choice then whether you live with your father or with me, but until you reach that age, you're under my care and protection—and I'm going to do what I think is best for you both. Whether you hate me for the moment or not, at this time in your life, you need me and I need you. We will stay together."

They stood at the departure gate as the small plane for Munising was readied. There were only two other passengers. Barbara kissed her children and then put her arms around Ted and hugged him.

The wind was blowing slightly and her hair was loose and pushed back with the wind. She looked young and vulnerable. "I'll call you three every night. Everything is just the same as when we're all at home together. Same rules. Same program. Your father knows it all. And study for your tests Monday. You're building good records for college.

"And don't forget your dentist appointments tomorrow. Your father has the schedule." The children groaned. "I'm sorry I have to leave you, there's so much to talk about, but we'll do that when I get back."

The last call for the plane boarding came over the airport PA system. She stood with her back to the plane, facing the three of them. The children were standing on each side of their father and they seemed very much a family.

Barbara had to brace herself. She hated good-byes, even for short separations. She loved her children more than anyone else in her life. More and more she realized how they were growing away from her day by day. It was inevitable but many times she wished they would stay children and she would always have them. Had she made the right decisions? As she photographed them in her mind, her children standing there with her husband, her husband for fourteen years, all of her old doubts ricocheted through her mind.

Melly picked up her mother's feeling. She stepped away from her father and hugged her mother for a last good-bye.

"I love you, Mom," she said softly.

"And I love you, baby, always." She reached out for her son and pulled him close to her. "Both of you. Remember that. More than anyone else in the world. I love you."

The children and their father stood waving good-bye as she reached the small airplane ladder and went up into the cabin. The plane readied for takeoff.

11

Munising, Michigan

The small commuter plane hit the runway, bounced three times, and finally jarred to a stop.

An attendant walked languidly out from the airport shack and shoved the short ladder steps up to the passenger compartment.

Michael Garibaldi stood out on the lip of the tarmac waiting for her to appear.

He hadn't slept in the sixteen hours since his father had come backstage after the preview performance for his world concert tour. Michael had waited an hour for Christina's plane to arrive. He hadn't seen her for two years, and he had just heard from his father that she had become addicted to dope.

How was it possible? She had been the health fanatic in the family. Perfectly conditioned. No "poison" of any kind in her body. Working out every day, in addition to her regular ballet lessons and performances. She had studied nutrition in school and kept up with it. The most superbly conditioned athlete he had ever seen.

As he watched Christina come down the steps from the plane, a wave of guilt swept over him. They had been too close when they were growing up. She had been a very young girl when their mother had died. Their father had been working long hours and was seldom home. Her sister had done the best she could for Chris, but it had been Michael to whom she had turned. He had been her protector. When you were very young, eight years' difference was important. He had become, in a way, her father, her confessor, her confidant.

They had had wonderful times together. But when she began to grow into a woman, and a very beautiful one, Michael had backed off. They'd never really talked about it. They were jealous of each other and possessive, and when they embraced or held hands as brother and sister, there was something more. They both sensed it. He was the leader. He had to be the one to back away. That's when he had gotten involved with the Haitian girl in school. He saw less and less of Chris and she had turned completely to her world of ballet, until the accident.

He had his own problems now. God knows what was going to come out of this family reunion at the Bay House. He hadn't been there for five years. But as Chris came toward him, the old emotions swept over him. She had been the person he loved most in the world, the other part of him, the constant in his life, with adoration and support that were never questioned. He had missed her deeply all these years. He realized that even more, as Chris caught sight of him and came running. She was dressed in a white parachute silk traveling suit. She was still the most beautiful woman he had ever seen.

She was in his arms, clinging to him.

"Michael, oh Michael!" She was on a high. Michael recognized it immediately. Her eyes were over-bright, her breath quick and excited.

"Michael." She ran her hand through his dark hair and put two fingers on her mouth with a kiss and then placed her fingers on his mouth. It was an old kind of pledge with them—"blood brother and sister."

He returned her kiss with his fingers. Gently.

"I've missed you, Chris."

She stepped back and looked at him.

"You've gotten even better looking, brother." She said "brother" a very special way. It was the voice of a sister and yet it was an expression of more.

He put his arm around her and started for the airport shack to pick up her baggage.

"Are Dad and Barbara here already?"

Michael nodded. "Do you know what this is about?" Michael asked. "No."

"Dad came to my show. The first time he ever saw me perform, Chris. I really shouldn't have left New York this weekend but he told me some things and he insisted we all had to be here. What really got me to do it is when he told me about you—that you were coming, that you were in trouble."

"What the hell is he talking about?" Christina snapped back. "I'm fine. I just came in second in the finals at St. Moritz."

"You're not supposed to ski anymore. You know that," Michael said. "It was one of the most important rules the doctors laid down after the accident to your leg. Remember what he said if you hurt it again?"

Christina tossed her head irritably. "I never listen to rules—and you didn't either—that was something we shared."

Michael took her by the arms and looked closely into her face. "You can't kid around with me," he said. "You're on a high right now. How long have you been on it?"

"I'm not on a high," she said. "I don't use anything anymore. I'm just in perfect health." She began to tremble slightly. "And I don't need any inquisitions from you." Her voice was louder, "Or from anyone else."

"You are talking from the top of the mountain. You think—I know the feeling, Chris; I've been there and we always have the same question—'What do we do when we come down?' 'How long can we keep it going?' More and more of the stuff until you crack up. I'm telling you: There are no happy endings. Coke and crack and free-basing and all the rest of it will destroy you. Half my band was involved in it with me. My drummer died. He OD'd. That's when I swore off. I won't allow any drugs in the band anymore. One joint and they're out. It's death, Chris."

The trembling of her body had increased. She lit a cigarette. Michael closed his two hands around her cupped hands, which were shaking too violently to control her lighter. He studied her until the cigarette was lit. Then he kept his arm around her, forcing the shaking out of her body.

"It's not going to kill me. It's not even going to slow me up. It just makes everything easier and better. When you're scared, like I am now, it makes you less scared."

"Illusion," he said. "That's all it is. Realistic until it wears off. You can trust me, Chris, I'm not judging you. Who am I to judge anybody? I'm just trying to survive in the war out there—and find something that makes sense. But I can tell you one truth. You matter to me, Chris. You are important in my life. I won't stand by and watch you destroy yourself. That's the main reason I've come home—to see you."

"I don't think I can make it anymore without getting high." Her voice was a whisper.

"I've got a doctor coming up tomorrow," Michael said. "The same guy who helped me get off drugs. He's gentle and he's smart."

Chris drew away. "I won't see any doctors," suddenly flaring again and regretting that she had admitted the truth. "I don't need a shrink. If I want to stop doing drugs, I'll stop. It's not that big a deal. All I have to do is make up my mind and I'll do it."

"That's what I thought until I almost killed myself free-basing. Chris, if anything happens to you, part of me goes, too. Maybe the best part." He picked up her bags and took them to the station wagon. It was old and weathered, a relic from the past of the Bay House. He got in the seat beside her. She moved close to him. Suddenly, she seemed very young. Her assurance had disappeared.

"I haven't been back in three years," she said.

"I know," Michael said, as he stared at the road.

"I've had a lot of fun," Christina told him defiantly.

"The fun wears out. I've been through it, Chris."

Christina's eyes lowered and she nodded her head.

"Okay, well, that's where I am now, Michael. I have nothing. Look at you, and Barbara, and Dad—everyone in this family is important—doing something important—except me."

"You're the most talented of all of us. You just had a bad break, that's all, but it doesn't mean you can't do something else."

"There's nothing else I'm good at except dancing," Christina grimly shook her head. "I'm scared, Michael. I'm scared to see Barbara and Dad. I was scared to see you."

Michael put his right hand on her knee and pulled her closer to him.

"You're going to get your confidence back. We all failed you, all three of us—we've all been too busy to listen. Remember the pact we made after Mother died—you were nine and I was seventeen—in the boat house, where you danced six hours a day?"

She looked up at him. "I remember, Michael. We promised each other to be best friends forever.

"Blood brother and sister—the old tradition of the Bay Indians—and we cut our fingers and mixed our blood. It was already mixed but I'd wanted to do that because I'd heard about it from some of the old Indian medicine men around the bay and I'd seen it in the movies."

"You're never going to feel alone again," Michael said. "If I could kick drugs, you can. You always were stronger than me, really."

The car turned a corner toward the bay. An old rambling house loomed up at the end of the road.

It was seventy years old, and it was built on a soft curve that followed the edge of the bay. A long pier ran from the house down to the water and there was a large boat house with a slanted roof and gabled doors and windows.

"Everything looks the same," Michael said.

"Just the way it did when Mother died," Christina answered. "Oh, Michael, if she were only here waiting for us. Like the old days. She could put this family back together again."

12

Mt. Angela

*T*he old cowboy stood tall at the top of the hill. Eric Garibaldi could see him waiting. Franco Carboni. How long since he had seen him?

The checks went out every month for the care of the Bay House and he knew that Frank would have everything ready when any of them came home.

Franco touched his hat on the brim. Eric saw the same old easy smile. The same glint in the eyes. It hit him hard.

Eric's wife had hired Franco right after the Centurion was launched. Franco had grown up in the lumbermill town of the bay. He was one of many people who had revered Eric's wife.

It was Franco who had named this highest of the foothills surrounding the bay. Mt. Angela he called it, and he had put up a modest sign on the little plateau at the top. Through the early years, this hilltop was where Eric and his family had come for their picnics, their horseback rides, their family get-togethers, their celebrations.

Eric saw the sign as he eased off the Arabian horse he kept at the Bay House. It was at the crest, freshly painted every year by Franco Carboni. MT. ANGELA.

The old cowboy returned Eric's double embrace. He was as tall as Eric with the slim grace of a man born to live and work in the outdoor world.

There was a fire going in the rock barbecue. Eric saw that Franco had dug a hole in the ground for his own dutch oven. There were going to be Franco's specialties tonight, starting with the dutch oven biscuits and the ribs on the spit.

The past came flooding over Eric. He looked around as though he expected to see Angela appear. It was then that he saw the surrounding hills, half exposed in the mist that was rising up as the sun went down. Everywhere, all around them, there were the same ravaged hillsides. Not a tree was standing of the tall pines of the Munising Mountains.

The old cowboy followed Garibaldi's gaze. Franco shook his head and knelt down on his heels to check the dutch oven. "The trees are gone," he said. "All of them. Pressure's been worse since you last came back to the Bay House to get more and more lumber out of here in the last few years. We tried to warn them but it didn't do any good. The prices were up and the profits were big and there were more forests to the north. They didn't replant."

"Nothing?" Garibaldi asked.

Franco shook his head.

"Nobody did anything?" Garibaldi continued to question.

"Sure," Franco said as he checked the biscuits. "They cleared out. Most of them. You won't believe it when you go into town, because half of it's just standing there like a ghost place. Only a few families stayed."

Garibaldi looked at him for a moment. "You stayed."

"I told Angela I'd take care of you and your children as long as you came back here—though lately, I began to think I'd never see any of you again. I thought you'd left too, like the people in town." The old cowboy stood up and stretched. The two men looked at each other and Eric stooped down and picked up a handful of the soil on top of the hill.

"Everything changed when my wife died. I wanted to come back to see you and ride Cherokee over there and go fishing in the bay, but there were too many memories. I think it's the same for the kids. We're all going to be together this weekend, though, for the first time in a long while." He let the handful of earth slip through his fingers. "She was the earth, Franco. Nurturing all of us. I didn't realize that when she was alive as much as I should have—I never really told her." The old cowboy followed his gaze out across the hills. His voice was hardly audible.

"She knew. Are you going to be here long?"

"Just a few days," Eric answered. "We've got problems. I wanted to come back here to try to work them out. I guess I needed to feel Angela with me. I need her."

Franco looked at him gently. "You'll find her here. She's never gone away. I know. I talk to her once in a while myself. Watch the coals, will you? They should be ready in another hour. Think your kids will be here by then?"

"They should be," Eric answered. "We were supposed to meet up here by sundown."

The old cowboy put some potatoes on the grill inside the dutch oven, just over the biscuits.

Eric smiled. "Smells great. Just the way it used to . . ." His voice died away. He looked up at Franco. "Is your family still together? All of them?"

"My wife and I are still in the same house two miles down by the bay. Right next to us on both sides our kids have places with their families. We built them together. There wasn't any money after the mill closed, but we'd saved the trees around us, and there was a place for the kids. There's just enough work for all of us. We like it this way."

Eric studied him. "You mean you've got three families living next to each other—all your own blood?"

"My two children," Franco said. "One son-in-law, one daughter-in-law, five grandchildren. Everybody's on their own but we can get together real easy when we want to. It helps me figure out some things, seeing my grandchildren grow up. Talking to my kids like friends. Living away from the city has been right for me. I need to feel the earth under my feet. I need the horses. I need to smell the grass, taste the wind now and then."

Eric took the saddle off his horse and began to rub him down. "Ever feel you've missed anything? Ever get an urge to go around the world to see every place you've heard of or read about?"

Franco shook his head. "I always loved the bay since I came here as a boy. There were twenty of us from Milano. Your father was with us. When we saw the bay and these mountains filled with those tall pines, we never wanted to leave."

"Did you ever hear of *Peer Gynt*, Franco?" Eric asked. Franco shook his head. "It's a play—a Norwegian classic. It's about a man who leaves his home to go all over the world to search for himself, and never finds what he was looking for until he comes back home. You remind me of him, only you saved yourself all those years of traveling and trouble."

13

The Reunion

The moon overhead was almost full. The fire in the charcoal pit had turned to embers. The horses were grazing on the other end of Mt. Angela, and Franco Carboni had packed up and started down the hill to the house on the edge of the bay an hour ago. The family was finishing off the last of the coffee.

They had laughed and reminisced and told favorite stories of the past.

Christina's eyes were burning with cocaine. She talked in bursts, her voice high and intense. Michael sat beside her.

Angela was gone. And her beloved circle of hills were stripped bare. They looked eerie in the moon-shadowed darkness. A patch of scarred hillside appeared here and there momentarily.

"I had to wait till Franco left," Eric said. "I'll give it to you as straight as I can. There are millions of people who voted for you, Barbara, but there are some who don't want to see you go to Washington."

"I'm aware of that," Barbara smiled.

"I'm sure you are," Eric answered. "But there are serious developments you're *not* aware of. A group of people who don't want you to take office have had our family under intensive investigation by private detectives for more than six months. I just found out about it. That's why I called all of you. Each one of us has secrets we've never shared with each other, but we have to now. They are going to be revealed to the press worldwide if Barbara doesn't resign her Senate seat—immediately."

Barbara sat stunned.

"That's why we're all together," Eric continued. "It took the threat to each one of us to bring us back here, and I'm not proud of that. But that's the way it is. So, I want you to hear my story before you read about it.

"You all know about my first car, the Centurion. Only you, Barb, were around then."

"I remember," Barbara replied. "I still think it's the most beautiful car I've ever seen."

Garibaldi looked at all three of them. "What you don't know is I took a million dollars from the company I worked for to build that car. I stole it."

14

American Airlines Flight 740, New York to Los Angeles

"Nine days of shooting and we're already in trouble. According to the schedule you're four and a half days over now. And Gregson and his boy, Clune, are on top of us. Can you make up the time, Steve? Because if you can't, Gregson will close us down as soon as his lawyers tell him he's in the clear."

Danny Chiaverini, the accountant and budget expert on the film, was sitting across the aisle from Magdalena and Steve. The key members of Steve's team were grouped together in the front of the plane.

"I had to get these locations to give the picture reality. When we're shooting on the stage and control all of the factors, we can make up time."

"I hope so," Chiaverini said. "I've been getting calls from Gregson, and Spartan, too, because you changed the schedule around. This trip was supposed to come later."

"I never would have gotten it later, Danny. If I didn't shoot any locations and did the whole film with plates and process on a stage, it would lose the reality. As it is, I have to shoot some of the end of the picture with plates."

"You've got me covered, haven't you, Boris?" He turned to Boris Peters in the seat behind him.

"From every angle. We can re-create every location, even Mt. Angela, if we have any retakes there. No one will know the difference now that you've established the real places. I agree with you, Steve. It's the only way to do the movie. And it's coming together. I had real doubts about the Monterey boy and Stephanie, but not after the scene at the bay airport. There's something interesting going on there. Something pulls them together. And breaks them apart."

Steve's tense face relaxed. "They've both got great defenses and those defenses are working for us."

"Where do you figure the cost to complete, Danny?" he turned to Chiaverini.

"About four to five hundred thousand over budget, if you don't go off the schedule again."

Steve looked at him, surprised.

"How long do you think it will take Gregson to come up with that 'cost to complete' figure?" he asked.

"A week at most," Chiaverini answered. "We're slowing up the billings as much as we can. But Gregson must realize you're almost five days behind."

Gaylin spoke up. "Maybe Gregson will ease up when he sees what we shot. Everybody's going to relate to those scenes, one way or another. Remember Harry's assistant on props—his daughter, Mary Anne? She was with us twice."

"Of course I remember her," Steve smiled. "A hard worker—intelligent—sensitive—I'd hoped my girls would turn out like Mary Anne."

"Not anymore, you wouldn't," Gaylin answered. His chiseled marine face slid into sadness. "She's on coke. Her family's tried everything. Those scenes with Stephanie at the Palladium—she played them like she was really addicted. I could see Mary Anne in her. And when she shot herself up in the john—I've seen Mary Anne do that at a Christmas party. I can't get it out of my head. She's just the way Stephanie is, playing Christina. There are so many Christinas out there these days."

"Christina is based on a real person, Gaylin," Steve said. "She's taken from real life."

"She sure is," Gaylin said.

Roberto Bakker joined in. "I didn't agree with this location trip, Steve, because I knew we'd go over budget. But I understand your decision now. We really do know these people, in our story—their problems are problems we all know of in one way or another. Gregson's got to see what this film could be."

"No," Lieu spoke up, "he won't. He has an absolutely closed mind on *The Rest of Our Lives*. It's a vendetta. Not just against Steve, but against any kind of story like this. He's made a success out of catering to the lowest common denominator. He kills off our film, he kills off many of his own fears.

"I'm excited about what we shot on these locations—the performances are there—and the story. And the story relates to all of us.

"I have two young boys—Cambodian boys—from a different culture. Since I got them out of the war zone they're growing up and looking for things in America to believe in. A film like this could get to them because it's showing things like they are for us and for our children, instead of illusions and fantasy.

"The better *The Rest of Our Lives* looks, the harder Gregson is going to try to close it down. If we get the picture, he loses, not just with Steve, but in his own career."

Lieu turned to Boris, Roberto, and David Thayer. "Is every department within its budget from this point on?"

"My department's going to be over a hundred thousand dollars at least," Boris said. "I'm building the interior of the Bay House to an exact replica on the stage. I can't cut it anymore. Unless we eliminate the pier and the boat house."

"No," Steve said, "that's out of the question. The boat house is part of the heart of this film—the scene between Rayme and Stephanie there is absolutely key."

Boris nodded his head. "I agree with you and I've got everything arranged so you can start with the boom shot. With the plates I have of the lake and the shore and the way the night lighting will work— even with the moon—it will have an extraordinary look. But if I cut the cost, I can't do it."

"I'm going to talk to Spartan as soon as we get in," Steve said. "We've got to come up with another five hundred thousand. Spartan will understand after he's seen the rushes."

"He's seen them," Lieu said. "I talked to him last night. He thinks they are suspenseful, well done, beautifully directed—but he's also furious at you for going over the extra days on location. He's going to meet us at the airport and he wants to have dinner with you."

"He wouldn't even wait until tomorrow?" Steve asked.

Lieu shook her head. "No. He said it was something personal between the two of you and that he had to get to the bottom of it. I've never heard him so upset."

Steve sighed and the fatigue came back into the lines of his cheekbones and the set of his jaw. A small crescent scar on the left side of his forehead turned red when he was tired. It was livid now.

The others were waiting for him to figure some way out of the dilemma. Steve glanced at the faces encircling him. Magdalena smiled at him encouragingly. "You'll find a way," she said.

"I've got one idea that may sell Gregson in spite of himself, particularly if we do it with an audience and his own executives there," Steve picked up enthusiasm.

He started back to where Rayme was sitting with Montango.

"Rayme, I want you to do me a favor," he said.

15

Trader Vic's Restaurant, Beverly Hills

"*H*ow the hell could you do this?" Spartan asked. "We're partners, and you didn't even check it out with me. I'm fighting every day to keep Gregson off your back, and the very first weeks of shooting you go over budget, just like he predicted you would."

"I had to do it, Spartan. It wasn't a rash decision, believe me. I thought about it and I thought about it and there was no other way. This isn't a glossy story. It begins quietly. You know that. And the only chance to grab you, to make this family believable, from the start, was to put them in real locations, almost in dramatic documentary form," Steve said.

"You're shooting a theatrical feature film, not a goddamned documentary," Spartan shot back.

"These are strange times, Spartan—slickness and glitz are in. Content is out. But when someone has the guts to take his best shot on what he feels, the way Oliver Stone did with *Platoon*, if you touch the truth, there's a hunger for it in audiences everywhere. There's an audience for films they can relate to, just as much as there's one for black comedy, and farce, and super action heroes.

"That's the kind of movie we have to make, Spartan. We have nothing else to fall back on. We don't have Stallone or Eastwood or Eddie Murphy or Redford or Dustin Hoffman. We have what we have, and we have to pull it off."

"You had everything planned out, didn't you?" Spartan asked. "It was tricky, Steve. We've talked about this before—you insist on going for perfection when it isn't necessary. Now you've made us sitting ducks for Gregson."

"I knew if I told you what I was doing, you'd react exactly like this. And you're right. But right doesn't always get the best film. I couldn't wait until the end of the picture to go on location. You know damn well that Gregson would have said we were over budget and that would have been the end of it."

"At least we would have had a completed film."

"We'll get the extra money."

"I'm worried, Steve. *The Rest of Our Lives* has become an obsession with you, and you are an obsession with Gregson. A man like Gregson needs something to destroy every day of the month—and he's got you penciled in for most of those days this year."

Steve nodded. They were in the Cabin Room of the new Trader Vic's. It was one of the few places in Los Angeles that stayed open after midnight.

Oswaldo had given them a corner table where they could talk. Steve took a sip of his drink and another shot at Spartan.

"Let me ask you a question, Spartan, now that you've seen most of the rushes. What do you really think of what we shot on location?"

"No question about it," Spartan answered, "it looks real. It grabs you. And the people—they are all interesting and involving. I began to forget they were superstars. Some of it is documentary real.

"I relate to Garibaldi. I want to know what he's going to do for the rest of his life. I'm getting toward his age and I'm facing those questions myself.

"I want to see how this family makes it. I guess you could say I'm hooked."

"That's the point," Steve said. "I'm living twenty-four hours a day with everything I have riding on this picture. The locations jarred my actors out of their Hollywood environments right into the place I need them to be. I wanted to get the tensions going. I've got things to work with that I never would have with process shooting on a stage. I had to go for it, Spartan."

"But why didn't you tell me? I'm your partner. We don't keep secrets from each other. We're like a good marriage, you and I. Have I ever stood up against you?"

Steve shook his head. "Never."

"Well, I won't now either," Spartan said. "And I hate to put another voice in your head, but I've got to have this straight right now between us. I can't work with you under these kinds of circumstances. I'll back you up, Steve, every inch of the way, but I don't want any more tricks. Nothing like that. It's lying by omission. I have to know exactly where I am with you and this movie on a daily basis. If you get an idea that affects this picture or the cost, I've got to know about it at the time."

Steve looked at him, chagrined. "I apologize, Spartan. You're right. I know this is a problem for me."

"I'm either your partner or I'm not," Spartan said.

"I don't know what I'd do without you," Steve replied. "I remember how it was before."

"Good," Spartan said as the waiter came up with more drinks.

"Now, the way I read it, Steve, we've got about three or four weeks to make up almost half a million dollars in cost or raise half a million to keep the cost to the studio at the six-million-dollar maximum. Gregson has got to let the film run for a few weeks and then see where his 'cost to complete' is. I think I can keep the whole thing alive that long, if you don't go over budget in any way again.

"Meanwhile, I've got to run down every possibility for the extra half million. The problem is that everyone will ask why the studio won't increase the budget if the rushes coming in are any good. That's the strange situation.

"And I can't go around trying to sell the whole production for six million dollars until the picture is finished. If I tried to do that in the midst of everything else, well, there are just too many legalistics. The film would never get finished. Gregson would love that. He'd write it off and you off, too.

"I wish you'd reconsider my offer, Steve. I'm willing to put in the extra half million if I have your word that you won't go another hundred dollars over budget without checking with me. I know I'll get my investment back."

"I can't do it, Spartan. I won't risk bringing you down in any way. I appreciate it, but I won't do it."

"Well, then," Spartan said, "I'll start down the list tomorrow. Everyone who has ever approached us about investing in one of your movies.

"It's not the way I like to work, Steve. You've got too many things to think about. But this time we're caught. Just remember what we talked about before the film began. Within these money restrictions, you're as free as Ingmar Bergman making his films with Swedish government financing, and no questions asked. Nothing is for nothing, right?"

"I had one idea on the plane," Steve said. "See what you think of this. We take over the Dome theater on Sunset Boulevard for one night. We get Gregson and his executives there with a live audience from Westwood. Then we have Rayme—and he's already agreed—and, well, this is the idea . . ."

16

The Dome Theater, Hollywood

*T*he huge curved projection screen inside the Dome theater on Sunset Boulevard carried the images of Rayme Monterey in concert, multiplied in size one hundred times. His eyes, the sharp angle of his jaw, his prominent nose, the sweat glistening on his forehead.

Steve and his editors had cut the film daringly. Even at this first stage, four days after it had been shot, the footage was exciting.

Steve sat with Spartan behind Jack Gregson and his studio staff. The rest of the audience at the Dome was mostly young people. They were rocking with the music, clapping their hands, some of them singing the words. The theater was buzzing.

Suddenly, at the peak of the song, the close-up of Rayme went dead. The screen went black with the music still continuing in the background and these words flashed on the projection screen:

"This is an assembly cut of one sequence from Rayme Monterey's first film, a new motion picture now in production, The Rest of Our Lives. We will appreciate your filling out a card with your comments and your reactions to this scene, which we have shown as a special preview tonight. Thank you. The Management.

It was eleven-thirty when everyone collected at Spago's. The owner and chef, Wolfgang Puck, and his wife, Barbara, had prepared one of their best pasta combinations. Steve, Spartan, and Jake Powers sat around the table with Gregson, Jerry Clune, and three others of Gregson's entourage.

Spartan finished stacking the preview cards in separate piles. He looked at the group with his intense dark eyes. "There are, gentlemen, three hundred forty cards. Two hundred and ninety-five raves. Forty fairs. Five negatives. For a four-minute rough cut."

Spartan looked at the notations on his yellow pad. "Two hundred and forty-five of the three hundred forty, gentlemen, are in the fifteen to twenty-two-year-old age group. You've just plugged in to the generation you're always trying to find. You're right in the heart of the buying baby-boom market. And Rayme Monterey is going to be the new movie idol of that big young audience."

"Four minutes is not two hours," Gregson snapped. "You've been in production sixteen days and you're already over budget. I've asked Jerry here to be on top of the accounts. Your cost to complete doesn't look good. What are the figures, Jerry?"

Clune was icy. "Close to five hundred thousand over."

Steve fired back, "Look what you've got now. You told me that Rayme Monterey was a bad risk. That he'd never done a picture before. That his fans wouldn't come to the theater. You've just seen standing room only to look at the *first* piece of film on Rayme.

"The manager told me and Jake Powers that without this special preview with Rayme being advertised, the Dome wouldn't have been half filled tonight. This is just a forerunner, Jack. Rayme Monterey's your insurance policy on this picture. He'd be money in the bank even if the picture cost ten million."

"It's not going to cost ten million, or nine, or eight, or seven. Not one dollar over six," Gregson answered. "And if you don't come up with a solution for this five hundred thousand additional cost to complete, by the time you're halfway through the production, I'm going to close you down. I want to see what cuts you're going to make in the schedule and you'd better not pull any more surprises on us, Wayland, like extra days on any location."

Gregson's shadow, Jerry Clune, cut in. "That opening location trip to Michigan and New York cost the production four days and most of the five hundred thousand."

"Have you looked at my rough cut on those sequences?" Steve asked. "They give size and quality to the film."

"The picture's a sure shot at six-five, Jack," Jake Powers, Steve's publicity man, said.

Gregson shook his head. "No six million-five. Six. Not one dollar more."

"You're wrong, Gregson," Spartan spoke up. *"The Rest of Our*

Lives—and remember what I'm telling you—is going to be one of the big films next year and you'll have it for an investment of only six million plus an additional five hundred thousand we need now to finish off the schedule the way it should be done. Match *The Rest of Our Lives* with your regular studio operation and you couldn't do it for twenty million."

"If you believe in this project so much, Spartan, why don't you put *your* money in it?" Gregson asked.

Spartan looked back at Gregson quietly. "I have. Five hundred thousand for preproduction. Match me, Gregson. My five hundred for yours. We'll all make money."

Gregson stood up and knocked over the pile of cards in the center of the table. "I don't give a fuck about these cards. Anybody can shoot a rock concert and get four good minutes out of it. *You* worry about the money to finish this film, Wayland. It's your baby. And as far as I'm concerned, your baby's going to be retarded.

"I'm telling you now, don't bother to put through any requests to up the budget." He pointed to Spartan. "Don't you put any more pressure on me. I'll close the studio to you. And if you and Wayland don't cut half a million out of the cost to complete in the next few weeks, I'm going to foreclose on the whole picture."

"You agree to sell us the picture for six million dollars—right?" Steve said. "I want it in writing, like you promised."

"Pick up the agreement at my office tomorrow, Wayland," Gregson laughed as he went out. "And where in the hell are you going to raise six million dollars?"

17

Together

agdalena was waiting for him at his home. It was Saturday night and there were thirty hours before they had to begin another week of shooting.

Steve had told her to catch up on her sleep, that he would see her on Sunday. But she had stayed up for him.

There were two places set in the dining room and a fresh bottle of wine, iced. She had made chicken sandwiches the way he liked them, with Worcestershire sauce, and his favorite dessert, crème caramel.

When Steve had left for the Dome hours before, she had gone to bed to try to conserve her energy. She'd lain awake, thinking about what Steve was doing. She hadn't believed this plan would work, but she had said nothing. Having seen too many Gregsons in her life, she recognized in him the mania to destroy.

So Magdalena was not surprised at the defeated look on Steve's face when he came in the front door. She had never seen him look so tired. Underneath his tan, his face had gone white. When he saw her he tried to pull himself together. The tight, cornered look on his face relaxed. They clung to each other in the hallway.

Nothing had to be said. Four hours before Steve had left her with soaring hopes that the preview footage of Rayme would change Gregson's mind.

"We'll find another way," she said. She drew back from his arms and looked at him. "Do you want to talk about it?"

He shook his head. "I'm too tired," he said. "Thank God for you, Maggie."

"We won't talk about it then." She took him by the hand and led him into the dining room. She lit the candles.

"I don't feel like eating," he said.

"When the world is black and everything is going wrong, a good gypsy family will say to each other, 'Well, nobody's dead.' Now, you have to keep your energy up . . ."

She brought from the kitchen as she was talking the chicken sandwiches and then the crème caramel. She opened the wine and poured for both of them. She sat down across from Steve and raised her glass.

"To our finishing the film." They clinked glasses and drank. He took her hand across the table and touched his lips to it. She held on to him tightly.

In the background, Barbra Streisand was singing "People" from her "One Voice" concert.

"Do you know gypsies really do have an intuitive gift?" Magdalena said. "I think it's something I inherited from my mother. That's why I've been on the set so much, even when I'm not shooting—I've been watching you and the others."

Steve gave her a questioning look. "I've liked that, but I know you're still tired from all that flying we did."

"I feel wonderful tonight," she said. "I took a nap while you were gone."

Steve shook his head. "It's amazing—we just got blown out of the water by Gregson and I've never seen you look happier or more beautiful. How do you do it?"

"It's simple," Magdalena said. "Tomorrow I have a whole day with you and your children after my fitting."

"Remember, I've got to go in for that dubbing session tomorrow night," Steve said.

"But I can go, too," she said. "You promised me and you promised the girls."

A vague smile came over Steve's exhausted face.

Magdalena went on, "Darling, I've made thirty-two films. With every kind of actor and every kind of director. My intuitions have almost always been right. And what I've felt on your set—I can tell you from the bottom of my heart, Steve, this film is going to work. It's going to work in a big way. I know it.

"I can't say I know exactly how we're going to finish it, but I know, beyond a shadow of a doubt, it's going to be as special as you dreamed. Take this and believe it from my gypsy blood."

18

Western Costume

"No, it can't be a designer dress. I know Barbara Garibaldi," Magdalena said. "She comes from big money but since her divorce she's out on her own. She's put her money into her career. She's running her home on a budget and supporting her children. It's very important to her that she be financially independent from her ex-husband and her father. That means supporting herself and her children on what she earns. And her job, until she goes to Washington, stays the same as it has been for four years. She's a teacher at Michigan State."

Magdalena looked at her dress designer on the film, Bill Thomas, and the fitter and the seamstress at Western Costume. They were in the large, mirrored reception room with the dressing rooms up a level and behind the basic fitting area.

A long rack of clothes was in the center of the room. On it hung a group of selections to choose from.

"How do you feel about this scene?" Bill asked.

Magdalena looked at him thoughtfully. "It's with her father, you know. She's always idolized him. She tried, in a way, to be wife and mother to the family when her own mother died; she's never felt quite good enough. She's a competitor who inherited her drive and her will from her father. She has to look her best in this scene, but still within her budget. I want her style to be soft and feminine like her mother was, but with a definite flair—*her* flair." She nodded at the rack. "Could she afford these dresses?"

Bill gestured at them. "I got these on approval from Robinson's and Saks and Bullock's. Medium price range. Your colors. Barbara Garibaldi could afford to buy any of these. Pick what you want, Magdalena, and then we'll do the alterations here."

She fingered through the dresses on the rack, almost taking a turquoise silk one, but then rejecting it as too attention getting. That was the Magdalena she was getting away from in *The Rest of Our Lives*.

When you were on a budget—she remembered from her early Paris days—the cost of cleaning was important when you thought about clothes. You didn't pick white or light colors.

She took a midnight blue dress, a simple sheath with long sleeves. It looked plain on the hanger. Bill Thomas smiled. He glanced at the fitter and the seamstress.

"Her eye is so good," he said. Magdalena held the dress up against herself and looked in the full-length mirror.

"What do you think, Bill?" she asked.

"I was sure you would pick that one. It won't really say anything until we fit it. And it will be simple. But with your hair and complexion and your figure, it'll be ultrafeminine. Slip it on, darling."

"All right." Magdalena took the dress and went into one of the dressing rooms behind the large, mirrored wall surrounding the fitting area. She turned back toward the designer for a moment. "Bill, do you think Steve will like it?"

Bill Thomas stepped up to the platform that was used for the individual fittings. He brought his voice down so that the fitter and seamstress couldn't hear him.

"Ever since I've known you," Bill said, "I've waited to see you look this way. In the space of one second, when you thought about Steve and asked that question, you had a look—you have it now—that tells me everything. He's in love with you, too, Magdalena."

"Has he talked to you?" she asked.

"He doesn't have to. I've done six pictures with the man. There've been women around him, but I've never seen him like this—the way he is with you. We've all been noticing that. Steve is very easy to read."

Magdalena leaned over and kissed Bill on the cheek. "Thank you for telling me. It's a new experience for me, and I'm not very secure with it."

"You should be," Bill said. "Just go with it. Trust him, Magdalena."

She pulled the dress around her once more. "You don't think I'll

be overdressed?" she asked. "I really don't want to look like a movie
star, Bill, I want to look like Barbara Garibaldi."

"I understand," Bill said. "You know how much I'd like to be
working the way we always have—creating an entire wardrobe for the
picture, one ensemble after another—but that's not the way this film
is. This time the 'ensemble' is the picture.

"And I'm not fighting it. It's a challenge for me to work like this.
Now, go slip on the dress so we can pin you."

Magdalena stepped inside the dressing room. Bill went back toward
the reception area of the room, where the fitter and seamstress were
waiting.

Many great stars of motion picture history had been fitted here. The
floors of Western Costume could outfit a corps of Bengal lancers, a
house of geisha girls, a marine parachute company, a Scottish brigade,
or a line of Radio City Music Hall Rockettes. For more than sixty
years, they had costumed drama, fantasy, history, and adventure from
all over the world.

In this main mirrored fitting room to the left of the entrance, the
finest tailors and seamstresses analyzed their clients. Following the
requests of the designers, they added inches and subtracted pounds.
They made a bust line where there was none. They made a graceful
curve to the hip where the hip was flat. Or they flattened the hip
where it was too curvaceous. They added length to legs and took away
excess weight from calves and thighs.

Bill lit a cigarette as he spoke to his old friends.

"It's the first time I've been this involved in a film in years," he
said. "It's like old times."

The head fitter spoke up. "From the first time you brought her in
here, I thought she was different from most stars. She's paid her dues.
. . . She's certainly much thinner now. We've got to watch that when
we fit the dress." Bill nodded.

The dressing-room doors opened and Magdalena came out in the
midnight blue sheath. She wore no jewelry except a double strand of
pearls around her neck. She had pinned her hair on top of her head,
the way Barbara Garibaldi had done when she was finishing getting
ready to go to the capitol for the nomination press conference. Her
makeup was clear and simple, no eye makeup at all. There was an
increased vulnerability about her.

She turned in front of the mirror, taking in the look as Bill and his
fitter and seamstress checked the dress from every angle. "It's loose
around the chest and the waist," Magdalena said.

"Around the hips, too," Bill said. The seamstress followed his gestures and quickly pinned the dress.

"Thank the Lord," Magdalena said, jokingly.

"You'd have an argument from me on that," Bill replied. "Don't lose any more weight, Magdalena." He looked at the dress again as Magdalena stood for the fitter. The seamstress, following the fitter, tightened the dress slightly in the places Bill and the fitter had indicated.

With the dress pinned, Magdalena turned slowly, checking the side and back views.

"I hope Steve—" she started to say, but then, suddenly, she faltered. She tried to cover it, but she had to sit down. She felt a weakness in her muscles and a rush of fever came over her. "Could I have some water," she said. Her voice was shaky.

"I'll get it," the fitter said.

Bill bent down to her. "What's the matter, darling?"

She shook her head. "Nothing. I just felt a little faint for a moment." She forced a smile. "You know, the location trip was very rough. It's always tense getting started and this was harder than usual."

The fitter came in with a glass of water and Magdalena drank it down. She wiped the beads of perspiration off her face and eyes. "Bill," she said, "would you mind if we took a little time out here? I'd like to rest a moment. I don't know what came over me," she said.

"You have to be careful, sweetheart. You don't want to wear yourself out. Are you still shooting this scene the first of the week?"

She nodded. She got up slowly and put the glass back on the table. "I'm going to lie down in the dressing room for a few minutes."

"Take your time. We'll wait out here for you. The dress is going to be fine. If you feel like it we can go through some of the rest of the clothes."

Magdalena went through the door and closed it behind her. There was a full-length mirror in the dressing room, two chairs, and a chaise longue. She stretched out on the chaise. "God," she whispered, "you can't let it happen now. Please."

From the outer room, Bill looked after her worriedly. He turned to the others. "She was looking so well."

"She's just overworking," the fitter said. "I've seen it happen so many times. And you know how she is. Once she gets into something, she gives everything she has."

"She's got a hard schedule on this picture, that's for sure," Bill said. "There's no time for days off and rest. And," Bill shook his head, "we're already behind. It's going to be a horse race to finish this film on schedule as it is—not to mention within budget."

"Are you saying Mr. Wayland might not get to finish this picture?" the seamstress asked him.

"That's what I'm saying," Bill answered.

19

The Dubbing Session

ichard Portman, master rerecording artist, Academy winner, and a wild man, sat behind the computerized recording panels. He had built the system himself for Gordon Sawyer's sound department at the old Goldwyn Studios, now belonging to Warner's. Regarded as an inventive genius by Steve and many other filmmakers, Portman, who came to work and toured the town on a racing motorcycle, dressed in a leather suit and helmet, had put his experience and imagination into the construction of these panels. There were forty-two different sound channels. Each channel carried synchronized reels of picture, sound effects, musical effects, electronic effects—every possible sound requested by the director.

Portman handed out minutely detailed yellow sheets to his sound effects editor, Ted Bariken, and to his music editor, Don Roberts. John Hammell, the music editor, explained some of the music channels to Don.

"Rayme," Steve called to the seats right behind the huge instrument panels on the raised platform, "move in beside Don over there. I want to get exactly the feeling you put in the music for this scene. You don't mind, do you, Don?"

"It'll only help," Don said. "Remember, I haven't heard any of these tracks before. This isn't a final dub, right, Steve?"

"No," Steve answered. "It's just to get a trial up there for the mood I want around the Bay House. Rayme and Stephanie have to play a very difficult scene there later in the schedule. And we're going to have to do it with plates. We can't go back to the location. We want to tell a great deal of the story with the sound effects and the music. We want it subtle, Richard. Just the way you like it."

He sat down beside Portman. "Touches of the sounds Frank Warner recorded on the edge of the bay."

Magdalena came in with Kathleen and Lorelei. They were carrying sacks from McDonald's—Big Macs and Cokes, milk shakes and French fries.

Richard Portman embraced the girls. "Hi, kids," he said. "You're growing up too fast. Makes me feel old." He looked from one to the other. They had a special rapport with Richard because his hair was long, his manner rebellious and filled with humor—they knew how talented he was from what their father had told them.

"Could we sit up here with you and Dad? We wouldn't bother anybody. Behind you, I mean," Kathleen said.

"We've never gotten to see this before," added Lorelei.

Portman touched them each under the chin.

"As long as you're very quiet. Some of these sound effects your father wants you can hardly hear."

"We'll be quiet," Lorelei said as she sat down behind him and next to her father. She put her hand through Steve's arm.

Steve smiled, then turned to Kathleen, who'd sat down on his other side. "This location trip seemed like months without you two."

"There're no more locations on this picture—I mean, away from home—are there, Dad?" Kathleen asked.

Steve raised his right hand in a Boy Scout salute. "No more, I promise."

Magdalena and Stephanie laughed from the back of the room where they were sitting together. Steve turned and went back to them. Portman was instructing the projectionist, Walter, to play the reels, one by one, until they were all synced up and ready to roll together.

He flipped the communications switch, which connected him directly to the projectionist.

"Walter, I want to see and hear what we've got. Then we'll predub some of the channels together, so we won't be working with so many different ones. We'll bring it down to seven or eight channels." He turned back to Steve. "How's that sound, boss?"

Steve said, "I want to be sure I hear every one before we put them together."

"Right. Let's get set up, boys," Richard said to Ted and Don.

"Rayme," Steve called to Rayme, who came back to join Steve, Stephanie, and Magdalena, "I wanted to have this little dubbing session to give me time to think about the scene that's coming up for you in the boat house in a few weeks. It's the subtlest scene in the picture."

"It's such a beautiful scene," Magdalena said. "I can't wait to see you two do it."

"I hope I can give you what you want," Rayme said. "I felt I touched it a few times at the airport when I was meeting her. I felt very drawn to you," he said to Stephanie.

"Really?" Stephanie asked. "I felt you were moving away from me."

"But that's what I would do in real life—that's what I have done, I guess, since the night we met."

"That *is* what you've done," Stephanie answered. "There've been so many times I've wanted to talk to you, wanted to go over our lines together, or discuss a scene, or just hang out. But I thought you didn't want to. So I left you alone."

"This is exactly the relationship in the film," Steve said. "I've seen you two feeling your way with each other since that night at the Roxy— defensive as hell—and that's the key to Christina and Michael. Growing up, they were the closest of friends. But then they got worried about their feelings for each other and they backed away. I really *found* this interpretation of the characters from watching you both at the Roxy that night.

"The obvious attraction and then how you walked away from it.

"That's the delicate line and that's one reason we're doing this dubbing. That's why I asked you both to be here tonight. I want you to watch this continuation of what we shot when you first came to the Bay House on location. This is the first time you've both been back to where you lived when you were so close, and before you grew apart.

"I've heard your music for this scene, Rayme, and I like it. It's different from anything you've done before.

"All right, Richard," Steve said. "Let's start with the picture and the first three sound effects reels."

The screening room darkened after everyone had finished his hamburger. Kathleen and Lorelei had passed around the bags of French fries twice. Now they were settled, and Steve went to his place right in back of Richard Portman. The girls were holding on to him excitedly.

The leader, the empty film with no images, went through the projection machine. The film that was being projected on the screen showed six big dots leading up to the actual start of the footage. The same dots clicked through reels three, four, and five of the sound effects.

When the picture started, all the reels were exactly even, to the hundredth of a second percentage point. This synchronization was monitored by the computers. There was a row of computer dials in front of Portman. He controlled sixty monitoring signals. Ted controlled another thirty-five and Don an equal number.

The sequence started with Michael and Christina Garibaldi pulling up in the station wagon to the old gabled house on the bay front. As they got out of the car and Michael took his sister's bags, you could hear the distant seagulls on the lake. They moved in and out on sound channel three, weaving through the soft wind on sound channel four, and the rustle of falling leaves on channel five. Portman, never taking his eyes from the screen, motioned with his right hand for Ted to bring the tracks down.

On the screen, the scene moved ahead in a medium long shot. Christina and Michael were framed against the background of the old boat house and the late afternoon sun over the bay behind them. Christina glanced back at the boat house. "Let's go down there after dinner, Michael. It was always my favorite place here, maybe because it was Mother's. I so loved the way she fixed it for us."

Michael glanced at her. "I remember watching you practice there— it was like a special play with a special star just for me. You would have been the best. You know that, don't you?"

"No, I don't know that," Christina answered. "I know I had a chance. And I would have really worked for it—always—as hard as I could."

They went up the steps of the wide porch that surrounded the gabled house on the bay. It was of another time and another place.

The wind was a little stronger now as Steve handed a written note to Richard that he'd like to hear it dialed up. Richard motioned to Ted, who edged up the very sensitive dial that brought in a stronger wind.

Steve handed Richard another note to dial up the seagulls in the distance. As the camera moved in close on Christina, Ted turned up the gulls, and the wind was strong, coming off the bay.

The camera was moving in, in an unbroken shot, to a large close-up of Stephanie. In exact perspective, Ted dialed up channels three, four, and five, the seagulls in the distance, the wind in the near trees, the leaves falling softly in the evening breeze.

The sight of the old Bay House and the sounds so long forgotten were deep within Christina. The tears came naturally to her eyes, but she checked them. She could not let herself remember too much.

The camera drifted slowly around to her right profile, and only two feet away, Michael's face filled the screen behind her, but not facing her. Nothing had to be said between them. They were people who loved each other, but they were separated in this shot, as Christina and Michael were in real life.

"It's so strange," Michael said to Christina, "to come home again."

Christina didn't look at him. "We were happy here, weren't we, Michael? All of us."

The film ran out. "Now, let's hear the rest of the effects," Steve said to Richard. "Crickets. I want a suggestion of crickets. But *very* quiet. Okay, Ted? And I want to hear the faraway sound of a train— a haunted sound. Let's run up the reels one at a time. Did you get a predub on that, Richard?"

"Got it on ice. Run it anytime you want."

"That's unusual footage, Steve. I don't get it yet. I want to see more."

"Just keep feeling that way," Steve smiled.

Magdalena was already talking to Stephanie. "This is the first time I've seen you on the screen," Magdalena said. "You're lovely. And you moved me. I really feel for this girl." She pointed back at the screen, now empty.

She called across to Rayme. "Rayme—you're so wonderfully quiet up there. I haven't seen that quality since Montgomery Clift. You're not doing anything, but you're doing everything. The relationship works."

She turned to Steve. "It works."

"Can we stay until you finish?" Kathleen asked.

"School's tomorrow," Steve said.

"Please, just this once," Lorelei pleaded. Her eyes were shining. She glanced at Rayme. "We haven't even heard the music yet."

20

Magdalena's Home, Bel Air

*M*agdalena glanced at the luminous face of the clock on the bedside table. It was past four in the morning and she had to be in the studio at seven. She hadn't slept.

This was going to be a difficult day. She dreaded and, at the same time, looked forward to it. She was approaching today from inside the thoughts and feelings of Barbara Garibaldi. Magdalena had become another woman.

She turned to look at Steve, asleep, but in torment. He was grinding his teeth while he dreamed. His eyelids flickered. His face was drenched with sweat. It was like this every night now.

They lived in fear that Gregson would shut down the picture. Every night, Steve and Spartan were somewhere, meeting with someone in the financial world, trying to raise the $500,000 they needed for the film.

Every day, Gregson or his number-one man, Jerry Clune, was on the set. Every night, there was a meeting with Danny Chiaverini, the picture's accountant, and Clune. Every financial commitment was checked. Every bill, day by day. And they were nearing the halfway point. Any time after that, Spartan felt, Gregson might close down the picture. They had to find the $500,000.

She looked up at the ceiling of the room. In a few hours she would be facing Robert Montango in one of the key scenes of the film. He was a completely different man in *The Rest of Our Lives* than she had known before. He had always been flamboyantly dramatic. And this was the character the public had seen in so many pictures.

He and Steve, working together, had maintained his power, perhaps increased it in a subtle way, Magdalena thought. She had seen, step by step, Steve winning over Montango to a different kind of character interpretation. Steve wanted the "inner" man. Now there was a new quietness in Montango's scenes. His emotions were in his eyes.

Eric Garibaldi had many of Robert Montango's qualities as a man, but he was complicated in a different way. He was an American "giant" facing the possible destruction of everything he had built and everyone he loved.

Steve wanted Eric to reveal these shadows and fears, and probe deep into himself.

Montango had become edgy and irritable. Magdalena had watched Steve use this in his scenes. It was working for the film, she thought. But not for Robert Montango.

He had been pulled out of his familiar characterizations, repeating things that had been successful for him for so many years. He didn't like feeling tentative and insecure. He was fighting Steve every inch of the way, and he was very distant toward Steve; they rarely spoke offstage. The company noticed it; they were waiting for an explosion. It was up to her, Magdalena thought, to play this scene as Barbara Garibaldi would live it with her father.

She would stay near Robert Montango, as much as he would allow it, between takes. That was one of her commitments for this day. Keep Robert Montango talking. Keep him center stage.

She thought about dinner the night before, after they'd left the editing room. The owner of El Cielo, Pasquale Vericella, who had become their friend, kept his personal table by the patio fountain for Steve and Magdalena. This was one of the few places they stopped sometimes on the way home from the studio after working late. No one bothered them there. They'd sit and discuss the day's work, the problems, the hopes and fears, soothed by the running water of the lion's head fountain and the flickering candles on each table.

The warm and colorful maître d', Georgio Rutovich, prepared special dishes that weren't on the menu, a succession of Italian salads and pastas, and some native dishes from his homeland, Montenegro.

Last night the chef had prepared for them his special ziti with marinara sauce. They hadn't eaten lunch and they were starved. They had two dishes each and a good wine.

They kept nothing from each other now. Most of last night they had talked about Robert Montango and the work of the day ahead. Steve knew what he needed from Montango in this scene. Eric Garibaldi had to show guilt. A sense of loss. Pervading loneliness. These were not standard elements in a Montango characterization.

At the very end of the dinner, just before they left, Steve had said something that was in Magdalena's mind now—what he had learned out of his own experience as an actor. "You just have to love your actors through it," he said.

Magdalena turned toward Steve again. He was even more restless in his sleep. Careful, so as not to wake him, she put her right arm around his head and eased him over onto her breast as though he were her child.

She had never felt the kind of maternal feeling that was coming into her love for this man. She could be angry at him, irritated with him, frustrated by him, but when he was in pain, when he was as exhausted as he looked now, even in his sleep, when he looked vulnerable, all her unfulfilled maternal instincts came out.

She had never had a child of her own. But now, this tense, on-edge man twisting in his sleep belonged to her. She put her right hand against the right side of his face and pushed back his hair gently. She had come to know a circle of love around her man that she had never experienced before. Once again, it came to her mind that she was facing, quite possibly, the end of her life. Perhaps this love was a gift to her now, at the very end. She clung to him.

He awakened. He held her close and didn't move. It was as though he wanted to go back to sleep, entwined in her arms, and not wake up for a long, long time.

She soothed him back to sleep. Magdalena felt his need—a deep need he openly spoke about often. Thank God he was a man who could admit his feelings. They were, in a way, she thought, truly the opposite sides of a oneness. They were both strong. They both had fought all their lives. They were both independent.

She had to do the scene tomorrow for him and get through it with Robert Montango. She thought of what Steve had told her when she was preparing for her very first scene in the film. He had spoken about what a star really had for the audience: the power to involve the audience with their feelings and their problems.

"You have that power, Maggie. You've always had it. Audiences care about you. They sense your vulnerability. Use that power for Barbara Garibaldi."

21

The Bay House,
Munising

"You should never have run for the Senate anyway. What makes you think you can solve other people's problems when you can't even handle your own?" Eric Garibaldi lashed out at his daughter.

"You're in the minority. I've got the majority on my side this time," Barbara fired back.

"I don't give a damn about the majority. I've been around a little longer than you have. I've seen a lot of women mess up whole families with their ambitions."

"You're not going to give me that old 'a woman's place is in the home' cliché—that's not your style, Dad—you've been wrong plenty of times, but you've got an original style. Where is it with me?"

"I'll tell you where it is with you." Eric leveled on her. "Neither one of your kids is happy. They miss you at home and they miss their father. They aren't a family anymore because of you."

"Look who's talking about a family!" Barbara said defiantly. "When I was growing up you were hardly ever around. We were lucky to have dinner with you once a week. We read about you in the papers."

"I took care of you, didn't I?" Eric blared. "You never had to worry about a thing. You knew where you were and you could count on things."

"Sure, Dad. I could count on being lonely after Mother was gone. I could count on no communication with you. I could count on being talked to when you felt like it, but never being able to talk back to you. You never learned how to listen. If you could have listened you would have known more about Mother. She never had a chance to try anything out there in the world. You've got to wake up, Dad. Things have changed—whether you like it or not."

"You're forty years old," Eric said, "and you're sleeping with a man who's ten years younger than you are."

"And you sleep with a woman who is twenty-five years younger than you are," Barbara faced him. "Dad, what's the difference? The only thing that matters is that people care about each other and support each other."

"Why wasn't your husband good enough?" Eric asked. "He's from one of the best families in Michigan—intelligent—money—position— hell of a good-looking guy. What do you want?"

Barbara's voice was quiet. "You gave me my image of a man. When I did see you, when Mother talked about you, when I read about you in the papers, well, you were my parade—big and strong and courageous with the crowds cheering.

"I remember two years when I hardly ever saw you. Always waiting with Mother for you to come home. Remember on Sundays Mother would take me to your warehouse and we brought lunch for you and your crew? I didn't know anything about cars but I felt the excitement. A new car was being built. The Centurion. You put it all together. That's the kind of man you are, with all your faults. And when that kind of man is your father, I guess you expect that from the man you marry.

"Ted's a fine man but the life we were leading was too damn easy. There was no juice in it, no fire."

"After your mother died I depended on you to hold our family together," Eric said.

"Mother died, Dad," Barbara replied, "and you put me into her place. I tried, but I had your guts and your drive. It's like when you went against all of them and left the company to build your own car. I was a little girl then, but I remember. I've lived around your guts and your pride—maybe I was meant to be a boy instead of a girl. Your son. Sometimes I think you waved your hand over Mother's belly and just *made* me *your* daughter.

"I want to be proud, too. I worked hard campaigning for the Senate. I can do a better job than Henry Calvin. I'm going to Washington to do the best I can to make my life count. Like yours. The seed of you is in me."

"You think your ambitions are worth the destruction of this family, of everything I built?"

"Now we're at the center of things," Barbara said in an angry voice.

"You always end up with the word 'I.' Can't you get off center stage
for once in your life? You're seventy years old, Dad, and you're still
running your company, and you're still the best there is in your line,
but I'm not like Mother. I'm not going to back off what I want and
what I've worked for. She gave up being a teacher because of you.
She loved you but she paid a hell of a price. She lived in your shadow.
I'm like you. I wasn't born to live in anyone's shadow."

"They're going after you, too—Calvin and his bunch—they've got
a list on each one of us. Michael's abandoned black son, Christina's
addiction, your affair with a mafia boss. And, of course, the million
dollars I took to build the Centurion."

"I'll take them on if you will," Barbara challenged. "I don't think
they can get away with this kind of blackmail. We've never backed
down from anything. That's one of the good things you've bred into
us from the beginning. I'm not going to resign my election, running
away from blackmail." She faced off with him. "And I don't believe
that you are really going to ask me to do that, are you?"

22

Goldwyn Studios,
Stage Six,
Warner Hollywood

"Let's get ready to do it again," Steve said.

"Reload," the camera operator added.

Robert Montango walked up to Steve quizzically. "What part are we going for again?" he asked.

"The whole scene," Steve said.

"Something wrong with the camera?" Montango asked.

"No," Steve said. "I'd like to try it a little differently. Robert, let's take a walk for a minute." Steve led the way to the side of the stage where no one else could hear them.

"Come on, amigo," Montango said. "What's eating you?"

"What we talked about before," Steve said. "You're too rich in there, Robert."

"You didn't like the scene?" Robert asked incredulously, his insecurity showing.

"I wrote this part for you," Steve said. "Not just you, the actor, but you, my friend. The person underneath all that success and experience. I want it to be the best you can do—and there's nothing better than that. But I'm not getting it in this scene, Robert."

"The hell you're not. Why did everyone come up to me as we broke and tell me what wonderful work I did?"

"I don't care what anyone else thinks, Robert—I know you and I know this scene. Eric Garibaldi has to slowly come apart here—we have to see there's much more than meets the surface with this man—we have to wonder if he truly loves his daughter or is he just worried about his own reputation. I want all those feelings in his eyes. And I want it subtle. Everything that unfolds about his character later is dependent on this. You're making the transitions too fast, too big.

"Remember how you look up there on the screen. When you become your theatrical self, you're so much bigger than life that many people believe that's great acting. The problem is, for me, in this story, it's too much. Played like this, we're watching an actor act; we're not watching a human being be."

"Are you saying you didn't believe me? I was playing my heart out."

"You were close," Steve said, "but not there."

"In your opinion," Montango said sarcastically.

"In my opinion," Steve said. "And on this stage, Robert, it's my opinion that counts in the end. You know that."

"Well, I don't agree with you," Montango fought back. "I think I know a hell of a lot more about acting than you do."

"I'm sure you do," Steve answered. "But not about my film, you don't. Every actor in the world needs someone looking on with a third eye. I've heard you say that yourself."

"And you think you're the third eye here?"

"For better or worse, Robert, I am. I want it the way I want it. And we're going to keep reshooting it until you give me what I want."

"Maybe I can't play it that way, maybe I don't want to."

"The eyes, Robert, my God, how many times I've seen you do it—transformed me in a theater with your eyes, with one look, with no eyebrows up in the middle of your head, and no violent gestures. You don't need a thing but that direct line from your heart and your mind to your eyes—that's motion pictures—and you know it—you've done it—and all I'm asking you is to do it once more, your best, Robert. I want the very best of you, no matter how mad you get at me. That's what I want and that's what I'm going to get."

Lieu delivered Steve's letter to Montango's home that night. He was finishing dinner on the patio of his penthouse, looking out over the ocean.

"You know what's in this letter?" Montango asked her.

Lieu nodded. "I typed it. He was going to write it longhand, but he was afraid you couldn't read his writing—none of us can."

Montango took the letter as though it were a dangerous explosive. "What's it say? Another lecture from the boy genius?"

Lieu said softly, "Do you want my opinion?"

"Yeah, yeah, I want your opinion. I don't want to open this if I'm going to get any more upset than I already am."

"How can you be upset when you did such a brilliant scene today? Everybody who was there is talking about it."

"I did it just as well the first time. So, what's the letter say?"

Lieu said, "It says, in Steve's way, how much he admires your talent and how much he loves you."

Montango looked at her, his eyebrows knitted together fiercely, and then gradually the tension went out of his face. "You like that son of a bitch, don't you?"

"I care for him in my way as much as you do, and for the same reasons. He's not perfect, we both know his faults, and he's got plenty of them. But this is a man who tries—and who cares."

Montango looked up at her. "Do you love him?"

"As my friend," Lieu answered, "yes. I'm not interested in any other kind of love at this point in my life."

Montango snapped back, "I don't believe that a woman who looks like you, with your body and your legs, and all that other mysterious Oriental stuff—"

Lieu looked at him steadily. "Aren't you going to read the letter, Robert?"

Montango opened the letter but did not unfold it. He looked at it and handed it to her. "You read it," he said. "I don't have my glasses." She took the letter.

Dear Robert,

I have two choices in directing you.

One is simply to let you go. No matter what you do on the screen, you're more interesting and alive than most other actors. You can work without direction, as you tell me you often do. It's easy to be afraid of you. A director can buy the big voice, the furrowed brow, those great looks you have. The man who is never afraid, a man who gets any woman he wants, who can win any battle, surpass any challenges.

But Robert, I know you. I know your humanity. I know your doubts and your fears. That's why only you can play this part and why I wrote it for you.

The second choice I have is to help you select the colors, nuances, the distillation of all the years of your living and acting—to always try for the best of Robert Montango. That's the choice I continue to make. Through you, I feel Eric Garibaldi's fears and pain. And I want to see his restraint and his reserve, the image of his character.

I won't let you settle for what's comfortable and easy for you. Our job together is to get you out into another place—and the key is simplicity. That is what we really argued about today.

You had the courage to go back and do it again. And you found the heart of Eric Garibaldi.

Lieu looked up from the letter and then handed it to Montango. Montango's eyes were filled with tears. "Jesus," he said. "Sounds like a fucking obituary." He took the letter, carefully folded it, and put it in his pocket, took it out again and gave it to her. "Lieu," he said, "I want you to have this letter put up in my dressing room in my trailer, in my wardrobe closet. Every time I prepare for a scene in this picture, I want to reread this letter—goddamn it, Lieu, that's the problem with that son of a bitch. He knows. He knows."

23

Mager-Golden-Lasky

A copy of the full production board was laid out in Jack Gregson's office.

Jerry Clune pointed out the course of the production of *The Rest of Our Lives*.

"Here's what's been done." He pointed to a series of slender strips of paper, each numbered and carrying the identifying details of various scenes shot during the day that the strip of paper represented.

"Approximately a third of the schedule has been covered," Jerry pointed out as he indicated a group of strips on the right side of the board, separated from the great mass of strips still divided into days and weeks left to be worked, on the left side of the board.

"What's the cost to complete, according to today's run?" Gregson asked.

Clune handed him a report from his attaché case. "This is straight from the computer. Accuracy tests out to be ninety-four point six on the eight productions it's handled for us so far.

"The cost to complete for *The Rest of Our Lives*, as of two o'clock this afternoon, is six million, four hundred and eighty-two thousand dollars."

"Is there any way Wayland can possibly make up the overage?" Gregson asked.

Clune shook his head. "Not unless he cuts down the shooting schedule that's left. It's a nine-week shoot, as is. The projection shows he can't finish under ten. He lost almost a week on the first location. And you know Wayland. He's not going to make changes because of the cost factor—God forbid."

"He will this time," Gregson said, "with everything he's got on the line. But I want him in a position where he can't finish the picture without going over budget, no matter what he does."

"He's almost there now," Clune said. "And if there were any interruption of the schedule, any change, anybody suddenly missing . . ."

Gregson cut in. "You mean like Monterey getting hit with another grand jury hearing?"

"Well, then, of course, it's all over," Clune answered.

"Jerry, have you got the report from our tax department? How much of the six million can we write off this year?"

"It's right here, Mr. Gregson," Clune answered. He handed him another sheet from a folder in his attaché case. "Seventy-six point eight percent can be written off."

"How much is he wasting by shooting on the old Goldwyn stage instead of using one of ours?" Gregson asked.

"Those figures are about the same."

"Not good for us, though, having a film shooting on another studio's stage."

"It's in his contract," Clune said.

"Wayland likes to think he was Goldwyn's protégé," Gregson said sarcastically. "The old man was already off his rock by the time they met. I'd like to see what he'd think of Wayland on this one . . . Okay, Jerry," Gregson said, "just remember, I want to close down Wayland absolutely, before he can finish the film."

"Right, Mr. Gregson."

As Clune left, Gregson stepped over to the production board. It was a complicated jigsaw puzzle: the names of all the cast on the left, the multicolored numbers across the days and weeks of production signifying every actor who would work on that day and in that week, the numbers of all the production departments that were responsible for different elements of shooting on each day. Gregson shook his head as he looked at the days already finished, only a third of all the mass of material yet to be shot, represented by the strips on the left.

He smiled and spoke softly to himself. "Not a chance, Wayland. Not a chance!"

24

Christina's Addiction

*C*hristina was soaked in sweat, shivering in the bed. She moaned in a half-comatose state, "Please—need—need—some—oh, my God—"

Barbara reached out for her sister. Christina drew away. "We're going to take care of you," Barbara said.

Christina's words drowned her out. "You left me. You all left me." Her voice was suddenly hysterical. Barbara ran down the hall to the doctor's room. He had arrived after dinner. She brought him back quickly. He was in his bathrobe, trying to shake off his sleep. He checked Christina's vital signs. Then he took a hypodermic from his bag.

"What are you giving her?" Barbara asked.

"She has to be sedated," the doctor answered. "If we take all the drugs away from her too fast, her body won't stand it. She could go into shock."

He was quiet and sensitive. Barbara had liked him from the moment Michael introduced him to the family. He was a staff member of the Menninger clinic.

"How long ago do you think this started? Can you tell?" Barbara asked the doctor as he stepped away from Christina.

"A full-blown cocaine addiction can happen pretty fast," he said. "But with a habit this size, and judging from the weakness of her vital signs and the deterioration of some of her organs, I'd guess this has been going on for at least a year."

"How could we not know about it?" Barbara asked incredulously.

"You would have if you'd been around her," the doctor said. "Cocaine addiction at this stage isn't very subtle. But I gather you all haven't seen each other much recently." He glanced at his watch. "It's almost morning. You were supposed to wake me hours ago."

"I wanted to stay with her," Barbara said. "She's almost like my own child. Our mother died when Christina was eleven and she lived with me for several years. We were close . . . then!

"Can you get her to stop?" Barbara asked.

"I'll be able to detoxify her from the drugs while I'm here," he said, "but addiction has a psychological side to it, too. For her to stay clean, we'll need to find out why she's trying to kill herself. And she'll need to be willing to get help."

It was still dark as Barbara went down the stairs and into the big country kitchen that had been a pride and joy of her mother's.

One end of the kitchen formed a large circular breakfast room so that there could be a continual flow of conversation from the kitchen. Some of the quotations that her mother had loved were still on the walls, along with framed snapshots of birthdays and Christmases. In that same breakfast room, Barbara had fixed Christina's hair, brushed it, and arranged it every day for school and Sundays for church. What possible connection was there between that lovely dark-haired, round-eyed little girl and the desperately sick woman upstairs?

She put on a pot of coffee, then turned as she heard footsteps behind her. It was Michael. Brother and sister looked at each other.

"I couldn't sleep," Michael said.

"Me either," Barbara answered. "I keep hoping it's all a bad dream, that everybody'll wake up from it in the morning and everything will be all right. Coffee?"

"Thanks. How's Chris?" Michael asked.

"The doctor's injecting her with some kind of sedative—she was hysterical most of the night, out of her mind, really—delirious." Barbara shook her head. "Unbelievable—so sick—so desperate—" A shudder ran through her body. "I should have taken her back home with me when she had to stop dancing. I should have understood what it meant to her, a member of this family losing her drive and ambition, losing her chance to be special in her own right. I was too busy with my own problems."

"Problems, problems. We're all eaten up by our own problems. We're all on that same old train trying to get somewhere, only we never get off long enough to look around," Michael said.

"I don't think there's anything wrong with goals," Barbara answered.

"Not if other people don't get hurt along the way. But that's another problem—they do get hurt.

"Look at Stephanie up there. Living in hell. I know, I've been there. She has a terrible need. When I left here as a kid I had a terrible need." His anger flashed out. "Don't you understand, Barbara, that's what Dad did to us. Christina needed to be special, like everyone else in the family. Christina could have been special, just like you are, but she got a bad break. I'm not a psychologist, but I've read enough on my own, and I've felt enough on my own to know that once that is ingrained in you—that you are supposed to be special, that you *have* to be special—you can't really shake it. And if you don't make it, you hate yourself. That's the way we were brought up.

"Neither Chris nor I made it, but you're the one who turned out special—the way you were supposed to be.

"But have you really? Don't you see how much like Dad you are? When I drove out of the Lansing airport, out the freeway and headed for the lake and saw all of your campaign signs—I liked them—they said something to me—and I liked the fact that you didn't have your name or your picture on them—they are good goals, Barbara, for all of us.

"But then I thought of the last time I saw your two kids. It's been a year and a half since I took them on that weekend fishing in the mountains. We talked all the time. They're carrying the same Garibaldi warp—straight from Dad to you to them. They *have* to be somebody—they *have* to make it. They *have* to accept Jim Reardon or anybody else you want them to accept—most of all they have to accept that their parents are separated and they'll never be one family again. They don't seem to me to be a very good reflection of what you have to say in your campaign.

"That's what struck me when I saw those signs. Is this campaign real? What're the motivations behind this driving ambition to be senator?" Michael asked. "What's really behind it, Barb? Center stage, your name in lights—you finally step out of Dad's shadow?" Michael looked at her directly. "I'm trying to decide, Barbara. I always was confused about you—are you a real person in your own right or are you just Dad born all over again in the form of a woman?"

"Where do you get off talking to me like that?" Barbara's anger flashed in her voice.

"Because I care about you," Michael answered.

"Oh yes, you care," Barbara answered. "I hear from you once or

twice a year on birthdays or at Christmastime—no telephone calls—
no communication. I could be dead and you wouldn't even know
about it until you came off some rock tour. . . . I'm proud of what
I've done."

"That's the trouble," Michael answered. "One of them. You are
too proud of what you have done instead of what you are supposedly
fighting for."

"I'm not Mother Teresa. I never said I was," Barbara snapped back.
"But what have you done?"

"Not much," Michael said. "I've thrown away plenty of years. I've
never even seen my own son. I didn't stand by the girl I loved. I've
been running—running away from the same thing that dominates your
life, and I think Stephanie's too. Dad's ambitions and work ethics are
ingrained into us—everything organized.

"God, I remember when we were kids. You were always so organized—your room, your work, your friends—everything. The perfect
daughter for Dad."

"But we're all responsible for what's brought us together now,"
Barbara said defensively.

"Christina's my fault, too," Michael said. "You know how close we
were after Mother died. She looked to me. We were bonded. I was
scared of it. We were so damned possessive of each other—the first
time she went out with a guy it was my best friend, somebody she
really didn't care about that much but she wanted to get to me because
I wasn't really there for her anymore."

"None of us were," Barbara said. "We haven't been there for her
or for each other, either—that's what I'm beginning to see. We've all
been too busy with our own lives to remember where we came from.
We lost what we had—we lost the meaning of our family. Remember
the talks we used to have? All of us, together, right at this table, about
everything under the sun?"

"That's when Mom was alive," Michael said.

Barbara's hand shook as she picked up her cup of coffee. "I don't
know how I'm going to get through this, Michael. One night with
Christina and I'm a nervous wreck—watching somebody you love
coming apart piece by piece. Disintegrating right in front of you—and
you can't do anything. We were brought up to fight. But you can't
fight someone else's battles."

"In a way, you can," Michael said. "When I got off drugs, I learned
a lot about addiction's being a family disease. . . . There'll be ways
we can help." He put his hand out to Barbara. "But you have your

own life to think about—you've done something that certainly no one in this family has ever done, against all odds, according to what I've read—and I don't think you should consider resigning your Senate seat to save the family reputation. Whatever that means."

Barbara glanced at him. "It means plenty. If they release the story about you and your little boy in Haiti, couldn't it really affect the band or the tour?"

"I don't know," Michael answered. "I guess they'll say I'm talking out of both sides of my mouth at once, that's for sure. Dad says they'll call me a racist and he's probably right. I'll be labeled a fraud. They have the contacts to do a job on me. They'll say I'm exploiting minorities, particularly blacks, and not putting it where my mouth is. I don't know.

"But don't resign because of me. I really mean that. Whatever else is happening we are making our beginning, all of us, in getting to know each other again—the only reason for you to resign is for yourself and your children, what is best for you and *your* family."

"They are threatening me, too," Barbara said.

"About your divorce?" Michael said. "For God's sake we've had presidents who've been divorced."

She shook her head. "Not the divorce. It's something you and Christina never knew about—before I was married. I was seventeen. For more than a year I had an affair with a famous lawyer. He was married. I knew that when I got into it but I was sexually obsessed with this man. I was warned that he was a famous front man for the mafia but I never saw that side of his life. Everything was exciting, romantic, and I never thought of where it would end. I just had to have this man and he had to have me."

"An affair here and there doesn't mean much in today's headlines," Michael said.

"This is something special—he's still very important in the underworld. There'll be questions and doubts. God knows what it will stir up on his side. It's not the best way for a new senator—a woman senator—to go off to Washington."

Michael shook his head. "I can't believe how little any of us really knew about each other. Even Dad. I thought this family used to talk once in a while, but we're four strangers now."

25

Hollywood Park Racetrack

"I've checked him out," Spartan said, as he turned the Bentley into the infield of Hollywood Park. "He's got the money to write a check today. But he wouldn't do a thing without meeting you face to face."

"At the racetrack?" Steve asked.

"The only place he'd meet," Spartan said. "He's semiretired now. When the tracks are open, he's there every day."

"I suppose he wants me to beg for it."

"I don't know," Spartan said. "But what I do know, Steve, is that Gregson is going to shut down the picture unless we can come up with five hundred thousand dollars by next week. I've covered every possible investor for you on both coasts. Orsini is the one shot we've got. I wouldn't bring you out here, Steve, if I weren't sure he could bail us out."

"What do we have to give him for it?" Steve asked.

"His people won't discuss it with me. That's why you had to come and talk to him directly."

"And just who is this Orsini? An Italian designer?"

"He's Italian," Spartan answered, "but he's not a designer. He owns a variety of businesses. He's known for quick decisions and fast action."

The valet attendant took their car, and they joined the stream of people walking toward the clubhouse entrance.

"Spartan Lee and Steve Wayland," Spartan said to the cashier, who thumbed quickly through a ready box, and drew out two guest cards. He pushed them through the barred window.

Spartan looked at the blue sky above. It was a clear day in Los

Angeles. Far to the east, the snowcapped mountains of the San Bernardino range were in sight.

"A perfect day," Spartan said.

"I'll decide later," Steve muttered.

He was watching the racetrack crowd standing in the clubhouse as they approached the headwaiter in the clubhouse dining room.

Steve looked at the people spread out at tables in front of the entrance and beyond it, eating and watching television sets, checking the constantly flashing betting boards which appeared every thirty seconds. There were racing forms and booklets of tips on every available surface. People watched with intensity, waiting to win money on the speed, effort, and training of the horses and their jockeys.

A few of the people in the clubhouse dining room really seemed to be watching the horses and the pageantry of the track. But mostly Steve was reminded of Las Vegas—that obsession with the bet, whatever it was. Most of these people weren't seeing the majestic animals for what they were, or measuring their past records and their generations-back heritage. It was the odds, the tips, the bets.

The headwaiter, in a sleazy tuxedo, inclined his head when he heard their names. "Mr. Orsini is waiting for you," he said.

He led them to a table in the corner with a good view of the track and two television sets, one aimed at each side of the table, which was set for eight people. Six places were already filled.

In the middle, at one side, a big man sat devouring a bowl of fish stew. A white bib was tied around his neck and extended down over his enormous chest and stomach. His face was unforgettable—a slab of granite with a fearsome smile painted on it. The mouth made the smile. The eyes shot bullets.

He was not young anymore. Pouches fell under his eyes into sacs hanging from sacs. His nose was long and broad, the cheekbones high, the chin prominent. His graying hair was thin on the top and his eyebrows were jet black, framing a stare that went right through you.

The mouth of the granite face went into action. "Hello, fellas." He looked at his watch as he nodded at Steve and Spartan. "You're right on time. I like that. We'll have time to talk before the next race."

He quickly introduced the other men by their first names. "Leo, Antonio, Walter, Happy, my partner, Stanley." One was his lawyer, another one his accountant; the others merely friends. They looked like an average group of businessmen, conservatively dressed, two with glasses, all with a subdued manner, and all catering to the mountainous man who made the introductions.

Nobody bothered to shake hands. It wasn't that kind of meeting. Orsini eased into another smile. The granite face slipped, and the thick lips pulled back to reveal a sparkling row of flashing white caps. Orsini's teeth looked like new spark plugs in an old car. Steve couldn't take his eyes off them.

Steve was already making his mental notes. This man was a character to remember. The eyes were ice, but smart ice. Street-smart ice. They were cunning, superior eyes that had lived with power a long time. Steve had seen the same eyes in certain studio executives.

A man came up to Orsini just as he was about to speak and whispered in his ear. Orsini whispered back. The man looked relieved and left.

Orsini chuckled. "That's a doctor friend of mine. He always comes to me for tips on horses. I don't know anything about the races, but he thinks I do." He nodded to a form by the side of his plate. "He saw me put my finger on a horse, and I give him the finger." He chuckled with what he thought was a joke. The laugh wasn't real, either—a stage piece.

Orsini took a mouthful of his bouillabaise; some of it slipped off onto his bib. He ate with his mouth partially open, which increased Steve's fascination. He ate like a crushing machine.

Orsini fixed his eyes on Steve.

"You're in trouble, huh?"

"My picture needs money to finish the way it should," Steve said.

"That's trouble, isn't it?" Orsini asked.

"Yes," Steve said.

"Five hundred thousand trouble. Is that the right number?" Orsini asked.

Steve nodded. "That's what the accountants tell me."

"When do you need the money?" Orsini asked, taking another mouthful of his bouillabaise.

"This week."

Orsini laughed. "Or they shut you down. That right, kid?"

Steve was taken aback at how he'd been addressed. He didn't feel like a kid. He felt older than this man—and tired. What the hell was he doing here with this gargantuan slob? Who was this guy anyway? Steve didn't like the smell of the food or the company.

He spoke quietly. "Mr. Orsini, I understand from Spartan you have a reputation for putting it straight. Here's the straight story. We've got a special picture. There's a personal conflict between the head of the studio, Jack Gregson, and myself. For his own reasons, he doesn't want the picture to be finished. If it isn't finished, I lose everything I've got. Even if the picture goes one dollar over budget."

The granite face went right on stuffing itself. "You know the main reason he's out to get you, kid?" Orsini said. "It's your woman. Magdalena Alba. He's been after her for years. He's never made it. Can't get into her pants."

"Watch your mouth," Steve snapped. Spartan swallowed.

"No offense," Mr. Granite smiled, his eyes deadly. "Look, I was complimenting the lady. She doesn't fuck around. That's the information I have."

Orsini continued. "I've got some old beefs against Mr. Gregson myself."

He nodded toward Walter, who was prepared. He handed over a checkbook and pen.

Orsini made out a check and laid it in the middle of the table, so everyone could see it after he signed it. Steve and Spartan glanced at it. It was a check for five hundred thousand dollars, made out to Steven Wayland.

Granite laughed, a frightening sound.

"The check is good, don't worry about that. But there's one promise from you that goes with it. If you agree to the only condition I have, you can pick up that check and go bail yourself out."

Steve looked up at him and waited. Orsini went on eating. Nothing interfered with his eating.

"I want an option on your next picture. I want to finance the whole thing independently. You can pick the distribution company.

"I have some companies on the big board. Some of them are perfect shells for your picture operation. We don't have to wait six months for Securities and Exchange clearance, we move right in on something that's already established and has partners. You'd be the general partner. We'd be the limited partners."

"Can we have approval of the partners?" Spartan asked.

Granite laughed, and nodded at the people around the table. "These fellas are partners. We supply twenty limited partners and let's say you furnish ten partners. They don't have to come up with a cent. We'll put up the money in their names."

He wiped his mouth with his bib. "You see, the banks are getting tougher all the time. You can't walk in with five hundred thousand dollars or five million or ten million and not put down on paper where you got it. You have to put down the mommies and daddies of the money. They don't accept bastard dollars anymore.

"I've got money coming in from different foreign sources. That money needs mommies and daddies so that we can use it and make the really good investments that we want to make. Like an investment in you folks. You furnish yourselves and eight other partners, solid business people, prestigious, and then we'll have good mommies and daddies for all the money we'll need. Get the picture?"

Spartan said, "I think so. You need 'mommies and daddies' with unquestionable records to join your twenty partners—some of *them* might be questionable—this way you can keep them in the background and move your foreign assets around more freely. Tell me, Mr. Orsini, if there's ever an investigation to find out whether the mommies and daddies of some of this money did, in fact, put up their own money, who has the answers? The general partner has to come up with those, right?"

Granite laughed again. "Well, you fellas are going to decide what to do with the money and how it's used and how it's put out. As general partners, you'd have complete control of the films we'll make. You can't get a deal like that anywhere in the business. Isn't that right, Mr. Lee?"

Spartan said, "Just about."

"Well, maybe if you're Spielberg, or Eddie Murphy," Orsini said. "We're giving you a legal setup, ready to go, with something fair all the way around. The only kind of deal I like to make.

"You get money to make your picture, and we get a company. We get mommies and daddies for our money and the money from our friends." He rubbed his hands together, drying off the grease from the bouillabaise. "We split the profits fifty-fifty. Beautiful, huh?"

Steve said, "What about this check? If they ask me, I'm going to have to say who the daddy was."

Granite laughed. "You're smart, kid. I like that. This is all in the books. Just tell 'em that the money is from Kenny Orsini. They can come to me if they want to, and we've got everything down just right.

"When I heard you were in trouble, I thought this out. We could give you something you needed and you could do the same for us. I've checked you out—you're an honest man. And so is your partner here, Mr. Lee. You're the kind of people we like to do business with. Honesty's very important to us."

Steve said quietly, "I can imagine." He stood up from the table. His eyes had turned cold. Icy, like Granite's.

Granite nodded at the check, still on the table. "Forgetting your check, kid?"

"I want twenty-four hours to decide," Steve said.

Granite picked up the check and put it in Steve's pocket. "You'll decide and you'll have the check to take to the bank. Don't disappoint me. We have a string of movies to make together."

Spartan stood up. Nobody shook hands.

"Wish you boys would stay for lunch," Granite said. "This bouillabaise is real good. And I'll let you have my tips for the races. I win most of the time." He laughed again.

Steve answered, "Thanks, but I've got to get back to work. We're in the editing room this afternoon."

Granite smiled again. "Sunday, too? People don't know how tough your business is."

Steve looked at Granite. "Tougher all the time."

26

San Diego Freeway

As teve gazed out the window as Spartan headed home. The landmarks of the freeway passed by, billboard after billboard, many of them proclaiming new pictures that were coming. Expensive pictures from various distribution companies. So much depended on luck and timing —two goddesses Steve had chased all his life.

Neither man spoke. Steve felt a depression sinking in, old self-doubts. He couldn't get the five hundred thousand he needed except through the mafia. It would be almost funny, if it weren't so sad. He took out Mr. Granite's check, tore it up, and watched the wind outside the car blow it away.

His mind flashed back to the giant sign on Broadway over the site of the old Astor Theatre. The biggest motion picture sign in the world, a block long. When he had made *Tomorrow* five years before, and it looked like it would be a big hit, Paramount had rented that sign for the New York run.

Steve remembered walking down to Broadway after he checked into his hotel and standing there in those Broadway night lights, looking up at that sign. It was a clean, stylized ad, one that he had worked on with the ad company, and there was his name. A Steven Wayland film. He had felt like a little boy who suddenly had a vision of his dream coming to life, a giant-sized dream that dwarfed the boy and his world.

He had finally arrived. He was somebody.

And then, *Tomorrow* had opened. Paramount had thought that it was going to win the Academy Award that year. The studio had put big money into the advertising. Steve had been stroked more than he ever had been in his whole career. The picture had a big premiere, and a party on the Waldorf roof afterwards. A week later, a premiere at the Village Theatre in Westwood in Los Angeles, and a premiere party in the International Ballroom of the Beverly Hilton.

But the planning had gone wrong. The picture was not the kind that all the critics were going to review well and back for an Oscar. It was a poetic allegory, in a category all its own. Either you loved it or you hated it. It was an allegory of individualism, of striving and searching.

In a time of black comedy, spaceships, action/adventure, and films made directly for the teenage market, *Tomorrow* found only part of an audience. The grosses were shaky. It was not the box-office hit Paramount had expected. The movie had finished with four Academy Award nominations, but didn't win one.

On the night before *Tomorrow* opened, Steve had looked incredulously at the huge sign stretching over an entire block. His name was one story high.

Weeks later, the night before he was to fly back to Los Angeles after a month's publicity tour, Steve had asked the taxi driver to stop; he had caught sight of the sign as his car passed the corner of the old Astor Theatre. There was something wrong with it.

There, in the twinkling lights of Broadway, a group of painters was working. The huge poster of *Tomorrow* was fading out, like a long dissolve on the screen. A new picture of Burt Reynolds was dissolving in. The huge gun in Reynolds's hand was the first thing you saw. And there, in the block-long sign, as Steve watched it, Burt Reynolds's gun was coming through on the new poster, obliterating the printing of "A Steve Wayland Film."

In one moment, the rejection hit Steve like a blast from Reynolds's gun. Your name, what you fought for, if it didn't make money—big money—was washed out overnight by new films standing ready in the wings. If you weren't earning the bucks, they wiped you out, literally and figuratively. It was a sight he would never forget.

Spartan turned off the freeway on Pico. He had to pick up some papers at Fox. The gateman at the studio knew both Spartan and Steve, and gave them a polite salute. They pulled around to the main administration building, and Spartan went in to pick up his package.

Twentieth Century-Fox. Another milestone in Steve's career. Fifteen years ago, he had walked to that same administration building, in the midst of the same sound stages, looking at the complicated numbering system of the preferred parking spaces. He had walked by the movie stars' dressing rooms. Paul Newman. Dustin Hoffman. Robert Redford. Barbra Streisand. Gregory Peck.

He was trying to make it as an actor and had just done a screen test with Gregory Peck for a motion picture to be made from a best-seller. It was an important film of high quality. Today was the day he was going to hear the results. Peck had treated him with kindness and respect, and Steve had been grateful.

Steve's agent, Mitchell Wertz, had spoken to Peck the day before. Peck had liked Steve's work in the test.

Steve and Mitchell had been ushered into a beautifully furnished office. At the end of the office, a well-groomed man in his sixties, who had once been a star of silent pictures, waved them into chairs.

Ben Wyman didn't shake hands, but nodded to Steve and Mitch. He gave his secretary some papers and turned his attention to his visitors. He looked at Steve. "You did a good test, Steve. You're a good actor."

Mitch took a drag on his pipe and leaned back in the armchair comfortably. "I told you, Ben." He gestured with the end of his pipe. "I've got a nose for it. This isn't some Johnny-come-lately off the beach. Steve's a pro, an educated man." He smiled again. "It takes one to know one."

Wyman looked at both of them. Mitch was smiling. This was the kind of time that he loved the most, to find a new talent, get the person tested, get the person under term contract. A steady flow of money coming in for the client and a steady flow of commission for the Wertz Agency. This could be a seven-year deal with options every year, and he probably could get it started at five hundred bucks.

Wyman looked directly at Steve. "Goddamn it, it's not easy to see."

"*What* isn't easy to see?" Mitch asked.

Wyman kept on looking at Steve. "The cock in his eye," he said.

Mitch stopped puffing on his pipe. "What are you talking about, 'cock in his eye?' Those eyes of his are going to be his fortune. Every girl in my office is in love with Steve's eyes. Bedroom eyes, that's the thing that's going to make him. I'll *bet* you. Every still I've seen—"

Ben interrupted, "I'm not talking about stills, I'm talking about motion pictures. His right eye is cocked."

Mitch jumped out of his chair and bent over Steve, peering into his right eye. "The hell you say. You trying to be funny, Ben? Look, this guy's worked hard. He might not understand your humor."

"I'm not trying to be funny," Wyman said. "Sometimes this happens. You find somebody that can really act and then there's something wrong with the face. Particularly the eyes. You've got to accept the truth. Steve can't be a leading man in films."

Mitch turned on Wyman.

"Cut it out, Ben."

Wyman replied, "No joke." He looked at Steve. "I'm telling you," he continued, "if Steve had a cock in his pants as big as the cock in his right eye, he'd be the biggest star in Hollywood."

Steve sat, frozen. His guts squeezed in a knot. Three months he had fought for that test, and when he'd finished it, the crew had applauded, and Gregory Peck had congratulated him. He was a sensitive new actor. Peck was going to recommend him at the studio. And he'd done so.

After that interview with Ben Wyman, Steve had gone into a depression, shut himself away.

What was he going to do with the rest of his life?

Now Steve felt that same kind of depression, as though everything in between meant nothing.

Spartan interrupted Steve's thoughts and memories.

"You want me to drop you at your place or Magdalena's?"

"My place, please," Steve answered. "Maggie's there with the children."

"They're getting along well?" Spartan asked.

"She's great with them. They idolize her," Steve said. "She spends real time with them. Not just buying them things or taking them out for an ice cream cone, but the tough things. Playing their games, watching their television programs, really talking to them and listening to them."

"She never had any children, did she?" Spartan asked. It was a question that didn't really need an answer.

Spartan looked at Steve as he pulled up to Steve's house. "I'm sorry about Orsini. I know how you feel. This is your moment of truth, as Robert Montango would say, isn't it? All your life has come together at one time. Your children, a woman you've been looking for forever, the house that you've built and put on the line, your dream film.

"Steve, let me sign for the five hundred thousand bucks. It's not going to break me. I want to do it. You're carrying too much, Steve. You're going to burn yourself out."

Steve shook his head.

"I can't, Spartan. I've signed the contract. I agreed to the budget. If it comes down to it, I'll just have to make some cuts in the picture. But I'm grateful. You're a real friend." He shook hands with Spartan and waved at him as he pulled away. Then, he turned around and started up the walk to his home.

It was almost twilight. The tall elm trees cast their long shadows across the lawn and against the front of the house. Steve loved those trees, they reminded him of Chicago and the countryside. When he turned up Mapleton Drive, off Sunset, the jungle fight seemed to fade out of existence. Mr. Granite was already a long way back. Everything was there inside his home at that moment, Magdalena and Kathleen and Lorelei and AGW, waiting for him.

Steve swallowed. Nothing could ever take away his family. And he knew they would be there at his side. Magdalena, too, even if he lost everything, even if he lost his house to Jack Gregson. This house wasn't his home. These people were his home.

No, he had been wrong, he thought. You can't put your roots in anything material. Because he was finding out, right now, it could be taken away. But people you love and who love you, those people in that house, his mother in Chicago, and his friend who had just driven away, nothing could change them. He fought off his depression and went into his house, calling out to his family.

27

Magdalena's Home,
Bel Air

*M*agdalena was waiting for Gregson in her library. It was a circular room she had decorated herself, in emerald and white. There was white English paneling, six-foot-high built-in bookcases, an emerald green carpet, and emerald green velvet drapes.

Two white Louis XIV couches upholstered in emerald silk faced the fireplace. A Sheraton coffee table was inlaid with white leather, and in one corner was a Louis XIV desk inlaid with emerald leather. Outside, the lawn sloped to the columned poolhouse and the oval pool.

Sara had fixed a fire, and the lights outside were just going on, as she ushered Gregson through the tall double doors into the library. Across from the entrance, above the mantle, was a large painting of Magdalena dressed in emerald velvet, with her emerald necklace, bracelet and ring. In the portrait she was standing, half turned around, as though she had been facing the other way, and turned to look at someone.

As Gregson entered the room, which he had never seen before, his eyes went straight to the painting.

"Thank you for coming, Jack." Magdalena's throaty voice pulled his glance to the window. Framed in the light that was still coming from the dying sun, the real Magdalena Alba stopped him cold. He was used to beautiful women, to seeing them, buying them, and having them any time he wanted. But there was something about this one. She had always been unapproachable. Now she welcomed him in her emerald velvet hostess gown, wearing Steve's diamond heart around her neck.

She was thinner than in the portrait, and thinner than Jack remembered her. But her face was even more haunting, with the high cheekbones, the oval eyes, the creamy color of her complexion. He took in the full swell of her breasts beneath her hostess robe and the voluptuous hips which curved out from the waist. He could see the shape of her famous legs through the slit in the robe.

Magdalena crossed to the couches in front of the fireplace and offered Gregson a seat opposite her. "Sara, please serve the tea now. Jack, would you like something to drink?"

"Tea is fine for me," he said.

Magdalena looked at him directly and smiled. "All right, Sara, thank you."

Gregson was nervous. He had agreed to come, because he had never been asked to Magdalena Alba's home before. Hardly anyone in Hollywood was invited here. And she had called him the day before from the set. He knew instinctively, with the intuitive sense of the street fighter he was, that something was wanted of him in connection with *The Rest of Our Lives*.

Steve Wayland was in deep trouble, and Gregson knew he'd been invited here because of that. He was going to enjoy every minute of it.

"Have you seen any of the rushes?" she asked.

"A few, of the location work. I don't really have time . . ."

She finished the sentence for him, "—and *The Rest of Our Lives* is not one of your favorite projects." She smiled. "I know that, Jack. I want you to know I'm not a game player. If I were, I couldn't possibly compete with you. I hear from every side that you're the best at what you do."

"It's a hard business."

She looked at him intently. "But it's also more than that, from what I understand about the past. I saw an interview last night with Katherine Hepburn. She was comparing Hollywood at the time of her life with Spencer Tracy with the way Hollywood is run now. Maybe you saw that piece."

Gregson shook his head.

Magdalena continued, "She said the studio heads of that time were tough businessmen, but they felt the romance of making motion pictures—really loved picture people, and cared a great deal about them. She said that now she found all of that romance and passion gone, replaced with balance sheets, computers, market sampling, technical data. She felt this has had an effect on the quality and the entertainment value of motion pictures. What do you think?"

Gregson answered, as Sara brought in a tea tray. While he talked, Magdalena served him. The room, the silver service, the woman, all reflected the romance she had just spoken about. Gregson seemed awkward with the small plate of sandwiches and the teacup.

"I certainly respect Miss Hepburn. She's a fine actress and a great lady. But the time she speaks of is long gone. That was before the technological revolution—before the massive use of TV, cable, and videocassettes we have now. It's much more difficult today. It costs more to make pictures, costs more to release them, and every picture is a gamble. There's no place for a romantic attitude."

Magdalena smiled at him as she poured herself a cup of tea. "Or for a romantic person?" she asked.

Gregson shrugged his shoulders and almost unbalanced his teacup. He was increasingly ill at ease.

"Not as head of a studio," he replied. "You can't let personal feelings enter into it."

Magdalena smiled and gestured with both of her hands, a feminine gesture of happiness. "I'm so glad to hear you say that, Jack!" she exclaimed. "I thought you would be too intelligent to let that happen—although," she paused, and then continued, "you see—I had heard that you really don't want *The Rest of Our Lives* to turn out—that, in fact, you dislike Steve Wayland, and that if he goes over budget you're going to take everything he has, his writings, his house, everything." She smiled. "I never believed that, Jack, because no one who's in your position could afford to feel so personally about a project financed by your own studio. As you said, you can't let personal feelings get into it."

Jack Gregson looked at her, then dropped his eyes.

She still had her smile, but she stared him down. "I'll come right to the point," she said. "I believe *The Rest of Our Lives* is an important picture. I think if you gave us a chance, we could finish something very valuable, in your own terms—a money-maker—a plus on the ledger sheet—and another credit to the legend of Jack Gregson.

"*The Rest of Our Lives* is going over budget. It wasn't budgeted high enough in the first place. You know that. We all know that. But whether you like Steve Wayland or not, Jack, you can take my word for it—I've made over thirty films, and some of them with the finest directors—Steve Wayland is an original. He doesn't copy anyone's style, nor does he attempt to be a pseudoartist. He doesn't belong to any school of 'in' film people—in New York, in Europe. He does it his way, follows his own vision, Jack. Not many people in Hollywood do that."

"He loses money."

Magdalena replied quickly, "Not always. And the film we're making is this man's life. You have to admit, no other filmmaker in this town has signed over all his personal assets, all he owns, to make a picture."

"Only a fool," Jack Gregson said.

Magdalena shook her head. "He's not a fool, Jack. And people like him, men and women like him, they are the people who make your job possible. Name me a single picture that has become a classic that hasn't had someone with passion standing behind it. The person who dreamed it, the person who made it."

She paused, and put her tea down. "Jack, no one knows I'm meeting with you. That's the truth. Do you believe me?"

Gregson looked at her. "I believe you," he said.

Magdalena continued, "You know that we need at least five hundred thousand dollars to finish the picture properly. Your computer people figured it out."

"At least five hundred thousand," Gregson replied. "Next week I'm giving notice of cancellation and I'm going to foreclose on Wayland. I warned him, at the beginning. We're almost at that point now."

"But what if you have the extra money? What if it comes from outside the studio? Will you make a pact never to reveal the source of the money, no matter what?"

Gregson put down his cup. He looked at her incredulously. "Depends on the deal. What's wanted for the investment?"

"No percentages, no points, no interest. The picture earns the money back, the five hundred thousand is paid back after the studio is even. If not, well, as you said, life is a gamble. But you can't close the picture down as long as it doesn't go any further over budget."

Gregson looked at her intently. "There's another way, Magdalena. I don't want you to put your money into this film. You'll lose it."

"That is my decision, Jack."

He waved off the interruption with his hand. "Give me a chance here. We're two sophisticated people. We've been through a lot. We've each come up the hard way. I've always admired you. You're not only a beautiful woman, but you have something so hard to get on the screen or off—class—quality." He took her hand across the coffee table. "I would like to come here from time to time, and see you.

Evenings, when you have no scenes to shoot the next day. Evenings when we could have dinner together, and talk and get to know each other. I'd like that kind of arrangement. And if we agree on that, I'll see that *The Rest of Our Lives* is financed, up to a limit of the extra five hundred thousand dollars."

Magdalena stood up, never taking her hand from Gregson's. She looked at him directly, without a trace of antagonism. "I'm flattered, Jack, that you would choose me, and that you could place such a high value on my friendship. I would suppose that most of the women in the world—most of the beautiful women in the world—certainly are available to you. But I also know that you are a man of class yourself. You're a man of taste and distinction. And certainly you wouldn't want an affair with a woman who has no love to give you.

"If we had met before—but that would be another story. I'm in love with someone else." She withdrew her hand from his. "And I know that you will accept the five hundred thousand dollars from me. I've already made the arrangement with my lawyers. If you should choose not to accept it, then I'm afraid that the details of your handling of this film, not to mention refusing to accept an investment which could complete a company picture, would somehow get out into the public's ears, both here and on Wall Street—well, I'm sure that wouldn't be desirable for you.

"You will have the money at the studio—a certified cashier's check from the California Bank—on Monday morning. Simple but legal papers will be attached. You will return them to my attorney and I will have made my investment in your picture, in complete mutual secrecy. I think it will be a good investment. We will see. And when *The Rest of Our Lives* is a success, Jack, perhaps we will drink champagne together, and toast our arrangements."

She walked with him to the library door, putting her arm through his. She turned as Sara came through the living room to show Gregson out. Magdalena smiled at him with a deferential air.

"Jack," she said, "I understand why you are head of the most famous motion picture studio in the world. Thank you for your time and your assistance."

Gregson looked back and forth between her and Sara, as though he had something important to say. But nothing came out. He turned and followed Sara across the spacious living room toward the front hall and the door of Magdalena's home.

28

Rayme and Stephanie

tephanie was the last one to leave the stage. Some nights, tonight being one, she stayed in her dressing room until everyone had gone. She liked to walk through the set of the Bay House that Boris had built. The big gabled house with its movable walls, the sections that could be pulled away so that every room on the two floors of the house had one side open, allowed the camera to pick up, with various lenses and angles, the smallest aspect of every room.

Every detail of the Bay House as it had been on location was the same. All the props were there, family photographs, the old playthings of the children, the awards won by various members of the family, soft, feminine touches of Angela Garibaldi everywhere.

Stephanie used these late nights alone on the set to walk again through the rooms of the house where Christina Garibaldi was living— to absorb the aura of the Garibaldi home, to become continually more familiar with the physical elements of the Garibaldi story. She always kept her script book with her, filled with her notes on every scene.

They had left the lights of the set on for her. Steve knew of these times at night that Stephanie spent on the stage, and many evenings he would come down from the editing room where he was working at night to have a cup of coffee with her and talk. She was aware that he watched over her all the time. That was part of his job. She counted on him, but she was beginning to learn that she had to depend on herself.

Two nights a week she met Pearl at her apartment. She was continuing to write down everything she could remember about her life.

Now she had to, as Pearl put it, "reprogram" herself. It would take a long time, but if she could get through this film . . .

She walked through the Garibaldi living-room and into the library. She had thought she was alone on the mammoth stage with only the security guard outside, but she saw someone else in the library. Rayme Monterey was walking back and forth in front of a projection screen for a 16 mm camera. The camera was on top of several thick books placed on the library table across from the screen. Stephanie had never seen the screen or the projection machine on the set before.

Rayme seemed embarrassed that someone else was there.

"I'm rehearsing for the scene tomorrow—just walking through," he said.

"I'm sorry to bother you," Stephanie said. "I didn't know that anyone else was here. I do this once or twice a week . . . I like being here alone and spending time in these rooms with all the pictures and props. It helps me."

"That's what I was hoping it would do for me," Rayme said. "I'm worried about tomorrow. I've got some tough moves all through the scene. I'm afraid I'll be thinking about where I'm supposed to be instead of what I'm supposed to be and who I'm supposed to be."

"Would you like some coffee? I've got half a thermos left."

"That's a good idea—I've got cobwebs up here," he gestured at his head, "like I'm split down the middle. Rayme Monterey on one side and Michael Garibaldi on the other."

Stephanie sat down in one of the chairs in the library and took out the thermos from her carryall.

"They're not that far apart," she said. "Michael Garibaldi and Rayme Monterey—that's happened to all four of us—I think the better Steve knows us the more of us he's bringing into the film. We're a mixed breed now—at least I am. Sugar? Milk?" She gave him a spoon to mix it up.

Rayme stirred his cup. They both looked up at the high ceiling and then through the open doors of the hallway.

"This is the best time of all," Stephanie said. "It's still like a dream for me—this big stage and this house of our own."

"And the view," Rayme added. "When they put those photographic plates up and light them, it looks like a forest from one window, the fields from another and the bay out beyond the boat house. . . . It *is* a world of magic. . . . Well . . . how are things going for you so far, Stephanie? Have you seen any of the rushes?"

She shook her head. "Only that night at the dubbing studio, the scene where you and I get out of the station wagon at the bay and go up on the porch."

"I haven't seen much more than that," Rayme said. "A few scenes that need different pieces of music which John Hammell, the music editor, and I are working on, when I have a day off."

"All time has come together for me," Stephanie said. "It's like there was another world before this film began, and another world after it ends—only when I think of it ending, I get scared. I want to run."

"I thought you were probably out every night, dancing up a storm somewhere with your boyfriends."

"I don't have any boyfriends," Stephanie said.

Rayme looked at her curiously.

"Never?"

"Never now. Before I did. I was married once. I didn't get involved for two years after that."

"Then what?" Rayme asked.

"I made a bad mistake. So I retired from the ring."

He looked at her.

"You're different than I figured. When I saw you dance that night at the Roxy . . ." he broke off.

"You thought I was hitting on you, didn't you?" she said.

He shook his head. "I was worried about myself—you're a beautiful woman, and I don't want to be involved."

"I saw you and Marny in a concert once at the Forum in Los Angeles," Stephanie said. "I was sitting about four thousand miles from the stage but close enough to feel what was between you when she came onstage at the end. Is Marny the reason you've backed off from me, even when we're all together, just talking about our parts? I never thought about trying to take Marny's place . . . nobody could."

He didn't answer.

"We're safe with each other," Stephanie said. "I don't want any more pain. At least I don't want to ask for it—and I know you don't either. We don't have to worry about each other."

She screwed on the thermos top and left it on the table between them. "I'll leave the rest of this for you. And, Rayme, I'm sure tomorrow will come out well."

Rayme shook his head. "It's my second scene with Robert Montango —he scared the hell out of me first time around—he's so damn strong."

"So are you, Rayme. See you."

Rayme watched her walk through the stage lights, down the steps of the porch with the photographic plate lake in back of it. In the night light it looked very real. He watched her disappear toward the boat house.

29

Christmas at the Bay House

The screen flickered with the images of the family at Christmastime at the Bay House. The living room was decorated on every wall and a large pine tree stood in the corner. It glowed with the strings of colored lights and the glistening of shiny bulbs. There were old-fashioned ornaments, too, ones that had been handed down through the Garibaldi family in Italy.

Eric Garibaldi was on the screen, twenty-five years younger, and his wife was handing out the gifts to the circle of her husband and her children. Angela Garibaldi looked strikingly like her daughter Barbara. They had the same eyes, the same forehead, the same graceful carriage, the same slender neck, the same kind of voluptuous body.

"She was so beautiful," Christina said. In the film she was a baby sitting on Barbara's lap. On the screen there were exclamations as the children opened their presents and then embraced their father and mother in the old home movie reel.

Only Michael was quiet. Suddenly he stood up, his shadow blocking out a part of the images on the home movie screen.

"Where are *you* going?" his father growled, as he stood at the back of the room operating the projection machine.

"I don't like these home movies," Michael said. "I'm going into town."

"No, you're not," Eric cut in. "You're going to stay here and watch with the rest of us. I want you to remember the way this family was when your mother was here—and the way we should be today—at least, for her sake."

Michael pointed at the screen, silhouetted by the flickering projection. "But we're *not* like that, goddamn it!"

His father walked into the beam of light from the projection screen. Only a part of the Christmas of twenty-five years before was visible. The living room was divided between the past and the present.

"We can be again."

The two men faced off against each other, both silhouetted in black against the flickering scene of Christmas at the Bay House, long ago.

"It wouldn't be the same today, Dad, even if Mother were still here," Michael said. "That day is gone. Families aren't like that anymore. The world's on a faster track. Either you get on the track or you're shoved off. We'd all like to go back to that time, but we can't. And goddamn it, you're just screwing us up emotionally, showing these scenes, surrounding us with Mother."

"She loved you," Eric said defiantly.

"And I loved her!" Michael shouted back. "We all did. But she's dead and none of us can bring her back to life. And when she died something went out of this family. The soul of it. We haven't had it since."

"The hell we haven't," his father said. "Maybe we haven't been as close as we were before. Maybe we don't see each other very often, but goddamn it, this is a family. It's still a family. And that's why we're here. To stand up against the people who would like to ruin us—" He grabbed hold of Michael and jerked Michael to him. "Don't you feel any of that, son?"

Michael lashed out at him. "I'll tell you what I feel. I feel free now. I walked out of all of this when I was seventeen because you were smothering me to death. I knew what you wanted me to be—your son, your heir, your image, your successor, a goddamn chip off the old block. I tried to tell you so many times. But you never listened. You never really listen to any of us."

He gestured to Barbara and Christina. "You lived all those years with our mother and you never learned one damned thing from her about really loving. About loving children for themselves, and helping them fulfill themselves. You wanted us to show *you* off, reflect *your* life, *your* success. Well, screw your success. I'm not so sure what you've contributed to the world."

Eric slapped him hard across his face.

"That's right, Dad, you still think you can take me, don't you? Well, maybe you can. That doesn't mean anything. I didn't grow up to beat my father in a fight."

"Oh, no," Eric said. "You grew up to get a black girl pregnant, let her go off to Haiti and have your child, and kiss the whole thing good-bye. After you got a lousy doctor who made a lousy try at an abortion. And you never told any of us. Well, now that's going to come out and you've got some things to face up to. How do you think it's all going to look to your United Nations band? And your fans? And especially, Michael, how's it look inside *you*?"

"I don't like the way I acted when Lissy got pregnant," Michael answered back, "but you know what was choking me from what I really wanted to do? I wanted to marry that girl and have that child. I loved Lissy. But the fear of you stopped me cold. The image of the Garibaldi family. I didn't have the balls to face it, but that was a long time ago. You told me when I walked out that you were cutting me off as a member of this family. That I didn't deserve you. And now, in one weekend, you're trying to put it all back together again."

Eric's voice was quiet. In the background, the old family Christmas scene was still running. "That's true. I am. I want it back."

He turned to Barbara and Christina. "I know things have changed for all of us. It's a different world, as Michael says, different real-ities. No family can just go off by itself and shut out the world. The whole damn thing is connected, whether we like it or not. What I hope can come out of this weekend is that we can save the things your mother—" He gestured at the screen, and his voice broke. "—the things that she lived for and brought to every one of us. Strength, courage, integrity. Loyalty. Kindness." His voice quivered. "Forgive-ness." He put his arm around his son and reached out his other arm to bring Barbara and Christina into a circle. "Don't do it for me. That lady up there—" He nodded at the screen. "She's in you, each of you. Still. Don't shut her out for the rest of your lives."

30

The Sound Tape

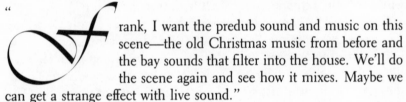"rank, I want the predub sound and music on this scene—the old Christmas music from before and the bay sounds that filter into the house. We'll do the scene again and see how it mixes. Maybe we can get a strange effect with live sound."

Steve was talking to his sound effects editor, Frank Warner, behind the camera.

Frank looked at him. "I'm still putting the tracks through the filters to get them just right on the dubbing stage—" He pulled a call sheet out of his pocket. "The predub won't be finished until tonight. It's here on my call sheet. That's the way I planned it. You didn't plan for it to be used today."

Steve exploded. "Goddamn it, Frank!" The whole crew went silent. Steve never raised his voice on the stage, but he was raising it now, loud and clear. His anger flamed. "You mean to tell me you can't give me that predub—when I want to try it for this scene and we'll never get another chance to repeat it?"

Frank was paralyzed. He and Steve had made three films together. There were many sequences they had done together when no soundtrack had been taken. Frank had created an entire sound-effects track from different tapes he had made for one film. It was an exceptionally detailed job and Frank was an acknowledged master. He was stunned by Steve's attack.

"Do we ever go by the exact schedule, Frank?" Steve ranted. "Aren't we always prepared to shoot late or shoot early or shoot whenever it's right—isn't that the way you and I work—always?"

Frank was quiet. "I'm sorry, Steve. My department's trying to keep up with you. Ordinarily we wouldn't be doing sound effects now. I have to go by your instructions day to day. We can fix this scene with any mixture of effects you want when we do the final dubbing."

"But the only time I can *shoot* everything together for this scene is now—and you're not ready—you should have figured out this possibility for yourself. I count on your not having to be told everything to do. I count on your doing your own job."

David Thayer, Boris, Gaylin, and Roberto were all watching Steve. They had never seen him like this.

Steve drove on, "I've got enough to worry about, Frank, I can't worry about your job, too!"

"I'm really sorry," Frank said.

"That's not good enough. We'll shoot the scene anyway," he said to the rest of the crew. "We'll have to fill in the sound effects I was counting on afterward. I wanted to give the actors a chance to react to the real thing—but Mr. Warner isn't prepared."

Warner turned and walked through the people around the camera and out the door of the stage. No one in the crew knew what to do. They moved away from Steve. This was a new element. Steve was in a pressure cooker—it was getting to him in ways they'd never seen before. Who would he turn on next? Where was this picture headed?

31

Goldwyn Studios, Stage Six, Warner Hollywood

t was early the next morning. Eight A.M. start. Steve called the full crew around him.

"I've called you all together this morning because I want you to hear this." Steve looked over his crew, and then at Frank Warner.

"The way I acted yesterday, Frank, was inexcusable," he began. "I had no right to do that. But I get worried and tired just like you and yesterday I was really strung out. It's happened to me before and will probably happen again. But I don't believe in treating anyone in the way I treated you, Frank, tired or not. You know you are one of my closest friends and one of my finest collaborators. Forgive me, Frank."

Frank put his hand out and clasped Steve's, and then patted Steve on the back.

"I want to share something else with all of you. Somehow, somewhere, the money we need to finish has been given to us. If we stay on schedule for three more weeks, we're going to finish our film."

He couldn't contain a smile as he said, "We've got a long day, so let's get moving."

32

Le Cirque,
New York

*J*ack Gregson had a corner booth held for him at Le Cirque whenever he was in New York. This was a two-day trip, but it was a critical one.

Gregson watched the District Attorney following the maître d' to the table. Gregson didn't shake hands. If it was possible for him to go into a meeting with greater leverage than the other person present, he projected a chill from the very beginning. He had spent a lifetime mastering the art of fear. And it worked. When people wanted something, he'd found they'd become desperately afraid that they couldn't get it, or, if they already had it, that they would lose it. By the time the district attorney sat down and the maître d' had taken their drink order, he was at Gregson's mercy.

"I want you to know from the beginning," Gregson said, as he turned away from the man only long enough to nod to a studio executive who was coming in with his wife, "I flew all the way here to *see* you. Nothing's the same on the phone. I want you to look me in the eyes and tell me *when* you're going to ask for a second grand jury investigation of Rayme Monterey and *when* you're going to serve him with a warrant."

"I'm almost ready," the district attorney said. "But this isn't your movie company, Jack—I'm an elected public official, and—"

Gregson cut him off. "You hit the key word, my friend—elected. Elected is what you are now. Elected is what you are not going to be this fall if the New York party chiefs aren't with you."

The drinks came and there was a pause in the conversation. The district attorney drank a third of his scotch as Jack Gregson watched him without touching his own.

"The way I see it, *Mr.* district attorney, you and I both have a lot riding on the Rayme Monterey case, but you have more. Mine is a personal matter. Yours is a political career. I'm not asking you to do anything illegal. I'm not trying to bribe you. I'm trying to be a friend. I have many friends in the party. I have many favors to call in. Owed to me. I am endorsing them over to you, your chance for the governorship."

He leaned toward the district attorney and his voice went to a whisper.

"I can't wait long. There are only three more weeks of shooting, and I need that warrant served on Monterey by the end of next week. No more discussion. No more footsying around. I want the warrant served, and I want Monterey locked up. Just like the last time, only this time, at least, you talk the judge into refusing to set bail. Monterey goes to jail and stays there until the grand jury hearing.

"Once he's arrested and in jail, *The Rest of Our Lives* is shut down. But no warnings—no publicity—no leaks—until the day you announce to the press the second grand jury investigation.

"Then we'll help you with publicity breaks across the country. Your name will be prominent in every press release to television, to radio, and to the newspapers—that's a promise. The indictment and the warrant next week, and then it's your turn. I can make you a star, buster."

33

Magdalena

The needles had been inserted into ten muscle areas of her body: her arms, her legs, her shoulders, her back, and her neck.

Dr. Arms stood by her bed in the UCLA wing built solely for the study and treatment of dermatomyositis. He was holding Magdalena's hand as he explained the examination.

"This electromyography—we call it an EMG for short—is based on the same idea as an electrocardiogram for your heart. The EMG studies the electrically measured activity of the muscles by using these needles that have been inserted into muscle areas of your body." He pointed to the complicated monitoring machine to which all the needles were attached.

"We can find out with this test, Magdalena, exactly what reactions your muscles have. It helps us diagnose not only the muscles but the peripheral nerves and the spinal cord.

"I want to warn you before we do it—when we run small electrical charges through the wires into the needles and back into the machine, every individual reacts differently. At the very least, it is uncomfortable. At the very most, it is painful. But you can stand it."

Magdalena looked up at this doctor she had grown to trust. He was honest with her and gentle. He also gave her confidence. She needed it now. The attacks of muscle weakness were getting worse and the blood tests showed elevated muscle enzymes, steadily increasing in her blood. The muscle biopsy test Dr. Arms had been making every two weeks showed that her condition was worsening.

She looked up at him.

"I have a low threshold of pain."

Dr. Arms smiled and shook his head.

"That's another point of disagreement between us, Magdalena."

"I'm ready. Let's get it over with." Her grip tightened on his hand.

He nodded to the nurse standing by the dials of the electrical unit. The nurse carefully moved the electric current dial.

Magdalena felt the currents surging into her body. It was like a hundred needles in every part of her. Her body reacted even before the full pain hit her nerve centers. Millions of tiny exploding pains raced out from her brain centers until agony seized her. She bit her lip to keep from screaming, and her fingernails dug into Dr. Arms's hand.

Magdalena's consciousness was ebbing now. Terrible racing thoughts split her head. Was she dying right then on the table? The picture would never be finished and she couldn't say good-bye to Steve. She was losing track of where she was. She couldn't see Dr. Arms anymore. The pain was too excruciating to see anything.

She was floating now—outside her body. The pain had gone. Was this what it was like to die?

But there was that voice again. So sure, so comforting.

"It's over, Magdalena. You'll have some reaction to this test. But in a few days the soreness will be gone."

She was back inside that needle-marked body. In that hospital bed. Dr. Arms's face dissolved into view.

The thrill of fighting off death, still being alive, surged through her. Dr. Arms was smiling at her.

"Rest here as long as you want, then get dressed and come into my office." He patted her hand and went to the machine to get the test sheets on the electromyography from the nurse.

Dr. Arms was studying the tracings of each needle that had been inserted into her body when she came into the office. For a moment he couldn't believe this was the same woman he had seen a short while ago in great pain on a hospital bed in his research wing.

Her hair was freshly combed, her makeup was redone, her eyes sparkling with hope once again. She was dressed in a fuchsia flowered print, and she looked like the California spring to him. New and glistening. Her hair was tied back with a ribbon of matching material. Her only jewelry was the small diamond heart she wore around her neck.

She sat down across from his desk.

"Well?" Magdalena said, "did I pass or fail?"

Dr. Arms had a mannerism of putting the tips of his fingers together when he was thinking. She noticed they were together now. Her voice became anxious.

"Remember your promise, Doctor. Always the truth."

"The truth is just what I thought it would be—what I told you it would be when you went into this difficult work schedule. You should be in a hospital right now, or, at the very least, getting rest and treatment every day. I could do so much more for you, Magdalena, if you would concentrate on this problem of the dermato."

He glanced down at the tests.

"Your muscle strength has weakened. This EMG shows it very clearly—just what the biopsies have been telling us. The periods of the attack of the disease are getting longer, and the periods of remission are getting shorter."

"We have just three weeks left," she said.

"Are you getting all the rest you can? Do you go home right after work? Do you rest on the days you don't have to shoot?"

Magdalena smiled.

"Well, Doctor, I won't lie to you. I'm living every precious minute I have. Finally I'm getting a chance to play a real woman, not an illusion. And finally, Dr. Arms, I'm getting a chance to *be* a real woman—not an illusion."

34

Stephanie

"This is a turning point in the film," Pearl said, "but more important, it's a turning point in your life."

Pearl watched Stephanie pace like a trapped animal in the kitchen of her apartment.

"When you're this scared—well—you've only got a few ways to go. You can get high, and find out as soon as you come down that you're still scared, you can quit the movie because you're too scared to go on, which is just a fancier excuse for you to get high, or you can accept that you're scared, like all of us are sometimes—of our jobs, of illness, of each other—and we show up anyway. You can walk through your fear, Stephanie. And if you do that, just this once, you'll never be this afraid again. I promise you."

Stephanie turned to Pearl and held out her hands. They were shaking.

Pearl took her hands to steady them, and sat her down at the kitchen table. She poured camomile tea from an old-fashioned English teapot, added honey to Stephanie's cup, and set it down in front of her. "Drink," Pearl said. "It'll help calm you."

"Right now, I don't think I know what that word means." Stephanie took a few sips of tea.

"Very often," Pearl said, "when you've been out of touch with your feelings for a long time and then they come upon you, like this, you don't label them right."

Stephanie gave her a quizzical look.

"Everything you're feeling isn't necessarily fear. You might be lumping your excitement into the same category . . . Pulling off this kind of emotional scene in a major motion picture, it's appropriate for you to have deep feelings about this. Aren't you excited, Stephanie? Even just a little?" Pearl smiled.

Stephanie took a moment to consider, and looked a little less terrified.

"This scene tomorrow, Pearl—it's like it's my life—it's like our sessions—only you won't be there."

"Oh, yes, I will be there," Pearl said, with another smile. "I'm taking tomorrow off to be on the set. Steve asked me to."

Stephanie glanced at her quickly. "I don't blame him. He knows I can't do it, right?"

Pearl shook her head.

"He's sure you *can*, and thought my being there could give you maybe one more inch of security. Stephanie—you know, I still have trouble with your new name sometimes—when I think of you, I think of Mary Jane—"

"Call me Mary Jane then, it's okay if *you* do."

"No," Pearl said, "Mary Jane was your name once. But you've begun a new life now. Just remember, everything you are, everything that's happened to you, is built on the foundation of Mary Jane. It's earned from your past, from your pain—you can *use* all of it tomorrow, Stephanie." She nodded at the little dinette table in the corner of the kitchen. There was now a large stack of written pages on it.

"Look at those pages. All that suffering," Pearl took her by the arms, "it's all led up to this. Now you're going to make it pay off for you—everything you've ever been through—it's all part of the success you're building. Steve has told me over and over how wonderful you are in the film. Magdalena is raving about you. And I've been around motion picture personalities long enough to know that most stars don't get too excited about the younger competition."

Pearl looked at her tenderly. "Don't go back now, Stephanie. After tomorrow, it's all downhill. You have everything set well in your mind—tomorrow it will come from your heart."

35

Christina and the Doctor

"I won't do it," Christina lashed out at the doctor from the Menninger clinic.

The doctor stood calmly at the window, relighting his pipe. His voice was unthreatening.

"Afraid?" he asked.

She shot him a look. "Of what?"

"Of yourself?"

"Don't give me any of your mumbo-jumbo crap. I'm not afraid of anything."

"Is that why you take drugs?" he asked. "Why you're killing yourself? That's what you're doing, you know. And if that's what you want, you're sure to get what you want. I can't stop you. No one can. If you don't let go of the drugs, which means dealing with why you've had to use drugs in the first place, then you're guaranteed to die, unless, of course, you go crazy first."

Christina had heard enough. "Nobody can tell me what's going to happen to me. And nobody's telling me what to do." She walked up to him quickly and screamed into his face. "Nobody! Don't even try!"

"If you're not afraid," the doctor looked at her steadily, "I want to work a little experiment with you."

"What do these stupid little games mean?" She nodded toward the two chairs facing each other in front of the desk. The doctor had placed them there six feet apart.

"I want you to have a seat in one of those chairs, and talk to somebody who isn't in the room."

"That's kindergarten shit." She inhaled so fiercely she almost bit the end of her cigarette off.

"You tell me you're not afraid of anything," the doctor said. "You pursue danger. You love a good dare. And the truth is, some of the things I'm afraid of don't even daunt you. So what difference does it make to you to try this? It's a way for you to listen to your own heart. What's there to lose?"

"I know what's in my heart," she screamed at him.

"Tell me," he said to her. "I want to know."

Suddenly she ran out of breath. She shrugged her shoulders. "Ah, what the hell," she said, and sat down in one of the chairs. The doctor stepped behind her, completely out of her sight.

"I want you to imagine now," he said quietly, "that your mother is sitting across from you."

Christina's lips began to tremble. "Why my mother?" she asked.

"Because she's the one member of your family who isn't here. I feel her presence in this house. And I think you do, too. This is where you spent weekends and summers all through your childhood, isn't it? This is where you were born."

Christina's voice was hardly audible. "Yes," she said.

"Did you love your mother?"

It was a moment before Christina answered. "I don't remember her very well."

"I want you to imagine her," the doctor said, "sitting in the chair opposite you. You are alone with her. Talk to her."

Christina fired up again. "Are you out of your mind? How can I see my mother there? She's dead. She's been dead a long time."

"Is she really dead for you?" the doctor asked. "Look at her there in the chair. Is she dead or alive?" the doctor asked. "Is she dead or alive, Christina, to you?"

Christina turned in her chair, eyes blazing at the doctor. The doctor made a motion to her with his right hand for her to turn back around.

"Look at your mother, Christina. Look at her. She is sitting there opposite you. You have an imagination. Use it."

There was not a sound in the room. The seconds raced by. The doctor's voice came at Christina again.

"Try, Christina. Speak to your mother."

Christina began awkwardly. "Mother?" She paused, and then her voice began to change, to intensify. "Mother, I think about you all the time. In strange places, sometimes, too. On a dance floor at some nightclub where I'm trying to forget everything. On the trips up with the coke and crack—and all the trips down. Some memories come back more than any others. Like the time, I guess it was about a year before you died, and you weren't feeling very well and I was scared. I couldn't find out anything. I woke up in the middle of the night— I went to your room and you weren't there. And then I found you. We were here at the beach house for the summer, remember? And I found you sitting alone in your nightgown at the very edge of the beach—just staring out at the water. You didn't even hear me when I spoke to you. And this terrible chill went through me because I loved you more than anyone else in the world—and you were always there for me. And then—it was like you were behind a curtain—your own curtain—and you couldn't hear my voice—and you didn't want to." Christina's voice went up into a cry. "You didn't want to. And I went down on my knees in front of you and I grabbed you, and I shook you really hard. 'Mother, I'm talking to you,' I said. 'Don't you hear me? For God's sake, don't you hear me? What's the matter, Mother?' " Christina began to cry.

"Mother," she went on, "it's been so hard without you. I see you everywhere in this house. I think I was happy here—a long time ago—really happy. I remember how you worked with me on my ballet lessons, when we used to practice in the boat house. I can't remember a time when you weren't there watching and coaching me. And that time you convinced Daddy that I should go to Europe to study at the Royal Ballet in London. You were always there for me." Christina's face suddenly distorted. "And then you were gone—you left me!" She screamed out as though she were going to attack the chair. "Nothing was ever the same—ever—you were gone so fast, in one night!" Christina was sobbing. "You didn't even say good-bye—you abandoned me without a word. Why didn't you tell us you were going to die? Mommy?"

Christina's voice suddenly had the innocence of a child's. "I was never afraid as long as you were there, Mommy. And then you were gone." She was shaking. "And I hated you—yes—" she screamed out "—I hated you—for leaving me. You never came back. How could you do that?"

The words came through her sobs. "Oh, God, no—no, no, no, I didn't *ever* hate you. I loved you more than anyone in the whole world—I still love you—I can't stand it because you're not here. I'm so afraid—I thought if I could be the great dancer that we dreamed I'd be—you and I—then maybe I would keep you alive inside of me—

but when the dancing was over, you were gone, too. I look for you in other people—but I never see you. And I'm always afraid—oh, Mommy—come back. Please, come back."

She crumpled in her chair. She clutched her knees and buried her head.

36

Goldwyn Studios,
Stage Six,
Warner Hollywood

As tephanie was emotionally drained, but Christina was working for her now. She understood Christina. She never felt outside the part she was playing. Christina followed her everywhere, even in her nightmares.

She stayed in her trailer on the set for every meal period now. Steve had sent Catalina Lawrence, the script supervisor, to work with her on her lines and to keep her company at mealtimes.

Catalina kept detailed notes of every scene, exactly what had been shot in each master shot, in each close-up, in each over-shoulder. Her typed notes went every night to Steve, with details of scenes to be finished on another day. Steve had to know exactly what each actor was doing at each place in the scene, how far a cigarette had burned down, where the knife and fork were, where the middle of a yawn was, where there was a sneeze, where there was a hand gesture, thousands of little details of human activity. All these had to be marked down for the progression of every scene.

Stephanie was fascinated with Catalina's job and took notes from her script book on the progression of the scenes she still had left to shoot. If Stephanie had been smoking a cigarette in the long shot and was just taking it out of her mouth when the cut was made, then she had to smoke the cigarette in the same position, at the same length of burning cigarette, and with the same motion, on the medium shot, the over-shoulder, and the close shot, which were done as covers of the same scene.

At the moment, Stephanie was in her trailer, wearing a powder blue caftan, her hair pulled back in a ponytail, and she was drinking hot tea. On her stereo, Paul Young was singing "Every Time You Go Away."

Catalina used these lunch periods to calm Stephanie down. Catalina was in constant touch with Steve and reported to her on Stephanie's condition. Steve and Catalina, and Lieu, too, had tried to set up supportive elements on the stage for Stephanie. They tried never to leave her alone, and yet not give her the sense of being overprotected or shadowed.

There was a knock on the door of the trailer and Catalina opened it to look into the eyes of a funky-looking middle-aged woman dressed as though she were reporting for the part of Miss Marple in an Agatha Christie mystery. Her clothes were English and belonged in an English countryside, together with her walking stick, which she had used to knock on the door.

"What can I do for you?" Catalina asked in her friendly manner.

"I need to see Stephanie Columbo," the woman answered in a voice that was definitely Californian. "Here." She handed Catalina a business card that said LILIAN CHILDS, PEOPLE MAGAZINE. "I was told by Jake Powers that I'd find Miss Columbo here."

Catalina looked at Stephanie. Stephanie shrugged. If Jake Powers had sent this woman, she'd better see her. She hadn't been around long enough to know that Jake Powers would never let any kind of reporter go to a stage alone and knock on the door of one of the actors. Reporters were watched and escorted, not left alone to do as they pleased. Catalina was skeptical, but she had seen Lilian Childs on other sets. She decided to stay out of it.

Lilian stepped up into Stephanie's trailer. It was a moderate-size, nicely furnished standard studio trailer. Catalina kept it stocked with fruit and Perrier. Stephanie had resumed the very strict training of her Roman days.

Lilian made room for herself on the built-in couch opposite from the table where Stephanie was eating.

"Can I get you something?" Catalina asked.

"Well . . ." Lilian said as she looked around, ". . . do you have any dessert—that is, something nice and fattening? That's what I feel like today. I hear so much about nutrition. Everywhere I turn I see versions of 'You Are What You Eat'—well, look at me. I am what I eat and I'd like some more of it right now."

Stephanie laughed. She liked this lady. So did Catalina, who was good-sized herself.

"No," Catalina said, "but I can get you something. Be glad to at the commissary. They have some wonderful spice cake."

"Thank you," Lilian said. "À la mode, please."

Catalina laughed, and mumbled as she stepped out of the trailer, "I could use some of that myself."

Stephanie looked at the older woman. Her clothes, her manner, and her walking stick had thrown Stephanie off. What she found now was a pair of the sharpest, most searching eyes she had ever seen, staring at her through spectacles.

Lilian pulled out a notebook from her cavernous purse and put it on the table, took out three sharp pencils, and straightened herself on the couch. She glanced around the trailer. "I wish my magazine would fix me up with one of these things."

"I love mine," Stephanie said. She nodded at her books and records. "I have my own things here and . . ." Her voice wandered off. "I can get away from the pressure."

Lilian picked it right up. "And you can always get away from any unpleasant things that happen on the set—any unpleasantness, any fights." She paused before "fights."

"I mean my own pressures," Stephanie answered. "You have to train hard to dance and I've got both dancing and, I hope, acting in *The Rest of Our Lives.*"

"And you're playing the romantic lead opposite Rayme Monterey, isn't that right?" Lilian asked, as she made some notes on her yellow pad.

Stephanie spoke back immediately ."No, that's not right. There are no 'romantic leads' in this picture in the way that you're describing. But you'll have to talk to Steve Wayland about the part I'm playing. None of us is supposed to discuss the story and I'm sure Jake has explained that to you."

"Oh, of course he did," Lilian answered. "It slipped my mind, we set this up days ago—in fact, I'm surprised he's not here. I thought he'd be waiting for me."

"I'm surprised, too," Stephanie said. "Jake is so detailed about everything. But he's very busy. He's always got forty people waiting to see Rayme and not very many of them get through."

"Tell me something," Lilian Childs looked at her with those piercing eyes. "What do you really think about Rayme? You know, we're going to do a big cover story. It could go either way. It might be Rayme but it might be you, too. You know what a cover story could mean for you—a cover story in *People*?"

"I'm sure it's a big thing," Stephanie said.

Lilian corrected her with a definitive statement. "A *very* big thing. With our circulation it's probably the number-one break a young actor or actress can get. And I have an angle—the woman's angle—I think we can get the cover for Rayme and you together." She smiled at Stephanie. "And I'd rather it be the two of you than Rayme alone, because I hear you're talented, and I don't like Rayme Monterey's attitude."

"What attitude is that?" Stephanie asked.

"He won't give me a story. That's number one. He says he doesn't care to be on the cover of *People*."

"I don't think he does," Stephanie said. "He doesn't like to be exploited."

"I want to tell you something, dear. *People* magazine doesn't *exploit*—it *grants*. Remember that. We're the ones who are pursued for interviews. By everyone, the world over.

"But this film interests me. Millions of girls all over the world are in love with Rayme. He's becoming the Prince Charming of this era. He's Elvis come back again. He's Jimmy Dean thirty years later." She coughed. "You see, Stephanie, I'm old enough to have seen them all come and go."

She leaned forward over the yellow pad, close to Stephanie's face. "You give me the story I want, I promise to quote you correctly, not change any statement, and it's fifty-fifty that I can get you on the cover . . . Stephanie Columbo on the cover of *People*, soon to be seen in *The Rest of Our Lives*. That's worth a great deal to you, dear. Ask Jake."

"What do you want to ask me?" Stephanie said. "What is the story you want? I'm sure it's not about me."

"In a way" Lilian said, "it is about you. Since you're the woman in *The Rest of Our Lives* who has so many scenes with Rayme Monterey, you can answer questions that *People* considers very important for its readers."

"Like what?" Stephanie asked.

Lilian leaned back and lit a cigarette. Somehow, the cigarette didn't fit with her tweeds, her scarves, and her strange English countryside hat.

"Our readers want to know what it's like for a girl to work closely with Rayme day after day. What's it like to be alone on the set at night, like you were the other night, rehearsing with him? What kind of man is he? You know, when two people grow close on a set like that, there's usually something happening. Our readers want to know exactly what's going on.

"What's your impression of Rayme Monterey? Is he still in love with Marny? Does he talk about her? Is he scared of another hearing coming down from the grand jury in New York?

"What's the future? What's he want to do? What songs is he writing? Do you go out with him? Where? When?

"Those are the things our readers want. You answer them, and I'll get you the cover. I know I can. Half the women in America would give anything to trade places with you."

"I don't think that's true," Stephanie answered. She stood up from the table angrily. "I'm going to call Jake Powers. I'm not going to give you any answers, because I don't have any. I can't talk in a personal way about a man I'm working with."

"Why not?" Lilian asked, blowing out a long string of smoke rings. "Everybody does in this business."

"No, they don't," Stephanie said. "I've worked around these people for weeks now. Steve and Magdalena and Robert and Rayme—the whole group of them—they don't gossip about each other."

Lilian kept after her. "Do you think Rayme's coming off? You've played several scenes with him now."

"He's got power. You feel that playing a scene with him," said Stephanie.

"Do you like Rayme?" Lilian asked.

"Of course I like him," Stephanie answered.

She pushed back the table and stood up. "I've got to study my lines now."

At that moment, Catalina came back through the doorway with two plates of spice cake à la mode. She took in the scene—Stephanie standing up angrily and Lilian still at the table, calmly smoking.

"Well . . ." Lilian said, ". . . I'll just take that along with me." She nodded at the cake. "But you should think it over, Stephanie. I'll give you a day because we'll be going to press and we've got some great pictures of you. This may be your first and last chance for the cover."

Stephanie turned to Catalina. "She wants me to talk about Rayme," she said. "That's all. It's another proposition. Give a story on America's lover boy: how does he look? how does he act? how does he play the guitar? how does he make love?"

Lilian picked up her notes and her large tote bag, and said, "Sooner or later, you're going to give someone that story. I know you will.

Why not let it be me? Ask Jake about me. I do everything in good taste. *People* magazine never exploits anyone."

"I'll never give an interview about Rayme Monterey," Stephanie said, her eyes flashing. "And if you make something up and say you're quoting me, I'll sue. I have nothing to tell you about Rayme. That's what you're looking for. You think we have some kind of relationship. We don't. We're working together. We're both private people. He happens to be exactly what he says he is—and thank God for that."

Lilian paused on the threshold of the trailer just as Skeeter Thomas walked by. Skeeter and Stephanie exchanged looks. Skeeter was headed for Rayme's trailer on the other side of the stage, carrying their lunch.

"Why don't you tell me the truth, Stephanie?" Lilian said. "It's written all over you. That's the story I came to get. You're in love with Rayme Monterey."

Stephanie's alarm showed in her eyes. "Practically every girl in America thinks she's in love with Rayme Monterey," she said. "We've grown up with him. He belongs to us. It's our dreams he's singing about. That's all it is. And I'll tell you one thing—and you can quote me on this. There's not a phony thing that Rayme ever does or says. He is what he is. He tells you what he thinks and he answers to no one. For once, there's a legitimate American hero. That's what Rayme Monterey always was to me when I was growing up, and that's what he is now."

Lilian looked at Stephanie and smiled. As she began to walk away, taking the first bite of her ice cream and spice cake, she said, "I'll save your pictures, Stephanie. This still might be a story someday."

37

The Forum,
Los Angeles

It was a hysterical night at the Fabulous Forum, Los Angeles' giant Greek temple of sport and fun built by Jack Kent Cooke. Home of the Los Angeles Lakers, home of the Los Angeles Kings, home of rock concerts, the circus, and the rodeo.

This was a first night for the heralded new rock band Lone Justice, and their lead singer, Maria McKee. The band had been playing the hinterlands and Maria McKee, the twenty-two-year-old unknown, had the star buildup behind her. They had moved from a supporting role to full stardom in their first headliner at the Fabulous Forum.

Rayme, Skeeter Thomas, and the rest of the Norfolk River Band had friends in Lone Justice, and they had been impressed with Maria McKee when they had seen her in supporting bills around the rock circuit.

In the front row of the loge, well-disguised and with two friend-bodyguards in tow, Rayme, Skeeter, and the Norfolk River Band gave Maria McKee a standing ovation.

Skeeter had tried to talk Rayme into inviting Stephanie to go with them. Rayme had looked at him as if he were crazy.

On the way to the Forum in the limousine, Skeeter had spoken privately to Rayme, sitting in the front seat of the car with the limo driver.

"We should have brought Stephanie, like I said, man."

"C'mon, Skeeter," Rayme answered. "I don't want to get involved with anyone, you know that. I ask a girl out and the press is all over us."

"Rayme," Skeeter grinned, "ever since that first night at the Roxy, when Badlands was playing, you been thinking about her, but every time she's around, you get quiet and take off, like she's another chick lookin' for a free ride. She's not like that at all.

"Man," Skeeter said, "most of the time I back you up all the way. You know that. But when you don't see yourself straight, somebody's got to tell you. That somebody is me. You like this girl and you feel guilty because of Marny.

"We all loved Marny," Skeeter went on. "She was special. But Rayme, she's gone. And she wouldn't want to see you like this. I knew Marny. She wouldn't want to see you turning away from somebody you like—especially when that somebody likes you—for yourself."

"What the hell you talking about?" Rayme turned on him again.

"You're so blockheaded sometimes, Rayme," Skeeter said.

"Are you saying that Stephanie—" Rayme started.

Skeeter cut him off. "I was coming back from the commissary with our lunch yesterday, and I walked by her trailer. One of the big writers for *People* magazine was coming out. Catalina was with her. They were talking—something about you. So, I stopped at the end of the trailer to listen—and they didn't see me.

"Stephanie was being offered the cover of *People* if she'd just talk about you. Professionally and personally. You know, the story of Rayme Monterey's leading lady—how does he really look—is he really romantic?—is he comin' on?—we hear there's a romance—all that bullshit.

"Stephanie answered their questions exactly the way Marny would have. She wouldn't give them a thing."

"Are you telling me that Stephanie Columbo turned down the cover of *People* magazine because she wouldn't give them a story on me?" Rayme asked.

"That's right," Skeeter answered. "Jake wasn't around, either. Obviously, that reporter just barged in and tried to take advantage of a new actress. And I heard Stephanie say that she was going to call Jake about what had happened. Check on it yourself.

"I'm not just talking about the romance department, Rayme. I'm saying Stephanie is a friend. She's one of the few people who could really hurt you, if she wanted to make up a story, or even tell the truth about some of your bullshit on the set—because sometimes you've been rude to this girl. I've never seen you act like that with someone you just met—and from what Charlie Tuna told me, that night at the Roxy when you first met her, you cut her dead.

"But when she had a chance to really get at you, she talked about you exactly the way Marny talked about you. The same. What do you get out of that, man?"

Rayme started to answer Skeeter, but the facts had sunk in. He hadn't told anyone about the night he and Stephanie had been alone on the set. He'd been thinking about her more than he'd like to admit.

He was quiet the rest of the trip to the Forum. And Skeeter knew him well enough to leave him alone.

Just before the end of the concert, Rayme, Skeeter, the rest of the Main Street Band, and their two muscular "friends" slipped out. They were lost in the crowd that was demanding an encore from Lone Justice. They went out on the opposite side of the Forum, where all the limousines were lined up.

Rayme was slipping off his wig and moustache on the way to the limo when he saw them. They were rounding the curve of the Forum, running from the same door Rayme, Skeeter, and the band had left. There were four of them. They looked like IBM machine men in matched gray flannel suits. Rayme sprinted for the limo with the band. The gray flannel men sprinted after them.

Rayme slid into the front seat, Skeeter right behind him. The limo's doors were still open when the driver gunned the car. The leader of the four gray flannel men reached the driver's door just as the limo took off. One of them had blue-backed legal papers in his hands.

38

Chasen's Restaurant,
Beverly Hills

A young blond girl with long hair flowing down her back had taken over the front room of Chasen's. She was bursting out from an orchid-colored cocktail dress, cut low in the front, almost to the edge of her nipples. No one knew who she was, but before the night was over, every man in the room would make an effort to find out. The biggest tips in many a night would be handed out for that information.

She sat between Jack Gregson and Jerry Clune in the booth facing the entrance into the front room. The number-one table was the only one Gregson would accept. On his regular Thursday and Sunday nights at Chasen's, table one was held for him.

The blonde already had one film credit. She'd been spotted on a farm near Bloomington, Indiana, and brought to Hollywood to be one of four stars in a *Playboy* film called *Farm Girls*. She hadn't had any other parts as yet, just two center spreads in *Playboy*, standing invitations to Hugh Hefner's mansion, and all the luxuries that came with being Jack Gregson's mistress. In two short years she'd come from the dirt roads of the outskirts of Bloomington to the center of the fast lane.

Julius, the maître d' at Chasen's, brought a phone to Jack Gregson's table.

"It's the call you've been waiting for, Mr. Gregson."

"Thank you, Julius," Gregson said. He was easy and relaxed. The girl sat very close to him. Her hand was on his leg teasingly as he talked on the phone. "Hello," he said. "this is Jack Gregson—" He paused. "He's been served, huh?"

"No, he hasn't," came a voice on the other end of the phone. "He wasn't easy to find. Your tip on the Forum was right, but he had a good disguise. Seventeen thousand people in that place—all rock fans— and none of them recognized him."

"Goddamn it," Gregson said. He straightened up in his seat and he pushed the girl's hand away. He was back in the ring, punching. "The makeup woman from the picture probably fixed him up—I didn't think of that."

"We finally did spot him," the voice on the phone said, "but he and his boys left early. We just missed them."

"Technically, then," Gregson went on, "he hasn't been served with the grand jury hearing papers and until you do find him and serve him, he's under no obligation to appear in New York. Is that right?"

"Absolutely right," the voice said. "We have people waiting at his house now and at the studio. I'm sure we'll have him served before morning."

"The morning papers will have this story," Gregson said. "And TV. Anyway, he knows about it now if he saw you there. He knows he's being chased. This will stop the picture. No question about that. Call me at my home as soon as you know anything." He hung up. The girl leaned on him.

"Are you talking about Rayme Monterey?" she asked.

"None of your goddamn business," Gregson said.

She didn't understand what had happened. She nuzzled him. "Don't be mad, Jackie."

"And don't call me Jackie either," Gregson snarled.

"You've got such crazy moods. One minute we're having a beautiful dinner, the best champagne, with the whole night ahead of us, and then, one phone call, and you act like you don't even care about me."

"Shut up," Gregson snapped. He turned to Clune. "Wayland will have to shut down the picture and wait for Monterey. None of the film insurance will cover this hearing. And there's no way Wayland can replace him. What would you say that does to the cost to complete, Jerry?"

"The film would be millions over, if Wayland had to wait."

"So we can shut down legally, foreclose on his collateral, and come out ahead. That wraps it up. *The Rest of Our Lives* is dead the way I called it, and the operation won't cost us a cent," Gregson smiled.

Gregson's mind switched channels. What would happen to Magdalena's five hundred thousand? That was a point for negotiation. A negotiation he'd enjoy personally. Everybody had a price!

39

Goldwyn Studios, Stage Six, Warner Hollywood

The red light was on outside the towering doors of Stage Six. A studio guard sipped on a cup of coffee, protecting the gate. Three crew members waited patiently for the light to go off, signifying the end of a shot that was in process.

Jack Gregson approached from his waiting limousine, Jerry Clune with him. He walked by the guard and up to the gate and started to pull it open.

The guard nodded at the light. "But, Mr. Gregson—" he said.

Gregson cut him off. "I saw the light," he said, as he swung the door open and walked onto the stage.

There was an intricate boom shot starting over the open top of the boat house at the end of the pier, moving down into the room to a close-up of Christina, dressed in ballet clothes. The moves and the timing were critical.

On the giant boom, David Thayer and Steve were perched on two catbird seats on either side of the Panaflex camera, moving in an exactly charted path toward Christina's face.

The camera was moving in on her when the stage was flooded with daylight from the open door which Jack Gregson had entered.

"Cut! Goddamn it—who opened that door? You think the light ruined it?" Steve asked his cameraman.

David shook his head. "Can't tell till we get the lab report—I didn't see the light in the lens but I did from the side of my eyes. What the hell happened?"

The crane came to a resting place and was secured. Steve jumped off the seat. "Who the hell did that?" he said angrily. "We have a special guard on that gate. Who the hell—?" Steve broke off as Gregson came up to him with Clune hovering behind.

"Didn't you see the red light on? Don't you know what that means?" Steve asked angrily.

"This is my stage, Wayland. I'm paying for it."

Steve yelled at him, "This is my stage. Get out."

"We have a difference of opinion on that point," Gregson said smoothly. He was enjoying this. "It's no longer your stage. As of now, I'm closing down *The Rest of Our Lives*. I'm going to dismiss your crew and the cast."

"Like hell, you are. Get off my stage or I'll throw you off."

"I wouldn't advise you to do that. My orders are from New York!"

"We're not out of money!" Steve yelled. "We've got enough to finish the picture, and you know it."

Realizing that the cast and crew were gathering around now, Gregson played the scene the way he had prepared it. "We can't continue shooting without each of your four stars—and there's a warrant out for the arrest of one of them. You knew this was a possibility when you started the picture," Gregson said smugly.

Steve was in shock. "Rayme? I didn't know anything about it."

"They're serving him today," Gregson snapped. "The district attorney's office just called MGL in New York and asked us to cooperate."

"And you didn't even try to get us the two weeks we need," Steve said. "You've pulled off a lot bigger things than that, Gregson."

Gregson shook his head. "I had no reason to try. We don't have any more commitments with you now, and the overages and losses are yours. Six million dollars of studio money, and the picture's unreleasable, Wayland. You can't fight the city of New York, and you can't fight the law."

Gregson turned to Clune. "I want this stage cleared by tomorrow. I don't want to pay one more day's rental."

"But my sets," Steve interrupted. "My God, we've got hundreds of thousands invested."

Gregson glanced again at Clune. "The sets should add to our tax write-off." He turned back to Steve. "I've run most of the rushes now. You don't have anything anyway. How the hell do you sell a story about issues and ethics? It's a hell of a way to go out."

Steve looked at him. "It's the way you hoped."

Gregson nodded. "People find their own level, Wayland, and you've found yours." He turned and walked off the stage.

40

Goldwyn Studios, Stage Six, Warner Hollywood

One by one, the arc lights on Stage Six illuminated the darkness. Eight big arcs and hundreds of smaller lights from the beams above the stage lit up the Bay House.

Steve stepped out of the darkness and walked up the steps of the house into the front hallway. Tomorrow the same crews that had erected this set would tear it down, as though it had never existed.

The Rest of Our Lives would never be finished. He was through making films. More accurately, they were through with him. He was burned out, emotionally and financially.

He was not the man his two girls idolized. His father had been right, he was a failure. He had had his shot, and he had failed. The wife he had loved was gone. The woman he loved now, more than any woman he had ever loved in his life—he had failed her, too.

He walked up the stairs to the bedrooms. They were still dressed and lit. He had been scheduled to shoot in Barbara's room tomorrow. But that was all over now. This was the last time he would ever set foot in a movie studio the rest of his life. Where would he go?

A voice called out from the darkness surrounding the set.

"Steve."

Magdalena came walking toward the pool of light around the set, from the doorway of the stage. She looked up at Steve, standing in the bedroom set.

She smiled. "Are you coming down?" she asked. "Or do I have to come up? I've been looking everywhere for you, calling you at home, your office, Robert's house. Mr. Pavetti told me you left hours ago."

"I wanted to be alone," Steve said, as he came down the stairs.

"We're going to finish this picture, Steve," she said, as she faced him at the front of the stairs. "I never expected to see you give up. What would Winston Churchill think?"

Steve shrugged. "I've tried to find some way we can keep Rayme for two more weeks. I talked to Ed Wilson in San Francisco two hours ago. They can lock up Rayme without bail until the hearing, once they serve the warrant on him. The law gives the district attorney that power."

"But they haven't served him yet," she said. "He's at Lieu's house. Robert took him over with Stephanie. They'll never think of looking there."

"We still can't shoot the picture, Maggie, don't you understand? We can't shoot it here. Here, or anywhere—" Suddenly, in mid-sentence, Steve stopped. "Wait a minute—wait a minute!"

In one flash of thought, Steve went from a defeated man to a man who could hardly keep up with his racing brain. "Maggie—we might just pull it off. Ed Wilson told me nothing can happen to Rayme until he's actually served—he's free until then. What if they can't serve him? What if he were out of the country? I don't think they have the legal right to extradite him. He could finish the film if we had somewhere to do it out of the country. We could do it anywhere—all that's left are two exteriors—the rest are interiors—it's crazy but it could work—come on, Maggie."

They went into his trailer and flicked on the lights.

"I'll see if I can get Priscilla's plane. It'll hold the cast and crew."

He picked up one of the phones. "We have to work fast," he said. "I'm going to call Ed, double-check the legal situation, and notify Spartan of what's going on. You call Lieu. Tell her to get everybody packed and check on passports. We have to take off before they find Rayme."

Magdalena dialed Lieu's number. "Take off for where?" she asked.

"I've got an idea," Steve said. "There might be one place where we can finish the picture . . ."

41

Studio Vault,
Samuel Goldwyn Studio,
Warner Hollywood

I t was fourteen minutes past midnight by the clock above the security desk at the vault. The security guard on the graveyard shift nodded pleasantly as Steve came in with his cameraman.

"Good evening, Mr. Wayland, Mr. Thayer," Jim Conlon smiled. He was one of the old-line security men in the studio, and had been forty-five years in the security system. He took the graveyard shift at the vaults where all the negatives were stored and where many work prints were held. He liked the shift because he was still a beach enthusiast. He had come to California for the weather and he still wanted to enjoy it in the daytime.

"How's the golf?" Steve asked.

Conlon smiled at the recognition of one of his chief avocations. "Down to a fourteen handicap now, Mr. Wayland. I play every day when I'm on this shift."

"I envy you," David Thayer said. "Never work for Mr. Wayland, Jim. You'll be on the graveyard shift like I am, and every other shift, too, and Sundays. You won't play a day of golf for a year."

Conlon laughed. "That's why I never tried to get promoted around here. My old lady always pushed me, but I inherited my dad's Irish good sense. I've buried too many of those bright young guys like you. Workaholics—competing till they wear themselves out—I was a boy here when Mr. Thalberg died. Mr. Goldwyn always thought he was the best. He had it all, but so what? I wouldn't trade."

"You're right," Steve said. "Jim, we want to go to our vault. We've got to take the work print out to do some work tonight . . . some problems on the picture."

"When I came to work tonight, the scuttlebutt was that *The Rest of Our Lives* had shut down." Jim's words had a question in them.

Steve smiled. "Shut down, Jim, but not stopped. We've got two weeks to go, and the studio can't afford to write off the picture. That's what David and I are going to do tonight—look for some shortcuts."

Jim took his keys off his police belt, locked the main door, and took them in an elevator to the second floor. He left a note on his desk that he would be back in five minutes.

As they walked along the hall that looked like an immaculate cell block—with steel doors every few feet, an endless row of overhead lights, and simple blocked-out numbers on each door—they came to vault seven and unlocked it.

"We're going to need a rolling rack," Steve said.

"They're down at the storage room at the end of the hall," Conlon pointed.

"I'll get one," David said.

"Okay," Conlon said, "because I've got to get back to the desk. You know, we're not supposed to let any of this film out without front office approval—during the night, I mean."

"Go ahead and call one of Mr. Gregson's people. But I hate to see you get your head bitten off for calling so late," Steve said.

"Well, after all, it's your picture, Mr. Wayland. I'm sure everything's okay. Stop at the desk on your way out and sign out, okay?" Conlon said as he started down the hall.

David came back with a long carrying cart on four wheels.

It was almost one o'clock before Steve approached Conlon's desk again. He covered, in part, David, who wheeled the carrier by, loaded with film cans and cardboard boxes full of reels of film.

Conlon's eyes followed David as he pushed the film outside the main door. "Christ, you've really loaded up," Conlon said. "That's a hell of a lot more than the work print."

"We've got the outtakes and opticals, other stuff we've been doing. We're going to try and sort through most everything."

"I don't know—I'd sure hate to get into any trouble. You know how Mr. Gregson is. Everything down to the last detail."

"Call him," Steve said, "if you're worried."

Conlon glanced at the phone, then started to look for a phone number in his massive black book.

"I think he's at the beach. The number's 555-3289, at the Colony."

Steve looked at his watch, then glanced at the big clock above the desk.

Conlon followed Steve's glance at the wall clock, started to punch in the number on the phone, decided against it. He hung up.

"I woke him up once," Conlon smiled, "and it almost cost me my job. I don't think I'll try it again. But you put down there exactly what you took, will you, Mr. Wayland?" He put a receipt form in front of Steve.

"I'll be responsible," Steve said, as he signed the form. "I'm taking everything out on my own responsibility. I'm putting that down here."

"Thanks, Mr. Wayland," Conlon said. "That makes me feel better. How's the picture looking to you?"

Steve looked at him directly. "Good, Jim."

"I'm glad," Conlon said. "I remember what Mr. Goldwyn thought of you. All the old hands around here are pulling for you."

"Thanks, Jim," Steve said. "Good night."

David Thayer already had his station wagon half loaded. Steve helped him pile in the cans and boxes of film.

"Let's move it," Steve said.

The studio guards passed on the station wagon with only a wave.

42

Burbank Airport,
Los Angeles

n the faint light of a private hangar at Burbank Airport, the gleaming silver nose of Elvis's plane, *Lisa Marie*, glistened. The name of Elvis's beloved daughter remained written in script on each side of the plane.

Priscilla Presley had had it completely renovated after she had achieved her own national prominence with her co-starring role in *Dallas*, and her best-selling book, *Elvis and Me*. She and Steve had become friends, and called upon each other in times of personal and professional crisis.

Quietly, almost like a commando movement inside the hangar, the heart of the cast and crew of *The Rest of Our Lives* was arriving. Bags, wardrobe racks, props, light equipment, the photographic plates for the Bay House and the Michigan state capitol, and David Thayer's personal camera equipment were being loaded into the hold of the *Lisa Marie*.

Steve approached the loading deck hurriedly, talking to Lieu, David, and Roberto Bakker on the way, dispensing them to last-minute jobs.

"Lieu, get the girls on the phone—we'll have to wake up their mother's house, but it's better than leaving without calling. Come and get me when you have them. David, all the film on board?"

"Right," David said, "labeled and tagged."

"Good." Steve paused a moment. "Maggie here yet?"

Roberto Bakker shook his head. "She left her house two hours ago in our limo."

"Keep calling. Rayme and Stephanie, Skeeter, and the boys?"

David nodded. "Here."

"Montango?"

"He's here. All the cast, Steve. Everybody had a passport."

Steve walked up to the pilots. He gave them a note. "This is where we're headed. Carrying a full load of fuel?"

"We're fully equipped. Gassed up," one of the pilots nodded. "Your lady, Lieu, stowed in the food and drink. We'll wait for you in the cockpit, Mr. Wayland," the co-pilot spoke up.

Lieu came up to him. "They're on the phone, Steve. Kathleen and Lorelei."

The girls were half asleep.

"Where are you going?" Kathleen asked, the pain of separation in her voice.

"Europe."

"How long will you be gone?" Lorelei asked.

"I don't know," Steve answered. "But I've got an idea. When we're finished shooting, maybe you two could meet me in New York on your vacation. Would you like that?"

Kathleen shouted excitedly into the phone, "Please, Dad!"

"Promise?" Lorelei asked.

"You know, Lor, this isn't just a one-way street. I miss you as much as you miss me. Remember, I love you with all my heart, always."

"Love you, Daddy. Good-bye, Dad," they said, almost in chorus.

Steve heard the click on the phone as he glanced up at Roberto. "Any news yet on Maggie?"

43

West Los Angeles

*M*agdalena waited for Dr. Arms to assess the checkup she had arranged on her way to the airport in Burbank.

The doctor came in from his laboratory with the muscle biopsy. He was in evening clothes; she had reached him at a medical benefit dinner dance honoring Jonas Salk.

"I can't let you go, Magdalena," he said. "You're getting weaker, step by step. Now the strain, the added stress, it's all going to wear you down even more—and you'll be away from what little care I can offer you. You can't rush off like this—God knows where—I don't understand it—you never told me there was another location trip."

"I didn't know before, but all that aside, Doctor," Magdalena replied, "I'm going. They can't finish the picture without me. And, as I've told you, it's become a very personal thing to all of us."

"And I'm sure if Mr. Wayland knew that you were sick, he wouldn't let you go, either," Dr. Arms said.

"But that's my agreement with you," Magdalena spoke up. "He can never know."

"Is he in love with you?" the doctor asked her point-blank, looking into her face with concern.

She smiled. "He is—and I've never known anything like it. He has his faults, but he loves me. Like children dream about—like I dreamed of when I was very little. Life hasn't spoiled him yet. He is a believer."

Dr. Arms looked at her. "Can you tell me, Magdalena, that you think it's worth your life to finish this picture? Because it's your life

I'm talking about. If you go away with these additional pressures, and for that additional amount of time—the dermatomyositis will intensify. By the time you finish the movie, it may be too late to help you."

"But you see, Doctor," she answered, "this picture is the one thing of value I can leave Steve. I love him. I want to leave him something."

44

The *Lisa Marie*

*T*he *Lisa Marie* was ready for flight. Everyone was aboard, except Steve, Lieu, David, Roberto, and the missing Magdalena.

As her limousine pulled up to the private embarking area, Steve rushed up to her, took her in his arms. "I was so worried," he said. "I thought there'd been an accident."

Magdalena kissed him as Roberto took her baggage from the trunk. "Well, I'm here," she said.

As the sun slipped over the edge of the horizon, Steve led Magdalena up the stairway of the *Lisa Marie*. The motors revved up, and the huge plane shivered into motion. The *Lisa Marie* rumbled down the runway, picked up speed, and lifted off into the dawn of a new day.

The
ISLAND

Book III

1

The *Lisa Marie*

"We're in a hell of a spot and we have to fight our way out of it," Steve said. "I want all of you to know exactly where we stand. Before we left, I was assured by my lawyer that you are not running any personal risk by coming with me, that the legal risk we're running is mine alone.

"We'll be landing outside of Paris in another hour. Two buses are waiting to take us to Cannes where we will take a ferry to an island called St. Venetia just off the coast. It has its own government, and the governor is a man I've known for years, René La Grange, the former light-heavyweight boxing champion of France, and one of the youngest soldiers in de Gaulle's Freedom Fighters. He became part of the French Resistance after he saw his mother and father killed by the Nazis in Corsica.

"He's a hell of a man, and he's invited us to St. Venetia. It's a beautiful island with one hotel and some buildings and locations that can work for us.

"We have fourteen days left to finish our picture, even under the best of conditions. Now, we have to get through those fourteen days without sophisticated equipment, a full crew, and without our sets. We've got to put together new sets, interiors and exteriors, that match with the rest of the picture we've already shot. We'll have to do it with illusion, and with impressionistic techniques.

"We'll have to live together and work together as the creative family that we've talked about. We're through, at least for this picture, with conglomerate board directions and committee decisions. Every one of you is going to have to make decisions on your own.

"There'll be no time to check with me or Roberto or Gaylin, Boris or David, on every single thing. We've got to spread out and cover the field, try and work one or two days ahead, hopefully with a cover if it rains.

"We're going to have to improvise. And don't forget—we'll be setting some kind of precedent. We're either going to be a bright page in motion picture history or a dark one.

"Our only way out is to make *The Rest of Our Lives* work so that it has a chance to be a profit picture. That's the bottom line, as you all know. All the yelling and screaming in New York and Hollywood today and tomorrow and in the next weeks, and the clusters of lawyers and Wall Street maneuvers—they won't matter if *The Rest of Our Lives* makes money.

"No one but us will ever know what we'll be going through during these weeks in St. Venetia—what we don't have—how difficult it is— what we invent—what we have to make work. No one will want to hear about the hard times. All that counts is the result up there on the screen.

"So I'm asking you to throw away the rule books. Everyone here is a member of a union. I belong to three. A few of our crew didn't come because they were afraid of union problems, and I respect that. But for all of us left, there's no union and no studio. No capital. No labor. No sides.

"I want to tell you something interesting. My lawyer, Edmund Bradford Wilson, is researching this question. It's never come up in motion pictures before. Everyone here has a percentage in *The Rest of Our Lives*. The question is: when different people have percentages and ownership in a picture, does the production studio have the power to stop such a film and write it off as a tax benefit and give the rest of our budget to another film? That's Jack Gregson's intention.

"We've had a letter for two months, a signed letter from Gregson, saying that we can buy back *The Rest of Our Lives* for the total cost of the picture, which they project as half a million dollars over the six-million-dollar budget. Gregson's idea was to stop the film, write it off as a tax loss, and scrap it.

"I can guarantee you one thing. With the publicity all over the world this picture will now get, it will be profitable if we can finish it. But we have to finish in the fourteen days we have left. That's the most time we can possibly pay for, using every credit line we have.

"We've taken on the system and we've burned our ships behind us.

"We'll be shooting seven days a week—probably fourteen hours a day. We'll try to give you enough rest, but we won't always make it. And we'll try to have the meals ready but I'm sure there'll be some meals we won't get.

"In one day we have to push a quiet, slow-moving island into a fully organized motion picture location. We'll have to win over the people.

"I want to assure you that you're going to be paid. Lieu and Barbara, during the flight, have made out commitment letters to every person here. Everything I have is pledged against those commitments.

"Now, let me tell you what equipment we've been able to bring. We have David Thayer's rented Panavision camera and two Arris. We have David's box of lenses and gauges.

"Gaylin has built eight hand reflectors. We won't have any arcs or lamps—and the only electric light we might have is the electrical power of the island. We don't have the money to rent or buy stage lights from any place in Europe.

"We don't have any kind of tracks for the camera, no crane, obviously, no Panaglides, no special equipment for the hand-held, only the crab dolly we brought.

"We have the basic wardrobe but no extras.

"Martha has a pair of movieolas and two splicers. We won't have any of the modern editing equipment.

"For sound equipment, we have three Nagras and body mikes. We have only one basic sound unit.

"I can't think of any situation in filmmaking that could be tougher than the one we're looking at—or more exciting.

"We're all professionals. We know it's going to be hard. We're going to be overworked and overtired. We're going to get angry and discouraged. But we're a team.

"We wouldn't be here now if it weren't for each one of you, and I'm grateful to you. I know what it means to you to be away from homes and loved ones and to leave on such incredibly short notice. You had the guts to do it. You believe in what we're trying to do together. Don't forget for one minute that this is your motion picture too. Whatever happens, I'll always remember what you've given to *The Rest of Our Lives* and to me."

2

Governor's Office, St. Venetia

The governor's office in the small village of St. Venetia was on the second floor of the government building in the heart of the city square.

Behind the large desk that was over three hundred years old, and battle-scarred on all sides, were the flag of France and the flag of St. Venetia.

On a wall on one side of the desk was a collage with the memories and the history of the French Resistance. There were faded newspaper clippings and pictures, framed photographs, and in the center, a photograph of de Gaulle decorating a twelve-year-old René La Grange.

On the other wall, to the left of the desk, was a boxing collage, the highlights of Rene La Grange's ring victories in story and photograph.

The desk was covered with memorabilia. Photographs of his wife and two children, a signed photograph of de Gaulle, a commendation from General Eisenhower. There were also three boxing trophies, small replicas of the Eiffel Tower and the Statue of Liberty, a bust of Napoleon, a signed photograph of Gigi Jeanmaire, and an open, velvet-lined box in which rested the official medallion of the governor of St. Venetia.

In one corner of the room was a well-stocked bar that looked as though it was continually open.

René La Grange was five-eleven and two hundred and twenty pounds, sixty pounds more than his fighting weight. He was powerful, heavily muscled in the upper body, yet moved with the grace of a cat.

The man was one of the last of a breed, a true military hero of France. He looked back on the war years and his boxing triumphs as the great days of his life. It had been a long time since there'd been any more great days for René La Grange.

After he had retired from the ring, he'd begun to spend his vacations in St. Venetia. He liked the peace and beauty of the island as a place for his family, for his children to grow up. Paris, the city of his heart, was too expensive for him now. More and more, St. Venetia had become his home. And he was the celebrity of the island. No one nearly as famous as René La Grange had ever come to live there permanently.

It was a matter of course that he had been nominated for governor and elected almost unanimously. That had been seven years ago. Every two years, René La Grange was reelected. Most people on the island assumed he would be governor for the rest of his life. So did he.

But the excitement had gone out of his life. Since the day he had joined the French Resistance, René had been a street fighter. He had lived by his wits and his fists. He was a recognized public figure in every club in Paris and in the surrounding French countryside. Much of his life had been spent on the edges of the underworld which controlled boxing and boxers.

René was a favorite hero of the showgirls, the call girls, the prostitutes, the pimps, the joints, the back alleys, the early-morning markets, the night worlds of theaters and Montmartre nightclubs. Like most sports heroes, he had been a favorite of the wealthy and the jet set. But when his championship days were over, these people dropped René La Grange and he returned to the streets of Paris, where he was still a king.

St. Venetia was a harbor for his family, but René had grown restless. He needed the power and prestige that the governorship of this little island gave him, but he'd begun to drink too much and sample French pastries too often. He was heavier than he should be, out of condition, and there was disappointment in his bright green eyes.

He was still a handsome man, and his attractiveness was increased by a three-inch scar along his right chin line. There were stories it was from a knife fight. He claimed that it was an injury in the ring, but he always had a twinkle in his eye about it.

When he was drinking, or if there was trouble at hand, René was still a vicious fighter. And when there was no excitement in St. Venetia, René tried to find it in a bottle.

Now, as he listened to his friend's story, René smiled and nodded his head. Their relationship dated from a time when Steve was in Paris and René had taken a short stint as his limousine chauffeur, in the lean days after the boxing championships were gone. Steve had known about his career and asked him questions about it. When Steve was alone, he sat in the front seat with René. They drove through Paris and the surrounding countryside together as Steve scouted locations.

René knew every village, every innkeeper, every restaurateur. It amazed Steve to see how the people in a little village would flock to him as soon as word got around René La Grange was there. He was an imposing figure and immediately recognizable.

He refused to wear the hat of the limousine service, and that had twice cost him his job. He still didn't wear it. He was not a man to be put in a uniform, unless it were military.

René and Steve had developed an interchange of dialogue between them. Rene had started it by calling Steve "Mon Capitaine." Steve had responded by calling him "Mon Député."

As René sized up his friend, he grinned and poured two glasses of wine. René raised his glass to Steve. "Mon Capitaine," he smiled.

The phrase lit Steve's memories and he lifted his glass. "Mon Député," he answered.

René laughed to himself and shook his head. "Every time I've ever seen you, there's trouble. Trouble with the motion picture. Trouble with women. Trouble with something. I love it. *Mon Dieu*, I love it. It's so goddamn dull around here."

He glanced at Steve. "I've heard the generalities. Now tell me the specifics. I already know from what you've told me every minute counts—and you're on an island, with my people, where time means nothing. I tell you, I love it. There's going to be trouble and it's been too long on this island without trouble. What are the specifics?"

Steve looked out the broad windows of the governor's office at the lights of the little village that extended out to the horizon of darkness.

"How much authority have you got, René?"

"I never looked it up in the governor's rule book, but I run this place—what there is to run."

"I'm sure you do," Steve said. "The ferry's the only way to get here from Cannes. Is that right? There's no place to land a plane?"

René shook his head. "No place. No planes. You either come in on the boat or you don't come in."

"And you've got jurisdiction over anyone who comes on the island?"

René looked at him. "No one's going to come on this island if I want to keep them off—they'd have to go through days of legal processing over on the mainland. My rules get stricter according to how much I don't want someone here. Think they'll be coming after you?"

"You'll be reading about it in the Paris papers. This thing's going to shake up every movie capital in the world. They'll try anything to take me off this island, René. If I go, in this case, the picture stops and everybody goes—because the rest of the picture is still in here." He pointed at his head.

René laughed. "You've always been crazy, Mon Capitaine. That's why I love you. I'll never forget that night—oh, well, we'll talk about that later. I see your face. Back to the specifics. What's the next thing you need?"

Steve gestured out the window. "All that light. What do you have here? One main generator?"

René nodded. "And it goes out pretty regularly, every couple of months—"

"Then the island is used to being dark sometimes?" Steve asked.

"Yes, it is. Why?" René said.

"Because I've got to tap into your generator or I can't finish the movie. We can make it during the days if the sun is up there with enough light and long enough—but we'll have to do some night shooting. We have no cables with us, so we're going to have to have every cable on your island. We've got to tap into your generator lines to have enough light to do anything once the sunlight is gone. It's the single most important thing I need, René."

"You'll have it," René said. "I have two engineers in this town. They'll be here anytime you say, to meet with you.

"I'm going to put out an official proclamation." He laughed. "That's one of the luxuries of this office—every time you feel like it, you can put out an official proclamation, with all the ancient seals of St. Venetia and so forth, and you put them up on the bulletin boards and tell the people what to do."

Steve looked at him. "You've got more power here than the president."

"Why do you think I'm here?" René laughed. "I got used to the power—I missed it. So I'd rather be a big man on a little island than a little man on a big one."

Steve laughed. "How about the people of the island? We're going to need them to build sets, cook, sew, play parts, fill in my crew, for transportation, every kind of thing. I've got to have five or six different labor pools and have them available for my key people for each department—men, women, children, too."

"They'll love it," René said. "I mean, filling in as extras, playing bits, just being around a film, you know how people are about movies—

but this is a very special public. These people live a very casual life. They're not used to the pressures of your work. They're not used to getting up early, working all those hours and taking orders—no, they would have made a very, very bad company in the Resistance, unless they were attacked. That's a problem, Steve."

Suddenly René slammed his fist into the desk. The old desk rattled. René grabbed for the bust of Napoleon, which almost toppled over.

"Why not?" René asked, his green eyes coming to life and his body resting on the balls of his feet as it had always done in his fighting days. "These people need something, Steve. I need something. The days go by and the years, and you wonder why you're alive. Like that song of your singer, Peggy Lee . . . 'Is That All There Is?' I think about the words of that song all the time here. About myself, too.

"You know, there was the Resistance, and then driving for some people like you, and then the island—but more and more it seems like everything's in the past. And I keep saying, is that all there is?

"I think that's what's wrong with this island. And I've never had any way to change it. I can't make a proclamation and tell people to see more, and question more, and feel more, and fight more. Fight for what? For another day just the same?"

René gestured toward the French flag behind his desk. "Scratch deep enough in a Frenchman, you find that flag—you find Napoleon—you find the great memories. They're there, if you can get them fired up. The people of this island will never know what hit them. I'm going after them. I want you to give me a list now of everything you need."

He went behind his desk and sat down. "So, we screen strangers who come in. We don't let any roving bands of tourists on the island. The generator. The work groups. Every piece of transportation that can roll. Right? What else? How's the hotel? It's the only one we've got, you know. They said they could take care of all of you, somehow."

"It's going to work out," Steve answered. "I've got the crew settled in—we've got a meeting at midnight."

He looked at his watch. "We have to shoot tonight or we'll lose a day. I wish you would speak to the hotel, though," Steve added. "We have to have early breakfasts for the crew and we'll try to get hot meals out to them when we're working on location. It's important. And, of course, the dinners at night. My manager's getting some money in here—all that we've got for the hotel. To get them paid ahead."

"Will my people get paid?" René said. "I don't care for myself, you know, but they're going to ask about that. Everyone thinks that a motion picture company is made of money."

"I'll give you a real reason for them to help us," Steve said. "One they'll understand. By now, all over the world, there are headlines in the papers, at least in the film sections, about what's happened. About kidnapping, stealing, exile, and rebellion.

"And what will every single story say? Every story in the world, when they know where we are, will be talking about St. Venetia. For the next few weeks, every story on *The Rest of Our Lives* is either coming from St. Venetia or it's about St. Venetia.

"Not so many people in the world know about your island, but everyone in the world's going to know about this. Whatever happens, St. Venetia's going to become a tourist attraction of unbelievable growth in the next two or three years. And if the picture's a hit, can you imagine the people that will want to come here and see where it was filmed and where we stayed and, by the way, hear about the governor? You and the island and the people are going to be rediscovered, René."

René's face lit up. "*Mon Dieu*," he said, pacing up and down, "you're right. Now that's a proclamation. One of my best. It will be posted all over this village and even on some key homes within twelve hours. And I'm calling in my emergency staff of one. He's a boy and his senses haven't been dulled by too many easy days yet."

"What's his name?" Steve asked.

"René La Grange the second." Rene held up two fingers like a fighter. "I'm going to attach him today as permanent liaison between you and me, Mon Capitaine. You can count on him."

"Then he's just like his father," Steve said. "Now, in four hours, I need to start shooting. Is this office near the central generator?" Steve asked.

"Two hundred yards away, Mon Capitaine."

"We're going to turn your office into a dining room of the house on the set we left in Hollywood. It's the only room in that house we hadn't filmed in yet, so we can take some liberties. We have the props. One thing, though—we're going to have to take out part of a wall so that we can move a camera around outside the room while we're shooting the people inside at the table."

René looked at him quizzically.

"We'll put it back exactly the way it was, replaster and repaint—will you let us do that?" Steve asked.

René shrugged his shoulders with a smile and glanced around his office.

"The whole thing needs to be painted anyway," he said.

"We're going to tap into your generator from here and we're going to need your best engineers right away," Steve said.

René poured two shots of whiskey and gave one to Steve.

"We'll have the generator lead-ins in four hours. We're going to wake up the whole town tonight to watch the first movie location in St. Venetia. Let's drink to it, Mon Capitaine."

He clinked his glass with Steve and drank down the shot. Then he smiled. "I will never forget tonight. And nobody else on this island will either."

3

The Dining Room
of the Bay House

A painting by Andrew Wyeth hung over the mantle, depicting a Pennsylvania family of mother and father and two children working together in a wheat field below their farmhouse on a ridge in the distance. Wyeth had painted it near his home in Pennsylvania.

One hour before, René La Grange had brought in the painting proudly. It was famous all over the island and had a place of honor in the home of St. Venetia's wealthiest citizen. It was now on loan to the movie company.

Boris Peters put it into place. It was a finishing touch to the set he'd created in four hours.

The governor's office had been revamped into the dining room of the Bay House. The scene to be shot there had originally been planned for the library, but that library was thousands of miles away on Stage Six at the old Goldwyn Studio, waiting to be dismantled.

René La Grange, Jr., a slender, handsome boy who resembled his father, and five citizens of St. Venetia had worked with Gaylin and Boris, slicing off one wall of the governor's office. The camera could now shoot in three directions in the room, covering almost every angle. The room could be photographed with depth, and the Panavision camera could be moved in on the crab dolly for closeups.

Steve was talking to Clare, the makeup lady. Magdalena, Montango, Stephanie, Rayme, and the doctor were gathered around him.

"No makeup, Clare," Steve said. "We're getting near the end of the weekend. Every one of the Garibaldis has been under pressure for three straight days. No one has been getting much sleep. All their hidden fears and resentments have been coming out." He glanced at his actors. "You're all tired from the flight; let's use it in this scene. I don't want to cover the exhaustion in your faces. Nothing is resolved yet in this family. I want the tension to show."

He turned to the actor playing the doctor from the Menninger clinic. He had brought him on the plane for this one scene he had left. There was no way to substitute for him.

"Clare, it's different for the doctor. He's a professional and used to dealing with all kinds of trauma. I want him to have a light makeup, just to ease the tiredness in his face from the plane trip.

"Let's get it very quiet now," Steve said to the crew around him.

He turned to René. "We're going to start shooting in a few minutes, and it's extremely important that everyone be still. No one moves around. No one talks."

René took the St. Venetia workmen off to the side and gave them their orders.

Steve walked back to Magdalena, who was standing in the hallway outside the governor's office. He nodded at Rayme, who was standing in the furthermost corner of the room, his back to the other people, concentrating, alone.

"Look at Rayme over there, Maggie," Steve said. "He's watched you and Robert prepare for your scenes—go into yourselves. In the midst of all this confusion, with the lights and people and equipment, even in this limited space that we're working in, there's Rayme, off by himself. He's gone inside."

René came walking up to them. "Steve, we're going to try the power lines. My boys have got them connected all the way back to the generator. We're about ready to cut in. Keep your fingers crossed."

René nodded to his son. "All right, son, go downstairs and give the signal."

Just at that moment the lights in the room and all over the village went out. Robert Montango's roar came from the makeshift coffee stand René Jr. had set up down the hallway. "What's happening now? You blew the whole village, amigo!"

Montango was looking out the window. The village was dark.

René went to the window of the newly created set.

"René," he called out to his son, who had gone down to the generator control center.

His son's voice came up from below. "Yes, Papa?"

"Let's try the switch now. All the cabling checked?" René's engineer nodded.

"All right, son, tell him to cut it in." René looked up to the sky. "Well, God, are you up there?"

Miraculously, light flooded the dining room of the Bay House.

David Thayer had made a light board holding placement for eight high-powered bulbs. They were the only extra lighting equipment the company had. They blazed in the bright light.

"My God! It works!" David said, as the eight bulbs came on.

Steve led the applause for René, his son, and their engineering crew.

Montango came in with his coffee mug. He nodded toward Thayer's makeshift board of eight high-powered light bulbs.

"What the hell are we doing? Making home movies here?"

Steve laughed.

Montango knew that Steve needed two things: a good start at a new location under these improvised conditions, and for his "family" to relax. Everybody was on edge. It was beginning to sink into the whole company exactly what had happened.

Steve had, in effect, taken the film company out of the country and challenged Gregson—perhaps had even stolen the film. That was something that could well end up in court. No one knew what would happen tomorrow.

"Let's line up the lights, David," Steve said. "Roberto, everybody off this set except those you absolutely need. Let's bring in the actors."

He glanced at the doctor. Clare was finishing his makeup.

"That's good, Clare," Steve said, looking at the doctor closely. "I can hardly tell he's got any makeup on at all," Steve motioned to the head place at the dining room table, "but he doesn't look as tired as the others."

"Doctor, you're there, just as we rehearsed it on Stage Six at the studio."

Steve turned to Gaylin. "I want coffee on the table and the family china."

"Ready," Gaylin said.

"I'd like coffee and cake, like we discussed on the plane. This hasn't been a regular meal. Some of them have eaten a few bites of the cake. Everybody has had coffee. Now they're on their third cup. That's the way we come into this scene.

"David," he said to his cameraman, "now that we've got this original Wyeth, thanks to you people," he glanced at René and his St. Venetia crew, "I'd like to change the opening shot. Let's start on the Wyeth, close, fill the screen with it, and move down over the group at the table as the dialogue is already going on."

He turned to the actors. He was already moving into the world of the Garibaldis.

"Eric, Barbara, Christina, Michael," he called his actors by their names in the film, "we are going to do this scene the way we rehearsed it two days ago on the set.

"Eric, you're next to the doctor. Barbara, you're next to your father and on the other side of the table. Christina, you're on the doctor's right, and Michael next to Christina."

Steve stood in the open passageway where one wall had been removed. The camera was at his side on the crab dolly. The wheels of the dolly allowed it to be turned in every direction, and it moved forward and backward without tilting the camera.

He studied his new set. It could have been in the Bay House. The white walls had been freshly painted, and Boris had found a handsome old buffet table with René La Grange's help. It did not match the dining room table they had brought from Rene's house, but the two pieces of furniture were harmonious together; they were both old, and had polished surfaces which had been worn down with time. There were other pictures on the wall now, the props they had brought with them from the real dining room in the Bay House, a small statue of Damon and Pythias, and an old wooden platform table.

Boris had found these in the mad scramble when they were setting up the room. Part of his talent lay in his ability quickly to switch his vision, even when it had already taken shape over weeks of preparation. In this case, he had found some plants from the governor's secretary's office and brought them into the corner. He had left Rene's side table, which held his liquor chest, in almost the exact place it had been. All of René's photographs and collages had been taken out, and the holes the nails and picture hangers had left had been puttied up and painted over.

It was an immaculate room now, simple, solid, and old. Like the Bay House itself. Steve looked over his shoulder at Boris, Gaylin, Roberto, and the crew.

"It's incredible. I believe this room. You are the best. All of you."

The actors were taking their places around the table. Magdalena came by Steve. She kissed him on the cheek as she glanced around the room. Already, the discipline of Steve's set was falling into place.

"It's going to work, darling," she said. "It's a miracle."

4

A Family Disease

The camera was moving down from the close shot of the Andrew Wyeth painting as the doctor talked to the Garibaldi family.

"Addiction is born out of a person's emotional and physical environment—the family in a large sense. So let's don't talk about Christina alone. All four of you have a part in Christina's disease, and also are affected by it.

"I don't care how little she's seen you. You're her family and she can't cope anymore. Underneath Christina's confidence, underneath the wild and racy trend setter is a shy and vulnerable young girl desperate for recognition and affection."

The doctor looked at the others. "A family with the ambition and drive of this one is very hard to measure up to. I've learned that Christina could have been a great dancer. But that gift was taken away from her and nothing was put in its place. She lost her mother, she lost her dancing—" he looked at them "—and along the way, she lost the rest of you. She didn't feel she belonged anymore. And, as she lost her reason for living, she found comfort in the pursuit of immediate self-gratification—sex, alcohol, and drugs. What little self-value she had was quickly destroyed.

"I want to work with Christina, which means working with all of you. Substance abuse is a family disease. I'd like Christina to come to the Menninger clinic for a six-week recovery program—during which time each of you will be asked to participate in the process. There will be private therapy sessions and family counseling as a group.

We'll give you a safe place to vent your feelings about each other and Christina's drug addiction.

"I hope you will decide to come. Between us—" his glance went to Eric, Barbara, and Michael, and then to Christina "—I know you can be free from drugs, and have a full life ahead of you."

5

District Attorney's Office, New York City

The Rayme Monterey story had broken wide open. And now *The Rest of Our Lives* was front-page news.

Rayme had eluded service of the grand jury warrant. Rayme and the Norfolk River Band had disappeared.

The movie company of *The Rest of Our Lives* had flown away in Elvis Presley's plane, and taken their film and much of their equipment with them.

The New York Daily News hit with a big headline: "*The Rest of Our Lives* Film and Cast Kidnapped." *The New York Times* reported it more conservatively: "Singing Idol Rayme Monterey, Director Steve Wayland, and Cast of *The Rest of Our Lives* Leave Hollywood in Mysterious Circumstances. Will Renew Production in France."

The New York District Attorney had called in the press. Five television cameras and crews had been set up. More than two hundred photographers were there.

The district attorney had fallen into a doubleheader. His name and image were everywhere in the papers and on television. And, as the sudden fair-haired boy of his party, he'd been getting calls from politically powerful people all day.

He was expertly linking himself with the cause of honest, decent people against the excesses of Hollywood.

The stage was set. Spartan Lee and Edmund Bradford Wilson came in just before the district attorney's entrance. They worked their way through the reporters, answering the rapid-fire questions with "No statement." "No statement today." "I have nothing to say." "All we know is that they're on an island off the coast of Cannes. St. Venetia."

"No, we're not in telephone communication yet."

"We'll gave our press conference tomorrow," Wilson said, as he and Spartan broke away from the crowd and, protected by two police officers, took a position in the front of the room.

District Attorney Clement Mahoney made his entrance flanked by five assistants. He had taken an advanced course in public relations. He had learned how to dress, how to wear makeup for television, even how to read the TelePrompters, almost as well as the president did.

Television cameras focused in on him, and the reporters and photographers crowded around him twenty deep.

Clement Mahoney glanced around at the crowd. He wore his most serious mien. He had served time in many insignificant places on his way up the tricky road of New York City politics. Now, at thirty-nine years of age, he was ready to make his political move.

He expected the present governor to consider running for the Democratic nomination for president. The timing seemed to be right for his own ambitions. The path might even be open for White House consideration. He was a communicator.

"Ladies and gentlemen. We have two cases, two warrants for arrest, to announce here today.

"Representatives in this Hall of Justice," Mahoney said, his voice ringing with drama, "were sent to California to personally serve a warrant for arrest for Rayme Monterey, relative to the new grand jury hearing that has been scheduled.

"However, Mr. Monterey, moving in the opposite direction from his pose as a spokesman for justice, yesterday eluded the representatives of this court and flew to France with the movie company making his film, to escape the legal processes of the country he proclaims to love so much.

"When he returns to this country, an official warrant for his arrest will be waiting for him.

"I also announce, at this time, that a warrant is being issued by my office for the arrest of Steven Wayland, the director and producer of *The Rest of Our Lives*. Charges have been brought before us of theft, perjury, transportation of processed film without permission, unlawful entry, and contractual violations."

He nodded toward Jack Gregson, who was standing a few feet away on his right. "Mr. Jack Gregson, president of Gregson Films International, whose studio is the actual owner of *The Rest of Our Lives*, is here to answer your questions.

"In the opinion of this office, these two entertainment figures have exceeded not only the law, but all due proprieties of respect and decency. We will pursue both these men relentlessly to serve notice on the entertainment profession in general that fame and money cannot buy special treatment and cannot avoid due process of law in the state of New York. Thank you."

There was a rapid exodus, with each reporter and each television group hoping to get the news out first.

Jake Powers came up to Spartan and Ed Wilson. "My God, the D.A.'s going to make this picture a household word. We ought to put him on our staff."

Wilson nodded, as Spartan gestured toward the crowd of reporters surrounding Jack Gregson. Gregson was making statements about American justice, dramatizing the outrage of his position, the vulnerability of production companies like his to the superegos of the entertainment world.

"Gregson call you back?" Wilson asked Spartan.

"Of course he did—he couldn't wait. Sounded like he's counting his chickens."

"Good," Wilson said.

Powers smiled. "What kind of garden trail are you leading this guy down?"

"We'll make our statement tomorrow," Wilson said. "Make sure everything Gregson says gets in the papers and the weeklies. I want everyone in this country to hear his story."

He looked at Spartan. "Do you know how long I've waited for a real case, Spartan? Something dramatic like this that's in the public eye?"

"Where do you want our press conference to take place?" Jake asked Wilson.

"Gregson wants the meeting tomorrow in the corporate office of MGL here in New York. He's setting up the biggest press conference ever held by the head of a major studio. He's always wanted to be famous, in fact, he once had political ambitions—and maybe still does. This is his shot. What do you think about making *our* statement on *his* grounds?"

"It's a good idea," Jake said. "It looks like we don't have any position if we agree to make our statement over there, like we've been called in on orders from Gregson.

"I'm sure he's planning to whiplash all of us in his statement. It's a perfect stage for us. Every single thing that's said tomorrow will have major network breaks. The stockholders of the company are going to be following this case.

"Now we have some leverage," Jake stated. "Spartan, when you got through to Steve, what'd he say about finishing the picture over there? I don't see how he can do it without the equipment and God knows what else."

"He'll do it," Spartan said. "His professional life's at stake, and his personal life too."

"He really thinks he can finish the picture on that island?" Wilson asked. "Then we're fighting for time—it'll mean pulling out every technicality in the book."

"He needs eleven more days," Spartan said.

"Gregson will go for an injunction to stop the film—that's the only road he has open—get it in New York—force the French government to enforce it—" Wilson said.

"Has he got a shot at that?" Spartan asked.

"It's a legal chess game. He moves. We countermove. Keep the ball in the air for eleven more days.

Spartan turned to Jake. "Jake, day by day—I don't have to tell you what to do with this. It's the dream story of your career. And if we win this case—" His voice trailed off.

Wilson picked up. "Gregson's managed to forget we have a signed turnaround agreement. He's forgotten we have the right to buy back the film for six and a half million dollars. If Steve can pull this picture together fast, with a temporary score and dub so we have a work print, we can bring it to New York when the showdown comes and try to pay off Gregson and MGL. Once Gregson is paid, his case collapses. He'd be in court for years and it would just fizzle out."

Spartan spoke up. "I want to announce in the trades a week before it happens and in every newspaper in New York and Los Angeles that we'll have one single showing of the film," Spartan said. "A reserved section for the critics and a reserved section for every distribution company in the world. They'll all come now, with the notoriety the picture already has. And that day we sell it to the highest bidder. They'll have four hours after the film is finished to put in a sealed bid.

"It will be a giant story, Jake. The first of its kind in motion picture history," Spartan added. "And I'm asking you on the strength of this campaign alone, even if the picture doesn't come off—what do you think the chances are that *The Rest of Our Lives* a month from now can get back at least six and a half million dollars in this auction?"

"Do you know what that would do to Gregson's career?" Jake asked. "Right now he's gunning for the favor of whoever buys MGL. This is the time for Gregson to come off a big winner and impress everyone bidding for the studio. His whole career is on the line against Steve's. And if he can't close down *The Rest of Our Lives*, and if the film can be cut together, if it has anything at all, Gregson's down the sewer. Wall Street will flip around—how often we've seen it happen."

Wilson spoke up. "Let's get a drink. I want to find out from you how the hell Steve is going to finish the picture over there on that island. With no studio, no equipment, no sets, nothing to make a location work."

Spartan said, "I can tell you there's nothing on St. Venetia to make a motion picture with—except some naturally beautiful locations. But I wouldn't bet against Steve Wayland. Whatever else is going on, he'll be shooting right now."

6

The Beach of St. Venetia
at Sunset

*T*he sun had already begun to slip into the ocean on the
far horizon of St. Venetia.

Boris Peters, Roberto and Gaylin, and a labor force
of fifty locals worked feverishly to complete the pier
structure out into the ocean and the framework of a boat house built
in the exact likeness of the real one on the edge of the Bay in Munising,
Michigan, and reproduced on Stage Six in Hollywood.

René La Grange and another task force, including René Jr., had
cut again into the island light source emanating from the one main
generator in the center of town. There were small lights hidden along
the pier, and David Thayer's board lights, three sets of them now,
were ready to work in the interior of the boat house.

Steve had asked Rene for the only "cherry picker" on the island,
which was used for street light repairs, telegraph pole work, and any
other odd jobs that needed a high, movable piece of machinery.

The cherry picker had become Steve's crane, the only conceivable
way that he could get a high, moving boom. David, with his handheld
camera, was already lashed onto the top of it. He was testing the moves
controlled by the cherry picker operator on the ground. The machine
extended high over the top of the framework boat house.

David was rehearsing Steve's opening shot, coming down literally
out of the sky into the interior of the boat house, which, like the boat
house on the bay, had a ceiling that could be rolled back for warm
days and nights. The lighting effect David had created inside the boat
house was one of natural light and shadow. By using the three boards

with eight globes shining from each, a natural moonlight effect had been created.

Every citizen of St. Venetia who could walk or ride was on the location. René had given orders that none of them was to approach within twenty-five feet of the boat house. They would not be able to watch the actual shooting. The scene was too difficult to have any onlookers who weren't closely involved in filming it.

The crowd was caught up in the wonderment of the cherry picker, the cameraman actually tied to the very top of it with his handheld camera, another position just under the cameraman prepared for the director. It all seemed confused, crazy, but exciting. It was magic time on St. Venetia.

Far down the shore Steve walked away from the crowds with Stephanie and Rayme, near the edge of the water. The last rays of the sunset streaked across the sky. The voices of the workmen and the crew and the crowds could no longer be heard, only the movement of the ocean and the last of the gull feeders swooping down to try to find their final meal of the day.

Stephanie was tense.

"The first shooting schedule said we'd do this scene the third week. Then it got pushed back, and pushed back again. I can't believe we're finally shooting it."

"The reason I kept pushing it back was to give you two more time," Steve said. "This is one of the most difficult scenes in the film. It has a delicate line—one we've talked about all the way through—it culminates in this scene."

Rayme looked at Stephanie and back at Steve.

"Michael really would like to make love to her," Rayme said. "He can't quite admit it but there has always been that attraction for him. That's what I get from the way we've been developing these characters—Michael and Christina have always had this thing for each other—it's built into them—and this is the moment when it almost happens."

"But, of course, they can't really become lovers," Stephanie said, looking at Rayme. "They know that—they've accepted that—and still, they can't stop the feelings."

"That's exactly what we have to have on film," Steve said. "Their underlying passion for each other—and the subtle way they defend themselves against it. Your relationship—the relationship between Michael and Christina—is only part of this complicated family—and what family isn't complicated?

"This is all we're going to shoot until daylight comes," Steve went on. "We've got ten hours.

"I'm going to cover everything tonight. The master shot. Over-shoulders. Close-ups.

"I'm not going in any particular order. When I feel that you both have it, I'm going to move in for the close-ups right then, because this sequence is going to be emotionally exhausting for you.

"If you get tired, tell me. We'll rest. If you are uncomfortable with any move or any line, tell me. I'll listen to your ideas and I'll try to work out something that is good for me and comfortable for you.

"And forget all these people around here. I couldn't tell them that they had to leave because they're part of our crew now—our support chain—and we couldn't keep filming without them.

"But inside that boat house, every person not working, I'm going to ask to leave the set. I want you to screen out every one of us—me included.

"This is you two—Christina and Michael—and," he glanced at both of them, "Stephanie and Rayme. Use your relationship—what you both have been through—what you both feel," he paused, "or don't feel—about each other. Just be open and let it happen. Do you trust me?"

"Sure," Rayme answered.

Stephanie looked at him.

"Completely," she said.

"I wouldn't lie to you. I've never tried to con you. In spite of the fact that this is the first film you've ever made, both of you, I had this strong feeling about you. I felt you were right for these parts and that you would understand Christina and Michael Garibaldi, feel for them, and merge with them. I've delayed this scene until I felt you were ready for it. I know you're ready now. You can give me everything I need on screen. You can capture what's said—and, more important, what isn't—" He paused.

"Remember, the camera picks up every thought, every feeling. Michael and Christina belong to you now."

7

Mayerling

ichael recognized the theme from *Mayerling*. The music was coming from the boat house at the end of the pier at the edge of the lake; he knew what it meant. She was there. *Mayerling* had been Christina's favorite ballet, perhaps because she seemed born to play it. She had been only two years younger than the tragic heroine of the real story when she danced it with the American Ballet Company with Baryshnikov as Prince Rudolf. It had been just before her crippling accident.

Michael hadn't walked down that pier since he'd turned his back on his father's plans for him and gone out on the road, on his own, as a hired guitarist in a rock band.

The boat house had been Michael and Christina's playroom. Their mother loved to spend time there, too: she would play the piano and they would all sing different songs—the old classics, funny songs, the popular hits of the day. Angela was musical and had passed that onto her children. Barbara had played the piano with her mother; Michael, guitar; Christina, electric guitar and banjo.

As Michael walked down the pier, the music grew louder. What was she doing there? Only a few hours before, she had been in a half coma. The doctor hadn't lied when he'd said she'd only be mildly sedated!

The glass doors facing the lake were open to the water and the sliding frame ceiling of the roof had been pulled back so that the night sky and the moon and the stars were directly over the boat house interior.

Michael saw the faint image of a woman in white spinning in nearly

perfect ballet form past the window. He remembered the steps he'd
seen Christina practice when she was a little girl. It had been their
mother's dream, as well as Christina's, that one day she would dance
the part of the lovely and tragic young Austrian girl, destroyed by her
own passion, in the true story of *Mayerling*.

Was this the way it was going to end for his sister? Lost in a tunnel
of confusion, grabbing desperately at memories, her spirit broken? He
was scared. He knew where the course of her disease would take her
if she didn't accept help. Christina, like himself, was an addictive
personality, which meant that if it weren't cocaine, it would be something else. Alcohol, pills, a new drug mixture or invention—they were
all interchangeable once you'd crossed the invisible line into drug
addiction.

Michael had seen it all from the time he broke in with Janis Joplin's
band. He had played a year with Janis and another two years as fourth
guitarist for Jimi Hendrix. Everywhere he turned, there were drugs,
and he, too, had fallen for their seduction. The powerhouse of un-
resolved feelings between him and his father, the unmet expectations
that his father would give him his blessings, if not his support, everything left unsaid between him and his sister, his guilt over abandoning
her and Lissa and his little boy in Haiti—all this and more became
much less painful when the drugs hit his bloodstream, much less
important, much less real. But Michael quickly found it to be only a
temporary euphoria. He'd sought help, and gotten off drugs for good.

Alcoholism and drug addiction were an accepted way of life in the
entertainment profession. So many dead, like Janis and Jimi. So many
stupefied out of their senses. So many brilliant talents extinguished.

He hadn't known that Christina had become a drug addict. He
hadn't seen her for more than three years, and he knew he'd stayed
away from her purposefully. God, if he'd only had an inkling. Now
he felt tremendously guilty that he could have done something before
it had gone this far.

He and Christina had been opposite sides of the same coin, different
only in age. How many times they'd talked about it, in this boat house,
at night, just like this with the ceiling pulled back and the seaward
doors open. Playing their records, dancing together, blending their
guitars—blending their lives.

But when Christina had begun to grow into a woman, the quiet
passion of their relationship frightened Michael. Somehow, his feelings
as a brother had been dwarfed by his feelings as a man. And there was
no one to talk to about it.

He had rushed into affairs with girls at school even when he was very young. But no one compared to Christina.

She had hated the girls he went out with. He remembered that now, and couldn't understand why he hadn't gotten help for both of them. They had never made love, but the bond was there—strange and frightening.

He had been shocked by the extent of his feelings when Christina had told him she had made love with his best friend, Jimmy Keefer. The thought of his sister being intimate with any man, especially his best friend, was unbearable to Michael.

And he remembered in this boat house the day he confronted her with it and she had said, blazing at him, "You did it, so I did it, too. You didn't like it, well, I don't like you sleeping around either. I always thought you'd wait—for someone who deserved you, someone beautiful and elegant, who really loved you. Someone who'd be part of our family. But you couldn't wait—well, I couldn't either."

Michael had looked at her helplessly. He didn't understand what they were feeling. What he did know was that they were too close, and that he couldn't handle it.

This relationship had driven him away, the fear of it, the fear of himself. He hadn't called Christina when he was on the road all those years. Once in a while he wrote a letter, but he'd had to put it all behind him and find himself.

Now, home again after all this time, all of his family brought together by the threat to their careers and their personal lives, he had found everything between him and his sister almost unchanged. When he saw her on fire with the drugs, refusing to eat, her violent mood swings and her defensiveness about everything, his emotions took him back into their childhood, and he knew that he still cared more about Christina than he did about anyone else in the world. Looking at her was like looking at himself. Her pain was his pain. Her defeats were his own.

Michael walked around the edge of the boat house. The moonlight was streaming in through the open space and down through the open ceiling.

She didn't see him. And the view of the room, where so much that he remembered of his childhood had taken place, with Christina dancing through it, deeply moved him.

The furniture was the same. Numerous family photographs—of holidays, the sailboat on the lake, everyone grouped around the piano with their instruments.

Christina in her first tutu. Christina at the Balanchine School. Her first meeting with Mikhail Baryshnikov. His mother and father on their wedding day. He'd forgotten how beautiful his mother was. His father waving at the wheel of the Centurion. Barbara graduating from high school, her large, serious eyes staring out at the world. Michael only skirted over photographs of himself. It was as though if he stared hard enough at the pictures of the others, he could bridge the gap of these years they'd all been strangers.

On the wall, preserved and framed, were Chris's first ballet shoes. His eyes went to his sister's feet, as she spun around in her satin slippers. He shifted his gaze upward. She had on one of her first ballet costumes—she could still fit into it—the one from *Mayerling*, which had been kept along with all her leotards and shoes in her own special closet in the boat house.

Suddenly, Michael realized she was dancing at full strength, on a short-lived high—the crest of the cocaine still in her bloodstream.

She was in a dream. Her knees would hold up for one performance, the last act of *Mayerling*. Her own life had blended with the classic story, and she was dancing out her death in ballet.

Michael stood in the shadows, looking at the beauty of his sister, and the grace and fragility of her dancing. The critics had raved about "the most delicate, pure, and fragile dancer since Gelsey Kirkland." She and Gelsey had been the bright, promising prima ballerinas of tomorrow before the sensational debut of Alessandra Ferri. Gelsey Kirkland, too, had become addicted to drugs, but that was after, perhaps even a result of, her great success. For Christina, there'd been one missed step, and her career had been over.

Now she was before him, dancing in and out of the rays of the moonlight, dancing in their playroom, surrounded by memories.

Michael stayed in the shadows as she came to the climax of the ballet. Her death in *Mayerling* was unforgettable; Kenneth MacMillan had staged it. In the final build of the music, Christina soared upward, an airborne figure of the sky, like a fragile and delicate bird that had been shot. She seemed to pause, suspended in the air. Then, in middair, she disintegrated, limb by limb, her breath coming faster.

There was a gasp in her throat. Her eyelids trembled. The corners of her mouth pinched in. She was fighting to live. But a tremor shook her body as she fell to the ground, killed by her royal lover, in the famous double suicide.

She lay on the floor, quite still. The ecstasy of her love was in her face. The music died away, too. Only the softness of the wind coming off the lake and the sounds of the night birds high in flight could be heard.

"Chris," Michael whispered. She opened her eyes slowly, still in the mood of *Mayerling*, not quite sure whether she herself was alive or dead. She looked at Michael as though he were an apparition. He knelt by her side and took her in his arms.

"Are you really here?" Christina asked.

Michael nodded. There were tears in his eyes. "That's the most beautiful dance I've ever seen." He embraced her and she clung to him. He picked her up in his arms and carried her to the edge of the porch, looking out over the lake.

"Are you going away again, Michael?" she asked. "Are you all going to leave me again?"

"I'd only heard about how much fun you were having. My famous jet-set sister, whom other women admired, and envied, and copied. I thought you were on top of the world, Chris, looking down on the rest of us."

Christina's eyes met his. "But I never even really left home. I never left the boat house."

"You won't be without your family again," Michael said. "We'll be behind you."

"But you see, it's too late," she said. "The rest of you have made something of yourselves—you're doing important things—you're winners—and I've already lost."

"No," Michael said. "No, you haven't." He started back along the pier toward the rambling old house on the lake. He carried her close.

8

New York

The head table for the press conference was divided into two sections. Jack Gregson was on one side, flanked by four lawyers, his own, MGL's counsel, and two other specialists. On the other side of the platform, Spartan Lee sat with Edmund Bradford Wilson, Jake Powers, and a research specialist from Wilson's office.

Gregson was finishing a long, carefully structured tirade against Steve Wayland. He was not going to attack Rayme Monterey; he had let the district attorney do that the day before. But now Gregson was giving in to his hatred.

"Steve Wayland has, in effect, stolen a film that belongs to the studio and is in the process of being made with studio money.

"I want the stockholders at MGL to know that we are serving notice with the Steve Wayland case on all filmmakers who think that they have free access to other people's money. We're serving notice on those superegos of filmmaking who believe they can get away with anything no matter what the cost.

"I can tell you for certain, ladies and gentlemen, that *The Rest of Our Lives* will not be a loss to MGL because we have a completion bond of over two million dollars worth of Steve Wayland's property—that's the only way we'd let him make the film. And that's the way I believe in handling these superegos. If they want control of a motion picture, then they've got to put their money on the line.

"Frankly, I don't think there's any way that this film will be finished. Now the production is without studio money or equipment.

"To the stockholders I say this—with this film, we have written off two other commitments with Wayland which could have cost us another twenty million dollars. That was a contract I inherited. I would never have made it.

"Between the tax write-off of the losses from this picture and the money that we will collect on Wayland's properties put up for completion, we will not cost the stockholders of MGL a single dollar, and we will have saved twenty million.

"Today, in Hollywood, Wayland's collateral is being legally seized and put into escrow until the end of this story. It cannot be sold or mortgaged.

"We expect, with the cooperation of the New York District Attorney's office, to have a warrant for arrest served and executed on Steve Wayland in St. Venetia within the next few days."

The press was in an uproar. This was a story almost as spectacular as the district attorney's the day before. The room gradually quieted as Spartan Lee stood up. He acknowledged the greetings of several reporters in the front rows whom he knew.

"Ladies and gentlemen, I believe this conflict represents much more than a single motion picture. I have many interests and several careers that have survived moderately well." There was a whisper of amusement among the reporters. Spartan continued. "Many great experiences were given to people all over the world by MGL and the other big studios for admission prices that even people as poor as my family could afford. Many of the most memorable moments of my life surround us here today."

He gestured toward the large photographs of classic MGL films on the wall.

"As this great company has been ripped apart by one conglomerate competitor after another, as the magnificent trademark tiger's teeth have been sawed away and his tail tied down, I as an observer and a member of the world film audience have been shocked.

"That's what this case is about, ladies and gentlemen. Some of the assumptions of conglomerate management are going to be brought to the test.

"We intend to challenge high-handed acts by certain executive heads of motion pictures against what we have heard here described as the egomaniacal filmmakers.

"History proves, ladies and gentlemen, that all the way up the ladder, from a family, to a company, to a country, and ultimately in the world political arena, ethics must become an equal value on both sides. Integrity must be present on both sides. I'm remembering a recent issue of *Time* magazine. The cover story. 'Whatever happened to ethics?' the cover read. 'Assaulted by sleaze, scandals, and hypocrisy, America is searching for its moral bearings.'

"I think what we're discussing here begins with the question of ethics." He turned to Jack Gregson. "Mr. Gregson—Edmund Bradford Wilson, who will be Steven Wayland's defense attorney, representing him against all the charges you have brought, has some very interesting questions to raise about this case."

Wilson stood up to speak to the press.

"I'm sure every one of you has heard of 'best efforts,' " he said. "They long have been an integral part of most motion picture contracts. Artists are promised best efforts. Accounting procedures are described as best efforts. Studio approvals and time limits are covered under best efforts.

"I don't believe I'm exaggerating when I say that this case which has sprung up so suddenly among us that we've not yet had the proper time for research and study—" he turned towards Gregson, "—is going to be a legal catalyst in the motion picture industry. I'm glad it's taking place in New York City, with easy access to Wall Street and the great money-managing concerns which traditionally have invested in and backed motion pictures.

"But beginning clear back in the early part of this century, when a group of inspired men fell in love with motion pictures, mostly men without money, many of them not fully educated, but all of them bright, street-smart, and carrying a dream, motion pictures began in New York and traveled west. The linkage between the East and West in motion pictures has always been fragile. The business end has distrusted the creative side. The creative side has distrusted the businessmen. There rarely has been a superstructure covering the coast-to-coast activities."

Wilson gestured to three large stacks of memoranda on his desk in front of him. "I have here on the desk in front of me, and there will be copies for all of you, a statement from my office, which is based on the research of my top analysts, Bruce Wiseman and Kevin Burke." He gestured to the two men on his right.

"Mr. Wiseman, Mr. Burke and their staff have been analyzing the contract between Jack Gregson Productions, Inc., Mager-Golden-Lasky, and my client, Steve Wayland, and his company, Steve Wayland Productions. This report takes into consideration the original contract that a previous management of Mager-Golden-Lasky signed with Mr.

Wayland, as well as all the agreements up to the present moment that
have been attached to it since its inception.

"Mr. Gregson—" he turned towards Gregson again, "—has taken
the posture both yesterday, at the district attorney's office, and today,
in this Mager-Golden-Lasky conference hall, so vibrating with the
illustrious past of this company, of a man in the right who has been
outraged, lied to, and robbed. He has talked about *his* company, *his*
picture, *his* money.

"This document, ladies and gentlemen—" he picked up a copy and
gestured with it, "—this document raises serious questions about Mr.
Gregson's statements.

"Do you know, for instance, that there are fifty-two owners of *The
Rest of Our Lives* apart from Gregson Films International, and apart
from MGL and all its stockholders? According to the contract signed
by Jack Gregson, Steve Wayland Productions, Inc., owns fifty percent
of *The Rest of Our Lives*. Mr. Wayland has divided that percentage,
which is his contractual right, into fifty-two shares. Every member of
the cast and crew of *The Rest of Our Lives* has a percentage of ownership
and net profits in *The Rest of Our Lives*.

"Here we have, then, a motion picture which is owned not by Mr.
Jack Gregson personally, or Mr. Steve Wayland personally, but, on
each side, in fact, by many people, including every company share-
holder," he glanced at Gregson, "to whom Mr. Gregson is accountable.

"Mr. Gregson, who is so possessive about *The Rest of Our Lives*,
owns a very small percentage of the film as a stockholder of Mager-
Golden-Lasky. His company, Gregson Films International, owns a
sizable amount of stock, but his own percentage of the whole is min-
imal.

"We will challenge legally that the contracts with Mr. Gregson do
not give him control over the people who have ownership participation
and net profit participation, and who own the copyright.

"If our position proves to be correct, Mr. Gregson will be sued, I
can promise you, by my client and his company for his failure to meet
contractual obligations, and, additionally, we will seek punitive damages for a staggering amount of money.

"We are going to get to the bottom of the very foundations of ethical
practice in this case, ladies and gentlemen. We are going to call for
the record books and the accounting books of three other pictures that
Mr. Wayland has made for this company. We are going to delve into

every detail of this contract. We are going to determine a legal definition of 'best efforts,' and then the law—the law, ladies and gentlemen, *not* Jack Gregson—will determine whether or not 'best efforts' have been applied ethically in the best interests of *The Rest of Our Lives* and *all* of its owners.

"We intend to prove that Mr. Jack Gregson never wanted to make *The Rest of Our Lives*. That he tried to prevent the picture from being made. That he is presently trying to keep the picture from being completed. That he has already recommended to his staff and to his company that the film be written off as a tax loss and that procedures be instituted immediately to foreclose Mr. Wayland's home, his screenplays, his story rights, and his residuals in the films he has made in a fourteen-year career.

"We intend to prove that Mr. Gregson is, in fact, waging a personal vendetta against Steve Wayland. We will show that in doing so, in attempting to destroy a respectable career and to damage a man's reputation in the community at large as well as across the country and abroad, Mr. Gregson has betrayed the intent and prestige of the company he works for.

"Severe charges have been made against my client. Sufficient testimony has been given to the district attorney to obtain a warrant of arrest on the charges. The leverage of Wall Street and conglomerate and computerized big business has been used by Mr. Gregson without full disclosure of the facts.

"Can one single man, one filmmaker without exceptional power, stand up against the Jack Gregsons and the corporate steamrollers behind them, and fight for his legal rights? That issue is at stake here."

He turned to Gregson again. "Yes," he said, "Mr. Gregson, yes, it is the right of a single man to stand up and have his chance and his day no matter what the powers are against him. The law, which I am proud is my profession, deals in truth and justice and ethics at its best. Sometimes the people that execute the law fail. But the law is still there.

"Ladies and gentlemen, I can tell you that I believe that my client, Steve Wayland, is completely innocent, in general terms, of each of Mr. Gregson's accusations. Not serving the company shareholders to the very best of his ability? Absolutely not. Not trying to make *The Rest of Our Lives* a profitable and good picture for the studio? Absolutely not. He has put everything he owns on the line for this film, for himself and for everyone who owns one single part of it.

"In a case like this, American law allows severe punitive damages.

I've already stated that we will seek to be redressed. And I want to assure you, Mr. Gregson, that we will go for every dollar.

"You have said that it is your purpose to eliminate a 'minor irritation,' as I believe you call him. You call Steve Wayland a minor irritation—those words will come back to haunt you, Mr. Gregson. Mr. Wayland may be on trial, but I predict there will be a different kind of finish to this case.

"This case goes beyond Mr. Wayland. This case relates to every man or woman in the world of motion pictures, in the world of art, who doesn't have great power but who cares about his work and is willing to take chances, on his own, to create something of value.

"Mr. Gregson, you say that Steve Wayland will never bring back a film that can be distributed. You publicly labeled *The Rest of Our Lives* a disaster before it even started. You have done everything to slander the film and destroy it as a commercial enterprise for your own company, to which you are accountable.

"And to accomplish your purpose of disgracing Steve Wayland, you have deliberately forced him to leave the country to finish his film. You say he won't finish. Ladies and gentlemen, we shall see!"

9

St. Venetia

The thunderous storm struck St. Venetia hard. The television reports coming in from Cannes and the French government channel in Paris said it was going to get worse before it got better. The Paris anchorman said it could grow into hurricane proportions.

Barricades and temporary dikes were going up all along the French coast. The wind was blowing at gale speeds. The temperature was dropping. There would be no ferries between Cannes and St. Venetia.

On the second floor of the government building, Steve was watching René's blurred and interrupted television set. Roberto, Boris, Gaylin, and Lieu were with him. René Jr. sat beside his father.

Everyone looked at Steve. No one in the room had to say what they knew was a fact. *The Rest of Our Lives* couldn't afford to lose one day in its schedule, much less a week. And a week's storm was what was being predicted. Steve leaned back in his chair.

"We've only got the cover sets for today. Not enough."

He turned to René Sr. "René, have you seen it this bad before?"

"Twice," René said. "Once the water came over a good part of the island. The other time the storm rained out just before it became a hurricane."

"How long?" Steve asked.

"Five days," René answered.

Steve went to the big window of the governor's office where he had first looked out on the lights of St. Venetia. He opened the window. The wind blew rain into the office. Steve slammed the window shut. He turned to Roberto.

"Is David ready to shoot?" he said.

"He's expecting our call," Roberto said. He turned to René Jr. "That truck you got us this morning, René, the grocery truck—it really worked well. It's now our camera truck and it's packed with everything we have." Roberto glanced at Steve. "David told me before I left the hotel, 'If I know Steve,' he said, 'we'll be shooting tonight in this storm, just around the time everybody'll have decided it's impossible.' "

Steve laughed. "Well, we've got to try. Roberto—Boris—this rain has one advantage for us," he said.

Boris scowled. "What, for God's sake?"

Steve pointed to the window. "Look out there. If we're shooting in this stuff, you could be anywhere. You could be in New York City, Los Angeles, or St. Venetia. We need these opportunities.

"Roberto, we're going to do two scenes tonight with Magdalena. Tell Bill Thomas I want everything he's got to keep her warm—one of the scenes is exterior. Two eighty-one."

Roberto made a quick notation in his notebook. "Long underwear if possible—whatever size—it doesn't matter," Steve continued. "I won't be shooting her feet. I want her insulated under this rain.

"When she starts out in the station wagon, I want her perfectly made up and her hair done. Tell Clare I want the makeup so that it will come apart and wash off her face in the rain—not too quickly—would you tell Clare also that I want her with us all night. And the hairdresser we picked up from the village, too."

Boris spoke up. "How are you going to shoot her driving the station wagon? We don't have any mock-ups and we don't have any dollies."

"Oh, yes, we do," Steve said. He turned to René Jr. "Did you finish those triple sleds for me with the roller skates underneath?"

"The workmen finished an hour ago," René Jr. said.

"Did they put rubber wheels on the outside of the skating wheels?" Steve asked. René Jr. nodded.

Steve walked toward the door. He looked at René Sr. "Your crew number three hasn't been called on yet. Can you get them to work all night? I need a constant flow of people—like a human chain—between the hotel and where we're working on the road. Hot soup, coffee, tea. We've got to keep our people as warm as possible." He turned to René Jr. "How many beach umbrellas do you have?"

"Ten," René Jr. answered.

"Roberto will show you where we're going to shoot. I want the road to the point, Roberto, the one that leads to the Chapel of St. Thérèse. We'll start there with the truck. We'll use the sleds for dollies. We'll use them when Magdalena gets out of the station wagon and starts to walk. Try and tie down some of these umbrellas for the camera crew and the actors.

"Boris, do you have the gravestones in place?"

"The family plot has been prepared," Boris answered, "and one side of the church exterior revamped. In this rain it will look like the Bay Village chapel if you only shoot it from one direction."

"I'll watch it. Thanks, Boris. Let's go—we're wasting time."

10

Hôtel La Terrasse, St. Venetia

The driving rain outside the large, double-doored windows pounded into the glass like bullet shots. Barbara Garibaldi was on the phone, pacing the width of the room.

"When did she go on the hunger strike, Ted?" Barbara asked.

"The night you left," Barbara's ex-husband answered over the phone. "She's refused to eat since then. The old symptoms are coming on strong now."

"Did you call the doctor?" Barbara asked.

"He was here last night. He says there are two choices now. Hospitalize her again, or the promise of extended time with you. When you can set her mind at rest about everything that's happened."

"Is that really what he said?" Barbara asked.

"I wouldn't make up anything at this point, Barb. Both children were counting on this time with you—of course, Melly needs it more than Stewart does right now, but they just don't know what's coming up. School is hell for them. All the notoriety and questions—I'm keeping them out until you come home."

"But their tests," Barbara said. "You know how important . . ."

"I know one thing is important right now," Ted answered. "For the kids and you. Time. Do you realize, Barb, how little time they've had with you, one on one, in this last year of campaigning? Your demands and expectations are already there, talked about and written about. But they need to know you believe in them and love them no matter what. That's what they're missing, Barb, and what they've been missing, really, for a long time."

"I've tried my best to be a good mother, Ted," Barbara's confidence in herself was slipping. Her voice lacked conviction. "I've been there for them."

"Not always, Barb. There have been times when they needed you and you couldn't be there. You were on the road and you were going after what you wanted—but the doctor says this is a kind of crossroads now, with what happened with your election—moving to Washington—separating from their friends—changing schools—most of all not knowing where they stand with you. You've got a new job and a new boyfriend and a new life—they have to know what their parts are. Barb, I'm telling you, you've got to come home."

"I've got to make some important decisions tonight. Tell them I will be calling later and that I love them." She hung up the phone. She stared out at the rain. She was shaking. There was a knock on her door, and then her father came in.

Eric hadn't slept all night. They looked at each other. Neither one wanted to open the conversation. They both looked haggard.

"I've got Bill Donnelly coming in tomorrow. Whatever you decide, he'll carry out the details." Eric paused. "Have you decided, Barb? You know how important it is for all of us."

"I'll decide before Bill gets here," Barbara answered. "I feel like I'm cracking up. I was so sure before this weekend—now I just talked to Ted. I thought the children were in really good shape but they're not. I'm questioning everything I've worked so hard to accomplish but, I hate to admit it, I don't want to give it up either."

"Barb, I've made so many mistakes—they all seem to have come home to me this weekend, too," Eric said. "Gut level, I've never known any of you three children—maybe not your mother either—I thought I did—but this weekend it's . . . well, it's like we're all talking for the first time—from inside—and I realize now that all I really have left are the three of you. Susan is there but she's not my heritage— you children are—and your children.

"I thought I had a family, but it's been in name only. I can't go back. I've missed so much all these years because, well, I just don't know how to say what I feel to the people I love. I never have been able to do it, just to say a simple 'I love you.' I can barely get the words out."

Barbara looked at him. "You just said it."

"What do we do, Barb?"

"I thought I knew, too," she said. She suddenly burst into tears as she embraced her father. He held her close.

11

The Storm

arbara was trembling as she steered the station wagon through the driving rain.

Boris and his crew had redone the station wagon so that it matched, from certain angles, the one used at the Bay House location in Michigan. The wheels had been taken off. Gaylin and his St. Venetia workmen had placed the body of the station wagon on four wooden boxes at exactly the same level as if the tires had remained on the car. He and Roberto had manipulated two headlights with cords on a flat wooden piece, separated the exact distance as car headlights. They passed the headlights back and forth, rehearsing a rhythmic path which they varied every few seconds. The effect of passing cars was perfect.

David had lined up his camera outside the windshield. Steve stretched out on the hood of the station wagon body, his face just behind David's camera.

"Frank," Steve called to Frank Warner, "Frank, I'm not going to try live sound sync with the camera. So it's all your creation. I want you to record every sound you hear in this storm."

"I've already been over on the other side of the island this afternoon," Frank answered. "I've got a hundred tracks of this storm locked up."

Steve turned back to David. "Will the sleds work? Can you tie down the hand-held on it?"

"I just tried one," David said. "It's going to be a little tough, but we can move."

"We've got to have a close lens on her when she gets out of the station wagon. This sequence must be from the inside out. What does Barbara feel?"

He turned to René a few feet away. "Your men ready?"

A smile split René's face and his green eyes twinkled.

"Thought you'd never ask, Mon Capitaine," René answered. He motioned to the three other men who were standing behind him sipping coffee. He gestured to them and they went to the car with him, two on each side.

Steve slid off the hood and put his face inside the car, through the narrow slit of window space left open. "Are you warm enough, Maggie?" he asked. She nodded.

Steve slid back up on the hood of the car. "Windshield wipers," he said. One of the crew from St. Venetia put the plug in. Steve smiled when the windshield wipers worked perfectly.

He called out to René. "René, just a soft roll, the way a car does on a night like this as the wind's blowing it. Don't make it too big. Let's see what you can do."

René and his crew of three picked the station wagon up off the wood blocks.

"Not that much," Steve said.

René motioned to the men and they lowered the car back, then started to roll it softly.

Steve looked in the finder. "Gaylin," he shouted through the night rain, "let me see the light board now." Gaylin moved the light board in an irregular pattern. Perfectly spaced headlights picked up the reflection shooting in the windshield.

"Looks good. Put the pins on." In the lens, Steve saw the pins light up Magdalena's eyes. David had fixed them on the lower part of the dashboard. No matter where she moved her head, sitting there, the pin lights hit her eyes.

"Everybody ready?" Steve asked. All points checked in: Roberto, Gaylin, Charlie, René with his team of weight lifters, Boris.

"Roll," Steve said. David flicked the camera switch to begin. René and his men started to roll the car. Gaylin moved his headlight light board in a realistic pattern.

Barbara turned the car on the road. The rain was hitting the lens of the camera. David watched as small capsules of water burst open, turning many colors in the golden, reflected lights and through it. Barbara's face, sometimes clear, sometimes through the rain itself, according to where the windshield wiper was, was touched with every kind of diffusion. It was an effect that no gauze could duplicate, no special filter could match. It changed constantly, bubbles of soft pastel light tracking across one part of her face, sometimes obscuring it but never covering the eyes because of David's pinpoints.

Frank Warner was stretched out on a sled mounted on wheels. He was moving under the back of the car, out of sight of the camera, but recording every possible variation of the storm: the storm hitting the car, the storm hitting the windshield, rain driving into the ground.

Steve saw him from the corner of his eye, his feet pointed upward, his sound equipment resting on his chest, while Roberto pushed his sled underneath the car.

Inside the car, Barbara saw none of this. There were forty people from the original crew out there and twenty-five from St. Venetia. It was two o'clock in the morning and St. Venetia was in the center of a storm of hurricane proportions.

Barbara was stopping her car. As Steve orchestrated it with his right hand, René and his men brought the station wagon out of exaggerated movement till it was still. Gaylin kept swinging his light board in varied rhythms. Other cars on the road were moving. Barbara's station wagon was "parked" on the side of the road.

She reached into her pocketbook and took out a scarf. She tied it around her chin, pulled her raincoat up around her, and moved to her left to get out of the station wagon.

"Cut," Steve said.

He looked at David.

"I think it was terrific. How'd it look in there, David?" he asked.

The hardest part was coming. She would have to be out there on the road in the driving rain, her hair and makeup destroyed, her clothes heavy and soggy on her back. Her eyes would have to tell the story.

12

The Chapel Hillside

arbara came to the crest of the hill where the chapel stood high above the edge of the water. Steve kept her between David's handheld camera and the one revamped wall of the church.

Boris and his group of St. Venetia craftsmen had built a wooden-framed side in the early-American style of country chapels. It had the look of American primitive. The rust of the aged French chapel was not visible in the driving rain and the edges of the other sides of the chapel were kept out of frame by David Thayer.

There were over a hundred tombstones in the churchyard of the chapel. They were only shadows in the storm, grayed and blackened with years of weathering. Here and there, a solitary tree swayed in the wind and rainstorm.

David looked at Barbara Garibaldi as she made her way toward the small family plot that Boris had prepared. He was making a medium shot, with Gaylin guiding him from behind, steadying his body as he moved through mud on the strips of wood buried slightly below the surface of the ground. The camera was tied to him with a Panaglide harness. Gaylin had tied extra ropes from the sides of the camera across David's chest so that the camera could resist the full impact of the storm.

Barbara came to the edge of the Garibaldi family plot. David moved in close on her face, step by step, Gaylin guiding him on the wooden planks underneath the mud. Barbara's face filled the camera frame.

She looked down at the headstones. The wooden frame of the bay chapel was etched in the night sky behind her. You couldn't see the details, but the feeling was there. The feeling of age, tradition, continuity of generations. Families gathered there in the final resting place known to this existence, but together, in a defiant gesture that said the feeling of a real family went on and on—that traditions were passed down—legacies, not only of property, but of love and faith.

These deep feelings were in Barbara's eyes, as she looked down at her family's graves. Two generations of Garibaldis were there now. It was the largest plot in the small graveyard. There was room for the family that was alive, and generations to follow.

David's handheld camera followed Barbara's eyes and moved from headstone to headstone. The Garibaldi past. An immigrant family, buried together, as Americans, in their country of choice. The headstones were aged and weathered like the stones that marked the other graves.

David's camera moved in slowly on the gravestone marking the last resting place of Angela Garibaldi. David let the rain wash out the colors in his camera finder in a dissolve, and then he moved his camera slowly up to Barbara's face. Her makeup had been completely soaked away. Her face was alabaster white. Her hair was dripping underneath her scarf.

Her eyes were filled with the memories of her mother. Her mouth formed the words. The beams of light faded in and out with the rain. The effect was not unlike the coming and going of memories over Barbara's face.

David moved into a tight shot of Barbara's face that would fill a projection screen.

"I don't know what to do, Mother," she whispered. "I need to talk to you. I need your help with this decision.

"I'm proud I won—I worked hard—I fought hard—I know I have some good ideas—I think I can be useful. I think I can leave a legacy like you did for me. You're alive, Mother, through all of us you touched. You changed our lives. Finally, I think I've found a way to help other people, too—but how can I hurt Dad, and Christina and Michael—how can I do that? Whatever they want to drag out about me, I'd go with it—I wouldn't look forward to it, but what they've got on me is all in the past, and what I did, I did out of feelings—I could talk about that—I could even answer questions about it—but about my family—I don't know—I've asked myself, 'What would *you* do, if you were here?'—and that is the answer I need to have—if I can only feel that I'm doing what you would do . . . ."

13

Beverly Hills

"There's only one solution, Jack," said the short, gray-haired lawyer who had represented Gregson for many years, as he leaned back in his chair, pushed his glasses up on his forehead, and rubbed his eyes. "You can't let *The Rest of Our Lives* be completed in any kind of final form. It's all over the industry now. Very few pictures this year will have the publicity this film is getting. I spoke to Paris, London, and Rome this morning. Film people are talking about nothing else. I understand reporters literally from all over the world are waiting in Cannes for the storm to subside so they can get over to St. Venetia. This picture is going to be covered, everything about it.

"You know how jaded this business is—and here they have a story that's fresh and exciting—the sad truth, Jack, is that you've given Wayland an opportunity to become a martyr, a hero, to the outside world and to the film industry itself. He's got the best kind of legal advice, and Spartan Lee and Edmund Bradford Wilson give a legitimacy to this whole thing. They wouldn't be supporting a crook or a bum. You have to recognize that, Jack."

"But everything collapses," Gregson said, "if Wayland can't finish the picture—if there's really nothing of any releasable nature to show."

The lawyer turned to his left and gazed out the window. He always did that when he was worried. Gregson picked up on it, and it didn't help to reassure him.

"If he has some kind of film to auction off for distribution on the date he's set—" began the lawyer, but Gregson cut him off.

"He can't have anything ready to show in two weeks—how the hell's he going to score the picture? How's he going to dub it? No way."

The lawyer swung his chair back from the window and faced Gregson.

"I don't know anything about the mechanics of making a picture. But I've talked to Lee and Wilson myself. As I said a moment ago, you don't win the belief of men like that without balls, Jack. I think we've got to face it. Wayland just might bring it off.

"You know damn well the whole MGL organization has been in turmoil for years. It's been dribbled around the economic world like a goddamn basketball. And people are angry. More than any other company, MGL has always had a huge family out there, and I'm not talking about stockholders. MGL has been Hollywood, all over the world. And people who went to MGL movies felt they had a stake in that studio. There's going to be a lot of trouble, I think, about MGL—if nothing else, a definite effect on the public. After all, motion pictures owe the public something. And they need to give it to them if they're to hold a big part of their audience," the lawyer said.

"Now you don't know what the hell's going to happen to MGL and I don't either. I know personally of two big foreign groups that are bidding to buy the studio right now."

"Jack, you can come out of this as a brilliant executive who had the courage to close down a picture that couldn't pay off for the studio. But if the picture works, with that buy-back letter Spartan has, if somebody comes up on that auction day in a few weeks and puts up the cash MGL has in the film, and if by some chance the picture should turn out as a success for another company, you'll be backed in a corner.

"This is developing into a Rocky story. The picture simply must not be in any shape to play at that auction. With all the publicity—" he lifted his hands, "—you know your business better than I do, Jack, but you can see for yourself what the newspapers and television are making out of this. And it's a hell of a story!"

Gregson stood up. "By your own admission, you don't have any concept of what it takes to make a picture, even when you're shooting at the studio and you've got hundreds of people helping you. Wayland can't possibly finish the movie on some godforsaken island. 'St. Venetia!' There's not a goddamn thing *on* it, Balcomb."

Gregson shook his head. A smile came over his face. "Just got an idea. Wayland's already made one serious mistake." He looked at his lawyer. "You can't even show a work print of a picture if you haven't got developed film. Everything he's shooting now on St. Venetia has to go to one of the European labs. I would expect Paris because it's the closest. I'll have MGL in New York contact the key labs in Europe. When Wayland's film comes in, it will be held under injunction. He won't get it back till this case is settled. No developed film, no finished film, no option, strikeout."

The lawyer glanced up, settling his glasses back in place on the ridged top of his nose. "MGL has the legal right to do that?"

"They have agreements with every major lab in the world. And they have lawyers everywhere, as you well know," Gregson replied. "In a few days, the film will show up at one lab or another.

"If MGL can get those injunctions, the labs can freeze the film. They'll be afraid if they don't, they'd become involved in a lawsuit. They will just sit on the film until they get legal instructions from their own attorneys. And you know how long you lawyers take to move—"

Balcomb stood up from his desk. "Get going on that, it's important, obviously. Every day is vital. If Wayland and his people can't get any film developed, the clock will run out on him and the whole thing will collapse . . . You'll finish the winner you've always been."

14

Governor's Office,
St. Venetia

partan Lee was calling from Los Angeles.

"That's the whole story," the voice came over the phone. "Gregson sold MGL on these injunctions to all the labs in Europe—where have you sent the film, Steve?"

"I'm glad to say we had to wait until the storm was over," Steve said. "We have seven days' worth of film to go into Paris tomorrow."

"For God's sake, not Paris," Spartan said, "That will be the first place they'll serve an injunction on."

"But I have to get the film developed," Steve answered. "If we're going to get a showable work print of any kind two days after we finish here, we've got to have this developed film back the day after we shoot it. Wait a minute, Spartan," he said, "the governor's waving at me—"

He turned to René. "René—back in your underground days—if film had to be developed and the enemy was looking to intercept the deliveries, and they had the power to prevent any laboratory from developing it, what would you do?"

René's green eyes tuned up again.

"Mon Capitaine," Rene said, as he rubbed his chin. "We should deliver the film to one of the obvious places."

"What do you mean?" Steve asked. "That's just what they expect us to do."

René smiled. "If no film arrives anywhere, Mon Capitaine, the enemy will be searching for an answer everywhere—the enemy will not sit back and relax and feel safe. That's what you need, for the enemy to feel safe, for the enemy to believe they've beaten you. Right?"

"Go on," Steve said.

"We send film," René answered. "I will take it myself. These are the things I do the very best. I will take the film to one of the big laboratories. Wherever you say, Paris, London, Rome, Stockholm, wherever. And we will let them refuse to give that film back to us, refuse to even develop it.

"But that film is just the waste footage that you cut and don't use every day. Martha, your editor, puts all those pieces together, and that's what we ship. The negative you've already eliminated. They will think they've stopped you, and then you can go on shooting here till you finish."

"But where does our film go?" Steve asked. "The real film, the film we have to have developed?"

"You leave that to me. Do you remember Picasso was a friend of mine? He made a special experimental film with René Clouzot. It's just being shown, I heard, in the United States right now. It was at the Cannes Festival years ago. It's called *The Mystery of Picasso*. The two men made a gentlemen's agreement and they made this film for fun, really.

"I spent a few days in Mougins, you know, the village where Picasso lived. And he talked to me about the film, and that they had done everything in an experimental way. They'd used a little laboratory privately owned, not far from where they were filming. All the work was done in this little laboratory. They generally handle documentaries and things like that.

"That's where we take our film. I'll take it myself. I don't believe the big American companies have ever heard of this laboratory. I will get all this information from Mme. Picasso. Between Mme. Picasso and myself, the laboratory will respect the confidential nature of this situation."

Steve looked at him in admiration. "It's a brilliant idea."

René smiled. "You don't grow up in the underground for nothing."

Steve turned back to the phone. "I think we have an answer, Spartan. Expect to hear that Gregson and his boys have located our first shipment in Paris. They will have located it, but it will be the wrong shipment."

"When can you finish shooting altogether?" Spartan asked.

"I need another six days to shoot and a day and a night, at the very least, to finish my temporary scoring and dubbing job on the picture so that the work print can play."

"I'll do the best I can to keep the authorities off your back," Spartan said. "Ed Wilson is throwing up every obstacle he can think of. We're fighting for days now, and Gregson is frantic that you might have something.

"I'm going to stay here, Steve. I think you need me more to be here than with you. I'll continue to pick up anything I can and feed it over to you," Spartan added. "And Steve—is there any way, really, that you can have music tracks on this picture and a temporary dub job that fast? We really don't have a chance of this auction coming off otherwise."

"I'm working on it," Steve said. "We're building music themes with Rayme, and Dick Portman is with us. They've got one movie theater here where we can run the film. Dick thinks he can make it work for a rough dubbing job."

"How's everybody holding up?" Spartan asked.

"Tired," Steve answered. "We're working long hours, you can imagine—but no one's complaining. I'm a little worried about Maggie, though. She worked all night in the hurricane three days ago and I think she's picked up some kind of French flu. She's a little more tired than the rest of us. I've got a doctor checking her."

"Sorry to hear that, but I'm sure she'll be fine. Well, I'll try to call you every two days. All the best, Steve." The phone clicked off.

Steve turned to Lieu. "I want the seventeen rolls of negative that we've shot delivered up here to René." He turned to René. "When do you plan to go?"

"Today," René answered. "I'll take them to Clouzot's lab after I see Mme. Picasso.

"To Operation Picasso," René said. He poured three glasses of wine. "Too bad the old man didn't live to see this. He would've loved it. He probably would've made a painting of the seventeen cans of film."

15

Santa Monica, California

t was after nine o'clock at night when the call came through to Kathleen and Lorelei. They hadn't known when to expect to hear from their father next, but every time the phone rang at night, they rushed to answer it. They knew there was nine hours' difference between where their father was in France and their mother's home in Santa Monica.

The minute Kathleen picked up the phone she knew it was her father, because the line had that funny overseas sound to it. The call seemed to be passing through several different lines, and the operator's voice was muffled.

"Miss Kathleen Wayland and Miss Lorelei Wayland?" she said.

"We're here," Kathleen said excitedly.

Their father's voice came over the phone.

"Kath—Lor?"

"Hello, Dad," Kathleen said.

"Daddyboat!" Lorelei exclaimed.

They talked for a moment of how much they missed each other. Then Kathleen's voice turned serious.

"Dad, I don't like to tell you this, but I think you should know. Mother drove us by our house the other day, and there are signs on both gates that no one is to go into the house and something about an injunction, I think that's what you call it. Are they taking our house, Dad?"

Steve said, "No, they're not. It's all going to be decided in court. Those signs are a legal technicality, because, as I told you, I put the house up for the picture. But they're not going to take our home. I feel sure of it.

"Girls, do you remember I told you at the airport before we left that I'd try to have you come over? You tell your mother that I'm asking her to let you meet me in New York in eight days—you and AGW— then we could be here—all of us together. I want you with me."

16

Hôtel La Terrasse, St. Venetia

Magdalena woke up gasping for breath. It wasn't a dream. She felt a strange sensation. It was as though a vampire had sucked the blood from her body in the night.

"Is this it?" she asked herself. "My God, if something happens now, what will happen to Steve's picture? What will happen to Steve?"

It was the first terrible, wrenching fear she had felt since Dr. Loussard had told her about dermatomyositis. She had been feeling progressively worse for the last few weeks. She had had periods of renewed strength, but each downward turn of the disease took her closer to death.

Then it struck her. This was the first real crisis of her life, a life-and-death moment, in which her first instinctive thoughts, straight from her heart, had been of another person. Her thoughts had been of Steve. Of his life, of his dreams.

She sat up on the bed, trembling. She looked at the clock. It was five o'clock in the morning. Should she call a doctor? No. It would be all over the island and then to the press, then to New York and Los Angeles, and it would be the finishing blow to *The Rest of Our Lives* and to Steve. No, there was only one way to do this. By herself. Either it was simply another down spell, or this was it.

Magdalena did something she hadn't done since her childhood, when it was a matter of form, an expected way of behaving in certain surroundings, particularly in the Catholic Church, in which she had been raised by her father.

She realized she had been hoping to find something she could believe in under the terrible pressure of this illness. At first, she had been able to let it pass from her mind. She had felt too well, she had been too happy, her face and body were unmarked, and she'd decided she had beaten the disease.

But then, as she'd begun to have spells of weakness, fever, and pain, and after her periodic visits with Dr. Arms at UCLA and at his home, she knew that this withering disease was there, lurking inside of her still.

Gradually, through the shooting of *The Rest of Our Lives*, she had come to a new spiritual consciousness. She was still afraid. She didn't have that gift of absolute faith that comes to people who, without reservation, believe in a life after death. But Magdalena had long ago reasoned out for herself that there was no explanation for the universe around her unless there was some universal power. Where did the great ideas of mankind come from? Where did the deep feelings of mankind come from? Why had man, since the beginning of recorded time, questioned who he was, why he was, and what was the meaning of his existence?

Through the years Magdalena had investigated most of the traditional spiritual beliefs of the world.

Organized religion, particularly the Catholic beliefs, did not answer her tests. Neither did the highly formulated Protestant religions. She was drawn to the concepts of reincarnation and karma, because those were the only explanations she could find for the injustices of the world.

Her nature was never one to simply accept and say, "What I'm expected to take, I will take—what will be, will be." She was too independent, too aggressive, too fiery, too determined to carve out a place for herself in the world.

But now, as she turned her heart to the universal power in which she was beginning to believe, to "her God" was the only way she could express it, she thought of how meaningless all wealth and fame were now she was facing a disease that could take her life. Everybody had to face the end. Was anyone ever ready?

Why should she be ready at thirty-eight, in the prime of her beauty and success, with so many victories won, and for the first time in her life deeply in love?

That was her hope. She had thought of Steve first when she woke up in terror. Maybe—just maybe she was on the spiritual path that was right for her.

She bowed her head, the way she'd been taught to pray as a child, put her hands together on the top of the bed.

"God—whatever you are—whatever that power is that gives some meaning to this world—that power that generates the universe—the earth and the sky and the sun and the moon and the stars and the planets—I know we all must be part of something. I know I must face what I have to face. Help me. Help me to do it with grace and dignity. I am so afraid."

She trembled and then she pulled herself up. The strength had gone out of her legs. She felt as if she might fall at any time, but she didn't. She got dressed quickly, threw a coat around her shoulders, and tied a scarf around her hair. She got the keys at the desk. She passed by the door to the dining room on the way out.

Lieu was helping the St. Venetia cooking staff prepare breakfast for the crew. Every table in the dining room was laid out. Magdalena didn't think anyone saw her as she took one of the hotel cars and drove away.

She knew the island by heart now. It was so small the company had already shot almost every conceivable location, and now Boris and Roberto and Gaylin were revamping places where they'd shot before.

Magdalena drove along the road to a point of the island, the Chapel of St. Thérèse, where they had filmed the Garibaldi graveyard in the rain. It was an old village chapel and garden, consecrated in the name of the beloved French working girl who had become a nun and who had died in her twenties. Magdalena had decided to see Father Peter Ciklic, who was one of three priests living on the island, and who was assigned to the Chapel of St. Thérèse.

It took her twenty minutes to drive there. She could still see the tracks, hardened in the road, from the grocery truck that had become the camera car, and from René's motor home.

She was calculating quickly in her head if she had shot enough scenes in Los Angeles and on St. Venetia that Steve could finish the film some way without her. If—if—if, if?

The chapel was empty. She made the sign of the cross, then went down to the altar. To one side of the altar was a marble statue of St. Thérèse. Magdalena looked around the chapel.

She was moved by the simplified Catholicism of this small chapel. There was absolute peace in the church, a stillness, that settled her.

She was kneeling in front of the statue when a priest entered from the side. He was not in his professional clothes. He wore corduroy work pants, a plaid wool shirt, and a navy pea jacket. He was in his late sixties, over six feet-four, with a distinguished face and a shock of black, wavy hair just beginning to turn gray.

His blue eyes looked at Magdalena inquisitively. "I was in our garden to get some flowers for Thérèse. It's Sunday—I saw your car—I don't mean to disturb you but I just wanted to be sure that there wasn't anything you needed."

Magdalena stood up and faced Father Ciklic. He smiled. There was something about this man; he had an aura. She had never believed what she read in some articles and what was being discussed by so many "in" groups, the science of the occult, the abundance of auras of different colors telling us different things surrounding different people. Supposedly, they'd even photographed some of these auras. But she'd never seen one and didn't believe in it.

Then what was it that was surrounding this man? It was a presence, and she felt it throughout her body. He seemed to pour strength into her. Her trembling stopped. The man spoke again.

"I'm Peter Ciklic."

"Father Peter Ciklic?" Magdalena asked.

The priest nodded. He smiled at her again. "Would you like some coffee? I have some very good fresh rolls from the village." He opened the side door of the church, led her out across the patio and into the small house on the point by the side of the ocean.

It was the simplest of parish houses. There was a tiny living room, a study cluttered with books and papers, a bedroom, bathroom, kitchen, and breakfast room. Everything was crowded together, but the ceilings were high.

Father Ciklic led the way to the kitchen, pulling a chair up to the kitchen table for Magdalena.

"Please sit down," he said, "the coffee is already made." He poured her a cup and one for himself, got the sugar down from the shelf and the cream from the refrigerator. Magdalena looked around. The room was neat and scrubbed. Everything reflected the simplicity of this man's life. There was no space wasted.

He took some croissants from under a glass cover, put them on plates, then went to the refrigerator.

"I have some homemade strawberry jam. Would you like some?"

"Thank you, I would," Magdalena said.

He put the jam into a dish and put it on the table. Magdalena looked at the dish in admiration. It was crystal, completely out of keeping with the simple china pottery that was on the table.

Father Ciklic noticed her glance. "That was my mother's." He smiled. "I always think of her when I use it—I only use it for company—and what beautiful company I have this morning. You're Magdalena Alba, of course."

Magdalena looked at him, surprised. The priest laughed.

"Don't be surprised. Movies are one of the passions of my life." He spoke with a definite accent. "Anyway, everyone on the island knows you now."

Magdalena looked at him curiously.

"I am Czechoslovakian," Father Ciklic said. "I've lived in so many places, my accent is polyglot. I see your ears trying to make sure you're hearing what you think you're hearing."

She smiled. "It *is* an unusual accent . . . So you like movies."

"Very much," he said. "They're an escape and an adventure for me. I see about half the things that come to the island here, and then twice a year I go to Paris, once a year I go back to visit my family in Czechoslovakia. I've been to three film festivals—all by myself."

"Really?" Magdalena said.

"I know you well, Miss Alba—on the screen. I haven't seen all your films, but quite a number. I can honestly say that you are one of the people I like the most in movies today. I always believe you. And that's very important. If I don't believe the actors in a movie then I don't like it . . . I don't feel anything. I was on the set one day when you were filming," Peter Ciklic continued. "I saw you and your director working through the scene together—each of you using all your experience and all your imagination. I don't think there was anyone on that set who didn't know you two were in love. It wasn't that you called attention to it, it was simply there." He smiled at her. "I'll never forget it."

"Father," she said suddenly, "I'm dying."

Father Ciklic put down his coffee and his eyes clouded over. "I can't believe that. How is that possible? What is it?"

"A very strange and unusual disease. They call it dermatomyositis."

"I know dermato," he said, "but it's possible to live with that. I had a parishioner in South America who had the disease. He's still living—"

"The treatment," Magdalena said, "I can't live with. It destroys your looks. You swell up, maybe forever. I can't accept that, Father. Anyway, it's too late now. I was supposed to be in intensive treatment four months ago, just after they discovered it."

She got up and walked over to the fireplace. She turned around and warmed herself. "Father, I need help. That's why I came to see you. I was born a Catholic, but I have not been a Catholic. I cannot believe in all the things a Catholic has to believe in—I can't do it. But I have heard on this island that you are an exceptional man—not just a priest but a man with his own ideas, his own faith. You see, Father, in these last four months, off and on, when the disease would hit me again, I have tried to work out my own way of prayer. I have needed to believe in something, in someone—in God."

Father Ciklic never took his eyes from her. "Of course," he said.

"And I had to do it my own way," Magdalena said, "and I thought I would have enough time—but this morning I suddenly woke up, an hour ago, and I felt like I was dying. My strength was gone, I was in a fever, with a strange tingling sensation you get in your muscles and ligaments. I know all the symptoms by heart. But I've never felt them so strongly as this morning. I could hardly drive out here.

"And then, in the chapel, when you came in, I've got to tell you, Father, I felt something so powerful and good coming over me and quieting me—and now I feel it here, in your kitchen, drinking coffee with you, I feel it again. I'm not afraid now."

"What do you want me to do?" he asked.

"Father, let me ask you a question. Love is such a common word, and yet so powerful. I really want to know that what I feel for this man I've fallen in love with, and what he feels for me, is finally the end of my search—I don't want to face death without knowing what real love is. Will you tell me your opinion?"

"I never thought about a definition of love, except the one from St. Paul that we all learned, all of those who are in the church. Paul said, 'Love knows no limit to its endurance, no end to its trust, no fading of its hope: it can outlast anything. It is, in fact, the one thing that still stands when all else has fallen.'

"But I guess if I were to try to define it right from the top of my head, one thought comes to mind, I don't know from where, but it's the one thing I think of. 'Love is a competition in giving.' "

Magdalena looked at him and said nothing for a moment. She tried to grasp that thought, to absorb it, to protect it against all her testing mechanisms. "Love is a competition in giving." She said the words softly after a moment. "Yes, that's a complete way to say it. That seems to satisfy all my questions.

"Actresses are not very well equipped for a competition in giving," Magdalena continued. "Usually they have been deeply hurt. They have fought hard, competed hard, and they have taken much. They are not usually giving people. If I had heard your definition a year ago I wouldn't have rated very well. But now, this morning, when I felt I might be dying, I thought of the man I love before anything else—I think I'm learning, Father."

"No question about it," Father Ciklic said. "Do you know how few people in this world can really do that? Think they are dying and think of another person before their own existence? Whatever has happened in the past, Magdalena, you have learned to love."

"If that is true, Father, and I must trust you that it is, then I can face death." Her shoulders trembled. "I hate the sound of that word. I can hardly say it. We all go through life dodging it, stamping it out, refusing to hear it, putting hands over our eyes, not wanting to see it—but, Father, do you really believe in life after death? Absolutely. With no question. The Catholic doctrine."

The priest took his pipe from a tray on the kitchen table, and filled it. "Yes, I believe that there is life after death. I don't believe in all the explicit descriptions of heaven or hell. But I do believe that life goes on in some area of existence, or spiritual consciousness, if you will, that we cannot really have a concrete idea of—there has to be that or all life is a joke, and a very bad joke. I don't believe that.

"When I look at a woman, a world-famous, beautiful, talented actress, across my kitchen table, and I see that she cares more about the possible loss for the man she loves than she does about worrying about her own illness, I don't believe this just happens. There are things moving inside all of us that we cannot comprehend. I believe what I see, and I have seen again and again in my life the power of love to overcome every kind of human tragedy, the power of love to deal with it, to comfort, to sustain. Actually, I don't care what religious name you want to put on it. When you get down to it, Magdalena, every major philosophy in the history of man that I know about has, at its center, love. It's as simple and complicated as that.

"Take love out of the world and life is not worth living, and then I would believe that there was no God." He paused. "You have to come to the very center of existence," Ciklic said. "At least that is what I believe, and that is what you have asked me. And at such a time as this is for you, dogma means nothing. I have to try to share with you what I believe."

It was amazing to Magdalena how much stronger she felt. There had been some kind of physical transformation within her in the last hour.

"Father, do you think I could be given enough time to finish this film? It's much more than that—it's Steve's career and everything he owns and his own belief in himself."

"It would be wrong of me," Father Ciklic said, "to tell you blindly that everything is going to be all right. You wouldn't accept it anyway. But I will pray for you and Steve both, every day, and I will come and pray with you when you come to this chapel. I believe in prayer. I absolutely do. However it's done.

"I believe in keeping a constant line open, if you will, with what we call God. I believe in talking to him all through the day—whenever I need to—in the car, in my garden, in my pulpit, with my parishioners, everywhere.

"Over the years, that relationship has become a constant in my life. And I can tell you this. No one can give a definite answer to any of the unanswerable questions. But I know, just for myself, my God is with me, lives with me, is here in this kitchen this morning as we have coffee and rolls and as you share so much of yourself with me. I can feel the presence of a force infinitely stronger than I am. And I ask that force to surround you, and go with you to protect you.

"When I was in London last year I saw a powerful musical play of Victor Hugo's *Les Misérables*. The most important line in the play has come to my mind as I've been talking to you—'To love someone is to see the face of God.' That has happened to you, Magdalena."

17

Magdalena and Lieu

Magdalena was waiting for Lieu as she came along the path to her room from the dining room.

"Lieu, it's a beautiful night. Would you walk a little way with me?"

"Of course," Lieu said. "I'd love to."

They walked silently along the shore before Magdalena said anything.

"Lieu," she said, "I want you to give me your word that you will not repeat to Steve or anyone what I want to tell you."

Lieu looked at her. "You have my word. What is it, Magdalena? I know that something's wrong. I saw you leaving the hotel early this morning. You looked very upset. Is there a problem we don't know about?"

"Lieu, with all the years you've worked with Steve, he says he still really doesn't know what happened in your life. You are a very private person. So am I. There are some things I cannot share with any of you."

"Even with Steve?" Lieu asked.

"Even with Steve," Magdalena answered. "There are some personal things in my life that I have to straighten out. I'm going to have to fly back to Los Angeles when we're finished. I can't go to New York with all of you.

"I have to know there's someone close to Steve who will be there for him. His children will be, of course. And his friends. But Steve needs the love of a woman. A woman he can trust. That's part of his creative life. You can't separate love and creativity, certainly not in him. He has tremendous needs. I know them now. I know how much he has to give if he is in harmony with his talents.

"I watched you the night we were together in Los Angeles at the Ray Charles concert. I saw you when you didn't think anyone was looking at you. That moment told me that you love him, too."

Lieu started to speak. "Magdalena, please don't—"

"Woman to woman, Lieu, I know. And I respect your love for him. I admire the way you keep it unknown to him. Could I resent it, could I resent someone or dislike someone because she loves the man that I love?"

"I'm just asking you, Lieu, because I love this man as I have loved no other in my life, to be ready—and never betray my confidence, and to stand by him. Believe me, Lieu, he will need you. For me, please, you will, won't you?"

In the half light of the terrace lights near the ocean, Lieu made her pledge to Magdalena.

18

Plaza Athénee Hotel, New York

athryn Manning's voice was coming over the phone. She and Spartan Lee were together in a meeting in New York. Two executives from the new ownership of the network, Capital Cities, were there, as well as Roone Arledge, the Executive-in-charge of ABC News.

"Steve," Kathryn's voice came through to him in the office of René La Grange.

It had been Jake's idea, and Spartan had carried it out. Every network wanted a top commentator and interviewer to go to St. Venetia and personally interview the leading figures in the biggest entertainment story of the year, in the few remaining days of shooting. Steve knew that if they all came, he would have no chance to finish in time. But they had to be accommodated, accompanied, and won over, if possible. The coming auction of the film they had planned needed media attention and buildup.

So Jake had come up with the idea that the networks should draw from a pool. The winning network would send a commentator it selected. The coverage of *The Rest of Our Lives* was to be shared by all, but the winning network had priority.

ABC had chosen the person generally respected as one of the best interviewers on television, particularly with entertainment people.

"I'd like to come on Wednesday. I plan to spend two days interviewing, for an ABC special, the cast, your production manager, your accountant, and the governor of St. Venetia. And of course you, Steve . . . Can I count on your full cooperation?"

"Absolutely," Steve answered. "We want you to come. But I hope you realize the situation we're in. We'll be working day and night. You can talk to anyone you want, and be with us on location any time you want."

"Can I see some of the film that you've shot on St. Venetia?" Kathryn asked.

"No," Steve said, "no one can see any of this film until the auction in New York. You know what we have at stake, Kathryn."

"I hope you'll change your mind on that, Steve," Kathryn said. "If I saw some of the film, I definitely would talk about it on the air. I'd like to run at least one minute of it on the program—and I'll let you choose the minute."

"I'm sorry, Kathryn," Steve said, "but if we start running clips from this film, anything can happen. Rumors can start, stories can be made up, the whole auction concept could be undermined."

"Keep an open mind, Steve. I'm excited about coming. I've interviewed Magdalena before. She's one of my favorites. I've been turned down four times to do a story with Rayme. But this time, Spartan tells me, he's going to talk to me."

"I'm sure he is," Steve said. "He has a big stake in this film, and I think he wants to talk about it."

"Good," Kathryn answered. "Thank you very much, Steve. See you Wednesday morning."

19

Emperor Theater, St. Venetia

athryn Manning's show was rolling.

Boris Peters had helped her crew arrange a comfortable living room set on the stage of the Emperor Theater. There were couches and chairs arranged around a coffee table.

Her crew had miked the set to allow Kathryn and her "guests" an easy, at-home atmosphere. Steve was seated across from Kathryn, with Magdalena, Montango, Rayme, and Stephanie sitting separately in chairs next to the couch. Roberto Bakker was there, Danny Chiaverini, and René La Grange.

Kathryn looked at a paper, an excerpt from a magazine in her lap. She was handsomely dressed in a black Chanel suit trimmed in crimson velvet. She had brought her own hairdresser on the flight, and she'd had a two-hour rest period at the Hôtel La Terrasse after she'd collected her notes, talked to Steve, and had a short tour of St. Venetia. She had been captivated by René La Grange and had asked him to be present for her taping.

Now Kathryn was ready, having absorbed every fact available to her in New York, Hollywood, and St. Venetia.

"I have in front of me," Kathryn opened the program, "the March issue of *California* magazine. It is highly regarded in business circles, and its research department is well respected. The title of this article is 'Power in Hollywood.'

"The researchers have broken down power in Hollywood into different categories—A, B, and C groups. The owners, the operators, the so-called foolproof talent. Producers, directors, writers, agents, wives—"

her voice raised in intensity, "—animal trainers. There are lists of those directors most noted for handling difficult performers, scene stealers, restaurants, churches, children's schools, and psychiatrists.

"For example, actors on the foolproof box-office list: Clint Eastwood, Dustin Hoffman, Eddie Murphy, Tom Cruise, Robert Redford, Barbra Streisand, Bill Murray, Michael Jackson. There's a little footnote attached to this list that says, 'Most projects proposed by these people will get made and make money, but only if they stick to their images.' "

She turned to Steve Wayland. "Have you seen this list, Steve?"

"No, I haven't," Steve answered.

"Have you heard about it?" she asked.

"Yes," Steve said.

"Do you know that you're not on the list of writer-producer-directors—not on A, B, or C?" Kathryn asked directly.

Steve smiled. "My manager told me."

"How do you account for that?"

"I don't think I'd ever be on a power list in Hollywood, because I don't have the power. It's that simple," Steve said.

"Do you think you belong on any of these lists, Steve?" Kathryn asked with that direct, probing way that made her a feared interviewer.

"I don't live by lists like that, Kathryn. If I did I would've quit long ago."

"You're aware, Steve, I'm sure, that you've become, in these ten days since you escaped out of Hollywood with your cast and your company, the biggest maverick, possibly, in Hollywood history. 'The Rebel with a Cause' is the label your friend Spartan Lee has put on you.

"You're getting blamed, castigated, praised, hero-worshipped, depending on where you are and whom you're talking to. In the press, you've become a superstar. Do you realize that if *The Rest of Our Lives* works, you, Magdalena, Rayme, Stephanie, and Robert would jump onto the 'A' lists?"

"And you realize, Kathryn," Steve said, "what will happen if we don't have a picture—if the auction ten days from now doesn't work?"

"If you lose, you're probably through as a director, you'll lose everything you have and face a big lawsuit from Jack Gregson and the studio."

She turned to Danny Chiaverini. "Dan, I was talking to you earlier today on the set. You're writing the checks and the IOUs for *The Rest of Our Lives*. Nobody understands how you're moving forward with no money from the studio. They're not paying any of the bills?"

"No," said Danny, "nothing."

"What was in the picture's account when it was shut down in Hollywood?"

"A little over two hundred thousand dollars. The night we left, we paid it all out to cover the bills we had."

"How's the company living here at the Hôtel Terrasse, where I'm staying—over forty people—and how are you paying all of the people of St. Venetia? I understand from the governor here, René La Grange, that everyone on this island is working for *The Rest of Our Lives.*"

"That's correct," Danny said. "We are giving out individual promissory notes for each day's work. The same for the hotel. In addition, Steve Wayland has given the hotel his personal note."

"Who signs the company notes to the working crew?"

"Steve Wayland," Danny said.

Kathryn turned to René. "From what I hear, you've turned over your island, your home, your office, the equipment of the island, your telephone communication system—everything—to Steve Wayland and to *The Rest of Our Lives.* Why?"

René loved the idea that he was going to be seen by perhaps forty million Americans on a program that would be translated into many languages and shown to millions more abroad. He gave Kathryn his best smile. He'd already talked with her that afternoon, and he enjoyed the match. They played evenly, and they understood each other instinctively. Underneath the experience and polish, they were both street fighters.

"Mademoiselle Manning," he said with his most charming accent, "Steve Wayland is my friend, 'Mon Capitaine.' He is like my brother. And besides, his movie is going to be very profitable for everyone on the island."

"You're not afraid that all these notes to your villagers may bounce, Monsieur La Grange?" Kathryn asked. "What if Mr. Wayland loses his fight for his picture? What if the film is a disaster? Where will the money come from?"

"Mademoiselle Manning," René answered, "I am not in the film business, but I've been around French films for many years. I have many friends in the industry. I've seen many films.

"I have watched what has been filmed here and how it is being filmed. And I have told my people in this village these notes are going to be good. In addition, Mr. Wayland has set aside some of his own profits to be divided evenly between the people of this island. Every person of St. Venetia who is working on the movie has a stake in it. Do you know what that means for this?" René patted his heart. "Do you know what that does to a man or a woman or a boy or a girl, to have a personal participation in an American movie?"

"Ah," René continued, "that is everything to a Frenchman. A Frenchman either is a part of the troops, as we say, or he is not. See for yourself in the time you are here, Mademoiselle Manning. I don't think any other village in France today is as alive and full of spirit as St. Venetia is right now.

"And certainly after the comments of such a famous telecaster as yourself, our tourist business should multiply many times."

Kathryn turned to Roberto. "Mr. Bakker, it's your job, as I understand it, to have everything ready to shoot every day and night, to have sets that fit the rest of the picture made in Hollywood—keep the one main camera you have going and the one Nagra sound unit—you're shooting a six-and-a-half-million-dollar film and you don't even have the full equipment for an educational short. How are you doing it?"

"I've made forty-two pictures," Roberto said, "in all parts of the world. A film being made develops its own personality, you have a gut feeling about it. It's like a child. You nurture it, you work for it, you wait for it to wake up, you put it to bed at night, you know more about it than anyone else in the world.

The Rest of Our Lives is completely different from any other picture I've ever worked on. I don't know what will happen to box office. If anyone knew that he would control this business. But I do know it's going to be seen and studied and written about and, thanks to people like you, talked about. When it is ready, the picture will speak for itself."

Kathryn turned to Magdalena. "Are you glad that you agreed to make *The Rest of Our Lives,* now that it has become the center of a raging controversy growing every day, with troops of lawyers on every side, and claims and counterclaims being voiced across the country? Tell me honestly, wouldn't it have been better for your career and your own life to have accepted Jack Gregson's offer of the starring role in *Victoria?*"

"This was the best choice of my life," Magdalena answered. "I have made so many pictures that really have contributed nothing. And then I've had my favorites: *Anna Karenina* was one, *Madame Bovary* was another—pictures that stay with you after you've seen them. Pictures that make you think, deepen your awareness. Most of all, move your heart. *The Rest of Our Lives* does all these things, at least to those of us who are making it. This film is very personal to me, more than anything I have made in my life."

Kathryn smiled at Magdalena. "Is it true, the rumors about you and Steve Wayland?"

Magdalena smiled back.

"I've never seen you look as beautiful, Magdalena," Kathryn went on. "And you look happy. I think for the first time I'm seeing you really happy. Is that true, Magdalena?"

"Yes, and before you start asking me why, Kathryn, and when, and where, I will simply tell you—" she glanced at Steve, "—the rumors are true. I'm in love with Steve Wayland. So, fortunately for me, the greatest professional experience of my life has come together at the same time with the love of my life."

Kathryn turned to Rayme Monterey. "Rayme, the word is that you have a contract of absolute approval of everything you do in this film. Is that true?"

"That's right," Rayme said.

"Is that the only way you'd make the picture?" Kathryn asked.

"Probably," Rayme answered, "but I didn't have to ask. That's what Mr. Wayland offered. I didn't believe it either, at first."

"Have you seen any of the film that you've shot here on the island?"

"Some of it," Rayme said.

"From what you've seen so far in Hollywood and here, Rayme, is there any part of your scenes or any full scenes that you're going to ask Steve to eliminate?"

"I don't think any more about it now," Rayme said. "Let me explain something to you, Kathryn. When I saw Huey Buis in Hollywood a few weeks ago, it was at the Golden Globe Awards dinner. Huey was up for an award and I ran into him at the Century Plaza. I was having a meeting there with Spartan Lee.

"Huey saw me and came over and spoke to me before he went downstairs to the ballroom for the banquet. He was asking me if I was going to do the picture and I said, well, I didn't know for sure.

"He said, 'My God, I thought the music business was corrupt, but from some of the things I've seen around Hollywood the few days I've been here, the music business looks like Alice in Wonderland. What would you do if you made a film here, how would you stay out of it?'

" 'How do you stay out of it in the music business?' I asked.

" 'Well, I've got my band,' he answered.

"I told Huey the same thing. If I make a picture, well, I've got my band. Your guys, the guys you've come up with, the guys you've been on the road with, the guys who've been with you when people have walked out on you, and the guys who've been there when the people are cheering. That's what I depend on, Kathryn. Skeeter Thomas and the rest of my guys.

"I can tell you there isn't one of us who even thinks about the approval clause anymore. We're not approving or disapproving someone else's picture, this is *our* picture.

"I don't want any of those guys in New York trying to stop this picture thinking Steve is going to have any problem with me. And I'm going to be in New York at that auction with my boys. We own part of this picture, and so does everybody else here."

"You know that a warrant for your arrest is waiting for you the minute you step foot in the U.S.A.?" Kathryn asked.

"I can't worry about that now. I've got to finish what I started here. My lawyer will speak for me on the grand jury hearing. For now, I have nothing to say on that."

Kathryn turned to Steve. "Please reconsider and let me see just one minute, and you pick the minute, let me put one minute of *The Rest of Our Lives* into this program. Let the public see what these people are talking about. I can't wait to see something myself."

Steve shook his head. "It's only eight days before we show the whole picture, Kathryn. I wouldn't know what minute to select. Any way we cut it, it would be like a trailer for the auction. Maybe something we'd like wouldn't strike the distribution companies the same way. It's not the way to play the hand, Kathryn. I'm sorry, we can't do that."

Kathryn's engineer was signaling to her from the side of the stage. The television cameras continued to roll.

"That's the end of my story for today, ladies and gentlemen. I regret we cannot bring you any film from the most talked-about motion picture in America today, *The Rest of Our Lives*. You can make up your own minds from what you've heard tonight what is the truth about the so-called 'kidnapping' of the film and the 'resurrection' of *The Rest of Our Lives* on St. Venetia island. This is Kathryn Manning for ABC saying good night."

20

MGL Studio,
Hollywood

*J*ack Gregson and Jerry Clune stayed late at the studio to watch the Kathryn Manning telecast. Fifteen minutes into the telecast, Jack Gregson was pacing the floor. Then when Rayme Monterey said he had seen film that had been shot on St. Venetia, Gregson turned ashen white.

"How could he have seen any film shot there?" he asked Jerry Clune. "Tell me, Jerry."

Clune shook his head. "I have no idea."

"Call the lab in Paris."

"It's five-thirty in the morning in Paris. We won't get anyone but security people."

"Call them at home. I want to know why they processed the film and returned it to Wayland on the island. Somebody crossed us, Jerry. I'm going to get his balls for it."

Clune got through to the home of the president of the Paris lab.

"While I'm on this call, get the D.A. on the phone!" Gregson fired at him.

"What the fuck's going on over there at your Paris laboratory?" Gregson yelled. "You told me that the film had come in from St. Venetia to the Laboratoire Français." Gregson murdered the French pronunciation.

"That's correct, it's been coming in every day. We have over sixty thousand feet there now under impound," the Frenchman answered.

"Then for Christ's sake," Gregson yelled, "how come I hear on Kathryn Manning three minutes ago that Rayme Monterey has seen, in the theater on St. Venetia, developed film shot on St. Venetia?"

"Impossible," the Frenchman answered. "We've never developed one foot of Mr. Wayland's negative. It's locked up in our vaults."

"Then develop a sample can of negative and express it to me. And call me when the next negative comes in. Any time of the day or night. We haven't any time to waste."

Gregson hung up and took the waiting connection with Mahoney, the New York district attorney.

"Listen," Gregson said, "this picture's going to be finished in five days. It's going to be auctioned here in New York in eight days. You've got to make the French authorities serve an injunction or warrant or something—even if you just tie up the picture for a few days—stop the filming—delay any auction—we can win this thing—if not, this whole thing can kill you off, Mahoney. So move it!" Gregson hung up the phone.

"How the fuck is Wayland getting his film developed . . . where?" Gregson muttered to Clune.

21

St. Venetia

René La Grange's camper had become the camera car. Gaylin had put three different camera mounts on the front and back of the camper, attached with his special grip equipment so that they would hold firm and not sway or bounce with the movement of the car. Long pads had been borrowed from the chaises around the pool at the Hôtel La Terrasse and tied down in front of each of the camera mounts.

David Thayer was lying on one now as he lined up Steve's shot on the station wagon. The angle of the camera was downward from René's camper, through the windshield, focused on Eric Garibaldi. Eric was driving Bill Donnelly, his lawyer, toward the Bay House.

This was one of the few exterior shots Steve could do on St. Venetia. The surroundings could not be differentiated from either the exact location at the bay in Munising, Michigan, or the exact replica of the boat house and the pier Boris Peters had built on Stage Six at the Goldwyn Studio in Hollywood.

Steve was on the side of the beach road that circled the island. The foliage was not unlike the actual bay area in Michigan. Steve had walked off with Robert Montango while Gaylin was fixing a final camera mount on the right window of the front seat of the station wagon. This angle could cover Eric Garibaldi close for a two-shot of Bill Donnelly and Eric, Bill's profile in the foreground.

"I'm counting on you, Steve," Montango said. "I've always wondered why this scene was even in the script. I was sure you would let it go over here with the time pressure we have—but when I saw it on the call sheet yesterday, I went over in my head everything we've shot. I thought again about what this scene means for Eric—he doesn't have anything important to say—he's just marking time—but inside, this is really my scene—not Robert Montango's, but Eric Garibaldi's. That's why you're shooting it, isn't it?"

Steve nodded. "How often I've heard you say, Robert, that the best actors are reactors—and that reacting is the hardest—"

Montango nodded. "All night, in my mind, I was running this scene, listening to Bill Donnelly—I was listening as a seventy-year-old man, in the film, and in real life.

"When we were rehearsing a few minutes ago, did you see the looks on the older people in our crew when we played back the soundtrack? They were feeling what I feel in this scene. They were listening to what Donnelly says—not just as conversation in a film. It meant something to them. I've got to get that over in my reactions to Bill Donnelly. So watch me, Steve, I don't want one eyebrow slipping up without my knowing it—no ridges in my forehead. I don't want to be unconsciously biting the side of my mouth. I want it clean. I want these reactions pure—because they're true—I found that out last night."

Steve lined up the tight two-shot with the camera shooting from the right front window of the station wagon. Bill Donnelly's right profile was in the foreground, Eric Garibaldi's face in the background. During most of the conversation between the two men, they were looking straight ahead. Occasionally one would turn to look at the other as they headed toward the Bay House. The station wagon was moving forward now.

"I've been away from the Bay House a long time, too," Donnelly said.

"Like the rest of us. Too long," Eric answered.

"This has been a hard decision for you, I know that," Donnelly said.

"For all of us," Eric answered. "Did you bring the documents?" he asked. Donnelly patted the briefcase he held in his lap.

"Right here, ready to be signed."

"Good," Eric nodded.

"Eric," Donnelly went on, "I wanted you to know before it was officially announced, I'm retiring from the law firm at the end of the year."

"You're too young to retire. You're ten years younger than I am, and I never thought about retiring," Eric answered. "If I retired, I wouldn't know what to do with myself. Life would be over."

"Not necessarily," Donnelly said. "I'm retiring to do something else."

Eric glanced at him quizzically.

"You've been my friend for over thirty years and a client for twenty-five," Donnelly said. "We've traveled," he glanced at the road, "many roads together—I want you to understand what I'm doing.

"Don't worry about you and your family being taken care of. The firm will go on and I'm turning your affairs over to the best people in my office. If there's any specific matter you want me to handle for you, I'll come back and do it, you know that.

"The only way I can think of to explain this to you is to tell you exactly what happened. I was flicking through the television channels one night a month ago, when I couldn't sleep. Usually television can do it for me when I'm restless or worried. This was a live interview with a Rabbi Harold Kushner on some talk show."

"The writer?" Eric asked.

"That's the one," Bill said. "I almost passed over that channel, but then I heard something in one of his answers that caught my attention. He said, 'I don't believe that the point of life is to win. I think it is to grow.'

"And then he went on," Bill continued. "He was talking about making a difference. He said, 'Sometimes in my talks around the country, and with my books, I really don't reach many people. I've been in the middle of important speeches for me, lectures, and I've known that I'm not getting through—sometimes you feel inspired and sometimes you don't—but what brings me back is that after I finish, four or five, sometimes fifteen or twenty, sometimes more, but at least four or five people, come up to the lecture platform as everyone is going out. They tell me that something I've said or something from one of my books has helped change their lives—that I have touched them. And that keeps me going. The power of any of us to touch other lives, I think, is the greatest power of all, and any one of us can have it if we want to. I really believe that.'

"And then he was asked a question by a man in the audience. Actually, it was him and his wife together. They had their marriage, had children, he had had a successful career. They had money to live out the rest of their lives reasonably. They had taken some of the trips they'd always wanted to. They had read. They had played golf. But something was missing. Something they had had before. So he asked Rabbi Kushner, 'When you get older, and you've either realized some of your dreams or not, when you know that life is in its last years, what is there to live for? Isn't it all over? Youth is gone—passion is gone—'

"Right then, the rabbi—I can see him now—interrupted them. He couldn't even wait for them to finish, because passion was such a key word to him.

" 'Passion,' he said to that older couple, 'the juice of life—the thrill of doing something that is meaningful to you—like a picture I saw a few years ago called *Flashdance*, a line I remember from it—a true line—'Lose your dreams and you die.'

" 'I'm glad you've asked that question, because here's what I think all of us can do with whatever life we have left—and who knows ever how many days or weeks or years that is? Coming to the last part of your life, like I am, is something we all have to face, but I have found—and I speak to you truly, I'm not trying to idealize—I don't like getting old any more than you do. I don't like a lot of things about it—but I do know this. Every one of us can look at the last chapter of his life like the last chapter of a book, where everything comes together . . . what we have known and experienced from all our mistakes, our regrets, our disillusionments, our pain. We can put all our knowledge and our feelings into the rest of our lives. Find a way, a dream out there,' he said, 'and put everything you are into it. There is such a need in our world for people with a dream, I don't care what their age is. Find yours!' "

Donnelly went on. Steve had told David Thayer to move in very slowly past Donnelly's face, at this point, into a tight close-up of Eric Garibaldi. Donnelly's voice was over Eric's face. Eric was listening intently. His thoughts were in his eyes.

"I made up my mind that night, Eric," Donnelly went on, "that I was going to retire and commit myself to the causes that I believe in—not just give money to someone else to do the job, but to try to do my part of the job myself—to get up every day knowing that what I'm going to do might make a difference.

"Even thinking about it made me feel younger. You know, Eric, when we used to talk about the law when you were working on the Centurion and I was building my practice? What was really in my head was the hope that someday I might be responsible, with what I did in my practice and in my theories, to contribute to the law as it changes here and there—to try innovative cases—to expound little-known facets of the law and how it should work for *all* people.

"Somewhere in these twenty-five years that dream didn't get done. I was too busy—I was too successful—I won, as the rabbi said, but I don't feel I've grown. That man challenged me. He changed my life and I'm going with it. I feel better than I have in a long time."

22

The Boat House,
St. Venetia

"Barbara, you've got to resign the nomination. That's the only answer there is." Bill Donnelly leaned forward at the table in the boat house interior Boris Peters had reproduced. It had to be shot at night so that it would look like the actual boat house set they'd left behind. Eric, Barbara, Christina, and Michael were grouped around the circular ship's table. David Thayer had raked his lights, so that the room was almost completely in streaks of light and darkness.

"That's not fair," Christina said, trying to force the thought through her clouded mind.

"Nothing's fair," Donnelly said. "What matters are facts. And the facts are that each one of your careers is threatened, maybe wiped out if Barbara goes ahead. You can get out now, Barbara, without hurting the party too much."

"And Henry Calvin steps in just like that?" Michael asked. "I've got another idea. Why don't we go to the FBI with all this, or even the police? Dad, you've got the clout to get to any of the authorities. This is goddamn blackmail."

"That's what it is," Donnelly said. "But it's very careful blackmail. There's no way to prove a thing."

"Why don't we go right to old man Calvin then?" Michael went on. "He'd never stand up against you face to face, Dad!"

"He won't see me face to face," Eric said. "I tried to meet with him before I flew up here. He's gone to Hawaii for a complete 'rest.' He's seeing no one. Supposedly, he's brokenhearted because of losing the Senate seat."

"I'm sure you're right, Bill," Barbara said. "There's nothing else to do. I won't have my family torn apart if I can prevent it."

"And be assured they are ready to let go on you, Barbara. It's going to be a nasty story and they'll spread it everywhere. They've got photographs and they've got love letters from you to D'Angelo. It's not the stuff great Senate careers are made of."

"Calvin must really hate me," Barbara said.

"He doesn't even know you, except on television," Donnelly replied. "This has nothing to do with love or hate. This is politics. And like in love and war, anything's fair. We've had the whole office on this, trying to think of any way to fight it, but we can't come up with a thing."

"How about some of the stories on that son of a bitch? Henry Calvin's got skeletons, I'll guarantee you," Eric said.

"What he has is pretty mild, and it's all a long time ago," Donnelly said. "We've covered that angle, too. But you must understand that Calvin never has been front-page news. You four—this family—have been in the headlines for two generations—you've been called one of America's dynasties, and a dynasty is big game, vulnerable, colorful, always big news. When you have the kind of sensational material they have on each one of you, they've got hot stories. They can break careers and people."

"Bill," Barbara said quietly, "I'd like you to call my campaign manager. Tell him I want to have a news conference at the capitol tomorrow night. That I can't talk to him about it yet. I've got to think everything out. Just how I want to handle this—and with my children."

"I'm sorry, Barbara," Eric said.

"So am I, Dad, but there's no other way. We'd better do this fast before these stories leak."

"I brought the documents, Eric," Donnelly said. He took an envelope from his briefcase and handed it to Eric.

"I want you to stay here for this, please," Eric said. "You're the family attorney, and you and your firm will be handling these things for me."

Eric looked around at his children. "I asked Bill to make up a new will yesterday and bring it with him.

"This family's been growing further and further apart, and it's my fault. It wouldn't have happened if your mother had been here. Anyway, it's happened now, and we all know it, but we can make it different from here on out.

"None of us ever knows about the future—God knows this thing has pointed that out clearly—and the Garibaldi Automobile Company is worth a lot of money. Your mother and I owned all the stock in the beginning, and she left hers to me when she died. I still have enough stock to control it."

He took out of the envelope five matching long legal documents, each backed with blue paper. "I've seen so many families in Detroit split apart by money. That's not going to happen to us. This is my new will, and I'm signing it now." He passed down copies around the table. "I want each of you to have a copy and keep it. I want you to know everything in this will. The secrets end here. There won't be any surprises after I'm gone. We either trust each other and love each other or we don't. I'm betting on you, each one of you.

"I'll tell you the main points, you can read your copies later yourselves. Bill, please correct me if I'm wrong.

"Each one of you will inherit one third of my stock in the Garibaldi Automobile Company, and each one of you will inherit one third of everything I have.

"I want you all to have an equal chance." He looked at Christina. "And I'm betting on you, Christina, just as much as the others. You've got a problem that's hard for me to understand, but it certainly is part of our time. Millions of people have the same problem. We haven't been with you on this."

"You didn't know about it," Christina said. "You can't take any of the blame." She was trembling.

Barbara put her arms around her. "Oh, yes, we can. And we do. It's not your problem alone. It's ours to fight—and beat—together."

"That's right," Eric added. "Christina, I want to give you the responsibility, starting right now, for something that's very important to me. Your mother loved this place. She loved these mountains when they were covered with pines. She loved the lake when it was pure and uncontaminated. She redid the house, built this boat house for all of us. I felt her presence here all weekend and I'm sure you have, too.

"I want this house and this community to come alive again—I'm going to put the Garibaldi Company behind it and you're going to get the money you need, Christina, to do what it takes. Franco will be your liaison with the town itself. What's left of it.

"It's a mammoth job, to replant these forests, to bring this town to life again. But it's become a little like our family to me now. Once it was a beautiful and shining place where we loved to come and be together, and now it seems to belong to the past. We haven't protected it, we haven't done our share. We're going to bring the mill back to life as a project of the Garibaldi Company, and you're going to be president and in charge. The CEO, we call it, Christina. We'll all help, but you will have the authority and the responsibility.

"And the state commission, by the way, will agree to let us change the name to Angela Bay. Beginning in a few weeks, it will be in the official books by that name.

"Christina, this is going to take every bit of creativity and imagination that you have—and you've always had more than most of us. But it's going to take time, patience. Someday those forests will grow tall again on those barren hills, and someday there will be a clear lake.

"But I can't possibly—" Christina broke off.

"Yes, you can," Eric said. "And we're going to be with you all the way. We've got to start giving back, and you're going to be the one who speaks for us and works for us. And one last thing—" he paused for a moment, "—my children—we take a pledge here that no matter what our commitments are, what are our problems or our pressures, the four of us, and your children, too, are going to be at Angela Bay for at least two weeks every Christmas, and a few weeks in the summer if we can.

"I ask you to pledge this in the name of your mother. In the name of the Garibaldi family."

Eric put his right hand in the center of the table and, one by one, Christina, Barbara, and Michael reached in and covered his hand.

"We're a family," Eric said. "We know we're not perfect people. We know we've pretended many things to each other and hidden many things from each other. But no more. There are pressures in the world on every side that would destroy the family—would eliminate loyalty and honesty and work and courage and belief in a dream.

"It's true, we all know, that the family unit has to change in these times. We're no longer living on ranches, prairies, farms, or in little towns. The world itself is in the fast lane. But when it comes down to it, when life gets rough and we don't know where to turn, with all our faults, we have a family—we've found that out this weekend, for sure.

"I'm not a very religious man, you all know that, but I do believe in something. There has to be something. And I want this family, each in our own way, to hang on to each other for the rest of our lives."

23

St. Venetia

Clare, the makeup lady, completed reworking the face and body of René's secretary. Clare stepped back to look at the woman with Lieu, Steve, René, and Barbara Carr, Steve's research specialist.

"Mon Dieu!" René exclaimed.

"Let me see your pictures, Barbara," Steve asked.

Barbara opened her research book and showed him the pictures she had brought from the hospital files.

Steve looked back at the woman with the marks all over her body that Clare had created. He went back and forth from the book, the medical close-ups of the spots, then back to the woman's body and face, even the marks on the hands.

"No doubt about it," René said, "it's smallpox." He turned to Barbara. "First case in how many years?" he asked her.

"Forty-three, according to the hospital," Barbara answered.

"Well," René's eyes were twinkling, "it's happened again, right here in the middle of the village."

"That means no one can come on the island?" Steve asked.

"That's right," René said. "No one will want to, either. Not even the French police who said they'd be on today's ferry to investigate what was going on over here."

"Could they possibly close us down?" Steve asked.

"Not if they can't set foot on the island." René laughed and pointed at his secretary in the bed. "We could be in the midst of an epidemic, don't you know that? This is the most deadly kind of smallpox. Look at the pictures."

"If you can hold them off a day and a half, we'll be finished—and all the negative shipped to Mougins," Steve said.

"I can keep this going that long. You know the bureaucrats. The law moves slowly in France, and each district is supposed to respect the laws of the others."

He turned to the woman in the bed. "Did you type up that new page for the law book of St. Venetia, the one I dictated to you, about the power to quarantine the island in case of contagious disease?"

The secretary smiled between her smallpox spots. "Yes, it's in the master book on your desk."

"Did you age the paper a little to match the rest of it?"

"I did," she said, "the way you showed me."

René turned to Steve. "The book'll be ready, and Michelle, here," he nodded at his secretary, "she's going to have a two-day vacation. The only thing is, Michelle, you have to keep the makeup on, and Clare'll check it every day. You better stay in the hospital, too, because you're going to terrify our neighbors if you walk out of the hospital that way.

"Steve," René added, "I'm getting my new doctor outfitted at your wardrobe department. He didn't look prosperous enough to be a doctor in his own suit. He's learning his lines, too. I wrote them for him," René said proudly. "He's going to scare the hell out of anyone who comes to check on what I say.

"First I'm going to show them the law book, then I'm going to introduce the doctor, and the doctor and I will bring them over to see Michelle there. I think they're going to leave you alone for days."

René, his new doctor, and St. Venetia's two fiercest-looking policemen were at the dock when the ferry came in. Two French plainclothesmen were in the bow of the ferry.

René La Grange stood at the point of disembarkment. He called for his friend, the captain of the ferry.

René gave a shattering performance. The island was in peril. Everyone was under quarantine. It was a severe case of smallpox after forty-three years without the dread disease. He had the new "doctor" fill in the details. He gave a fluent, highly technical, Latinized explanation.

"Don't get too close to me, Captain," René said soberly. "You know how small this island is. We've all been exposed."

The doctor added with great seriousness, "It spreads like wildfire, this is the worst kind—the damn plague is back."

René lowered his voice as the two French police officials spoke between themselves, and he stepped a few feet away with the ferry captain.

"Captain," he said in a low voice, "don't worry, you won't lose a day's salary. How long have we known each other, fifteen, twenty years at least? You're going to be paid off handsomely if you do just what I tell you. For two days, no one's going to make this ferry trip, except me. You're going to come for me at night and bring me back."

"But you've been exposed," the captain said. "You said—"

"I've been exposed but I'll take my chances. You just pick me up and bring me back every night. Stay away from me so you won't catch anything."

The captain looked from René to his new "doctor."

René stared through him. "Now I'm going to take you to the hospital to see the victim. Bring the two Paris investigators with you. My men will stay here and prevent anyone from leaving the ferry."

The captain introduced the investigators to René. They greeted him with the deference a French hero deserved.

Twenty minutes later, the captain returned, shaken. He and the two investigators walked far apart from René La Grange.

The captain gave the instructions to cast off. He stayed on the stern of the boat, looking back at St. Venetia, now an island of doom. He and the investigators, surrounded by questioning passengers, described the pitiful victim they had seen in the hospital.

24

The Night Before the Final Day's Filming

It was long after midnight and Rayme was stalking the beach alone, walking at the very edge of the water. He picked up a stone and hurled it out across the waves. He stared after it. He tried to sort out his own feelings. He had always hated good-byes. And tomorrow his new family would be breaking up, getting back to their lives outside the film that had consumed them all.

Edmund Bradford Wilson had cleared the way so that he could fly back to New York in peace, until he hit the reporters. Ed Wilson had posted a bond for him. Rayme would stay in New York until the grand jury heard his case. At least the film was finished. He felt he had done something of worth.

He threw another rock, looping it as high and far as he could throw over the surface of the ocean. He watched it drift downward in the night sky, disappearing. Was everything about *The Rest of Our Lives* going to disappear too?

What hit him the most was Stephanie. He hadn't realized until they did their last scene as Michael and Christina what she meant to him. Not to see her again, not to work with her again, not to be building something together.

He turned from the edge of the beach and walked back toward the cottages of Hôtel La Terrasse.

Stephanie came to the door of her room. She hadn't been able to sleep either. The sliding doors were open to the sea in the back of her small cottage. She had been writing and there was a large stack of papers on the table in the patio.

They stood there looking at each other. Rayme took her in his arms. She clung to him. They were one movement, one feeling.

Rayme carried her to the bed and let her down.

"I've waited for you so long," she said. "Make love to me, Rayme. I need you."

They held each other long after their love making.

Stephanie searched Rayme's eyes, looking for the answer she had to have. He didn't move away from her now, as Charlie Heckert had always done, and Bobby Slater, too. "It's like the first time ever for me, Rayme, honestly—looking at you now—I see what I was afraid I wouldn't see."

She kissed his face from one side to the other, his eyes and his mouth, then looked at him again.

"This is the beginning for me, as if I've never been with a man before—and in a way that's true. What I see in your eyes, Rayme, makes me pure again. I think I have love to give now, or at least I'm able to try."

He brushed her hair back with his hand as though he couldn't get enough of her soft, vulnerable face.

"I've changed, too. I think I've got things straight," Rayme said. "What there was before has nothing to do with what is happening now. I felt it every day on the set—I was falling in love with Christina."

"And I was falling in love with Michael," Stephanie said. "Michael let me fall in love with him. Rayme Monterey wouldn't.

"You know something funny, Rayme—I mean funny-strange, not funny-funny? Everytime you spoke up in our scenes when the family was together, I could feel the take-charge in you. I could feel the strength you have—I felt you would protect me. I need that, Rayme, I need that badly right now. Please don't hurt me, Rayme."

He kissed her. "I'm going to be there for you—you can count on it."

"Stay with me all night. I want to stay this close to you, holding each other. Please. All night."

25

The Last Day of the Film

Steve pulled the worn black cowboy hat down to shade his eyes from the rising sun. A man who had helped him get started in his chosen profession, who had treated him like a son, almost like Mr. Goldwyn had, had given him that hat from his favorite film, *Red River*—for good luck, when Steve had left for Arizona to make a picture, *The Challenge*. John Wayne had encouraged him to fight to make his own film. The "Duke."

Steve had worn that hat on the opening and closing days of every film he had made.

He needed luck today to finish the last two scenes of *The Rest of Our Lives*. He needed one extra day. But there was no way to get it. The money was gone. There were only three thousand feet of negative left.

He looked at the first location they'd shoot this morning. On an empty lot in the middle of the residential section of St. Venetia, the set was roped off and guarded by René La Grange's son and two young friends of his.

Boris Peters had worked all night to finish the construction of an old gabled house with a wide front porch—just wide enough to fill the camera lens on a medium shot, shooting toward the house. Boris had worked all night nearly every night they'd been on St. Venetia to come up with the impossible.

And there it was. The last set Boris had had to duplicate stood there exactly as he had reproduced it on Stage Six at the Goldwyn Studio —a "slice" of the front of the Bay House in Munising. Steve went to the spot the station wagon would be in the shot, and looked at the slice of the Bay House with his viewfinder. Against the blue sky of the island in the far background, the set was no different from the Bay House matching front in Hollywood.

He heard footsteps behind him. He turned around; it was Magdalena.

"You shouldn't have come so early," Steve said, embracing her. "You're exhausted. I've been worried about you, Maggie, how tired you've been—and you're losing weight."

"I'm fine," Magdalena said. "We're all worn out, but it's worth it. I'm so proud of you. I can't believe we're here—the last day."

"Never would have happened without you, Maggie. You've kept me fighting. I would have given up if I'd been alone."

"Never," she said, shaking her head. "That's not the way you are. That's why I fell in love with you." She kissed him. "This is the real beginning for you, Steve."

"For *us*," he said.

26

The Garibaldi Family
Leaves the Bay House

ichael carried Barbara's bags out to the station wagon that Franco had brought around to the front of the Bay House. She had to be back in Lansing to prepare for the announcement of her resignation as United States senator from Michigan.

She was going to say nothing in advance. She had simply asked Jim to call a press conference at the state capitol, and to let the rumor get out to the press that it was important and personal. She didn't have the energy left to argue her decision with Jim, so she'd kept it her own secret.

Franco put the bags in the back seat. The others were scheduled to leave later in the day. They had wanted to accompany her to the airport, but she had talked them out of it.

"I hate airports and I hate good-byes . . . but I know I'll see you all soon."

Barbara embraced her father and then her sister and brother. She stepped toward the front seat. Franco was holding the door open for her. She had the thought that it would be good to have a few minutes' drive with Franco. Talking to him would take her mind off tonight.

As she looked at her family, the image flashed through her mind of four days before at the airport in Lansing, when she had faced her two children and their father—saying good-bye—leaving again—always leaving with the conflicts pulling inside of you. She would have to have some time with her children after she went to the state capitol tonight. She wanted them to understand what she was doing and why. She worried about their reactions. She knew they had become more proud of her than they'd ever been, and they were enjoying their celebrity status with the other children in school.

Her father, her sister, and her brother felt a deep sadness as they looked back at her. Eric wondered if it could be true that his elder daughter, in these few days, looked more like her mother than ever. Maybe he simply was shaken up by the events.

"Barb," he said, as she turned to get into the car. Barbara turned back toward him.

"Dad?"

There was a silent moment between them.

"You are the earth," he said. Barbara had heard him say that once to her mother. During an anniversary celebration at the Bay House. She saw tears in her father's eyes.

She knew she had made the right decision. How could she put her personal ambitions before her family's well-being? And that family included the two children whom she would see in a few hours.

She got into the station wagon quickly and looked back at the Bay House and her family only once, for a last wave good-bye.

27

Barbara Garibaldi Resigns

*S*teve had shot photographic plates of every angle of the interior capitol rotunda, the stairway, hallways, and reception hall, while the company was on location in Lansing, Michigan. Roberto and Gaylin had been working for a week on the installation of these plates behind the stairway of the St. Venetia Historical Museum. It was more than a hundred years old, and the stairway, if it was diffused by David Thayer and Steve was close on Magdalena with the camera, could pass for the stairway of the capitol in Lansing. You wouldn't really see it, but you would feel it, a suggestion on screen.

David Thayer had large plates already projected on all four walls of the reception hall upstairs. They could get away with the impressions of the real capitol hall in Lansing if almost every shot Steve made was in close. They wouldn't know for sure how it would work until they saw the developed film.

Steve looked at the lights massed into the old museum. Everything they had was there, lit and burning. The heat was intense.

Clare, the makeup lady, came up with Catalina behind Robert Montango. "You would be perspiring in the real situation, Mr. Montango—Steve wants to see it." She approached him with her spray of make-believe sweat.

"I make my own sweat," Montango snapped. Everybody laughed, and Montango joined in. The tension eased.

Steve took Magdalena aside.

"You don't say the words here, but this is your scene—just the way we've rehearsed it. The circle of *The Rest of Our Lives* completes with you. Barbara Garibaldi is a different woman from the one she was when our film began."

"So am I," Magdalena said.

28

The Press Conference

The reporters and photographers followed Barbara Garibaldi up the steps of the state capitol rotunda.

She knew them all on a first-name basis now. The same reporters and telecasters had covered much of her campaign. The rumors had gotten out that she was going to release a statement to the press, so the national newspeople attached to the press services in Michigan were there, too.

They were grouped around her as she went up the staircase of the rotunda. These were the same stairs she had climbed only five nights before to accept her election of United States senator from Michigan. She would never serve even one day in Washington, she thought, as she neared the top of the stairs. But she had made the right decision, she was sure of it now.

Jim was waiting for her at the door of the reception hall. She could hear the conversation of the crowd within. Jim embraced her, and the photographers were on them.

"Are you sure?" Jim whispered in her ear. She nodded.

"I can't believe it," Jim whispered.

"I'm sorry," Barbara said softly. "Let's get it over with."

"There's no written statement?" he asked her.

She shook her head. "I didn't want to make a canned announcement."

Barbara glanced around her as the doors opened and the large assembly of press photographers and party members inside turned toward her. She waved at them with Jim at her side. "They," she nodded at the crowd of people moving toward her, "deserve more than that."

The room was the same as it had been five nights before. The giant banner was still on the wall with the huge words spelled out on one line, WHAT ARE WE GOING TO DO WITH . . . and on the second line THE REST OF OUR LIVES? The only difference was there was no music now. No victory shouts. No political literature spread out on tables through the room.

The members of the party crowding the room applauded. It was a spontaneous moment, and she took it in. She tightened her grip on Jim's hand. How could she tell them? How could she do this so that they would still believe her campaign had been honest—that she had meant what she said?

In the center of the large crowd, with camera and television lenses pointing at her, microphones in a circle around her, Barbara spoke quietly. The crowd of people grew silent.

"I have a statement to make to you, ladies and gentlemen of the press, and to all of you loyal people here and within the sound of my voice who have supported my campaign, believed in me, and elected me as the first woman to serve as United States senator from Michigan. I will never forget this honor, and the respect and kindness you have shown toward me.

"I have come here tonight to tell you—" Her voice was interrupted by a murmur that ran through the crowd. The circle around her made way for five people who had just entered the reception room.

"What's going on?" Jim asked her. "You didn't tell me your family—" His voice cut off as Eric Garibaldi, flanked by Christina and Michael, came up behind Barbara, with Barbara's children, Melly and Stewart. The photographers and reporters immediately closed in on the four of them. Barbara looked at her family, stunned.

The press was clamoring. "Can we have a statement?" "What is the announcement?" "Is there a press handout available? We don't know what's going on," a reporter said to Jim.

Eric Garibaldi put his arms around his children and faced the camera. He didn't answer Barbara's questioning looks.

"I'm Barbara Garibaldi's father. This is her sister and her brother. Barbara's going to have a lot to say in the months to come. This is the last time I'll ask to speak for her.

"You were called here tonight to hear Barbara resign her election to the United States Senate. We have been threatened, and we don't know for sure what group or individuals are behind it. We're making no accusations. I don't think we need to.

"We were told, by anonymous callers and messengers, that unpleasant and damaging, but documented stories about each one of us would be given out to the press if Barbara did not resign. Five days ago, we were given one week to make this decision.

"Every big mistake we've made, each one of us, promised to make great listening and great reading. These are things in the past. They are not situations we had revealed to each other. We certainly didn't want to see these things spread around Michigan, much less the rest of the country.

"But my daughter has started something here which really concerns all of us. As she said in her campaign, 'What are we going to do with the rest of our lives?'

"We have been together for a long weekend, our first in years, all four of us, to decide what to do. None of us wants to see our mistakes, our personal skeletons, become public knowledge.

"But this is a time in our lives when every one of us is facing questions about values and ethics. It's hard to find anything to believe in anymore, and we decided we could believe in two things—ourselves and the truth.

"Barbara came here to tell you that she was going to resign, because she wanted to protect us. When we last saw her earlier today that was the family decision.

"But it wasn't right. It's not that easy for the Garibaldis to give up. Her brother and sister are with me on this, and so are her children.

"We've come here tonight to tell Barbara—" he looked at his daughter, then back at the circle of spellbound faces, "—and all of you— we'll face whatever dirt is thrown at us. There are no questions we won't answer. The whole truth is what you're going to get, and we don't know what will happen as a result. Maybe our family secrets will spoil everything that you and Barbara have worked to build together. But nothing can spoil the idea, the idea up there on the wall that caught fire in this state: 'What are we going to do with the rest of our lives?'

"I can only tell you what this family is going to do. We're together and we're here to tell any of you who are interested that we stand as a family—proudly—for the election of Barbara as United States senator from the state of Michigan."

29

St. Venetia

Lieu was getting ready for bed after the last day of filming. Even though she lived alone and slept alone, she prepared for bed every night of her life in a kind of symbolic ritual of her own feeling as a beautiful woman and her own self-respect. She remained a woman of great pride.

In a shimmering pale green nightgown and peignoir, she brushed her long, dark hair. She never wore it long publicly. It was always done in an Oriental style, parted in the middle and bound at the back.

Now as she brushed her hair in front of the mirror, the years fell away, and in the soft light of the candles in her room she seemed to be a young girl again. An exquisite Oriental woman with the femininity, intelligence, and sensitivity of thousands of years of Oriental culture inculcated in her.

There was a knock at her door, and she looked up, suddenly taken out of her thoughts and memories. She called out, "Yes?"

She recognized the voice that answered. It was Robert Montango. "Lieu," he said, "I need to see you."

She closed the front of her peignoir around her and opened the door.

Robert Montango was coming apart. She saw that in an instant.

"Would you like a drink?" Lieu asked.

"Whatever you've got," Montango said.

She went to the refrigerator and brought out a bottle of white wine.

Montango watched her curiously as she engaged in another ritual of sorts. She put a cloth over the table, put some crackers on a beautiful plate, and brought out a fresh Edam cheese. He reached for the wine to open it. She gestured delicately for him to stay where he was, then she put a cloth around the wine and opened it herself. She brought two glasses from the kitchen cupboard and poured the wine. It was a simple act of everyday living made into a graceful, sensuous motion.

Montango looked at her. She was always so unapproachable. Throughout the picture his desire for this woman had mounted.

Steve had told him of her background, but Robert and Lieu had never really talked. He had watched her the way he watched every woman, but of all the women in the picture, including even Magdalena, she was the one who challenged him.

Montango looked at her, his wine glass raised, and he tried to find his voice, a voice known around the world. But that voice wouldn't come out. He sounded more like a boy, unsure. The strength was missing. And his hand was trembling.

Goddamn it, his hand was trembling, lifting a glass to toast a beautiful woman. What the hell was happening? He knew what was happening. He'd felt it before, it was different this time. Maybe this was his last film. Maybe this was it.

"I want to say something to you," he said. "I've been wanting to tell you through the whole picture. Lieu—" his voice was low, "—I've fallen in love with you."

She didn't laugh at him, as he half expected. There was no ridicule in her eyes. Here was a man who had said those words to so many women in so many places, in so many pictures and so many locations, and in so many real-life scenes that it was a cliché with him. This woman seemed to understand him.

"That is a great compliment," she said, "for any woman. To be told that honestly by any man. Thank you, Robert. Somehow, that's a beautiful closing note to what has been an extraordinary day and an extraordinary film."

They both sipped the wine.

"I don't want it to be a closing note," Montango said. He looked at her. "Lieu, I've got to tell you something that nobody knows, but I'm feeling so strange."

Lieu's voice was compassionate. "I think we're all feeling a little lost tonight, Robert."

He stood up and started to pace. His voice came in sputters and pauses. "I don't mean the same as everyone else. Yes, we're all sad about the picture being over; we're all excited; we're all exhausted. We're all having emotional catharsis. But Lieu, let me ask you something, are you scared?"

Lieu shook her head. "Why should I be?"

"Because of life," he said. "I know you've lost everything you had. And as far as I know, you don't have a husband or a lover . . . by choice. Don't you want that? Aren't you afraid of being alone?"

Lieu shook her head. "I have had my pains, like everyone else, Robert. But I have found peace. I wanted so many things when I was young.

"I met a wonderful Indian woman, the mother of Zubin Mehta, an extraordinary woman, Tami, whom her son worships. And she told me once that she had learned that, for her, happiness was peace.

"I've remembered that. I try to keep from wanting too much anymore. I have my children. I have my work with Steve. And I have friends in the Cambodian community in the United States. There's so much needed there. And I'm needed there. So, no, I'm not afraid."

Montango turned on her. He drained the wine and she filled his glass again. "I'm scared, Lieu. I'm scared all the time. When I'm working hard, when I've crawled inside someone else's skin, behind someone else's eyes and into someone else's mind and tongue and heart, I'm all right. I'm at home.

"Then I have strength. Then I know who I am. I'm that person. And I'm that person for as long as the filming lasts.

"But when shooting ends, like today, then I'm Robert Montango again. And I tell you the truth, Lieu, I don't know who Robert Montango is anymore. He's lost somewhere back in his childhood in East Los Angeles. In a little house where there were no windows, so my father painted beautiful scenes of exotic foreign lands in little rectangles in the room, and that way we'd be looking at something, because we couldn't look outside.

"I'm lost somewhere in a mixed Mulligan's stew of jobs—cab driver, boxer, bricklayer, waiter. I didn't really do all those things, but when I tell my life story in an interview or something, I don't even know what's true and what's false anymore.

"There's Robert Montango out there, who's written about and reviewed and talked about, and then there's the real Robert Montango, me. And the closest I can come to him, in words, is that he's a little boy who doesn't really approve of the other Montango. You know, I swear to God, Lieu, I swear to God, when I stood on stage, accepting my Academy Award, I said that I didn't believe in competition among actors. But even then, I could hear the voice of that little boy inside me, saying, 'Who the hell do you think you are? You're nothing. You think you're a big man because you won the Academy Award? What have you added to the world? Who are you? You've lied, you've cheated, you've pretended, you bragged, you've gotten drunk, you've been in love with a lot of women—' Pardon me, Lieu, pardon me. But I don't want to go back inside the old Robert Montango.

"Now, today, I can tell you, Lieu, this film—I don't know what it is, I don't know what we've got in the film, I don't even know what I've done. All I know is that somehow Steve got inside of me, and I put something on the screen there without artifice. I think I let the little boy come through—and I don't know what the hell's going to happen to my career now.

"And I've got to have a career because I don't exist unless I'm inside a part.

"Do you know what kind of life that is? When I go back to Hollywood, go back to my sculpture and my painting, I'll put on all the trappings of Robert Montango again. But at night—until I have another part—until I know when I'm starting another picture—I'll be in a cold sweat, wondering if the phone will ever ring. Wondering if I'll ever be wanted again. Wondering if I'm too old—" He stopped.

Lieu said, softly, "I don't think anyone thinks of you as ever growing old, Robert. You're like a fixture in the firmament. Something that's always there, something that does not change."

Montango knelt beside her, trying to feel her warmth without touching her. "God, I wish that were true, Lieu, but you know, I see it. I see it on the screen, I see it in the mirror every morning. I feel it in the way people look at me. The face—" he ran his hand through his hair. "My hair is getting older. I have to use more and more of the goddamned rinse—and I know no one escapes it—"

He stood up and looked at her. "Lieu, I'm getting old. You know something strange? I don't feel any different inside than I did when I started acting. Fifty years ago. I have the same instincts, the same desires for everything. I have the same lust for life—for life, Lieu. Not only women. I know everybody talks about that, but that isn't all.

"I want to experience everything, and there just isn't time. I remember a line from a film I made with Steve. This rejected man says, 'I'm going to go everywhere, I'm going to know all there is of life.'

"That line rang home to me, because that's the way I've felt all my life. That's the way I feel now. I've never felt more alive, more anxious, more excited, more on edge, as this strange, and, I hope, wonderful picture comes to an end.

"That's when I thought of you. If there was any woman who could understand this, who could see beyond my face changing and my body aging, and understand the dreams that are still inside of me . . . if any woman could do that, you could. You could understand, because you have the wisdom, as they say, of the ages. I'm sure, looking at you."

He put his hand under her chin and lifted her face toward him. "That's why I came here. I'd hoped you weren't asleep yet. I had to tell you this. I couldn't hold it in any longer."

"I understand, Robert," Lieu said, quietly. "I'm flattered that you came to me. A woman needs to be needed."

He took the sides of Lieu's face in his hands. "Lieu, I swear to God, I know there are a million stories about me, and most of them are true. But this is different. This is really different. I respect you. I admire you. I look up to you. I really need you."

Lieu said softly, "I think I understand you, Robert. And I will try to be here for you when you need me." She took his hands from the side of her face, and put his hands together, like a child's, and kissed his fingers tenderly. "As your friend," she said.

He looked at her quietly. "I want you as a woman, Lieu. I love you."

She kept holding his hands, clasped together. "I think we have a different definition of love, Robert. I have been through the love of eternal pledges, impassioned nights, of possessiveness and longing. And holding inside of you the seed of the man you love and worship. Giving birth to your children, and his children.

"And then seeing the imperfections and inconsistencies and selfishness of some people eat away at that love until the whole experience is destroyed.

"I've learned what I think love is. Robert, for me, love is caring when you're sick, seeing the beautiful in someone who is tired and worn, uplifting someone when life has broken them in two, putting your hands—" she tightened her hands on his, "—on the wounds that life brings.

"Love is as complex, for me, and as simple as 'being there'—being there with all of your heart and your mind and your soul.

"Love, for me, is not a beautiful speech or a passionate letter, or arguments and reunions. Robert, real love is rich and mature, and passionate, and serene. And does not change with the aging—" she put her hand on his cheek, "—of the face, or the changing—" she ran her hand through his hair, "—of the hair.

"I have seen love like that—rarely, but I know that it can exist. And until I find such a love, if I ever do, I will never be with a man again. I made that vow to myself. To my Buddha.

"When my husband deserted me and went with many women, and disgraced me in front of my people, for whom I was a symbol, I took off all my jewelry. I had an exquisite collection of jewelry, Robert. You've never seen me wear even one piece, have you? I put away my fur coats. I did away with all the trappings of a life that I was never to have again. I went back to start life again on the basis of knowing myself, expanding my horizons, devoting myself to my two boys and my people.

"I won't deny that it is lonely. I feel your need, and I want you to know the truth. I don't believe, Robert," she raised his face until his eyes were level with hers, "that's the kind of love you're searching for. I want you to know I think you're an extraordinary man, a great talent, and because that little boy is alive in you, and needs so much comforting, you are very appealing. The little boy would win my heart long before the bullfighter.

"Please be my friend. I have needs, too. I need the friendship of those who mean much to me. You are one of those people, Robert."

She put her arms around him tenderly. "I'm proud that you came to me. Very proud."

He held her for a moment, then turned back to the door. He seemed to revive and his voice was strong again.

"Good night, Lieu. Thank you for being here!" he said, and closed the door behind him.

30

St. Venetia

agdalena and Steve walked along the edge of the beach, barefoot, under a moonlit, star-filled sky. They were arm in arm, and for a long time they said nothing. Magdalena stopped to embrace him.

"Did you ever see an old English film, Steve, it's on late television now and then, it's called *Cavalcade?*"

"Sure—I've seen it two or three times—"

"Do you remember," Magdalena said, "that moment when the young couple who have just been married are standing on the bridge of the ship, and the woman is so happy, so unbelievably happy, and her world is so perfect, so absolutely perfect, and she says to her husband, 'I almost wish that life could stop right at this moment, because I could never be any happier than I am right now, and nothing could ever compare to what I feel. Everything would stay forever, just like this moment.'"

She smiled. "That's a rough translation. I'm not sure of the words, but I am sure of the meaning."

Steve said, "And then the camera moved down from the two lovers on the railing of the ship to a round life preserver and the words on it were 'S.S. *Titanic.*' That was a great piece of moviemaking."

Magdalena nodded. "And a great piece of reality, Steve. That's the way I feel, right now." She turned and put her arms on his shoulders. "I've known it all, now. I've had total, wonderful love with you."

Steve kissed her eyes. "Correction," he said, "you have. H-a-v-e. No past tense. We're going to go on and on, Maggie, just like this ocean." He looked across the ocean to the horizon. "We are forever, Maggie."

Magdalena looked at him steadily for a moment and then kissed him. "Forever," she whispered.

Her mood suddenly changed. "Steve," she said, "let's go for a drive. I don't want to waste one hour sleeping. Let's go back to every place we've been, every place we've filmed across 'our' island."

Along the roadside near the beach, a herd of horses galloped in the fenced-in field. They were racing horses, and their shining, sleek bodies glistened in the moonlight. Magdalena put her hand on Steve's arm. "Steve, let's get out here—for a moment—"

Steve pulled his car over onto the shoulder of the road. Magdalena slipped out of the seat and walked to the edge of the fence. Beyond it was the high grass and, in the distance of the night, there was the movement of the horses grazing.

She took Steve's hand and led him through the fence gate and into the field.

They gazed at each other. "We are part of all this," she said. "And I want to remember it. The film brought us all back to the earth."

"I was born close to the earth, Steve, and now you've brought me full circle—every star, every hilltop, every meadow like this—every blade of grass—has a meaning for me now that it never did before."

A horse running full out suddenly passed close by them, half hidden in the tall grass. Steve pulled her to him. She trembled, but not with fear. They walked toward the center of the field. Now the grass was lower.

Suddenly Magdalena turned to Steve, put her arms around his neck, and pulled him down close to her. Steve picked her up and put her on the soft green-covered meadowland.

"Please—here—now. I want you more than I've ever wanted you," she said.

Steve eased himself onto her, her legs wrapped around him, covered in their long silk stockings. Her blouse was open. She moved her hips under him till he was deeply into her. She looked up at him, covered with the umbrella of the night and the star-sprinkled sky. There was no one else in the world. They were alone, God's creatures.

Steve moved slowly within her. "Together," she whispered. "Together, mi amor, mi vida."

Steve burst within her, and their passion throbbed until they were quiet, side by side, holding each other closely. Enfolded in each other's arms, they embraced the sky.

31

Charles de Gaulle Airport

A shimmering summer rain clouded the Charles de Gaulle Airport on the outskirts of Paris. René La Grange and Lieu had arranged for a special permit for Magdalena, as well as themselves, to go beyond the security check and the passport control desk, out to the actual embarkation point of Air France flight 738 for New York.

Magdalena stood in the shadow of the giant plane as the cast and the key members of the crew started up the steps. This had to be her best performance. She prayed that it would be.

She looked enchanting standing there in a powder blue trenchcoat with matching rain boots, holding her Parisian umbrella, a burst of spring colors. As Steve came hurrying toward her, having checked through the last of his "family" for the flight to New York, he warmed at the sight of her.

She looked stronger, even though they had been up all night. In the last few days her pale complexion had become flushed by the summer sun of St. Venetia, and she actually seemed sunburned, almost as if she had a high fever. She exuded happiness and good spirits. He had no way of knowing that the "sun" on her face was, indeed, the flush of the burning fever that had risen in intensity almost day by day the last week.

He had tried again to persuade Magdalena to go with him to New York, but she'd said she had urgent business in California. He had tried to send Lieu with her, but Magdalena had refused. She didn't want to cause any change of plan, as the auction would be the following night in New York. Steve promised to call her the minute he had the news. She had said, "I'm glad, in a way, that you won't have to worry about me in New York. You should have your full concentration on the picture."

"Kathleen and Lorelei are going to be there, even AGW. Why shouldn't you be there, too?" Steve had answered.

"I've had you to myself in many ways these last weeks. Your children deserve to spend some special time with you, and I *know* you'll be celebrating together. If I were worried about the result of the auction, I would come with you. Just settle everything, and don't feel sad because I'm not there. Promise to call me after you open all the envelopes on Tuesday night."

"You're very confident," Steve answered. "*All* the envelopes? You're counting on us having several offers?"

"I know it," she had said. They were in the limousine on the way to the airport. "You've won, Steve, you have fought an incredible fight." She leaned over and kissed him and pushed back his hair from his forehead.

Steve began to walk slower as they approached the plane. He was watching this woman who had become part of his life. He didn't want to be away from her for one single day. He had seen her every day for three months.

It seemed that another old cliché was true, that he had known her such a long time. She had crowded every other woman he had ever known out of his memories. With Kathleen and Lorelei, Magdalena had become the center of his life. He would go to New York, take whatever was to come, and pray to God that Magdalena's expectations were right. He wasn't afraid of the results, whichever way they went. He knew what he'd done. He knew what he and all his "family" had accomplished. They had done the best they could.

He had stayed up all night with Dick Portman, finishing the temporarily dubbed work print. He had hardly thought of the lawsuits waiting for him, and even a warrant for his arrest. Ed Wilson and Spartan were handling those problems. What if the auction failed? The house of cards would collapse.

He knew that he loved and needed this woman with all his heart. She was the other part of him, the completeness of him, his friend, his confidante, his lover, his woman, and soon, as soon as she set the time and the place, his wife. He was so proud of her. What a magnificent person she was!

What a joy, the constant give-and-take between this great performer and her director. And, incredibly, she had seemed to be increasingly humble as the picture progressed. Her slight irritations, her rare flashes of arrogance, her egocentricities had declined steadily, particularly on the island. Increasingly, she had gone out of her way to give of herself, not only to him, but also to Stephanie, to Lieu, to Robert Montango, to Rayme, and to all the crew who were now boarding the plane to New York.

He came up and stood beside her in the rain, thinking of a portrait of her that Robert Montango had painted and how much he would like to have another portrait of the way she looked now, with the almost pastel rain of the Paris summer falling on her umbrella, her face bright and smiling, her eyes shining with affection as she said good-bye to the people who had become her family, too. He thought, for a moment, how strange it was that her eyes were so full of light. They looked as if David's pin lights were shining directly into them.

Magdalena wondered if she could hold it together. It would be just another minute or two. The baggage and the food carts were pulling away from the plane now. They were getting ready to leave. Lieu embraced Magdalena, then she drew back and looked at her with tenderness. "You are a great woman," she said.

Magdalena hugged her. "I've learned so much from you, Lieu. Patience and humility." Then she whispered in Lieu's ear, "You won't forget our talk, will you?"

"I'll remember," Lieu said. She looked at Magdalena quizzically. What was the mystery? Lieu went up the stairs and into the plane.

From the top of the stairs the stewardess called down. "Sorry, Mr. Wayland, but we're ready to go."

Steve nodded. "I'm not ready," he said to Magdalena. "Promise me something, will you?"

"If I can," Magdalena smiled. Oh, God, she thought, let me do this right, the way I've planned—let me send him off the right way. Give me the strength. "I will if I can," she said to Steve.

"I don't ever want to be separated again," Steve said. "Not even for a day. I don't want us working in separate places. If it's your career, I'll go with you. If it's my career, you be with me. I've seen too many people break up with the separations of our work. I need you. Nothing is the same without you. I want you to promise me that we won't be separated again."

"Don't you think," Magdalena said, "that I want to stay as close to you as I can? There's no life for me either, Steve, without you."

He kissed her again as the stewardess called out, "Mr. Wayland."

Steve turned toward her for a moment. "I'm coming," he said, "right away." He turned back to his woman, holding both her hands.

"I love you," he said. "Forever."

"Forever," she answered.

They looked at each other for a moment.

Magdalena had broken out in a sweat. The fever was on her stronger than she'd ever felt it. Please, God, get me through one more moment, she prayed.

"Don't forget to call me right after the auction," she said, as he went up the stairs to the plane.

"Don't worry, I won't," he said, and then he turned at the very top of the stairs, framed in the curved doorway of the main cabin.

She stood there in the soft summer rain, a vision of pastel colors, her eyes fever-bright, looking up at him, her left hand in the air, almost frozen there, as though she was straining to touch him one last time.

Steve couldn't understand why he felt so depressed. After all, it was only going to be a few days. But she was part of him, like Kathleen and Lorelei. Nothing was the same. He gave her a last salute as the stairs were pulled away and the stewardess was preparing to shut the door.

The tall figure in a dark blue coat, smoking a pipe, walked up behind Magdalena. She turned toward him as she heard the footsteps. "Father Ciklic!" she exclaimed. "I can't believe you're here!"

Peter Ciklic embraced her and she buried her head in his shoulder. She was crying now.

"Steve called me," he said.

"I didn't know that," Magdalena said.

"He wanted me to be with you. My taxi was delayed in the rain," Father Ciklic said.

"Thank you for coming. I've got to pull myself together. I don't feel very well," Magdalena said. "And I know Steve. He's going to be watching from the window. I can't see him, but he'll keep looking for me while the plane taxis away. I've got to be here in the same place, just as he left me. He'll know you're here and he won't be so worried about me."

"He doesn't know?" the priest questioned.

She shook her head. "No, thank God. And this is one of my really bad days. I didn't think I could do it."

Father Ciklic kept his arm around her. They were both facing the plane and waving in its general direction. Magdalena knew that somewhere inside that plane Steve was pressed against the window for one last moment with her. She waved and forced a smile.

He probably couldn't see that clearly from the small window, but just in case, she thought. "No matter what happens now," Magdalena said, "Steve has his picture."

"And you," Father Ciklic said. "I've rarely seen a man so completely in love."

"Will he be all right, Father?"

"In time," Father Ciklic answered, "because he will find that you are within him. When a person really loves, nothing can change that."

Magdalena turned toward him. "You really believe that, Father?"

Peter Ciklic nodded. "Yes, Magdalena, I do."

The plane began to rumble toward the takeoff, and they turned back toward the airfield, waving their good-byes through the rain against the gray-blue sky of Paris.

Steve, sitting in the front of the plane, was pressed against the window of his seat. He saw the two tiny figures receding in the distance with their arms waving. He waved at the window, although he knew they couldn't possibly see him. He framed that picture of Magdalena in his heart. Magdalena standing there in the Paris rain, her eyes shining, her hand raised, stretching out toward him.

He began to count the days and the hours and the minutes until she would be back in his arms again. This was the last time they would be separated, ever. She had promised him.

The SEARCH

Book IV

1

Sutton Theater, New York City

The auction of *The Rest of Our Lives* was to be a unique event. Spartan Lee had rented the Sutton Theater on the East Side for the evening.

Steve had given the work print to the care of Roberto Bakker. Ed Wilson would be with Roberto when it was delivered to the projection room of the Sutton. Ed had explained to Steve that it could be seized and held if Steve brought the film in himself. Possession was still nine tenths of the law. By the time Roberto and Ed delivered the print to the Sutton, Wilson's office would have a restraining order preventing the seizure of the film by anyone until the screening and auction were over.

The screening of *The Rest of Our Lives* was by Spartan Lee's invitation only. Every major distributor was there.

Neither Jack Gregson nor Steve Wayland came to the theater.

Gregson was in his suite at the Pierre Hotel with Jerry Clune and the rest of his entourage. Gregson could not believe how big this thing had become. How in the hell had Wayland ever thought of sending the cans of unusable negative to the Paris lab, throwing him off the track?

Gregson had thought he had it all wrapped up before Kate Manning's show. Then he had ordered one can of developed negative at the Paris lab sent express to him at MGL.

He had screened the developed film with the head of his editorial staff. Gregson had hoped desperately that this jumbled collection of shots, half-finished, lights failing, Steve walking onto the set while the camera was still rolling, were part of a crazy Steve Wayland collage. But his editor had assured him that this was the way any can of unusable negative would look if it were actually developed. This can and the other hundred cans like it had been deliberately sent to the Paris lab as a ruse.

The truth had finally come out. A little lab in Mougins, France, where Picasso and Clouzot had developed *The Mystery of Picasso*, had done all of Steve's work. The negative had been secretly taken there and the developed film secretly taken back to St. Venetia. It was an undercover work of art.

Who the hell had ever heard of Mougins, France? Gregson thought. Or René Clouzot, either, for that matter. No wonder they hadn't been able to find out where the film was being processed. Wayland had made a fool of him, but he was going to pay in full this same night. By midnight the auction would be over. And Steve Wayland would be finished. Gregson was sure of it. But why the hell was he sweating? Why did he have those shooting pains in his gut?

Edmund Bradford Wilson had taken service of the warrants of his clients, Steve Wayland and Rayme Monterey. Monterey was to go before the grand jury in four weeks. There would be a pretrial conference on Steve Wayland's case in three weeks. It would be years before all the legalistics were over if it went to trial. But Steve's personal fortunes could be settled by midnight.

Wilson had a plan to have all Gregson's charges against Steve dropped if the auction worked. He'd need the right leverage, though, which only a successful auction could give to him. Six million and interest for the studio. Five hundred thousand to the Bank of California, representing the anonymous investor.

Spartan Lee's invitations had been carefully screened. He had worked closely with Jake Powers and Lieu.

They had taken a key cross-section of all their New York premiere lists. Opinion makers. Prestigious leaders in the city. Writers. The top literary agents. A few critics who made a signed agreement that they would not review the picture until it was officially released. Anchormen. Columnists Spartan could trust. The society crowd. Fashion designers. Celebrities. They had all come out to be a part of the first audience ever to see *The Rest of Our Lives*.

Spartan had limited the photographers. All photographs had to go through him. The crowd was covered, but in Spartan's own selective way.

At five minutes before six, Spartan had two men on his personal staff close the doors to the theater. No one else was to be admitted, no matter who it was. Everything was precision-timed.

At four minutes before six, the officially announced starting time for the screening, Spartan walked out onto the stage of the Sutton Theater. He spoke into a microphone.

"I want to explain, briefly, the rules of the auction," Spartan said. "There will be no exceptions.

"In exactly four minutes, *The Rest of Our Lives* will begin. This is a work print with temporary recording of music and sound effects. As you know by now, everything was completed in St. Venetia after seven weeks' shooting in Hollywood, Michigan, and New York.

"The ownership of *The Rest of Our Lives* has not been clearly defined by law. There are literally hundreds of people involved in the ownership, including the producer, director, and writer, Steve Wayland, his cast, his crew, the owners of Jack Gregson's company, and beyond that company, the parent company, Mager-Golden-Lasky, with all its stockholders.

"There is a contract which requires Mager-Golden-Lasky to distribute the film, but there is also a signed buy-back letter from Mager-Golden-Lasky to Mr. Wayland and his company.

"The facts are simple. Six and a half million dollars is the cost of the film. Some seven weeks of intensive postproduction are still necessary.

"*The Rest of Our Lives* is the first film in motion picture history to be auctioned in this way. As in any other auction, the highest bidder, or the company with the best conditions to offer Mr. Wayland, or a combination of both, will gain the worldwide distribution rights to *The Rest of Our Lives* in all media, as well as fifty percent of the net profits. All bids must be in excess of six million five hundred thousand dollars."

"Sealed bids will be received at my office at the Plaza Athénee Hotel between eight o'clock tonight, when this screening is finished, and midnight. Everyone has an equal opportunity to compete, if they care to do so. Thank you for coming."

Spartan Lee would never make a special plea for anything, to anyone. It was his tradition to be in a position, or, at the very least, to play out his hand as though he had a position, of strength. He catered to no one.

The lights began to dim.

* * *

Steve Wayland was stretched out on the bed in his suite. The phone was on the table beside him. He turned out the lights. He wanted to be alone during the sweat-out.

He glanced at his watch. Six thirty-five. They were into it now. How many people were walking out? For a moment, he wished he were there. And then he knew that Spartan had been wise to urge him not to attend the screening.

He thought of how you watched like a hawk when you were sitting in an audience seeing a first showing of your film. Your peripheral vision was never better. You sensed anyone in the theater who got up. You saw whether it was a man or a woman, even in the darkness, and what they were wearing. And then the sweat began to ooze out of you. You waited and waited, hopefully, and then if that person who had gotten up and gone out came back in, it was like you'd been given an extraordinary gift. Simply because a man or a woman had gone to the restroom and not out of the theater.

And then there were those who didn't come back. You'd lost them. How many more would there be? You couldn't really watch your picture. It was a torture chamber.

No, Steve was thankful that he wasn't there. There was no political game he had to play. No one he had to speak to. He didn't have to look into a face and know that that person wanted him to fail, was hoping he would fail. Not because he was Steve Wayland, but because that's the way it was.

"The only award worth winning, in the end, is the one within yourself."

That remark of Sam Goldwyn's came back to Steve now. He wanted to evaluate for himself how he felt inside, before he heard the reaction of others to the screening and before he and Spartan sat in Spartan's penthouse office in the hotel and waited for the bids. If there were any bids. He wouldn't know anything for another two hours. All the years that had brought him to this point in his career and his life crowded together in his head. His love affair with motion pictures. It had come full circle.

Steve had been seven years old when his mother and father had taken him and his brother to the foremost theater in Chicago, the palatial Loew's State, for their first movie.

Steve had been awed by the massive lobby with its Italian marble statues and art objects. The white Carrera marble he would see again someday in Michelangelo's *Pietà*. The elaborate fountain at the center of the lobby was from Milan, his mother and father told him. He had no idea where Milan was. Everything about the Loew's State was bigger than life. The ceiling seemed almost as high as the sky.

Clearly, this place had been built for kings and queens—red velvet seats, red carpeting on the aisle floors, the red velvet and gold brocade curtain covering the large screen at the front of the theater. Young men and women dressed in starched red uniforms, shining flashlights ahead of them, took you to your seat.

Steve had read about movies, heard about them, but he'd never seen one. Some of his friends at school had. Finally he was to see this movie after many months of pleading with his mother and father.

They had told him it was the story of a great French writer, Victor Hugo. It was called *Les Misérables* and starred one of the top leading men in Hollywood, Fredric March.

And now the lights were going out. Steve loved the way they faded so slowly at the same time the huge red velvet curtain was parting, and the brocade was being pulled back in a graceful curve by the gilt ropes.

It was like opening the cover of one of his treasured books, like *Robin Hood* or *David Copperfield*. But this was even better, because it was so big and beautiful in there and he felt warm and secure sitting between his mother and father.

He could not stand it when the captains in the galley whipped Jean Valjean. He stood up out of his seat, clinging to the one in front of him.

He wanted to do something, he wanted to help Fredric March up there on the screen. What a fine-looking man he was. And they were beating him cruelly. He hated those galley captains.

And then Jean Valjean was finally released from his prison sentence. He was a young man, but he could hardly stand up. His clothes were rags. He had a long beard. And he was still in pain from his injuries in the galley.

He was a frightening figure on the road. No one would touch him. He was an outcast. Alone. That terrible feeling. Alone. Steve had grabbed onto his mother and father for support. He never took his eyes from the screen.

Now Jean Valjean was hungry and he had no food. And he was turned away from many doors. But then the priest, that kindly-looking man who reminded Steve of a Sunday-school version of God the Father, opened the door and asked the filthy Jean Valjean into his home. And he had his housekeeper serve Jean Valjean a full meal.

The man ate like an animal, like the dog that lived next door to

Steve. He kept his mouth close to the plate, and his eyes were raised in suspicion. But the priest sat there and talked to him just like he was any other guest at the table.

Jean Valjean looked at him scornfully. Poor fool. Giving away his life to a God that didn't exist. A God who would allow you to go into the galleys, who would let you be imprisoned for stealing a loaf of bread, a God who allowed you to be beaten until you were almost dead, until you'd rather be dead. God! Jean Valjean looked like he was going to spit in the priest's face.

The night went on, and the priest and the housekeeper went to bed in their sections of the house. The guest room had been given to Jean Valjean. He listened until he could hear the priest snoring, then he got out of the bed. He'd never taken off his filthy clothes or his dirty boots.

Where was he going? Oh, Steve saw, those silver candlesticks that had been on the dining room table. He'd seen Jean Valjean looking at those. Now he understood why. That was because something was going to happen with Jean Valjean and those candlesticks. Jean Valjean looked at them, measuring how much they might bring him in money with which he could buy food and clothes. He put both the large silver candelabras in his filthy bag that he carried over his shoulder, and he made his way out into the night. Jean Valjean had robbed that man who looked like God. What would happen now?

The priest was awakened by the police at his door. They had Jean Valjean handcuffed. They had seen him come out of the priest's house and they had found the silver candelabra in his bag. They needed the priest to state that they were, in fact, the priest's candlesticks, then they could write up a report and put Valjean in jail. They knew that Valjean was on parole, that he had been a galley slave, and his sentence by law would be to go back to the galleys for many more years.

The priest's face didn't change. He smiled as he spoke to Jean Valjean and said that he had hoped that he would stay until morning so that he could have a very good breakfast before he started his trip. As for the candlesticks, the priest said, as he turned to the police, "No, you've made a mistake, officers. The candlesticks don't belong to me. I gave them to Jean Valjean last night. After dinner." The police officers had looked at the priest incredulously.

"You gave them to him?" one officer asked.

"Yes," the priest said. He glanced back at Jean Valjean and looked him in the eyes. "This man is my friend."

Reluctantly, almost, the police unlocked Jean Valjean's handcuffs, and Jean Valjean stood at the doorway of the priest's home.

"Won't you come in for breakfast, Jean?" the priest said.

Jean Valjean glanced behind him until he saw the policemen disappear. He reached into his bag and took the candlesticks out again. He handed them to the priest, but the priest put up his hand.

"I meant what I said, Jean," the priest said. "The candlesticks are yours. Now come in. You should have a good breakfast before you start on your journey."

Jean Valjean didn't move for a moment, and Steve would never forget the look in Fredric March's eyes, burning with intensity. A passionate man! He put out his hand and clasped the priest's hand in both of his.

"I will never forget you," he said. "I will keep your candlesticks as a symbol of what I want to be. I will never curse God and His heaven again. I will never doubt there is a God. I have found someone to believe in."

Steve was crying now. His mother was sorry they had brought him to the film. She had tried to tell his father that he was still too young. But Steve had won his father over. Everyone at school was talking about the film, and the teacher said it was one of the great stories in all literature. Steve would even be reading it in school in a few years as part of an assignment. So why couldn't he see the movie?

The years flowed by in the film. Jean Valjean kept the priest's candlesticks wherever he lived and worked. He had new clothes now. His beard was shaven. He was in love with a beautiful blond aristocratic woman. He was the best-looking man Steve had ever seen.

There he was on the screen. A god. A god whose face and figure were magnified fifty times on the screen in this royal palace. And the woman was perfect-looking, too. They belonged together, you knew it the first time they met each other on the screen. They were two perfect people in an imperfect world.

And just as their happiness seemed complete, an old technical charge on Jean Valjean's record came to the attention of the greatest manhunter on the Paris police force, a man named Javert. Jean Valjean was a man of wealth now, of position. And suddenly the shadow of a long-ago minor charge, never officially made part of Jean Valjean's record, began to overtake him.

Javert was a relentless pursuer. And when he thought he could prove that Jean Valjean was the criminal he was looking for, it became an obsession with him.

Steve hated Javert. Charles Laughton was such an extraordinary actor that he made you feel whatever he wanted you to feel.

Javert was the symbolic villain. An interesting, three-dimensional, complicated villain with his own code of ethics.

It was the hero against the villain, good versus evil, the classic confrontation.

Steve loved Fredric March and hated Charles Laughton. But when, in the end, Javert could not bring himself to arrest Jean Valjean and therefore failed his own ethics and killed himself, Steve felt sorry for the homely fat man up there on the screen. He understood something about what had happened and why the man had committed suicide.

But then he was so glad that his beloved Jean Valjean was safe. The hero had won. It was a happy ending.

In one night in that royal palace of marble and gold, red velvet and brocade, Steve had been transported from the reality of a difficult life of a relatively poor family to the magical storybook world of heroes, villains, and beautiful ladies, and a priest who looked like God, and right winning against wrong, beauty against ugliness, truth against falsehood. All the right people, and all the right things, had conquered.

Was it ever that way in real life?

Steve switched on the light and looked at his watch. It was five minutes after eight. The film should be over. He was drenched in sweat. There was a knifing pain in his stomach.

Lieu got through to the phone around the corner from the Sutton Theater at exactly twelve minutes after eight.

"I don't know what to tell you, Steve," she said on the telephone. "It's bedlam. Everybody's talking and some people are getting mad at each other."

"How many left during the show?" Steve asked.

"Seventeen people went out and eight came back. So we lost nine."

"Any of the main distributors walk out?"

"Not that I saw," Lieu answered.

"Was there applause at the end?" Steve asked.

Lieu swallowed. "No, Steve, there wasn't applause. Everyone was absolutely quiet for about a minute. I don't know whether they were waiting for the credits that we don't have on yet, or whether everybody was thinking his own thoughts."

"Did you stay out in the lobby and listen?" Steve asked.

"I just left the lobby now," Lieu answered. "It took me five minutes to get through it. Everybody is standing around in little groups, talking, arguing, some of them yelling at each other. It's very strange."

"But most of them haven't left yet?" Steve asked.

"No," Lieu answered.

"Is Spartan with you?"

"He's on his way to you now," Lieu said. "He asked you to meet him in his penthouse."

"How did he feel about the reaction?" Steve asked.

"I don't think he knows what to think either," Lieu said.

"He looks worried, then?"

"Spartan never looks worried," Lieu said. "Especially not in front of this crowd. He walked through these people as though he already had twenty bids in his pocket.

"Steve," Lieu added, "I don't care what anyone says, it's an unforgettable film. You feel—you identify with the family—and you have to talk about it—word of mouth is going to be incredible—something happened to all of us in the theater."

2

Plaza Athénee Hotel, New York City

*S*teve was waiting for Spartan Lee in his penthouse at the Plaza Athénee. He had gone down to the dining room to have a cup of coffee with Kathleen and Lorelei and AGW, who were just finishing their dinner. The girls had jumped up as he came in the blue-and-white Magic Room, and he had told them he wouldn't know anything until midnight. He had explained to them exactly how the auction worked, and how he would be upstairs with Spartan.

"When I know, I'll come and tell you."

"Even if you don't know till after midnight, Dad, wake us up," Lorelei added. "We don't care, we want to know."

"We won't be asleep," Kathleen said. "We've already made a promise with AGW. We get to watch television until we know what happened from you. But we'll make up for it tomorrow. Right, AGW?"

Spartan came in quietly and went for the bar. Steve followed on his footsteps. "Well?" he said. Spartan broke out the champagne. He didn't show any emotion.

"It's hard to talk about it. You made me forget our problem and think about the family in the picture." He shook his head. "The picture gets to you—slowly but surely—it surrounds you—you begin to see yourself and your family in the Garibaldis.

"It's hard for those people, distributors anyway, to disassociate what they're seeing from everything they've heard about the picture, pro or con. When they came to the theater tonight, they all brought their own preconceptions about *The Rest of Our Lives*. They want to talk to other people, trade opinions, trade ideas. Not many people in a controversial situation want to speak right out. We're going to come out all right."

The telephone rang. Steve looked at Spartan sharply. "It's probably Magdalena," Steve said. "I promised to call her as soon as I knew."

Spartan picked up the phone. "Yes, this is Spartan Lee." Pause. "Yes, Mr. Kagan . . . we'd be glad to talk to you . . . Come right up."

Spartan Lee hung up the phone. He turned quizzically to Steve. "Ever hear of a motion picture man named Jeffrey Kagan?"

Steve shook his head. "I don't know who he is," Steve said.

"I don't either," Spartan mused, "but obviously it's something to do with *The Rest of Our Lives*. Let's hear what he has to say."

Spartan opened the door of the suite. A short, slight, young man about thirty-five years old, with a sensitive face, put out his hand. "I'm Jeffrey Kagan, Mr. Lee."

Spartan shook hands. "Call me Spartan, please, and if I may, I'll call you Jeffrey. It'll make things a little easier."

Steve walked into the hallway. Spartan introduced them.

"Steve, Jeffrey Kagan."

"I've seen you before, Mr. Wayland. Don't bother trying to remember, because I was one of many students who attended two lectures you gave at UCLA."

"Would you like a drink, Jeffrey?" Spartan asked.

Kagan shook his head. "No, I'm sure there are going to be many offers flooding in here quickly. I wanted to make mine face to face. I may not be able to offer as much money as some of the others, but I can offer you conditions I think you'll like."

Kagan pulled out a piece of paper from inside his pocket. There were five names, addresses, and phone numbers typed on it. He looked at Spartan and Steve. "You may want to check me out. Those are five home numbers of my bankers in San Francisco and Los Angeles. They'll all be at home tonight to verify your calls."

Spartan glanced at this list. "I know three of these men."

"Ask them anything you want. You'll get full disclosure," Kagan said.

"Now let's talk about the money first. My new company, Kagan

Communications, Inc., will pay you ten million dollars advance for worldwide distribution and the fifty percent of *The Rest of Our Lives* that Jack Gregson and MGL have now. We believe the film should be released with great care, in the pattern of *Out of Africa* and *Platoon*. We want to release the film in November of this year and wage a campaign for Academy Award consideration. We think *The Rest of Our Lives* can be an award contender.

"You will have approval rights for key city distribution, both here and abroad. And we want you, Steve, to go with your film to the openings here and to the major foreign cities.

"You will have basic advertising approvals in all media."

"Who will distribute the picture?" Spartan asked.

"A new company," Kagan said. "It's going to be announced in the *Wall Street Journal* tomorrow. They're holding the copy now. I promised to let them hear from me at midnight.

"If you accept, the announcement goes in a centerfold spread. The name of the company, which is a subsidiary of Kagan Communications, Inc., is something I heard you speak about, Steve, at UCLA. You were asked about the integrity of accounting practices throughout the industry.

"You said you were trying to sell a policy to one of the majors right then. You called it the 'Open Book Policy.' Your idea was that one of the nationally known accounting companies would keep the books for each film made and distributed by the motion picture company. Every dollar spent and every dollar that came in would be tabulated by the accounting company.

"Every dollar earned by a film would come from the accounting company, whether it was to the major studio or to the production company making the picture or to profit-sharing creative talent. Every single expenditure would be backed up by receipts. There would be no floating accounts. It would be set up like General Motors or U.S. Steel. The practice of keeping three sets of books, two to show and the real one that's never disclosed to anyone outside the distribution company—this practice, accepted and expected in many parts of the motion picture industry, would be eradicated.

"You told us that night that if any major company instituted an Open Book Policy like that, where not one dollar could be questioned, stolen, misrepresented, or triple booked, within a very short time every major independent filmmaker would be distributing through that company. You felt it could revolutionize one side of motion pictures, because every production company, every independent filmmaker, every profit participant would get an exact share of the proceeds.

"We've named our company the Open Book Distribution Company. Perhaps it's overly simplified, but it gets the point across. And that's what we want. *The Rest of Our Lives* would be our first film, if you'll agree."

"How much money are you putting into the distribution system?" Spartan asked.

"Twenty-five million to set it up," Jeffrey said. "We have a consortium of private and corporate money.

"I've been watching for this picture ever since it was announced. I wasn't surprised by what I saw tonight at the Sutton. Not everyone in the audience realized it but they saw an important picture—it's about every one of us—handled well. *The Rest of Our Lives* can do a sizable gross in the international market.

"I know you've never had a real box office winner. That's cut down your power in motion pictures. But this film can go all the way for you. Don't get me wrong, it won't be the biggest grossing picture of the year. But it's going to be a profit picture, especially considering its cost.

"I know you go by the rules, Spartan. You're going to wait until every bid is in. I respect that. I wouldn't be here if I didn't. But I don't care how much money anyone else offers you. I want to be a part of what you two are building. My company wants every picture you two can make.

"We'd like to announce a long-term relationship, no options on our side, but options on yours. This is your time and we're going to be proud to be there with you.

"Spartan, you can choose the accounting company for our distribution of *The Rest of Our Lives*. If you decide for us, call me at the Stanhope. I'll be there waiting for your call. Contracts have already been drawn."

"You're very sure we'll be signing with you, I see," Spartan said.

Kagan smiled at Spartan. "You know when I first heard about making out the contracts ahead of time, with all the numbers figured in, because the deal was right, right for both parties? The contract we have waiting for you is a Spartan Lee contract. It's clear, it's simple, it's not filled with legal terminology."

"My own words coming back to haunt me," Spartan said. "We'll call you, Jeffrey, when the returns are in."

They shook hands and Kagan left.

"Spartan, tell me I'm not hallucinating," Steve said. "Wait a minute. No, no, I'm sure, forget it."

"Thinking about checking the references he left us?" Spartan asked.

Steve nodded. "I don't have to check him out. I believe him. I've been waiting for Jeffrey Kagan to walk through that door all my life."

3

Plaza Athénee Hotel, New York City

*T*he written bids lay open on the table as the tall, blue-faced antique grandfather clock in Spartan Lee's suite struck twelve. The bidding was closed.

It was hard for Steve to believe, but Spartan wasn't surprised. He'd been confident that the worldwide publicity about *The Rest of Our Lives* would produce at least a $6.5 million bid, enough to get Steve out from under and pay the California Bank on behalf of the anonymous $500,000 investment. Most of all, he had wanted to see Steve's house saved, his properties, and his future.

The Rest of Our Lives had not been a smash hit at its special screening at the Sutton. And everyone connected with the making of the picture had known that it would be debated and pulled apart. But most of the cast and crew were too close to the film really to anticipate the way it would be received.

Spartan had had more distance from the picture. He had not been present for several of the final weeks on St. Venetia. But he had seen the work print early in the morning at the Emperor Theater on St. Venetia, the day they flew to New York.

Spartan knew that Steve had pulled it out. Only he and Steve had been at that screening. It was a test run to see if the print was as clean as possible and Dick Portman's temporary dubbing track playable. Both men had sat together at the theater at six o'clock in the morning and run the film. They were so nervous that they sat a good distance apart and never spoke until the film was over.

Inside the Emperor Theater in St. Venetia, thirty-six hours ago, Spartan had been fulfilled in his association with Steve Wayland. Of course he cared about the opinions of everyone else who could influence the success of *The Rest of Our Lives*. But within himself Spartan knew that *The Rest of Our Lives* was original in thought and in content. And it was certainly "today."

The reality Steve had strived for was there. The story was there, reaching out at you because it was true to life.

Spartan motioned toward the table. "There are fourteen bids here, besides Jeffrey Kagan's," he said. "Five of the majors. Three of the smaller distributors. And six foreign conglomerates, including two Chinese companies, Golden Harvest and the Shaw family. The guarantees go as high as fourteen million dollars, including the ancillaries.

"Three of the majors, Warner, United Artists, and Fox, are willing to give us a gross distribution deal—our percentage would begin from the first dollar at the box office and go up as the earnings of the picture increase.

"The two top cash offers are for a complete buyout of all your rights.

"I've put this all together quickly on one sheet of paper—cash, ancillaries, distribution—take a look—it's your call." Spartan glanced at his watch. "You have to decide fast if we're going to make the *Wall Street Journal*."

Steve took the paper and studied it. Then he smiled. "We've got a promise to keep. Let's call Jeffrey Kagan."

4

Magdalena's Home, Bel Air

She'd almost finished packing when he called. The huge Bekins storage boxes, seven feet tall, stood like sentries in a circle around her bed. They extended through the door and into the dressing room area and the bathroom. All the mirrored closets were open. Sara was finishing packing the clothes from the last ones.

"It's him, Miss Magdalena," Sara said. "From New York."

Magdalena took a moment to collect herself before she picked up the phone. Sara, watching her, stepped out into the hallway and closed the door.

"Hello, darling," Steve said.

Magdalena smiled. She knew from his voice what the answer was. "You got the bid, didn't you, Steve? I can tell from your voice."

"Fifteen of them in all. And the one we're taking is a whole new future, for all of us. I'm coming home tomorrow night. I can't wait to tell you about it. I miss you so much."

Magdalena stood at the foot of the bed, looking out over the circle of packing boxes. She was holding on tight to the phone; this had to be her greatest performance. She didn't have many more of them left in her, after the good-bye at de Gaulle Airport in Paris.

"Could you come to the airport for me?" Steve said. "Pan Am flight 8. Gets in about six-thirty. Have Sara call a car from the studio. Maybe we can have dinner together on the way home. Or better yet, maybe Sara can make a little something for us. Maggie, I can't believe it. Our luck has changed."

She felt two emotions at the same time—responses to his luck, and to hers. There wouldn't be any more "ours." She fought to control herself.

"Maggie, are you there?"

"Yes, Steve, I'm here. I'm so happy for you."

"For us," Steve answered. "Will you be there tomorrow night?"

"I don't know."

"What's wrong?" he asked. "Are you all right?"

She twisted the phone cord in her hand. How could she do this? What was the best way for him?

"Of course I'm all right. But Steve, you know how it is after a picture. I didn't realize how completely drained I was. You get on an emotional high, you work with people day in and day out, you live together. Then suddenly it's all over. You know we've both been through this many times, but it doesn't get any better. It's depressing. It will take me a few days to get over it, that's all. And then I'll be ready for you."

"But Maggie," Steve's voice came over the phone, "it's not over for us, it's never going to be over."

Magdalena swallowed hard. "Steve, why don't you stay in New York for a few days? You've won. I was sure you would. I know you and Spartan have a lot of business to do there. And Ed Wilson has to deal with the lawsuits. Just stay there. Until you've done what you should do. You've earned this."

"Spartan can handle everything here," Steve said. "This is his time now. He's the best in the world at what he does. He and Ed will work out the legal problems. I want to come home to you."

She made a decision and turned away, as if she were turning away from Steve's voice.

"We both need some space right now. You just as much as I."

Steve was becoming alarmed. "To hell with space. We belong together. Maggie! Tell me, I know something's wrong. What's going on?"

Her voice started, then stopped, and then started again.

"I've been alone for many years," she said. "You know all the things you have to do to stay up there as a movie star. A lot of it bores me, but it's something I have to do. I don't think I could accept losing my position. I've fought too hard."

"What position are you talking about, what are you going to lose?" Steve asked. "Everyone agrees about one thing in this picture—the performances. Especially yours, they're all raving about you. Call Spartan if you don't believe me. Or Jake."

"I believe you," Magdalena answered. "But—"

"But what?" Steve cut in. "You're going to be bigger than you ever were. You'll have your choice of projects. Maybe we can do another one together. I want to."

"It's been fun to have all the wonderful times we've had, Steve . . ."

"Don't you love me? Don't you want to get married?" Steve cut her off. "I've never heard you talk like this. I need you. What's all this about? I don't want a life without you. *We're* more important than either your career or my career. Maggie, I want to marry you. You know that."

Magdalena's throat closed up. She didn't answer. Her love for Steve was in her face, but the knowledge that it had to end was there, too.

She walked down the row of boxes. Every drawer and every closet was open now, and all her things were packed away. The room was as empty as she felt.

"Steve," she said, "I need time."

"What do you mean?" His voice sounded angry now. "We've already set the date, at the end of the month. You wanted to arrange everything. The Church of the Wayfarer in Carmel. Everybody's coming. I'm counting the days. You were, too, when I left you. I knew something was wrong. What's happened?"

She pulled herself together. Her jaw set. "I need a few days, darling. That's all. You know how vain I am. I don't want you to see me when I'm not at my best. And I've just kind of collapsed, Steve, after all these emotional weeks. I want to pull myself together."

"Do you love me?" Steve asked.

"Of course I love you," Magdalena answered. She had thought of a way. "But I had this little plan, you see, and now you're not going to let me go through with it. I wanted to go to the Golden Door for a few days, and when you got back from New York, I'd be here to meet you looking and feeling my best. I want to be at peace, Steve."

"Oh," Steve's voice was gentle again. "I thought there was something else. Yes, I can hear it now, you are worn out, it was selfish of me. I didn't think of you, I only thought of myself. One of my old problems when I'm angry. But you have to admit I'm getting better."

"Yes, you are." Magdalena's eyes were filled with tears. "You are getting better, Steve. So much better." She forced a laugh. "We women are so caught up in the way we look, particularly for the man we love."

"Go ahead, Maggie," Steve said. "Go to the Golden Door. I understand. I'll come in after the weekend. You want to look and feel your best for the wedding. I just didn't put it all together. I'm sorry I sounded upset. It's just that I don't ever want to be separated from you again. You haven't forgotten your promise at the airport?"

"No, Steve," Magdalena said, "I haven't forgotten."

"I'll call you at the Golden Door. And Maggie," Steve added, "don't ever forget how much I love you. And I'm so very proud of you. I think yours is one of the finest performances I've ever seen."

"That's because of you," she said.

"No, Maggie," Steve replied, "it's us. We're right for each other. We have so many things to look forward to, the doing together, the sharing. I can't wait to make another picture with you."

Magdalena's voice was low now. "I hope you know how much I want to do that."

"We will," Steve said excitedly.

"Thank you for understanding. It's very important to me, Steve, that you always understand."

"Maggie," Steve said on the other line, "when are you leaving?"

"Tomorrow, I think," she answered. "Tomorrow afternoon."

"Then I'll call you tomorrow night about this time. Try to get rested. I'll be thinking of you. Everybody here sends their love."

"Give them mine, darling. All of you are very much with me, and you always will be. I love you, Steve. Good-bye!"

"Good night, darling." Steve's voice came over the phone tenderly, and then there was the sound of him hanging up.

Magdalena held the phone for a moment. It was her last contact with the man she loved. The phone had somehow become the man himself. She wanted to keep him alive in her life as long as she could. Slowly, she put the phone down. Her eyes flooded with tears, and now she cried openly.

"Why?" she said. "Why now, when I've only found you?"

5

UCLA Medical Center, Los Angeles

"He must never know . . . *ever*, Alfred," she said. "He would blame himself. It has been my own choice. You have it written down in your journals of my case. I chose to be with him as long as I could without any treatments that would change my appearance. My conviction has never wavered from the first time I saw you. Isn't that true?"

"Yes, but—" Dr. Arms started.

Magdalena cut him off. "There are no 'buts,' Doctor." Her voice didn't falter. "I'm going to do things your way now. I never thought I would. I'm going to go—" her voice almost broke, "—to this island, take the treatments, and accept whatever comes. On the one condition that my identity is never publicized—that I am listed on the Pukhet Hospital records as Sara Martinez.

"Miss Martinez is my housekeeper and she's agreed to let me use her name, so we will be transgressing no one's privacy. Everything has been arranged to cover my tracks and take care of my business and my property.

"The time has come for Magdalena Alba to disappear from public life."

The doctor nodded. "I understand. But don't give up hope, Magdalena. It may not be too late."

She shook her head. "Whatever comes, I never cared that much for life until—"

He finished the sentence for her, "until now."

"And I've had it all in these few months, Alfred," Magdalena said.

Her eyes filled with happiness. "I know that it is possible for life to have meaning—love is possible—and forgiveness. I have known forgiveness.

"I have your permission and Dr. Cahill's that I can stay on the island for the rest of my life? And be 'lost?' I will try to find some way to serve the little community and not be a burden. I don't want to be a burden. I never have been, and I'm not going to start now," Magdalena said.

The doctor nodded, "The arrangements have been made, and Dr. Cahill and his staff are all grateful for your generous contribution. A new children's wing will be built on the island hospital with the endowment you have given us."

She looked at him quietly. "Anonymously. And that wing will be completed, whether I live or not. It's in my will."

The doctor smiled at her. "That's our agreement, Magdalena. But you're going to be there for the dedication, after it's built. I feel sure you will. And one day, we'll talk about your coming back home."

She smiled at him. "We'll see, Doctor. But I appreciate your encouragement." She picked up her purse. She was dressed in a white suit, white cashmere sweater, and long white patterned stockings, and she wore the small diamond heart around her neck.

She was even thinner now, as the disease made its inroads. Her cheekbones were more prominent and she was more striking, in a way, than she had ever been before.

"Alfred, you must keep my secret. Steve has so much to give the world. And he'll get over this. I will not see him dragged down and his career finished, taking care of an invalid or standing a death watch. He is too good for that. You understand, don't you, Doctor?"

"Yes," he nodded.

She kissed him good-bye on both cheeks.

"Alfred, if we shouldn't meet again, please remember how much you have helped me. I know now how few people ever truly love—and are truly loved in return. I will never forget what has been given me."

6

Jack Gregson's Suite, Pierre Hotel

Jack Gregson used his suite at the Pierre Hotel in New York for the "special" business he wanted to conduct away from his office at Mager-Golden-Lasky headquarters in Manhattan. The suite, with a maid and a butler, were part of his "business expenses," paid for by Mager-Golden-Lasky.

When he was going to stay longer, he brought his mistress from California. When he was there for a quick trip, he utilized an exclusive "escort service" which featured the best-looking collection of call girls in New York, continually tested for AIDS as part of their up-to-the-minute service. It was all as confidential as it was efficient. And Gregson liked variety.

He had dismissed last night's companion before the auction showing of *The Rest of Our Lives* at the Sutton Theater had finished.

Gregson had drunk steadily the night before, until he began to get the results. The early edition of the *Wall Street Journal* laid it out there in black and white. He couldn't believe it. He knew from what he'd heard when his people had gone to the showing that *The Rest of Our Lives* was a much better film than he had ever expected. His entourage had tried to talk around it, but Gregson's street intuitions had picked up the vibrations.

Now, at nine o'clock in the morning, the *Wall Street Journal* was spread out on the coffee table in the living room of his suite and there were more than twenty calls waiting to be put through.

But, by God, he wasn't done yet. Wayland had been nailed with the warrant when he stepped off the plane.

Spartan Lee and Ed Wilson had been prepared for this. The district attorney hadn't set the bail, the judge had. The judge had decided to wait until the auction was over to name the bail. That would be sometime today.

Steve Wayland would be able to pay it, even if it was exorbitant, but he would still be on trial in a few months on ten different charges that Gregson had brought against him. Jack Gregson would have his day in court!

Jerry Clune came in from the office of the penthouse.

What is it that's different about Clune? Gregson thought. During the last two weeks he had seemed different. Just a shade less deferential. Just a shade more confident of himself. Gregson was wary.

Clune spoke to him quietly. "Edmund Bradford Wilson is downstairs."

"I don't have an appointment with him," Gregson snapped.

"He didn't feel he needed one," Clune replied. "I told him to come on up."

"You what?" Gregson stood up from the table.

"We're getting calls from all the media. They want statements from you, Jack. I'll hold them all off until after you've seen Mr. Wilson."

"What the hell do you think he's going to do—change my mind about Wayland and his picture?"

"I guess we'll find out," Clune said, and went to answer the doorbell.

Edmund Bradford Wilson came in, shook hands politely with Jerry Clune, and then nodded at Jack Gregson. He put out his hand in a friendly manner. "Thank you for seeing me."

Gregson looked at him with a perplexed frown. What was coming off here? Wilson sat down on the couch. Gregson sat down across from him.

"I don't have much time," Gregson said.

"I know you don't," Ed Wilson said, "and I'm not going to take much of it. I'm going to make a suggestion, that's all." He took a legal document out of his pocket and put it on the table between them.

"I came here myself to serve you with this lawsuit. It's for seventeen million dollars in damages, harrassment, and mental and emotional cruelty. And all the other dots and dashes to go with it. It's a standard, straightforward suit, Gregson, and one I warned you about several weeks ago. If we win, punitive damages are possible—very possible. Your estimated worth is seventeen million dollars. We are going after all of it, exactly the way you have gone after all of Steve Wayland's property."

"What the hell are you—"

Ed Wilson stood up and cut him off.

"My suggestion to you, Gregson, *today*, is to take another look at the lawsuit you served on Steve Wayland. Look at your charges specifically in the light of MGL being paid off today, in full, the six million dollars, with interest, and the California bank representing the anonymous investor who put up the five hundred thousand dollars being paid off today, in full, with interest.

"Remember, you and your studio were free to bid for the picture yourselves last night, and you were one of the major studios that did not. You are exactly where you wanted to be, Gregson. No more picture commitments with Steve Wayland, and, as for *The Rest of Our Lives*, you and your studio are not out one single cent.

"So look at the charges in your lawsuit, and imagine for yourself how it's going to appear in court with the evidence we have. No one was kidnapped, as you charged. Everyone has been paid, as of today, everything owing to them. All equipment belonging to MGL and Panavision has been flown back to Los Angeles. The raw stock has been paid for. The laboratories have been paid. Item by item, everything in your lawsuit. And I would imagine the judge will bear all these facts in mind when he sets the bail for Steve Wayland.

"But if you want to have it out—all of it—don't take back any of your charges. Don't ask the judge to forget the bail. And for sure, don't call off your suit against Steve Wayland. Steve and I are looking forward to those days in court with you, Gregson. Every detail of what happened will come out. With witnesses. Good witnesses. How many people do you think will be there speaking for you, Gregson? Think about it."

Ed Wilson left Gregson sitting frozen in his chair. Then Gregson screamed out. "Jerry! Where in the hell are you, Jerry?"

Mahoney, the New York District Attorney, was waiting as Edmund Bradford Wilson was ushered into his office. He had seen the famous attorney during many trials, but he had never been lined up on the opposite side of a case from him, much less two cases.

This was supposed to have been the situation to have catapulted him into New York politics and onto the national scene. Gregson had thrown all his leverage behind Mahoney's cause. His campaign had been riding high. Mahoney's picture was everywhere, and his mastery of modern television political communication was evident in every appearance. He was becoming a celebrity figure, and the notoriety of *The Rest of Our Lives* had only added to his newfound fame.

Until last night.

Gregson had assured Mahoney, over and over, each step of the way, when they had failed to stop the filming of the picture, for instance, that the film couldn't possibly *buy* its cost back, much less *earn* its cost back. There had to be prints and advertising put up by somebody even to distribute *The Rest of Our Lives*. And the auction would prove him out. There wouldn't be any bids. Gregson had staked his professional reputation on that.

Mahoney had been in the audience at the Sutton Theater. He had fought the mood of the film. He didn't want the performers to interest him. He found everything possible wrong with the film as it moved along. And then, about halfway through, the film was so political in part of its story that he began to relate to it. That was what he'd been talking about on TV, after all—issues—America's lost morality— where had American ethics gone?—the country seemed to be getting more and more addicted to drugs—and then the AIDS problem, spreading rapidly now in the heterosexual area—the dire predictions from the scientific medical studies—what was *he* going to do with the rest of his life?

Before it was finished, *The Rest of Our Lives* was no longer a motion picture to Mahoney. It was a face-to-face confrontation with himself, with his life, his family, his ambitions, his career, his entire belief system.

Mahoney hadn't contacted Gregson when he had left the Sutton the night before. He had gone alone to a small bar and restaurant on a side street near Columbia University, where he had gotten his law degree. He'd gone to that bar when he was cramming for finals and waiting for his grades.

He knew all hell would break loose now with both the Rayme Monterey and Steve Wayland cases. Warrants had been served on them. Their bail amounts would be set tomorrow by the judge.

The Rayme Monterey case was in his power. He had worked for and asked for the second grand jury hearing, and he had the power to ask for a delay. A delay based on more study of the evidence, and perhaps, even some more new evidence in the medical studies of the three men who had been wounded and lived through the subway shooting.

Whatever else he knew, Mahoney was sure that after the release of

The Rest of Our Lives, Rayme Monterey was going to be that much more famous and idolized by the young people of the country. Anything to do with Monterey would be blown out of proportion.

He should study the case more, Mahoney thought. Let it take time— a long time—he could control that. And in the end he could either go ahead with his request for the second grand jury hearing—or he could let the Rayme Monterey case fade out.

What did he really believe himself? Did he buy the argument that the three subway assailants still alive had had no premeditated malice toward Rayme Monterey and Marny?

"Thank you for seeing me," Ed Wilson said. "I know your calendar is crowded."

"And so is yours," Mahoney said.

"Right," Wilson said. "We both know what we have to talk about. The ball is in your court, Mr. Mahoney. Hard ball."

"I don't like pressure from anybody, including you," Mahoney said. "I have respect for this office. I want to do what the law asks me to do. No matter who likes it."

"That's exactly why you have an excellent political future," Wilson smiled at him. "Your reputation is around. You can't be bought. Anyway, I don't try and buy anyone. I merely came here to ask you for clemency."

"Clemency?" Mahoney said, surprised.

"That's right. My client, Rayme Monterey, has been through a great deal. You know that. I am not going to argue in this office whether he is guilty or innocent of any of the charges you brought against him. We both know how we feel.

"But I don't think you've got the chance of a snowball in hell getting any jury in this country to bring down an indictment against Rayme Monterey, and then a conviction. You're never going to be able to lock him away, Mahoney. And I don't think you should. All that aside, you and I don't decide the law. We just argue our beliefs in it.

"But why not let this whole thing cool off for a while? You have the power to delay the hearing for a long time, until all the publicity has washed out. You know how quickly the public interest tires and changes to something new.

"That will happen with regard to this second grand jury hearing— and the Rayme Monterey case. I think it is important to at least consider a postponement—a time for all of us to think it over—for the public to forget the heat of the moment. I suggest to you that the right tack for you to take, in the best interests of everyone concerned—not to mention your own political career, Mr. Mahoney—is for you to soften up on this thing. Postpone the grand jury hearing. Take another look at it in a year or two. Your handling of this case is very important to the public here and to the people of this country. Protection against violence is a leading issue now. Persecuting a national idol at this new height of his popularity—I don't think I'd hang my political hat on it, would you?"

The judge made his decisions on bail late that afternoon.

Rayme Monterey's bail was set at $100,000. The grand jury hearing was delayed. The district attorney had requested an indefinite postponement, to consider possible "new evidence."

In Steve Wayland's case, the judge took into consideration his countersuit against Jack Gregson. He waived the necessity for any bail and set court dates on next year's calendar for both lawsuits.

Gregson was alone in his suite at the Pierre Hotel when he heard the news telecast. Jerry Clune had promised to call him from the courthouse. But Jerry Clune had disappeared.

7

MGL Studios, Culver City

*J*ack Gregson pulled into the parking lot at MGL and headed for the position that was always kept for him, right inside the gate. It was car space number one.

Gregson circled his yellow Rolls-Royce around and headed in, then suddenly stopped.

The number-one space was taken by a black Porsche. Gregson pulled into number two, furious at the mistake of the security policeman who was in charge of the parking lot. He picked up his attaché case and went directly to the security station opposite the entrance of the parking lot.

"What the fuck's going on here?" he lashed out at the security man. "Who did you let park in my place? You know you're supposed to keep that clear for me. You make that mistake once again and you'll be out of here."

The security man just looked at him, and then he gave a strange reply. "Really?" He didn't even add the obligatory "Mr. Gregson."

What the hell was getting into people these days? Nobody knew his place. The smart-asses were everywhere. Well, that man would be gone tomorrow. He'd give the order immediately.

Gregson walked up the steps of the Dana Building. He'd rushed back to Hollywood after the turmoil in New York. Why the hell had he ever given Spartan Lee and Steve Wayland that goddamned buy-back paper? He hadn't thought anything about it when he signed it. How the hell was that film ever going to get a six-million, much less six-and-a-half-million, advance from any other company? The whole town had heard about Wayland and *The Rest of Our Lives*. They had laughed about it in the executive dining rooms.

He walked by the girl at the reception desk. She was just out of college, and he'd picked her himself. It was important to him who represented MGL, particularly if you could get a hell of a good-looking girl with great tits and a good ass. The people coming in noticed that, and it reflected on the studio. And more than that, some of the girls felt indebted to the people who picked them. So Jack Gregson made sure that he had a hand in the selection.

He hadn't made a mistake when he picked this girl. He was in a foul mood, but the sight of Terry's breasts jutting out there in her white blouse, with no bra, revived him. He hadn't taken her out yet, but he'd talked to her about it. He knew she was waiting for him and that she would pay off for a better job.

Her usual big smile was missing.

"Hello, Terry," he said.

"Glad to see you, Mr. Gregson. I didn't know whether you were coming back or not."

"What do you mean?" Gregson asked.

Terry covered. "Well, I just heard somewhere that maybe you'd be staying in New York or something."

"Then who the fuck would be running the studio, Terry? This is my studio. Remember that. And next week we'll have that dinner."

"I'll be waiting, Mr. Gregson." She gave him a smile and breathed her tits out toward him.

He took another look and wished it was another day. He would've taken an early lunch and it would've lasted three hours. Well, next week.

Jack Gregson walked along the corridor leading to his office, traditionally the office of the studio head. It was the same corridor that Steve Wayland had walked down six months ago.

The same unforgettable stills from great classics lined the walls of the corridor. One memorable film moment after another. He didn't even look at them. He never had.

Fucking actors and actresses. He hated all of them. Just because they were born with good looks or something that came across on the screen, they got the best money, the best lays, the best of everything. Today, top stars had even more power than the head of a studio. What did those cocksuckers know about it? Stuck-up bitches, arrogant bastards.

He walked in his office, punching the door open. "Hello, Betty," he said as he walked in.

Betty's number-one reception mood was gone; she had on her number-four face and the number-four tone was in her voice. It stopped him dead. Betty had been his right hand for a year. She orchestrated his life with his mistress. She covered for him with his wife. She lied for him in the business.

Betty was sitting there like a stranger. She didn't even stand up, the way she always did when he came back from a trip. She simply looked at him and said, "Mr. Gregson."

"What's the matter with you, Betty, is the whole world screwed up this morning?"

"There's nothing wrong with me, Mr. Gregson." The year of servicing a man she did not respect, a man she didn't like, a coarse, vulgar, cutthroat operator, a man who belittled women, a man who treated her like the most menial servant, a man who never asked her about *her* life, her problems; and he was asking her what was wrong with her!

"My calls?" Gregson asked.

"There haven't been any calls," Betty said.

"No calls? What are you talking about? There are hundreds of calls in here every day. I want your special list and then the ones that don't count. Now."

"There are no calls," Betty said.

Gregson shook his head and started for his office. He was brought up short again. The office door was closed. There was a new, elaborate bronze sign on it, just like his. Only his had said MR. GREGSON. This sign said MR. CLUNE.

"Wait a minute," Gregson said. He turned back to Betty. "Am I going crazy? What's Clune's sign doing on my office door?"

"Why don't you ask him?" Betty said.

Gregson opened the door without knocking. Jerry Clune was sitting behind Gregson's desk. Except it was a new desk. His antique French desk had been replaced by an early American George Washington copy.

His furniture was gone, his paintings were gone, and some of the MGL Oscars that had been won for pictures before he had ever been there were gone. He had taken the awards out of the glass display cabinets in the lobby of the Dana Building and placed them on the table behind his desk. Now they were gone, too. Even the carpet had been changed. His had been brown. Now it was navy blue.

What in the hell had happened? He'd only left for New York four days ago. He looked at Jerry Clune.

"Get the fuck outta my chair, Jerry."

Clune smiled his easy smile and shook his head. "It's not yours anymore, Jack. Everything of yours has been sent to your home."

"I don't get it," Gregson said.

Clune leaned back in his chair. "You're through. Fired. Hung and strung up."

"I just came from New York. Nobody told—"

Clune cut him off. "Nobody told you because they had the meeting about it when you left for the airport. They didn't want you around. You stink, Jack. They don't want your stink anywhere around, even in the board room when they vote."

"You mean I'm out?" Gregson said. "No notice, no call? Nothing?"

"This is the way they wanted it handled, Jack, and I handled it. You shouldn't be surprised. I learned how to do this sort of thing from you. I've seen you do it to directors and producers and writers. A clean sweep overnight. Well, as they say around town, what goes around comes around. And it's come around for you, Jack."

"All this over Wayland's fucking little picture?"

"Not all over that. But *The Rest of Our Lives* was the last straw. You made all the wrong choices. If you hadn't done that, you'd still be here, Jack. You took a little picture and beat the hell out of it. The only trouble is, it kept on growing, just like the virus in *Alien*. And that little picture grew and grew and now it's the talk of the industry. You know the rest. You went out of your way to broadcast your personal opinions and to destroy Steve Wayland. He didn't destroy so easily."

"But what about you?" Gregson questioned. "You were with me the whole time. Feeding me the figures, supporting me; you never believed in the picture any more than I did," Gregson said.

"Balance," Clune said. "You've got to learn balance. That word doesn't exist in your vocabulary, Jack. People and projects are either yours or they're out. I was never yours. You thought I was, but I saw your flaws. I knew sooner or later you'd kill yourself here, and there'd be one person left who knew everything that was going on, and the studio would have to hire him. You were replaceable, and you've been replaced."

Gregson charged toward the desk. "You little shithead—you couldn't run a studio, not in your wildest imagination! You've got no balls, no style, no nothing!"

Clune stood up. He had punched a button on his desk. "By the way, Jack, I've taken over the production of *Victoria*. The New York office has asked me to try and sign Steve Wayland to write and direct it."

A security man stepped into the room. Jerry Clune looked at him and nodded at Gregson.

"Tom, would you please show Mr. Gregson out. Just the way he came in. I want you to leave instructions with your men that Mr. Gregson is never to be allowed to come into the Thalberg Building again. He's not allowed to go on the stages. He is absolutely barred from MGL. Do you understand, Tom?"

"Yes, sir," Tom said. "Better come on, Mr. Gregson."

Jack Gregson spit at him. "Don't you tell me what to do, you dumb blockhead! Who the hell are you? You never had enough brains to be anything but a cop. Get your hands off me!"

Tom had gently taken Gregson by the elbow. Now he put his hand in the middle of Gregson's back and shoved him toward the door. The guard was six-foot-three and two hundred twenty pounds of muscle; not too many years ago, he had been a defensive back on the New York Giants football team. There weren't many chances for a little action in his job, and he liked action. He had never cared for Gregson; Gregson had never even learned his name.

Gregson started back toward him and Tom just put out his hand, full against Gregson's chest.

"You swing at me, Mr. Gregson, and I'm going to knock the shit outta you. And I've got a witness here that you started it, so you can't even sue me. You better just walk along."

Gregson looked from Tom to Jerry Clune. He turned around and walked out of the office. Betty gave him that new look, the look of hatred and disdain. It was worse than a number-four look—it didn't even *have* a number on it.

Gregson passed the cop in the security post across from the entrance to the parking lot. The security man was smiling.

Gregson had it all in his mind now. He'd have it done before the day was out. He was going to sue everybody. MGL, Jerry Clune, even this cop who was walking behind him. They'd all pay, every one of them!

Tom stood outside the door of the yellow Rolls-Royce and watched Gregson get into it. Across the lot, out of a Ford station wagon, came a man in a shiny blue suit. He was walking directly toward them. Just as Gregson put his key in the ignition of the yellow Rolls-Royce, the man in the blue suit quickened his pace and stepped to the door of Gregson's car. He stood right next to Tom. He pulled out of his pocket a blue-backed, folded document and dumped it in Gregson's lap. He turned to Tom.

"Can I have your name? You're a witness to the service of a lawsuit."

Jack Gregson unfolded the blue-backed document. It was the service of a suit for palimony by his mistress, the ex-*Playboy* centerfold. He liked her; she kept her mouth shut, and she was always ready for him. His terms, his hours, his needs. She'd never given him an argument in the three years that he'd known her. How the fuck could she be suing him?

"Palimony." He looked at the name of her lawyer on the document. Marvin Mitchelson. The king of alimony, palimony, friendimony. Mitchelson covered them all. He and Gregson often ran in the same Hollywood social circles. The lawyer always had a cigar and a big smile. He even had his own press agent, Gregson had heard. Mitchelson talked a lot about his wins.

Now, Gregson thought, this is going to be all over the papers. The whole family's going to be splashed. He didn't care so much about his wife, but he didn't like it coming right now in the community. It was like getting hit by a shotgun. New York, Wall Street, MGL, Jerry Clune, studio cops, and now a palimony suit from his quiet, gentle mistress, handled by Marvin Mitchelson.

He flicked the ignition switch of the yellow Rolls-Royce, but it wouldn't turn over. Even his battery was dead.

8

Bel Air

*S*teve's limousine reached Magdalena's home just as dawn broke over Bel Air. He hurried up the lawn and across the gardens to the front door. The outside lanterns were on. He rang the bell; there was no answer. Then he reached into his pocket, took out his keys, searched for the right one, unlocked the door, and let himself in.

It was a ghost house. Everything was gone except the carpet and the drapes. He couldn't believe it. He went from room to room, calling names at first, but no one appeared. He even went to the servant's quarters, the back of the first floor, but they, too, were empty. Sara was gone as well.

He took the steps four at a time. His heart was racing now. He knew that something terrible had happened, but he couldn't imagine what it was. He burst into Magdalena's bedroom. Only the bare mattress was left and the elaborate satin quilted headboard. Even the blankets and bedspreads were gone. The closets were empty. Everything had been taken away.

He went from her bedroom to her bathroom, stunned by the fact that nothing remained except the bare furniture. He pulled out all the drawers, opened the closet doors. Every trace of the woman was gone.

9

Santa Monica Ironworks

As teve found Robert Montango at the forgers. The sculpture *Woman* was in its final stage, being forged into bronze from which the final sculpture would emerge, subject for the last rubbing-in of the patina and the coloring by the sculptor.

He spoke quietly. Somehow he felt Robert knew.

"She's gone," he said. "You knew, didn't you?"

Robert nodded. Steve grabbed his arm and twisted him around to face him.

"Where in the hell did she go? She never showed up at the Golden Door."

Montango looked at Steve with tenderness.

"She didn't tell me, amigo. She wouldn't."

"I don't understand," Steve questioned.

"She said she told you on the phone," Robert said. He looked probingly at the younger man. "She said she had commitments she had to take care of."

"Where?" Steve asked.

"She didn't tell me," Robert answered.

Steve glared at him. "Do you believe her?"

"I believe it for her, maybe not for you, amigo," Robert answered.

"Why wouldn't she tell me?" Steve asked.

Montango raised his voice to speak over the sound of the fire. "She's tired from the picture, Steve, she never worked this hard. She's drained. You pulled everything out of her and she's numb right now. You're a director, you ought to understand that. You did it.

"Nobody gets anything for nothing—that's one old cliché that's true—you touched perfection, Steve. But you scared the hell out of all of us. We don't know what to do with our imperfections anymore. We don't know what's real—what we see in the mirror or the work we did for you. Both sides are part of us, or are they? Is one thing ourselves, or the other thing, the vision you created, is it really you, looking through our eyes, speaking with our tongues—ah, to hell with it, I don't know—it's the most extraordinary experience I've had in a hundred and seventy-one films."

"Robert, I'm begging you, I think you know where she is. I've got to see her," Steve pleaded. "Maybe I did push her too hard. It's my fault, I guess."

"You've given her something no one else has given her," Robert answered. "She went beyond what she ever dreamed she could do. Now she's had to make some decisions. You think I know where she went? What she's doing? She wouldn't tell me because she knew that I'd tell you—I couldn't stand that look on your face—you look like someone's run a knife through your gut."

"She has," Steve said.

"You'll get over it, amigo. I've been there."

Steve looked at him after a pause. "I won't get over it. I don't even want to think about living without her. All my life I believed that a real relationship was possible between a man and a woman. I finally found that, Robert, a meaning in life. I can't lose it now."

Montango looked at him compassionately. "All I can tell you is, she must love you, in her own way. She gave you your film."

"What do you mean?" Steve asked.

"She put up the five hundred thousand dollars for the extra days you needed. Just before Rayme's problem gave Gregson his opening. She never wanted you to know. She swore the bank to secrecy. But I have friends there. One of them made a slip just after I got back. I kept after him until he told me the truth. What matters is, she gave you everything she had and her last words to me were, 'You and Lieu look after him. He'll need you both.' "

10

Island of Pukhet, Thailand

*T*wilight rimmed the island of Pukhet on the edge of the China Sea.

Magdalena Alba sat in the prow of Dr. Cahill's boat. Behind her were suitcases, a Thai nurse called Noi, and a small but powerfully built Thai man named Komson. Komson steered the boat toward the Pukhet camp harbor. Several beautiful islands offshore from Pukhet in the China Sea stood like lonely sentinels in the ocean.

Serenity was in the sky, in the tides of the ocean, and in the patient faces of the natives.

Magdalena wore simple clothes, and her diamond heart around her neck. Strangely enough, this piece of jewelry had been inspired by the folklore of the land to which she now was coming for the first time.

Dr. Cahill was gradually becoming a world figure. Few people had ever met him. He had been a protégé of Dr. Albert Schweitzer's and had spent years serving as an apprentice with him at his hospital in Lambarene.

He had established on Pukhet, with Guggenheim and Rockefeller grants, the first research center in the world for the dread disease of dermatomyositis.

Now there were research centers at UCLA and three different medical centers in Europe. But in far-off Pukhet, Dr. Cahill could do controlled experiments. Four young doctors were in residence concentrating on this one field of illness.

There was a good story here, and several journalists had picked it up. A young Dr. Schweitzer, coming of age in the mysterious country of Thailand, on the almost deserted island of Pukhet. The story had taken on mystery, and the place was becoming the source of legend.

Dr. Cahill was forty-five years old, and already decorated by many governments; he had received a Medal of Freedom from the President of the United States for outstanding service to his country.

He was Irish, red-haired, good-looking in a rugged way—perfect material for legend-making stories.

His ways of staffing and running his Island Medical Center were informal but strict. They were set up in much the same way as Dr. Schweitzer's hospital, and Cahill had adopted Schweitzer's philosophy of "reverence for life" in any form. No animal life on the island of Pukhet was allowed to be killed.

It was into this atmosphere that Magdalena Alba came, as Sara Martinez, to undergo intensive treatment to stop the disease that was attacking her body. She had left a tearful Sara behind at the Los Angeles airport, having sworn her to secrecy. Sara was to have an extended vacation in her home in Argentina. Magdalena had deposited $100,000 in Sara's bank there, in trust. She was afraid that if she gave it to Sara directly, the woman would know that she might not ever see her again.

They had been together for twelve years, and Magdalena knew her place in Sara's life.

She wanted to go into this new world absolutely alone. She would face what she had to face alone. But she had carefully prepared everything. She was certain Dr. Arms would not give away her secret. He was the only one who knew she was taking a new identity, from which there probably would be no return.

She gazed across the edge of the China Sea as the little boat came into the harbor, pulled in to the wooden pier by four native boys.

Dr. Cahill's nurse, Noi, who had met Magdalena at the airport in Bangkok, helped her up the pier's ramp, to the pier itself. She could hardly climb up, so rapidly was her strength diminishing. She wavered on her feet in the high humidity, and Noi steadied her.

That night she moved into a simple cottage, a solidly constructed building with the barest of furnishings. Her quarters had a bed and a bathroom the size of a small closet, with just room enough for a stall shower.

There was a small living room with a few simple pieces of furniture made on the island.

A handsome picture of the king and queen of Thailand hung in the living room; it was a sacred object in Thailand and never to be touched.

A Thai guitar had been left in the living room for its new inhabitant.

The short walk from the house passed four other small cottages and the hospital. The hospital was sixty-five feet long and divided into four rooms.

One room was called the sick call room.

The second room was used as an office for Dr. Cahill and his staff.

The third room was for the nurses.

The fourth room was a modern operating and testing room, built and sponsored by grants from famous foundations. Everything was clean, handwashed and handrubbed.

A thatched hut in the complex contained nine bamboo cots. This was the isolation ward for the rare leprosy cases.

Noi showed Magdalena around the compound. While they were looking at the hospital, Dr. Cahill came up to meet them. "I've been waiting for you, Miss Martinez," he said. "I want to start treatment tonight. I have a full report from Dr. Arms."

Magdalena studied the man in whose trust she now placed her life. He was bigger than she'd expected, and more rugged.

"Doctor, I have read two books about you. Your island has been called 'a compassionate candle in the darkness.' That is a wonderful thing to have said about something you are involved in."

The doctor shrugged. "This is no Shangri-La, Miss Martinez. It is an undeveloped Asian village, alive with disease. But we have isolated this one island so that we can study dermato. I hope you'll understand that I have to be brief, there's so much to do. And I want to get started with you right away.

"You've taken a great gamble by not being treated as soon as your disease was discovered. I don't understand that, but we'll talk about it later. What's important now is that we do what we can, as soon as we can."

He took her by the arm and guided her toward his office. "There's no time for bedside manners. Dermatomyositis doesn't wait for that. Let's get started."

He squeezed her arm. "Have you felt any shrinkage in your arms?" he asked.

She nodded. "In the last few weeks."

He made no reference to who she really was, and whether or not he had even heard of Magdalena Alba.

His manner was direct; he instilled confidence. Clearly, he was not used to losing.

"Take off your clothes," he said gently. "I know you're tired, but I want blood samples and scans done tonight."

He called to Noi to get the scanning machine ready.

The next morning, Dr. Cahill gave Magdalena her first injections of cortisone.

Noi had prepared the sick call section of the main building; she had screened the area off. Magdalena lay on the table under a blanket.

Dr. Cahill spoke gently. "Now, Sara, this is going to hurt a little, I'm not going to mislead you. I'm giving you as much as possible in these cortisone shots. The dermato has a head start on us with you, so I have to.

"I know you're worried about the swelling, and you probably will swell up. I don't know where, everyone is different. But I also want to tell you that there are cases where the swelling goes down—not all of them, but some, when the disease is arrested. Let's just take it one day at a time."

"Do you think I'll be around when the hospital is finished?" she asked quietly.

"We've got a chance, but you have to help me. Courage has a great deal to do with beating this thing. Medicine doesn't have all the answers. I've seen recoveries where there were no possible medical answers. And I've seen people slip away with very little wrong, actually. The will to live is a big part of treating dermatomyositis or any other disease."

11

Holmby Hills,
Los Angeles

portrait of Magdalena Alba, standing in the rain at the Paris airport, hung over the fireplace in Steve's living room. Robert Montango had painted it for him.

She looked out at him every time he came in the room, and the living room had become his favorite room in the house now. He felt Magdalena's presence there. They had planned to live in this house after they were married.

Now on many evenings, he had his dinner there, and on the weekends, or whenever he had Kathleen and Lorelei, they often ate in the living room on small tables that AGW had bought when she realized the changes in Steve's living pattern.

He spent a great deal of time at home alone now. Most of the day and part of the evening he was in the editing rooms at Goldwyn Studios, finishing *The Rest of Our Lives* and preparing for the final dubbing of the film.

Jeffrey Kagan had made the $10 million purchase as soon as the papers were signed. Six million had been paid to MGL and $500,000 to the California bank, in escrow for the "anonymous" investor. Spartan had it in a special money fund earning a top return, as the money had not been claimed yet. Steve called there every day; every day he was told the same story. They had no contact with Magdalena Alba, and no knowledge of her whereabouts.

Spartan's preproduction investment of $500,000 had been repaid.

All the liens on Steve's screen properties, his residuals, and on his house had been lifted. He was financially beholden to no one.

The cast and crew of *The Rest of Our Lives* were collecting their percentage of profits of the remaining $2 million and would collect their share of all the money to be earned in excess of $10 million. The story of that was all over Hollywood.

Everything was being handled by Open Book Distribution Company. Exactly, as by contract, every cent that was being paid out went through Price-Waterhouse. Every dollar was accounted for. All the profit participants had separate accounts with Price-Waterhouse.

It was summer vacation, so Kathleen and Lorelei were with Steve. They had dinner with their father almost every night. They went on trips with him on the weekends.

His friends were worried about Steve. He had brought his career to the best point, the place where he had economic security, backing for the next few years, and an Academy Award-contending film if the rumors were right. Yet Steve's fire had gone out.

He was working hard, he was editing and scoring, but even his professional collaborators noticed that his sense of humor was gone. He didn't want to see people, to socialize with friends. He stayed by himself night after night.

Sometimes, when AGW would awaken in the night, she would sense that someone was up. She would go downstairs, and there Steve would be sitting on the couch, in the dark, except for one light—the one shining on Magdalena's portrait.

Steve's detective contacts had been hired the day after he realized Magdalena had disappeared. They had been looking for her all over the world for two months.

Airplane passenger lists had been checked. Steamship line lists. International cruisers, and the transatlantic liners, as well as the Pacific cruise ships, had been checked.

Sara, Magdalena's housekeeper, had been questioned in Argentina. She had absolutely nothing to say except that she had been let go, with a handsome bonus, and that Magdalena Alba was the "finest lady I've ever known."

There was not one clue as to what had happened to her. Through Spartan, it was arranged for the police department to take on the case without publicity. A thorough investigation in the Los Angeles area came up with nothing. She had vanished.

Everyone came to the same conclusion—Magdalena Alba was dead.

Steve refused to accept this. Every ring of the telephone, every car that drove up to his house, every mail delivery could be some word from her.

It was Steve's mother's birthday. She was almost seventy now, and was making a courageous fight to recover from the death of her husband of forty-three years. The marriage had had its ups and downs, but it had been real, and it had always been there when a crisis hit.

Steve remembered a poem by Elizabeth Barrett Browning he'd read in his English literature class when he was a junior at Princeton. He couldn't remember the name of the poem, but he remembered what he'd felt about it. He had wondered how you could write this way about a person you loved—it had to be more exciting, more romantic, than she had expressed. There was one key line that Steve recalled.

Elizabeth Barrett had wanted her husband "to the level of each day's quiet need."

That was the level, the essence of what Elizabeth Barrett had written about Robert Browning. "Each day's quiet need" did not excite Steve Wayland at that point in his life. But for some reason, there it was, now, stuck in his mind. Wasn't that what he was longing for—Magdalena, "to the level of each day's quiet need"?

The children brought in his mother's birthday cake. The outline of Point Lobos in Carmel was the background of the cake, and an almost exact likeness of his mother's favorite picture of her husband and herself was in the foreground. There was a house with a gate there, and on the gate was a sign that said WINDSWEPT, his mother and father's holiday cottage in Carmel.

"You have to make a wish," Lorelei said.

"Close your eyes," Kathleen added.

Their grandmother closed her eyes tight.

"Have you got your wish in your head, Grandmother?" Lorelei asked.

Their grandmother nodded and smiled. "I'm thinking of it," she said, "right now."

"Take your time, Grandmother. When you're ready, be sure you get them all."

Steve's mother smiled at both girls, took a deep breath, and then, with AGW watching, she blew out all ten candles the girls had decided to put on the cake.

Steve looked at his mother thoughtfully. She was happy there at his home. Everybody could feel it. She was part of a family again.

Steve glanced at Kathleen and Lorelei. Kathleen looked at him excitedly. "Now?" she said.

Steve nodded.

"Grandmother, it's time for your present. We all went in together this year for the same one."

Their grandmother smiled again. "I know I'll love it, whatever it is. The cake was enough."

Kathleen took her grandmother's arm gently and urged her out of the chair.

"We can't bring the present to you, Grandmother. You have to go to the present."

"Well, well, well," Mrs. Wayland replied, with the phrase that she used so often and that they all laughed about with her. Each one of the family had imitations of her "Well, well, well," and they competed to see which one their grandmother thought was best.

The children took her, arm in arm, out of the dining room, down the steps, and across the study, to the study door that led outside to the back yard of Steve's house. The lights were on, the fountain was working well for a change, and the two statues in the garden that Steve had bought in Italy stood soft and lovely in the rose garden. In the center of the back yard, the large oval pool shone deep blue in the night lights.

As the children took their grandmother outside, she laughed. "What could my present possibly be doing out here? I hope it's not a dog, girls," she said with a slight edge of worry in her voice. "You know I don't have any place for a dog in my apartment."

"It's not a dog," Lorelei said. "That much I can tell you."

"Not even a cat," Kathleen added.

They took her around the edge of the pool and then stood before the pool house. Steve walked past them and opened the door with a key.

"Shut your eyes, Grandmother," Lorelei said.

"Absolutely shut, Grandmother, no cheating."

"What in the world?" their grandmother said.

"You'll find out," Kathleen replied. "Now, just take a few steps forward."

Steve turned on the lights while his mother's eyes were still shut. The present was the pool house, completely done over.

Steve and the girls had had it made into a bedroom suite for Mrs. Wayland.

Steve had had some of her own things sent out, her pictures, her books, her writing desk, even some of her clothes. He'd had it all done secretly after his mother had left Chicago to come west. The girls, AGW, and Lieu had worked on it with him.

They all knew the way Grandmother would like it. Her mother's needlepoint chair, a little cabinet for her collection of music boxes, which Steve had sent her from all over the world. The Lincoln bookends standing on each side of a leather-bound copy of each of Steve's films, inscribed to his mother and father. A mezzotint of the University of California at Berkeley, his mother's school. Pictures of her mother her sister, and her brother. A painting of her husband over the fireplace, the one from her apartment.

Her keepsakes, little mementoes through the years, were carefully spread around the pool house. There were fresh flowers on the coffee table and towels in the bathroom that the girls had picked out. They were powder blue, Grandmother's favorite color, and in dark blue, each towel had sewn into it in script the word GRANDMOTHER.

There was a handmade sign taped over two of the windows, which faced the patio. HAPPY BIRTHDAY, GRANDMOTHER, AND WELCOME HOME it said.

"You can open your eyes now, Mother," Steve said.

His mother hardly took it in at first. She was surprised, shocked, and heartwarmed all in one moment. She turned to the girls and Steve and AGW in open-mouthed wonder.

"How did you do this?" she asked. "I don't understand."

Kathleen hugged her. "You're going to move here, Grandmother."

"And live with us all the time, or at least most of the time, as long as you want," Lorelei added.

Steve embraced her, too. "We don't want you to go back home, to stay. Your life is here, Mother, with us. We want you to gradually close down your apartment in Chicago, however it's best for you, or if you want to keep the apartment, fine, whatever suits you. But this is your home."

"That's right," Kathleen said.

"You have to read to us every night," Lorelei looked up at her. "Promise?"

Steve's mother couldn't help it now. She broke down and cried with happiness. AGW hugged her, too. "We all want you to come, Mrs. Wayland. We've been planning it a long time. Happy birthday."

"Oh, Anna," Steve's mother said. "I can't believe it. Thank you, thank you, thank you." His mother turned to Steve. "But I can't move here, son. You have your lives to lead. You can't have an old woman—"

Steve cut her off. "I don't want to ever hear those words from you, Mother. You're not an old woman. You're a vital and sensitive woman. We need you in our lives. You have much to give all of us.

"There's a whole new attitude coming in this country, Mother, completely different from the way it's been. In other countries, families stay together, and there's a continuity of the generations, values handed down, a traditional family structure that contributes to a sense of morality, to a society where everyone has his worth. People are beginning to look at that in this country, and thank God for it. Just because a person gets older doesn't mean they're useless, or not needed, or not loved.

"There are no secrets between us, Mother. You know you're lonely in Chicago. I realize you've got many friends there, but it's not the same, with Dad gone, and Junior and his kids back there. It's got to be tough on you. There're too many reminders."

He kissed his mother.

"You're going to live with us. We need you, and that's the truth."

"Yes, Grandmother, please," Kathleen said.

"Daddyboat's going to make you do it anyway," Lorelei said. "We've talked about it, and we know what's best for you."

Steve's mother bent down to hug the girls.

"How can I possibly fight you all?"

Everyone was asleep now. Steve was slumped on the couch, having a last cup of coffee. Only the painting lights were on. He looked at Magdalena's portrait. She seemed so alive. She was alive in him. He shared every special moment, like tonight, with her.

Steve, looking at the painting of this woman he loved, held on to his hope. She had to be alive, somewhere. There had to be an explanation. He had to find her.

12

Buddhist Temple of Pukhet, Thailand

The massive carved figure of Buddha was over a hundred feet tall and seventy-five feet wide. The impassive golden face looked out over the columned temple.

Buddhist monks paced out their solemn and reverent steps. In the background, singers chanted their reverberating monotones.

Magdalena Alba sat by herself near the back of the temple. This was the only house of worship of any kind on the island. She hadn't thought about going there when she first arrived.

She prayed as she had begun to on the island of St. Venetia with Father Ciklic. It was not just a routine, as it had once been when she was a very little girl. It wasn't something you did before you went to bed, or before you ate a meal. She prayed continually throughout the days and nights as though she had an invisible friend whom she could talk to, or laugh with, or confide in, or confess her fears to—it was a force that was there with her.

Magdalena smiled. George Lucas's phrase "May the Force be with you" in *Star Wars* hadn't meant anything particular to her at the time, it was simply a good, wholesome expression of hope and optimism, that there was good to combat the evil, that there was hope to combat despair.

But Magdalena marveled as she watched the people on the island, the working people who were not patients. The Thai men, women, and children seemed to have a natural sense of peace, a happiness and tranquility as they went about their daily work. All of them were Buddhists, and their religion was part of their daily life.

Magdalena had gone to the temple, finally, to listen to the chants, and to hear the prayers of the people. She didn't understand them, but she felt them.

She watched the men and women and children, coming into the temple. Each one went to the front and brought a candle to offer to the great Buddha. They knelt before the towering figure, lit their candles, placed them at his feet, then bowed their heads in prayer.

How strange, Magdalena thought; it did not seem dissimilar from the practice of the Catholic Church. She felt somehow that there must be a link between the great spiritual beliefs throughout the history of mankind. At the center of most of them was one common conviction. Love. As Peter Ciklic had said. To love was to have meaning in life. Love did not die.

She thought of Steve and wondered about him. She was sure that the pressures of his work, now that he had made *The Rest of Our Lives*, were great, but his success and fulfillment at long last must be exciting for him.

She was thankful that she had been able to complete the film, that it had been her last picture, that she had done her best work in it, and, most of all, that she had done it with the man she loved. She could face her fate now with the conviction that she had finally lived fully. She had loved with all her heart, and she had been loved in return.

She put her hand up to touch the diamond heart.

She watched two young girls go forward and put their candles at the feet of the giant Buddha. Maybe that's what she would do with the time she had left—work with the children of the island. Maybe she could start a class and teach the children stories—some of the stories she had worked on as an actress. Maybe she could even read some of the great works to them, a little at a time. She would talk to the doctor about it. He was anxious for her to get involved in something to take her mind off the painful treatments.

Magdalena followed the line of people approaching the altar. She took two candles and, as was the custom, left coins in the bronze receptacle to pay for them. She knelt and looked into the Buddha's impassive eyes. And then she lit the candles, one for Steve and one for herself.

13

Steve's Journey

teve went back to the beginning. The flamenco-haunted gypsy caves of Sacre Monte. He wanted to walk in her footsteps. Perhaps somewhere there was a clue, an answer.

He stood where her mother had first danced for her father in the gypsy caves. Gypsies were still there and there were those who could speak to him with the help of money, and hired interpreters, about the legendary "Bastarda."

It was gypsy legend now to be told and retold from one generation to another, by the campfires, in their gypsy civilization that seemed to reach back hundreds of years.

The stories had grown, twisted, been added to, gossiped about, exaggerated and minimized, but they all agreed on one thing. Magdalena was the one person who had ever been born in the gypsy caves of Sacre Monte and gone forth to become known all over the world.

They loved to tell, in excited voices, of her return, when she was twenty-two, after she had starred in four motion pictures. She had come back to the caves to appear before the tribal council of Sacre Monte gypsies. She had come back to accuse those people who had abandoned her after her father had died, and who had refused to protect her in the gypsy tradition.

She had waited eight years to come back. She denied all gypsy traditions and heritages. The gypsies' most famous representative on the world stage had resigned in front of the gypsy tribal council, had turned her back on her half-gypsy blood, and, in gypsy tradition, left forever her gypsy tribal family.

Steve watched the gypsy dancers and remembered there in the heat of the night, with the gypsies dancing together just as they had done generation after generation, just as they had done when Rodrigo Alba, Magdalena's father, had come for the annual "fair" to represent the Spanish government.

He thought of how Magdalena had danced for him at El Cid after the Academy Awards. He longed to see her coming toward him again, her magnificent eyes flashing.

Steve followed her footsteps on his pilgrimage. He flew to Paris. He had breakfast every morning in the Plaza Athénee coffee shop. He watched the waitresses there. Many of them were young, pretty girls supporting a career in the theater or in the arts by working as waitresses as Magdalena had done. He could picture her going from table to table as a young girl, in the stylish, starched designer dresses of the Plaza Athénee coffee shop.

He went to the old Truffaut office, where Magdalena had auditioned for her first part.

Everyone in Paris knew Magdalena Alba, and the gossip was rife. But Steve could find no one who could give him a clue as to where she was or what had happened to her, not even Sylvia, her former secretary, or Yves St. Laurent, her designer in Europe.

The caretakers of her apartment in Paris had not heard from her.

There was no record of her location in her former Paris bank. Her accounts had been closed even before *The Rest of Our Lives* had begun to shoot.

Steve flew to Switzerland to see Magdalena's best friend, Sophia Loren. Sophia had heard from Magdalena when they were on St. Venetia, but nothing since then.

He flew to London to meet David Lean at the Connaught Hotel. She had made one film with him. David Lean had not heard from her.

The final part of his search was to Buenos Aires to hunt for Sara. He had found her finally in a remote village in the gaucho country, just outside of Mar de Plata. She greeted him warmly, but said she had no knowledge of where Magdalena had gone or what had happened to her. She had given Sara a sizable trust in the Bank of Argentina, and Sara's love for her mistress was clear. Sara felt that Magdalena was dead.

There were no more leads for Steve to follow. For three months he had flown to most of the world, talked to everyone Magdalena had known well. He had found no trace of her.

Steve flew home for the Academy Awards, alone, depressed and defeated.

14

Academy Awards, Dorothy Chandler Pavilion, Los Angeles

*T*here was a burst of applause from the audience as Magdalena Alba's face came on the screen. Among the starstudded crowd, Kathleen and Lorelei, on either side of their father, squeezed his hands.

Seated next to Kathleen, Lieu glanced at Steve. AGW was seated next to Lorelei and holding her hand tightly.

Sitting in front of Steve, his mother and Spartan Lee glanced back at him. They knew this moment would be difficult for him.

It was Academy Award night. Over one billion people were watching on worldwide satellite television. Only those communities which had no television were outside the reach of this program; and Pukhet was one of them. One segment from each film for which an actress was nominated for Best Actress was shown on the giant screen at the Music Center.

At the end of the five nominations, Robert Redford came to the microphone. He was given the envelope and looked out at the audience for a moment before he said the words.

"The winner is Magdalena Alba. She is unable to be here tonight. The director, writer, and producer of *The Rest of Our Lives*, Steve Wayland, will accept for her."

There was a spontaneous outburst from the audience as Steve made his way to the stage, because the love affair between Magdalena Alba and Steve Wayland, and Magdalena's subsequent disappearance, were known to everyone in Hollywood. It had been talked about around the world.

"Magdalena," Steve paused, as though he were speaking to her directly through the television network, "our prayer is that wherever you are and whatever has happened to you, you will know that your picture and your performance have been honored tonight. Your family sends you, in the hope that you will somehow hear us, our deep respect, and, for always, our love."

As Steve backed away from the microphone, the Academy audience rose to its feet. The applause was deafening.

15

Pukhet

The children's wing of the hospital had been begun. It was the central topic of discussion on the island. No one knew where the money had come from. But there it was, going up in the wild countryside of Pukhet. Everything had to be brought in. The lumber. The cement. Most of the wood, the pipes, the wiring, the generators, the electrical plant, the water purification system, the sewage system, a small compact modern city in the middle of the Pukhet jungle.

The Thai people were watching the building grow step by step. Many of them were working on it. The children's wing was their pride, and their hope.

The children of the village were playing in the school courtyard. There was an old but sturdy slide, two seesaws, two swings, and a circular turntable which spun fast when enough of the children pushed it before they hopped onto it. This particular morning the turntable was spinning very fast. It was recess time and the children were playing with their teacher.

The turntable slowed down and the teacher got off with several of the children. They pushed it again for the rest of the children to have a second ride.

The children who had gotten off clustered around the teacher, asking her to play. She was a slender woman, too thin. Her long blond hair was pulled back from her face and tied with a ribbon. Her face was round and tan from exposure to the sun. Her nose was straight and her forehead full. Her cheeks were out of proportion to her face. Her cheekbones were lost in the somewhat swollen flesh.

She picked up one of the children, the smallest, to give him a hug. "What are you going to read today?" he asked her.

"King Arthur," she answered.

The little boy clapped his hands. "And the Knights of the Round Table?"

"That's right," she replied. "I like it as much as you do. Right after recess."

The little boy reached over and kissed her, then scrambled to the ground and ran back to the merry-go-round.

The woman he knew as Sara Martinez looked after him. Her eyes shone in the sunlit day, the unforgettable eyes of Magdalena Alba. The face was changed, swollen; it had lost its fine angles. But there was something more in the expression and beauty of her eyes. There was a steadiness, a certainty, a love that seemed to extend like open arms to the world, to all that she saw or felt or touched.

Wherever she walked on the dusty roads and in the steaming heat of Pukhet, along the edge of the China Sea, in the quiet of the hospital compound or amid the cries of the very sick and dying in the hospital ward, Sara Martinez had become a special person in Dr. Cahill's medical encampment in Pukhet.

There were rumors everywhere in the compound that she was dying, because the fear was so great that she would. She had a severe case of dermatomyositis, well advanced, and it was said there were heart complications. Those who had been there when she had come, eight months before, recognized how much weight she had lost. She had still been a voluptuous woman when she had arrived. Now she was extremely thin.

Dr. Cahill was working at his desk late one night when Sara Martinez came to see him. He greeted her with affection.

"Sara, what a nice surprise. I was getting so bored with these reports. My God, how I wish I had three secretaries, instead of half of one."

Magdalena sat down across from him. "Could I be of any help?" she asked.

He shook his head. "No, Sara. We need you with the children, just as long as you can . . ." His voice trailed off.

Magdalena filled in. "I think the time has come, Doctor. I'm very tired."

The doctor replied quietly. "Everything we know about the tests shows that the turning point is here. That doesn't necessarily mean you'll go down, Sara. Let me tell you something."

He sat down on the couch opposite her. "I think you're going to make it—and you know I never deceive. When you came here, I didn't think you would—I thought the disease was too far along. And I didn't think you really had the will to live. You acted as though your life was over, and you were already resigned to leaving it.

"But you've become deeply loved here. You *know* that. We've never had a teacher like you. The whole village wants to come to your night classes on the theater. They love your readings, even if they don't understand very much of what you're reading."

She smiled. "I've seen *you* there once or twice."

"Every chance I get," he replied. "Sara, your will to live is coming back. We've never talked about it before, and I think the time has come to do so. I know who you are, of course, and about your career, but I didn't think you wanted it mentioned. And that's the way it's been. No trading on the past, a completely new beginning or ending. That's what you wanted."

She nodded.

"You've had it. But now I think it's up to you," Dr. Cahill said. "We're very close to arresting the spread of dermatomyositis inside you. If your body doesn't give up first, and if you want to live hard enough, you're going to have to force yourself to stand when you feel like falling, to walk when you feel like sitting, to run a few steps when you feel like walking. You've got to do it, because the disease is reaching its last real drive at you. If you make it through the next few weeks you're going to live.

"And I want to tell you something else, speaking as a man. Yes, the cortisone has swollen your face and your legs a little. No one on earth can tell you whether it's going to stay that way or go down. But I can tell you this: you were a beautiful woman when you came here, and you're a beautiful woman now.

"When I look at you, I don't look at the swelling—I can't get past your eyes. And your eyes, Sara, make you the most beautiful woman I've ever seen.

"I know what your beauty has meant to you and I understand what it means to see that beautiful body change, and that face, well, that incredible face, change, too. And it *has* changed. Something has been taken away, but something has been added, and *you've* added it. It's *you*, Sara. Anyone can be born beautiful, but to grow into the kind of beauty you have now, that's the person—that's the *woman*."

"Your island changes people, Doctor," Magdalena spoke quietly. "It's so different from the outside world. You look at things differently. People look at you differently. All the values are different."

He took her hands. "I'm going to be behind you. Sometimes you're going to hate me during the next months. But I am not going to let you give up."

Sara was burning hot. It wasn't the tropical sun. It was a red-hot river inside her skin. She didn't think she'd get through the day. She had the children out by the pier to watch the sunset, just as she had seen it on her first night's arrival at the harbor of Pukhet.

She wished Noi were with her, as she usually was. She would have liked to send the children back home with Noi as it grew dark. She would have liked to lie down right there, away from everybody, and just watch the ocean, where there didn't seem to be any difference between life and death. Where the whole world joined in the endless horizon. Where the importance of a single life didn't seem to matter, against the endless centuries of that mysterious ocean and the infinite height of the sky. Where there seemed to be no time, no space, but only some unfathomable universal truth.

It couldn't all be for nothing. The endless seasons, the turning of the planet, the development of life, the centuries of man.

Here on the edge of the China Sea, in the tiny village of Pukhet, the driving forces of material ambition seemed pointless, the sacrifices of health and friends and the lust for money and power—here, at the edge of the China Sea, was perspective. A view of the world from the edge of the world. A view of civilization from the footsteps of primitive man.

Here you could let life and memories, and even breath, slip away without such a terrible struggle.

Magdalena's life flashed through her mind. The memories, faces, fears, ambitions. The evil she had done. And the good.

Everyone had at least two selves within. Good and evil. Sacred and profane.

Here, in Pukhet, Magdalena Alba summed up her life.

The search—the agonizing, lonely, tearing-at-the-soul search for a place in the sun.

Was it to be better than anyone else, richer than anyone else, more beautiful, more envied?

Or was it simply to find a place alongside your fellow man—a place to serve in the endless chain of mankind's struggle for meaning? She thought of the brilliant Austrian psychologist Viktor Frankl, who had lived through the Holocaust in Germany to come back and build a new family, a new psychology called logotherapy, based upon the will of a man under the worst conditions possible to find a meaning, something of value.

She looked out over the ocean. That must be Komson with Noi coming with a new patient who would try to find a life on the island. It was hard to see now, but yes, she was sure that it was Komson, sitting with one of the sailors in the prow of the boat where she herself had once sat, with the new patient across from them. The setting sun was going down on the far horizon just behind the boat.

Yes, now she would send the children home with Noi. And she would stay there, at the edge of the ocean, to wait.

If this was the end, she would face it. Her will to live, to fight the pain, was almost gone.

The sun sank down below the rim of the ocean. The moon already hung low in the tropical sky.

Yes, Magdalena Alba felt she could reach out and touch eternity here. Her hand went to the diamond heart on the hollow of her throat.

She went to the edge of the pier, where two sailors had thrown out a rope to the boat and were pulling it in.

She waved at Noi and Komson, and then suddenly she froze. Standing beside Noi was Steve.

She was sure that the fever in her blood was giving her hallucinations. Maybe she was dying right there. She had read so often about split-second flashes of your life passing before your eyes. But she didn't want to die right here in front of the children. A scream stopped short in her throat. The children strolled to the edge of the pier to greet Noi.

Steve swung onto the ladder and moved quickly up to the floor of the pier.

He had aged five years in the eight months since she'd seen him. His face had tension lines at the eyes and at the corners of his mouth. There were dark circles under his eyes. He had a haunted, desperate look as he took hold of Magdalena.

"Maggie. Maggie. I've looked everywhere for you."

Her hands tightened on his arms, and then she touched his face. She couldn't believe he was there. She felt his strength surge into her.

"Oh, my God, Steve! Steve!"

"I saw a snapshot. One little snapshot from a *Time* magazine story on Dr. Cahill."

"But they didn't take any pictures of me," she said. "They didn't even know I was here."

He put a finger on her lips, and then kissed her. He clung to her.

He whispered to her, "A little boy, a doctor's son, had his own Brownie camera and he took several pictures. He took one of the school children.

"Their teacher is barely there in the background, but one thing is clear. I had it blown up over and over, again and again. The teacher was wearing a diamond heart. Then I studied the face, and I saw you, Maggie, I saw you."

She turned her face up toward him. "I tried so hard for you not to find me, for you not to see me like this. I didn't want it." She was crying now. "I didn't want it," she said again.

"You couldn't lose me, Maggie, I need you," he said, his voice finding itself. "Not just a perfect face. I need *you*. Maggie, do you know anything about your success in *The Rest of Our Lives*?"

She shook her head. "I didn't want to know anything about the world I left behind. I really didn't."

"Well, you won all the awards. New York Critics Circle, the Academy, National Board of Review—all of them," he told her.

She smiled. "I'm so happy for you. And did you win?"

He shook his head. "Nominated. All my life, Maggie, I wanted to win an Academy Award. I wanted to be recognized.

"But then I got there and without you, well, it didn't matter. And you can't send me away. I'll never leave you again. We either go back together or we don't go back. That's what the picture was all about. We have to try again."

Magdalena's voice broke as she smiled at him, her eyes filled with tears.

"Oh, Steve . . . darling . . . I never thought I'd see you ever again. You *do* really love me . . . for *me*."

Steve drew her to him.

"Everywhere I went, you were there, Maggie. Your face . . . your voice . . . your eyes . . . your heart . . . they never left me . . . we belong together, Maggie. Always."

Magdalena kissed him. Her voice was a whisper.

"Oh, yes . . . yes . . . my darling. We'll be together. We are forever."

HALL BARTLETT is one of the most independent and most honored of American filmmakers. He has directed, produced, and written sixteen major theatrical films, including *Jonathan Livingston Seagull, The Children of Sanchez, The Caretakers,* and *The Search of Zubin Mehta.* These sixteen films have won seventeen Academy Award nominations for Hall Bartlett and more than one hundred international awards.

Hall Bartlett is a graduate of Yale, Phi Beta Kappa. He presently resides in Bel Air, California. He has two daughters, Cathy and Laurie.